Frances J.
Eckart

THE MIRACLE OF THE BELLS

*W*E'RE OF ONE FLAME—*all kin of stars and sun.*
The brothel's beacon—altar's candle—one.
The sluggard's lamp—ambition's raging fire.
Saint—sinner—sage and fool—Life's deathless pyre.
The Christ who cried to One in agony—
The thief who cursed Him from the neighboring tree—
All God's—Who out of Darkness ordered Light
And gave man's soul the miracle of Sight!

Verse found by William Dunnigan
among Olga Treskovna's papers.

The MIRACLE
of the
BELLS

By

RUSSELL JANNEY

New York

PRENTICE-HALL, INC.

To the real Olga

WHO LIVES I KNOW AMONG HER BELOVED HILLS

ACKNOWLEDGMENTS

To Dr. Edmond Pauker for encouragement, to Gorham Munson for valor, my sincere gratitude. And grateful appreciation is expressed for permission to use the words "A Pretty Girl Is Like a Melody That Haunts You Night and Day" from Irving Berlin's copyrighted musical composition

THE MIRACLE OF THE BELLS

I

A TALL FIGURE of a man stepped down from the last day coach at the end of the express train from the West. He carried a heavy, much-traveled suitcase. He looked about as if the surroundings were not familiar, then proceeded along the lengthy platform toward the front end of the train. He passed several more day coaches, three Pullmans, and arrived at the two baggage cars, from the open doors of which some trunks were being unloaded as well as numerous sacks of mail. As he reached this point a long box was pushed from one of these cars onto a waiting hand truck.

It was a mid-afternoon in late August. The tall man put down his suitcase and gazed about impatiently. The railway station (its name was on a sign across the end of the platform's half-roof) was that of Wilkes-Barre, Pennsylvania. The long box obviously contained a coffin.

"Are you Mr. William Dunnigan?"

The words were spoken by a stocky fellow with a stolid, expressionless face, who now approached the tall stranger.

"I'm Dunnigan. You the Coaltown undertaker?"

"Yes sir. I got your wire from Los Angeles," and the shorter man produced a yellow envelope as proof thereof.

"O. K. Here's the coffin and here are the papers. That your hearse over there? Good. Attend to things and let's get going pronto. I want to be away from here by tomorrow night."

"I'll have to take these papers to the station master, Mr. Dunnigan."

"O. K. I'll wait here. Make it snappy."

The tall man watched the long box being wheeled to the near-by baggage room, the undertaker following. He himself moved to the waiting motorized hearse backed up in the adjacent station-drive-way. He took a cigar from his vest pocket, bit off the end, spat out that end, and lit the cigar, scratching the loose match on the under-side of the hearse.

An observer would have given this tall figure a second look. Per-haps a third. As did several loungers about the platform who were not especially observant. They looked at him instead of at the long train now plunging eastward once more.

His athletic frame was clad in a perfectly fitting suit of pale red and blue checks on grey. His contrasting shirt was a brilliantly dark royal purple, though the four-in-hand tie was black. The shoes were also black and highly polished. But it was probably at the two extremes of the figure—the head and the feet—that the loungers especially glanced. The man wore a snappy black derby tilted at a rakish angle on his slightly greying hair. And the black shoes were topped with white spats—somewhat soiled from the train trip, but still white. His face was ruddy and handsome in a rough-and-ready way. The keen eyes were a steel-grey.

Presently the undertaker reappeared and the long box was pushed into the hearse compartment.

"How far to this Coaltown?" asked the man with the cigar.

"About ten miles. My name is Orloff. James Orloff."

"Yes, I remember. I'll ride with you, Mr. Orloff, if you don't mind."

"I expected you to. Only way you can get to Coaltown unless you wait for a bus by way of Nanticoke. It's a rough ride."

"Lots of damned hills, aren't there?"

"Yes sir. Mountains. Eats up plenty of gas. But at Coaltown we got the highest breaker and the biggest slack pile in the Valley."

The tall stranger seemed unimpressed by this compensation for the presence of hills. He answered somewhat wearily as if regret-ting he had mentioned the subject at all.

"O. K. Get going. As I said, I want to get away from here to-morrow night."

2

*I*T IS WELL that we have a "preview" (as Mr. Dunnigan would have called it) of "this" Coaltown. In its own private valley, for a full mile it stretched an ugly, one-street length through the stark loveliness of the Wyoming Valley hills—Exhibit A (a philosopher might muse) of how man can place his greedy imprint on Nature's best. Even to the making of hills themselves. For behind the houses along this Coaltown street there were two kinds of hills. Hills made by God. Hills made by man. The former were green with pine and maple and spruce and cedar, and in the springtime flowers bloomed at the roots of the trees. In the autumn they wore a mantle of every shade of red and yellow and orange, and in the winter the ermine of the snow.

The other hills—the hills praised by the undertaker—were black; spring and fall and wintertime. Great mountains of "slack," the waste ore from the mines that could not with profit (even with the labor of boys and girls) be turned into Company dividends—mountains accumulating through the years until their man-made, rounded shoulders rose almost as high as Nature's own handiwork. No trees grew on them, nor any springtime flowers. Iron rail tracks constantly bridged their tops, so that more and even more refuse could be hauled up and heaped up.

Smoke rose from them in the spring—some sort of combustion of inflammable elements where the sun struck the hottest. Any flower would be summarily destroyed. Any cloak of snow also, for the heat lasted into the winter. It seemed they would remain black and smoking until the trumpet of Gabriel sounded the end of Time.

Gabriel, however, did not yet rule the destiny of Coaltown. That office was held by the Breaker—the "highest," as Mr. Orloff had stated, in the entire Wyoming Valley. Almost as high as the hills it raised its head at the top of its black, wooden tower. It could smile indulgently when cities boasted of their skyscrapers. Long before these steel-supported wonders, it was standing there, unaided, where the town begins, as you approached from the direction of Wilkes-Barre. Tower and sloping body looking not unlike a prehistoric dinosaur, its erected fangs spitting into the heavens, its sloping, swollen body trailing down to Mother Earth. By day and night one heard its voice—the grinding and crunching of a vast internal machinery that swallowed the freshly-mined coal ore at the top (where small, stubby cars from the mines fed it on an endless chain), chewing and separating and digesting this raw food into hard lumps of pure carbon power.

Its excrement formed the "slack" of the man-made hills.

This Breaker, and the mines that fed it, devoured men also—men and children who were early put to work in them—took greedy toll of their strength each day while planting a dark, sinister imprint of life-bondage inside each human lung. Workers rarely lived beyond a middle age.

So—as if somehow to indemnify for all this unlovely and grim business of living—at the faraway other end of the street, but up a steep incline and around a sweeping bend, were the five cemeteries— as restful and beautiful as the Breaker was ugly and horrific. Small cemeteries, only a few hundred yards square, three on one side of the roadway and two on the other, but each in its center had a raised wooden cross bearing a life-sized image of the Blessed Saviour crucified, gazing down on the green mounds and their grey-white headstones in painted compassion and understanding.

The cemeteries were on a sort of plateau high above the town, a plateau surrounded by distant hills. There were farm lands in between the cemeteries and the hills, where corn and wheat was grown. Coaltown and its works seemed far away, though a walk of five minutes brought you there. Only if you went to the far edge of one of these cemeteries could you see the human habitations below, and then their ugliness was hidden. House roofs—even of Coaltown—had a pleasant look. Only the Breaker reared itself in ugly silhouette.

There were five cemeteries, because in the town there were five churches scattered along Main Street. Two Polish, one Czech, one Russian, and one Protestant. Five splotches of near beauty in the dreary lines of "company houses." Three of the churches were of brick—all had grass plots around them; and the black dust from the Breaker seemed to respect these holy oases. Four of them even had small, round beds of flowers—tulips in the spring, geraniums when these were gone.

Some twenty-two other buildings also punctuated the monotonous row of miners' homes—not exactly splotches of beauty. Coaltown's twenty-two saloons.

There was also Nick Orloff's "Dance Palace" with a square false-front, an "American Store," a "Funeral Parlor" (which we shall presently enter) with a pool and billiard room at the back, and the Wyoming Hotel. This last was avoided by any traveling salesman who had once spent a night under its grimy roof—even if the buses had stopped running and one must pay a dollar and fifty cents for a Ford to get back to Wilkes-Barre. For, as undertaker Orloff had also indicated, Coaltown had no railway station. Just freight tracks for guiding coal cars to the nearest main lines.

One word more. You have guessed that people lived in Coaltown, as well as came there for burial. Poles and Russians for the most part, the older ones straight from the immigrant boats, and still, after many years, clinging to motherland customs and language. They married, had children, ate, slept, worked, got drunk on Saturday, went to Mass on Sunday. You met the men in the early morning on their way to the mine shafts in grime-stiff overalls and tight-laced miners' boots, rudely moulded Slavic faces beneath the hard, visored caps with light-fixtures projecting at the front. These men went deep into the earth—one thousand, fifteen hundred feet— to blast with dynamite at the black wealth that was there. Sometimes there were accidents. Eventually "miners' asthma got you"— if the accidents "passed you up." Doctors called "miners' asthma" by another name. Tuberculosis. But the Breaker had to be fed.

And children were bred as rapidly as possible. It did not mean "more mouths to feed." It meant more hands to bring home "pay" —as soon as those hands were large enough to work. They could "pick coal" on the slack piles almost the first day legs could take them there. They could sit astride the shoots in the Breaker at ten. Boys could become "helpers" in the mines at twelve. Girls—if they could not earn money—could be married off at fifteen. Three years at school was enough for anyone. That is, until a heretofore vague thing called "the Government" stepped in and insisted on more education and no child labor. But "the Government" was slow in dis-

covering Coaltown. It was off in the hills in its own private valley
and had no railroad station.

In the years that Olga Treskovna grew up there, the Breaker was
the Government.

———————————————————————————— *3* ————

*S*UCH WAS THE COMMUNITY that William
Dunnigan of Hollywood and Broadway was now rapidly approach-
ing, riding arms folded in the dusty front seat of Mr. Orloff's hearse.
Mr. Orloff was the brother of Nick who operated the dance hall.

The body in the box inside the hearse was that of the aforemen-
tioned Olga Treskovna.

This saga is indeed about this girl, the "Breaker Girl." But Mr.
Dunnigan's appearance calls for a paragraph.

Bill "White Spats" Dunnigan. For his striking bit of foot adornment had attracted the attention of others besides the loungers
about the Wilkes-Barre station. It was known in fact from coast to
coast, from Montreal to Mexico, in theatrical, sporting, and newspaper circles, since this somewhat conspicuous pedal accessory had
long ago attached itself to the name and fame, as well as to the
shoes of its wearer.

"Spats" was a celebrity in his sphere. A genius perhaps. One of
the ace "press agents" of the show world. An eccentric genius who
had been hired and fired by practically every purveyor of amusements in the land. Product of New York's East Side; graduate of
"promotion" for Dance Halls and Burlesque, the race track and the
prize ring and the circus into the most astute representative of the
finest of musical spectacles. Broadway's top ace, since the year he
trumpeted to world renown, and (what is more difficult) kept there
for a decade, the name of a certain great "revue" producer whose
series of girl shows had held the spotlight for that (theatrically
speaking) lengthy period. With the death of this producer, Dunnigan had reached what seemed to be the climax of a success career
—a lucrative Hollywood assignment. Up until one week ago he had

been no less than chief drum beater of the domain of Super Pictures, Inc., ruled by another great architect of public entertainment, Marcus J. Harris.

At this moment, however, riding toward Coaltown in the Orloff hearse, he no longer held this enviable and exalted position. He had been fired—emphatically and conclusively fired—by the great Marcus Harris himself. The catastrophe that brought it about was doubtless already Broadway gossip, and would prevent his securing any future jobs with picture companies or indeed in the regular theater.

So both the present and the future looked anything but bright—as dead, it seemed to Dunnigan, as the foreboding countryside through which he was now riding with an undertaker and a corpse.

He was at bottom "low" in both mood and estate. He was "broke," despite the three-hundred-and-fifty-dollar bank roll still reposing in his wallet. For that bank roll was the "residue" of the estate of his late friend, the girl in the wooden box, and he had promised her to carry out certain sacred tasks.

He felt no resentment. What he was doing—what he had done—was for her. But he was very tired and very blue. Riding five days —and nights—in a day coach from California, eating meals from the baskets of itinerate sandwich and coffee vendors (for the money must be carefully conserved for the task ahead)—all this, with the funeral of a dear friend at its end, was not conducive to an elation of the spirit. Not at least to Bill (White Spats) Dunnigan.

The two men in the hearse had ridden the first few miles in silence. They could have continued in silence to their journey's end at Orloff's Funeral Parlor with its poolroom at the back as far as the press agent—or rather the *ex*-press agent—was concerned.

He had certain information to obtain, but it could wait. The stolid, expressionless face of the bullet-headed mortician who admired "slack piles" did not promise interesting talk.

That gentleman did not speak because he had learned it was good business to respect the "sorrow of bereavement," to use a trade term. Besides, he had to watch the none-too-smooth and always twisting mountainous roadway over which they sped. But he was consumed with a burning curiosity about this strange bird who had climbed down from the trans-continental express at Wilkes-Barre.

Finally Mr. Orloff could endure the suspense no longer. Moreover, he was wondering just what he could charge this cryptic, flashily-dressed city gent from whom he had received a telegram marked Los Angeles, California, five days before. That the name on the papers for the body—Treskovna—meant nothing to him, added to the mystery. Why should such a man, obviously not a native of these mining valleys, travel all the way across the continent for the burial of someone whose name was also strange, although it did sound Polish?

"You the husband?" Orloff asked at last.

"No."

This reply was not encouraging, but having broken the ice the undertaker tried again.

"I don't recall ever seeing you around Coaltown before. Or knowing the name of this deceased." Orloff momentarily took a hand from the wheel in a combination gesture of crossing himself and jerking a grimy thumb toward the rear of the hearse.

Bill Dunnigan pulled himself out of thoughts of ironic frustration in a rotten world. "I'm just a friend," he said. "The girl came from your town. Wanted to be buried here. Olga Treskovna, the name on the papers, was her professional name."

"Professional?" Orloff made the word sound as if the dead girl had used an alias in some illicit business.

"The theater," said Dunnigan patiently. "It's often done. The name she was called here—what was it—Trocki—Olga Trocki."

Olga Trocki! The car slowed down perceptibly. Turning, Dunnigan saw the undertaker come to sudden life. Expression spread over the stolid face. Sullen, resentful expression.

"You mean Stan Trocki's kid?"

There was anxiety in the question that somehow did not have a kindly ring.

"Why, yes. I think she told me that was her father's name. He's dead, I believe."

"He certainly is dead," was the almost viciously prompt reply. "Nobody knows that better than me! I did a hundred dollar funeral for that no-good drunk on this girl's say-so and never got paid for it."

Orloff pulled over to the side of the road and stopped with a sudden screeching of the brakes.

"Four years ago it were," he proclaimed, his hands and mind now free to concentrate on a matter of such financial magnitude. "She left town right after that. Wilkes-Barre for awhile, and then nobody knew where. Sent me a money order for ten dollars once from Chicago, but that's the last I ever heard of her. So it's ninety she owes me now."

Orloff glared at Mr. Dunnigan. The undertaker was sore, there was no mistake.

"Well?" asked Dunnigan.

"If this deceased is Olga Trocki," and the gesture toward the back of the hearse was lacking in its former reverence, "I want cash in advance for anything I do. And I want to know where I stand about the old man's account."

Dunnigan really looked for the first time at his companion. He could easily (he believed) throw this moon-faced, overfed, macabre ruffian into the ditch beside his hearse. But he was too depressed in spirit to feel much anger. And he thought of the girl. He'd promised to see this thing through and he would.

"All right. Keep your shirt on, friend," he said. "You shall have your pound of flesh for the father. She made provision for it. And the present job too will be cash on the barrel head—on the coffin head I suppose we ought to say." His voice grew sharper. "By the way, the father's bill was only eighty dollars, not a hundred, according to the girl."

"It was a hundred," reiterated Mr. Orloff. "There was extras for flowers, and I had to pay the pallbearers. You see, her old man was no good and nobody wanted to be a pallbearer——"

"I know all about that too," Dunnigan interrupted. "Suppose we skip it." He realized Orloff made no move to start the car. "You mean, you want the money—right here?"

"I wouldn't mind seeing the balance on the old man's bill," said Mr. Orloff decisively.

This time Dunnigan felt the muscles twitch in his right forearm. He had to restrain a vigorous and well-trained fist connected with those muscles. He hadn't been press agent for six or seven world-championship fights without acquiring a more than superficial knowledge of a brisk and singularly effective uppercut.

But again he held himself in control. Olga Treskovna had told him, he remembered, that there was only one undertaker in Coaltown.

"O. K.," he said. "I'll pay that here and now."

He took out the wallet from his rear trouser pocket, and extracted a hundred-dollar bill, painfully conscious that only two more "hundreds" and one twenty and a few tens were all that remained. Abruptly he handed the bill to Undertaker Orloff.

"Here. And according to your figures, there's ten dollars change coming to me."

Orloff took the money but hesitated about the change. There was already a charge for the trip to Wilkes-Barre and back to his "parlor," and he was getting involved in a completely new transaction with the day-coach-traveling stranger—doubtless from his appearance also in the dubious "theater business." Still, he could not exactly unload a coffin at the roadside. He decided he must take a chance.

From an inner pocket he produced a fat billfold (he had noted that Dunnigan's wallet was very lean) and carefully extracted the necessary "ten."

"We talk the business part of this girl's job when we reach my place," he said, and stepped on the starter. "Understand—I ain't givin' no more credit. As a businessman—I take it you're also a businessman—you appreciate my position. I have bills to meet myself."

He steered back into the roadway and drove ahead again. He opened his mouth to launch further "business" dissertation.

"I have to help my brother pay for a new bar in his dance hall," he commenced, but his companion wished the matter of the Orloff family finances closed.

"Skip it, please," commanded Dunnigan. "Just keep moving. I've quite a lot to attend to. There's a church called St. Michael the Archangel—" he was consulting his notebook and thought, *what a ridiculously pompous name!*—"I've got to find its priest."

"It's just near my place." The shrug that accompanied the comment was not expressive of approval for either the church or anyone who sought it.

But Dunnigan's interest was only in its proximity.

"Good," he said. "Maybe you won't charge to point it out to me! I want the funeral from that church tomorrow. Want to leave here tomorrow night, as I told you. And don't despair. I won't ask for anything on the cuff. You'll be paid cash money—in advance. You can meet this week's payment on your brother's precious dance-hall bar. Don't forget, however, to give me a receipt for the father's bill. In full."

Again Dunnigan withdrew to his own somber thoughts—thoughts not brightened by an unfriendly and (to him) entirely bleak landscape. The cruelty of the people of the little towns! It had been as bad as the girl had said.

Her strangely sad, sensitive face was real and lifelike before him. Born to these damned scowling hills! She had to "take it" from people like this undertaker! God, why did she ever want to be returned here! Well, she had wanted it passionately, and it was little enough he was doing to carry out that wish.

Carry it out and get back to New York where even the faces of strangers were friendly, and where a ten-dollar bill was not a matter of life and death.

Poor little kid! This then was journey's end.

He felt more utterly and completely depressed (if that were possible) than when he had boarded the train in Los Angeles.

He lit a fresh cigar and realized that it was the last Regina Perfecto.

4

*P*OOR LITTLE KID! Come to think of it, that had been his thought, his audible comment, the first time he had laid eyes on her. But there was no despair then in the phrase. It was journey's beginning—and beginnings are times of hope. And it was in New York. The city of eternal hope.

It had been about three years before, on an April morning. Dunnigan had walked up Broadway from his hotel, and there was the first magic of a first spring day in the air. The water from the street sprinklers smelt fresh and clean on the asphalt; the bright, open space straight ahead that was Times Square blazed in the sunlight like a huge diamond. The tall buildings looked newer and more upright against a sparkling sky—like giant, belted, close-ranked

soldiers standing at smart attention along the canyon of the street.
Bill had even stood and gazed straight up at their trim lines—at the
sky toward which these bayonet-like lines seemed to rush with living swiftness. He did crazy things like that sometimes.

He had now reached Forty-Second Street and he did another crazy
thing. On impulse, he walked in through the front of the Venus
Burlesque Theater near the corner. He had no connection with this
theater. He had left burlesque behind him a long time ago. The
next day he was leaving for Atlantic City to prepare the way for the
out-of-town opening of Broadway's most famous yearly "revue."
But maybe one of his pals still was directing the numbers at the
Venus. Spring brought memories of old friends and old days when
he was trying to make the grade. There were always morning rehearsals at the Venus for the new show with which each Sunday
night started the weekly grind. He hadn't seen such a rehearsal for
years!

Dunnigan was inside now and walked down the dark aisle, his
shiny, white-spatted shoes crunching peanut shells and empty candy
boxes from the previous day's midnight show.

There was no feeling or smell of spring in the Venus Theater. A
single hundred-watt bulb on a short upright pipe coldly illuminated
a line of girls rehearsing in practice clothes on the bare stage. In
front of the line, a slender, tired, shirt-sleeved dance director was
showing the girls a new "routine." Over at one side the musical
director sat wearily at a battered upright piano. The rest was lost
in shadow.

"One—two—three—pivot! One—two—three—pivot!" the dance
director intoned. And the piano banged out "I Can't Give You
Anything But Love, Baby!" to which the musician added an occasional limp flourish of his own devising. He was a disappointed
composer.

"One—two—three—pivot!" droned the dance director again, and
then his voice rose angrily. "Stop! For the love of Mike!" In the
sudden silence his words hurtled out. "You—third from the end!
Who told *you* you were a dancer! Good God—don't you know what
pivot means?"   .

Dunnigan, unnoticed by the occupants of the stage, looked across
the dead orchestra pit at this third-from-the-end girl.

She was awkward and scared and looked at the director with ter-

ror in her eyes. Green at such work, Dunnigan saw at once. But
the cheap playsuit that she wore could not entirely ruin the clean,
slender, boyish figure—so slender it seemed almost undernourished.
And the terror could not hide the deep blue of her large eyes—eyes
wide apart in a beautiful, wistful face. Wistful and forlorn. There
was some unusual quality about her that held press agent Dunnigan
—trumpeter for the show that boasted "the most beautiful girls in
America." Maybe it was just that he was sorry for her.

"Poor little kid!" was what he said to himself.

The dance director broke the spell. "You're the new girl, aren't
you? Well, you're some lemon! This is a *thee-a-ter*, not a kinder-
garten. I'll give you one more chance to get it right!"

The girl, too frightened to answer, merely bowed her head. Her
hair was long, Dunnigan noted, and seemed a silken brown. The
cleanness of the outside springtime—*that* was her lure! A delicate
flower growing in a line of sturdy weeds. The other girls were hardened "chorines"; chunky of body, blank of face, hair bobbed, they
did their steps with a tired, professional precision. They were au-
tomatons—cold and bleak and lifeless as the winter that was over
and gone.

This third-from-the-end girl was Spring. Spring trapped in the
Venus Burlesque Theater!

The musical director had finished lighting his new cigarette from
the butt of the old one. The tinny piano burst into action again.
And Dunnigan's eyes watched his Spirit of Spring proceed to a new
debacle.

She was trying to watch the dance director, her own feet, the girl
next her, all at the same time, in her desperation to understand and
copy a "pivot." She stumbled and nearly fell as she tried this simple dance movement on the next count. To make it worse, she
threw out of step the girls each side of her. Dunnigan felt a curious alarm and sympathy.

Unfortunately for her, the mind of the dance director was not
Dunnigan's. It was not focused on any such abstractions as the
contrasting of Winter and Spring, of flowers and weeds. Nor did it
flow this morning with a generous, springtime sympathy for his fellow man—or woman. He had a new show to put on the boards by
Sunday night. And the old show to keep going meantime. Godal-

mighty! He wanted a "pivot" after three steps! His patience was exhausted.

"You—third from the end! Out! And stay out!" He spoke the words with a grim finality.

Dunnigan, watching the girl, thought he had never seen on anyone's face such a look of utter terror. And now she spoke.

"Please," she said, and the voice, though frightened, was low and musical. "I can do it. If you'll just give me a chance. I'll stay after the rehearsal and practice till I learn——"

"Sorry, sister."

Sometimes we do things we cannot explain. Things that change our entire lives.

"Tom!" called out Bill Dunnigan, and as the dance man wheeled toward the footlights and peered out into the semi-darkness, "Tom —give the kid a break!"

Dunnigan had no idea why he spoke up so suddenly. It was none of his damn business! It was as though he were listening to someone else say the words that tumbled from his mouth.

But the startled dance man could not mistake or forget that hearty voice.

"Bill! Bill Dunnigan!" he cried. He was suddenly all smiles. A younger man by a dozen years! The great press agent of the great five-dollar Broadway musicals—his old buddie, Bill Dunnigan— had not forgotten him! He had taken the trouble to come into a humble, fifty-cent burlesque house to say hello! "Gee! Is it really you! I'll be right down, Bill!"

He wheeled back to his line of girls. "Relax!" he shouted. "Take a smoke! This is my friend Bill Dunnigan, the king of press agents!" He was by this time half way through the wings.

Dunnigan saw the startled third-girl-from-the-end looking down into the dark void that was the orchestra. She could not discern clearly the exact appearance of this sudden interceder from Heaven. Except that he was tall, and wore a light-colored suit, and a dark derby cut at an angle across his forehead.

"Oh thank you, sir," she stammered. "Thank you so very much! I really can do it. It's just that——"

"Forget it," came back Dunnigan's voice from the void. "Relax. I'll try to fix it for you, kid."

The next moment the press agent stood wondering. Why the

hell should he be taking the part of a pathetic, amateur, starved-looking, entirely unknown-to-him chorus girl! Even if her eyes *were* big. It was the Spring perhaps. He'd better get to a bar and have a sobering Scotch!

"Gee, Bill, I read about you in *Variety!*" The dance director was beside Dunnigan, his hand affectionately on the press agent's shoulder. "You don't forget old friends! Most of 'em do when they climb out of this five-a-day stuff—comedians—advance men—prima donnas——"

"Shut up! We're all in show business," said Dunnigan. He had been fond of this humble dance man who really knew his stuff. But his eyes were again drawn to the stage. The line of girls had vanished into the wings for their "smoke." But the third-from-the-end stood there alone, uncertain of her fate, her eyes still pleading for a chance.

"This kid," Dunnigan said—he was in for it now—"You'll give her a break, won't you, Tom? She—she's a friend of mine. I know her people."

Was it again the intoxication of Spring that made him tell these lies?

"Sure, Bill, sure!" the dance man replied. "Any friend of yours can have anything I can give."

He turned and called up to the waiting figure on his stage. "You're still in, sister. Hang around. But learn to pivot. For God's sake, *learn to pivot!*"

He called toward the wings, "Nellie!" A bleached and scarred veteran among the dancers sauntered onto the stage.

"Nellie, take this new girl and teach her how to pivot. She's a friend of Bill Dunnigan's. Go on, sister—Nellie will give you the routine. And Nellie! Tell the girls they can take fifteen minutes. I'll be back at eleven-thirty, sharp!"

The third-girl-from-the-end wanted to say a word of thanks, but there was a choke in her throat. Besides, the two men had turned and were striding up the theater aisle in animated conversation. A side door opened; for a moment they were silhouetted against the bright outside light. The slight figure of the dancing man—the tall figure with a rounded derby cocked at its rakish angle. Angels come to this earth perhaps in strange guises! But the girl Nellie was at her elbow and pulling her aside.

"Come on," she drawled. "I'll show you how it's done. A friend of Bill Dunnigan's, eh? What the hell are you doing in this dump!"

The "friend of Bill Dunnigan" did not see him again. Not for a long time, at any rate. Bill didn't return to the burlesque theater after the drinks at the Astor Bar. He had the urge to speak about the girl, but how could he talk to the dance director of someone "whose family he knew" and yet of whose name even he hadn't the slightest idea! He left town early the following morning. And from Atlantic City he moved on to Boston, then Montreal, then Detroit. His big show needed more "fixing" than usual before its Broadway opening.

He thought of her at times—a strange thing for him to do, for his busy mind was not on women, except as they were part of the scenery of the productions he represented. Riding in a plane, or in his drawing room on a train, her face would suddenly appear before him. Sad and terrified and beautiful—as she had looked when the dance man discharged her.

Poor little kid!

When he finally did return to New York, he went again one morning into the Venus Theater. He told himself he was going to visit the dance director. He knew it was to find out about the third-from-the-end girl.

No luck. The house had completely changed hands. The dance director and his entire troupe had been transferred to a "stock" in Chicago. Dunnigan could only wonder if this girl were still with it.

"I hope she made the grade. I hope she learned to pivot," he said to himself as he moved on to his own resplendent show house.

He learned long afterwards that she had written him a note of thanks. The dance man had given her the name of a theater in Atlantic City. But with a constant changing of theaters during those weeks, the note somehow had never reached the ace press agent.

Time dulls all memories. Only it was a curious thing that ever so often Bill Dunnigan would see her eyes—feel her presence. Ah well, maybe he would run into her again sometime. Show business was like that!

"Poor little kid."

――――――――――――――――――――――― *5* ――――

*D*UNNIGAN was yanked back into the present by another sudden screeching of the brakes of Orloff's hearse. They had reached the "funeral parlor."

The town had no outskirts. One minute you were traveling in the countryside, the next you were on Main Street. The press agent looked out at the grimy building with its obviously false, second-story front. His spirits sank further, and he felt a fierce resentment against the whole place and the man beside him.

"My parlors," said Orloff.

Dunnigan climbed down to the roadway, lifted out his suitcase and crossed to the sidewalk. The large paving stones were cracked and dirty. Already his shoes needed a new shine. His famous spotless spats were a pasty grey, above which he watched for a moment several black coal flecks hover and then comfortably imbed themselves. His clothes needed brushing and pressing and he could feel fresh soot on his derby rim as he adjusted it to its proper angle. Soot like a non-melting black snow! It stuck to his fingers. What a place!

With hardly a glance about, he followed Orloff into the "office" of the "parlors." Here there was a smell of stale tobacco and stale beer. The unmistakable click of pool balls came from an adjoining rear room.

"My billiard parlor," said Orloff. "If you have some time to kill, make yourself at home there. It's twenty-five cents an hour."

So in Coaltown you came in at the same door to shoot a game of pool or bury your dead! Or you could combine these activities.

Dunnigan seldom bargained. Ever since he had been successful enough to be "in the money" he had paid for what he wanted without question—even if he knew the charge was exorbitant. "Keep the change" was his financial slogan. But when his anger was aroused he could be as close as any man. Also, paying the father's bill had been an unexpected, forgotten liability. He had to watch the bank roll or he would run out of cash.

He knew very well that the one hundred and fifty dollars first proposed by Orloff for the meeting of the train at Wilkes-Barre, transportation of the body to Coaltown, the "repose" of the body that night in the funeral parlor, the use of the hearse and one carriage the next day to the church and the cemetery, was an outrageous overcharge. But it took half an hour of haggling to reduce it to one hundred and twenty-five dollars. As he handed over the money Dunnigan insisted on an itemized receipt, marked "Paid in Full." He somehow did not have an implicit faith in the Orloff integrity.

He noted that he had now left in the wallet a hundred and thirty-five dollars.

"I forgot—there'll be a charge for pallbearers," Orloff added, as he handed Dunnigan a finger-marked receipt. "I don't think the deceased has any friends or relatives here. So the pallbearers will have to be paid. Somebody must carry the coffin out of the church and up at the cemetery."

"Well?" said Dunnigan, too disgusted to fight further. Orloff was the master at this sordid business.

"I can get six men to carry the coffin at two dollars a head," said Orloff. "That's twelve dollars. Then they'll have to wear black gloves. They're a dollar a pair—special funeral rate. That makes a total of eighteen dollars."

"You couldn't quite make up the twenty-five dollars, could you?" said Dunnigan, as he again produced his wallet.

"Huh?" said Orloff.

"Skip it," said Dunnigan. "You know what I mean. But we'll argue no further. We'll do it right—pallbearers, black gloves—a complete production." He extracted the twenty-dollar bill, and handed it over. "Keep the two-dollar change," he added. He even felt a repugnance to take money coming from this undertaker's clothing. "That's a tip for your consideration and courtesy."

Orloff pocketed the twenty. For two dollars he should worry about the obvious sarcasm of the last remark!

"But I want a receipt for that also," said Dunnigan. "Mark it, 'for six pallbearers and six pairs of gloves for same, paid in full.'"

"Why sure," said Orloff. If this city wise guy wanted to load up with receipts in exchange for folding money, he was quite welcome.

The undertaker wrote out and handed over another piece of paper. On this one the ink was smeared.

Business triumphantly concluded, Orloff changed his mood. "Have a drink," he smirked, and without waiting for an answer produced a bottle and two glasses from a drawer in his table desk.

"No thanks," said Dunnigan. "Thanks just the same." He felt the need of a drink, but not with Mr. Orloff.

"Suit yourself," said Orloff, and poured a shot and sipped it slowly. He was pleased with himself. He had collected an old account he had considered lost. He had extracted all the traffic would bear (he craftily surmised) from this stranger. A home-town customer would have paid fifty dollars for a similar job. His cleverness filled him with a pleasant sense of accomplishment. He guessed Dunnigan didn't have much more money left in his wallet, probably just about enough to take care of the "church part" of the arrangements. He hoped Dunnigan didn't think *that* was free! He mentioned it now, as his customer was placing the two receipts in his wallet.

"You'll have to arrange with the priest about the plot at the cemetery, and the grave digging and the burial service. That's their graft. I just deliver to the graveside and lower in. What church was it you said you wanted?"

Dunnigan once more consulted his notebook. That ridiculous long name again! "St. Michael the Archangel," he repeated wearily.

"Good," said Orloff. "You've picked the right one for this deceased. They'll do it cheapest. They need the money." He finished his drink and poured another. "It's across the street, down the block a little. The wooden one that needs painting. Father Paul is the priest's name. A poor sap. No business ability. His church falling to pieces. Spends his time praying, I guess, and visiting sick women. Doesn't know how to hustle for the dough."

A third drink from the bottle was putting the undertaker in a jovial and communicative mood. He continued, though he had to retain his listener by a hand on the arm. "Now take Father Spinsky up the street. The big brick church. There's a go-getter! Made friends with the mineowners. They live in Cleveland but come here once a year. Got them to put in a new organ last time. Preaches sermons about working hard and being happy with your lot. Ha, ha! A smart guy! You'd have to pay double if you were dealing with him! Yes—Father Paul's the right place for you——"

Bill Dunnigan clenched his fists, then slowly unclenched them. He had stood about all he could from this man, but he must not lose control.

"The hotel is where?" he asked.

"Two doors down. Has a veranda in front. 'The Wyoming Hotel' painted on a sign. Want me to introduce you there?"

"No, thanks. I'll find it. I'll leave my suitcase here, however, while I see the priest, if you don't mind. Where is the coffin now?"

"In the parlor. That's what you're paying for. Want to see it?"

"Yes."

Orloff got up and opened a door. Another dingy room that faced the street, but the blinds were drawn. Bill had picked up his suitcase and placed it by the box that stood on a long stand against the wall. The coffin was still in its shipping case of plain wood. He felt that his suitcase would keep it company while he was gone. That Olga Treskovna would know she had at least one friend in this dreadful town.

"I'll take the coffin out of the box," said Orloff.

"Let it stay as it is," said Dunnigan, "until we remove it to the church." He had a feeling that the more protection the girl had around her in Orloff's place the better.

"You're the boss," said Orloff with an indifferent upturn of his hands. "It won't cost you any extra. Of course, usually friends want to come here to pay their last respects to the deceased and leave flowers, but in this case I don't think we'll be bothered." A new, lucrative thought occurred to him. "Now if you want any flowers—that's another thing I forgot—I can provide them for whatever you can afford to spend——"

"No flowers," said Dunnigan. "Would you mind now just leaving me here alone?"

"Make yourself at home. And this evening don't forget—if you want to shoot some pool—or perhaps you don't play pool——"

The look on Bill Dunnigan's face was not a pleasant one. Mr. Orloff decided not to press the question. "I've got to put my hearse in the garage," he said, and withdrew.

Dunnigan stood by the long box that was the abode of Olga Treskovna. He touched it with his hand. He looked at the bare walls of the room. The horrible, faded wallpaper was broken only

by a small cross nailed just above where the coffin stood. There was
a framed motto on another wall, but it was in Polish and he could
not read it. It should read "Cash in Advance," he thought. But
he felt a little better just to be near her—alone with her.

"I love you, kid," he said suddenly. "It isn't much good to tell
you that now—but maybe you can hear me. Maybe you knew it all
along. We just didn't get the breaks, kid. You and me. Your star
went back on you. My luck ran out. But I'm still here, kid. I'll
get you out of this joint tomorrow and into that church, and then
where you wanted to be. I'll fight these Coaltown bastards—they
shan't gyp you out of *that*—they shan't hurt you any more! Coaltown shan't hurt you any more!"

And it seemed to Bill that he could see her, not in that pine-cased
box, but as she looked the time they really met—that second time—
smiling—lovely—and he lived over in a few seconds an evening
that had been burned into his memory.

6

*I*T HAD HAPPENED about two years after he
had first seen her in New York. Christmas Eve. In a certain mid-
dle-west metropolis that shall be nameless.

Dunnigan arrived in late afternoon. He was out "in advance" of
a trans-continental tour of his great revue, which was scheduled to
play that city for two nights the second week of January.

He arrived to find the local theater closed tight, having no attraction to offer that week. The manager himself was not even in
town. A bachelor, he lived at the hotel where Dunnigan registered,
and the advance agent was informed he had gone to the country to
spend the holiday with his mother. No telephone there.

The men in the city's two newspaper offices were strangers. This
was one city in which Dunnigan did not have a single friend, or at
least one friendly acquaintance.

Such work as he could do, visiting the papers and arranging his
railroading, he soon finished. He returned to the hotel.

The hotel seemed deserted. Even the usual downstairs gathering of traveling salesmen was missing. Apparently they had planned to be home on this day of days to be spent at home.

Dunnigan found himself the lone occupant of the solemn row of chairs in front of the solemn row of brass spittoons in the lobby. Brass spittoons, though decorative and companionable, were not good conversationalists, and the desk clerk, bitter that he had to work on Christmas Eve, had decided also to wrap himself in a mantle of silence. Even the always-dependable-for-a-chat girl at the newspaper and cigar counter had closed up shop at eight o'clock and gone to the bosom of her family.

Dunnigan left the hotel and started on a walk about the town. Late shoppers hurried past, friendly of face, but not for him. There was a civic tree in the main square, but its blaze of light seemed a mockery. He thought of his own Times Square and the Astor Bar! Half a hundred friends in every block! The warm-blooded city of hotels and restaurants and theaters.

This place boasted that it was a "city of homes." In fact, that was its motto. Dunnigan cursed this midwestern city. No one but a homeless man can understand the utter loneliness of a stranger on Christmas Eve in a "city of homes."

Two motion-picture "palaces" and one theater were still open. The theater was a burlesque house, according to the legend on its flickering electric sign. Dunnigan did not care for the tawdriness of burlesque. He had seen too much of it when he'd earned his salary from promoting its wares, but he cared less for the "double features" of the picture palaces. He bought a ticket and entered the burlesque theater. At least he would find there live actors behind real footlights! Not canned music—canned emotions.

He hardly had seated himself in the half empty orchestra before he saw her. She stood on the stage well down front, backed by the usual line of dancing girls, and she was singing a song.

His heart beat faster the moment he recognized her. She radiated that same sad beauty that had struck him so forcibly when he'd glimpsed her for the first time at the Venus Burlesque Theater on Forty-Second Street; but now she didn't look undernourished, nor was she awkward and unsure of herself.

Instead of that ill-fitting, cheap playsuit, she wore a daring, clinging gown of satin and rhinestones that accentuated her slender figure. Her eyes were made up now with mascara and shadow, and her painted lips were full and red. For a moment Dunnigan's heart sank —had she become a strip-tease girl?—but knowing his burlesque and sizing up her "spot," he decided she had not. She was the soubrette —the singer of songs who filled out the tableau numbers, the girl who acted as a foil for the comedians in the sketches.

The words of her song were pretty cheap, almost vulgar, and soon she was joined by a loose-trousered comedian who added to their vulgarity by suggestive postures and grimaces. But the girl was neither cheap nor vulgar. Even the comic could not make her so. She managed to give to the song a certain distinction—what Dunnigan called "class."

"The child has talent!" he thought. And then, "Poor little kid!"

He looked at the program to discover her name. His third-girl-from-the-end had a somewhat unusual name. Olga Treskovna.

"Nice name too!" thought Bill. He decided she was Russian.

He watched her through the entire performance. She played her part competently in several sketches. She sang two other songs. She was not rough enough for the complete pleasure of most of the audience, but they paid her talent the respect of a quiet listening. Bill Dunnigan got a thrill and a lift of spirits.

After the finale, Dunnigan went around and down a dark alley to the stage door. He scribbled his name on a piece of paper torn from the program and sent it in by a sleepy doorman. A twenty-five cent tip permitted him to wait inside the door as well as pay the messenger. It was growing cold outside; a flurry of snow had started to fall.

She came out more quickly than he expected. The make-up was completely gone from her face and eyes. The same wistful face with the large eyes. Her fur-trimmed coat and hat were in quiet taste. There was no polish on her fingernails. Dunnigan was glad of all that. He had an aversion to theater girls who carried their stage make-up and their stage-dress styles into the street.

"Mr. Dunnigan!" she said, and shyly held out her hand.

She, too, was noticing some things. That the derby hat he quickly removed cut an angle across his forehead. A rakish angle. There was a certain silhouette, framed in the side door of a theater back in New York, that such a derby had helped to make indelible. Bill thought there was a catch in her voice. He took her hand and held it a moment.

It was the first time he was close to her. He discovered that she was more lovely up close than at thirty or forty feet across the footlights. There was character in her face, a sense of proud loneliness in her clear blue eyes, and an alluring ruefulness in the curve of her lips.

"You remember me, kid?" he asked.

"I have remembered you every night in my prayers for two years," she answered. Her voice was low and sincere.

Bill Dunnigan had been remembered before—in curses, in newspaper anecdotes, in barroom stories—but never, so far as he could recall, in prayers! It was a trifle disconcerting.

He tried to turn it off with a laugh. "I guess you learned how to pivot that day in New York."

"If I hadn't, I would have had to learn how to live without eating!" she replied. "In fact, I *was* learning. I hadn't eaten for two days when you helped me that morning. I was just a little weak in the legs." She smiled.

Bright sunlight, it seemed to Dunnigan, sunlight and then shadow, for her face had a curious Slavic sadness. Gee! It was good to see her again! But he spoke of a practical matter.

"Speaking of eating, we're going to eat now," he exclaimed. "That is, if you are free. I'm not cutting in on some boy friend? No? Had your Christmas Eve dinner yet? No? Good! I don't know what we can find open at midnight in this locked-up burg, but we can try. You've saved my life, kid, you sure have! I was going batty from loneliness!"

Dunnigan's fears about dinners at midnight in that town were well founded. The hotel dining room was closed. The chef had gone home. The Palace Restaurant was closed. The Childs Restaurant had been closed since early afternoon. For this was a city of Christian homes.

Wait. There was still a light in Ming Gow's Chinese Restaurant on the second floor of a building across from the hotel. "Open All Night" was printed boldly on the window. Blessed words for two strangers seeking feasting and a little happiness on the eve of the birthday of Him who died to bring happiness into a locked-up, selfish world.

It remained for a "heathen Chinee" to bring that Christian feast and happiness to Olga Treskovna and Bill Dunnigan.

Ming Gow was a gentleman of the old school—a school that dated back five thousand years. One might venture to say that he was more of a gentleman than the president of the local Board of Trade (and the First National Bank) who had ruled that all public eating and drinking places owned by members of the "Association" must close on Christmas Eve—out of respect for the "sacred character" of the day.

Ming Gow was not a member of the exalted "Association." He was not even a Christian. He followed the ancient faith of his ancestors. So he remained open, in heathen ignorance of his impiety.

And he quickly understood the need of two strangers who knocked at his gate this Christ Day Eve, understood it not as a tradesman, but as one gentleman understands another, in spite of the language in which that need was expressed by Bill (White Spats) Dunnigan, who was by now out of his dumps and in the finest of press-agent fettle. For at the end Ming Gow refused, obdurately refused, to accept payment for his fare.

"Listen, old boy," Dunnigan said to the elderly Oriental, who always greeted his guests just inside the door at the top of the flight of steep stairs, "we are damned aliens like yourself, far from the homeland and the festive board of our fathers! We seek sustenance —in simpler words, food or grub. But not just ordinary grub. We look for a meal that will bring a glow to the heart and a thrill to the soul, as well as a mere filling of the belly! For know you, this is Christmas Eve, and not a damn Christian place is open in this Christian city of this Christian land of America the free! You alone, out of all the citizens of this town, burn the welcoming lamp in your window. You alone, by the insignia on your glass banner yonder, indicate that the yule log is blazing inside for any who shall enter at this hour! We accept your hospitality. We are here! Do you get me, kid? Can you do the trick? A Christmas Eve dinner de luxe!"

The solemn face of Ming Gow lit up with a broad smile. He took an immediate liking to this tall stranger in the plaid suit and the black derby at an angle. He liked the honest Irish eyes that looked straight into his. He liked the girl with the man—the girl who reminded him of a lotus flower. And he appreciated the speech of introduction, for he had been a diligent student of the curious American language for the ten long years since he had arrived from China.

"Cast aside your fears. Leave it all to me," Ming Gow said in perfect English. "I welcome you to my poor restaurant that is also my home. Please to consider that for tonight it is your home also. Be seated. Do not, I ask you, take up that printed bill-of-fare. I remove it. Such trash is not for you. Never before in America have I had guests after my own heart—guests who placed themselves at my feet. I humbly place myself at yours. I myself retire to prepare what you shall eat. I will try not to disappoint. I believe I can do—as you say—the trick."

And what a meal it was! Two servants brought forth and spread over the imitation-marble table-top a fine linen cloth embroidered with dragons and strange flowers. Ming Gow himself served them a cocktail, which was a concession to America, but it was unusual with fruit juices and the white of an egg added to its base of carioca rum.

Then the servants brought a soup brewed in a melon with lotus seeds and bits of chicken and ham and stuffed noodles. Then came an entrée of walnuts and shrimps in a casing of crusty flakes that melted to the tongue. Then spareribs of pork with a luscious sauce that had the fragrance of rare incense. Roast duck came next, the meat rich autumn-brown outside and tender and juicy beneath, all swimming in a sauce sprinkled with almonds. Fried rice appeared with this, and snow peas, and mushrooms, and hearts of bok choy. And for dessert, fresh pineapple in a wine sauce, and a preserve of ginger and melon and golden limes held captive for a year in honey.

So the two of them sat there in Ming Gow's Chinese Restaurant in a town they had never seen before and would never see again, eating and drinking on the blessed Eve of the Christ Mass; and it had seemed to Dunnigan that he felt warmer and friendlier and happier than ever before in all his life. They didn't talk much at first; they merely sat close together across the narrow table and concentrated on the wondrous food. And were content with all the world. Just as if they had known each other for years. But toward the end of the feasting they began talking of many things.

And then—between the spareribs and the roast duck—a startling idea occurred to Bill (White Spats) Dunnigan. It was such a startling idea that he felt his breath coming short. Was he in love with this girl out of burlesque, this girl whom he had seen only once before? Was he in love for the first time in his life—and was Olga Treskovna to be the woman?

-- *7* ----------

*I*T REALLY DIDN'T HAPPEN all at once. Looking back, Dunnigan realized the thought must have germinated when he had first laid eyes on her in the Forty-Second Street Venus Burlesque Theater. That's why her face had appeared before him on trains and in planes. And the germ, never entirely dead, had stirred to life when he touched her hand in the backstage hallway of that other midwest burlesque house an hour earlier.

And now it was blossoming in his mind, full-grown and developed, and Dunnigan was assailed by exhilaration and bewilderment.

He had learned a little about her. "You are Russian?" he had asked.

"No. Polish. That is, my father and mother were Polish. I was born in America. A little mining town in Pennsylvania that I'm sure you've never even heard of!"

"I don't believe there is a town in America I haven't been in," said the theater press agent.

"Then I will spoil your ever making that boast again," laughed the girl. "I'm sure you were never in Coaltown."

"Coaltown?"

"You see, I'm right! It's really there. But it isn't even a one-night stand!"

"I've been in Wilkes-Barre and Scranton. That's coal country. They used to be grand three-day engagements."

"You were very near my home then. It lies south and west of them. Off in the hills. I love the hills. Don't you?"

"I'm afraid I don't know much about them, except that they're hard on the knees when you have to climb 'em in cities like Albany and San Francisco! I was born in New York. I'm just a city guy.

Get more of a kick out of tall buildings than mountains. Know mountains mainly by the rough ride they give you when you have to travel them on a sleeper jump. But tell me—born way out there in those hills, how in the world did you ever get onto the stage of a burlesque theater in Forty-Second Street! Whatever made you want to 'go on the stage,' as they say?"

"I didn't exactly want that at first," she said. "I didn't even know about theaters! But I did want to give something worth-while to the world—something beautiful and clean and good—for everything I knew seemed the other way round. You must smile to hear this from the soubrette of Max Weinstock's Star and Garter Show. But I don't consider that I'm even 'on the stage' yet."

"But why, then——"

"Why did I pick burlesque? For an economic reason, I think you'd say. I'd heard the almost unbelievable story that girls in burlesque earned twenty-five dollars a week! That seemed a fabulous fortune when you were earning twenty dollars a month, even if your meals were thrown in."

"Twenty dollars a month?"

"As a waitress in a counter-restaurant in Wilkes-Barre. You see, I didn't make the jump direct from Coaltown to Broadway, or rather to Forty-Second Street. I guess that wouldn't have happened ever!"

"Even Abraham Lincoln made a stop at Springfield, Illinois, on his way from a log cabin to Washington!" commented Dunnigan. And they laughed happily.

"When I was a girl in Coaltown," she continued, "I thought I'd write—write songs and poetry about the hills. But my father died. My mother had died when I was born. I didn't have a relative in all America. I didn't want to work picking coal at the Breaker any more. The other girls in town already called me 'the Breaker Girl' because I worked there after school. You see, I couldn't always get the black dust out of my fingernails. Sometimes it even stuck behind my ears!"

"You mean as a child you worked down in the coal mines!"

"Not down in the mine. The Breaker is the outside part of it. The great black building that sticks up above all mining towns, into which the coal ore is poured and crushed and sorted. I got ten cents an hour. Oh, that was a lot of money, and I didn't mind. Ex-

cept on a June day sometimes, when I wanted to walk in the woods.
We were very poor. My father was—not well—some of the time.
Groceries had to be paid for. Even coal in winter. We had to buy
that from the Company. And while I could go barefoot in summer,
I had to buy shoes in the winter."

"I shouldn't have thought your father would let you work in
this Breaker!" exclaimed Dunnigan. It was then that the thought
staggered him. Was he in love with this girl? Why else this intense concern that she had worked for ten cents an hour in a coal
"breaker" at a time that he was making two hundred dollars a week!
Why this absurd resentment that he had not known her *then,* so
that he could have protected her!

He stopped eating. He swallowed hard. He had never been in
love with a woman. He was forty years old. There had, of course,
been women in his life. Romances—in the easy way of a gypsy existence. A dozen assorted blondes and brunettes and redheads. But
he had never for one instant imagined he was in love.

He had never concerned himself about the meaning and the texture of love. That was something that happened to other people
and usually brought them trouble in plenty! It was a "situation"
used by playwrights—hokum to stir audiences.

Maybe it really existed! What exactly was love? And why did
he wonder if he loved Olga Treskovna?

"My father didn't exactly like me to work in the Breaker," the
girl was saying rather wistfully. "But what else could I do in Coaltown and still go to school, and earn as much as three dollars a
week? Sometimes more! Oh, father had some fine qualities. He
could play beautiful music on his accordion that he brought from
the old country. He must have known a hundred Polish songs!
Some of them I've never heard anywhere else. I know most of them
too.

"Someday—if I can really study singing—I will give a recital of
Polish songs. When I was working in New York, I used to walk up
to Carnegie Hall late at night after our midnight show, and I'd
stand and imagine my name was on one of the billboards outside:
'Olga Treskovna—In Her Yearly Recital of Polish Folk Songs.' I
even planned the kind of dress I would wear—a peasant dress that
was my mother's—it was Poland's colors, red and white—my father
had a picture of her wearing it. Oh, she was beautiful! But it was

all foolish of me, wasn't it? Imagine me famous enough to give a recital in Carnegie Hall!"

"Not at all," Dunnigan said. The girl was surprising him with every new statement. "Maybe someday your name *will be* on the billboard at Carnegie Hall. And on other halls. But what did your father do besides sing these Polish songs?"

"Oh, he was a miner. All the men in Coaltown are miners. Except the men who run saloons. It wasn't too bad a trade, if father had been—been well. But there were times when he didn't bring home any 'pay.' The Company paid every two weeks. But these songs—there was a lovely one about a dying Polish soldier." Olga Treskovna hummed a strange Slavic melody.

Dunnigan stopped eating entirely and stared at her while she hummed the song. He sure liked the way she looked, the rueful curve of her lips, the throaty sincerity in her voice. All the tragedy and glory of the plains of Poland were in that voice. And it crossed his mind—was it artistry—talent—the old theater hokum that made him think he loved the woman he had met by chance only for the second time? Could that be it? Nonsense. He had listened to the greatest and they'd left him cold.

She finished humming the melody and smiled at him. Shadow and sunlight!

"That's beautiful," Dunnigan said. "I guess your talent as a singer would have drawn you sooner or later into the theater."

"I love music," she said. "I learned to play my father's accordion a little when I was hardly big enough to hold it. How he would laugh at me! I want to study it someday. I'd like to play the violin too. I don't think I could ever sing really greatly, but maybe I could make a violin sound like a great human voice.

"Or to be able to play an organ! There was a good pipe organ in my church in Coaltown. I went to Mass sometimes three or four times on Sunday, just to hear it. I found out when the organist practiced at night, and I'd sit on the church steps and listen. The organist was a blind woman. I thought if a blind person could learn to play, surely I could learn!

"The other girls preferred to listen to the juke-box music that came from the saloons. They would dance to it on the sidewalks. I guess I wouldn't have had such a trouble holding that job on Forty-Second Street if I had practiced with them!"

"How did you get to New York?" Dunnigan asked.

"The restaurant where I worked in Wilkes-Barre was near the old Wilkes-Barre Theater. It didn't get many plays by that time. But it booked burlesque two days a week. The girls from these shows came to the restaurant to eat. One of the girls took a liking to me. She had come from a small town, also, and was homesick. I got to know her. She gave me her name, and told me to look her up if I ever came to New York."

"And so you came."

"I had saved a few dollars. I didn't like the work in the restaurant. I didn't like the dirty dishes. And my boss. He began to notice me when his wife wasn't around. He was fat and ugly, and his hands were never quite clean. He frightened me. One night I just left. Put my three dresses in a bundle and took the midnight bus for New York.

"I couldn't find the girl who had given me her address. It was a little hotel off Times Square. She really lived there, but was away on the road. So I started to look for one of those marvelous twenty-five-dollar-a-week jobs! I went only to the burlesque theaters. Funny, I was afraid to go to any of the others. Just knowing that burlesque girl made me feel that I knew burlesque!

"Some of them wanted new girls, but not girls without experience. I could sing a little, but the dancing broke me. You saw yourself what happened when I got to that part! Never before had I gotten as far as the rehearsal line. I lied to your friend, the Venus dance director. I told him I knew dancing. I was desperate. My money had been gone for several days. The hotel manager told me that morning I would be locked out of my room unless I paid him or had a job. I simply had to get work!

"I was too proud to go back to Wilkes-Barre. It would have been a long walk, anyway! I thought I would have to try New York counter-restaurants where maybe I could hold a job without dancing experience! And perhaps the New York dishes wouldn't be so dirty! Then you saved my 'career.'"

Olga Treskovna smiled again. When she really smiled, it was radiant.

Dunnigan stared at her. Not at her eyes now—eyes could deceive —but at her firmly-rounded chin and her lips which seemed to express everything he valued in life. Pride, humble pride; honesty;

courage. No woman's lips could be curved like that unless she had experienced days of proud loneliness and deprivation which she had yet accepted good-naturedly; unless her mind had known bitterness and yet was not twisted by knowing it; unless she had sought out for herself the true values of life, and yet had developed no cynical worldliness in discovering them. It occurred to Dunnigan that never before—except for his mother—had he really listened to a woman talk.

Bill Dunnigan was an East Side slum boy with the instincts of a gentleman.

His relationship with women had always been courteous and respectful. He extended his considerateness even to the worst of them, "just because they were women," as gentlemen of an older day used to say. When Dunnigan saw a woman drunk, it was not funny. For reasons he never analyzed, an intoxicated woman always hurt something deep inside him. But women's innumerable monologues—the "stories of their lives"—had impressed him as little as the overtures preceding countless performances of his girl-studded musical shows. Now he was listening to a woman with desperate attentiveness, as though his life hung on each word.

What had come over him?

He pulled his thoughts back to their conversation—that "career" which her tone indicated was not yet setting the world on fire.

"Well, it *is* a career, kid," he said. "Don't you make light of it. You're leading numbers already, and only in it a year! I've known girls, talented girls, to work in shows for five years, and still not get a break. And when they did get that break they couldn't always make good. But what do you want to do next? Where do we go from leading numbers for Max Weinstock?"

"I want to get out of burlesque," Olga Treskovna said. "Oh, I'm not ungrateful for the work. And for the start it's given me, and the experience. But I've been studying. I've read everything I could find about acting. I've just finished Stanislavsky's book, *My Life In Art*. Have you read it?"

"I've heard about Art," Dunnigan laughed, "but I'm afraid I've never gone in much for it."

"Now you're laughing at me. And making light of *your* career. You are an artist. I've found out all about you, Mr. Dunnigan.

They say you're the best press agent in America—perhaps in the world."

"Nonsense. Anyway, there's not much art in it. Just luck, kid. I've had the breaks—hit shows. And I'm not laughing at you. You're on the right track. You're studying. I never studied. Just read the newspapers. And the dictionary. Found I had to learn more words than I knew when I got into this trade."

"I want to go to California," Olga Treskovna said. "And I'll get there now, I think, for our company is headed west. I want to try for pictures. I photograph better than I look."

"You're not especially hard on the eyes now," Dunnigan said.

"Oh, I'm not a raving beauty. I know that. But I've learned how to make up for the stage lights. I've bought books on that. Our company manager complains about the extra trunk I carry full of books! I've worked on pantomime. And with my voice. I've learned many roles in a lot of plays I've bought. When I had no money to buy books, I went to the public library and read them there. If I get that chance I want to be ready. I want to know how to pivot next time, if the director wants a pivot!"

They both laughed.

"Gee, kid," Dunnigan said. "I think you've got what it takes. That library stuff reminds me. I was once out ahead of Otis Skinner. That's about the nearest I ever got to Art. They hired me, I guess, because the play was about a bullfighter. Figured my circus experience would fit in. I'd just been out for Barnum and Bailey for two summer seasons. And I had a talk with this chap Skinner before I went on the road. He was regular. A great artist, but no 'art' when he met you man to man. 'How did you get to be a star?' I asked him. 'I had no competition as a young fellow,' he said. 'What do you mean by that?' I asked. 'I studied my parts,' he said. 'No matter how small they were, I went home from rehearsals and studied. I went to the library and studied. I went to the East Side and studied, if it was an East Side character. I went out into the country on Sundays and studied, if it was a country boy. I started in lurid melodramas and cheap farces—*The Maniac Lover* and *Slasher and Crasher* were the names of two of the masterpieces—but I secretly learned every Shakespearean role. No one else studied. They left their work in the theater. I guess I was a damn nuisance with all my studying, but I was determined to make good at my business!'

"And that lad sure did!" Dunnigan added.

"I want to make good too!" Olga Treskovna repeated. "There is a reason why I want to make good quickly. As quickly as I can."

Dunnigan looked into her eyes this time. A deeper shadow seemed to cross them for a fleeting moment.

"You can't be more than twenty-one! You've lots of time."

"I'm twenty. But there isn't time for the long years the regular stage usually takes," the girl said.

He wondered what she meant, but he did not ask. If she wished to tell him, she would.

She sensed his question. It seemed to Dunnigan she hurried on, as if to forget that phase of the subject. "I like pictures. I see all the movies I can. I study them. I go back to the hotels and act out scenes in front of the mirror—if the room has one! A bellboy once saw me and reported I was crazy. But I don't care. Do you like pictures?"

"I hate 'em," Dunnigan said with characteristic honesty. "But don't let that discourage you. There are a hundred million on your side. Only I don't know much about that business. I don't know any picture producers. Maybe I could help if I did—give you a letter or something. I wish I could help."

"Hating pictures as you do, I think you did your share!" she said. "For when I'm a great film star and they ask me to whom I owe my success, I'll say: To William Dunnigan, who spoke up and said, 'Give the kid a break,'—who made me believe that somebody cared in a unanimously non-caring world."

Dunnigan was embarrassed, for the girl spoke very seriously at the end. "Nonsense," he said. "Someone else would have helped you. You rated help—and when you rate help, you get it."

"Not always. There were plenty of times I needed help badly and there wasn't anyone like you for miles around! But we've only talked about me. What about you? I don't mean your work. My world knows all about that. I got my first chance at a number because somebody remembered that I was believed to be 'a friend of Bill Dunnigan.' Who—who is your best girl? What is she like? Is she your wife? Have you children, maybe?"

Dunnigan laughed. "Gee, kid, I'm not married. No children.

No best girl even. Know too many in my business, I guess. Found they smiled only when they wanted something. And I never met one who could measure up to my mother. She took in washing to put me through grade school—and a year in high school. I wasn't born in any palace either. A tenement on Houston Street. That's in New York's East Side. It was my *dad* who kicked off about the time *I* was born. I guess he hadn't been much good to my mother anyway. But we'll skip that. My mother was the real McCoy."

"They say boys are usually like their mothers. I think your mother must have been grand," Olga Treskovna said.

"She died after she got me through that high school term. I didn't realize how hard she'd been working—washing in the daytime, cleaning offices in a skyscraper at night. Oh, I worked, too, after school. Sold newspapers. Opened cab doors in front of theaters for tips. That was the start of *my* theatrical career. But I never should have let my mother work that way. She wanted me to be a priest! Some fine priest I would have made!"

"I think you would have made a very fine priest. Only I guess it was lucky for me you became a press agent instead. There are a lot of priests, but there seems to be only one William Dunnigan in this world." She spoke the words almost as if to herself.

Dunnigan reddened. His ruddy face, hardened from twenty years on the road, was actually blushing! He hadn't blushed since his teacher in the Third Grade complimented him publicly for keeping his shoes shined—a "sissy" business in the view of his fellow students of the male sex, aged eight to ten. He'd had to soundly lick four of the biggest ones to prove his manliness.

Olga Treskovna sat across from him, her eyes downcast, sensing that her words had unexpectedly affected him. In that moment of silence, Dunnigan thought that he no longer wondered if he loved Olga Treskovna. He thought he knew that he did. This was it— at last. They were meant for each other. He must tell her.

But Ming Gow suddenly appeared. While they were finishing their meal, he had changed from his simple smock to a long, ceremonial garment of great beauty—his finest dress. All green and gold it was. And in his hands was an earthen flask of rare brandy, a rice brandy more than fifty years old.

"May I humbly offer you this, my new friends," he said, "as a token of my pleasure in serving you?"

Olga Treskovna seemed relieved that Ming Gow had come. Should she have spoken to the great Bill Dunnigan as she had? Did he—the thought disturbed her—did he understand her simple sincerity? Her months of gratitude?

"You must sit and drink with us!" she suggested to Ming Gow.

"But please—" Ming Gow smiled in embarrassment.

"You bet he'll sit!" cried Dunnigan. He too felt a momentary relief from a too tense urge. He rose quickly and placed another chair from a near-by table. Ming Gow was shy, but he was pleased. He also had been a lonely man.

At his gesture, the servant brought three slender, crystal-clear glasses. Ming Gow opened the flask and poured out the liquid nectar.

"And you must propose the toast," said Olga Treskovna to him.

Ming Gow raised his glass. "To this new land that has given me peace," he said, "to the excellent United States of America—to my old land that gives me memories—my beloved China—may they always be friends as we are friends. And to you, Madam, your good health and success—and a Merry Christmas to all of us!"

They touched their glasses and drank.

Looking at these two men, in garb and background from the opposite ends of the earth, Olga Treskovna had an eery feeling that they were not unlike two of the Wise Men who came together outside a little town in Palestine nearly two thousand years before, that very Night. She felt that she was being permitted to watch a miracle—that there was Another Presence there—in this Chinese restaurant in a very modern town in Iowa.

The spell was broken, and yet not broken, when the Man from the East would take no payment for his wonder feast, and the Man from the West pulled out his pass book, and wrote complimentary tickets for the opening of his musical show that was to come in a couple of weeks. The exchange of gifts! Each giving of his very best. The girl found herself thinking—and it seemed no irreverence—that the Presence would also attend Dunnigan's "girl show" with Ming Gow that special night. Both as the Guests of a clean, unselfish man who was now really her friend.

They said good-by to Ming Gow, and Dunnigan followed Olga Treskovna down the stairs of this Chinese restaurant, feeling more excitement than he had ever felt in his life. He must hold Olga

Treskovna close to him and tell her that he adored her. There was not a moment to be lost. He must tell her at once, on this night, in this strange city.

And yet the instant they struck the clear, crisp night air, placed feet on the snowy sidewalk, doubts clouded his mind. He had been under a spell in Ming Gow's restaurant, an unreal spell that made him a different fellow from the one he knew he really was. Walking with her along the deserted streets to her hotel, some distance from his, he saw himself as he *really* was—Bill "White Spats" Dunnigan, rough theatrical press agent; forty years old; cynical, whiskey-drinking; his home a suitcase, his future a week-to-week salary check.

What right had he to speak of love to such a girl! She was so much finer than he—she had her career ahead. What happened when honorable people spoke of love. They got married. They had children. They settled down in a home. If they didn't have a home, the marriage usually went bust! He had seen plenty of such.

"Pull up your socks, Dunnigan. Think straight!" he said to himself.

"Is anything wrong, Mr. Dunnigan?"

"I beg your pardon?"

"You seem so silent," she said.

"I'm sorry. I was just thinking."

They were crossing an empty square. The night had cleared. The sky overhead was sprinkled with bright stars.

Olga Treskovna stopped suddenly and looked up. Dunnigan paused and wondered what she saw.

"Up there," she pointed, "is *my* star. That very bright one the color of a rose. I can always find it because it's near that V-shaped cluster. As a little girl I picked it out above Coaltown. It was above New York too. It's up there now, over this town. It follows me about, you see! I like to think that star has picked me out from all the people in the world to guide to success! Do you think I am very selfish and very foolish to believe that?"

"I think you are very wise for your years," said Dunnigan. "When I was your age, I didn't have the slightest idea what it was all about!"

Did he still?—he meditated.

They walked again in silence. They reached her hotel, a less expensive one than the place where Dunnigan was staying. They stood for a few minutes in the deserted lobby.

"I'm for you, kid," Dunnigan said. "I think you'll go places sure!" And after an awkward pause, "Well—I suppose this is 'Hail and Farewell.' I heard that in a play. You're going West in the morning. I'm going East. That's this show business! Let me know how you make out. If I can ever help, I'm at the other end of the nearest Western Union. The Ziegfeld Theater will always get me. Sorry I don't know more about the picture game. But if you change your mind and come back to the big town, I could help you get a better job there, I think."

"You're just like I thought you'd be," Olga Treskovna said. She started to tell him about her vision of the Wise Men and the Presence, but she stopped. Surely he would think it silly.

Instead, she said: "I'm glad I couldn't pivot that day, or tonight wouldn't have happened! My star is taking care of me."

"It always will," he said.

She shook his hand. "I'm really a friend of yours now. That's true, isn't it, Mr. Dunnigan?"

"My name is Bill to my pals."

"Good-by, Bill."

"Good-by, kid."

He went quickly. He must get a firm grip on himself. She was all too lovely—the touch of her hand was too electric.

He was not, he *must* not fall, in love. Or try to make her fall in love with him.

Dunnigan knew what their relationship should be.

He believed there was in the human heart a greater and deeper emotion than the thing commonly called love. It was an emotion free of the fierce attraction of body for body, that fateful chemical attraction that led to jealousy and suspicion. It was of the mind and the soul—and the heart too. But the heart part of it was a comradeship of sympathy and understanding.

It might be called friendship. Dunnigan had a better name for it. A stronger name. "Palship."

That was how he must feel toward Olga Treskovna, and how she must feel toward him.

8

*A*ND TO WHAT CONCLUSION had it all now come?

She lay in undertaker Orloff's bare room with the small cross and the Polish motto, and Bill Dunnigan's suitcase was by her side. She was in a friendless place where she was known only as the daughter of Stan Trocki, drunkard.

Was this then the end of star-dreams?

The room had a door opening directly onto the Coaltown street. Dunnigan moved to that door, opened it, and stood looking at this main thoroughfare where Olga Treskovna had walked and breathed as a child.

Again it seemed to him that he was not alone. Again he was holding a hand tightly in his own. The living Olga Treskovna seemed by his side. This was happening as it did in Hollywood, the night she died.

It was about five o'clock in the late afternoon.

The noise of the Breaker first attracted his attention. There it stood—the tall, black building half a block away.

"You see"—it was Olga Treskovna's low, vibrant voice that he heard—"That is it! The ore cars look like swollen ants, don't they, crawling up to its top? There's where I worked as a young girl."

The rumble of the grinding machinery smote Dunnigan's ears with a pulsing, metallic dirge. He could see murky sprays of dark dust issuing from what were apparently narrow windows, placed here and there up and down its straight sides. The whole building was a furnace of black dust stuffed with the choking vomit of the ore cars.

"Good God!" he said. "Good God!"

"—And over there, across the street, is Koepke's Bar and Grill."

Dunnigan knew he was himself reading the tarnished letters of its sign, but Olga Treskovna's voice was still speaking. Raucous "music" suddenly issued from the open door of its shadowy interior, and there was a burst of rough laughter and an oath particularly vile.

"They've got the biggest juke box in Coaltown! Its sides light up with blue and red when it plays. You can see it from here! I would sometimes watch those lights from the sidewalk. I thought they were magical! I should have practiced dancing like the other girls! Then I wouldn't have been such a trouble to you!"

More laughter and another oath from the saloon.

"Kid," he said. "Poor little kid!"

Several women were now trudging past, carrying bundles of supper marketing—women with expressionless, flat faces and flat bodies.

"These are the women of my town—they're not really old—it's the hard life—washing eternally mine-begrimed clothes—cooking over hot coal ranges for big families of hungry men—bearing children—one every twelve months——"

"You would never have looked like them!"

"Oh, yes, I would. They were pretty once. And maybe that's what I should have done. But I got to looking at my star—and dreaming. I wanted to get away and make something of myself. Still, even when I was away, and before I went, I always wanted to come back sometime. I dreamed that maybe I could cheer them up a little with a song—some poetry about the hills——"

"Olga, kid," he said, "I didn't realize. I didn't really know. Why didn't I find you then, my darling!"

"It's all right, Bill," she seemed to say. "You came along at just the right time. And don't mind all this. This is the town. I told you it wasn't nice. But the cemetery—wait till you see the cemetery. It's different. It is beautiful—just as I told you out in Hollywood—you'll see—"

The voice ended. Bill Dunnigan felt his hand relax. She was gone. She was in that coffin behind him in Orloff's "parlor." She lay there with the noise of the Breaker and the blatant tones of the juke box with the red and blue sides pounding against her unhearing ears. He knew that. He had known that all along. But this was where she had wanted to come. This—and the cemetery that went with it—was where she was to spend eternity!

                    *   *   *

The cemetery might be all right, but before he could achieve the cemetery he must go through the ordeal of interviewing another citizen of this miserable place—the priest of Olga Treskovna's church. The church with the ridiculously long name! He could see that church up the street and across the way. "The wooden one that needs painting," Orloff had said, and there it was.

This priest was doubtless another hopeless case—mean, lazy, letting his charges go to the dogs. "A poor sap," Orloff had described him. "Doesn't know how to hustle for the dough." But he would have plenty of financial acumen, Dunnigan surmised, when a stranger appeared—a stranger in city clothes. He'd get all the dough in sight!

Well, he, Bill Dunnigan, would gladly pay. So long as the cash lasted, he'd pay! He wanted no favors from such people. He just wanted to finish with it all and get away. Olga Treskovna would understand that. She'd be nearer to him even back in the Venus Burlesque Theater than here!

Would it have been different if he had taken her in his arms that night when they left Ming Gow's? Taken her East with him (if she would have come), let him care for her, protect her? Would it have been different even if he had answered her letters after that meeting in the midwestern city?

"Stop it!" he said to himself. What was done was done. She had wanted to accomplish certain things. At least she had had her try. And what a try! Even if it ended now in Orloff's Funeral Parlor. She would not have found happiness trouping with a press agent from city to city. Or alone in a hotel room back in New York— waiting—waiting. No. The other way was how it had been fated to be.

He had passed up the street and paused opposite the dozen wooden steps that led up a steep embankment—from the sidewalk on the other side—to the front yard of the Church of St. Michael the Archangel.

It seemed a pathetically small church, perhaps a story and a half high, topped by a triangular roof that met at a point well up above its center. This roof seemed too tall, too heavy—as if a too large hat were pushed down on the head of a fragile man. Being on a plot of raised ground, the building rose quite a bit above the houses that flanked it. It did need painting. Its shingled front was a dirty brown in color. And it seemed to set a little crookedly—to lean—as if it were very weary of it all and wanted rest.

It had wide front double doors. A square bell tower, that rose about as high as the roof ridge, was at the extreme right.

Dunnigan noticed that the cross at the apex of the church roof was clean and painted, as was a small cross above the front doors. The crosses were white. The whole edifice had once been white.

What was obviously the parish house—a two-story frame dwelling, with a narrow, railed veranda along its front—stood farther back on the lawn and at the opposite side of the bell tower. This parish house also needed painting and had a pathetic look of respectable poverty.

Dunnigan noted with some surprise that the grass was well kept, green and trimmed, and there were bright geraniums in the circular flower bed between the church and the parish house. But this—and the clean crosses—were the only touches of healthfulness.

Crossing the roadway, and mounting the rotted and cracked wooden steps (life seemed to him just such a stretch of rickety steps), the "last episode" of Olga Treskovna's career—the last "sequence" in their unique palship—passed (like the motion picture that was a part of it) before his mind.

9

THE EPISODE had commenced more than a year after the dinner at Ming Gow's, for the winter became spring, and another summer and winter intervened. What happened in between is quickly chronicled.

The first week after that Christmas Eve was a battle for Dunnigan. He found himself thinking too often of Olga Treskovna. Every telegraph office that he passed, every telegraph counter in the hotels cried out, "Send her a wire! Tell her what she really means to you!"

Every shining telephone instrument in his hotel rooms beckoned an invitation to ask for "Long Distance" so that he could presently

hear her voice. He was not sure exactly where she was—like himself, she was changing cities every few days—but he knew in a general
way the route of a burlesque company traveling west. He could
have quickly located her, if he had tried.

He had no urge to write. He never wrote letters. Had an almost physical abhorrence of correspondence. He conducted his
business entirely by telephone and wire. He had quit two good
jobs because his bosses wanted letters, complained of his large telephone accounts and two-hundred-word telegrams. He simply
could not be bothered writing to people—hunting for a place not
out of postage stamps—when there was an easier and quicker means
at hand.

Nevertheless, he fought this desire to communicate with Olga
Treskovna. He had made up his mind they were just good friends.
Pals. Pals in his world didn't phone each other every week, every
day. He might not hear from a pal for a whole year. Two years.
That didn't mean they were any the less friendly.

If only he did not feel so damn lonely when he returned to his
room at night. When he ate solitary dinners in the ornate hotel
dining rooms!

He was glad when, several weeks later, he was "home" again
near Times Square. Broadway was not quite so lonely.

There was a letter from her one morning, sent care of the Ziegfeld Theater. He had told her he would be back in New York in
about a month. He held the envelope in his hand and he knew
that his heart was beating faster. He knew the letter was from Olga
Treskovna because her name was written across the name of a San
Francisco hotel printed in the corner of the envelope. He let his
cigar completely burn out as he gazed at it.

He did not open the letter there. He went back to his hotel.
Alone, in his room, high above Broadway, he read it. It was just a
letter of thanks for the Christmas Eve dinner—"You're back in New
York now, and I want to tell you what a happy evening you gave me.
I shall remember it always"—and the further news that she had
given in her notice to leave the burlesque show in Los Angeles and
make that "try for a quick road to fame" in the pictures.

He read the letter over and over. He had never seen her handwriting before. It was a bold, legible, vertical script—strong and

sincere. "Like her," he thought. *She knew what she wanted to do. And she had the guts to tackle it!*

The temptation to put in a call across the continent was almost stronger than he could resist. He picked up his telephone receiver. But he crushed the temptation down. Instead of saying, "Long Distance, please," he ordered a highball. When he went out again, he did stop at the telegraph stand in the lobby and sent her a wire.

"Thanks, kid," he wrote on the yellow paper. "Keep your chin up! I'll be watching for your name on the screen billboards!"

She wrote him again two weeks later, giving him the address of a hotel in Hollywood. She was at last at her geographical goal, "my Mecca," as she said, and was going to start out the next day making the rounds of the picture studios. She sent him a poem she had written "about a girl and a star." "I don't mean that it's me!" she wrote, "for my eyes are blue, I believe. It's just that I get homesick for my hills. The hills that you don't like, because they make your knees tired! I like to imagine things that could happen to imaginary people back there."

Dunnigan read and reread the poem. He read it so many times that he learned it by heart, the only poem he ever committed to memory in his life. This was the poem:

AUSTRA

By Olga Treskovna

Austra—tall and strong and fine,
Somehow like our mountain pine.
Earthborn—but her dark, green eyes
Seemed to look beyond the skies.
"Austra" meant "a morning star"—
Star the Pine Tree loved afar.

Each dawn Austra climbed the tor
Where the Pine Tree loved the Star.
Blue shone in her dark, green eyes—
Blue and gold of morning skies.
There she stood with Tree of Pine—
Tall and strong and mountain-fine.

Mountain skies are thrill-shot blue.
Mountain storms are thrill-shot too.
Thunder bellows at the tor
As the Pine Tree seeks the Star.
Black are Austra's dark, green eyes
As they mirror angry skies.

Angry too the Thunder Lord,
Lightning in his upraised sword—
Envious of the calm, green eyes
Unafraid of storm-torn skies,
Struck them!—standing strong and fine—
Austra and the mountain Pine.

Strangers say she's sleeping there
By her Pine Tree—broken—bare.
Mountain folk have keener sight—
Folk who rise with dawn star-light.
Near the Morning Star they've seen
A new satellite—*dark green!*

Dunnigan did not answer this second letter at all. He really meant to, but he put it off from day to day. He was afraid to answer it. He was afraid to involve himself further with Olga Treskovna. She stirred him too deeply. And he now felt he would only be in her way—if she also came to care.

He knew nothing of "pictures." Olga Treskovna would doubtless make friends in Hollywood who could really help her. He, Bill Dunnigan, would just be a New York stumbling block to her progress—a Broadway millstone about her neck. He *must* kill off this love thing that somehow would not completely die in his heart.

And Olga Treskovna did not write again. She was a little hurt that he did not acknowledge her verse. Was it as bad as that! And —as he afterwards knew—there was nothing of cheer to write him about.

10

*I*N *HIS BATTLE* to forget Olga Treskovna, Dunnigan received some help at this time of an unexpected and tragic sort. The genius-producer of his yearly revue suddenly died. That ended the series. It was a personal blow. Dunnigan was devoted to this man, admired him greatly. They had been closely associated for ten years. He felt pretty bad.

After awhile, when the old office was closed and its affairs wound up, when the famous New York theater was leased to pictures, he went to work for a rival management. And swiftly, in one season, five consecutive musical plays Dunnigan press-agented failed miserably. Three of them did not even get to New York, after expensive, money-losing tryouts.

For years the white-spatted, derby-wearing press man had been considered good luck to any attraction. Bill (White Spats) Dunnigan "out ahead" meant a sure-fire hit. He began to worry. Could it be that fortune had turned thumbs down? Was he—of all people—now becoming that shunned, abhorred pariah of the show world, a "jinx"? He tried to laugh off the thought, but once he started thinking about it, it stuck in his mind.

And he knew that his Broadway associates sensed his worry, even if they never openly spoke of it. Was he, at forty-one, on the toboggan? Through? It might be so. He knew only too well what a fickle jade the theater could be! He knew too many guys who had been on top and were now borrowing quarters for lunch money.

This was the year (and we are now reaching the beginning of that final "episode" that concerned Olga Treskovna) that one of the wonder personages of the motion-picture industry was skyrocketing to fame—in that amazing industry that sometimes made talented impresarios of humble pants pressers.

Marcus J. Harris had left the company he (and his deceased brother) had founded, and of which his name was still a part, and formed his own Super Pictures, Inc., Marcus J. Harris President. His first new independent production, "Gone with the Sunrise," was a tremendous financial and artistic success. Harris, whose humble origin and lack of formal education had been the butt of numerous jokes at first, soon won approval of critics and public. He was a natural artistic and financial genius, with a sure instinct and taste for the best.

Now he was about to launch a second epic venture on his own, a picturization of another best-selling novel, *The Garden of the Soul.* For it, he had engaged and was bringing to America for the first time, the noted Polish actress, Anna Gronka. She spoke English. Harris had seen her in two London-made films. The star role of the new story required a Slavic type.

And Marcus Harris wanted a special publicity campaign for this great foreign star and for what he felt was the finest story he had ever produced. He was dissatisfied with what was being done by his regular staff.

He was told there was one man who could do justice to Anna Gronka and "The Garden of the Soul." The late revue producer's ace press agent, Bill Dunnigan. This press man had made and handled sensationally a dozen great stars. He knew all the tricks and invented new ones. He might bring new angles into the picture game. He might do for the name of Harris what he had done for the name of this musical show producer—and for half a dozen other Broadway figures.

Marcus Harris in Hollywood sent a telegram to William Dunnigan in New York.

Marcus Harris received no answer. He sent a second wire, saying he would be in New York the next week, and requesting Dunnigan to appear at the Super Pictures, Inc., offices in Radio City at eleven-fifteen the following Tuesday morning.

Dunnigan, of course, received both telegrams. The Harris organization did not send wires to wrong addresses. What happened was that the Broadway press agent ignored them!

He simply was not interested, in spite of his worry about whether he was becoming a jinx. As Dunnigan had told Olga Treskovna and most of his friends, he disliked motion pictures. Jinx or no jinx, he would fight it out in his own "legitimate" field.

But Marcus Harris got what he was after, whether it had been

the pants of all the male inhabitants of a certain apartment building, or—in his present business—a story, a star, a press agent. When
Dunnigan did not appear at the august New York offices at the appointed time, Harris telephoned the Dunnigan room at the hotel
where the press agent lived. Dunnigan happened to be in.

"I want you," said Marcus Harris, "to handle Anna Gronka and
my next picture, 'The Garden of the Soul.' You know I want you,
and I know you are disengaged at the moment. So, that being the
case, the only question is, do you start for me today or tomorrow?"

"Thanks," said Dunnigan, and he could not but smile, "but I do
not start at all. I don't like Hollywood. I hate pictures."

"I don't like Hollywood myself," said the imperturbable Harris.
"What is your salary?"

"More than you'll pay," Dunnigan retorted. But he couldn't
help admiring this calm voice that calmly went after what it wanted.
It reminded him of his late employer.

"I ask you, what is your salary?" Marcus Harris repeated quietly.

"Three hundred a week," Dunnigan fired back, raising it one
hundred more than his real fee. That would end the conversation.

"I'll make it four hundred and you started work yesterday,"
Marcus Harris said.

Dunnigan laughed. "Don't be a damn fool!" he said to himself.
To Marcus Harris he said, "You win, boss. I'll be at your office in
an hour. I start work then."

"I don't think I'll still be here in an hour. I have a Wall Street
meeting with my bankers. But go to my publicity department.
They'll expect you. I'll see you later in the day. And Dunnigan——"

"Yes, boss."

"I am sending a messenger with your first week's salary and a
hundred dollars expense money. Wait for it, please."

He hung up.

Dunnigan shrugged his broad shoulders and hung up also. Then
he had a good laugh—at himself. He'd always heard the picture
business was screwy. It sure was! Well, he was in it now. He'd
crossed the Rubicon or the Tiber or whatever the name of that
river was! His word was as good as his bond.

Maybe it would change his luck. You just couldn't turn down a persistent guy like this Marcus Harris. He'd give it a couple of summer months till the regular theater season started.

Incidentally, he was on a spot. He was always on a spot because he had saved no money. That is, he had not saved any sum he considered worthy to be called "money." He lived well and gave freely. The expensive suits and shirts and neckties and shoes would have dented a larger salary. Ten to fifteen Regina Perfectos a day at forty cents each could be quite an item. He was known as an "easy touch." Just before his revue producer had died, Dunnigan had had a lucky afternoon at the race track, and deposited five hundred dollars in a branch of a Dime Savings Bank in a remote section of Brooklyn. "Deposited the money in a foreign country so it will be hard to go and get—it will pay for my funeral," he explained to an intimate. "Don't want them passing the hat when I croak."

Now he was down to that five hundred, and quite healthy! Only yesterday he had dug out the bankbook and put it in his wallet. He did not like the thought of journeying to darkest Brooklyn. The "hated" pictures were saving him *that* hardship!

II

MARCUS HARRIS had an immediate sample of the dynamic bill of goods he had bought in Bill (White Spats) Dunnigan.

When the ace press agent reached Radio City, conscious of five hundred throbbing simoleons lining his impoverished wallet, he did not even ask for Mr. Harris.

"I'm Dunnigan," he announced. "Where's your publicity department?"

He was taken there.

"I want the facts about this Polish dame," he told the gentleman in charge, "and what you've done already. If you've got a brief synopsis of your yarn—what is it?—'The Garden of the Something-Or-Other'—that will help."

The office publicity head was a Harvard graduate. He had been engaged to give a supposedly desirable "literary flavor" to Harris releases. He stared in some amusement at William Dunnigan.

"Madam Gronka, who is to be the star of 'The Garden of the Soul,' arrives tomorrow at eleven from Europe. The French Line. We have covered it thoroughly. Sent out formal notices to every paper."

"O. K., kiddo! Give me half an hour to look at your stuff. I might still have a suggestion or two for covering it," smiled back the cigar-puffing man in the plaid suit and the white spats, with his black derby now pushed to the rear of his head. And he gave the Bachelor of Arts (who had also taken a postgraduate course *cum laude* in "public relations") a hearty, comradely slap on the back.

In exactly half an hour—from the cloud of the second Regina Perfecto going double blast—the hurricane started.

Dunnigan got the Polish Embassy in Washington by long distance. He persuaded the Ambassador himself to fly to New York next morning. It would 'put his country in the news—help cement friendly relations.' (Dunnigan sensed that the Ambassador had always had a secret yen to meet the great Gronka.) Dunnigan next phoned City Hall and talked with his good pal, the Mayor. Certainly! His Honor would be glad to welcome Gronka "officially" at noon, if Bill would bring her to City Hall from the boat. "You know, there's a lot of Polacks in this town!" said Bill. The Mayor knew it, and that they had votes. That gave Dunnigan another idea.

He remembered seeing some of these "Polacks" in the Memorial Day parade, dressed in their picturesque peasant costumes. He located the headquarters of their largest society. 'Could a hundred of them be at City Hall at twelve to welcome a famous countrywoman, meet their Ambassador, as guests of the Mayor? And oh yes—could they wear the grand uniforms in which he'd seen them marching on Memorial Day? And could they bring their band? Wouldn't it be nice to march up Broadway and to the Waldorf for a reception and luncheon in Madam Gronka's honor?'

The voice at the other end was gasping and eager with excitement. 'They certainly could!' Maybe the voice 'could get together two hundred? Could the wives and children come?'

"Why not!" said Bill Dunnigan. "But have all of 'em in those swell costumes. It will make Madam Gronka feel that she is among friends!"

Back to City Hall again, via the ever busy telephone wire, rushed the new Harris press agent to secure the permit for the "parade" and a detail of mounted police to lead it. "A few motorcycles and their sirens to clear traffic would also be appreciated." And to his friend Oscar at the Waldorf: "Hold the grand ballroom and be ready to serve a luncheon to about five hundred. By the way— decorate your joint in whatever the colors of Poland are—you know —where the Polacks come from—and hang out a Polish flag or two over the Park Avenue entrance. Marcus Harris' Super Pictures, Inc., will foot the bill."

Oscar—smiling—knew what to do! He had helped out Bill Dunnigan on short notice before.

Now to the newspapers—the city desks, the dramatic critics, the film critics! The syndicates and the newsreels! Telling each personally what was cooking, and inviting all and sundry, in the name of Marcus Harris, to the Waldorf reception. To the ship news boys at the Battery—he'd have a special tug to go out and meet the incoming French liner at quarantine. The newsreel lads were also invited on this trip, and the staff photographers. A call now to his friend Fred Dalzell, who controlled the tugboat business in the harbor. 'Sure! Dunnigan could have his newest tug! It was a Diesel-engined jim-dandy!'

Meantime, the somewhat groggy Harris publicity staff was rushing page-long telegrams to the innocent editors of every large newspaper in the entire country. Telegrams announcing Gronka's arrival for the new Marcus Harris film, describing the "momentous excitement" in New York over her arrival, the plans for her "official reception"—a glorified summary of the lady's career abroad.

Action! That was exactly what Dunnigan needed to pull him out of his damn slump. He'd show 'em if he was "through"!

Marcus Harris wasn't able to meet his new publicity aid. He had to fly to the Coast the next morning without seeing him. By the time his new boss returned from Wall Street that day, Dunnigan was personally "making" all the newspaper offices, carrying under his arm photographs of Gronka and separately typed and slightly

differing copies of her life history. Turning loose that infectious
Irish smile on the hard-boiled among the editors.

But Mr. Harris read the morning papers before he left. Lengthy
news stories in every one of them. Front page in several. The
Ambassador's coming and the City Hall reception had turned the
trick.

The newspaper boys liked Dunnigan. He had "color." They
had all heard rumbles about the "jinx." There wasn't one of them
but would stretch a point to put him in the running again.

Before he left, Harris did talk with Dunnigan. Called him on
the telephone from his home.

"I've got to leave at nine," he said. "Just learned there is
a chance of borrowing Victor George for our male lead, if I am on
the ground. Can you see me off at the airport in three-quarters of
an hour?"

"Haven't time, boss!" said Dunnigan. "Due at the Battery in
half an hour."

Harris was disappointed but pleased. He, too, liked action in
a business world too often cluttered with big talk and no performance.

"Well, good luck. I leave it in your hands. You seem to be
doing all right with the morning papers. Congratulations! Make
my apologies to Madam Gronka for not meeting her. Bring her
on to the Coast tomorrow if possible. The office will charter a
plane. We've got to start shooting at once. Everything's ready
there, if I can land this leading man."

"O. K., boss," said Bill. "See you in movieland tomorrow night!"

Astute Marcus Harris was still smiling when he boarded his plane.
For his first-week's investment of five hundred dollars he knew he
had already received five thousand dollars' worth of free space in the
morning New York papers. Why hadn't he discovered Dunnigan
before!

And the day had only started!

Gronka's actual arrival was spread through the evening editions.
Illustrated by two and three column group photographs of the star,
the Ambassador, and the Mayor. Pictures, also, of the "welcoming
parade," which included some four hundred stalwart Polish-Ameri-
cans in gala attire.

For Gronka was driven up Broadway and Fifth Avenue behind

screaming, red-lighted police motorcycles, a band, a regiment of her fellow "Polacks." She spoke "to America" on the city-owned radio from the Waldorf. That night she and the Polish Ambassador were the guest stars of a famous coast-to-coast weekly program. Citizens, who neither read newspapers nor listened to the radio, saw sky-writing airplanes scrawling a huge "WELCOME GRONKA" across the noonday heavens—a last thought of Bill's early that morning. Dunnigan passed up no opportunities.

The Harvard graduate of the Harris office moved about in a flustered daze. "Don't mind me helping you a bit, kiddo," said Bill. "You know, we simply can't *sneak* the old gal into the country! It wouldn't be polite! She's temperamental, and her feelings might be hurt!"

The next morning Madam Gronka, her two maids, and Bill (White Spats) Dunnigan were speeding at a hundred and fifty miles an hour in a special plane toward the West Coast film capital. And in Radio City the auditor of Super Pictures, Inc., contemplated a charge of fifteen hundred and eighty dollars from the Waldorf, and nearly eight hundred dollars in Western Union due-bills. The bill for the sky-writing was not yet in.

"I suppose Mr. Harris knows what he's doing!" he said in dubious alarm to Miss Feinberg, the secretary.

"You poor stiff!" replied that lady. "You couldn't buy what Mr. Dunnigan's landed in the papers alone the past two days for a hundred thousand dollars!"

Miss Feinberg was all-out for the new press agent, who was already calling her his "petite passion flower."

One thing disturbed Dunnigan as he sank back in his comfortable plane seat and tried to rest. Gronka did not look unlike Olga Treskovna. She was much older and not so fine of feature. But the resemblance brought back a loneliness that the theater press man had almost succeeded in killing.

"Poor little kid!" He wondered if she were still in Hollywood. What had happened to her? He'd look her up right away.

She'd laugh when she heard *he* was in pictures!

—————————————————————— *12* ——————

THE TRUE ARTIST—and in spite of his denials, Bill Dunnigan was that—finds joy in any creative work. Motion pictures won him over. They had almost won him over in New York, the two hectic days before he boarded the Coast plane. Established in a suite at the Beverly Wilshire Hotel in Beverly Hills, with a fancy office at the Super Pictures Studios, he was, to his surprise, entirely happy about his job.

For the first time, Dunnigan had unlimited money to carry out his ideas. His press releases were sent, not only to newspapers in a single city or state, but to the press of the entire country. To the entire world almost—for the world was the market for a good film. He found many old friends in Hollywood: writers, actors, business managers, who, like himself, had been in the "legitimate." The Brown Derby was not quite as homelike as the Astor Bar, the steaks at Chasen's didn't seem quite as thick as those at his favorite Gallagher's, but like Mercutio's wound, they would suffice.

And there was no further need to worry about being a jinx. These million dollar pictures did not fail! Some were better than others; some played longer and to bigger receipts than others, but the thousands of motion-picture theaters (although they sometimes gagged a bit) gulped and digested them all.

He had meant to look up Olga Treskovna at once, but he did not. Each day he found himself thinking of her and wondering where she was. She might not have remained in California. But he fought against taking the simple steps to find her. Instead, he found excuses. His first weeks *were* pretty fully occupied over conference desks with authors, actors, directors, and Mr. Harris himself. Setting up with expert thoroughness his publicity campaign for "The Garden of the Soul."

The little picture tycoon, Marcus Harris, was "good copy" and interested Dunnigan even more than the actors. He was a new type to the press agent. Clever businessman and great artist all in one.

Dunnigan syndicated a story across the country, building up Harris as the "Napoleon of the Industry." This clinched the faith of the film executive in his new press agent. Even the greatest of us have our weaknesses, and Harris had a weakness which he was later to regret—a weakness for Napoleon.

Dunnigan came upon Olga Treskovna suddenly—through the lens of a camera!

The great, new picture was to be filmed in technicolor, and the Marcus Harris technicians were experimenting on one of the stages with Anna Gronka's costumes. A girl engaged as her "stand-in" stood against a setting while the cameramen turned their photographing eyes on her. Dunnigan, that day devoting himself to what he called "getting the low-down on the camera angle" of his exploitation task, asked if he could take a look. He found himself looking at Olga Treskovna.

***

13

OLGA TRESKOVNA wore a colorful peasant's skirt and blouse, and yet seemed more regally beautiful than any woman Bill Dunnigan had ever seen. His heart literally stood still. The moment he looked at her he knew it was no use pretending any longer. She wasn't his pal. She was the girl he loved. He would fight against that love no longer. He would tell her he loved her.

His first impulse was to call out her name. "Olga kid! Olga Treskovna!" But he thought better of it. He stood aside and waited while the cameramen finished their test. And he repeated the phrase that always seemed to come to his lips when they met. "Poor little kid!"

For although the "stand-in" for a great star like Anna Gronka was not a bad job, and doubtless paid adequately for board and room, it meant that Olga Treskovna merely posed in position for Anna Gronka while the lenses were being focused, or made costume tests, as she now was doing, to save the Great One's strength under the hot lights. It did not exactly give the holder of the job a chance to carry out the acting principles of Constantin Stanislavsky of the Moscow Art Theater! It gave her no chance at all.

This was certainly not "making good quickly." It was, in fact, becoming a mere shadow of someone else, or, to change the metaphor, it was being shunted onto a siding while all the opportunity trains dashed by.

Even if you played a "bit" role, you had a chance to act, and there was always the hope that your "bit" would escape the cutting-room floor and stand out in the finished picture, attracting the attention of a director or a producer. But a "stand-in"! It saddened Dunnigan. He'd have to do something about that.

When the test was ended he moved down to her. He felt exuberant, boyish, as he pushed his way through the crowd of technicians and property men. Life was good once you were sure of something! He must tell her he loved her here and now, this very moment, come what may! It seemed incredible that he had spent a lifetime without her. He would make up for lost time.

She turned and saw him coming. The moment she recognized him he saw her face light with that radiant smile he remembered so well from their Christmas Eve meeting a year and a half before. The smile that was like sudden sunshine.

"Mr. Dunnigan!" she cried.

The cry was joyful, but he felt it was the cry of a drowning person at the sight of the lifeguard. Well, he was there.

"Hello, kid! I'm mighty glad to see you again!" He grasped her hand. "And I told you once before—my name is Bill to my pals."

"Hello—Bill." She held tight to his hand. Bill's was a large, strong hand.

He stared at her, his mouth slightly agape. He had so many things to tell her, yet all the words were stuck in his throat. "I'm glad you're set in a good job here," he said finally.

For a moment weariness came into her blue eyes. Sunshine—then shadow!

"It isn't a very good job—Bill." She spoke his name awkwardly, as though she were being presumptuous to address him with such familiarity. "It isn't what I dreamed of you finding me doing. I read the other day you were in Hollywood—I didn't want you to see me as a stand-in——"

"Stop it, kid," he said. "I'm down a few pegs myself. I work here. In pictures. Me!"

"You haven't become an actor!"

"No. Haven't fallen that low! I'm still an honest publicity man! I'm hired to handle this picture 'The Garden of the Soul.' I suppose they have to have names like that. I've really come to like it here—except for the picture titles."

They both laughed.

Now—*now* he must tell her! But they were already being pushed around by scene clearers. The light men were shouting orders. He couldn't tell her here! And he suddenly realized he was still holding her hand. Holding to it for dear life. He let go, embarrassed.

A young assistant director moved in and told Olga Treskovna to report to another set. "You extras keep off the stages till you're wanted," he said to Dunnigan.

"You see," laughed Bill, "I don't mean a damn thing here either. He thinks I'm an 'extra'! What about dinner tonight? I'll come for you if you'll tell me where."

She smiled. Sunshine once more. "It's my turn for dinner. I've got a flat and a kitchenette. It's time I did something for you. I'll cook it myself."

"Why go to all that trouble? Why not step out? The Brown Derby or my hotel——"

"Don't be so frightened," Olga laughed. "I *can* cook! Even if no one here seems to think I can act!"

She told him her address as she moved away. "It's in the telephone book also," she said. "I thought all the studios would be wanting to reach me!" She was gone.

Dunnigan watched her walk toward the stage exit and it struck him that she was one of the few women he'd ever seen who walked gracefully. Eleonora Duse walked that way. And the famous Follies beauty, Dolores.

When she was entirely gone he stood alone, smiling dreamily to himself. The die was cast. Tonight, after their dinner, he would take her driving to Malibu. The Harris Studios had supplied him with a car from the first day. They would park facing the beach.

They two together facing the timeless ocean. Then he would tell her.

People had homes here. Even show people. They settled down and still had careers. He had been welcomed to several such homes of former globe-trotting guys like himself. They had children.

He would ask Olga Treskovna to be his wife. He would never be lonely again!

"Didn't I tell you to move on!" It was the efficient assistant director.

"Sorry, pal," said Bill. He was on a mountain top! On the top of the Empire State Building! He sang a snatch of a Follies song he'd always liked, "A pretty girl—is like a melody—that haunts you night and day—" "Here, buddy!" he addressed the irritated assistant director and pressed something into his hand, "here's a dollar. Get yourself a big lollipop! Smile!" And he strode off the set, still singing.

A prop man laughed. The officious assistant director was not popular. He stood there furious, Bill Dunnigan's dollar note in his unwilling hand. "Some fresh extra!" he sputtered, "I'll see that he's fired!"

An electrician spoke up. "I wouldn't worry about that, brother. And I'd keep that dollar bill as a souvenir! That's White Spats Dunnigan, the Broadway press agent. I saw him when I worked the New Amsterdam in New York. He's nuts sometimes but he's a great guy, and he's out here for the Governor on this new film!"

Even this youthful assistant director had heard of "White Spats" Dunnigan. And like all assistant directors, he was ambitious to get ahead. What a terrible mistake! "Mr. Dunnigan! Mr. Dunnigan!" he cried after Bill, and rushed off the set.

But Dunnigan was out of sight. Halfway to his office—walking rapidly—almost running.

His office? He was halfway to Paradise!

14

*B*UT DUNNIGAN did not, on that night, tell Olga Treskovna that he loved her. Startling things happened this time to prevent it.

The evening commenced propitiously. The girl's one room, kitchenette-and-bath, furnished flat in a small Hollywood apartment building, seemed to Dunnigan a pretty good substitute for Paradise.

Olga Treskovna had added much that was personal to its original cold furnishings. Her books lined the walls in low cases she had bought for a song at an auction room. And the pictures were hers —good reproductions of good paintings. Bill noticed they were mostly outdoor scenes and the streets of little towns. Hilltops and church spires.

There was a picture of another genre showing the dark interior of a great cathedral, the altar a blaze of light at the far end of the center aisle, and in the foreground a figure of Christ standing in a soft glow against the tall, Gothic columns. It was called "The Presence," and there was a verse in small, fine script just beneath it. It read:

> ". . . and lo, I am with you always, even unto
> the end of the world.
> > St. Matthew, xxviii, 20."

"That picture always reminds me of our Christmas Eve dinner," she told Bill Dunnigan.

"Why?" he had asked.

"Sometime I will tell you," she smiled, "when I know you better."

Bill thought, "I must never lose her again!"

She wore a simple, light blue house dress and her white apron had small blue figures.

"A home!" thought Bill, "a home with her!" That would make life worth the living!

She made him sit in a chair by the window while she prepared and served him an Old-Fashioned.

"I hope you like it," she said. "I can't make any other cocktail.
And I don't like shaking things in a tin container here. It would
sound just like a hotel then. I'm so tired of hotels."

He knew that he also was tired of hotels. Well, please God, he
wouldn't have to live in one much longer!

She held up her own Old-Fashioned. "To you and me, and to
Ming Gow," she said. "I wonder if he ever thinks of us?"

There was hope for him then! The girl *must* care a little, if she
treasured so vividly the memory of their first dinner together.

What a clever woman can conjure from those tiny compartments
in a wall, optimistically named "kitchenette," is one of the marvels
even of this age of efficiency! Olga Treskovna produced from hers
their second dinner together. This time it was an American home
dinner.

Bean soup with the fragrance of the open garden, fried chicken
with plenty of milk gravy and steaming hot biscuits, corn on the
cob, and baked sweet potatoes. Thick apple pie with cream and a
big cup of coffee that Dunnigan called "just right" for dessert.

Olga Treskovna knew how to cook. She had cooked for her
father when she was eight years old, and now she confessed to Dunnigan that before she got the job in the Wilkes-Barre restaurant
that finally landed her on Forty-Second Street, she had worked as a
cook for a well-to-do family in the Pennsylvania city.

Dunnigan insisted on helping her with the dishes after they finished dinner. He had done this for his mother always. Only now
it was not a patched-at-the-elbow sweater jacket that he took off
when he rolled up his shirt sleeves, but a Fifth Avenue tailored coat.
And the shirt sleeves were of the finest Sulka linen.

And like his mother, Olga Treskovna insisted on putting a great
apron down over his head to protect his vest and trousers. Had he
not been in love with her before, that simple, maternal act would
have won Bill Dunnigan's lasting worship.

"Gee, kid," he said, when the dishes were finished, and he sank
back in her Morris chair puffing at his Regina Perfecto, "Gee, kid, I
never knew before what it was to be absolutely content!"

He almost decided to tell her then that he loved her. But no—he
would presently propose that they drive to Malibu. It was a beautiful, clear, early-summer night. Her star would be shining down on
the beach. Under her star he would speak his mind.

Her telephone rang.

"It's for you!" she said in some surprise.

"Must be the Studio," he said in asperity. "They started shooting the picture late this afternoon. Mr. Harris' secretary here asked me to leave my number if I left the hotel. What in God's name do they want at this hour!"

"You'd better take the call," laughed the girl. "I wouldn't want to make you lose your job! I'm afraid it wouldn't help if I said, 'Give the kid a break.'"

"Well?" said Dunnigan into the telephone. Couldn't he be let alone on this of all evenings!

It was Marcus Harris himself who was put on the wire. "That you, Dunnigan? Come to my office as quick as you can get here!"

"Why?" countered Dunnigan. He had grown fond of Harris, but he wasn't quite used to being given peremptory orders.

He gasped, however, when he heard the news. Anna Gronka had quit! Left the Studio flat!

The full details of the historic blow-up between Anna Gronka and Marcus Harris need not be a part of this history. Dunnigan didn't learn them all just then but he heard enough over Olga Treskovna's telephone.

Marcus Harris, it seemed, had dared to open his mouth to make a slight suggestion concerning certain mannerisms Madam Gronka affected in playing the first scene to be filmed. This "common American businessman" whose energy and genius had merely found the story, the money, the writers, the actors and directors to produce "The Garden of the Soul" had had the effrontery to tell Anna Gronka—the first theater personage in all Europe—how to act! Her righteous rage, starting with a dissertation on the crudeness of Americans in general, rose swiftly and culminatingly to a not-too-flattering description of Marcus Harris' ancestry, features, mentality, and, finally, his religion.

The break had been pretty final. The lady had stormed from the set and was flying back to New York in an hour, where an unsuspecting producer had made her a lucrative stage offer. She wanted no more "Hollywood insults."

"I'll come," said Dunnigan. He hung up. He sighed bitterly. He looked at Olga Treskovna and told her what it was all about.

"I'm not surprised," the girl said. "One of her Polish maids has been talking to me. Anna Gronka is temperamental. She's had rows with managers before and walked out. Left one that way in London in the middle of a picture. And she's nursed a special grievance against Marcus Harris."

"What grievance?" asked Dunnigan.

"That he didn't personally meet her in New York when she arrived. She said the whole city turned out and the Polish Ambassador came on from Washington and the Mayor himself greeted her, and yet Harris didn't think her important enough for a personal welcome—sent an underling to her boat——"

"The underling was me," said Dunnigan, "and as for that 'whole city turning out' and the Polish Ambassador and the Mayor——"

He stopped. Dunnigan never boasted of his exploits. "She's just a damn fool," he said, and let it go at that. "But I'll have to go and see Harris. Maybe I can patch things up between them."

"If you don't, I suppose it means the end of my stand-in job," said Olga Treskovna. "I shouldn't think selfishly of myself when you and Mr. Harris have all this trouble on your hands, but it did pay better than 'extra' work."

"Look here, kid," said Dunnigan, "I was going to talk to you about that. And about something else. I'll have to run now, but let me come back later. Tonight, I mean. Wait here for me, will you, kid?"

His earnestness surprised her, but she agreed. "I'll read, as I usually do," she said. Did he detect loneliness in her voice? Well, that should be remedied. Aloud he said, "You're still buying books, I see."

"I'm reading history now," she said. "I've got the idea that if I study people, real people who have lived, it will help me to act someday."

"You must write, also," said Dunnigan. "I forgot to tell you. I liked your poem about the girl and the star."

"Now I *will* wait for you!" she laughed.

"I'll be back as soon as I can. I have my car," he said and was gone.

His small roadster was parked in front of her house. Just as he was to start, he looked up to see if he could locate her windows. She was standing in one of them, and she waved to him. Gronka and "The Garden of the Soul" did not seem important. He must get through with Harris quickly and hurry back. Tomorrow would be time enough to face business problems. Tonight belonged to him and Olga Treskovna!

But the problem facing Marcus Harris was an urgent and a serious one. Dunnigan found him with his staff—his casting director, his studio manager, the name-director he had especially engaged. They had been in conference an hour.

What to do? Half a million dollars in sets already had been constructed. Another half a million in actors, authors, composers, technicians, were under play-or-pay contract. Victor George, the leading man who was to play opposite Gronka, was on loan-out to Harris from United Stars only for the next six weeks. Harris had flown on from New York to secure him, and paid the rival Studio a handsome bonus. Time was tragically of the essence. "The Garden of the Soul" had to be shot speedily, or else the fortune and prestige of Marcus Harris, Dunnigan-dubbed "Napoleon of the Industry," would wither and fade.

"Want me to try to patch it up?" said Dunnigan. He felt keenly sorry for this short, round-faced, thick-lipped, homely man, whom he had found generous and straight-dealing. "I probably know Gronka better than anyone. I don't like her, but I know her. I've patched up star and producer quarrels before."

"That is over," said Marcus Harris quietly. "I would not let her inside my Studio. I do not mind what people think of me, if they make fun of how I look and dress and talk. Maybe I am ludicrous. If it amuses them, they can laugh because my brother and I had a small tailoring shop on East Seventieth Street and pressed pants. It was my father's shop and he put us through school by means of it when he brought us here as small boys from Russia. They can speak of me personally as they wish. I know all the jokes. But when anyone attacks me because I am a Jew, I am through. I am not ashamed that I am a Jew. I am proud of it. My father and my mother were Jews. And their fathers and mothers before them. I can understand now what my father and mother went through before they came to this great country. That woman from over there has shown me."

Dunnigan had once managed a play about Sancho Panza. He thought of the courageous Sancho as he looked at Marcus Harris— Sancho the goatherd who became the Governor of a Province, ruled

it wisely, and, because he had been a goatherd, had to endure the
taunts of those who had not half his wisdom or were not half his
equal.

Marcus Harris, with his squat, ungainly body, his short fat legs,
his homely face, was a noble figure as he paced the floor of his domain and would risk disaster rather than crawl to an ignorant defamer of his ancient faith.

"I'll telephone the newspapers and the press associations at once,"
said Dunnigan. "I'll give them your side of the quarrel, Mr. Harris,
before Gronka gets to them."

"When I phoned for you I thought of doing that," said Marcus
Harris, "but I've changed my mind. After all, she's a woman. We
are gentlemen, I hope. Let her say what she pleases. We'll find a
way to carry on. If only we had more time!"

It was then that the idea came suddenly to Bill Dunnigan. It
struck him so forcefully that he half rose from his chair and opened
his mouth to speak, then caught himself. This was not the place to
spring it. At least, not before the whole Harris staff. He must have
Marcus Harris alone.

"I'll see the papers and simply say that Anna Gronka has resigned. She felt the role did not suit her talents," said Dunnigan,
trying to speak matter-of-factly, to hide his excitement. "I think we
should at least say that, and say it at once. Can I phone you later,
Mr. Harris?"

"Call me at the Biltmore if you wish," said Marcus Harris. "I'm
going to my hotel to think. Maybe I can think of some other star
to play the part. I've already tried Garbo and Dietrich, and half a
dozen others. They're all on assignments and not free for months!
It needs a foreigner. We'll meet at nine here tomorrow."

Dunnigan seized his hat and went out quickly. He leaped into
his car and started driving at top speed. But not to the newspaper
offices.

He raced back to Olga Treskovna's flat, his mind pounding as fast
as the engine of his car. He did not enter the self-service elevator.
He tore up the stairway, two steps at a time, to her third floor.
When she opened the door he just stood there for a few moments
panting, and held both her hands.

They were inside now and he had caught his breath.

"Listen, kid!" he said. "Do you think you could play Anna Gronka's role in 'The Garden of the Soul'!"

She stared at him. "Me—a great part like that!"

"Sure—you!" said Dunnigan.

"But I'm not a star——"

"Have you read the book?"

"I know it almost by heart."

"Could you play the girl—her name is Olga, isn't it?"

"I'd give my soul to play it—but——"

"But what?"

"This is crazy! I know how they think. They would never risk all that money on an unknown like me. They'll get Garbo or Ingrid Bergman or——"

"They've already tried for all the known ones. Nobody is available. There isn't a foreign-looking, foreign-talking star available for the next two months! And Harris has to shoot this picture fast. Right away. Or he'll lose a fortune."

Olga Treskovna sank into a chair. Her eyes were wide with excitement. *Her* heart was pounding. But her brain was clear—that woman's brain behind the face of a child, the brain that had gone through suffering and disappointment.

"You mean to tell me you're afraid to pivot now—after all this studying!" And Dunnigan swept his arm in the direction of the book shelves.

Olga Treskovna laughed. "Gee, Bill," she said, "do *you* think I could do it!"

"You're foreign looking. You're Gronka's height and size. The costumes all fit you. You've had most of them on already. And if you're not better looking and cleverer than that conceited, rattle-brained dame, I'll eat the printed novel of 'The Garden of the Soul,' cover and all! It would be some meal—it's five hundred pages long! I had to read the damn thing!"

"You didn't answer my question, Bill. Do you think I can *act* it?"

"Would I offer you the part if I didn't think so?"

"You're offering me the role?"

"Do you want it?"

"Do I want it! What do you think?"

"O. K. You're in, kid. Sit tight. Go to bed. Go to sleep. Get a good rest because you're going to have a busy morning tomorrow!"

He seized his derby and made for the door.

"But wait a minute!" she cried. He turned. "Does Marcus Harris know about this?"

"Not yet," Dunnigan laughed. "But he's going to hear plenty as quick as I can get back to him! So long, kid! Chin up!"

She heard him tearing down the stairs. From her window she watched the car start with a tremendous plunge. He had not looked back and up, as he did before.

She looked up at the night sky and there was her star, glowing like a rose near its group of little stars. Was it imagination that the star seemed twice as bright that evening? Was it madness to dream that Bill Dunnigan could persuade Marcus Harris to give her a chance at such a tremendous part? And that she could make good!

~~~~~~ *15* ~~~~~~

MARCUS HARRIS kept his real home in New York. As he had told Dunnigan in their first telephone conversation, he did not fancy Hollywood. But he had to work there, so he also maintained a suite the year round at the Biltmore in Los Angeles.

A half hour later Dunnigan was in that suite.

Harris was in pajamas and an elaborately-embroidered dressing gown. "My wife gave it to me Christmas," he said apologetically.

How Dunnigan really accomplished it he never could clearly remember. This was certain, few men could match him as a salesman when his heart was in his work. And he went to work on Marcus Harris with the deadly precision of a hawk attacking its prey.

Why not give the stand-in, Olga Treskovna, Anna Gronka's part? This was the refrain, like the beat of a tom-tom, that Bill Dunnigan pounded against the ears of Marcus Harris.

Harris listened. A secret of his success was that, at an early age, he had learned to listen. At last he said, "No. No."

Why not? Dunnigan persisted. Olga Treskovna was Polish. In many ways resembled Anna Gronka. But she was younger—much more beautiful. She looked Slavic. She had the low, Slavic voice. She walked with Slavic erectness.

"Have you ever seen her act?" said Harris.

"I have," said Dunnigan. The press agent did not as a rule speak of his "past performances," but he felt he must now tell Marcus Harris a couple of incidents that happened to have the merit of being the truth. "I saw a girl in a cheap stock company in Syracuse one matinee when I had an hour to kill. I wired my boss, George C. Tyler, about her. Remember a little item—" and Dunnigan named a play and its new star that had created a veritable sensation some years before. "I dragged Florenz Ziegfeld to a vaudeville theater in Jersey City to see a guy that swung a rope and told gags." The name the press agent then mentioned was not exactly an obscure one.

"I don't know. I don't know," said Marcus Harris. "I only know I have an awful headache."

"I tell you, this stand-in girl is a natural for the role," reiterated Dunnigan. "What if she is unknown? Didn't every soldier in the armies of Napoleon feel that there was a Marshal's baton in his knapsack? Wasn't that one of the things that made the little emperor great? *He* didn't have to let others find him leaders. He found them himself. He *made* generals."

The Napoleonic reference did it. That, as we know, was the weakness of Marcus J. Harris.

"All right, Dunnigan," he said. "I'll see what she can do. Bring her in at ten in the morning. I'll have the director try her in the scene Gronka made hash of. And now, for God's sake, let me get some sleep!"

"O. K., boss! She'll be there!" said Dunnigan. "And boss—she'll make good!"

~~~~~~ *16* ~~~~~~

*D*UNNIGAN drove back to his studio office. He had there a shooting-script of "The Garden of the Soul." He'd been culling it for press material. He found the scene Marcus Harris wanted Olga Treskovna to play. He read it over carefully. Of course she could do it. It was tailor-made for her.

He took a blue pencil and marked words in the margin opposite certain speeches. "Passion." "Fear." "Derision." "Hope." It was a help he had seen Otis Skinner employ in studying a role. It indicated the mood of the spoken line.

Then he removed the fasteners from the thick manuscript and extracted the latter part. It would not be needed. He bound up again the scene to be shot in the morning, and what preceded it. He placed this in a big manila envelope.

Once more Dunnigan drove back to Olga Treskovna's apartment building, this time through silent, empty streets. It was long past midnight. He took the trouble to stop his car gradually—no grinding of brakes. He got out and looked up. All windows were dark. The whole house was asleep, Olga Treskovna included.

Bill Dunnigan had made his plan as he drove along. He must not disturb her again if she had retired. A few hours' rest might mean success or failure.

He entered the small vestibule. With his ever-present blue pencil, which he always carried in a vest pocket, he wrote her name in large letters on the manila envelope.

Before him was the usual line of brass-doored letter boxes. The name "Olga Treskovna" was on one of them. His manila envelope was too large to go into the small slot of the letter box, but there was a sort of shelf above, and he placed the envelope there, in an upright position.

Dunnigan drove back to the Beverly Wilshire. It was three-thirty in the morning by the time he was in his room.

He was dead tired but he left a call for five-thirty, and another for five-forty, to be sure he'd be awakened. He took off his clothes and sat on the side of his bed.

The motion-picture business was assuming new proportions in his mind. It consisted now of a great electric sign covering the top of a block-long building back on his beloved Times Square. That sign flashed in huge letters "OLGA TRESKOVNA in THE GARDEN OF THE SOUL."

Bill Dunnigan went happily to sleep.

At five thirty-five he was phoning Olga Treskovna.

"Kid, this is Bill," he said to the sleepy answering voice. "Glad you've had some rest, but now comes the dawn and get yourself wide awake. This is important."

"I'm wide awake, Bill," she said.

"There's a manuscript of the first part of 'The Garden of the Soul' on the shelf above your letter box downstairs. Get it, and start studying the scene on page ten. I've marked it. You'll understand. You know the character—they have followed the novel closely. Get that scene into your head, for I'm coming for you at nine. At ten o'clock Marcus Harris will shoot a test of you doing that scene."

"Bill, you're not joking?" Her voice broke a little.

"I don't joke at five thirty-five A.M.," said Dunnigan grimly. "If Harris and the director like the way you do that scene, you're in. The director, Cecil Burleigh, is regular. He didn't like Gronka at all. This is your chance, kid!"

"Oh, Bill!" she gasped, and then there came a firmness in her tone. "Bill, I won't let you down!"

"I know you won't. Get that script, kid, and go to it. And don't forget to make yourself some breakfast. You know what happened before, when you tried to pivot without eating!"

"I'll eat, Bill," she said.

"So long, kid. Calling for you at nine."

Bill Dunnigan remembered he'd forgotten to telephone the newspapers about Gronka. He decided to wait. Maybe by noon the next day he would have a real story for the boys—a "stand-in girl" promoted to a star! He went back to bed, leaving another call for eight.

*S*HE HAD A CUP of coffee for him, bubbling in her electric percolator, when Dunnigan arrived at nine. She wanted to fix him some breakfast.

"Good lord, kid!" he said. "You're worrying about my breakfast when your whole future is in the making!"

"I think you've been doing some worrying about me," she said. "I was too surprised last night to realize it, but it must have taken a lot of doing to persuade Marcus Harris to give me this chance."

"He's in luck to have you on the lot," Bill said, "and I've had my breakfast at the hotel. You've eaten? Cross your heart? Good. But I'm grateful for this cup of coffee."

He drank it quickly. How different the gratitude of this girl from the absurd egoism of Anna Gronka! Again he was on the point of speaking of his love. No. He must do nothing now to upset her.

He looked at his watch. "Gosh—we must hurry! The make-up people are to have you ready by ten."

They did not talk as he drove rapidly to the Studio. The truth was, she was just a little frightened. Could she, a burlesque singer, step into one of the greatest parts ever written into a novel! But she looked at the man beside her, and knew she must not fail. His faith in her ability was so ardent! He seemed to give her of his strength.

If Olga Treskovna had analyzed her feelings for Bill Dunnigan she would not have called it love. It may be doubted if she dreamed that he loved her. And she would have considered it most presumptuous of herself to be in love with him. No, it was another emotion. She worshiped him. He was still her Wise Man from the West; he was still the heaven-sent figure that had suddenly spoken up in a Forty-Second Street burlesque house, "Give the kid a break!" She thanked God humbly that this great personage of the theater took an interest in her, believed in her!

Dunnigan had taken particular pains that morning. This day of days! The black derby was a brand new one. The plaid suit was his latest. The white spats had never been worn before. The maroon and silver-striped tie came from under a shirt collar of purple-blue. Were you crossing a traffic light and looked at him at the wheel of his car, you might have surmised he was a successful racetrack tout, so little do clothes really proclaim the man. The crookedest gambler on Broadway dressed like a banker. To the girl beside Dunnigan, he wore the armor of a Crusader straight from Holy Communion. Or he might be a knight in shining silver and black, straight from King Arthur's Court.

Dunnigan purposely did not talk to her about the part. She was intelligent. Let her do it her own way—with such help, of course, as the Harris director would give her. He knew the bad results of "lecturing" a player just before that player "went on." Olga Treskovna was about to "go on."

Marcus Harris with his director, his best cameraman, the sound men, the other technicians were on the big sound stage at ten. Dunnigan introduced Olga Treskovna to Harris and the director. They had really never noticed her before. It was obvious that they liked her looks.

She had been made up for the lights, but still wore her simple, daytime frock. "Play the scene in that dress," said Marcus Harris. "It's simple. I like it." Harris had thought all along that some of the Gronka costumes were too elaborate—that they would destroy sympathy for the character of the role.

"Let's go," said the director.

Dunnigan stood by Marcus Harris. Olga Treskovna stepped before the cameras. She looked at Dunnigan. "Go to it, kid!" she could almost hear him say with his steady eyes.

"Camera! Action!" The girl plunged into the scene—a solo in which she was talking alone. Dunnigan knew instantly she would make good. For Olga Treskovna turned on the pent-up emotions of a lifetime. The studying of parts in many plays, the practicing before hotel mirrors, the reading aloud in lonely hotel rooms, the holding of hundreds of impatient burlesque audiences with sheer charm and sincerity—all these things and many more helped Olga Treskovna on that day.

She had been asked to pivot and this time she was ready! And there was a burning determination not to let down the man who had won her this opportunity.

Dunnigan, watching Marcus Harris and his director, could see that they were pleased—surprised.

She was not perfect, of course. Harris made a suggestion. The girl grasped it instantly. The director suggested a change of gesture. Olga Treskovna was doing it before he had finished his sentence.

They kept her before the cameras for two hours. They tried several close-ups. The great leading man came at eleven and went through a scene with her. Finally, Marcus Harris spoke to his director, and the director said, "Thank you, Miss Treskovna. That is all. We will let you know."

Dunnigan went to her. "My office assistant is waiting in my car. He'll take you home. Get some more sleep. They want to see how you look on film. The 'takes' are already on the way to the laboratories. I'll stick around. I'll phone you."

"How do you think I was?" she asked.

"Apparently they're never sure how people will photograph," he said. "If we make that hurdle, there's nothing to it. You can act, kid, you can act!"

Olga Treskovna went home in Dunnigan's car. Bill went back to the Studio offices with Marcus Harris and the director. Harris had tried for still other known actresses with no success. It was a particularly busy time at all studios. Contract players were all occupied.

The three men had lunch in the Studio canteen and at two o'clock Dunnigan followed Marcus Harris into the producer's private projection room to see the "rushes"—the developed films just as they came from the sound stage.

Dunnigan was spellbound when he looked at Olga Treskovna on the screen. She was photogenic to a remarkable degree. She was more than just beautiful. She was heartrendingly appealing. She reached out and drew you into her scenes—into her heart.

Her voice also recorded well. Rich, deep, thrilling, sincere.

Dunnigan looked at the other two men. Was it his love for her that made him think Olga Treskovna was ten times better than Anna Gronka? Had putting an apron over his head (as his mother had done) touched him so that it warped his cold judgment? Or fried chicken and hot biscuits?

"Dunnigan, I think we've got something!" said the director. His voice was a little unsteady.

"Mr. Dunnigan found several new stars for Broadway," said Marcus Harris. He was smiling for the first time in twenty-four hours.

"When do we start on the picture again?" asked the director. He was like a race horse at the barrier.

"We start tonight," said Marcus Harris. "I've lost a precious day already." To Dunnigan, "Who represents this girl? What kind of deal does she want?"

"She's on your pay roll already," said the press agent. "I don't know what you pay stand-ins, but that's her salary now. I think she'll leave the increase to you."

"All right," said Marcus Harris. "We'll see that she doesn't go hungry. Tell her there'll be a car and a chauffeur at her disposal. And a studio maid. We'll have to work fast, and long hours. If she don't fail me, I'll do the right thing in the way of a bonus when we get it all on film."

Dunnigan knew that Marcus Harris would keep his word. The main thing was for Olga Treskovna to make good. Success in the star role of a film like "The Garden of the Soul," and her future was secure!

"May I go back to my job and tell the papers about it, boss?" said Dunnigan.

"Shoot the works," said Marcus Harris. "What was it you said about every soldier of Napoleon carrying a General in his knapsack?"

"Carrying a Marshal's baton in his knapsack," laughed Dunnigan.

"Well, whatever it was they carried, get that prop into the story to the papers," said Marcus Harris. "And Dunnigan——"

"Yes, boss."

"Don't get the Polish Ambassador here this time. I think that fellow is hard luck for us!"

"Olga Treskovna is American," said Bill. "Born in the great state of Pennsylvania. It was only her father and mother that came from Gronka's Poland."

"I'll not hold that against Treskovna," smiled Marcus Harris, "so long as it don't make her object to my watching a scene occasionally! Explain to her that I've got quite a bit of money tied up here, and am sort of interested in what goes on."

And the little man pressed half a dozen cigars on Bill Dunnigan —a sure sign that he was happy.

Dunnigan telephoned the newspapers. The story of an unknown "stand-in girl" getting the assignment opposite the great Victor George in "The Garden of the Soul" outweighed in interest anything they had heard about the Anna Gronka row. Cinderella stuff always went, as Dunnigan well knew. It gave every girl in America a new hope.

He suddenly realized that he had not telephoned the good news to the person most interested—Olga Treskovna. She answered on the first ring. She could not sleep! She'd been sitting by her telephone. How could she do anything else!

"Kid, they liked your pivot!" said Bill.

He could hear her short gasp. Then, "Did it really turn out all right?"

"It turned out so well that you're in!" he cried. "You start on the real picture tonight at seven."

"Mr. Dunnigan—Bill—I can hardly believe it! I don't know how to thank——"

"Skip it, kid! Didn't you save me from suicide one lonely night in Iowa? We're even now! Get some rest and show up here at seven. The Studio will send a car for you."

"When will I see you, Bill?"

"You'll see me plenty, but tonight I've got to get busy myself! Change all my press stuff. Put a new name into the releases. Bet you can't guess whose it is! Chin up, kid! Hit 'em hard!"

"I'll do my best," she said.

When he had hung up, he realized that he had not yet told her of his love. What had happened to the drive to Malibu, to the declaration to be given under her guiding star!

He'd gone into the star-business for her himself now! He must give her every help in making good. There would come a better moment for romance than at this anxious time.

—————————————————————————— *18* ———

*T*HEY COMMENCED FILMING "The Garden of the Soul" at breakneck speed. Victor George, the star leading man, had to be returned to United Stars in six weeks. Olga Treskovna was at the studio by six-thirty each morning. Her hair was dressed, her make-up applied, her costumes fitted. She worked before the cameras till five in the afternoon.

Dunnigan haunted the stages the first week. He neglected his publicity work. Marcus Harris watched closely also. Dunnigan knew that even now it was not too late for the picture producer to change his mind. But the "rushes" that were daily run off in the private projection room carried only one message. Olga Treskovna was a ten-strike "find."

Twice Dunnigan took her to a quiet restaurant for dinner. But he knew she must have rest after long hours under the lights, and he drove her home immediately after and left her at her door. She had to study and commit the lines of a dozen new scenes each evening, to be ready for the next day's shooting.

He suggested she might prefer to live at a hotel while the picture was being made, to free herself entirely of house work. That did not appeal to her.

"I'm really just a home girl," she said. "I'll work better if I come back to a place of my own at night. I get rest and peace and strength. My studio maid is sending me a woman who will come at four in the afternoons, clean the apartment, have a simple dinner waiting for me. That is all I need. That—and your confidence in me."

She smiled her radiant, sad smile as she said the last sentence.

Dunnigan's heart was overflowing, but he said nothing of his love. The girl was giving her heart and soul to the work. Not entirely selfishly either. "I'll die before I'll let you down!" she said to him. He remembered those words later.

The theater-wise press agent knew how important it was that she have no outside emotional disturbance. She was fond of him he knew—intensely grateful also—but suppose she did not "love" him as he loved her? Suppose she would feel that she must now accept his love because of the great chance he had secured for her. No. Dunnigan wanted nothing like that. He would wait till the cameras stopped turning on "The Garden of the Soul."

Olga Treskovna would then, he felt certain, be an assured star. Her future secure. She would never have to worry again. She would not need him to help her. Then—*then* if she wanted his love; that would be happiness for him and for her! Meantime, work—hard work for both of them.

Work can be a substitute for love, if that work is for the one we love. At the end of the first week of "shooting," Marcus Harris flew back to New York for ten days. That meant he was fully satisfied. There was no danger of Olga Treskovna's being let out.

And Dunnigan, conscious that his anxiety had caused him to neglect his own duties, dug into his publicity campaign with a consuming vigor. He was careful not to say too much in praise of Olga Treskovna. He put emphasis on the story, "The Garden of the Soul." He knew the danger of an extravagant advance ballyhoo for a new star. Let the critics find it out for themselves. Let the public acclaim her. That would make her a *real* star. Meantime, by making the name of her vehicle—the story—a household word, he would have the public in a receptive mood to grasp a new film personality.

He began toiling at his Studio office from early morning till late at night. He did try each day to go at least once to whatever stage Olga Treskovna was working on. And he would have a few words with her. He felt that she understood. It was imperative that both she and the picture get off to a right start.

Hard work always agreed with Dunnigan. He became ruddier, healthier. And it was not until the end of the fourth week of shooting (Marcus Harris had returned, stayed a week, and gone back to New York) that it occurred to Dunnigan that the relentless grind was not affecting Olga Treskovna in the same fine way it did him. Watching her on the set late one afternoon, he suddenly realized that she was thinner, much thinner. Perhaps it was the heat—it was now July, and a wave of intense, humid weather had set in. He waited for her and asked that she go to dinner with him.

"No," she said, "you come home with me. I'm too tired to go anywhere. I'll telephone my 'cook' to make enough for two."

"But that will be a lot of trouble."

"No trouble. Martha can go to the corner and get you some chops. We always have plenty of vegetables in the icebox."

The meal was simple but good. And it was good to be alone with her. When the middle-aged Martha had stacked away the dishes and gone, Dunnigan put his worry into words.

"Olga kid—do you feel well? Are you working too hard? Aren't you losing weight?"

"It's the hot, damp weather," she said. "Next week we're going on location—up to Yuma, they say, for the desert scenes. I'll be all right then! We're nearly through with the studio shots."

"I know they're driving you," he said, "but it can't be helped. They want Victor George back on the United Stars lot. A sequel story to one of his roles, and they can't start till he is through here."

"I'll be all right," said Olga Treskovna. "My star is very bright every night! I look at it just before I go to bed."

"I don't want you up there with that star—like the girl in your poem!" exclaimed Bill, and he thought that he saw again a strange shadow move across her eyes. "I'll tell you something to cheer you," he added quickly. "Marcus Harris wired me yesterday that he's buying another great story just for you!"

"I don't know how I can ever show my gratitude to you," said the girl.

"But I'm going to insist that Harris let you take a rest, before they start you on another one," continued Dunnigan. "Maybe you'll let me take you to Palm Springs. Maybe I can get a week off too. I've been driving pretty hard myself, only I gain weight! I eat like a horse out here! My vests are all getting tight. I'll be as fat as Marcus Harris if I don't take care!"

He had lit his cigar, and was standing in front of the print called "The Presence." Olga Treskovna came to his side.

"Bill," she said, "I'll tell you why that picture reminds me of our Christmas Eve dinner. In that restaurant I thought that you and Ming Gow were like two of the Wise Men—you know, in the Bible story—who met on Christmas Eve—and it seemed to me there was Someone Else there too—a Presence—like in my picture—and that

He would go to your revue with Ming Gow on the night you gave the passes for."

Dunnigan was moved. This was another time it was with difficulty he kept from taking her in his arms—telling her of his love. When he had mastered his impulse he said:

"If He was there, it was because of you! I think you're something very fine, kid, just about the finest thing this side of Heaven!" And that was as near as he came to telling her that he loved her.

"I wish Flo Ziegfeld could have heard you say a thing like that," he continued quickly, to cover his urge to speak of more personal matters. "Ziggie produced 'girl shows' but they were always inspiring, as well as sensuous. Like a clean flame! Beauty was a sort of religion with him. That's why he went on, year after year, and never failed with them. That's why he will be remembered. That's what all his imitators did not understand. And they lasted a season or two and dropped out of sight."

"I'm glad 'The Garden of the Soul' is a clean story and an inspiring one," said the girl. "I suppose I would be playing in it no matter what kind of story it was, and grateful for the chance, but I'm glad it's what it is!"

"Things that are good always find each other," said Dunnigan. " 'The Garden of the Soul' just could not have *been* without you."

"Or you," said Olga Treskovna.

Driving back to his hotel, Dunnigan felt again the acute loneliness. Could he ever measure up to her? He could only try, if she consented to link her life with his.

~~~~~~~~~~~~~~~~~~~~~~~~~~~~~~~~~~~~~ *19* ~~~~~

*B*UT THE NEXT DAY Bill Dunnigan was faced with as heartbreaking a decision as any man could have.

Olga Treskovna had a coughing spell on the set, ruining a lengthy scene. The director called time out, and she retired to her portable dressing room. Dunnigan rushed over from his office when he heard the news.

She opened the door of the dressing room herself, and came out smiling. "Hello, Bill," she said. "I've just ruined a scene. But I'm all right now."

"Are you sure?" said Dunnigan.

She laughed. "Some of the big words I have to say must have stuck in my throat. These novelists surely like to use big words! It's silly of me to do a thing like that. Now I'm going back to work."

The director, who had followed Dunnigan, sighed with relief, but the press agent frowned. He felt a presentiment. She wasn't fooling him with her laughter and light dismissal of the coughing spell. He recalled there was something she once told him that tied in somehow with all this. He wracked his brain, but couldn't solve the puzzle.

The scene was re-shot, and Olga Treskovna played it with consummate skill. Bill watched awhile, but had to return to his office. He had an important appointment with a famous newspaper "special writer" who was visiting Hollywood. He had invited the man to dinner.

But dinner over and rid of his guest, he had a keen sense of uneasiness. All at once he remembered. It was something she had said to him on that Christmas Eve, when she spoke of wanting to go to Hollywood. *"There's a reason why I want to make good quickly —as quickly as I can. There isn't time for the long years the stage usually takes."*

He had not asked her to explain the reason. Now he wished desperately to know what it was.

He was in his hotel room. He lifted the receiver and called her number. The woman Martha answered.

"Miss Treskovna has not been home. Telephoned me she would be late."

"Did she say where she was?"

"No, sir. But I expect her soon."

Dunnigan was disturbed. He knew that Olga Treskovna usually went directly home. He went out hurriedly and drove to her flat.

The woman Martha was just leaving as he knocked at her door. Again he had ignored the elevator and rushed up the stairs two steps at a time. This time it was in alarm and fear.

"I must go," said Martha. "It is nearly nine o'clock. I have my children to put to bed."

"I'll wait awhile, if I may," said Dunnigan.

"I guess it's all right, Mr. Dunnigan," said the woman. "When Miss Treskovna comes in, please explain. Her dinner is in the oven. She can heat it just a little, in case she has not eaten."

"I will tell her," said the press agent. "And Martha," he added, "give me your telephone number. In case—well, in case I need you."

"I have no telephone," said the woman, "but I can give you a number in a candy store next door. They will come for me. My last name is Monahan."

Bill Dunnigan wrote it in his address book.

He had never before been in Olga Treskovna's room alone. He looked about at her pictures and her books. He stood in front of the picture called "The Presence." He repeated the first line of the poem she had sent him.

"Austra—tall and strong and fine,
Somehow like our mountain Pine—"

If only Olga Treskovna were as strong as she was fine!

What an imagination the child had! And then, "Poor little kid!" He had not had that thought about her for some time.

His eyes were drawn to several large films lying on her small writing desk. He had asked for some new "stills" of her. Perhaps these were the stills. But why films, not prints? He picked the films up.

They were not "stills." They were chest x-rays. There were the white lines of the ribs, the dark lung expanse. His heart sank. There was a letter in an envelope beside them. He could not help but see that a doctor's name was on the top corner of the envelope.

Dunnigan did not usually open and read other people's letters, but he took this one from its envelope and spread it open. It was from a Dr. Hiram Jennings in Los Angeles.

Dear Miss Treskovna,

I haven't had any luck in reaching you. And you haven't phoned me as you promised. I have just received the accompanying x-rays from the laboratory, and they

show you have a serious infection in both lungs. Your
case requires immediate hospitalization. Please come to
my office today without fail. I will be in this evening if
you can't come during the day.

Sincerely,

Hiram Jennings, M. D.

Dunnigan's impulse was to telephone Dr. Jennings at once. But
no. He had no right to telephone to Olga Treskovna's physician.
Not even to ask for her there. He had no right to take this letter
from its envelope and read it.

He read it again. Then he folded it carefully and replaced it in
the envelope, and placed the envelope exactly where it had been
when he picked it up. He put the x-ray films where they had been.

He understood now why she wanted to make good quickly, and
why she knew she did not have a lot of time. She had worked in
the Breaker in Coaltown too long as a child. The monster had
planted his black breath in her lungs. She knew her life would be
cut short. She had seen it happen to many others in Coaltown.
Hollywood had not made her any different. She was still the child
of the Breaker. "The Breaker Girl."

Dunnigan was glad she had not come in. He hoped he would
not meet her as he went out. He flicked off the lights and walked
out of the flat. The catch-lock snapped in the door. He descended
to the street, got into his car and drove back to his hotel.

He wanted time to think—to decide. He paced his room with
clenched fists.

He understood now why Olga Treskovna held herself aloof.
Aloof and lovely. He understood why there was such a sadness in
her eyes at times—those shadows that passed across her eyes. He
understood why there had always seemed to him something sacred
about her. She was a little nearer heaven than the rest of us, he
thought.

He could confront her with his knowledge, see this Dr. Hiram
Jennings, rush her off to a hospital. What then of her career?
What of "The Garden of the Soul"? Her heart was wrapped up in
it. It would kill her just as surely if she had to give it up. It would
ruin her. Chances such as she had barged into were few. She
would never get another one.

They were going to Yuma in two days. It was hot and dry there. Perhaps she could pull through. The picture finished, she could take a prolonged rest. They cured that sort of thing now.

Come what may, Olga Treskovna's life was her own. If she wanted to quit work on "The Garden of the Soul" and go to a hospital, she must make the decision herself. Even if she wanted to use her last strength to finish the picture, she had the right to do so. He hoped against hope—he must gamble—that she could finish it and still get well.

He went down to the bar and drank two highballs. Then he telephoned her from a booth. This time she answered in her firm, low voice.

"Olga, kid, how are you?" he said. "After what happened this afternoon, I was worried. I had a business dinner engagement. But I tried to get you. I came out to the flat and waited awhile. Martha was there."

"I'm quite all right," she said. "I was a little worried myself and I went to see my doctor. He says I'm fine. Just need a rest, that's all—and I'll get one now in another week."

"Palm Springs in another week?" asked Dunnigan.

"Palm Springs," she said. He knew then she had made up her mind to stick it out.

"Martha asked me to tell you your dinner is in the oven," he added.

"I found it and I ate, as you say, like a horse! I'm going to bed now for I am a little tired."

"Well, see you tomorrow, kid," said Dunnigan.

"Good night, Bill," she said.

Dunnigan did not go to bed. He went back into the bar again and stood alone in a corner and drank eight highballs in a row. But they left him cold sober.

— *20* —

OLGA TRESKOVNA put on a performance the next day that made even the stagehands applaud. It was an especially difficult scene and long, requiring almost ten minutes of uninterrupted acting before the camera. One wrong movement or inflection during those ten minutes meant that the whole would have to be retaken. She amazed the director by acting it perfectly the first time. He ordered the scene re-shot, merely for protection, and again a perfect performance by his new star.

"She's a marvel!" he said to Dunnigan who stood back watching her.

"Yes," said Dunnigan. He alone knew just what a "marvel" she was.

During the rest period the press agent went to her dressing room. "Kid, you were wonderful," he said. "Are you sure you feel all right today?"

"Perfectly all right. Never better," she said. He thought she was looking at him curiously.

"I'm for you, kid. We're all for you," he said. "But please take care of yourself." He turned and went back to his office. It hurt him too much to watch her. He did not trust himself not to blurt out what he knew.

That evening, Olga Treskovna and the company of "The Garden of the Soul" left Los Angeles by special train. They were headed for "location" in the desert country near Yuma, Arizona, to shoot sequences which were supposed to happen in the great Sahara. Dunnigan could not go along. Marcus Harris was returning to the West Coast the next day, and there were to be important conferences.

The director telephoned the Studio daily, reporting on the progress of the film. Dunnigan talked with him several times. The director's enthusiasm for Olga Treskovna's work grew with each day's filming.

"Never," he said, "have I found an artist so responsive to suggestions. The girl has brains as well as looks. It's like playing on a Stradivarius after struggling with chain-store violins! She will go far, Dunnigan, I prophesy!"

"How is she standing up under the work?" Dunnigan asked. That was the important matter to him.

"She's grand! Seems to be losing weight even, and that's good! We're doing the part of the story where the girl is lost in the desert for a week—not supposed to get more buxom in the process! Last year I did a picture and my heroine gained twenty pounds while I was shooting scenes where she was in a prison on bread and water! It was hell! But this Treskovna is an artist!"

The director also was an "artist," his mind on his film story, not the health of such impersonal things as actors. "Don't worry about Treskovna. It's hellish hot here. A hundred in the shade today. I've lost some weight myself!" he added as a reassuring note.

Dunnigan was not reassured. He was worried—tragically worried. On Friday he again had premonitions of disaster. These were well founded, had he known. That day Olga Treskovna fainted during a scene, but she had quickly recovered and carried on. She would not give in. When she felt close to the breaking point, she set before her eyes a tall figure, as she remembered it in an empty burlesque auditorium—a figure topped by a black derby at an angle. And she heard again a voice that said, "Give the kid a break!"

She had said to the director as she recovered from her fainting spell—a spell he attributed to the intense heat—"I must not let Mr. Dunnigan down!" And she also, when she realized what she had said, found the same excuse, "He was a friend of my family."

By Friday night Dunnigan had decided to fly to Yuma the next day. He could stand the anxiety no longer. But word came that the whole cavalcade would return Sunday and Marcus Harris had called a conference Saturday afternoon. Dunnigan decided it was best not to run away.

He sent Olga Treskovna a telegram. "Will meet your train Sunday, kid. Chin up. It's almost finished and in the can, as they say here. I'm making reservations at Palm Springs."

Dunnigan had some photographers at the arrival of the train. He intended sending out a story about the "Garden of the Soul" desert scenes being the real thing, not studio stuff. He lined up the large company and working staff on the station platform, along the side of the ten-car train. Olga Treskovna stood between Marcus Harris and the director.

The girl was indeed noticeably thinner and seemed pale. Dunnigan thanked heaven that in a few more days she could rest. For several studio re-takes was all that remained to be done.

He drove her to her flat in his car. They were both silent during the ride. He looked at her and her eyes were closed. She was very tired.

He went up the elevator with her to carry her small handbag, but he would not stay. The woman Martha had only prepared food for one. He used that as an excuse to leave Olga Treskovna to herself and to her rest.

"I still eat like a horse!" he said. "I'll go back to my hotel. Call me if you want anything. You need a good night's sleep on your own bed. That always fixes one up. I know. See you tomorrow, kid."

"My star was over Yuma—it followed me there too, Bill," she said, with a smile, as they parted. It seemed a forced smile to Bill Dunnigan. The sunshine was missing.

There would perhaps be another day of it. Then she must rest for a month or two. So thought Dunnigan as he drove away. Not Palm Springs but a hotel-sanatorium in Arizona. He had friends there. She would have the care of specialists—get well and strong again.

She seemed all right the next morning at the Studio. The re-takes were soon finished. By one o'clock they had a party on the set, and everyone concerned with the picture ate little sandwiches and drank coffee or liquor out of paper cups. Even Victor George, who was not the most gracious of male stars, had fallen under Olga Treskovna's sway. "I propose a toast to the greatest little actress I have ever played opposite, and I have played with the best!" That was quite an unbending for Victor George. The hundred-odd prop men, electricians, grip men, cameramen, wardrobe people, extras, actors, and actresses cheered.

"Speech! Speech!" they cried.

Olga Treskovna stood up. To all of them but one, she was the great new star of "The Garden of the Soul." To Bill Dunnigan she was a shy, frightened girl standing on a burlesque stage in Forty-Second Street.

"I don't know how to make a speech," she said. "I have to have
my lines written for me. I can just say, 'thank you all from the
bottom of my heart!' You have all been so very kind to me. And if
you wish, I'll recite you a little poem a friend of mine wrote about
a girl in a small town where I came from. It's a sad poem. But
maybe you won't mind. This is a sad time for me—to leave you all."

This was the poem Olga Treskovna recited. Bill Dunnigan later
found a copy of it among her papers. But he knew as she was saying it that she had written it herself. It was like the other she had
sent to him. "Things that could happen to imaginary people in her
town." Or was it imaginary? She seemed to be saying the poem to
him and for him.

SYDRA

Sydra neither moaned nor cried
On the day her father died.
Sydra whom he loved the best
Stood apart from all the rest.
Smiled—and felt her yellow hair.
He had loved his fingers there.

Sydra wore no somber gown
When they bore him through the town.
She alone in dress of red.
"Heartless!" all the neighbors said.
Sydra felt its crimson breast
Where *his* head had loved to rest.

As the box sank under sod
Sydra spied some goldenrod.
Laughed—and plucked its shimmering blade
As the others shrieked and prayed.
"What a minx!" "She does not care!"
He called goldenrod God's prayer.

On the day they read the will
(Leaving her the farm—the mill)
Sydra was not even there
On a straight-backed, parlor chair.
Trout swam in the pool that day—
He had loved to watch trout play.

Sydra never climbed the hill
Where the grave lay, brown and still.
Brought no wreaths, no flower-filled pots
To outdo the neighbors' plots.
Then one dawn they found her there
(Never was her smile so fair)
Dew had gathered on her hair.

Many of the studio people came from little towns. With simple artistry Olga Treskovna had sketched a vivid scene that took them "home" again. There was silence—then applause. Bill Dunnigan thought again, "How fine she is!"

When the crowd thinned, he approached her. "Could we have dinner tonight?" he said earnestly, for it was very important to him.

She seemed to understand. "Yes," she said. "I would like that. But at my flat. I'm going there now to rest all afternoon. Martha will fix dinner. Please come about seven o'clock. I want to talk to you."

"I want to talk to you too," said Bill. He thought, *"I will tell her tonight. I must not wait any longer."*

21

*O*LGA TRESKOVNA WENT HOME to her flat and collapsed on the floor. For two weeks she had been working entirely on her nerve—her determination to finish the picture and not to "let Bill Dunnigan down."

The woman Martha found her an hour later when she came to clean and prepare dinner. She was a calm, level-headed woman, and she got the girl onto her daybed couch and forced some whiskey between her pale lips. Then she called Dr. Hiram Jennings.

Dr. Jennings rushed an ambulance to the apartment building and they took Olga Treskovna to the large hospital with which he was connected. After a quick examination, he told the nurse his patient had only a short time to live. He ordered a blood transfusion. Dr. Jennings was provoked that the girl had ignored his advice about entering a hospital two weeks before.

Olga Treskovna asked for just one thing—to see William Dunnigan, publicity executive at Super Pictures Studios.

It took a while to find Dunnigan. He was not at his Studio office. He was nowhere on the "lot." He was not at the Beverly Wilshire Hotel.

Dunnigan had driven out to Malibu. The sight of the sea always steadied him. He picked out the spot on the beach where he would take Olga Treskovna that night, after their dinner together. The sky was clear. Her star would be shining. Then she should know—and he would know.

He drove back to the Studio for a "still" photograph that he wished to show her. In it, the girl was standing at a convent doorway in her peasant dress, looking straight ahead; and in her lovely, uplifted face was reflected the faith and hope of all mankind.

So thought Dunnigan, and he planned to make posters in color of this "still"—three sheets—eight sheets—to look out from every billboard in every city where "The Garden of the Soul" was shown! He would have it painted on the twenty-story sidewall space of that building on Times Square which was used for advertising.

The girl who tried to imagine that her name was on a single Carnegie Hall billboard, standing there unknown and alone at midnight, would have not only her name but her image on the fronts of half the theaters in America!

At the Studio they told him that Olga Treskovna was at a hospital and asking for him. He rushed out of the building, leaped into his car and drove recklessly past all traffic lights. Somehow he arrived without accident or being stopped by traffic police. It was about seven when he reached the hospital corridor down which at the far end was her private room.

He forced himself to be calm. "Miss Olga Treskovna's room," he said to the nurse behind the floor desk.

"What is your name?" asked the nurse.

"I'm William Dunnigan. She sent for me."

"Yes. We were told to let you see her. Are you a relative?"

"A friend and business associate."

"Has the patient any relatives?"

"I think not. Why?"

"Dr. Jennings left word you should notify any relatives. It is a very serious case."

"I am the only one close to her," said Dunnigan. He somehow felt that this was very terribly the truth. Terribly and yet blessedly the truth.

"You may go in. Room 618. You must not remain too long."

Dunnigan knocked lightly on the door of 618, his throat tight with anxiety. A nurse opened it. He took the few steps to the bedside of Olga Treskovna.

She had the type of beauty that seemed still more lovely with paleness, and now, lying motionless in the hospital bed, she was as pale as any living woman could be. He looked down at her and drank in her unearthly, haunting loveliness which he would never be able to forget.

She opened her eyes. A sad smile came to her lips. The shadow and the sunshine were there at the same time. Sunshine through a darkened cloud.

"Hello, Bill," she said almost inaudibly, "I'm sorry I can't make good about the dinner."

He found his voice. "Gee, kid," he said, and put his hand on hers. She took his hand and held it tightly, and he sat on the chair by the bed. "I sort of thought you weren't looking so strong since you got back from Yuma. But don't worry. Chin up! A good rest and you'll be as fit as rain again. It's going to be a great picture. You're grand—better than Gronka ever could have been! That studying sure was the right dope."

She shook her head. How fine her hair was! The silken brown he had first noted when she bowed her head on the Forty-Second Street burlesque stage. And how wide apart her eyes—and how blue!

"No, Bill," she said. "I'm done for. I know it and I know that you knew. You saw the letter from Dr. Jennings and the x-rays the night you came to my apartment."

Dunnigan's face turned red. "I saw the letter, kid. But that doesn't matter now. All that matters is for you to get well——"

"Bill, thank you for not saying anything. For not telling the director or Mr. Harris. I just had to finish the picture. I was afraid that you would tell them."

"That was your business," said Dunnigan. "I had no right even
—oh, just skip it, kid. We've got to concentrate on pulling you
out of this."

"Remember, Bill," she said dreamily, "I told you I had to make
good quickly. Well, it's come faster than I thought. I won't live
very long. I won't even live until tomorrow."

"No, no!" Dunnigan said. "If these damn doctors told you that,
they're crazy. They don't know half the time what they're talking
about! I had a friend once——"

"Nobody told me," she said, "but I know that's what they think.
This time they're right."

She had a coughing spell that brought the nurse running to her
side. Then she lay quite still for a while. Bill Dunnigan looked
at the grave face of the nurse and understood. He was stunned.
He wanted to fight on but he felt utterly helpless.

She opened her eyes presently and spoke again. "I'm not afraid
to die. It's my lungs, Bill. The Breaker dust. And I caught a
bad cold just before we went to Yuma. I knew I should have
stopped, but I didn't dare stop. I had to go on, had to get this
picture done. My first and my last."

"You're going to make a lot more pictures," Dunnigan said, but
his heart had sunk. "And you'll do plays too—in New York.
You're going to be O. K. Don't worry about anything. Let me
worry from now on. After a few weeks here I'll take you to
Arizona. I know a sanatorium there. It's really like a big, fine
hotel. You'll have a lot of fun. While you're getting well you
can write more poetry. I liked the one about the girl and her
father. I knew you wrote it yourself."

"Thanks, Bill. But I'll not be going to Arizona or New York—
or write any more poetry. I want to go back to Coaltown——"

"Sure, kid. I'll take you to Coaltown too, if you wish."

"You're the only one to take me where I must go. It's not the
town—it's the cemetery—the lovely cemetery above the town—
among my hills."

"No, kid, no!"

"Please listen, Bill, there isn't much time. There's five hundred
dollars in my flat. It's in a glass jar in the bookcase. Behind the
Stanislavsky book. Please take it. I think it will pay for what I
want you to do. You'll do what I want, won't you, Bill?"

"I'll do what you want—anything, kid—only——"

"I want the funeral from the church. St. Michael the Archangel is my church. The undertaker's name is Orloff—James Orloff—write it down, Bill—he's the only one there. I know, for I still owe him eighty dollars on pop's funeral. Pay that first. I own the cemetery lot where pop is. It cost twenty-five dollars. I managed to pay for that when he died. But there's no stone on pop's grave. The priest can locate it though—they have a map. Stanislaus Trocki was pop's name. That's my real name—Trocki. Write that down too. I'll spell it out. T-R-O-C-K-I. Sometime later maybe you'll get a stone and put my name on it—and pop's? Make mine Olga Treskovna, though."

"Kid," said Dunnigan, "you mustn't talk like this!"

"I must," she said. "Please listen to me. I want you to buy something for the church. I don't know what. Something they need badly. They *must* need something that I can buy. I burned a candle once for pop and didn't put in the nickel for it. I had no money that day. It was All Souls' Day, and I just had to burn one! And I want the organ played—by the blind woman if she's still there. And Bill—I want the bells rung—rung for me and pop."

"What do you mean—the bells?" asked Dunnigan.

"They always ring the bells of the church for a funeral, for ten or fifteen minutes, like they do every evening at six o'clock. But it costs five dollars. By the time I paid for pop's grave plot and some other things, I had no money left to pay for the bells. Pop always loved the sound of bells. I felt terrible when I couldn't afford to have them rung for him. So promise me you'll have the bells rung for pop—and me."

"It's a promise," Dunnigan said.

"I think that's all, except I want some little girls with white paper wings—they wear them at Confirmation—to stand by my coffin during the Mass in church. I always wanted to do that for other people, but I never could. I couldn't afford a white dress, or the wings. You'll laugh at me for all these childish wishes."

"I'm not laughing," Dunnigan said, and blew his nose.

"I didn't tell you before," she continued, "but now I'd better tell you, for you'll find it out anyway. My father drank. He really was a grand man, but he got drunk—terribly drunk. He'd stay drunk sometimes for a whole week. He'd get fired from his job. And I'd have to see the foreman to get them to take him back. The fore-man liked me. I'd let him kiss me and then he'd take pop back. But that's why we were always so poor. That's why I had to earn what I could in the Breaker. Pop tried hard not to drink, but he couldn't help himself. Pop should have been a singer, not a coal miner. I guess he didn't have the luck to know someone like you when he was young. Someone who'd say, 'Give the kid a break.' "

She looked hard at Dunnigan. He was holding her hand so tightly it almost hurt. Again she smiled. Sadly—dreamily.

"Don't feel sad, Bill. It won't be bad at all sleeping there among my hills. Down in the town—no. I wouldn't like that. Where the other kids used to laugh at me because my legs were so skinny, and there were big holes in my shoes. One day a gang of them followed me all the way to our house and chanted: 'We saw your old man drunk today! We saw your old man drunk today!' No, I wouldn't want to sleep in the town. But the cemetery—it's way above the town. The hills are all around it. Guarding it. You'll see.

"I used to go there at night, even before pop died. I was safe there from everyone. Even the older people were afraid to go there at night. But there's nothing to be afraid of. It's beautiful, Bill, especially in the moonlight—just like a scene in fairyland, all misty and silvery. And the fireflies dance over the graves and the whip-poorwills sing. I think I'll like to hear the whippoorwills every night."

"Olga—Olga kid," Dunnigan said, "I hope—I know you are all wrong!" He stopped short. The look in her eyes stopped him.

"You'll attend to everything like I wish?" she asked again.

"I promise," he said.

The nurse came over and gave him that look of "You're staying too long."

Olga Treskovna understood the nurse's glance. "I won't talk any more," she said.

Dunnigan stood up. He bent down and kissed her white, thin hand. "So long, kid. I'll be here to see you early tomorrow."

"I'm depending on you, Bill," she said. "I guess I've always depended on you."

Her brave smile again. Then the shadow.

Dunnigan walked out of the hospital. He left his address at the desk at the end of the corridor.

"Call me," he said, "if there is any change for the worse."

He drove back to his hotel. He went to the bar. He drank two double whiskies. Then it dawned on him that he still had not told Olga Treskovna that he loved her. He felt a desperate urgency to tell her before it was too late.

Would they let him in the hospital again that night? He telephoned and asked for the desk on her floor.

The hospital was just trying to reach him. The girl had had a relapse. She had asked for him again. For him and for a priest.

He raced back to the hospital, cursing himself that he had ever left. "She must not die! She must not die!" he found himself repeating.

But the moment he saw the face of the nurse who stood outside Olga Treskovna's room, he knew he was too late.

She had died five minutes before. A priest was in the hospital visiting another patient and had administered the last rites. No pain in her final minutes, the nurse thought. She had just closed her eyes and died.

"She left this letter for you," continued the nurse, and handed Dunnigan an envelope.

He opened the unsealed letter. It was on hospital stationery, and the body of the letter was not Olga Treskovna's writing, but the signature was in her bold, upright hand.

"I took it down while the priest was here," said the nurse. "She dictated it to me. It is witnessed by the priest, an intern, and myself."

Dunnigan read:

This is my last will and testament. I have no relatives. I leave my possessions entirely to my dear friend, William Dunnigan. I want him to keep my books and a picture called "The Presence." The other pictures, my clothes, he can give to Martha Monahan who takes care of my flat. Pay her the week's wages that will be due tomorrow. Mr. Dunnigan is to take charge of my body which I want buried in my native Coaltown, Pennsylvania. He understands fully all my wishes.

"What do I do now?" asked Dunnigan. It was a sweltering night, but he was cold all over. He felt numb.

"Come back in an hour," said the nurse. "We have sent for Dr. Jennings. He will sign the death certificate. We will call an undertaker. Here are her keys. She had them under her pillow. I was to give them to you."

Dunnigan walked dazedly down the hospital corridor. He stepped into the big elevator and went to the ground floor. He got into his car and drove slowly to Olga Treskovna's apartment house. He pulled up at the familiar curb. He did not immediately get out. He took out Olga Treskovna's "will" and read it again. He stared straight ahead. It was a quiet street and deserted. Suddenly he dropped his head on his folded arms across the steering wheel.

Bill (White Spats) Dunnigan of the dance halls, the prize ring, and the "girl shows," sobbed as if his heart were breaking. It was the first time he had cried since he was a small child.

22

*W*HEN HE RECOVERED from this burst of grief, Bill Dunnigan became strangely calm. There was much to be done, and he was the one to do it. He had never sidestepped responsibility.

He realized that he had eaten nothing but one of the small picnic sandwiches since breakfast. He drove around into a near-by main thoroughfare and entered a small bakery restaurant. There was a public telephone sign on its window. That was another thing he wanted. He ordered a beef stew and then, consulting his notebook, dialed a number.

He was calling up the woman Martha. He was glad he had that candy-store number through which he might find her—the number he had asked for the night he discovered that Olga Treskovna was ill. He wanted Martha with him when he went to her apartment now. There were things he wanted a woman to do.

He held the wire until her voice came at the other end.

"Martha," he said, "this is Mr. Dunnigan. Miss Treskovna has just died. At the hospital. I'm eating dinner at a restaurant near her flat. I have to go there and I would like you with me. Can you meet me there, downstairs, in half an hour?"

The woman said she could and would. She was not surprised. She was the one other person who knew about Olga Treskovna's health.

Dunnigan forced himself to eat his beef stew. Then he drank three cups of coffee. He had no desire now for liquor. He wanted a clear brain.

Olga Treskovna was dead. He was thinking about her with a detachment that surprised him. He would never see her again, except in her coffin, perhaps. He would never hear her low, vibrant voice. He would never watch that radiant smile break through the Slavic shadows of her face. She would never know that he loved her. He would never know if she loved him. He would never have that home, with her or anyone else. That last he was sure of. No one else would ever take her place in his life. It would be pretty lonely.

But he *would* hear her voice, see her again! The film "The Garden of the Soul!" He'd forgotten that. There she was, on some ten thousand feet of film, back in the Super Pictures laboratories. That must be his great work now—to make that picture a success—the greatest success any motion picture had ever achieved —a monument strong as granite to her talent, her beauty, her goodness.

It struck him that on her deathbed she must have experienced a satisfaction denied to most of us. Most of us die knowing we have accomplished little or nothing. Nothing at least that will go on living. But this girl of humble beginnings was presently going to give to the world a great new joy and warmth!

And she knew it before she died. As little a thing as the "party" toast of Victor George must have given her an assurance that she had completed a good job. So, perhaps to her, death had not been so heartbreaking. She had done the thing she had wanted to do in life, and done it well.

And he, Dunnigan, could take comfort in the knowledge that he had helped her do it, given her the "break" that had made it possible. Thank God he had not ruined that work of hers by speaking the knowledge that might have prevented the finishing of the picture. Even if he were doomed to loneliness. Even if she was now dead.

He paid his check and drove back to Olga Treskovna's flat. Martha was waiting for him downstairs.

The woman had good sense. She did not slobber grief. "I'm sorry, Mr. Dunnigan," she said, and let it go at that. Dunnigan was grateful.

They went up to Olga Treskovna's apartment. "I have her keys," said Dunnigan, and unlocked the door. He threw on the light switch in the small vestibule.

"Sit down, Martha," he said, "I want to read you her 'will.' It concerns you and me alone." He took from his pocket the hospital envelope and read its brief contents aloud.

The woman wiped her eyes when Dunnigan finished. "She was a good girl," she said, "and always considerate. I never worked for anyone so thoughtful and considerate."

"I had a talk with her this evening before she died," said Dunnigan. "She told me there was five hundred dollars in a glass jar behind a certain book. It is to pay for her funeral. We will now try to find this money."

He located the Stanislavsky book, a thick, dark-covered volume. The jar was behind it and the money, in a neat roll, was inside. Dunnigan counted the money and placed it in his wallet.

"I am taking her body back to Pennsylvania. I'll leave tomorrow if I can. I have a good deal to do and must ask you to attend to things here. I don't want any strangers in the flat."

"Just tell me what you wish done, Mr. Dunnigan."

"I believe the books and the pictures and her clothes are all that belonged to her. The furniture went with the apartment. Get some carton boxes tomorrow. You can probably find some at the grocery stores near by. Pack all the books in them, and have an expressman bring them to me at the Beverly Wilshire Hotel in Beverly Hills. And that picture called 'The Presence.' I will tell the hotel to expect them. Her papers and letters I will collect and take with me tonight. The other pictures are yours. I hope you will treasure them. They are good pictures."

"It's mighty proud of them I'll be! And my children will enjoy looking at them. I'll hang them in my parlor. I have three rooms."

"Now her clothes. Can any of your children wear them? I wouldn't want them sold, or given away to strangers."

"My oldest girl is in high school. They will fit her, I know."

"Good. Let's look at her clothes now, if you don't mind. I want her to be buried in a certain dress. A blue house dress. She wore it the first time I saw her here, before she found you. She cooked a dinner for me herself."

"I know the dress you mean." And the woman opened the door of the clothes closet in the vestibule.

There hung Olga Treskovna's wardrobe. There were not many clothes. A dozen dresses. Several simple coats. Dunnigan recognized the grey cloth coat with a fur-trimmed collar, the one she had worn that Christmas Eve in Iowa. It made him feel very sad. A few hats were on the shelf above, and in shoe holders fastened to the inside of the door were half a dozen pairs of shoes with their trees.

"I'll want you to go back to the hospital with me. We will take the blue dress. And maybe you will pick out the under-things that go with it. I suppose they're in the bureau drawers over there."

"I will know what to take," said the woman, "and I'll take also fresh stockings and a pair of black shoes."

"We'll stop and see the house manager as we leave. I'll tell him you are in charge, and pay him if there's any rent due. But I don't think there is. The month has another week to run, and she probably took the place by the month and paid in advance."

"She paid in advance. I took the money down for her this month."

"Good. Make a bundle of what we want and we'll go. Come back in the morning and attend to the rest. She owes you for this week. How much does she owe you?"

"It's twelve dollars, but I'd rather not take it. With all these beautiful things she is giving me——"

"I want you to take it," said Dunnigan and pulled a roll of bills from his pocket. "Here it is. And here is twenty dollars to pay for boxes, the expressman, and anything else you have to put out money for. Whatever is left, please keep."

"Thank you, Mr. Dunnigan. You can depend on me."

While the woman was collecting the things for the hospital, Dunnigan took the papers from the small desk. They were mostly receipted bills for rent, groceries, milk, a hairdresser. The large x-ray films were still there, and a large envelope in which they came. Dunnigan put the films and all the papers in this envelope.

There were several sheets of paper in her handwriting that seemed to be poetry. Lines were altered or crossed out here and there. "Poor little kid!" said Dunnigan. He put the poetry with the other papers.

Just before they left he stood in front of the picture called "The Presence." It was not a large picture—only about two feet square in its frame.

He had not really read the small script in the lower corner of the white margin. He read it now.

"... and lo, I am with you always,
even unto the end of the world."

Bill Dunnigan was not religious. He had never given any thought to such things as immortality or what happened to us in the Great Beyond. And it was then for the first time that Olga Treskovna seemed to be beside him. She was holding his hand. She was saying the words that were written there on the picture she wanted him to have. "I am with you always, even unto the end of the world."

A wave of content swept over Bill Dunnigan. He was not alone any more. "Kid, I'm still working for you!" he said aloud. "We'll put it over with a bang!"

"What did you say, Mr. Dunnigan?" called the woman Martha from the bedroom alcove.

"Nothing," said Dunnigan. "But I think I'll take this picture with me tonight."

He lifted it from the nail holder that supported it by a short wire at its back. He took a newspaper from the table and put it around the picture.

Then he and the woman Martha left the lonely apartment.

*   *   *

Dunnigan spent the rest of the evening arranging about the body of Olga Treskovna. Although the tasks were tragic, his heart was not heavy. They were together now and would be together always.

The hospital had sent for an undertaker. The body was already gone when Dunnigan and Martha returned there. He paid the hospital bill. He went with Martha to the undertaking establishment.

Martha disappeared with the woman attendant to dress Olga Treskovna. She carried the blue dress Dunnigan wished the girl buried in. Dunnigan selected a simple coffin from the showroom. He filled in and signed the papers necessary to take the body out of the state. He paid the bill from Olga Treskovna's cash in the glass jar. He had used up his own cash money, although he still had an uncashed salary check in his wallet.

He realized he was very tired. He went back to his hotel. In the morning he would arrange about getting a week off to take Olga Treskovna back to Coaltown. Then he suddenly remembered that he had not telephoned the one man besides himself to whom Olga Treskovna's death might be important. Marcus Harris. Well, he needed sleep. He would telephone early in the morning to the Biltmore. No use upsetting Marcus Harris tonight.

And by morning he would have a plan for handling the publicity. Much would have to be changed. He must work out in his mind the best way of breaking the story in the newspapers of Olga Treskovna's death.

23

*D*UNNIGAN WAS AWAKE at seven o'clock the next morning. As he opened his eyes he felt unreal, as though he were some person other than the Bill Dunnigan who was press agent for "The Garden of the Soul." What was wrong? Then it swept over him like a flood.

Olga Treskovna was dead. It was like a knife to his heart. Why was he still alive, now she was gone? Then, the next moment, she was really not dead. She was not dead because every expression of her lovely face, every grace of her slender body, every tone of her voice was recorded in a picture story that would live—a story that he, Bill Dunnigan, was left behind to help make live.

And she was not dead because he had felt her standing by him in her flat, when he had read the lines printed on the margin of that framed gravure.

He got up, went through the customary setting-up exercises a very great fighter had taught him, took a shower, shaved and dressed. All the time his brain was working.

He would tell the truth to the newspapers. That would be thrilling enough! Olga Treskovna had given her life to make that motion picture. She had been like a soldier going out to battle—a soldier who did not falter, although he knew that quick death awaited him. But in that death—victory.

"I'll put it over, kid," he said. "Just watch my smoke! I'll put it over!"

That was how he would explain it to Marcus Harris and he must telephone Mr. Harris at once. Perhaps Harris had already heard the news.

Dunnigan first ordered his breakfast sent to his room. Orange juice, toast, bacon and eggs. And a pot of coffee. He must stoke up for a busy day. Then he asked for the Biltmore and to be connected with Marcus Harris.

"Mr. Harris, this is Bill Dunnigan."

"Yes, Dunnigan. What gets you up so early?"

Harris then did not know. Dunnigan knew Harris was an early riser and might have seen something in the newspapers, if the news had already leaked out. Apparently it had not. So far, so good.

"I have some unpleasant news for you, Mr. Harris. Are you prepared for it?"

"In this business I'm always prepared for it." And Dunnigan could see the little man's wry smile. "What is the trouble now?"

"I would have waited till I saw you at the Studio, but you know Napoleon said, 'Wake me to tell me bad news—the good can wait.'"

"That is the proper way," said Marcus Harris.

"Olga Treskovna died in a hospital last night."

There was a silence at the other end. An ominous silence, Dunnigan thought. Why didn't the man say something?

The silence held and Dunnigan had to continue. "I believe I know how to handle matters so that it will even help, not hurt, the picture," he said.

"You are telling me this girl is dead?" Harris had spoken at last, as if he had not been able to believe what he had heard. There was a strange tone in his voice.

"She is dead. I was at the hospital."

"At what time did she die?"

"It was about nine o'clock."

"Why didn't you telephone me last night?"

"It was a bitter shock to me. I was her best friend. I did not feel like talking about it. I had to attend to her affairs. Make arrangements at an undertaker's. But I will come now to the Biltmore if you wish. It may sound cold-blooded, but Miss Treskovna would understand—we can help the release of the picture with a proper build-up about her death and——"

Marcus Harris cut in. "At what hospital did she die?"

"The Cedars of Lebanon. Her doctor was a Dr. Jennings. I will be right over——"

"No. Meet me at the Studio at nine. I prefer to see you there."

"Yes, sir."

"I should have been told about this last night."

There was a sharp click. Marcus Harris had hung up. He had not even said "Good-by."

Dunnigan had a premonition of trouble. It had not occurred to him that Harris would be angry because he was not notified immediately. Suppose Harris had been back in New York as he might well have been?

Dunnigan was so disturbed that he did not eat his breakfast when it arrived, as it did at that moment. He drank the pot of coffee and paced the floor smoking a cigar. He took the picture of "The Presence" out of the newspaper and set it on his bureau, but it seemed cold and dead. He put it away in the top bureau drawer. Whatever trouble there might be with Marcus Harris, he would face it alone.

He put on his hat and went down to the lobby and bought the morning papers. There was nothing in them of Olga Treskovna's death. In fact, there was a press story on the theater page, which he had telephoned around the afternoon before, about the "party" on the set and the shooting of the final scenes of "The Garden of the Soul." They spoke of Olga Treskovna as if she were alive. One paper even used one of her photographs.

Dunnigan walked to the hotel garage, ordered his car, and drove slowly to the Super Pictures Studios. He had known really big men to be upset by small things. He did not mean Olga Treskovna's death. He meant the fact that he had not communicated with Marcus Harris immediately the night before. Perhaps he had been wrong in not doing that. Marcus Harris had a great deal at stake. He would apologize to him.

He was asked to wait in the outer office of the picture producer's room. That was unusual. He had always walked directly in. He waited ten minutes—fifteen minutes—past the time of his appointment. He smoked half of one cigar, then lit another. Several other studio executives had gone in and out of the sanctum, and Dunnigan thought they regarded him curiously.

At last the buzzer rang—the reception girl picked up the inter-communication phone.

"You may go in now, Mr. Dunnigan," she said.

Dunnigan entered the private office of Marcus Harris. The pudgy man sat at his desk. Dunnigan thought he looked pale and older. Harris did not rise from his desk as he usually did. There was no smile or gesture or word of friendly greeting.

"Sit down, Dunnigan," he said.

Dunnigan sat in a chair opposite the desk. "I'm sorry, Mr. Harris, that I did not telephone you last night. I was very upset. I apologize."

Then came the bombshell.

"I did not ask you to come here to discuss that, although it is customary in my organization to inform me at once of any unusual happening. It makes no difference now. The only matter of interest is that the star player of 'The Garden of the Soul' is dead, and I cannot release the picture. I shall not even cut it. I have ordered all work on it stopped. I have canceled all booking contracts with theaters."

Dunnigan was stunned. He could not believe his ears! He rose unsteadily from his chair. He stood and looked at Marcus Harris as if he were regarding a crazy man. "You surely do not mean what you are saying!" he exclaimed.

"I mean every word of it," said Marcus Harris.

"But you cannot do such a thing!" Dunnigan cried. He was almost inarticulate. It was as if he were drowning.

"You are telling *me* what I cannot do?" Marcus Harris spoke quietly, in contrast to Dunnigan's agitation.

"It's not fair! It's not right! And you'll lose a fortune!" Dunnigan heard his own voice rise almost to a shout.

"I was under the impression that it is my picture and my money."

"Of course, but——"

"It will just about ruin me. All the profits of my other successes are in it. And more. As you say, I will lose a fortune. I will have to start again. Don't tell *me*, Dunnigan, what is right and fair."

"I mean it's not fair to this girl! She gave her life to finish this picture! You shan't rob her of her work! You've got to finish and release 'The Garden of the Soul'! I know how to handle the matter——"

He was standing over Marcus Harris. He was crying out the words like a man possessed!

"Sit down, Mr. Dunnigan," interrupted Marcus Harris. "You are no longer 'handling the matter,' as you put it. I am running my own business from now on, and I'm not running it to promote any actress or actor. Particularly this girl. She was evidently sick when I hired her. When *you* persuaded me to hire her," he corrected. "I must have been insane not to have investigated her."

"Investigated?"

Dunnigan was again on his feet. What could that mean?

"Since you so kindly telephoned me this morning I have checked with her doctor through the hospital where she died. She put one over on me. I don't know if you knew. I give you the benefit of the doubt that you did not, and that she put one over on you also. She had advanced tuberculosis——"

"I knew," said Dunnigan.

"You knew! You persuaded me to spend half a million dollars to back an actress on the road to an undertaker!"

For the first time the voice of Marcus Harris was raised, and there was amazed anger in it.

"What difference does all this make?" cried Dunnigan. "She

gave a great performance. You admitted that. Your director admitted it. Even your leading man! I have seen all the rushes and so have you. I'm no picture expert, but I don't believe there has been a finer performance recorded on any film!"

"I am not in a mood for discussion or argument, Dunnigan," Marcus Harris broke in. His voice was coldly calm again. He regarded for a moment the evident distress of the man who stood opposite his desk.

"I am not a hard man. I feel sorry for you," Harris continued, "and I'll tell you something, although there is no reason why I should tell you. This same thing happened to me once before. My brother Irving was alive then. It was one of our first big pictures. The star died. He released the picture. It failed. That season everything else went wrong for us. The banks would not renew our loans. A theater that we owned burned down. Some people who were injured started legal actions. Our financial troubles killed my brother. He committed suicide. He was alone. I had my faithful wife and somehow kept on. But I am not going to make the same mistake again."

Dunnigan afterwards said he felt horribly weak. You cannot combat a stone wall!

Marcus Harris had spoken with the same finality as when he had refused to have anything more to do with Anna Gronka.

The press agent groped for his chair and sank down, staring at Marcus Harris. He had read once of a charging soldier having both legs suddenly shot off from under him and the man remained fully conscious. Thought he was still charging forward. That was how Dunnigan felt.

"The public does not want to see a picture with a star who has died," continued the voice of Marcus Harris, and Dunnigan realized this idea had become an obsession with the picture producer. "Maybe—after a year or so—I will film 'The Garden of the Soul' again. I'll find a star who won't kick out or drop dead while I am doing it! I'll find a press agent who won't put something over on me—sell me a bill of damaged goods——"

"What do you mean by that?" said Dunnigan. He was on his feet again and flushed.

"You have told me you knew she was ill."

"I knew it only two weeks ago," said Dunnigan.

"Well—that doesn't make it quite so bad. I apologize for what I just said. But I may as well come to the point. You and I are parting company, Dunnigan. I was warned about you back in New York when I bullheadedly hired you, that you were bad luck to any show. That you were a jinx. I didn't listen because I was greedy for fame. That is, my wife is greedy for me to have fame, and I love my wife. And I knew how you had made the names of several Broadway producers famous. I thought you would do the same for me. I always admired Napoleon. You happened to use that idea. I fell for it. It pleased my childish vanity. Maybe it serves me right that I have got a kick in the pants! Maybe I was getting too big for my pants!

"But I can't take on your bad luck—your jinx—any longer. First the Gronka row! Then Treskovna dies! What next?

"If there is any money owed you, the treasurer will pay it. If your union requires that you have two weeks' dismissal salary, take it. I'll gladly pay you a full month's salary. I brought you on from New York—I will give orders to pay your fare back there. I'm leaving for there myself tomorrow, to beg the banks not to put me in jail. Not because of little money, but big money.

"That's all, Dunnigan. I'm sorry, but I really don't want to see you again."

Bill Dunnigan stood there feeling completely crushed. It was the word "jinx" that had crushed him. He felt it was true! Marcus Harris was right. Whatever he, Dunnigan, now touched, withered and died. Olga Treskovna whom he loved, Anna Gronka whom he despised, Marcus Harris whom he respected—they all got it in the neck the minute he, "Jinx Dunnigan," came actively into their lives!

He pulled himself together.

"You can keep your two weeks' salary or your month's salary, Mr. Harris," he said dully, and said it not in anger. "You owe me nothing, not even railroad fare to New York. If I had it, I'd return all the 'little money' you've paid me. I'd give you back the 'big money' you've lost because of Miss Treskovna."

He turned and walked out of the studio offices of Super Pictures, Inc. He did not get into his car. "Have it taken to the garage," he told the guard. "I don't need it any more."

Dunnigan walked to the street and hailed a taxi.

He went first to his hotel. At the desk he cashed his previous week's salary check which he had been carrying in his pocket. He asked them to make up his bill, and arranged for the boxes containing Olga Treskovna's books to be received and stored until he sent for them.

He consulted the porter at the time-table rack and found that a train going East and connecting with Wilkes-Barre, Pennsylvania, left at noon. He figured out when he would arrive at Wilkes-Barre and wrote a wire to the undertaker Orloff at Coaltown. He found there was no telegraph office there, but telegrams were sent by messenger or telephoned from a place called Nanticoke. He had written Orloff's name in his address book, and he jotted down the new name "Nanticoke."

He called up the Los Angeles undertaker and asked to have the body of Olga Treskovna at the station in time for this train. He would be there half an hour early to get the necessary tickets and attend to the checking of the coffin.

Up in his room he quickly packed his large wardrobe trunk. In years it had never been entirely unpacked. That, he would have the porter ship directly to New York. It had been so shipped to Hollywood, for no plane would carry such a large trunk. He put what he would need for the next week in a suitcase. There was a box of fifty Regina Perfectos still unopened. Thank God for them! He tossed them into the suitcase. He sent for a porter and had his baggage taken downstairs.

In the lobby again, he entered the bar for a last drink in California. He reflected, as he sipped it, that he should never have come to Hollywood. Pictures were not for him. No—if he hadn't come, Olga Treskovna might have died as just a "stand-in." At least the poor kid had had her fling. Six weeks of happy achievement! And she'd died believing her work would live.

Perhaps death was the end anyway. A long sleep into oblivion. So that it did not matter now to her what happened back here. Dunnigan hoped so. God, what a rotten, disgusting world to be stuck in! He finished his drink.

He intended to carry out Olga Treskovna's dying wishes to the letter. He took a taxi to the railway station and was just a little alarmed when he found that after buying the two tickets required by rule—one for himself and one for the corpse—he had only some three hundred and fifty dollars left in the wallet. They were coach

tickets at that. He decided he'd best forgo the luxury of a sleeping
car. He had no idea what the funeral expenses at the Pennsylvania
end would be.

His money and hers had disappeared like water—two hundred
and fifty dollars to the Los Angeles undertaker, the hospital bill,
the railroad tickets, his own sizable hotel bill. He had, of course,
the Brooklyn Dime Savings bankbook. It had lain in a drawer in
his trunk and he had transferred it to his wallet when packing.
Well—he could eat for a week or two when he finally reached New
York.

He bought a couple of early edition afternoon papers. There was
a brief announcement, evidently sent out by the Harris organization. "Olga Treskovna, player of a leading role in 'The Garden of
the Soul' has died suddenly. Marcus Harris will shelve the picture."
One paper mentioned briefly that this was the second setback for
"The Garden of the Soul" and recalled the Gronka incident. As
for Olga Treskovna, she was not yet well enough known for the
papers to play up her death on a bare announcement. Dunnigan
could have handled it, but now——. Poor little kid!

At noon Bill Dunnigan boarded his coach train. He had not
phoned any of his friends to say good-by. He traveled alone, except
that (like the refrain of the old ballad) the body of his dearest pal
was "in the baggage coach ahead."

"Low" did not adequately express his mood. "Lifeless" might
have. He speculated no more on life and love and eternity. He
gave up utterly trying to figure out what it was all about. To hell
with it!

------- *24* -------

*T*HE MIND of William Dunnigan had wandered
back to fabulous Hollywood, but his feet were now mounting the
wooden steps that led up to the raised lawn of the shabby Church
of St. Michael the Archangel and its adjoining parish house in un-
fabulous Coaltown. Again he was yanked into the present, as the

heel of his shoe caught in a jagged space where part of a step was missing.

The press agent swore, and focused his attention on the buildings before him.

They did not improve with a face-to-face view. Undertaker Orloff had spoken of the church as "going to pieces." In a physical sense it did seem to Dunnigan that the disintegration was the result of poverty rather than purposeful neglect.

He had noted from across the street that the grass lawn was well kept and green. The geraniums in the circular flower bed between the two structures were bright red, and the sod about them had been newly spaded. A quaint border of small, white flowers was carefully planted around this bed.

It was the wretched frame buildings themselves that needed repair and a coat of paint. Several coats. He saw why the church seemed to lean—like an unlovely tower of Pisa. The stone foundations along the parish house side had sunk too deeply into the sod.

The front of the small, dingy parish house was not on a line with the church but several yards back from the embankment. The front of the church was separated from the top of the wooden steps only by a concrete walk, from which several stone steps, flanked by a wooden handrail, led up to the church doorway.

Dunnigan followed around the narrow, concrete walk, and crossed the several yards of lawn to the side door of the parish house, which seemed to be its used entrance. There was a dark scowl on his face.

He did not relish the task before him.

Bargaining with an undertaker had been sordid enough. Now, with only a small sum left in his wallet, he must bargain with a worthless priest, to arrange for the final details of Olga Treskovna's funeral.

There was something especially obnoxious about haggling with a priest. It seemed almost indecent.

He hoped this Father Paul was in. He already despised the man and he wanted to get through with the unhappy business quickly. Anyway, some hundred and fifteen dollars was all that he could still pay—all that remained in the wallet to be wrangled over!

Dunnigan mastered his distaste, mounted two more steps to a

small side veranda, and looked for the bell. It was not an electric
bell, but an old-fashioned knob that you pulled outward.

He gave this bell-knob a vicious jerk and could hear the prolonged jangle inside. He stood waiting, impatiently.

25

*T*HE BELL'S JANGLE disturbed the thoughts of
a youngish man seated in a small, bare room just off the entrance
hallway on which this side door opened. He wore a long, black
cassock. He was seated at a narrow desk, which, with the exception of two folding chairs, was the room's only furniture. He had
been sitting there for the past hour, and held in his hands a sheaf
of bills. Unpaid bills. The top one was for church candles, went
back several months, and amounted to some sixty-odd dollars.

The state of mind of this man was not much different from that
of the one whose ring disturbed his thoughts—except that the depressed thoughts of the priest had nothing of bitterness in them.

This priest was Father Paul. If you had given him a second
glance, which you would not, you would have described him as "in-
significant." The thin, undersized body was topped by a small
head for which the prominent nose and ears were a size too large.
And the chin was not strong enough for the nose.

Since his church served the Polish population, he was a Pole. He
had been born and reared in near-by Scranton. He looked to be
and was about thirty years of age.

He had not been thinking of the unpaid bills he held before him,
except as they were a tangible evidence of his life's inefficiency. He
was thinking that as a priest he was a complete failure.

How much longer could he go on?

He had had every chance, he told himself, as he now reviewed
his "career." His widowed mother had used most of her meager
earnings as a "dressmaker" to prepare him for entrance into St.
Joseph's Seminary for the priesthood. How proudly she had watched

when he was ordained and said his first Mass at the Cathedral in their native Scranton! He knew that she had visioned through misty eyes her son as someday a Bishop—a Cardinal—even (if God were good) a Pope! So dream all mothers and there is no folly in their dreams. In that great democracy of the Church, peasants have worn the Triple Crown!

He—the Pontiff of Christendom! Not that Father Paul himself had ever had any such lofty dreams or ambitions. His ambition was a simple one—to serve his fellow man. What was wrong? Why was he such a failure? He really did not know. He only knew he had not even "made good" as a parish priest!

Father Paul was almost glad his mother had not lived to witness his present state.

This mother had known that her son had faith. That he wanted devoutly to live like, and carry out the teachings of, the Master. What more was needed! It disturbed her a little when less fervently religious but more personable young men moved ahead of her son up the golden ladder. Were sent to thriving parishes. It had disturbed Father Paul also. To be pure in heart, to be humble, did not seem to be enough in a practical, commercial era. But the mother's basic faith never faltered. She prayed each day to that Blessed Mother who would understand the hopes of mothers. And at last, the Bishop, whom she knew and whom she had never ceased to importune, told her he was giving the lad a church in Coaltown where an elderly priest had died.

The Bishop did not tell her it was an unwanted church, so run down at the heel that it might soon possess no heel at all! It would not have mattered if he had. Her son would at last have a parish! Her boy was on his way to high advancement! She had died feeling the certainty of a dream fulfilled.

The dilapidated state of the affairs of St. Michael's in Coaltown did not at first matter to Father Paul. He had one feature that told of an inner fire of which the outer face and body gave no trace. The eyes were unusual. They mirrored his ardent, unselfish soul. They mirrored, also, this inner flame for God's tasks.

He saw in the run-down condition of St. Michael's his opportunity—his life work. He would first, of course, administer to the spiritual needs of his flock. But besides that, he would work for their physical welfare and their mental progress. He would search out unhappiness, illness, unnecessary poverty, and not just wait till they came to him. He would start at the root of the drab existence in these mining towns. With better sanitation and health knowledge, with some cultural interests even, he would show these people how to lift themselves out of their black environment. Did not the Master start with the healing of physical needs? Then, with clear lungs and alert minds, these people would breathe more deeply of a spiritual life.

It was a Quixotic dream. There was plenty of unhappiness, illness, poverty to tilt at, but the contented possessors of these attributes entirely misunderstood Father Paul's solicitude.

His rounds of calls were considered prying into personal affairs. His kindly questions and suggestions the further proof of it. Was he trying to find out how much money they had? Why couldn't he stay in his church where he belonged! When they wanted him they would send for him. He need not snoop around and give advice about health. He looked none too healthy himself!

Father Paul could cook, liked to cook, and when he had the temerity to suggest that pork chops fried in deep lard were not the ideal diet for an ailing child, it was going too far! Coaltown had cooked in deep lard for years.

Worse was yet to come. It was reported one day that Father Paul had given some sort of "absolution" to a dying Jewish peddler, for there was no Rabbi in the place. He had heard of the man's illness and called at his shack at the edge of the town. Perhaps this young priest was not even a good Catholic! He had attempted to justify his action to a "committee" that questioned him about it by saying that the peddler believed in the same God they did—was going to meet the same God that would greet them!

Attendance, never large, for the church was a small one, fell off steadily. Parishioners transferred their worship to other churches whose priests spoke ardently of hell-fire on Sundays and who let them alone the rest of the week.

Thus, the practical result of three years of effort was near financial disaster to St. Michael's. The collections consisted mostly of pennies. The building became more weatherbeaten each year. There was no money to repaint it. There was no money to rebuild its foundations which were sinking because a mine shaft had been driven beneath them. There was not even money to pay the bills for altar and shrine candles.

Coaltown had almost crushed Father Paul—defeated him. Just as it had tried to crush Olga Treskovna. Just as it was crushing Bill Dunnigan.

You could not fight the Breaker and its works!

* * *

Such was the man and the disconsolate reverie that the ring of a very irritated Bill Dunnigan interrupted. Father Paul sighed, put the unpaid bills down on his desk, arose from his chair, went to the door and opened it.

Dunnigan surveyed the unattractive priest. The irritation in the press agent's steel-grey eyes hardened to contempt. He was thinking: *So you are Coaltown bastard Number Two that I must traffic with!*

"Are you Father Paul?" he demanded aloud.

"Why, yes—I am Father Paul."

As this priest only stared back and made no move of invitation to enter, Dunnigan abruptly stated his business.

"My name is Dunnigan. I have the body of a girl, who was a parishioner of your church, across the street in the undertaking place. She has a plot in your cemetery where her father is buried. Paid for in full—she told me. I want to arrange for what you call a church funeral tomorrow. How much do you charge?"

The truth is that Father Paul, usually calm, always courteous, had been very much startled by the appearance and the abrupt demand of this stranger. Startled and alarmed.

On first opening the door he had thought he was confronting an aggressive salesman or a bill collector. Salesmen came occasionally with wares that ranged from church supplies down to assorted brushes and "investment securities." None-too-polite collectors had been appearing lately with more than comfortable frequency.

He quickly became himself. "Come in," he said in a friendly voice. He led the stranger to the small room. "Please have a chair." He indicated one of the two folding chairs opposite the desk, and Dunnigan sat down stiffly, holding his derby in his lap.

Father Paul was trying to be courteous, but he did not care for the harsh, almost insulting tone of this stranger when the man had stated his errand. Still, in the midst of financial chaos, here was someone demanding to pay money! A practical mind (even of a religious turn) would have seen the heaven-sent answer to some of those bills on the desk. It did flash across the little priest's consciousness. But only for a second.

What disturbed him now was that there had been a need in his parish—an illness—a death—that he had been entirely ignorant of. He hastened to say, "I did not know there had been a death in my parish! I am sincerely sorry to hear it. Had I been informed of the illness, I would have been at your service, sir, before."

Father Paul had seated himself behind his desk and was leaning forward in his anxiety.

"Oh, she died in California," Dunnigan answered impatiently. He did not like the intense way the priest looked at him. In all likelihood he was again being sized up for what he was worth. He noted that his financial question had not been answered.

"I arrived in Coaltown with the body only an hour ago," he continued with rising irritation, "telegraphed your local undertaker who met me at Wilkes-Barre. The girl's father's name was Stanislaus Trocki. Hers, Olga Trocki. If there's anything due on the father's funeral service—it was four or five years ago—I'll square it before we talk business about the daughter's job."

He produced his wallet and placed it sharply on the edge of the desk. The name of "Trocki" in Coaltown seemed to call for a show of currency. What he wanted out of this priest was—*How much?*

The unpaid bills lay before Father Paul. His eyes were drawn toward the top one. Across its bottom was stamped in red, inside a blatant red square of heavy border, the words

OVERDUE!

PLEASE REMIT!

Dunnigan could not help but see these large words across the small desk. A mental sneer lowered the corners of his mouth. Even religion in Coaltown seemed primarily concerned with money and accounts!

Father Paul noted the direction of his visitor's glance and frowned. He took up the bills hastily, folded them, and placed them in a drawer.

"I was looking over some accounts when you came," he said, and then, as if he must explain, "It is a part of my duty."

"I'll do my business strictly on a cash basis," snapped Dunnigan. "The father's account first."

Father Paul was now really annoyed by this ill-mannered stranger's persistent references to money. However, he did not change his tone.

"It was not God's will that I serve here four years ago," he said quietly. "I would not know about a service then. I recently destroyed a book I found containing a list of money due the church from its members. I did not care to have it in my desk. I am indebted to my parishioners, not they to me."

Dunnigan eyed the priest. He did not quite understand Father Paul's last statement, or the challenge in the calm eyes. Perhaps the crafty priest wished to pretend generosity regarding any old accounts, in order to charge more for a new one! The press agent wanted the all important money question answered. How much?

He now gave that question to the priest in such vehemence as would end fencing.

"I believe there was nothing due anyway about the father's burial service," he barked. "The church got its! I just wanted to be sure. Now we can get down to our present business."

"Please do," said Father Paul.

"I'd like to know your cash charge for a Mass, a funeral service, and—let me see—" (again Dunnigan looked at his notebook) "the organ to be played—and perhaps you priests understand this, 'six girls with wings to stand beside the coffin.' I'll pay in advance for all of it, without bargaining, if the amount isn't beyond my means. And perhaps you will be kind enough to make me out a bill."

Dunnigan took his wallet and significantly tapped it on the priest's desk. He wanted this distasteful transaction completed without further delay.

Father Paul, taking cognizance of this gesture, and the implications in the words preceding it, raised his eyes to those of Bill Dunnigan, and the press agent noted for the first time their strength and depth. And the flash of anger, also, that flared within them.

It was not only the people of Coaltown, thought Father Paul, who could not understand! This outsider even—with his insulting rudeness——

But hold. Maybe it was his own fault. Maybe that was what was wrong with him as a priest. He just did not have the grace to convey his meaning to others.

The anger subsided, and intense sorrow replaced it. Sorrow for himself. Sorrow that there were so many people in the world who could not believe in brotherly love—in honesty—in helping your neighbor as you yourself would be helped.

When he spoke at last there was no anger, but his voice held a quiet strength and dignity.

"For whatever I can do—for whatever my humble church can do —there will be, if I may use your words, no cash charge. So I'm afraid I cannot make you out a bill."

"You mean you do not get anything at all for the Mass? And for the use of your church?"

"I make no financial charge."

There was such a bewildered look in Dunnigan's eyes that Father Paul now really felt sorry for the man. He felt that he must ease the situation by the mention of something that could be paid for.

"I believe our organist receives three dollars for playing at a funeral," he said. "You can pay her directly. But I have found that she will gladly play without charge, if no funds are available. My organist is a blind woman, but very talented. I understand, as a priest and a Pole, what the departed one meant by 'girls with wings,'" and a brief smile lit up the eyes. "It proves a true Polish birthright. It is one of our most happy customs brought from the older country, and used when a child is confirmed. We had such a Confirmation last Sunday. I am sure I can find six children who will be glad to serve. These children do not charge, sir, for their services."

Father Paul's lips seemed now almost ready to smile, but the matter brought no humor to his caller.

"I didn't mean that the children would charge!" exclaimed a flustered Dunnigan, "but you yourself—*you* must charge something! There *must be* a funeral fee!"

This was completely cockeyed! And Dunnigan knew he was trying to defend his own brash manners. He felt his face becoming very red.

Father Paul realized Dunnigan's acute embarrassment, and now he really smiled—an open, friendly smile. "If you desire to make an offering to the blessed Saint Michael—he is our Patron Saint—"

Father Paul indicated a colored Polish lithograph of the winged Saint clad in his armor, which hung framed on the wall at Dunnigan's back—"my church will, of course, receive it, and be grateful. But I assure you, it is entirely voluntary. There is no obligation on your part to do so."

The hard-pressed priest really meant what he said! This was no "act." Turning back from the poster-like picture of Saint Michael and looking into the clear, glowing eyes of the living man of God opposite him, Dunnigan could not doubt it for a second.

The press agent's own eyes lowered and lit on the wallet he had so cynically placed on Father Paul's poor desk. It was a long, handsome wallet of dark, tooled leather. It had often been admired. But it seemed a monstrous, ugly thing in this tiny, bare room whose furnishings were three folding chairs, a desk, and a cheap lithograph. Something out of place and of no consequence. He took it up hastily and replaced it in his pocket. Bill's knowledge of the Bible was fragmentary, but there flashed into his mind a long-forgotten Sunday School lesson about the money changers being cleared from the Temple. And he, Bill Dunnigan, down to his last hundred bucks, was in the role of a money changer!

"I beg your pardon, Father," he said. "I had you all wrong! Please forgive me. I ask your pardon. You see, I have just come from making certain financial arrangements with a Mr. Orloff across the street."

Dunnigan realized he had been acting like the cheapest heel. Rasping at this priest like an East Side hoodlum, insulting him, insulting not only his cloth but his church, his religion! Father Paul should have ordered him to leave. But instead of throwing him out, this gentle person, beset by God alone knew what worries, had listened patiently, overlooked insults, smiled, was willing to do what he could to help, and wanted nothing at all for the doing!

"That is quite all right," Father Paul was saying, "the best of us often makes mistakes—just forget it. I can understand why you spoke as you did, but do not blame Mr. Orloff or hold it against him. He runs a business which has many expenses, and people sometimes forget to pay when it is all over."

Remembering the papers he had seen the priest thrust out of sight, Dunnigan wanted to ask, "Haven't *you* expenses also, and don't people *always* forget to pay you when it is all over?" But he refrained. He was forming a liking for this funny-looking priest guy who even tried to defend a character like Orloff.

"I'll certainly make an offering and I'll not forget it," said Bill Dunnigan impulsively. "All I can afford. Father, I——"

Again Dunnigan had to check himself. He was on the point of blurting out the whole story to this man he had been despising only a few moments before. How he had met this girl, how brave and determined she had been, how she had dreamed of putting some happiness into the world, of bringing some happiness even to this miserable Coaltown, and how she had been cheated out of her dream by the obsession of Marcus Harris connected with releasing a picture with a star who was dead. How he, Dunnigan, felt that somehow he was to blame for it all, because of the "jinx" that seemed to pursue everything he undertook to do. How he'd drawn nothing but kicks in the face since he had broken the news to Marcus Harris, until he had come to the conclusion that everybody in the world was as selfish and mean as Orloff the undertaker.

Had Bill Dunnigan only known how Father Paul would have thrilled because a fellow man wished to open his heart to him!

But the press agent did not know. He thought that he had no right to unload troubles on this priest who already had plenty of his own, if observation, and what the undertaker had said about St. Michael's church, were true. And there was something cheerful he could say—if this priest would not misunderstand.

"Father—" Dunnigan started again, "there is one thing I *must* ask you to let me do—for you and your church. Please understand how I mean it. It has nothing to do with the funeral service. This girl wanted to buy something for your church. Something you need. It must be simple, I'm afraid, because she did not leave very much money. But she felt there must be something she could buy."

"That was thoughtful of her," said Father Paul.

"You see, she told me that once, on All Souls' Day, she burned a candle to her father and mother without putting down the jitney to pay for it. She was very poor, Father, when she lived here——"

The priest held up his hand and smiled again. It was an embracing smile. It was like a firm, warm handclasp. Bill's liking for Father Paul went up another notch.

"I rejoice that she did not forget the holy day and burned that candle," Father Paul said. "And I think the blessed Saints rejoiced. I don't think they were worried about that—ah, jitney."

Dunnigan caught a twinkle now in the eyes of the priest. And he caught the friendly repetition of the slang word he had used without thinking. This priest had a sense of humor! An all-right guy for sure!

"Don't mind my vocabulary, Father," he said. "I'm new to this church talk. But you see how it is. I *must* get something for you! I've got to! I gave my word I'd do it. Something your church needs—something you yourself really want your church to have!"

He was conscious he had added the last phrase himself. But he felt that Olga Treskovna, could she have known this priest, would have said just that.

The smile faded from the priest's face and was replaced by a look of longing. Father Paul did have a secret desire. It was a "vanity" and he had resolutely put it aside as such, when he had been tempted. But he had seen a picture of what he wanted in the catalog of a Philadelphia Catholic supply house. He had locked the catalog away in the lowest drawer of his desk, where he would not see it; but sometimes, alone late at night, he would take it out and gaze at the picture.

He did not mind the shabbiness of his own vestments. They would do for him, the servant in God's house. But his altar—the very floor of the Temple (as it were) of his Blessed Lord—should have only the best! What it had was cheap in texture and even repaired where it had been torn.

Father Paul wanted desperately a new altar cloth.

"I do want something," he said. "And if you care to provide it, it would give me great happiness. I need a new cloth for my altar. I know I should not dream of such a thing when there are more pressing needs, but I cannot help it."

Dunnigan hesitated. "May I ask—I *must* ask—just what this altar cloth would cost?"

He felt he had never phrased a more hateful question in his life.

"Ah, that is it!" said Father Paul. "Such things must be bought."

Dunnigan could see the priest gathering his courage to speak the ominous words—words that would probably end his dream!

"There is one that would be beautiful for twenty dollars. It is of the finest linen, and, I am sure, with care it would last for years. I would wash it and iron it always myself to be certain. There is another—ah, but that is too much to ask, I know—there is another, with long fringe and the Sacred Heart embroidered on it, for thirty dollars. But please—the twenty-dollar one would be quite sufficient. I should not even have mentioned the other!"

Bill Dunnigan looked into Father Paul's eyes. He had looked into many eyes that wanted things, in an active life of contact with his wanting fellow men—and women. Eyes that wanted money— eyes that wanted fame—eyes that wanted excitement—eyes that wanted lust. But never had he gazed into eyes in which the wish was so fervent, so intense, and yet so utterly pure, so selfishly unselfish.

He thought of the thousands of dollars that had been wasted, thrown aside, on the plays he had been connected with—on the picture Marcus Harris had just made! Enough to buy ten thousand altar cloths. And here was a man to whom just one such cloth (cost —thirty dollars), meant supreme happiness.

"I think we can manage it," he said. "One altar cloth or the other. I will know which one the bank roll can afford when we are all finished tomorrow."

"Thank you," said Father Paul. "Thank you with all my heart!"

"Besides the church service, I'm afraid I'll have to impose on you for some other help," commenced Dunnigan. There was real apology now in his tone.

"That is all right," said the priest. "That is why I am here." This stranger was turning out to be a different person from the one whose bell jangle had even sounded unfriendly—who had towered so gloweringly in the parish house doorway a short time before. If only Father Paul could convey to him his happiness to serve!

"We must find out right away about this girl's cemetery plot," the priest continued.

"Yes. I want to go to the cemetery next—if I can," Dunnigan said. "The girl told me that there was no stone on her father's grave, but that you had a map. I remember that especially, Father. I thought how strange a map of graves must be!"

"I will show you," said the priest. He opened a drawer of his desk and took out a large rolled chart. He unrolled the chart and Dunnigan pulled his chair closer and held down one end. It looked like the plan of a small town—streets, blocks, and smaller squares with names written in their borders.

"The last time I looked at a chart like this, Father," said Dunnigan (holding that chart seemed another friendly link between them), "it was the plan of the Dempsey-Tunney fight arena. Tex Rickard had the names of box-holders and ringside-seat buyers written in the spaces, and a lot of customers were phoning squawks about where their seats were located—" The press agent suddenly remembered where he was, and to whom he was talking.

"That was a good fight," said Father Paul.

"You! You know about it!" exclaimed Bill Dunnigan.

"I read about it. I was just a lad in school. I have always wondered about the 'long count.' "

"Gee, Father!" cried Dunnigan. "Gee!"

Now he felt that he really knew this priest! And it was a pleasure just to meet such a man and be in his company!

"What did you say was the family name of this member of my parish?" asked Father Paul.

"Why, Tunney—I mean Trocki. Stanislaus Trocki."

Dunnigan had been about to tell the Father his own idea of that count. But the priest was poring over the grave plan. Bill mustn't forget to tell him, however, before he left tomorrow.

Dunnigan pulled his mind back to the grave chart and bent over it with Father Paul. "If there was no tombstone, maybe the grave isn't even marked here! I suppose no one cared for it when the daughter left Coaltown."

"All my graves are cared for," said Father Paul proudly. "You see, I like gardening—maybe I should have been a gardener—and only last week the gravedigger and I, and a poor lad I get to help us, cut the grass where people had moved away or families died out. And every grave should be recorded—I've found it! Right there! That's on the north side, by the border fence. See! 'Trocki' is written in the space! We'll have no trouble now in locating it."

"She wanted to be buried by her father."

"There is room for a second grave, according to the plan."

"And who do I talk to about digging the grave? Gee, but I'm a lot of trouble to you, Father!"

But Father Paul's face was getting happier every moment.

"When we leave the cemetery we can stop at the gravedigger's

house. He's an old man who lives halfway up the hill. I had forgotten—you'll be able to pay out some money about that!" There
was that friendly smile twitching at the corners of Father Paul's
lips.

"Good!" said Bill Dunnigan and he too was smiling.

"There's a fixed fee that goes to this gravedigger. Seven dollars.
The graves used to be always seven feet long and he told me it was
figured a dollar a foot! Poor man, he earns his money, for our
mountain soil has many rocks—sometimes surface veins of coal. It
often takes a whole morning to dig a new grave."

"We'll have no argument about the seven dollars," smiled back
Dunnigan.

Three dollars for the organ. Seven for the grave. Total expense
with Father Paul—ten dollars! The money would hold out, with
the thirty-dollar altar cloth thrown into the bargain. And whatever
was left in the bank roll would go to Saint Michael the Archangel
(even if he did have a long name!)—less the press agent's hotel bill
and the cost of a coach ticket to New York. So calculated Mr. Dunnigan.

Yes, and when he got back to New York, he would turn that silly
Brooklyn Dime Savings bankbook into cash, and send back a money
order for whatever that red-stamped, "Please Remit" bill amounted
to that had troubled Father Paul when he arrived. And a photograph of the famous "long count" incident, of which Dunnigan had
always treasured several. He would even get the two fighters and
the referee to write their autographs across it!

He'd send the photograph framed! He wondered if it would be
proper to have the picture of a prizefight in a parish house? Why
not? This Saint Michael certainly looked like a scrapper—he had
a lance upraised in one hand and stood in a real fighting stance!

Anyway, this grand priest should not lose by this day's work!
And maybe Father Paul would forget what a loud-mouthed jerk he,
Dunnigan, had acted when he first came in.

— 26 —

*B*ILL DUNNIGAN and Father Paul started for the cemetery. The priest wore his long black cassock, and had put on the low-crowned, curled brim, "shovel" Roman hat that went with it. Under his arm he carried the rolled-up graveyard plan.

They made strangely contrasting figures—these two men of different worlds! Dunnigan was taller by a full head and shoulders. Though soiled from the five-day train trip, his nearly-new plaid suit of pale red and blue checks on grey bespoke the flashy Broadway atmosphere in which he moved. His derby hat was at its customary angle. A green silk handkerchief projected from his breast pocket. His white spats were smudgy, but they, too, were new, and the shoes that needed polishing were heavily heeled and soled, and shapely.

Father Paul's cassock was old and worn. There was an obvious darning at one tight elbow. His shoes were thin and bulged at the side—a small patch on one of them where the leather had cracked through. But the face of the priest was now eager and almost glowing. And his step was more firm and rapid than that of his companion.

Father Paul was doing the thing he wanted most to do—helping a fellow man! A thing that Coaltown had not often permitted him to do.

Dunnigan glanced sideways at the frail figure that matched his stride. He felt a sudden great friendship for this little man. And a great admiration. In spite of adversity, poverty, obvious frustration, Father Paul had not quit. He was battling on! He had not become mean and sour and bitter. He had even defended Orloff, and Orloff had called Father Paul a "poor sap."

In contrast, what about himself, Bill Dunnigan? He had taken it lying down from Marcus Harris. He had sulked and felt sorry for himself all through that long train ride. Next, he had let Coaltown make him as mean and petty as the meanest man in it.

He would now, as quickly as possible, bury Olga Treskovna, the only girl he had ever loved, and then slink back to New York and live in deadly fear of his jinx. At that moment he, Bill Dunnigan, who had fought his way up from the slums to the top of his profession, was without doubt the world's champion quitter!

It was the most disturbing thought the press agent had yet had. Further unhappy pursual of it was interrupted by a question from Father Paul.

"How old was the girl who died?"

"She was twenty-two," said Dunnigan. And with his answer a fierce bitterness again swept over him.

They had reached the end of the main street, past the rows of company houses, saloons, dusty stores. They were about to cross a small bridge over some railroad tracks that were submerged in a cut—tracks for coal ore cars. Mounting huge on one side was one of those man-made hills of "slack," and black smoke rose from it in several places. Loaded cars were bumping along the tracks below, and the dust from them shot up through the wide cracks between the wooden planks of the bridge flooring. The dust made both Father Paul and Bill Dunnigan cough.

"That was another thing, Father," said Dunnigan, "another thing that caused me to shoot off my mouth the way I did back at your place. This girl was only twenty-two, with all of her life ahead of her. And she had to die! She died because of this town, Father. Because of the coal dust that had damaged her lungs when she was a child here. She told me she worked in what you call the Breaker. She had tuberculosis. So in one hour I had come to hate this town. I regarded it as her murderer. How do people stand it here!"

Father Paul suddenly spoke as he had not spoken to any man. He bared to this stranger his own frustration—the thing that troubled his soul to madness.

"It can be cured—it can be prevented—it can be wiped out! Just as sin can be wiped out," the priest exclaimed. "This tuberculosis and the other things that go with it, I mean. The mining work must be done. Coal must be dug from the earth. But disease does not have to march with it. Disease and wretchedness and untimely death. That was one of the things I thought I could help about when I came here. And I have failed utterly!"

"Why couldn't you help about it?" asked Dunnigan.

"Ignorance—inertia—indifference—greed. Most of all—my own inefficiency. There should be a hospital here. There should be a nursing service. There is not even a doctor nearer than Nanticoke, six miles away! There should be new health-saving machinery in the Breaker, in the mines. The miners' families should be taught the simple rules of properly cooked food—fresh air—" Father Paul made a gesture of despair.

"I tried to talk to the people of my own parish. They thought I was attempting to interfere in their private affairs. I did persuade a Visiting Nurse Association in Scranton, where I came from, to send two nurses twice a week. The Coaltown people would not listen to them. Shut doors in their faces. The nurses soon gave up. The owners of the mines are not Coaltown folk. They seldom come here. Anyway, they do not care, so long as the mines make money. Why, only last week I was reading about a new drug called penicillin. They say it can stop the streptococcus germs."

Dunnigan looked at this frail man. This "poor sap" who didn't know how to "hustle for the dough." He felt that he was looking at a great man. He felt a great, tugging urge to help Father Paul. But how?

Bill Dunnigan, the jinx press agent, could not even help himself!

"Have you given up trying to do something about it?" he asked.

"I almost had," said Father Paul, "but I am not going to give up!" There was a moment's silence and then the priest continued under this impulse to complete confession, "I had wanted a new altar cloth for months. I had prayed for one. I had decided I would never have one. I had almost decided, God help me, that prayer was not answered any more. And then you came along, Mr. Dunnigan!

"The altar cloth is not important, but my faith is important, my belief in prayer. Now I shall start again. Perhaps I did not go about it the right way. I seemed to antagonize the people. Maybe there is another way. I must think hard and pray for guidance."

They plodded up the steep hill roadway. The sidewalks ended at the houses by the bridge. Bill Dunnigan was thinking hard.

"Gee, Father!" he said at last, "you make me very much ashamed of myself."

Now they had reached the top of the hill and swung around a sharp bend. They were, in fact, going back in the direction of the town but on this higher level. They proceeded a couple of hundred yards between pasture fields and, suddenly, there were the five cemeteries on both sides of the road. They passed the first on the left, and came to the iron gate of the second. The metal scrollwork in an arch above the gate spelled "St. Michael the Archangel."

They moved down the central gravel path between the green graves, past the high cross and its crucified Christ on a round mound at the center, and then they walked across the grass to the far side which overlooked the town. Father Paul opened his cemetery plan and they quickly found where Olga Treskovna's father was buried. There was room beside the unmarked mound for a second grave.

So this was where Olga Treskovna would sleep. Dunnigan gazed about at the plateau. It was indeed a wonder spot. Quiet, peaceful, breathtaking, majestic. The distant wooded hills ringed it like battlements, as if they would protect it from all the tragedy and sordidness of the world. The girl had felt that way about them, Dunnigan remembered. Farmlands stretched from the cemeteries to these hills. Dunnigan thought of the two poems she had written. And for just a brief second she seemed again beside him, holding tightly to his hand.

"Don't you think it's beautiful, Bill?" she seemed to say, "just like I told you!"

"Beautiful—but lonely, kid," he answered.

"Ah, Bill, it's just because your knees are tired, climbing my hill!" And there was her low, musical laugh.

"They sure are!" said Dunnigan ruefully.

"Did you speak?" said Father Paul.

"I—I was speaking to the girl," said Dunnigan. He felt that Father Paul would understand.

"She could not have a more beautiful resting place," said the priest.

It was now about six o'clock. The sun was performing its nightly miracle of slowly sinking behind the westernmost hills. The thin face of Father Paul was solemn as he gazed at it. It was a sight that had never lost its magnificence for him. He had seen it the first evening he had arrived in Coaltown three years before, when, after a tour of his sordid parish, he had climbed the steep roadway to view the last resting place of his newly adopted flock. There, on the plateau, alone with his God, far (so it seemed) above the grime and sin of the world, he had suddenly looked toward the western sky and viewed a masterpiece of Nature's painting.

That first evening the setting of the sun had stirred his soul. He had climbed the hill to watch it many evenings since. To gain strength from watching it. Now he could not help but point out to his new friend what it meant to him. Even after three years the priest spoke of it with deep reverence—haltingly—for mere words could not for him describe it.

"Look one moment, if you will, Mr. Dunnigan, toward the west. If I did not believe in God, I would now! Is that green mountain not like a great altar? Those pine trees are the giant candlesticks which the setting sun is lighting. See how they seem to drip hot flame on an altar cloth of hickory and birch. And listen!"

Suddenly the whole valley was filled with music—the vibrant ringing of church bells.

Bill Dunnigan had not been especially moved by the sunset. He only half heard Father Paul's rhapsody about it. Ziegfeld had put a "sunset effect" in the Follies one year that seemed just as colorful.

Bill, at that moment, was thinking of several, more personally vital things. Of Olga Treskovna. *She was not dead.* She had really stood beside him only a moment before. What could he do for her that he had not done? Of this gallant man of God. Could he do something to help this priest? Of his own life—what was he going to do with it? Wasn't it about time he stopped being a quitter? But he was startled out of all questioning reverie when he heard the bells. He almost jumped.

He had completely forgotten Olga Treskovna's most urgent request.

"What is that!" he cried. And something else besides Olga Treskovna's last, pathetic wish was pounding at his brain cells with a sudden, terrific impact.

"Our vesper bells," explained Father Paul, and wondered at the man's sudden animation. "Our five churches ring them together every day at this hour, and when they coincide with such a sunset as this, they are like a glorious Holy Choir singing a benediction for the weary day. Why, sir——"

But ace press agent, Bill Dunnigan, had grasped the shoulders of the priest. There was a wild look in his eyes, his heart was pounding violently, and his voice shook with excitement.

"Your new altar cloth, Father! Don't worry about it! It's in the bag! You're doing your stuff in front of it right now! The thirty-dollar one. One! We'll have half a dozen of 'em! A new one every Sunday! And those lousy bills of yours I couldn't help but see, and those plans you've made about doing good! They're on the make too! Olga Treskovna's funeral! She's not dead! I'm the guy who's been dead for a week! I'm the guy who ought to be picking out his own grave plot! But no more! Whoopee!"

"Mr. Dunnigan, do you feel entirely well?" gasped Father Paul.

"I feel like a million!" shouted Bill Dunnigan. "Father, you and me are going into partnership. We've both been fall-guys! Saps! Buffaloed by a phony jinx! But from now on we're going to chase those jinxes up the alley, over the hills, and show the world what a couple of alive, two-fisted, honest-to-God he-men with brains and guts can do!"

―――――――――――――――――――――――――――――――― *27* ――――――

*B*ILL DUNNIGAN had not suddenly gone mad. It was simply that what had been called the greatest press-agent brain in America was functioning once more—the brain that had ranged twenty-five circus elephants up and down each side of the Capitol steps in Washington at six o'clock one morning (the day of the Big Show's opening) for a startled, newly-elected Republican Congress to pass through—or not pass through. The brain that had painted the name of a certain "girl revue" very appropriately across the front of a notoriously graft-ridden State Capitol building. The brain that had not "sneaked" the ungrateful Anna Gronka into America.

The external cause of that renewed functioning had been the sound of the bells of the five Coaltown churches, ringing out clear and strong to fill the whole valley with their sound. The internal cause was a mixture of the determination to renew the fight for Olga Treskovna; determination to find a way to help this unselfish priest; determination to restore his own self-respect and courage, and, incidentally, his earning power as a self-supporting member of society.

"Father," said Dunnigan, and the priest was still startled by the dynamic change in the man before him, "I completely forgot the most important item in this funeral!"

"What do you mean?" asked the mystified priest.

"Those bells! I promised the girl to have the church bells rung!"

"We usually do that," said Father Paul. "It is another of our Polish customs."

"But it *costs money,* doesn't it? At least it used to cost money It's something that *can be bought?*" Dunnigan was firing his questions at the priest with the rapidity of a machine gun.

"That is only because we have to pay our sextons extra for this work."

"I know. And is five dollars still the union scale? That's what the girl told me it was when her father died."

"Why, yes—the bell ringer and the church get five dollars for ringing a wedding or a funeral."

"And how long do the bells ring for this five bucks?"

"Why, usually fifteen minutes. In the case of a funeral we ring them just before or just after the Requiem Mass."

"And suppose someone wanted the bells rung longer than the fifteen minutes—what would be the union scale by, say, the hour?"

"I don't know. I don't believe anyone ever had them rung as long as that!" *What was the man driving at?*

"But we could do it, couldn't we?"

"I suppose we could."

"And maybe get a wholesale rate—if we hired 'em rung for, say four hours—ten hours—twenty-four hours—maybe for four days?"

"Mr. Dunnigan, are you sure you know what you are saying!"

But Bill Dunnigan spoke even more rapidly and forcefully. " know what I'm saying and I've only just started talking, Father There are four other churches in the town besides yours, aren't there?"

"There are five churches in all in Coaltown."

"And each church has a head guy like you that we can talk business to—you know what I mean, Father—arrange about the bells?"

Father Paul drew back a step. "You mean you want the bell rung in *all* the churches!"

"Every one of 'em, Father! So that it sounds just like it doe now. You said yourself how glorious it is!"

"Yes—but—I really don't understand!"

"It's this way, Father." Dunnigan was filling in with bold, expert strokes his basic idea as he hurried along. "When this girl's pop died—that's what she called him—the poor kid was up against it—busted—broke—and there wasn't any priest like you around that did things free gratis, for nothing, without pay, just because he wanted to help people—and she couldn't have the bells rung at all —not even for five minutes or five seconds at *one* church, because that five bucks tax might just as well have been five million! Her pop loved the bells, Father. So she made me promise her just before she passed on, that I'd have all the church bells rung good and long to make up for the four years he'd been waiting to hear em—lying there waiting in his grave——"

"But Mr. Dunnigan, that would cost a fortune, even if we could arrange— Why, it would be twenty-five dollars if *all* the churches rang just for fifteen minutes!"

Bill Dunnigan broke in.

"You and I are through with ifs and buts, Father! We've got a job ahead of us and we're going to do it! And we haven't time to hang around watching any sunsets! Some other night will do for that! We've got to pull up our socks, step on the gas and go to town!"

"You mean that this girl really wanted the bells of all the churches rung for four days—because her father didn't have any at his funeral!"

"That's part of it," said Dunnigan, "but only part! Father, what a break it's going to be for all of us! And for your church! Just leave it all to me! Because we've got a hell of a lot to do quick! We got to move into high—and fast! These other priest guys—no offence, Father—lead me to these bozos pronto!" He looked at his watch. "It's already after six, and we must get the curtain up by ten! There's a midnight deadline I have hopes of!"

"A deadline?" said Father Paul blankly.

"Yes—but don't you worry about that either! That's my department. And don't be upset about these other Reverends stealing any of our show—they won't get any new altar cloths or any part of the credit for this funeral—you're my little prima donna and your church is going to be the Metropolitan Opera of Coaltown! And what an opera we're going to perform! Say, will those other pastors be home right now?"

"They're usually in at supper time, but Mr. Dunnigan——"

"Great! You see, we need 'em as a sort of chorus—just extra.
they are—to help fill up the stage!"

In his enthusiasm Dunnigan had reverted completely to the jar
gon of his trade, leaving Father Paul even more confused. The
priest returned to the simple problem of the bells.

"But if you really gave your word to do this, and if the other
pastors are asked to ring their church bells along with St. Michael's
some of them will want money—in advance, I fear."

"You don't have to tell me that, Father!" Dunnigan cried. "
know there's only about one Father Paul in this whole damn
country—maybe there's a couple more—but not in any one town!"
He continued with an intense determination: "I'm not flat yet
Father! And I've got a bankbook that's good for five hundred
simoleons more, and before that's gone—Father, look at me! I've
got a lot of faults—they stick out all over—I oughtn't to swear when
I'm talking to a priest—forgive me, please—but I've never yet le
down a pal. This girl was my pal. She's still my pal. I wa
walking out on her! Leaving her flat without lifting a hand! M
dearest pal! I'm not going to let her down! I see a way to get he
in the clear! You too—you are my pal, although I've only known
you for an hour—that is, I hope I may count you as my pal——

"I like you, Mr. Dunnigan, more than I have liked anyone fo
a long time," said the priest sincerely.

"That's fine! And I'm not going to let you down either! I'r
going to get you and your church in the clear too!" The loo
on the priest's face was so perplexed that Dunnigan felt he mus
add, "I'm supposed to be an expert at a certain thing, Father. It'
a damn crazy thing! It doesn't make sense half the time! I don'
think you'd understand it if I told you. But I'm supposed to b
tops at it. The cleverest guy in the game thought I was tops, an
paid me a top salary for ten years. But for a week now I've bee
down at the bottom of the heap. Bottom! I've been buried te
feet deep! It was meeting you that yanked me up again."

"I'm happy if I have helped you. I can't tell you how happ
I am!" Father Paul was not confused about that.

"All right! Just trust me, Father. I'm going to help *you* nov
We're going back to Coaltown to lick the hell out of that Breake
And all that the Breaker stands for. And some other Breake

that I've been up against that you don't know about. Lead on—
the lot of you—and damned be he who first cries 'Hold! Enough!' "
Bill Dunnigan shook a challenging fist in the direction of Coaltown
and Coaltown's black, towering master.

The press agent's quotation from the Bard of Avon may not have
been entirely appropriate. It was a remembrance of a few weeks
"in advance" of Robert B. Mantell. But it thoroughly expressed
the drive of Dunnigan's reborn fighting spirit.

We give trust sometimes without rhyme or reason. The heart
sees more clearly than the mind. Father Paul, looking at the man
before him, let his doubts and alarm be swept away. He did not
exactly understand what it all meant, what it was leading to. His
own brain was in a kind of excited turmoil, for it was impossible
not to catch this stranger's ardor. Instinctively, the priest seemed
to believe in Bill Dunnigan, to rely on him, to have faith that the
man meant well and good and knew exactly what he was talking
about.

"If your friend really wished all this—" he said, releasing his
last grasp on caution.

"I gave her my promise," said Dunnigan. "I give you my
promise!"

"Then we'll have to hurry," the priest declared, "if we are to
see the other pastors before they finish their suppers. And Mr.
Dunnigan—it's best you try not to swear when you talk to them.
Some of them are not very broad-minded, I fear."

"I'll watch my words," said Dunnigan.

But before starting, Father Paul knelt by the unmarked grave of
Stanislaus Trocki, father of Olga Treskovna. Bill didn't know
whether he should kneel or not. And as he was trying to decide,
there seemed to be another figure kneeling beside the priest. A girl
in a blue house dress, and the hair of her bowed head was a silken
brown.

Dunnigan just stood where he was. He had taken off his black
derby when Father Paul had knelt.

The bells stopped. The valley was silent. The priest rose and
the two men hastened out of the cemetery. They walked rapidly
down the plateau road, around the bend and down the hill, across
the railtrack bridge, back into the main street of Coaltown. And
part of the way, until they reached the bridge and the town, some-

one was on the other side of Dunnigan, walking with him, holding tightly to his hand. And in her uplifted face was reflected the faith and hope of all the world.

28

*I*T IS NOT NECESSARY to chronicle in detail each of the four ensuing interviews.

The other priests and the Protestant pastor were at home. Dunnigan watched his words. The ringing of their church bells was a customary ceremony during funerals. Also a source of revenue. As the press agent had rightly predicted, unlike Father Paul they were not averse to taking money for that or any other proper ecclesiastical service.

To be sure, no one before had wanted the bells of *all* the churches rung—or wanted them rung for a stretch of four and twenty hours! From ten o'clock that night till ten the next, was what Dunnigan first contracted for, with a hint that the ringing might be continued at an advanced rate for wear and tear, if everything was entirely satisfactory!

Ten dollars an hour was the agreed "wholesale" rate of each church. The press agent paid out his last hundred-dollar bill to give each church two hours cash in advance, insisting that Father Paul take his share with the others.

And he deposited with Father Spinsky (the priest so admired by undertaker Orloff) his Brooklyn Dime Savings bankbook as a negotiable guarantee of five hundred dollars more. That covered payment for twelve hours, or until ten the next morning. Another payment was to be made at twelve o'clock noon (this at Father Spinsky's insistence) to complete the initial contract.

Dunnigan explained that he had more ready cash coming from New York, and that it might not arrive until then.

So by eight o'clock it was definitely arranged with four somewhat mystified but entirely happy pastors (a windfall of two hundred and forty dollars each was not to be regarded lightly by any Coaltown parish) that their qualified bell ringers should start tugging their several bell ropes promptly at ten P.M.

This transaction left Bill Dunnigan exactly fifteen dollars in the wallet.

As they parted at the last parish house, Father Paul had another suggestion. "Mr. Dunnigan," said the priest, "the body of this girl should be moved at once to St. Michael's and placed in the center aisle of the church, before the altar, because the ringing of the bells will mark the starting of the burial service."

"I'll be glad of that!" exclaimed Dunnigan. "I didn't like at all the thought of her remaining at Orloff's place even for one night. I'm going there now to pick up my suitcase, and I'll have that undertaker transfer the coffin to your church right away."

"I'll be at the church to receive it," said the priest, "and I must locate my sexton about the ringing of our bell. We have only a small bell, but it was brought here from Poland, and its tone is very beautiful."

"I'm sure of that. By ten o'clock, Father, there'll be more music in this town than there has been for a long time!"

"I hope I am doing the right thing," said Father Paul. For while talking with the other priests there had again been brief moments of doubt—even alarm. This was such a strange adventure for him, Father Paul, to be a part of! But he had looked at Dunnigan's eager, sincere profile and allowed himself to be swept along.

"Everybody is satisfied! Just trust me, Father!" cried Bill. He wanted to give his valiant ally an encouraging slap on the shoulder, but maybe you didn't so slap a man of God. Instead he took the priest's hand in both of his and pressed it warmly.

"Chin up, Father!" he said. "That goes for both of us!"

"Chin up!" repeated Father Paul. And there was a lift in his voice also. Somehow life was taking on a new beginning!

~~~~~~~~~~~~~~~~~~~~~~~~~~~~~~~~~~ **29** ~~~~~~~~~~~~~~~~

*D*UNNIGAN HASTENED down the street toward Orloff's "Funeral Parlor." He half realized that the people he passed looked at him curiously—as well they might! For the press agent, his head thrown back, was singing to the world at large:

> A pretty girl—is like a melody—
> That haunts you—night and day!

But he stopped that song as he entered Orloff's place.

The undertaker was in his back room, playing pool with some customers. "Oh, it's you again," he said, as Dunnigan appeared in the doorway. "Decided to shoot a game?"

"No, thanks. But I want to see you right away."

Orloff completed his shot, missed, swore, and placed his cue in the rack. "Be back in a minute, boys," he said, and stepped to the doorway. "Did you make out all right with the St. Michael' priest?"

"Fine!"

"I hope you didn't let him stick you. When these priests need money they sometimes load it on."

"The business arrangements are entirely satisfactory. But I've changed my plans. I'd like the coffin moved over to the church at once."

"You're not going to have the funeral tonight!"

"No. Maybe not for a day or two. But I've made a special arrangement about the coffin."

"Are they charging you extra for this? Because if you wanted to wait another day, I'd make you a reduced rate for the extra time."

"Nothing extra. It's just that I want it that way."

"Well, it's after hours. I'll have to get out my hearse again from the garage. And it'll take a couple of men to help me with the coffin. Won't tomorrow morning do?"

"I want it taken there at once."

"You're the boss." A new thought caused a more cheerful look to come into Orloff's small eyes. Cheerful and shrewd. "Of course there'll be an extra charge for this overtime moving."

"How much of a charge?"

"Five dollars."

"But it's part of your bargain to take the coffin to the church!"

"Not on overtime. And I'll have to pay a couple of the boys extra for their work."

"Very well. Here is the five dollars." Dunnigan parted with
one of his three remaining five-dollar bills. "You'll take it at once,
please. Father Paul is waiting."

"I'll go get the hearse now. The boys playing with me will help
with the coffin." Orloff had already worked it out that "the boys"
would have to take their payment in poolroom trade. "Lucky for
you these fellows dropped in or I couldn't do it tonight," he added.

"Yes, I guess I'm lucky today!"

"There's one thing more."

"What is that?"

"I'd like a release," said Mr. Orloff.

"A release?"

"Well, I'd like it written down that you don't get a refund because I didn't harbor the body overnight. I'm perfectly willing to,
you understand, as per our agreement."

Dunnigan was relieved. No more money! He even had difficulty
in concealing a smile. "Very well," he said, "make out your release."
They moved into Orloff's office and the undertaker wrote out
another piece of soiled paper and read it over carefully. He passed
it to Dunnigan.

It read:

> I hereby agree that no refund shall be demanded because
> the body of one, Olga Trocki, name on papers, Olga Tres-
> kovna, was moved to St. Michael's Church, instead of being
> kept overnight at Orloff's chapel as previously agreed.

Bill Dunnigan smiled at the double identification of Miss Treskovna, and again as he came to the word "chapel." It took many
kinds of mentality to make up a world! Orloff held out the pen.
"I've got a lucky pencil. Think I'll sign with that if you don't
object," said the press agent. He produced his blue pencil from
his vest pocket and wrote "William Dunnigan" with a large flourish.
"I suppose it's legal—signed with a pencil?" said Mr. Orloff
doubtfully.

"We'll double sign it then!" declared Dunnigan. This time he
laughed out loud. And he took up the pen and wrote another
large signature underneath the first. "And you'll have to do the
same for me," he added.

"How do you mean?"

"I'd like a receipt for my five bucks.   Mark it: In full settlemen
for overtime removal of coffin of Olga Trocki, known professionall
as Olga Treskovna, to St. Michael's church, no further charge c
any kind to be made for taking same to cemetery and lowering i
the day of the funeral."   Bill smiled as he dictated the remembere
phrase "lowering in."

Orloff frowned.   This was undoubtedly a concluding, end-a
statement!   But the Dunnigan wallet looked about empty.   Notl
ing more to be squeezed from it.

The undertaker's frown became a smirk.   Another finger-marke
receipt was soon carefully placed in the wallet.   That wallet was n
out of place at Mr. Orloff's!

"At what hour is the funeral?" asked the undertaker as Dunniga
rose.

"I'll have to let you know in the morning.   I may put it o
a day."

"I must know in advance.   I can't get experienced pallbeare
on five minutes' notice."

"You will have ample warning," said the press agent with anothe
smile.   "Ample warning!   Now I'll get my suitcase.   I hope there
no extra charge for storing *it*."

"I'm always glad to accommodate a fellow businessman," replie
Orloff.   "And don't forget—if you feel like a game later——"

"I may at that!" said Dunnigan, as he stepped into the "chape
for his luggage.

He said just one word to the coffin as he lifted the suitcase.   "Ki
your star is shining again—and I think we've got that jinx on th
lam—ninety miles an hour!"

*   *   *

At the Wyoming Hotel Dunnigan registered and was shown
a room—a musty, spacious chamber on the second floor facing Mai
Street, the one room of the hostelry that possessed a private bat
He felt badly in need of a bath.

Before he took his bath he ordered sandwiches sent up and a p
of coffee.   He called down to the desk clerk over a speaking tut
in the wall by the door.   The room had no telephone.   He ordere
a dozen sandwiches.   Here was another day he had not eaten sin
early morning.   His appetite had returned!   He was the old Bi

Dunnigan again. He shed no tears for the Bill Dunnigan of the past week. That guy was dead and buried, he hoped!

He shaved, changed his linen, brushed his clothes. He got most of the coal dust off of the black derby. If only he had brought a fresh pair of spats! But the half-dozen extra ones were in the trunk that went direct to New York. He did manage to brush up the present pair a bit.

"We're stepping out, pals—we're going to show 'em some tall striding from now on!" he said to the refurbished footgear.

His sandwiches and coffee had arrived and he ate and drank ravenously. "Eating like a horse again, thank God!" he said to himself. Then he descended the narrow stairs to the lobby where he negotiated the purchase of five cigars—retail price six cents each or five for a quarter. They were highly recommended by the clerk.

"Where is the nearest telegraph office?" Dunnigan asked the clerk.

"Nanticoke," replied this gentleman. "But I can telephone your message from here over our pay-station wall phone."

"I don't want to send it just yet. Not till about midnight. How long is that Nanticoke office open?" Now Bill remembered the name "Nanticoke." That was the way his wire to undertaker Orloff had traveled from Los Angeles. Father Paul had also mentioned it as being the nearest town. Undertaker Orloff had spoken of a bus line—but that wouldn't be operating at midnight.

"The office is open all night. It's a railway telegraph office," the clerk was saying.

"Splendid!" Dunnigan did *not* mean the cigar he had just lit. "And this town is how far away?"

"About six miles."

"This is a very important telegram. I want to give it direct to the operator. Could I hire someone to drive me to this Nanticoke at midnight—and bring me back?"

"My son will be glad to earn the money. We have a Ford."

"How much for the round trip?"

"Would three dollars be too much?"

Dunnigan made a lightning calculation of expenses ahead and the funds in hand. A ten-dollar bank roll. Three from ten was seven. There would be enough left for the telegram.

"O. K.," he said. "Have your son and your Ford here at midnight. I can depend on it?"

"My son is as reliable as our Ford." The clerk spoke with the assurance of absolute confidence.

"That's good enough for me." The little, joked-about cars had saved his business life many times on the road, God bless 'em! He forgave the clerk the cigar.

So now, everything was arranged. The powder train was laid. The bells of Coaltown's five churches would, in another hour, ignite the fuse. Would it be a dud or would it set a certain world aflame? He could only wait and hope. Prayer was not yet a part of his equipment.

Dunnigan felt a need to be again with Father Paul. He went out and walked the short distance to the St. Michael parish house. How differently he had approached that parish house only a few hours before. What a wonderful thing it was to find a friend! He parked the cigar outside. He must not risk losing *that* friendship.

The priest was again in the small room used as an office. He'd just finished instructing his janitor about the ringing of St. Michael's bell. He turned over the entire twenty dollars Dunnigan had given him to this man, for the church was behind in paying wages. That he had received this back-money was all the janitor wished to know. And he would ring the bell till doomsday for the several dollars an hour that would be his share of the "wholesale rate"!

Earlier, the coffin of Olga Treskovna had been delivered and placed in the church before the altar, resting on the folding stand which each church kept for that purpose. Orloff had removed the coffin from the outside shipping case before delivering it. Father Paul had placed the three tall candles on each side. He would light them before the Mass the next morning.

For Father Paul was going through with it. In spite of any mis-givings! This stranger—now his friend—had reached out and touched an unused chord in the heart of the defeated priest—the chord of romance and adventure that is hidden in all of us. A new altar cloth—his church bills paid—even the possibility of having the church repaired and repainted—the money from the bell ringing might almost accomplish all these! And his own house in order maybe he could really try again with some new approach to do what he wanted to do for Coaltown.

A whole new world was opening! Help was surely sent in answer to our prayers. Strange help perhaps—but help nevertheless.

One thing did still worry him. He voiced that worry now to Dunnigan as the press agent again sat on the folding chair opposite his desk.

"Won't all this bell ringing attract undue attention? Perhaps even get into the newspapers?"

Bill Dunnigan swallowed hard. He prided himself that even in his wildest stunts he always told the truth. It might be a somewhat embellished truth, but it was the truth all the same.

"I've thought of that," he said without a smile, "and I give you my word, if the reporters come around I'm going to tell 'em to pipe down. I'm going to beg them to! This is a private funeral. I have to carry out the wishes of the departed. You wouldn't want me to go back on promises I made to a girl on her deathbed?"

"No, you couldn't do that," said Father Paul. "I only hope it doesn't get into the newspapers!"

"Father," said Bill Dunnigan, "I've spotted you for a grand guy. One of the best, there's no doubt about it! I'll place my last dollar on you! And that picture on your wall of the lad with the wings and the lance and the shield. Your Saint Michael. I don't like him at first because his name was so long—the Archangel part, I mean—but I sort of remember about him now. He was the real McCoy too!

"People like you two ought to be known! It wouldn't hurt at all if something *were* in the papers about you! I think it would help your church. No matter how fine things are, if people don't know about 'em, Father, where are they? Your Saint Michael was a fighter, wasn't he? A great fighter?"

"He was the chosen champion of our Lord," said Father Paul.

"O. K. A champion. But is he known like Jim Corbett or Jack Dempsey? No! And as for yourself——"

"But how could Saint Michael be made better known? I have preached several sermons entirely about him."

"I'll tell you how. There's a business that does just that. Makes people *known*. Worthless people most of the time. I know a guy in that business. Know him pretty well. Have influence with him. I'm going to see if he won't do something for two right guys like you and your Saint Michael. This fellow is called a press agent."

"A press agent?"

"That's what he's called. And you know, Father, I've been think-

ing. That's what you need! That's what your church needs!
That's what your Saint Michael needs! Maybe even your Almighty
God could do with a good press agent sometimes—who knows?"

——————————————— *30* ———————

*E*XACTLY AT TEN O'CLOCK the bells started
their ringing. The bell at St. Michael's rang out first—a clear, high
voice-like tone. Then Father Spinsky's St. Leo's joined—it was a
very large bell in D flat and might be called the bass of the quin
tette. St. Adalbert, the Czech church, soon followed, and the
Russian church of St. Nicholas and the Protestant church chimed in

It so happened that these bells were all cast in different keys
so that together, as Father Paul and Dunnigan had noted at the
cemetery, they gave the effect of a choir, of well-concerted chimes

At that hour of night, in the silence of the countryside, it was
an awesome sound. Dunnigan had gone to the corner of a small
side street where he could be alone, his watch in hand. He had left
Father Paul a little while before.

Father Paul had asked Dunnigan if he wanted to go into the
church, but the press agent had put that off until the next day. The
Olga Treskovna he was battling for was not *there*. He wished to
be somewhere alone, but on the sidelines where he could view the
"audience" when it all started—just as he always liked to stand by
himself at the back of the orchestra during the opening night of
his new shows on Broadway. Outwardly calm, he was far from
placid within. He had had a feeling also that Father Paul preferred
to be alone when the bells commenced to ring.

And as the mingled tones issuing from the five church towers
smote the night air above Coaltown, Bill Dunnigan felt frightened
for the first time in his life. A gambler all his years, he had never
before shot the dice for such vital stakes. He had never risked
everything that was dear to him on a single throw!

If a show failed, if a certain horse did not win, if the dice rolled
a "box-car," there were other shows, other races, other throws. Now

it seemed, all depended on this startling single cast—the future of Olga Treskovna, the future of Father Paul, his own future. For Olga Treskovna had a future also. Bill no longer thought of her as being dead.

He looked up toward the heavens. He was instinctively searching for Olga Treskovna's star. He found it easily; it was big and glowing near its little group. Brighter, he thought, than ever before. He did not realize that over a comparatively dark town, all the stars would be brighter. He only knew that its steady glow gave him courage.

"Your spotlight is sure blazing again, kid—and our curtain's up!" he said aloud.

He did not have long to wait for the first reaction. Father Paul's fears that all this bell ringing would "attract undue attention" had not been groundless.

By ten-three on Bill's watch, the assorted late patrons of the town's twenty-two assorted bars had left their drinks, their laughter, their argument, had disgorged onto Main Street, and stood gazing up at the black sky.

"What's happened!" "Where's the fire?" "Who's ringing all the bells?" A continuing bong! bong! was the only answer to the questions!

By ten-five the juke-box dancers at Nick (brother of undertaker James) Orloff's Dance Hall had left their gyrations and added a feminine flavor to the crowd, as well as a show of youth.

"What's doing!" "What's the row!"

From ten-eight to ten-ten there was a rapid-fire blazing of lights in the windows of every house whose occupants had retired for the night, and questions were shouted from open doorways by silhouetted figures (male and female) in various stages of undress and various assortments of night clothes.

The sound even penetrated to the night shift working in the Breaker, for at exactly ten-twelve, as if by previous agreement, that monster suddenly became silent, because its entire crew of more than a hundred men had stopped work and rushed into the street to discover the reason for this melodic clangor. The Breaker seemed to acknowledge momentarily the futility of raising its hoarse voice in competition with the clear, resonant singing of the bells.

The ringing even penetrated into the mine shafts, and workers dropped their tools and listened in wonderment. Only the night shifts, far underground at the two-thousand-foot lower levels, toiled on undisturbed.

It was quickly decided that this nighttime hubbub had nothing to do with the mines. There had been no accident in the shafts or at the Breaker. The bells were not ringing to give an alarm of fire. No red flames, except the occasional ones from a "slack" mountain, licked upward into the night skies. Nor was Coaltown being invaded by any foreign foe from Mars or nearer places, unless the invaders were the occupants of half a dozen alien motorcars, that had been loafing along near-by roadways, and who had hastened to Coaltown's Main Street to gawk with its citizens into the void of this unanswered auditory phenomenon.

It was the wife of the town's druggist, Cilka Shoen, who had the first sensible, the first brilliant idea.

Cilka was in a ferment. As she carried close to two hundred pounds of energetic avoirdupois, it was quite an agitation. For fifty years nothing had happened in Coaltown that she did not know about—usually well in advance. Now, here was a tremendous event, the happening of which, the meaning of which, she was in abysmal ignorance of! She was near to a mental crackup. No one else knew anything—that was her only saving anchorage to sanity. No other woman had beaten her to the kill!

Cilka, bringing to bear the powers of a highly acquisitive brain trained by a lifetime of ferreting out and analyzing other people's business, expounded her idea to the crowd gathered outside her husband's store. "This noise comes from the church bells! The church bells are in the churches! They don't ring by themselves, do they? *Someone* is ringing them! Someone in the churches knows what's up!"

Inescapable logic! Cilka started off in the direction of the near-by St. Leo's bell tower. Bells in Coaltown were rung *by men,* so praise God it was no other woman who knew the answer!

Even while Cilka was telling the gaping crowd her theory, Bill Dunnigan would have been pleased to know that the circles of his bell-sounding pool were reaching the outer world. Cilka's husband, inside, was answering a telephone call from the editor of the semi-weekly *Nanticoke Courier.* The bells were being heard in Nanticoke.

"What in hell's happening in Coaltown?" this editor demanded.
"I don't know," wailed druggist Shoen, who had a high-pitched
voice. "Nobody knows! But I know this. My wife will soon find
out! I'll ring you right back!"

Reaching St. Leo's at the head of a throng that might have posed
for a miniature scene depicting the march on Versailles by the
French patriots of the time of Marie Antoinette and Louis XVI,
the hefty Cilka bade them wait and climbed the steep ladder up
into the St. Leo bell tower. Head and shoulders projecting through
the trap door, she faced its sexton, who was very deaf. This sexton
was methodically tugging at his bell rope.

After much shouting, for the man would not stop his ringing,
Cilka only elicited that he "didn't know nothing!" Somebody had
died, that was all. It was some sort of special funeral.

"Who has died?" shouted Cilka.

"I told you I don't know!" shouted back the occupied sexton.

"But you *must* know!" screamed the frantic Cilka. "Who's paying you?"

*One thing was certain. This man would not be ringing his bell
without pay.*

"Father Spinsky—and he's not dead!"

"When do you stop ringing?"

"What?"

"When do you stop ringing?"

"I don't stop. I ring all night."

"*All night!*"

"You heard me. *All night!* And my brother takes my place in
the morning. All day tomorrow. That is, if this bell rope holds
out. If you see Father Spinsky, tell him I'm worried about this
rope! I hope it lasts, for my brother and I can use the money
we'll be getting——"

But Cilka was struggling backward down the ladder. You couldn't
get any satisfaction from such a dumb one whose only interest was
bell-ringing pay and the strength of bell ropes! Besides, her voice
was giving out against the shut-in reverberation of St. Leo's gigantic
D flat bass. She would have to brave the wrath of Father Spinsky
for an interview at this late hour. But when she reached the outside of the tower, her opportunity was gone and her followers had
escaped her.

Mary Spinsky, Father Spinsky's sister, who kept house for the St. Leo pastor, had lured them away with real, first-hand information, which she was now handing out in front of the St. Leo parish house. Dunnigan had extracted promises of silence from the four pastors when he made his arrangements for the bell ringing. "This must be a strictly private matter," he had repeated, which had somewhat reassured Father Paul.

But Mary Spinsky, a native of Coaltown like her brother, had probed from him all available data five minutes after the bells started. She, too, gave a solemn promise to be silent, but when she heard that Cilka Shoen was in the St. Leo bell tower, promises went to the wind. For years she had been trying to beat the druggist's wife to the draw in a duel of gossip. This was her hour of triumph. She spread the information to all who would listen.

So by ten-thirty, the following pertinent "facts" were established by the now wide-awake citizenry of Coaltown:

1. The daughter of the town's late drunkard, Stan Trocki's girl Olga, had died in California, and her body now lay in the church of St. Michael the Archangel.

2. She had become "immensely wealthy," because her body had been transported clear across the continent, and there was money enough to ring all the church bells in Coaltown for twenty-four hours—some said an entire week!

3. The arrangements for the bell ringing had been made by a New York millionaire—husband or friend (it was not certain) by the name of William Dunnigan, who had checked in at the Wyoming Hotel.

4. This girl, Olga Trocki, had "gone on the stage." She had actually been seen in a "show" in New York, a couple of years before, by two of the informants, sex male.

5. She had lately been in "moving pictures" in Hollywood and used a "stage name." Her salary had been ten thousand dollars a week.

So, by ten forty-five, almost everyone in Coaltown—with the exception of young mothers who faced the problem of coaxing their children back to sleep under the continued bell ringing—was in a high state of agreeable excitement. The one other exception was James Orloff, undertaker.

Mr. Orloff had been as mystified and made as curious as everyone else by the sudden booming of the church bells at ten o'clock. He had perilously left his game of pool—there was a dollar and a half at stake and he was winning—to find out what it was about. The only person, except for the five pastors, who had actually talked with this Mr. Dunnigan about the funeral, he was among the first to piece together the "facts."

When he realized their (to him) dreadful import, he grew pale, and his stomach had a very sick feeling. He did not go back to his game. He retired to his "office," locked the door, and poured himself a stiff drink. He contemplated a carbon copy of a bill for this funeral signed by him "Paid in Full." The bill was for one hundred and twenty-five dollars. And he had completely "released" the body for an additional five dollars. Released it both under her real and her professional name. This careful identification at his own suggestion! And that cursed final receipt he had given Dunnigan. Not a single loophole left!

That dirty city cheat! He had been dealing with a millionaire! There was no justice or honesty in this world!

Millionaire Dunnigan was not in his room at the Wyoming Hotel. The crowds on Main Street had become such that he felt it safe to join them, and he pushed his way along, a not uninterested observer of the growing excitement. There was a smile on his lips and a merry gleam in his grey eyes.

What a show! The bells sure sounded grand! In the still night air their chiming must carry for miles! He wondered if they could be heard in Wilkes-Barre and Scranton. Too bad New York and Philadelphia were so far away! And Hollywood! But he couldn't rearrange geography.

A crowd of two hundred or more soon gathered in front of the dark parish house of the church of St. Michael the Archangel. A miner, prodded by his friends, mounted the steps from the street and rang the jangling bell repeatedly.

Father Paul had gone to bed. But he was not asleep. He lay wide-eyed, listening to the clangor that burst through his open window—that seemed to be coming even from the walls and ceiling! At first he had been terrified but soon it sounded beautiful, even restful. He had a feeling that God's voice was at last speaking out in Coaltown. God's bells.

Then came the jangling of his own doorbell—a bell with no

heavenly sound! This caused a return of his fears, and at first he thought to ignore it. But when it continued, he got up, put on his cassock like a nightrobe, and descended in some apprehension to his door.

When he opened the door, a silence fell over the gathering that had followed the bold miner up to the lawn of the parish house. To arouse a priest in the middle of the night was not something usually done, except for approaching death. But overwhelming curiosity can break down all usages.

The miner who had so courageously pulled Father Paul's bell knob lost some of his assurance as he faced the apparently rudely awakened priest. He removed his cap and shifted from one foot to the other. "Father—we—" he stammered. He mistook Father Paul's alarm for anger.

A voice from the safety of the crowd spoke up. "What is it all about, Father?" and another, "Tell us, Father, are the bells to ring all night?"

"Yes," said the miner, "we just wanted to respectfully ask who had died—and if we could do anything." He added the last as if to explain their breaking in on the pastor's rest.

Father Paul's priesthood training of calmness before an audience stood him in good stead. He raised his hand.

"I appreciate your desire to be of service," he said, "but there is nothing any of you can do. Except of course to pray, as we all should, for the soul of the faithful departed. Her name was Olga Trocki—she left Coaltown before I was privileged to come here. have promised not to talk about her wish to have the bells of the churches rung. They will be rung all night, and I hope their music will bring thoughts of God to your hearts and minds. Her mortal body now rests in my church which is closed for the night. There will be the usual morning Mass at five forty-five. Go home my children, and God be with you always. And please don't trample my flower bed."

Father Paul made the sign of the cross and closed his door quickly. He was not quite as calm as he had pretended to be.

As he climbed the stairs to his room, he was again perturbed by all this agitation. At the same time he felt a curious elation in his soul. His church of St. Michael was at last an object of interest

People had come to its doors at this late hour. Perhaps more than the usual ten or twelve communicants would attend the early morning Mass.

When Father Paul closed his door, someone in the crowd suggested that they move to the Wyoming Hotel where this dead girl's friend was said to be stopping. The millionaire who was paying for all this—handing out "right and left" dozens of hundred-dollar bills! At least, it was so reported, and there was much debate as to whether it was the Trocki girl's money or his own. This stranger seemed the only remaining source of information.

The bells pounded on; the excitement mounted steadily.

31

*A*T ELEVEN-THIRTY, William Dunnigan strode into the lobby of the Wyoming Hotel.

There awaited him, besides more than three hundred townspeople, the editor of the semi-weekly *Nanticoke Courier,* four reporters from the three Wilkes-Barre newspapers and two from Scranton, and an Associated Press man and a network radio commentator from the latter city. There was a wild rush in the direction of the derby-topped figure even as the night clerk started to point out "Mr. Dunnigan."

The press agent found it difficult to suppress his exultation. His trained eye spotted the reporters at once. It seemed that Father Paul's great dread was about to befall—the strange happenings in Coaltown were going to "get into the newspapers."

Dunnigan received the newspapermen and the radio commentator, and as many of the Coaltown curious as could crowd around them, in the dingy parlor of the hotel. He stood by the mantelpiece, one arm resting just below a faded crayon drawing of "The Stag at Bay," and addressed solemn words to the gentlemen of the press.

"My friends," he said, "I beg of you not to make anything of this. I am only carrying out the sacred last wishes of a simple girl, born and raised in your beautiful hill country. We all, I suppose, want to find our final resting place where we were born and nurtured through childhood. No matter how far afield we go, we want to come home when the grim reaper calls."

"But the bells!" a reporter interrupted. "Is it true they are to be rung for a week!"

"Ah, the bells," said Dunnigan and sighed deeply. "Funeral bells are a custom here—a quaint custom brought from across the sea. I had hoped, gentlemen, they would not cause any undue stir. For there again we have the simple wish of a simple child. Though her story in this connection has its sad—its almost tragic background. Her dead father loved the sound of these village church bells. He wanted them rung at his own funeral when he passed away four years ago. But this poor girl could not then afford to have them sounded even for the usual quarter of an hour. Poverty bears down hard when death strikes. But fortune was bountiful to her. Out in the great world her talents bloomed and were recognized. But always, in her success, there had haunted her the bitter memory of not being able to carry out her father's dying wish. So what was more natural than that, when her time came, and she was now able to afford it, she should at long last do for her parent the thing he wanted most?

"And to make up for the four intervening years, she asked me to have the bells of your Coaltown churches rung for four days—rung day and night for her father and herself. Only four short days, gentlemen! A strange, whimsical wish perhaps, but I think that now this girl is happy, and that her father is also happy, and that his spirit and hers will rest in eternal content until the Day when greater bells than mortals cast will summon us all to a reckoning."

Bill Dunnigan was about winded. He took a deep breath and lit up a Wyoming Hotel cigar.

"This girl—just who was she?" the Associated Press man asked. Dunnigan thought he detected a note of skepticism. But the press agent was playing a game at which he was expert. He put forward no claims of grandeur.

"As I said, a simple country girl, well-known by many people here," he answered. "Her name was Olga Trocki."

A murmur arose from the crowd. The Coaltown people confirmed their knowledge of the name. They had been talking it for n hour. Dunnigan heard exclamations of "You remember Stan Trocki's kid!" "I told you that's who it was!" "Everybody knew her father. Why he—" which statement was usually finished *sotto voce.*

"She would, I know, have preferred to let it remain at that," Dunnigan continued, getting his second wind and eyeing the Associated Press man casually, "but sooner or later her real identity must leak out. She was on the stage, as you may have heard. There, of course, her professional name was known to the entire world—the name of Olga Treskovna. It was under this name that she had just finished starring in the making of the newest Marcus Harris million-dollar film, 'The Garden of the Soul.' Doubtless some of you recall the best-selling novel from which the picture was taken."

"I remember," a Scranton newspaperman said. "That was the picture where this girl stepped in to replace a foreign star named Anna Gronka. There was something on our movie page last week about Olga Treskovna's sudden death."

"I imagine the press services in Hollywood sent wires about that sad event," said Dunnigan.

The townspeople in the room were now really stirred. "A great movie star!" "It's true then!" "No wonder she was rich!" "Think of it—Stan Trocki's girl!" "Her death was in the papers!"

"It also said that Marcus Harris wasn't going to release this new picture," the newspaperman added.

"Yes, that is true," said Dunnigan. "So it is a double tragedy that this girl from your Wyoming Valley had to die; for the picture 'The Garden of the Soul' would have been the crowning achievement of her career. Please say nothing of the picture, please, for it will lie, figuratively speaking, in the grave with Olga Treskovna on your lovely hilltop."

"But why won't this picture be shown?" the radio commentator asked.

"Marcus Harris will have to answer that question," Dunnigan said. "He had a great admiration for Miss Treskovna's talent—he considered her the greatest find of his Napoleonic career, and when his grief over her untimely passing is somewhat conquered, he will doubtless issue a full statement——"

Dunnigan paused. Respect for the sorrow of Marcus Harris overcame him. And he noted from the corner of his eye that the local

newspapermen and the radio commentator were busily taking note
Even the A. P. man had produced a notebook and was unscrewing
fountain pen.

"I think that such a picture should certainly be released!" said th
radio reporter.

"It was a wow of a story—and had a lift," conceded the Associate
Press representative. He had heard of that million-copy runawa
as who had not? "The movies could do with less gangster trash an
give us a yarn like that," he added.

"With all due respect to personal grief and loyalty, they shouldn
deprive the public of a fine picture!" said the uninhibited radi
commentator. "I happen to know Marcus Harris. If I can reac
him I shall talk to him by telephone before my broadcast tomorro
evening. I speak at eight-thirty over the Green Network and——"

"Did this Coaltown girl leave a great deal of money?" This pe
tinent interruption from the Nanticoke editor.

Dunnigan noticed there was an eager straining forward to hea
the answer to that question. "I really do not know," he said. "
left California with her body a day after she died, before such ma
ters could be gone into. The lawyers there will, in due tim
divulge the contents of her will. Great artists expend as well a
earn huge sums of money. Their estates sometimes dwindle. He
estate is the inspiration of a magnificent career. I am here only t
carry out her dying wishes, for which she amply provided funds be
fore her untimely demise."

"Are you her husband?" a Scranton reporter asked.

"No. Olga Treskovna never married. She was wedded only t
her great art. She gave her life, in fact, to finish this picture, 'Th
Garden of the Soul.' Her doctor warned her to stop work, but sh
paid no heed. She carried on. Like the loyalty to her father's mem
ory manifest in the ringing of these church bells, so was her loyalt
to producer Marcus Harris, whom she felt was her artistic father.

"Did you hear that? Gave her life!" came the voice of a woma
in the crowd. Better still, Dunnigan observed the reporters wer
making note of it.

"I'm just a friend of Olga Treskovna's," continued Dunnigan, an
he realized again that he did not really think of her as being dead
"a friend who had watched her career and always believed that sh
would reach the heights. As she surely did. But now," and h

forced himself to think as his listeners must think, "all that is past. She's just a small-town girl—come home. Please keep it so, gentlemen, if you feel that some note of her passing must still be made."

Bill Dunnigan took another deep breath. That crowded room was strong for Olga Trocki—professionally known as Olga Treskovna—and a picture called "The Garden of the Soul"! There was no doubt of it! And from that room—well, great things had started from lesser places. What you could do to one room, you could do to a world of rooms!

Dunnigan spoke the end of his oration, and spoke it especially to the gentleman of the radio network. "What an inspiration it is for all of us here in America, to think that from the humblest beginnings—Olga Treskovna worked as a child in your coal breaker to earn her daily bread—she became the great actress she was! Each one of us has the same equal chance of success in this glorious, free land of ours!"

There was no question about the impression his oratory had made. There was a vigorous nodding of heads, and all reporters were very busy over their notebooks. The emotion-seeking radio man, his eyes flashing and his lips moving, was almost rehearsing his next broadcast then and there.

Dunnigan knew his hunch in Hollywood had been right—Olga Treskovna's story would find a reverberating echo in the hearts of the millions—as reverberating as the bells which now underlined each word that he had spoken.

"How do you spell her stage name?" the still skeptical Associated Press man asked. "I may as well get it correct."

"T-r-e-s-k-o-v-n-a," he spelled patiently. And he thought, "*How grand it's going to look in the electric lights! Even you'll believe it then.*" Aloud he said, "But please—just call her Olga Trocki, the Breaker Girl."

"The Breaker Girl!" another woman exclaimed. "I remember that name! And she could play the accordion and sing! She could sing well!"

"The Breaker Girl—good! Excellent!" repeated the radio commentator.

"That picture is 'The Garden of the Soul' produced by the same Marcus Harris who did 'Gone with the Sunrise'?" This from one of the Wilkes-Barre scribes.

"The same," said Dunnigan, "but, as I said, that picture, in its beautiful technicolor, its fidelity to the great novel from which it was taken, will never be released. And now, if you will excuse me, I am very tired. I hope you really don't put all this in your papers. Or you, sir, mention it over your broadcasts. It's just a private funeral."

"Thanks! Thanks!" came in chorus from the news gatherers and their radio associate. Even the doubtful A. P. scribe had been won over for, as Dunnigan mounted the stairs again, he saw this gentleman at the wall-telephone, calling for Long Distance and New York. And back in his room and looking from his window to the street below, he watched the other reporters jump into their cars and dash off for Wilkes-Barre and Scranton. Bill Dunnigan's face wore a broad, contented smile, and the sound of the bells, filling his room, was the sweetest symphony he had heard in years!

He gave the lobby five minutes to clear, then went downstairs. The Associated Press man was still very occupied at the telephone. Dunnigan could overhear "Treskovna—I'll spell it for you—Marcus Harris—Garden of the Soul—ringing the church bells for four days in memory of her dead father—gave her life to make a film—known as the Breaker Girl when she lived here—more excitement than there's been for years—I smell publicity, but it's real human interest stuff——"

Dunnigan moved to the night clerk.

"Your son?" he asked.

"Waiting at the curb since eleven-thirty sharp, Mr. Dunnigan!" There was a new respect in the clerk's voice. He admired millionaires. Here was the first millionaire he had ever known personally!

"Good," said Dunnigan. "See you when I get back."

The little car raced through the night. The bells seemed even louder and clearer on the hills outside the town.

How his old Broadway boss would have seized on an opportunity like this! How the great musical show producer would have thrilled at those chimes if they had been tied up with a show of his! Was Marcus Harris made of the same showman stuff? Would he relent in his obsession about a dead star? Dunnigan could only wait and see. It was now "on the knees of the gods," as somebody said in some play or other.

They were presently in the small city of Nanticoke and at the railway station telegraph office. The operator was standing in the doorway, listening to the distant clangor. He was in his shirt sleeves and wore the sleeve garters and the vizor-like green eyeshade that seem always to be the badge of his occupation.

"What's going on in Coaltown?" he asked.

"Just a little preliminary, warming-up, bell-ringing practice for the funeral of the greatest little picture star of all time!" said Bill Dunnigan. "Did I say funeral?" he corrected himself, "I mean birthday! My driver will tell you what Coaltown knows. And in five minutes I'll have a very confidential wire for you, brother. Give me a couple of blanks quick! And say, what's the name of the leading bank here?"

"The Miners' National."

"Good. Sounds reliable enough! Ready for you in five minutes!"

Dunnigan stood at the high window-counter and wrote his telegram. He had sent hundreds of telegrams in his career, but never one so important to all that life now meant for him.

Nevertheless, he wrote quickly and with a calm confidence.

MARCUS HARRIS PERSONAL
CARE SUPER PICTURES INC
RADIO CITY NEW YORK CITY
DEAR MARCUS HARRIS WILL YOU SHOOT TEN GRAND TO SAVE
YOUR MILLION IN GARDEN OF SOUL AND RELEASE A PICTURE
THAT WILL MAKE YOU ANOTHER MILLION QUESTION MARK
MUST HAVE FUNDS BY NOON TOMORROW STOP THERE IS A
MINERS NATIONAL BANK HERE IN NANTICOKE PENNSYLVANIA
TO WHICH MONEY CAN BE TELEGRAPHED TO MY ORDER STOP
AM STAYING AT WYOMING HOTEL COALTOWN SAME STATE SIX
MILES AWAY TRESKOVNA HOME TOWN BUT WIRE ME AT NANTI-
COKE STATION WESTERN UNION STOP LOVE BUT NO KISSES STOP
YOUR LATE PRESS AGENT BUT STILL PLUGGING FOR YOU

                         WILLIAM DUNNIGAN
P STOP S STOP ALSO IF POSSIBLE SEND IMMEDIATELY COALTOWN
ADDRESS HALF DOZEN PAIR WHITE SPATS STOP FRANK BROTHERS
FIFTH AVENUE KNOW MY SIZE STOP SIDEWALKS OF THAT TOWN
TERRIBLE ON SPATS

                                              W D

The operator came back, unlocked his office and stood inside the window.

"How much?" said Dunnigan.

The operator counted the words. "A hundred and twenty-five words. Full rate?"

"Full rate," said Dunnigan.

The man figured again. "Three dollars and thirty-two cents, including tax."

"Here's five bucks," said Dunnigan. "Get it off at once and keep the change. There'll be an answer for me probably about ten or eleven in the morning. If it gets here before I do, please hold it. If a new man comes on, tell him to hold it for me. You have my name on the wire."

"Thanks! Thanks very much, Mr. Dunnigan!"

"Don't mention it. The pleasure is all mine!" said Bill Dunnigan, and meant it.

Millionaire Dunnigan now had five dollars left in the world. Three would go to pay for this Nanticoke trip, with perhaps a dollar tip to the hotel clerk's son. Nevertheless he burst into his theme song—"A pretty girl—is like a melody—" and it seemed to synchronize with the distant bells as he rode back through the otherwise silent night to Coaltown.

32

*T*HE YEAR BEFORE, Father Paul had hopefully instituted a daily Mass at five forty-five A.M. so that such workers as desired could have the comfort of the Church before beginning the day's toil. He had reasoned that those toiling under a constant danger to health and limb with an occasional mine catastrophe involving entire shifts would welcome the opportunity to pray a little before each day's hazard.

As usual (so it seemed to him) his plan did not gain any overwhelming response. There had never been more than ten people in the church on any one morning, and half of these were housewives, not men. Sometimes there were only two or three persons in the pews. There had been mornings when not a single worshiper appeared!

It seemed that miners in need of assuagement or courage preferred to take it in liquid form through the side doors of their favorite saloon—since said saloons could not open legally till six A.M.

However, Father Paul had not given up his Mass. He might give up trying to persuade parishioners not to nail down their bedroom windows in the winter—to let the children bathe more often than once every month; but something that concerned the church, once started, must go on. So he arose each morning at five, and was ready before his altar at the appointed time, though it might mean going through the service for the benefit of the four walls of an empty edifice. Even the designated altar boy would sometimes fail to appear.

He awoke earlier than usual on this particular day. Sheer exhaustion had caused him to pass into dreamland the night before—a hectic dreamland of gorgeous thirty-dollar altar cloths marching down the church aisle arm in arm with six-foot-tall bills for candles marked "Please Remit" in large red letters; of men on ladders (they all wore black derbys at a rakish angle) painting the shingles of the Church of St. Michael; of his mother saying, "You've got a parish, Paul—a parish of your own!"; of a housewife crying "I've cooked in lard for thirty years, raised and buried ten children—I think I know what children should eat!" And under it all was a metallic sound—Ding dong dong! Ding dong dong!

He knew now what the sound was. For it continued as he emerged into wakefulness. The bells! The bells of the five churches. They were ringing steadily at this usually silent hour. What was it all about? Oh yes! The stranger from the West—the dead girl in her coffin in his church—the curious last request that she had made!

Panic again gripped him. Would all this be his final, great mistake? His supreme cataclysmic error. The climactic blunder that would drive the last worshiper from his parish!

He got up and looked out of his bedroom window, from which he could see the street and the front of St. Michael's. It was barely daylight—an almost full hour before the Mass. The morning star still blazed like a bright lantern high in the pale eastern sky.

A murmur of human voices reached his ears. He looked down. There were some twenty or thirty persons gathered on the steps and in the roadway! Why were they there? To reprimand him? To jeer at him? But the talk that floated upward was quiet, respectful.

The faces, insofar as he could make them out, were eager and friendly—more eager and friendly than he had ever seen faces in Coaltown. More people were joining those already waiting. They seemed simply to be waiting for the doors of the church to open! Eagerly waiting!

Again he was conscious of the bells. They were beautiful. But terrifying also. And it was typical of Father Paul that another thought came to his mind and blotted out all others—what of the elderly janitor who was valiantly tugging the St. Michael bell rope? Was this man near exhaustion with the all-night effort? Had he had anything to eat?

Father Paul plunged into the business of washing and dressing. He must hasten at once to the bell tower.

Just before descending from his room, he again looked out of the window. There were more than a hundred people now in front of his church doors! Waiting for those doors to be unlocked!

The priest entered the church by a rear entrance which he could reach from the rear door of the parish house. It was his usual route and led to the sacristy behind the altar where he kept his vestments, and where the altar boys met and put on their red and white gowns.

This door was not locked, and he gazed incredulously as he entered. Not one, but all six of his altar boys were on hand at this early hour! They were in the midst of a heated argument about whose turn it was to serve!

"Father Paul! Father Paul!" They were all speaking at once. "I missed one day last week! I want to serve it now!" "This is my day, Father Paul, as you know!" "No, I am the one to serve today!"

"I think we can arrange it so that everyone will be happy," said Father Paul. "All of you please stay!"

"Hurrah!" cried the lads in chorus. It may not have been a response prompted by ecclesiastical fervor, but it brought relief to the priest's anxious mind. If the children of the parish were in such a mood, all was well.

"I must go first to the bell tower. Wait here for me," said Father Paul.

He had a further lift of spirit when he entered the bell tower. And he could not help but smile. The bell ringer was there right enough, and so were his two sons, his cousin, and an old uncle. They were taking turns at ringing the bell! Someone had brought sandwiches and hot coffee! There was no hardship or discontent or antagonism here!

"Good morning!" said the priest, and from the excited way they returned his greeting, it was evident they were not worrying about the work. They considered it a privilege and an honor to be a part of this unusual funeral service. They would have something to boast about for days!

Father Paul walked downstairs and opened the front doors of the church. Again he stared in amazement. It seemed as though half the town was there, waiting to pass through the opened doors!

"Good morning, Father!" "God bless you, Father!" greeted him on every side. How it warmed his starved heart! His face became really handsome. He could hardly believe his ears, his eyes!

In a few brief minutes every pew was fully occupied. There were worshipers before every shrine. Dozens of candles were being lit, and the sound of metal dropping against metal told that these candles were being paid for as the coins fell into the offering boxes. Money was pouring in upon St. Michael's! People were soon standing in the aisles, with a solid gathering at the rear and out onto the steps through the open doors.

Father Paul went through the simple service of the Mass with a thumping heart! All six altar boys assisted, for thus he had settled that minor controversy. The responses from the pews came back low and strong and fervent. It was not a part of his dreams. It was really happening!

It had never been his custom to take up a collection at this Mass. But in the gathering were two of his vestrymen of more practical minds. One was the druggist and the other the owner of a garage. Father Paul had never seen them before at a weekday service. They knew only too well the state of the finances of St. Michael's. They reasoned this was an opportunity that might never come again. Of their own volition they came forward—took the long-handled collection bags and started down the crowded aisles.

For the first time in the history of this church, not only quarters and half dollars, but even dollar bills were dropped in plentiful confusion into the cloth pouches at the ends of these hopeful sticks!

From the first, all eyes had strained toward the closed coffin that stood on two stool-like supports in the center aisle before the altar. It was a plain, oak coffin with handles of white metal. Dunnigan knew that Olga Treskovna liked simple things. At each side were the three tall candles, in their tall, black funeral stands, which Father Paul had placed there the night before, and which he had himself lit before he celebrated the Mass. Candles not yet paid for, he had mused. It seemed that they would be paid for now!

And after the service, the great pilgrimage commenced—a pilgrimage past this coffin that was to continue without interruption during daylight hours for four days!

This was according to the custom of their mother Poland. It was deliberate and slow. Each observer knelt, on reaching the coffin's foot, and said a brief prayer. And after the prayer, one usually moved to a shrine to light a candle for the dead and pray again.

Soon every candle before every sainted statue was burning steadily in its tiny, cup-like container. Red and green and yellow and white were these containers and they gave their colors to the flame. The vestrymen—if not Father Paul—noticed that there was again a steady, pleasant tinkling sound of coins going into the boxes to pay for these candles. The alert druggist, remembering that there were half a dozen unused candle racks in the basement beneath the church, sped down to rescue them from their cobwebbed obscurity, and, with the help of the altar boys, they were soon filled with chunky wax cylinders and installed in extra spaces around the shrines. Father Paul's meager stock of candles was completely exhausted by the time all were filled.

His Mass over, Father Paul stood at one side near the altar. Never before had his Church of St. Michael sparkled with such a twinkling of tiny, holy lights! Never had its lonely atmosphere been so sanctified with the pungent odor of burning wax! Misty tears filled the eyes of this simple, grateful priest. And over all, the bells pealed on in an arousing chorus, as if the whole universe were crying praise to Heaven!

Father Paul felt proud and shaken. No matter what the reason, his church, his own beloved church, had at last been full to overflowing! Its walls had echoed to the responses of nearly a thousand human voices! If nothing else happened as a result of his acquiescence to Mr. Dunnigan's strange request, this alone was worth it all. His despised, neglected, early morning Mass had been crowned with at least one glorious gathering! One thing he had attempted in Coaltown was not a complete and utter failure!

He had forgotten to tell Mr. Dunnigan about this early Mass. Too bad! The great morning had passed. There would probably never be another one like it.

--------------------------------------- *33* -------

WILLIAM DUNNIGAN was sleeping soundly through these momentous events at Father Paul's church. Even had he known about this early Mass at St. Michael's, it is doubtful if he would have thought of it as the scene of any unusual happenings that morning.

The religious consequences of his project were still a vague thing in his mind and he could not have predicted any definite, concrete results, such results as he was counting on to happen in his own special field of knowledge. He wanted very much to help Father Paul. To put him and his struggling St. Michael's "on the map." He had discovered that any activity that caused people to talk favorably, or even sometimes unfavorably, about a place or a person would help to that end. That was his business as a press agent, and an uncanny instinct for creating news values had made him the success he had sometimes been.

That the Church of St. Michael would be crowded to bursting with worshipers at five forty-five A.M. the very next morning was beyond the calculations of a man whose day did not start till around ten.

The theater man had not really ended his previous day until a couple of hours before this morning Mass had taken place—namely, at about three in the morning. On his return from Nanticoke and the sending of the telegram to Marcus Harris, he had wandered along Coaltown's Main Street for awhile to listen to "his" bells. That street was then almost deserted, for hard-working, early-rising folk must go to bed and get some sleep regardless of unparalleled events. Especially since many had determined to be on hand for Father Paul's early Mass to get a first look at the reason for all this exciting bell ringing—the coffin of the great actress, Olga Treskovna.

For the daughter of Stan Trocki, town drunkard, was now esteemed great—at least so in her native town. And the lonely Olga Trocki would have been amazed at the number of "bosom friends" who suddenly remembered how they had shared her closest confidence and companionship. Just as the late Stan Trocki, were his ghost circulating in any one of the familiar twenty-two saloons (from all of which he had been ejected at one time or another), would have been mystified to hear what a fine fellow he had always been!

Dunnigan overheard scraps of such comment, as the late stayers drifted homeward from the closing saloons and the dance hall.

Then Coaltown once more belonged to the Breaker, the church bells, and the hovering stars. The bells had competition now. The Breaker night shift had returned to their grimy tasks and the town's one tall building roared on, as if to say to these bells, "You may have your hour, but I will be speaking when you are over with and forgotten! For I am eternal—as work and pain are eternal!"

And the stars looked down and said, "We shall outlast you both —we shall still be here when you and your little world-globe have disappeared into the void."

But press agent Dunnigan that night did not permit thoughts of the eventual omnipotence of either the Breaker or the stars to occupy his attention. He was concerned with a much more immediate and unpredictable problem.

What would the newspapers say, and how many of them, and with what space and heading would they say it? Would the A. P. man's story strike the city desks in New York as being of human interest and news value? Would Wilkes-Barre and Scranton papers send in special wires about it? Had so much else happened in the world the day before as to crowd his story off the pages? Or would the morning be one on which he might even make the front page? That sensation-seeking radio commentator—would he shout the saga of Olga Treskovna, "the Breaker Girl," across the air waves of his network?

Such was Bill Dunnigan's anxious preoccupation as he strolled the town and listened to the pealing of the bells of the five churches.

Newspaper and radio reaction, not anything he, Dunnigan, might wire or say, would impress Marcus Harris back in New York with the dawn of the business day. Consequently, he had purposely said nothing in his telegram as to what it was all about. He must give the impression that what was happening was so momentous, so tremendous, that it could not be ignored—that Marcus Harris would know all about it without any telling by the press agent.

Lacking immediate money from Marcus Harris, his whole promotional structure would collapse. Suppose the picture producer did *not* come through? Would Father Spinsky, who had seemed to doubt Dunnigan's solvency, have him arrested for fraud, if he could not meet his contract payment by twelve noon? Would the grand funeral he was building up turn into a grand fiasco—even a disgrace?

He had walked to a spot opposite Father Paul's church. All was dark in church and parish house. The starlight seemed to reflect on the clean, white cross at the top of the church. This cross stood out against the sky. And Dunnigan suddenly felt a great certainty and faith that his plans would this time come out all right. He was glad he had taken the risk, no matter what happened.

He was glad, also, that the body of Olga Treskovna was in Father Paul's church beneath that cross, and not back at undertaker Orloff's dingy "parlor." Even her first night in Coaltown was not entirely bad, though she was sleeping "down in the town."

Dunnigan returned to the Wyoming Hotel, observed the late hour, and asked the clerk to call him at nine and not disturb him before that hour. He, too, must have some sleep.

Just before going to bed there was another good omen. He had taken from his suitcase a well-worn deck of cards and dealt out on the bed cover half a dozen hands of his favorite solitaire known as "coon can." Bert Williams, beloved colored comedian of several Follies, had taught him that Harlem card game. It consisted of "beating the deck" in the matching of certain cards. He "won" four of the six games—a quite unusual proportion.

So finally, he went to sleep to the clanging lullaby that in the morning would lead to either fortune or oblivion.

34

*T*HE ONE ADJUNCT of modern origin in the equipment of the Wyoming Hotel was a large-faced, electric clock in its lobby. The hotel belonged to the mining company and so it had been pure accident that this lobby had acquired such an up-to-date time indicator. A similar clock had been ordered for the company's local office and two had been sent. The extra one found its way to the wall of the Wyoming Hotel.

The installation of this clock had had a curious effect on the long-faced, mechanically-minded night clerk, whose secret pride was that in appearance he resembled Henry Ford. The electric clock had made the clerk acutely "time conscious." If asked the hour, he gave it to the minute and second. And he took especial relish—by the aid of this clock—in arousing occasional all-night guests at the exact moment they had requested to be awakened. No sooner, no later. If his ancient building had caught on fire and a lodger had given orders to remain undisturbed till a certain time, it was believed this clerk would have seriously debated his duty between the guest's safety and the dictates of the mechanically-driven god on his wall.

As there were no telephones in the rooms, this service depended on an unfailing and highly skilled co-ordination of vision and touch. One eye on the clock, one finger on a series of buttons connected with each room, he pressed the proper button at the precise fraction of a second.

A terrific buzzing, calculated to arouse even the dead, resounded instantly in the proper room. If the sleeper did not immediately answer (via a speaking tube above a corresponding button somewhere on his own wall), the buzzing was energetically repeated.

Sleep-dazed tenants had been known to search five minutes on dark mornings, unable to find either speaking tube or light switch, in order to silence the deafening clamor. Later protests at the desk met with a polite but firm, "You asked to be called at six-fifteen, sir.

Our time is correct to the second." There was a glance to the place on the otherwise bare wall where this correct-to-the-second tyrant slid eternally along.

Guest William Dunnigan escaped this unique Coaltown experience. Something of even greater importance than exact, to-the-second punctuality occurred in the lobby below.

Never before had the clerk faced such a problem, or problems, of decision. This city man, a man apparently of considerable consequence, had been most emphatic that he should not be called before nine. The innocent clerk had smiled condescendingly. "Very well, sir." *As if you will be called one second before—or past—that hour!* He little knew how he must suffer and finally falter in the keeping of this trust.

For, starting at seven, there were insistent telephone calls for William Dunnigan on the lobby pay station. Mostly from newspapers, it seemed. The clerk wrote them down, but refused to wake up Mr. Dunnigan, or "the man who ordered the bell ringing," as he was more often referred to. By eight o'clock several strangers who "looked like reporters" had arrived by car, and were impatiently waiting. They were told they must be patient till nine.

But when at eight forty-five and three quarters, a certain personage appeared who had never before entered the hostelry, and asked to see Mr. William Dunnigan by name, the clerk decided in a mental agony that he must capitulate. With a glance that begged forgiveness of his idol on the wall, he mounted the stairs to A-1 front.

At least he had not pressed one of the sacred buttons at other than the designated hour!

"Mr. Dunnigan, sir," spoke the clerk, after a discreet knocking on the portal of A-1, and a sleepy "Well?" from within, "I apologize. I know it is now only eight forty-eight and three quarters, nearer four quarters; and you asked to be called at nine. I assure you I am breaking a strict personal rule in doing this. But Father Spinsky, pastor of our largest church of St. Leo, is waiting to see you! I apologize again—it must now be only about eight forty-nine and one quarter—but I thought you should be told. I hesitate to keep the clergy waiting."

"Thanks, pal. You done right. Tell the Father I'll be with him as soon as I can dress," replied the now wideawake Mr. Dunnigan. The name "Father Spinsky" had fully aroused the press agent.

"Well, what now?" speculated Bill, as he hastily got into his clothes. He had been obliged to make such hasty dressings many times to catch trains or to get off trains on sleeper jumps. He had a special technique for it—socks, shoes, spats, trousers—but that did not matter now. What mattered was: *Did this Orloff-praised Father Spinsky come swooping down to throw some sort of monkey wrench into the works?*

This priest's face, Dunnigan remembered, was solid and large and hard—as large and hard as Father Paul's was small and kindly —a large face on a large body that gave the impression of being made of some sort of expressive stone. It was he who had uncompromisingly set the twelve o'clock deadline about money. Moreover, he had examined even the unimpeachable Brooklyn Dime Savings bankbook most carefully and suspiciously before putting it in the drawer of his desk—a drawer that he carefully unlocked and locked. If there was any money owed Father Spinsky's church, Bill would wager *he* had not destroyed the record books thereof.

Well, there was no actual money due yet for the bell ringing, which, Bill noted, was proceeding merrily according to agreement. The bass note of Father Spinsky's St. Leo's was booming along with the four others. The ringing was all paid for till ten A.M. if the five hundred in the bankbook were counted. Dunnigan had assigned the bankbook to Father Spinsky. But Coaltown, though small, seemed able to produce surprises, and whatever had brought this priest to his hotel had best be faced quickly.

Fully if not carefully dressed, Dunnigan descended. He put off the persons who "looked like reporters"—four men and one woman —with a brisk "Good morning! I'll see you in ten minutes!" He greeted Father Spinsky who stood apart waiting, and these two proceeded to the hotel parlor. "My lucky room," Dunnigan thought, remembering the response he had gained there the night before.

When they had entered the parlor, Father Spinsky himself carefully closed the door. Bill thought for a moment that the priest was going to lock it, as he had locked his desk drawer, but the St. Leo pastor did not proceed to that length. He was, as indicated, a large, very solidly-built man, quite as tall as Dunnigan and much heavier. He wore a well-made black suit of good material and the Roman collar of his office. On his large, square-turned head was a black straw hat. His black shoes were heavily-built and well-polished. Bill thought: "He has not *walked* Coaltown's sidewalks to the hotel, that is certain!"

"I'm sorry to have kept you waiting," said Dunnigan. "I was not yet up. I hit the mattress—if it can be called a mattress—at a very late hour. What can I do for you, Father?"

"Be seated, my son," said Father Spinsky. Bill noted with relief that the voice was conciliatory. A little too conciliatory! It put the experienced Mr. Dunnigan on his guard. But at least the pastor of St. Leo's was not on the warpath.

They sat down by the table which furnished the center of the room. The priest continued: "I don't think last evening any of us realized, surely Father Paul did not realize, the importance of this funeral—the great numbers of friends this deceased girl and her—er—late father had in the parishes of our town."

"Well?" said Mr. Dunnigan with a slight smile. He had over-heard enough on the streets the night before to know about the sudden change of heart in Coaltown toward the tribe of Trocki. But why did it so concern this gentleman of another church? Quite evidently he wanted something, and Bill had a feeling this something was of a selfish nature and boded no good to rival Father Paul and St. Michael's.

"You see," continued Father Spinsky, "the Church of St. Michael is very small."

So that was it! Orloff had been correct. Father Spinsky was a "smart guy." An opportunist in a Roman collar. Already stretching out his greedy hands. But he was barking up the wrong tree to catch Bill (White Spats) Dunnigan, especially if what he wanted concerned a little fellow named Father Paul and a tumble-down church dedicated to the glory of a Saint pictured with childlike garishness in shield and armor on the wall of the office of that church's parish house.

Mr. Dunnigan, however, still wore his smile. "Miss Treskovna was a very small girl," he could not resist replying to Father Spinsky's indisputable statement of dimensional fact. "As I remember, only about five feet four."

Father Spinsky shifted in his chair. He was a serious man with no time for silly repartee. But you had to humor these city people who thought they made clever remarks—if you wanted something from them.

"I perceive that you have a sense of humor," he said. "That is not bad. It helps us to bear up in the hour of sorrow."

As Mr. Dunnigan waited in silence and made no comment on this platitude, Father Spinsky cleared his throat and continued.

"I was, of course, not thinking of the size of the coffin. Six feet of earth is all that we finally command in this transitory life—sinner and saint alike. I was thinking of the friends who will wish to attend the requiem Masses for her soul—of the friends who will eventually wish to attend the final funeral services."

"Those friends will be welcomed, I am sure, by Father Paul at the Church of St. Michael," said Dunnigan, eyeing the priest steadily. "Besides I am indeed surprised to learn that there is such an interest. From a conversation I had with undertaker Orloff, I gathered that the late Olga Trocki (as she was known here) and her—er—late father had not exactly won any popularity contests with your citizens."

"Ah, Mr. Orloff," sighed Father Spinsky and made a depreciatory gesture with large, stubby hands. "A worthy man, but with no sense, I fear, of the finer things of life."

"He seemed to be an admirer of yours—he spoke very highly of you," said Bill Dunnigan with a broad smile.

Father Spinsky looked hard at Mr. Dunnigan. But that usually frank and expressive face could assume a blank, almost inane poker innocence on occasion. This was one of those occasions.

"I have endeavored to merit the approbation of the businessmen of the community," said Father Spinsky with his best professional unction. "They are, after all, the foundation of the greatness of our country. But Mr. Orloff should have brought you to me when he learned the name of your departed friend."

"On the contrary, on learning that Treskovna and Trocki were synonymous, he was quite certain that Father Paul was my man," said Dunnigan. Bill was beginning to enjoy this interview.

Father Spinsky frowned. He shifted again in his chair which creaked dangerously under his weight.

"Yes, I know. I have just talked with Mr. Orloff. He is, I am happy to say, extremely regretful of his curt treatment of you, a stranger in our midst. In fact, the memory of it has made him quite ill."

"That is, indeed, too bad," said press agent Dunnigan blandly. "I hope he will soon recover. He has contracted to 'deliver the body to the graveside'—those were his words I believe—and 'lower in,' and to engage me six pallbearers with gloves, for which I have already paid him. I hope his suddenly failing health will still permit him to carry out these obligations."

Father Spinsky could not decide whether Dunnigan was very dumb or very clever. He was getting a little impatient, and the discussion of undertaker Orloff brought no happy thoughts. He continued to speak calmly however.

"I think you can depend on Mr. Orloff's carrying out his agreement," he said. "He is thoroughly reliable. It is only to be regretted that he cannot combine a spirit of Christian charity with his business arrangements. And speaking of business arrangements, I will return your savings bankbook." And he took the small, envelope-enclosed book from his pocket and placed it on the table.

"As between gentlemen no such security is necessary," he added.

Father Spinsky would never have understood that the sight of that bankbook did it! It swept over Bill Dunnigan all of a sudden, as if a theater electrician had turned on the great flood of a thousand-watt spotlight. The press agent did not reach for the book. He would not have touched it for a million dollars!

"Just how, besides returning this bankbook, do you propose to combine that spirit you speak of with whatever arrangement you have come to propose to me?" he asked bluntly. And he looked at his watch. He wanted to eat his breakfast and proceed to Nanticoke.

Father Spinsky eyed Dunnigan shrewdly. He, too, decided to beat around the bush no longer.

"I have come to propose—that is—" and he hastily corrected his phraseology, "I have come to offer the use of my church for these services."

As Mr. Dunnigan was silent, Father Spinsky continued his sales talk. "It is a large, new church, seating some two thousand people. My organ is the finest in the town. We have a choir of twenty trained voices and an organist who comes from Scranton. My altar is the most expensive in this part of Pennsylvania. It will provide a proper setting for such a service as I believe you wish to have."

Dunnigan knew, of course, that this was coming. The enormity, the unfairness of it, made him almost see red. But he was learning control in this school of Coaltown personalities and values.

"Have you consulted Father Paul about this change?" he asked smoothly, his narrowed eyes the only clue to his real emotions.

Father Spinsky did not realize the meaning of the narrowed eyes. The man was impressed, he felt.

"I have spoken to my colleague Father Paul—in fact, I just came from him. I think he would agree. He naturally had hoped to continue and carry through a ceremony starting in his church, but since he could scarcely accommodate the gathering at his early Mass—he admitted he was already out of shrine candles——"

Father Spinsky's voice was rising perceptibly, but the surprised Bill Dunnigan interrupted.

"You mean, Father Paul has already had a service!"

"Yes. I suspected you knew nothing of it. His 'five forty-five Mass'—an innovation which he undertook some months ago without consulting the other churches and which, until this morning, has been a ghastly, pathetic failure, bringing discredit on the whole Church body——"

Father Spinsky again checked himself. He realized he had let his pent-up resentment of this innovation of Father Paul's cause him to desert the character of brotherly benevolence. He returned hastily to his initial statement.

"I have come to offer you the greater facilities of St. Leo's. The funeral charges I will make purely nominal. And I will send Father Paul some proper proportion of the collections to recompense him for the trouble and expense he has already taken in the matter."

The collections! In spite of Father Spinsky's carefulness it had slipped out. Bill Dunnigan had really never thought of this angle of the enterprise. He did not then entirely understand, though come to think of it, churches *did* take up collections!

Here was a basic reason for the priest's generosity in offering his larger church.

Dunnigan hated insincerity. Especially sanctimonious insincerity. He would have had much more respect for this priest if he had come right out with it. "Father Paul has something of value that I want. I am willing to pay for what I want." But this smooth, unctuous hypocrisy, as it seemed. He stared at this heavy-handed "go-getter" in his Roman collar, and the press agent's soul revolted.

One thing it made clear, however. Coaltown was aroused. But Coaltown was a small place and what might move Coaltown might not stir New York; specifically it might not stir a certain office high in Radio City.

Since Coaltown was so small, Bill Dunnigan felt he must not risk making any out-and-out enemies here—at least not until he was standing on a solid financial rock in its midst, instead of the quicksand of less than a dollar in currency. If he were indeed destined to stand on a rock!

His answer to this crude proposal must of course be, "No," but he must frame that answer less emphatically, less embellished with a few choice and forceful expressions than he would have delighted to enunciate.

Dear, gentle Father Paul! Bill had no doubt the pastor of St. Michael's would acquiesce if he felt St. Leo's was a nobler place for Olga Treskovna's last rites. Fortunately (thought Bill), Father Paul now had a hard-boiled partner fully capable of dealing with the Father Spinskys of his world.

So Mr. Dunnigan spoke in his most dulcet tones. He would return hypocrisy for hypocrisy.

"I appreciate your kindness and the generosity that prompts it. But I am carrying out a deathbed promise. The late Olga Trocki specifically requested that she be buried from the Church of St. Michael. She even mentioned their organ and its blind organist. It seems they gave her inspiration and comfort when she lived here as a lonely child, and did not somehow realize the vast multitude of her friends. So although I am deeply grateful to you, I cannot accept your offer."

The face of Father Spinsky flushed and hardened. He was used to having his own way in Coaltown church matters. He had told both his sister and James Orloff that he would arrange to have this important funeral, that was attracting such wide and favorable attention to the unworthy St. Michael's, moved over to his own church. If he knew his sister, she was already spreading the information. It had not crossed his mind that an alert man from the city would not jump at such an opportunity. But there was no doubt the priest had been turned down.

Nor was Father Spinsky so dense that he could not detect something of the unsaid thoughts of the man opposite him, something of the sarcasm Dunnigan was not entirely able to keep out of his voice. Very well. This man would have to pay for his suave mockery and cheap banter, and pay well. The St. Leo's pastor arose and delivered his ultimatum.

"There remains then the matter of the bells. At twelve o'clock noon there will be due to myself and to my colleagues an additional one hundred dollars not covered by your bankbook, which, to protect their trust in me, I fear I must continue to retain."

And Father Spinsky reached out and recovered the book from the table.

"I would like that hundred dollars promptly by twelve," he continued. "It is bad enough that there will be delay in collecting this bankbook money. We also find that the price as arranged for the first few hours is not adequate to meet the extra expense of their constant ringing. I myself fear that I must install a new bell rope. Our price from now on, therefore, must be twenty-five dollars an hour, payable in advance."

If Father Spinsky expected argument or capitulation at this point, it failed to come. The eyes of the man opposite him only became a little narrower. The priest continued:

"The morning newspapers say our bells are to ring for four days. It was very unwise of you to make such an announcement without coming to a definite agreement with us. Four days at twenty-five dollars an hour will be six hundred dollars a day for each church. Twenty-four hundred dollars a day for the four. Nine thousand, six hundred dollars for the entire task—exclusive of what you may pay St. Michael's. I do not represent Father Paul.

"I was planning to waive a good part of this expense, could you have accepted my offer. I have influence with the other Catholic pastors also."

He paused, but Dunnigan, who was also standing, still made no move to speak.

"Since you decline," and there was open antagonism now in Father Spinsky's tone, "I fear I must have this money in hand by noon today. Otherwise our bells cease ringing. You are entirely unknown to me, sir. You seem to be known to Father Paul, but his financial standing and his judgment are hardly such as to give any weight to such a recommendation. I am being as generous as I can. If you change your mind, I will be at my parish house. I wish you good morning, sir."

Father Spinsky had been holding the bankbook in his hand. He now placed it securely in his inside pocket.

If the priest thought Bill Dunnigan would cry out at the loss of his bankbook, he was vastly mistaken. A very curious idea had been fermenting in the mind of the press agent. An idea that swamped his desire to assist the St. Leo's pastor's exit by a swift jolt of an entirely physical character.

That damn bankbook! *That* was the jinx! He'd had hard luck ever since he possessed it. His most loyal Broadway employer had died—new shows he had press agented had failed. The Hollywood fiasco. Nothing but misfortune!

Of course! The possession by him of such a book was an open distrust of Fortune—an affront to Fortune—Fortune who had always before been on his side! What business had he—Fortune's son—saving money? None whatever! Let this unpleasant Father Spinsky keep the damn thing and the bad luck that went with it! Father Spinsky would "get his" without any assistance from Mr. Dunnigan!

And Father Spinsky marched out of the parlor and the Wyoming Hotel not understanding at all (and somewhat worried by) the broad smile on the face of the man who politely opened the parlor door for him to leave.

Dunnigan's smile, however, quickly changed to a tightening of the lips. This was serious. The bells alone would now cost ten thousand dollars. He had wired Marcus Harris for ten thousand. If Harris came through—and maybe with the jinx savings bankbook gone he would—matters could somehow be managed. If Harris didn't come through, perhaps Father Paul's bell alone could be rung for the remaining three days.

The hundred he would owe by noon? He could at least get that. A collect wire to Charlie, the Astor bartender. To Mabel, the hatcheck girl at the Stork Club. To Tommy, the treasurer of the Lyceum Theater, who had been the revue producer's office boy. Some one of these humble people could and would shoot him a hundred, he felt sure. And an extra twenty-five to get back to town for a new start.

No more damn hoarding of good money in jonah savings banks!

He was hungry, but the thing now was to get to Nanticoke and be at that telegraph office. It was nine-forty. He went out of the hotel and into the main street of Coaltown.

There were more people on the street than usual. He could see Father Paul's church farther up and across the way. A line that looked like some two hundred persons was moving slowly through its doors. And those who had finished were emerging alongside this entering line. It reminded Bill of the queue at the box office the morning after a show had made a hit. St. Michael's was on the map already. Should he hasten there first and talk with Father Paul?

He stifled the inclination. The trusting priest must never know of the desperate financial gamble Dunnigan had taken. Better not see Father Paul until he knew how that gamble was coming out. On to Nanticoke to learn if he were "heeled" or on his own!

As if to second this decision a bus was approaching bearing on its front a plainly marked sign "NANTICOKE." He hailed it and stepped in. The state of the exchequer would not allow a journey there in style via the Ford of the night before.

He had escaped the reporters who were by this time talking to people in line before St. Michael's. That was best, anyway. Let the now not inarticulate citizens of Coaltown tell the press what was astir!

Aboard the bus Dunnigan heard more about Father Paul's early Mass. Two women seated in front of him were discussing it.

"The crowd couldn't all get inside St. Michael's," one was saying. "They were standing clear into the street. It was like Christmas Eve Midnight Mass! But I came early and was in the fifth row, right opposite the coffin!"

"They say the collection was nearly three hundred dollars! Druggist Shoen told my husband his side of the church alone gave a hundred and eighty dollars and forty-two cents!"

"The service was beautiful. Six altar boys. And every candle lighted!"

"Did Father Paul speak about the dead girl?"

"Only to pray for her soul—and all the souls of the faithful departed. Then just the Mass."

"When will the next Mass be, I wonder? They say the main service won't be till Friday."

"I heard that service is to be moved to Father Spinsky's. His sister told me Father Spinsky was seeing the millionaire about it."

"I hope they keep the funeral at St. Michael's. After all, that was her church. Olga Trocki's. Who would have thought she would become so rich and famous!"

"Father Spinsky usually gets his way. They'll move it to St. Leo's."

"I wonder who'll get this girl's fortune? The *Wilkes-Barre Journal* has all about her on the front page."

"I haven't seen a paper. We stopped subscribing last year. Do you think I can get one in Nanticoke?"

"Logan's Drug Store has them. I want to get another copy if I can, to send to my sister in Shamokin."

All of which was music to the ears of Mr. Dunnigan, until a terrible thought crossed his mind. What about Father Paul if the press agent could not carry on? If there were no answering telegram marked "William Dunnigan" at the railway telegraph office? If that telegram were a curt turndown? If eleven o'clock—twelve o'clock came—and still no telegram? What about Father Paul?

As regards any hazards of losing, Bill Dunnigan had been thinking only of Olga Treskovna and himself. He had thought that, however it turned out, Father Paul would benefit. St. Michael's would benefit. They had benefited already, not only in prestige but in a money way. This was confirmed both by Father Spinsky and the gossip of the women seated in front of him. But would not this initial success rebound like a bone-shattering boomerang if Dunnigan failed to meet his financial commitments!

Father Paul had trusted him. Had, in a way, gone bond for him. For, come to think of it, without Father Paul's presence, the other pastors might not have agreed to the ringing of their bells. The idea had been Dunnigan's, but it was Father Paul who had made possible its fulfillment.

And it was Father Paul who would suffer most if things went wrong. It was Father Paul who would be the laughing stock of the community. Another "crazy idea" of this priest's gone wrong. Another "innovation" bringing "discredit on the Church," as Father Spinsky had venomously recited.

The powerful Father Spinsky had it "in" for Father Paul. Dunnigan could see the St. Leo pastor's face, if he did not have his money by the stated hour of noon. The vengeful trip to the St. Michael parish house. The "I told you so." The "Now see what you have done." It would just about finish Father Paul.

Dunnigan looked at his watch. Noon was only two brief hours away!

A cold sweat broke out on the press agent's forehead. A paralyzing fear gripped his whole body. He had assured Father Paul he would not let him down. He hadn't realized when he spoke, when he had recklessly plunged into his plan, what its failure might mean to this priest. He only saw what its success could mean.

Nearly ten thousand dollars needed by twelve noon! What were his, Dunnigan's, actual resources? A watch that maybe he could pawn for twenty-five bucks. A pair of platinum cuff links worth a few dollars more. That let him out!

He had demanded with such assurance the name of the leading bank in Nanticoke. He should have asked for the name of the leading pawnshop—if there was one!

Ten thousand dollars! Dunnigan was not a financier. He had always worked on a salary. He had never tried to raise money. He had asked for publicity appropriations and gotten them or been refused, but that was a different matter. He could always borrow a "century" here and there, just as he had freely lent them, but he knew no one, except Marcus Harris, who could check out ten thousand dollars. And who else would anyway, since "The Garden of the Soul" was the sole property of Marcus Harris.

Panic seized him. Dreadful, heart-clutching panic. He was going to fall down on Father Paul.

He might let Olga Treskovna down, but to the world she was dead. He might let down his own resolutions, but he could return to New York where one day's events were forgotten the next. But Father Paul must face the music here alone, must remain in this gossip-ridden, vindictive, unforgetting Coaltown; Father Paul must meet these cruel, sneering people every day of his life, face Father Spinsky and the other priests whom he had helped to hoodwink.

Father Paul whom he had come to love as a brother in the past few hours! Father Paul who had unselfishly helped him and backed him up with scarcely a question!

There came before Bill Dunnigan's eyes the face of the little priest. His dignity when he had explained that he wanted no money for Olga Treskovna's church service. The longing when he had spoken of the dreamed-of altar cloth. The gratitude when Dunnigan had promised it. The hope and courage when he had reiterated his faith in the power of prayer. The determination when he had spoken of again trying to help the people of Coaltown.

Groping for some steadying support on the brink of this bloodchilling precipice, another image came before the press agent's eyes—the gaudily colored representation of Father Paul's Saint Michael on the parish house office wall. The Saint with the armor and the shield and the sword. And the face of a fighting angel.

And as Olga Treskovna had felt that she could approach the theater through burlesque, because she had met and known that burlesque girl in Wilkes-Barre, so Bill (White Spats) Dunnigan felt that he could approach his God through this fighting Saint, whom he had met at Father Paul's. Besides, he, Dunnigan, had always been a pal of fighters in life and on the stage—Jack Dempsey—a musical show about Cyrano de Bergerac—another about D'Artagnan—a play with Jim Corbett——

Anyway, riding on that bus to the town of Nanticoke, the press agent did a strange thing. A startling thing. Bill Dunnigan said a desperate prayer to this Saint. It was the first prayer he had said since he was a boy.

"Dear Saint Michael," he spoke almost aloud with tensely moving lips and with clenched fists, "I can't let down a right guy like your Father Paul. I'm not quitting anymore. I'm doing my damndest—everything I know how to do. Throwing leather with every punch. Please help me, Saint Michael—for I need help! Help me not to let down Father Paul!"

He remembered that you should say, "Amen" to a prayer, and he added, "Amen."

This prayer was not couched in proper reverential terms. The man who said it was sitting in a jolting bus, his black derby cocked at an angle.   But his mind's eyes were straining heavenward, and there was a great sincerity in his heart.

As Dunnigan was saying this prayer (it was now about ten A.M.), a short, stocky, round of face, thick-lipped, thick-legged man was entering his offices in Radio City in New York.

~~~~~~~~~~~~~~~~~~~~~~~~~~~~~~~~~~~~~~ *35* ~~~~~

*T*HE NEW YORK OFFICES of Super Pictures, Inc., Marcus J. Harris, President, might be written down as the realized dream or nightmare—depending on your taste in art—of a Salvador Dali enthusiast.   The word "modernistic" was archaic if used to describe them.

Marcus Harris was not to blame for this.   Dunnigan's "Napoleon of the Industry" was a homey man who liked to drink coffee from a saucer, bought his shoes and clothes plenty large, wore garters only on compulsion, and worked in his shirt sleeves.   He liked comfortable chairs.   His simple personal tastes had nothing whatever to do with the often flamboyant pictures produced by his stage directors.

Mrs. Marcus Harris was to blame.   She was a frustrated artist. Frustration in the realm of art can lead to direst consequences.   A certain disappointed paper hanger took vengeance on the entire world.   Frustrated vocalists and musicians have terrorized whole neighborhoods.   As a young woman, Rachel Harris had painted china.   The creative flame thus kindled only awaited its opportunity.

When that excellent provider and faithful companion, whom she had married when he and his brother were running a nickelodeon, became a producer and moved from Fourteenth Street to Times Square, she was silent.   But when he progressed from Times Square to the glory of Radio City, she asserted her secret passion. In a moment of weak affection Mr. Harris granted her full authority in setting up his new business abode. Unfortunately, he had been called to his West Coast Studios while this was being done.

He left behind a beloved roll-top desk, a swivel chair, the seat well-worn to his curves, a comfortable couch where he could take a brief after-lunch nap, and assorted roomy leather repositories for the bodies of his business friends. All this in a room of cozy, almost cramped dimensions—the friendly room of a friendly soul. On his desk was a lamp that looked like a lamp, with a green shade.

He returned to something that reminded him constantly of a thing he tried in New York to forget—his own picture sets. Thus did Fate avenge herself—thus was he hoist by his own petard into one of those grandiose salons in which his Hollywood designers placed the scenes of the simplest pictures.

His New York "private office" was now the size of a small banquet hall. A blond, flat-top contraption at the distant far end—it seemed a full half mile from the door—was his "desk," with nothing at all on top that he could pull down with a conclusive bang when he had finished the day's toil. He sat on a hard, blond object with a short, hard back. Other blond structures of wood and shiny metal, equally hard and uninviting, were for his visitors. The light came from upright pillars in distant corners, and was directed toward the ceiling.

"Now you have the most modern office in Radio City, Marcus, darling!" exclaimed the proud perpetrator of all this when, like Moses, he had been led up fifty stories to view the promised land. "It's just like your marvelous setting in 'The Billionaire!'"

Mr. Harris gulped and was staggered, but he controlled his feelings. He had always felt sorry for that "billionaire."

"It's beautiful," he had said, "I'm proud of you, Rachel." He loved his wife. He would not hurt her feelings for a world of offices.

She was an attractive woman. Marcus Harris often wondered how he had ever won her. She had stood by him through the early vicissitudes of the new business. She had been his one comfort the dreadful year they had released that picture in which the star had died, and everything else had then gone wrong—the business misfortunes of which had killed his brother. He knew that if he lost every cent he possessed, and had to go back to a tailor shop, "his Rachel" would be at his side.

If only she had not taken up china painting as a girl!

*   *   *

In spite of this love and gratitude, Marcus Harris had sometimes contemplated rebellion against the Radio City office. He came the nearest to open mutiny this August morning of the events just related in Pennsylvania. For, instead of a smoothly if dizzily-rotating planet on which events somehow clicked along toward an ordered fulfillment, his world had become a tumultuous, nerve-cracking, ignited bomb, that had paused and gone into reverse in order to bedevil Marcus Harris! If ever a man needed swivel-chair, roll-top-desk comfort, Mr. Harris was that man.

He was just off a plane from the Coast. He had been air-sick all the way. His journey thoughts had been: "My stomach gone, my capital gone, my peace of mind gone, my reputation gone!"

He had always blamed himself for his comparatively few business mistakes, but in this instance he blamed someone else—William Dunnigan! Trouble had started with the engaging of this press agent. It was entirely because of him that he now had on his harassed mind the problem of Olga Treskovna. He never would have heard of the wretched girl if it hadn't been for Dunnigan! Certainly he would never have put her, well or sick, into that leading role!

For this girl was still a problem. Harris thought he had dismissed it, ended it, even if it might break him financially, when he had announced that he was shelving "The Garden of the Soul." It had not proved as simple as all that!

His announcements had never before been questioned, but this one had brought down on his head a barrage of protest. That hostile bombardment had kept him three days longer in Hollywood than he had intended to remain. Others besides Bill Dunnigan were upset, and on the rampage.

First, his name director. On reading the announcements in the Los Angeles papers, this gentleman had verified their astonishing truth at the Studio and then tracked down Marcus Harris at his Biltmore suite. His protest was entirely selfish but no less forcefully proclaimed because of that.

"It's the best work I've ever done as a director!" he declared. "I was counting on its boosting my reputation and my salary. I turned down a year's contract with Metropolitan to give you my services!"

"But Olga Treskovna is dead, and I don't care to release a picture with a dead star," repeated Marcus Harris.

"Why not?" persisted his director. "Anyway, she's not a star. She won't be until the picture is shown. And that picture will get such grand notices nobody will care whether the actors in it are dead or alive!"

"I care. I have my own reasons."

"What reasons?"

"I don't wish to go into that."

"If you are afraid of adverse publicity, Dunnigan can handle the matter so that——"

But the unfortunate mention of the press agent ended that interview. Marcus Harris had said with rising asperity: "I'll not discuss it anymore. I have made up my mind. I will not release the picture."

"You are a fool!" shouted the director and stamped out of the suite and the hotel. He proceeded to the Studio to air his protest and opinion to all departments where he found there was a considerable underground of sympathy. Olga Treskovna had been liked. Bill Dunnigan had been liked.

The leading man, Victor George, was the next to raise his cultured voice in most uncultured dissent. It was also *his* best work and he certainly did not expect it to be shelved when he had agreed to play the role. His public was looking forward to seeing him bring to life the famous part of the lover Maurice. Must he now disappoint millions of ardent fans! *He'd be damned if he would stand for it!* Nobody would care who played the woman so long as he, Victor George, was there making love to her! "Though this Treskovna girl was damn good!" he interjected. This interview was at the Studio, and the actor left to consult his attorney!

Then there had come a long distance call from the literary agent of the well-known author of the novel. This agent also threatened legal action—and for well-grounded damages. Failure to release the film might be taken as a reflection on the value of the story. It might impair the picture value of this author's new novel just coming out. The Harris contract specified a definite release date. Had Mr. Harris forgotten that?

His chief cameraman, a really great artist who used lenses instead of oils, and who had been with Harris for many years, came to the producer with tears in his eyes.

"I have some close-up shots of this girl that Whistler, that El Greco would have thrilled to paint!" he exclaimed. "Never will I find another subject like her! To destroy that film, Mr. Harris, is sacrilege! It is like cutting up the Sistine Madonna! Or the Mona Lisa! And there are some exteriors on the desert where, for the first time, I get an effect like a Turner———"

"I am not destroying it. I simply will not release it," said a stubborn Marcus Harris. The plea of his cameraman troubled him more than the shouts of all the other complainants, but he had made up his mind.

Then came a telegram from his Wall Street banking connection.

"What is this we hear about not finishing 'The Garden of the Soul'? Our interest substantial. Advise you return New York and communicate with us immediately."

Very well—after three hectic days of Hollywood buffeting, of hard looks on all sides, he was back, and the prospective interview in lower Manhattan was not going to be a pleasant one.

Another most disturbing thing had occurred. A film-colony lady columnist, whose stuff was syndicated across the country in hundreds of newspapers, had printed a slur implying Marcus Harris had worked this young girl to death in order to save money. It had made Harris, a humane and kindly man, furiously angry. The fact that the accusation was a half truth did not lessen its sting.

He had not, of course, made the picture at lightning speed to save money. It had been because of the short time he had control of the services of Victor George. Nevertheless, the night and day toil in filming "Garden of the Soul" had undoubtedly hastened the ailing Olga Treskovna's death.

This stab in the back hardened his resolution to shelve the whole thing. At least the papers would not be able to say that he, Marcus Harris, was now going to try to make a fortune over the body of a dead girl!

All in all, it was a nasty mess, and for the thousandth time he blamed William Dunnigan. Why had it been destined this man should carry his jinx clear across a continent, straight into the Hollywood Studios of Super Pictures, Inc.? Why should this alien jinx take such form as to bring back the memory of that dreadful year when he had put out a picture under similar conditions, and misfortune upon misfortune had climaxed in the suicide of his only brother?

So thinking, Marcus Harris arrived from the airport at the tallest building in Rockefeller Center. He hardly spoke to the polite starter and the always polite operator of his elevator. He pushed by the smart girl who sat behind the outside, circular reception desk (a blond monstrosity! he thought—the desk, not the girl) without his customary brief but friendly, "Good morning!" Her "We're glad to see you back, Mr. Harris!" froze on well-rouged lips. Down the passage to his private office he stamped, stamped the endless distance to the flat-top desk. He could not sink into his chair. But he spread over its hard surface ingloriously, and his heart was bitter with the gall of unjust, unmerited censure and calamity.

He usually telephoned his wife the first thing on reaching his office, but today he delayed that custom. He did not want to talk with her until his mind was more at rest—if it ever was to be at rest again!

He must think, and think clearly and decisively. He must not let this thing destroy him. He had not been able to think clearly in Hollywood or on that plane.

The meeting with the bankers was the foremost problem. Could he make these money machines understand how his honor, his reputation, his loyalty to the memory of his brother demanded that this picture not be released? Would they bow to such sentiment and extend his loans until he could finance and get ready another film; or would they demand that their money be at least partly recovered, regardless of dead actresses and his personal feelings and reputation? Curse this press agent Dunnigan who had brought so much affliction in his wake.

Before him lay a stack of telegrams and letters. He mechanically opened the topmost telegram.

Fortune and his efficient secretary Miss Feinberg had placed Bill Dunnigan's wire on top. Mr. Harris unfolded it and read. And reading, his smouldering distress became a bursting volcano. His pent-up wrath could hold no longer.

"My God!" he cried, "My God!" He viciously tore the yellow paper across its middle and tossed it at his waste basket. At that moment Miss Feinberg entered from her adjoining room.

The slender, thirty-year-old Miss Feinberg, who had been with Marcus Harris for ten years, was usually standing by his desk to greet her employer on his return journeys from California. She always personally handed him his letters and telegrams, and had notes about any important matters that had come up since she had talked with him by long distance in Hollywood—as she did almost every day he was away. But on this morning she had been tied to her own office telephone by an avalanche of outside calls.

The International News Service, the Associated Press, the newsrooms of the three major radio networks—all the evening papers, had been on her wire asking for Marcus Harris and for details of the story they had received from Scranton and Wilkes-Barre about the late star of the new Harris film.

She had heard Marcus Harris come in. She told the switchboard to hold any more calls, and seizing a *Times* and a *Tribune* from her desk, entered the sanctum of the president.

"Miss Feinberg!" spoke Marcus Harris before the secretary could even greet him. "If ever that loafer Dunnigan tries to enter this office, have him thrown out! If ever he tries to telephone me, hang up on him!"

"Yes, of course, Mr. Harris," said Miss Feinberg, "but I want to tell you——"

But Marcus Harris was aroused. And voluble. He felt a need to spill some of his grief into a sympathetic ear. Miss Feinberg's ear had always been dependable in such emergencies.

"Not satisfied with ruining me, with ruining us all, with persuading me to put a sick girl who died on me in Gronka's role in 'The Garden of the Soul,' he now wires to send him ten thousand dollars at some godforsaken place in Pennsylvania where this Olga Treskovna lived!"

"It's about that matter in Pennsylvania, Mr. Harris——"

She got no farther. Marcus Harris continued: "Don't Dunnigan know he's fired! I discharged him four days ago in California. Discharged him inclusively! He killed 'The Garden of the Soul.' It's as dead as his lousy friend. He's nearly driven me insane! He's one person I never want to hear about or see again!"

Miss Feinberg realized she must use tact, a difficult personal matter when she herself was laboring under such excitement. But she knew Marcus Harris well and felt she could get him to listen with a little patience.

"I don't think you have seen the newspapers this morning, Mr. Harris," she said.

"No, I have not! I'm just off the plane. We were an hour behind schedule."

"You should see the *Tribune* and the *Times*, Mr. Harris," she said as calmly as she could.

"Why?" exclaimed Marcus Harris with a new burst of irritation. "Why should I see the *Tribune* and the *Times?* Stocks are down. Taxes are going up. Business is being ruined. I know what's going to happen to the country and to me without reading about it in the *Tribune* and the *Times!*"

"But something has happened that I don't think you do know about, Mr. Harris. Your name is mentioned———"

"My name!"

"Did you say Mr. Dunnigan's wire was from Pennsylvania?"

"I did. What's that got to do with it?" There was genuine alarm in his voice now and his flushed face turned ashen.

But Miss Feinberg's face glowed. "I knew it!" she exclaimed, "I knew it must be Mr. Dunnigan! That explains it! No one else could have thought up and stirred up such a break!"

"What do you mean—break? Unless you mean that I am broke with eighty thousand feet of film costing a million dollars going into the ashcan!"

"Mr. Harris," said Miss Feinberg firmly, "please look at the *Tribune* and the *Times*. It's on the first page. A two-column box in the *Tribune* and a good solid headline at the bottom of the page in the *Times*. And the telephones have been ringing ever since I came in—the evening papers—the radio newsrooms— Mr. Dunnigan's pulling something, up in this Pennsylvania, and it looks to me like dynamite!"

She held out the *Tribune* to Marcus Harris. He had been staring at her open-mouthed. His body sagged. He took the newspaper with shaking hands and a sinking heart.

What now? What further diabolical disaster could William Dunnigan invent to put Super Pictures, Inc., and its president completely into bankruptcy!

The black, capitalized headline focused his eyes. The words danced at first, but presently they were still and readable.

CHURCH BELLS RINGING FOR SOLID WEEK; DYING WISH OF LATE SUPER PICTURES STAR.

Special to The New York Herald-Tribune

SCRANTON, PA.—A small-town girl, who rose from deepest poverty to leading roles in Hollywood, and who died there last week after completing the newest Marcus Harris picture "The Garden of the Soul," is carrying out from her coffin the unfulfilled last request of her late father. There are five churches in her native mining settlement of Coaltown, and Olga Treskovna left a sizable part of her fortune to have the bells of all these churches ring an entire week, starting at ten P.M. last evening. It seems that four years ago——

Marcus Harris read through the glamorous, heart-tugging tale Bill Dunnigan was gambling would be recorded. He went back and read it a second time. It had the ring of truth. It touched even Mr. Harris. Poor child! At the end he was on the point of wiping a tear from his eye!

But wait a minute! This was about himself, his film, his star! There was that Pennsylvania telegram from Dunnigan. Where was it? It had landed ingloriously on the carpet just beyond the wastepaper basket. He arose and picked it up, pieced it together and reread it.

"It was announced on all the radio stations this morning!" Miss Feinberg was again speaking. "I heard Frank Singer on WOR at eight o'clock. He said these church bells could be heard for twenty miles and that the whole countryside was flocking to this town!"

"Let me see the *Times*," said Marcus Harris weakly.

Miss Feinberg handed him her *Times*. A heading near the bottom of the page read:

MARCUS HARRIS STAR, OLGA TRESKOVNA,
HAVING BELLS RUNG IN NATIVE TOWN
FOR FOUR DAYS

And the credit line was

"By The Associated Press"

That meant the story was appearing in every large-city newspaper in America!

"It's in the *Journal-American* also," said Miss Feinberg, "but on the second page. And the *News* has a large picture of Miss Treskovna on its back page and carries the story with big headlines on pages six——"

Marcus Harris was for the third time staring at the Dunnigan telegram.

"The *Mirror* telephoned they are sending a special writer by plane to this Coaltown; the *World-Telegram* wants to talk with you as soon as you come in; the Pathé News Reel has a man going there also by plane; NBC is broadcasting the sound of these bells over their network at noon today; the *Journal-American* has called three times, and is sending a reporter to see you here! I told them all you'd surely be in by eleven——"

"Miss Feinberg, get my wife on the private wire," said Marcus Harris. He looked at his watch.

Ten-twenty.

36

A NEW DECISION was forming in the turbulence of the picture producer's mind. It was not entirely because of what Bill Dunnigan had accomplished. It went much deeper than that. Dunnigan's work in Coaltown had simply brought everything to a focus, so that Marcus Harris now saw clearly what he had not been willing to acknowledge all along. Heaven—in Dunnigan's case—was, as the saying has it, helping someone who had tried to help himself.

But first Marcus Harris wished to talk with his wife. This was not merely a matter of releasing or not releasing a film. It concerned her also—it concerned his past and possibly his whole future.

Harris was a showman. He was also a very keen man of business. He realized what all this astonishing "publicity" could mean for any product, whether it was a new breakfast food or a new motion picture. One did not rise from pressing pants in a basement tailor shop on East Seventieth Street to the fiftieth floor of Rockefeller Center without an instinct for what would give the collective trousers of an indifferent humanity a swift and uplifting heave.

Jinx or no jinx, this resourceful press agent had, as Miss Feinberg said, "pulled something" that looked like dynamite! And the explosions so far created were only to the credit of Marcus Harris and "The Garden of the Soul." It was difficult, just as a showman, to cast aside wantonly such an opportunity.

But there were other factors that he realized had been prodding at the back of his conscience from the beginning.

The *Times* said the girl Olga Treskovna had given her life to make this film. Dunnigan, who knew her well, had declared this to Harris in Hollywood at that final interview. The girl's work had been magnificent. His own judgment told him that. His director had confirmed it. The leading man had confirmed it. His cameraman's unusual admiration. The enthusiasm of all the studio officials when they had viewed the "rushes," confirmed it. Harris knew the difference between mere "yessing" of the opinion of "the Boss" and spontaneous approbation.

And he was arbitrarily tossing into the discard all that this dead child had striven for—her single chance for fame!

And the cursed-out Dunnigan? The press man had behaved with dignity and generosity. Harris could still see him—his anguish, his stunned distress when told that the film would not be released. And here was not self-interest. It was for Olga Treskovna. Perhaps the press agent was in love with her. What of it? He had fought for her as a great artist. She had been that, unless his entire staff were wrong in their evaluations.

Dunnigan had only wilted when Harris had whipped the jinx accusation across his face. Was that a fair thing to have done? A manly thing? Kick a fellow when he was down? Harris knew it was not. He had had jinx periods in his own life. Everybody had. The quitters were beaten by them. The winners kept on. Dunnigan hadn't quit. He was keeping on.

And the commercial side of Harris had not forgotten the money part of that interview. Usually, when the producer had been obliged to discharge some employee, there were demands for contract salary, threats of lawsuits for the dismissal. Dunnigan had refused to take even what was rightly due him! And stated that he only wished he could repay what Harris had lost. Stated it so simply there was no question of the man's sincerity.

Marcus Harris, who prided himself on his fairness, knew he had been unfair to both Olga Treskovna and William Dunnigan.

Why had he been unfair? Because he was harping back to a jinx of his own. No wonder he visioned the world as rotating in reverse! He had let that bad year of other days overshadow and warp all other considerations. The two cases were not comparable. That other story had been an inconsequential one. It probably would have failed, anyway. Moreover, the star who had died had not been over-good in the role, or even sincere in her work. Parties and drink had killed her, not overwork.

Marcus Harris realized clearly that he had been afraid, not courageous, in his stubborn decision to give up "The Garden of the Soul." And, for this cowardly reason, he had trampled on a brave man who had been loyal to him, tried to load onto this jinx-ridden fellow man his own jinx of former years. His own experience and fear should have made him understanding, not vindictive.

And he was grievously wronging this dead girl.

The bell of his private instrument was ringing.

"Your wife is on the wire," said Miss Feinberg, and handed the receiver to Mr. Harris. She withdrew to her own office. She knew that Marcus Harris wished to talk alone when he spoke with his wife.

"Rachel darling," said Marcus Harris, "I am back."

"Yes," came the voice at the other end, "I was waiting by the telephone. For I knew you hadn't heard the radio this morning— all the fine things they have been saying about you, Marcus, and the new picture, and that new girl who died. Poor child! But you're going to make it up to her, I know, with what this great picture will do for her memory! I'm glad it's you, Marcus, made that film, and I hope she is glad!"

"Rachel," said Marcus Harris, "I am both ashamed and happy to hear you say that. I wasn't going to make it up to her. I was going to shelve the picture because she had died."

"Why?" asked the voice. "Why would you do that, Marcus?"

"Because I was a coward. Because of what happened to Irving ten years ago. It is almost ten years ago today it happened. Have you forgotten?"

"I've not forgotten. I was going to the synagogue this morning to set up a glass to Irving's memory. I was thinking he would be less sorrowful that on his anniversary you were doing something that was fine and noble. Perhaps, Marcus, he has even found happiness."

"Rachel," said Marcus Harris, "go to the synagogue at once. I would go myself but I have many urgent things to do. Talk to the Vilna Rabbi if he is there. He can explain to the dead. He could act as our advocate. Ask him to pray for us all. And for 'The Garden of the Soul.' And Rachel——"

"Yes, Marcus."

"Ask him to pray for a man named William Dunnigan. He's not of our faith, but he is a brave man that I have wronged and he deserves our prayers. Ask the Rabbi to help remove a sort of jinx that has hung over this man."

"I will do just as you say, Marcus," said the voice. "And don't be late tonight for dinner. I'm fixing you myself some gefüllte fish just the way you like it best, dear." The youthful china painting of Rachel Harris had not corrupted her skill as a cook!

When he had hung up, Marcus Harris pressed his buzzer for Miss Feinberg. He looked at his watch. It was now ten twenty-five.

*   *   *

Miss Feinberg was staring at a changed employer. The drooping shoulders had straightened. The troubled, dead eyes were alive. The thick lips were firm and authoritative. The chin had assumed its proper aggressive jut. So Napoleon must have changed when the troops sent against him on his return from Elba came over to his side. Even the decorative horrors of this New York office had receded into oblivion.

Marcus Harris was no longer afraid of a fear.

The voice that issued orders had the ring of mastery, of control—not only of his own destiny but the destiny of the world! The "Napoleon of the Industry" was again Napoleon.

He was holding before him the two pieces of the Dunnigan telegram. He said:

"Take these orders down quickly, Miss Feinberg!"

"Yes, Mr. Harris." The pencil was poised like a miniature javelin above the ever present shorthand tablet.

"First, have the treasurer go to The Manufacturers Trust and transfer twenty thousand dollars——"

"You said Mr. Dunnigan asked for ten thousand——"

"Are you taking dictation from Mr. Dunnigan or from me, Miss Feinberg?"

"From you, Mr. Harris! I'm sorry." Her face was beaming.

"—Twenty thousand dollars to the order of William Dunnigan at the Miners National Bank in a place called Nanticoke," and he spelled the name, "Pennsylvania. I'll sign the check at once. The money must be there before noon. Have the treasurer stay at the bank until its reception in Nanticoke is confirmed by telephone."

"Yes, Mr. Harris!" The expert fingers had been flying across the tablet even more quickly than her employer had spoken.

"Have one of the office boys go immediately to Frank Brothers shoe store on Fifth Avenue—look it up—and express parcel post special delivery half a dozen pair Mr. Dunnigan's size best white spats to our William Dunnigan, Wyoming Hotel, Coaltown, Pennsylvania. Better give the boy about fifty dollars to pay for them. They must be sent today. You please follow up that they *are* sent."

"Yes, Mr. Harris."

"And take this wire—go to the telegraph office yourself on the basement floor and get it off rush—give the operator a dollar to rush it special——"

"Yes, Mr. Harris."

"William Dunnigan, care Western Union, Nanticoke, Pennsylvania. What do you mean ten grand—exclamation point—Haven't you been with me long enough to know I'm not a piker—question mark—Shoot twenty grand and do whatever you are doing Grade A —stop—Money should be in designated Miners Bank by time you receive this wire—stop—Matter of spats receiving immediate attention—stop—Hope you can hold out until tomorrow as doubt if they will arrive Coaltown before then even with our most urgent attention—stop—See you made first page Times and Tribune but only inside page Journal American and News—stop—Trust you are not slipping—stop—Love and plenty kisses—Marcus J. Harris President Super Pictures Inc."

Marcus Harris again consulted his watch. It was ten-thirty o'clock.

In Nanticoke, Pennsylvania, a worried William Dunnigan was dismounting from the Coaltown bus.

─────────────────────────── *37* ──────

*T*HE BUS ON WHICH Bill Dunnigan had ridden from Coaltown ended its journey before a drug store in the main square of Nanticoke, a mining borough of some twenty thousand. There was a newspaperstand outside this store and from it he bought a Wilkes-Barre and a Scranton morning paper.

"The last two left!" said the woman who attended the stand. "I've sold out twice this morning. There is certainly some excitement over that movie-star funeral in Coaltown!"

There it was, spread over the front pages. Dunnigan read avidly. It was all that a diligent press agent could desire and more. If his fate had depended on Wilkes-Barre and Scranton! But those two admirable cities were not New York. Marcus Harris would judge solely by New York.

The New York papers did not arrive till one o'clock. And this stand received only the *Times* and the *Sun*. Dunnigan paid the woman for these two so that copies would be put aside for him.

After the bus fare and the newspapers there was eighty-two cents left in the treasury, which treasury at that moment was Bill Dunnigan's left-hand trouser pocket. He asked direction to the station telegraph office. It was a short distance down a side street a block away.

Over the daytime street noises the Coaltown bells could not be heard so clearly as the night before. But if he listened carefully, Dunnigan could hear them—a faint, distant, melodic murmur. He wondered if they would still be heard after the fateful hour of noon? People were pausing on the sidewalks to listen, and the conversation was all about the funeral. Had his mind been at rest, he could have asked for nothing better. But as we know, his harried mind was very far from being in repose.

At the corner where he turned to go to the telegraph office was a solid-looking, box-like brownstone edifice, with bronze doors and high, decoratively-barred windows. "The Miners National Bank" was cut indelibly in the cornice along its front.

Dunnigan paused a moment and read the sedate, stone-carved lettering. Would this austere citadel be his sanctuary? Was he destined to storm it presently, armed with an assenting telegram from Marcus Harris? Or would he never penetrate and view its cloistered interior? His predicament had its humorous aspect but there was an anguish in his steady eyes. The strain was becoming almost more than he could calmly endure.

And sure enough, on the other corner was a pawnshop. It was housed in a shabby building with none of the solidness of the Miners National Bank, but it looked very friendly and inviting. The usual gilded three-ball sign of the cult hung above its doorway. The door was wide open, so that all might enter without hindrance. And in its low and inviting glass window he could see, even from where he stood, the pathetic clutter of second-hand musical instruments, fishing rods, tools, shiny smaller objects, all once treasured by proud owners, now orphaned and unredeemed and waiting on the auction block for any who could buy.

Would that doorway under the nailed-up wooden sign "LOANS" be his more humble rendezvous with finance, there to exchange the watch a Follies company had given him for new funds with which to telegraph New York and try to raise at least the hundred dollars he would owe at twelve o'clock?

Never before in his whole life had mere money meant so much to him. Never had mere money been a matter of life and death. Yes, there had been the time when he had needed a quarter to buy the pig-tailed girl who sat in front of him at school a flower for her birthday. Alas, lack of that quarter had lost her forever!

Stupid, lifeless money, when there were great living projects astir —when there were splendid, heartwarming tasks to do! But lack of this money, he knew, would balk his plans.

He pulled himself together and walked rapidly to the telegraph office. He knew it was too early to expect an answer from Radio

City, but he must let the operator know he was in Nanticoke and waiting.

It was the same operator.

"My relief phoned that he can't come on till noon," the man explained. "Told me his grandfather was ill. Nuts! I know what he's doing. He's driven over to Coaltown to see the excitement!"

There was as yet no answering wire, neither "yes" nor "no." Dunnigan said: "I've not had breakfast. I'll get something to eat and be back." He felt he could not survive if he had to just stand there and wait. And his empty stomach might feel a little less jittery with some ballast of food. He had passed a counter restaurant a few doors below.

He went into this place and sat on a stool. It was devoid of customers, for the early morning rush hour had passed. The menu was posted in white, movable letters in a frame on the wall behind the counter. A mop of bright red hair was diligently rubbing the long counter-surface with a damp cloth—the sole attendant.

Dunnigan studied the bill-of-fare on the wall with special attention to prices. In fact, he looked at the prices first. Eighty-two cents was his limit—breakfast, tip, a nerve-steadying cigar. He took out his change and counted it to be sure.

The redhead had stopped its polishing, placed a glass of water before the customer and stood expectantly, hands on the counter, awaiting the order. One hand was near Dunnigan's two newspapers.

"Lots of excitement around here today! Puts everybody on their toes! Did you decide what you wanted, sir? I'd advise the Special if you haven't had your breakfast, sir."

Dunnigan lowered his eyes from debating between "Corned Beef Hash Egg 40" and "Special Ham And Eggs Toast Coffee 45" to the owner of the hair and voice. The voice was cordial, high-pitched, and emanated from the round, pug-nosed face of a very young lad.

"Very well—I'll take a chance on your Special. Let me have the coffee now. What excitement?" said Mr. Dunnigan without enthusiasm.

Redhead had whirled and was drawing the coffee from the faucet of the tall, nickel-plated container. The voice continued with gusto:

"The doings in Coaltown, mister! You should read about it, sir! Funeral of a big movie star! It will cheer you up, sir, if you feel a little down!"

The coffee was now deftly placed before the press agent. "Help yourself to cream and sugar. Take all you want, sir!"

Dunnigan regarded this eager dispenser of news and food, likewise keen observer of a client's mood! He was about to say, "Must you perpetually talk?" but he realized the topic of conversation was his own "show." He, Dunnigan, had really started it. He shrugged his shoulders.

"How can reading about a funeral cheer you up?" he queried. The tone carried the implication that no answer was required.

Redhead was not to be beaten down by any customer's bad humor. "That's right!" he replied brightly. "It does sound funny to say a thing like that!"

He had whirled again and was turning up the gas under a long hot-plate and with the same movement extracting the ingredients of the Special from the adjoining icebox. The flow of words continued.

"Guess you're a stranger here! Guess you've just gotten into Nanticoke! *Some* day to arrive here, sir!"

He now stood with his eggs and a slice of ham, regarding this obdurate case of morning dejection. "Want me to make the Special real good for you, sir! Fry the eggs in butter, sir?"

The intent of the eager face was too friendly to be denied. Dunnigan *had* to smile. But there was a problem in connection with this inquiry.

"Will frying the eggs in butter cost extra?" he asked.

The lad grinned. "No, sir! Not right now, sir! When the boss is around, he won't let me use butter—just lard. You'd prefer butter, wouldn't you, sir?"

"I sure would," said Dunnigan.

"Everybody would! Lard loses customers. I told the boss a dozen times but he don't believe me." The boy turned; a lightning extraction from the icebox, and there arose a brisk sizzling and the pungent odor of hot butter.

"I'd always use butter if I had my own place!" was tossed over the redhead's shoulder. Another quick movement and eggs were expertly broken and crackling on the flame-heated surface. Then the ham sent out its own special sizzle and aroma.

In spite of mental perturbation, Bill Dunnigan found himself becoming interested in this meal—looking forward to it!

"What I meant about cheering you up is the way it says this Coaltown girl made good!" The boy returned to his initial thesis, as he watched his ambrosial order progress to the right color and texture. "She's the star of a new million-dollar picture, and a millionaire is having all the Coaltown church bells rung for four days! You can hear them clear over here! Didn't you notice the sound, mister, before you came in?"

"My attention was called to it," said Dunnigan.

"All this for a poor girl that once worked in the Coaltown Breaker! You ought to *see* Coaltown, mister! Eggs turned, sir, or on one side?"

"Why—one side," said Dunnigan.

"O. K. Sunny-side up! Breakfast is ready!"

Dunnigan watched the expert transfer of eggs and ham to a platter which he now noticed the lad had placed so as to have it warming on the dry part of his griddle. Toast that had been crisping just beyond the eggs also appeared.

"There you are, sir! Hope it's as you like it, sir!" And the boy put down the platter, with a knife and fork and a paper napkin beside it.

"Like another cup of coffee, sir?" He noticed his customer had finished the first cup in two long gulps.

"Why, yes, I would!" Bill Dunnigan was brightening. The Special smelled and looked grand! "But how much extra is another cup?" he added cautiously.

"It's usually ten cents," came the reply, but Master Redhead was already at the tall container and fauceting a fresh cup of cheer. "This is on the house, sir. I see you like coffee. If it was my place I'd give everybody who ordered food two cups!"

"Thanks!" said Dunnigan. He knew his counting of pocket change had not escaped keen, understanding eyes and the inquiries about extra charges were understood. Kindness did still exist in spots in that district! He was glad there was enough change left for a generous tip this lad would not expect. He plunged into the animal joy of this surprisingly promising meal.

"It's what this millionaire said to the newspapers that has me all stirred up!" declared Red Hair, placing the second steaming cup and facing his customer again.

"What did this millionaire say?" inquired Bill Dunnigan between large bites of ham and eggs.

"He said that everybody has a chance in America, just like this Coaltown girl! I wisht I could talk to this man!"

Bill Dunnigan paused in his eating. The lad was not looking at him at all, but off into some horizon of Great Adventure. The eyes were wide, the lips parted, the nostrils of the stubby, turned-up nose almost quivering. But their owner quickly came back to present duties. Another friendly grin replaced the gaze into whatever soul-stirring Dreamland it was that beckoned.

"Is everything all right, sir?" he asked.

"It's fine, kid!" said Dunnigan as the fork conveyed an especially large portion of ham and eggs upward. "Never tasted better! Why would you like to talk to this—this millionaire?"

The lad looked wistfully at Dunnigan. "You won't laugh at me, mister, if I tell you? I do feel like talking this morning, and you being a city gentleman——"

"Go right ahead!" said Dunnigan.

"I want to own my own Quick Lunch! That is, my girl and I do! She works in a candy store now. We want to get somewhere in life —just like that Coaltown girl! She's Irish but I'm Polish. This rich man's name is Irish. And he's interested in Polish people. I came from Wanamee—right next to Coaltown. I worked once in the Wanamee Breaker but I got out of it. I've learned the Quick Lunch business. There's a big future in it, mister! I know I could run my own place! I've got a lot of new ideas about what to do!"

The words had come with a rush. The boy stopped as suddenly as he had begun.

"My girl says I talk too much," he commented and grinned. "She says I'm perfect, except for that!" and there was a still broader grin. "I guess you think I'm a little crazy! It's that Coaltown thing that's got me so excited! I cut out of the papers what that rich man said." And he produced a folded column of type from the pocket of his white work jacket. "Do you think I'm nutty, mister?"

Bill Dunnigan paused again. Here was a surprising new development of his Coaltown performance! He almost forgot his worries about what Marcus Harris was deciding perhaps at that moment.

"I think what you say makes very good sense," he replied to the boy's question. "You sure can cook ham and eggs! You've met a

nice girl. But where does this millionaire who's stopping in Coaltown come in?"

"I don't suppose he'll come in at all," said the boy, "but when I
read what he said and how he had faith in this Polish girl, I thought
if I could meet him he might help my girl and me—might back
us——"

"Back you?"

"We've saved two hundred and fifty dollars. My girl and me together. We need another two hundred and fifty. I've talked to a
lot of people around here. They think I'm nuts. They say I'm too
young. And the ones that have any money are tight. I guess I'll
have to find a pretty rich man to risk that much money—and someone from a big town with big ideas. That's why I thought if I
could only get to this millionaire over in Coaltown—the papers say
he's at the hotel there. Do you think he'd see me, mister?"

Bill Dunnigan took a gulp of his coffee. "You can only try," he
said.

"I want to have the finest Quick Lunch in America!" said the lad.
"Have it right here in Nanticoke!"

"That's a pretty high goal to shoot at!" said his listener.

"That's the only way I think. Aim high. Like the papers say
this girl from Coaltown did! I'll bet that millionaire aimed high
too, when he was young. And I've got a name for my place. A
humdinger! Want to hear it, mister? You won't tell it to anyone
else?"

"I'll keep it secret," said Dunnigan.

"Quick Lunch Heaven!" said the boy, and watched eagerly for
the reaction of his customer's face. "And I'd have painted under
that 'Two Cups of Coffee'!"

Bill (White Spats) Dunnigan, sometimes named America's greatest
creator of show slogans, paused in his meal. "I think you've got
something there, kid," he said. "Two Cups of Coffee! That would
hit me! Good stuff!"

"You really think so, mister!"

"I certainly do."

"Thanks! I wish my girl could hear you say that! We get awful
discouraged sometimes. And my coffee won't be like this. I'll make
it in glass percolators so that it's fresh for every customer! This old
way it cooks all day. I started this lot at six o'clock. I've tried to

get the boss here to change—it would be extra work for me—but he won't put out the money for the glassware!

"My girl and I have got a lot more ideas—salads—a frankfurter with just a touch of garlic and a little sugar in the rolls so that they're like coffee cake—and everything kept spotless clean! Mister—" and the boy leaned forward on his counter, his eager face cupped in his hands—"I'm off at four o'clock. I'm going to go over to Coaltown! It's only half an hour by bus from here. Wouldn't you advise me to try to see this millionaire before he goes away?" There was a boundless hope in his flashing eyes.

Mr. Dunnigan swallowed hard. "There's no harm in trying, my friend—try anything," he said.

But there would be harm. His own anxious problems had returned. Another trusting soul would be let down! *Some* millionaire he was right then, as he sat on that quick-lunch stool!

He pushed back his empty plate. Like Jack Sprat's famed dish, it was licked clean. And the coffee cup was entirely empty, also. To the final drop. The boy clipped a check from the metal-held pad at his belt. Clipped it opposite number forty-five. He moved to the small cash register near the door.

"I'd like a cigar," said Dunnigan rising. "Your best ten cent cigar. It would be a crime not to smoke after a meal as good as that!"

"Thank you, mister." The lad was smiling from ear to ear. "It's been a pleasure to serve and talk to a real gentleman. Take a Phillie, sir. Everybody says they're the best for that price. We haven't ones any more expensive, anyway!" he added, and held out the open box.

Dunnigan took a cigar, removed the cellophane, bit off the end. The boy had lit a match and was holding it ready.

Dunnigan took out his money. "Fifty-five cents," he said, and counted it out. There was a quarter left and a couple of pennies. He placed the quarter on the counter.

"I can't take a tip from you, sir, and that's too much, anyway!" The Quick Lunch dreamer pushed back the silver coin. "If—" he hesitated, then continued "—if you're short tomorrow, mister, and will come in about this time, when I'm alone here, I can let the check ride for a day or so."

"I'll be O. K. tomorrow," said Dunnigan, "and that quarter isn't a tip. One gentleman doesn't give a tip to another. You probably can't get much of a flower for twenty-five cents, kid, but that's to buy the girl friend a flower—a carnation—a small rose."

"Gosh! That will please her! Who shall I say it's from?"

"The name don't matter. Say it's *to* the girl who's landed the best Quick-Lunch cook in America! Good luck, boy!"

"Good luck to you, mister! And come again if you stay in Nanticoke."

Bill Dunnigan was in the street once more. He did feel a little better. A good breakfast certainly bucked you up! And a good cigar. The Phillie tasted almost as fine as a Regina Perfecto! The smile of that redheaded lad as he held the match had penetrated the tobacco, just as his smile had added to the flavor of the ham and eggs!

And his own press agent trade wasn't such a useless, phony profession after all. Perhaps it did count for something to spread courage and hope! If it was not spread in vain!

He stopped and listened. The Coaltown bells were still sounding. How much longer would they ring?

——————————————————— *38* ———

*D*UNNIGAN HEADED AGAIN for the telegraph office. He looked at his watch, a watch soon to repose (he feared) in the Nanticoke pawnshop. It was eleven-ten, and by eleven-twelve he was peering through the small, high window into the telegraph operator's room. It flashed through his mind how strange that this small room in an obscure town he had never even heard of a week before should be the most important place in all America that morning! In all the world!

"Something coming through now for you, Mr. Dunnigan," said the man within, looking up from his clicking instrument.

At last the decisive moment! Dunnigan said as calmly as he could: "Can I step inside? I mean, I'm very anxious. I'd like to read it as it comes over!"

"Sure!" said the operator, remembering the tip of the night before. And he pushed a button beneath his desk. "It's against the rules but come on in if you wish. I guess this has something to do with the Coaltown bells."

"It has!" said Mr. Dunnigan fervently.

The operator removed the cover from his typewriter, ran in a blank and a carbon, and started tapping the keys as his other instrument clicked out the Morse code of the telegram.

No commanding general ever watched a message from the front lines with more anxiety, no stock-market gambler was ever more glued to his ticker tape than Bill Dunnigan as he devoured the letters spelling out, on that yellow blank, the words of Marcus Harris.

There was a moment of terrible, crushing anxiety. At the end of the first line—"WHAT DO YOU MEAN TEN GRAND EXCLAMATION POINT" —the instrument stopped dead. Some interruption at the sending end. Bill Dunnigan died a hundred deaths. But the black key started speaking once more, and this time went through to the end.

The clerk had broken a rule in permitting Dunnigan inside his office, but he now carefully kept another rule. He ran the typed form from his machine, removed the carbon copy, carefully folded the message and enclosed and sealed it in an envelope. He very deliberately filled out another slip and passed it to Dunnigan, now champing at the bit in real earnest.

"Sign here," he said. Dunnigan felt that should this operator ever receive a message directed to himself, he would go through a similar ritual!

Bill Dunnigan signed the slip with a trembling hand. He received and tore open his envelope and read again the Harris message. It was really there on the typewritten form, word by word, backed by all the integrity of Western Union! He had won! And he was getting twenty thousand bucks from his picture producing boss! A piker indeed! Good old Marcus Harris!

"I can't give you another tip now, brother," he cried, "but just wait here! I'll be back! I may need you for identification at this Miners Bank. I'm going there now pronto!"

As he rushed from the telegraph office another thought came to him. There had been some able assistance in this matter, the kind of assistance we ask for and then forget to be grateful about.

"Good old Saint Michael!" he said aloud. "You got yourself a press agent for life!"

It was ten minutes later in the sedate sanctuary of the president of the Miners National that the Marcus Harris transfer came through. The identification was not difficult—his press agent's union card, his card of membership to The Lambs were almost sufficient. He had in his pocket his last bill at the Beverly Wilshire. The clinching proof, however, was the several receipts from undertaker James Orloff.

"Good old Jimmy Orloff!" Dunnigan even found himself repeating.

Bill Dunnigan took five thousand of his credit in "folding money" —not that he folded it, for the greater part was placed in a long, heavy envelope. Four five-hundred-dollar bills, twenty "centuries," the remaining thousand in fifties and smaller denominations.

"I'd like nine ones and a dollar in change," he said with a broad smile. "I'm all out of silver." The bank president little knew how entirely "out" was his new and apparently wealthy client!

The remaining fifteen thousand dollars Dunnigan left on deposit, and received therefor a bankbook and a pocket checkbook.

"Now please direct me to the nearest garage. I must have a car quick!" he asked the president who had personally supervised these transactions. Even the great Miners National was impressed by a client to whom twenty thousand dollars was transferred from one of the most important of New York City banks.

"There's a garage right off the Square. One of our clerks will go with you," said this official. "Opening a business in Coaltown, Mr. Dunnigan? That seems to be the center of activity today!" And then, before Mr. Dunnigan could answer, the name out of the front page story in his breakfast-table newspaper struck home.

"Of course! You're the Mr. Dunnigan the paper speaks of in connection with this funeral! A theater man, I take it."

The bank president had nearly said, "The *wealthy* Mr. Dunnigan." How fortunate this revered word had *not* slipped out! In his banking circles one only knelt to vast riches—never crudely enunciated sacred words to the holder thereof. Mr. Dunnigan sensed this sudden attitude of adoration although the president remained seated in his chair. And he wondered if this same gentleman would have staked him to a cup of coffee half an hour before!

"I have sure opened a business in Coaltown!" he smiled. "But it won't be operating if I don't get back by twelve noon!" He had again looked at his watch. Eleven-thirty already!

"I'd like to talk with you when you have more leisure," said the president. "There is room in Nanticoke for a first-class motion-picture theater, and some of us were thinking———"

"I'll be seeing you again and thanks for your kindness," said Bill, "but I'm already planning to back a Quick Lunch here in Nanticoke!"

"A Quick Lunch!" said the president in complete mystification.

"Yes," said Mr. Dunnigan, "Great future in that business! Two cups of coffee, you know!" and he rushed from Nanticoke's Temple of Money leaving behind some doubt as to his complete sanity. However, thought the bank president, these millionaires were often eccentric! He had known a wealthy mine owner who played and collected banjos!

The clerk assigned to pilot Mr. Dunnigan to the garage reported another erratic action. The new twenty-thousand-dollar depositor stopped briefly opposite the Nanticoke Loan Company and doffed his hat elaborately to that lowly and unlovely institution.

At the garage their best Packard car was selected and engaged in record time. Engaged with a driver for a week; paid for in advance with no argument as to the price!

"On to Coaltown!" commanded its new master, but there was a stop for a few moments at the telegraph office to dispatch another wire to Marcus Harris. Dunnigan had written it out on the back of a check while waiting for the Packard to be fueled.

"Thanks Marcus boss" (it read) "Money joyfully in hand stop I apologize stop That guy Maecenas was a tinhorn piker compared to you exclamation point Love and plenty kisses Bill."

He pushed the message with a ten-dollar note through the small high window. "Get it off quick—keep the change—keep mum!" he cried. "I'll probably be doing more business with you. No information to any newspaper reporters—understand?"

"You can count on me, Mr. Dunnigan!" replied the operator. He also had acquired a lift of spirit. He was intending to give up a correspondence course in radio and electronics. He decided then and there to keep on with it. The world was a grand place to be in after all! That nine dollar tip would pay for a month of those lessons. The flame of courage that Bill Dunnigan had started, Father Paul had started, Olga Treskovna had started, was spreading into unknown lives.

The Packard raced through the stark loveliness of the Wyoming Valley hills. They were no longer lonely and foreboding to William Dunnigan. They were no longer "damned hills." They were beautiful, magnificent, superb, heartwarming! All the adjectives he had ever used in his press stories! Father Paul was right. One must believe in God just to look at them! Even without a sunset flaming behind them. The sun was now overhead and every green mountain shone like a deep, rich emerald.

Halfway back, when they were at the very summit of a long, steep climb in the roadway and could look out over the valley for miles, he felt a slender hand touching his, a hand that then clasped his and held it tightly. He turned and there she seemed to be—her face radiant, her lips parted in that seductive curve he remembered so vividly from their Christmas Eve together.

"I'm depending on you, Bill," she seemed to say. "I guess I've always depended on you!"

"And I'm depending on you, my darling," said Bill Dunnigan. "Don't ever leave me for long! Come to me whenever you can!"

"I told you I'd be with you always. It's you and me, Bill, for ever and ever!"

She was gone as quickly as she came. The Packard was plunging down the last hill into Coaltown.

As they whirled past the Breaker, grumbling and roaring and fuming under the lashing of the bells, Bill waved a gay salute.

"Hi-ya! Old Bozo!" he cried, "Pull up your socks and pull in your stomach for you're going to get a punch right in the solar plexus! A twenty-thousand-dollar punch that you won't forget!"

He pointed out the brick parish house of St. Leo and the car pulled up in front of it. It seemed to Dunnigan he was not stepping down from a motorcar. He was leaping off a great black battle charger—like Richard the Lion Hearted or was it General Sheridan or Paul Revere! He wasn't quite sure—his history was a bit confused—anyway, he had galloped madly over the hills and the fight was saved—for it still lacked two minutes of being noon by the Follies watch.

It was high time he arrived. The enemy, in the robust form of

Father Spinsky, was just emerging from the St. Leo parish house doorway.

Father Spinsky had also noted the time. With tight lips he was on his way to stop the ringing of the bells, since the promised business arrangement had not been fulfilled.

-- *39* ------

*F*ATHER SPINSKY of St. Leo's was not an evil man. Judged by worldly standards he was in many ways an admirable personality, since he had for fifteen years conducted the business of his parish with the strictest integrity and a considerable success. He owed no one; he paid all bills promptly (always taking advantage of a discount therefor); he had accumulated a sizable reserve. He had accomplished this by not hesitating to speak from his pulpit of financial needs, by telling his congregation that if they did not meet these needs they were in danger of the displeasure of the Almighty. He also stressed the spiritual value of liberal contributions to collections and the box at the door. Nor did he overlook the suggestion that when death came, the good Christian would not lessen his claim to salvation by leaving savings to mother church.

This avarice, this "greed," as Bill Dunnigan had thought it, was not for himself. It was for his church.

But by "church" Father Spinsky did not mean that great spiritual structure of charity, solace, forgiveness, inspiration, that is the Church in the heart of the Ages. He meant the actual edifice of St. Leo's over which he presided—a tall, plain brick building of no particular architectural design, wide enough to boast of two great doorways across its façade, tall enough to have stained-glass windows of three-story height along its sides. So his religion had hardened into a shell of brick and mortar—into a marble altar as large and fine as any in the near-by large cities, into an organ the most expensive for miles around, into the great metal bell that was the loudest and deepest in that vicinity and which hung in a square brick tower rising at one side of his basilica.

The near-by ramshackle wooden structure of St. Michael's was a source of constant irritation. He felt that it should be torn down, removed, as one removed a dead limb from a tree. He had hoped it would be closed when its elderly, easy-going priest who had been there for years passed on to his reward.

But then came young Father Paul with absurd ideas of resuscitation—ideas about "helping the town." Worse, he attempted to enact these ideas without consulting Father Spinsky, who, although he had no authority over other Coaltown churches, felt that as the pastor of the largest and richest church he should be conferred with. And now this unworthy and superfluous and inadequate Church of St. Michael was the center of an intense and profitable interest not only from the town but from all the surrounding countryside!

When Father Paul had brought Dunnigan to him, Father Spinsky had thought of the four-day bell ringing as the whim of some obscure person. Let them have their whim if they had the money to pay for it! It would bring in some extra revenue which St. Leo's could well use. But he quickly discovered that this dead girl, far from being "obscure," was, in fact, identified with a great industry whose personages lent themselves flamboyantly to an appeal to the popular imagination. And the bell-ringing fee was going to be only a part of the financial returns. Perhaps only a minor part.

His own St. Leo's should be the center of any such publicity and acclaim. And revenue. Certainly it was a most distressing twist of fortune that all this should go to the down-and-out St. Michael's! And before it was over, Father Paul would make a bungling mess of the whole affair!

At any rate, in another five minutes St. Michael's would be the only Coaltown bell to continue its ringing. The payment deadline had been reached. And an unsecured arrears of one hundred dollars had to be collected!

There was a screeching of brakes at his curb. Leaping at him was the tall fellow who had on foot arranged for the bells, the fellow he had watched climb aboard a Nanticoke bus after their interview that morning, who had agreed to make further payments at this hour, but whom Father Spinsky had half expected never to see again.

Is there such a thing as transference of a mental attitude, or did Dunnigan unconsciously carry out his own imaginings in descending from the Packard? For it seemed to Father Spinsky also, for one brief second as he looked, that the tall man was getting off a horse! But he had distinctly heard the noise of brakes and it was surely a large, strange motorcar at his curb.

"I'm just under the wire, I know!" exclaimed Dunnigan as he strode toward the staring St. Leo pastor, "but I had to breeze from Nanticoke, and my driver says they enforce a forty-mile-an-hour speed law in Pennsylvania! If we can go inside, Father, I think we can settle all bets."

Father Spinsky withdrew his eyes from the curb and looked at his watch. It was one minute to twelve noon. He was a just man if not a lovable one. He led the way back into the parish house office.

"You say you arrived in a motorcar?" he asked doubtfully as they moved back up the walk.

"Sure did! Thought you saw me! Hired it in Nanticoke where I had some banking business," replied Dunnigan. And he wondered just what Father Spinsky meant by such a question. Perhaps he *had* made a rather agile leap to the curb, and if by any chance the priest were near-sighted——

"Great gallop it was over your high hills!" he added with a gesture of tugging at the reins. It amused Dunnigan hugely in his present elated mood to act just a little before this meticulous cleric. He noted that Father Spinsky took another quick glance toward the street curb.

Inside his office the priest felt on solid ground. Here there would be no optical illusions, for it was a solid room with a huge solid desk, a long solid table and solid chairs. Behind the desk were two tall, oak letter files; and a large safe with "Parish of St. Leo" painted on its front stood solidly by the files.

Dunnigan had been there the day before but had taken little notice of his surroundings. Now he observed for the first time a daily calendar with large numerals on the wall above this safe. It advertised the Miners National Bank. He and Father Spinsky were brother depositors!

"Be seated, sir," said Father Spinsky, as he lowered himself into his desk chair. Again he looked at his watch. The gesture indicated without further words what Mr. Dunnigan was expected to produce.

But in looking downward, Father Spinsky noticed for the first time Bill Dunnigan's spats. Their virgin white was now a dull grey—a steel grey. And they somehow reminded the priest of the greaves on medieval armor. He had made a journey to New York two weeks before and spent an afternoon at the Metropolitan Museum. The armor gallery had fascinated him. The garb of fighting men. Strength. That was Father Spinsky's religion.

Dunnigan, "heeled" (as he would have called it) with the twenty thousand bucks from Marcus Harris, at that moment radiated strength from toe to head. Having duly seated himself, and in so doing drawing up his trouser legs so that his spats were well exposed, the press agent was speaking.

"I came as quickly as I could, for I knew how worried you would be about your obligations to your colleagues." He took from his pocket the long, thick, manila envelope and snapped off the rubber band around it.

Father Spinsky transferred his gaze from the spats and watched with equal fascination the opening of the envelope. Free of the contracting influence of the rubber band, it sprang wide apart and seemed to contain enough large bills in good U. S. currency to cover the semi-weekly pay roll of the mines! A number of five-hundred-dollar certificates were plainly visible. It looked to Father Spinsky as if the whole envelope were stuffed with such bills.

Dunnigan, however, managed to find one of a smaller denomination—a humble hundred-dollar note. He placed it on Father Spinsky's desk. Money did not seem out of place on *that* desk.

"The hundred dollars for which you so graciously gave credit without security I now pay you," he said. "Since it is twelve noon —maybe a minute or two after that—we start again from scratch.

"You told me that from noon today the price went up to twenty-five bucks an hour. That seems a little steep, but it's O. K. I am instructed to be generous. And I realize you'll have to hire extra bell ringers, and all that, to go on for three more days. I want a first-class job and nobody down with bell ringers' cramp!

"It's now Tuesday noon. We'll have the funeral on Friday. Say we ring the bells till six o'clock Friday evening. Tuesday noon till Friday noon is seventy-two hours. From noon that day till six is six hours more. Total, seventy-eight hours. At twenty-five bucks an hour that makes one thousand nine hundred and fifty iron men. I'll pay each church direct, if you don't mind. Keeps my accounts straight that way. Do you want yours in cash, Father, or will a check on the Miners National of Nanticoke, which I see you also patronize, meet your requirements?"

He now dramatically drew from his pocket the new checkbook and flipped it open.

Dunnigan's rapid mathematical calculations of the hours and the payment therefor had taken both his breath and that of Father Spinsky. Bill hoped he hadn't made a mistake in his figuring! Father Spinsky, viewing resources so adequate and so lavishly to be dispersed, felt more keenly than ever the terrible mistake of this funeral's taking place anywhere but from his own St. Leo's.

He sucked a deep breath through tight lips and forced a smile. He would make one more desperate try.

"If you will look at my Church of St. Leo," he said, leaning forward, "I think you will realize how much better suited it will be to your purpose."

"I will gladly look at your Church of St. Leo when I have the time," said Bill gaily, "but not for the housing of this funeral. That attraction is booked solid with Saint Michael the Scrapper. That lad in the sword and armor has a run-of-the-play contract with me. I only just met him at Father Paul's, but we became pals right off, if I may say so without offence, Reverend. We saw eye to eye pronto! Saint Michael has sort of had a raw deal around here, but he's going to get a break from now on or I'll eat my hat! And his iron one! Which shall it be, Father, cash or check, for I must gallop along. The other three churches—I don't want them to worry or stop ringing their bells!"

Father Spinsky sighed deeply and uneasily. He had somehow known it would be of no avail. And his eyes had again been drawn to the steel-grey spats of his visitor. Why should they remind him of the armor room of the Metropolitan Museum of Art, and also of something else—he couldn't quite determine what it was?

"Your check on Nanticoke will, of course, be satisfactory," he said at last. "I have already sent your savings bankbook for collection, so I cannot give it back to you."

"That's O. K. also," said Bill. "O. K. and double O. K.!" he added with a laugh.

"I never doubted the authenticity of that book," said Father Spinsky quickly.

"I didn't mean that you did!" smiled Bill Dunnigan, "And what I do mean we'll skip. Little personal matter. I only hope your big church doesn't burn down or something! From what you say it would make quite a blaze! And I need your bell in my choir. Some basso profundo, that bell!" And he cocked his head and listened for a moment. "Reminds me of my old friend De Wolf Hopper. Well, here's your check—" Bill's fountain pen had been busy "—it will also serve as a receipt. I've written across it 'payment in full for bell of St. Leo to ring bass till six P.M. Friday.' So don't you dare change its voice!"

Dunnigan arose. "I won't ask for a refund, however, if anything happens to you. It won't be *your* fault. Now good day, Father, and no bad luck to you!"

Bill Dunnigan took up his checkbook, his envelope of currency, and his black derby. The first two (having re-snapped the rubber around the currency) he jammed into his inside breast coat pocket; and the hat he placed on his head at its most jaunty angle as he made an almost running exit.

Father Spinsky, Dunnigan's check still in his hand, moved to his front window and watched this athletic apparition leap down his walk and into the waiting Packard, which immediately lunged forward.

Again the priest had the sensation that he was watching a figure dash away on horseback!

~~~~~~~~~~~~~~~~~~~~~~~~~~~~~~~~~~~~~ *40* ~~~~~~~

THE PASTOR of St. Leo's knew now the other thing that those greave-like spats had reminded him of. The only Saint habitually pictured in full armor. Saint Michael the Archangel!

In his years of opposition to St. Michael's Church in Coaltown, he had thought of it only as a shabby, superfluous building, handled by inefficacious clerics. Its name, as such, did not enter into his antagonism. It might have been St. Anyone or St. Anything.

Churches had to have *some* name. St. Michael's external decrepitude and debts (which everyone knew about) and internal uselessness (as Father Spinsky believed) would have been equally obnoxious to him under *any* name!

But now an entirely new and alarming idea came into his consciousness. It had commenced to form while Dunnigan was speaking. Suppose it was *not* that shabby building he had been fighting, but the particular Saint for which the church was named? Saint Michael himself! The Captain of the Army of God! Suppose—at last aroused—Saint Michael himself were taking a hand! Suppose——

Father Spinsky wiped his brow. The idea was ridiculous, but he could not drive those silly, greave-like spats from his mind. He stepped into his well-stocked library and took down the September volume of his *Lives of the Saints*. He remembered September was Saint Michael's month. It was almost September!

The First Warrior of Heaven had made numerous appearances on this earth. He it was who had spoken to Moses on Mt. Sinai—delivered to him the Tables of The Law. He it was who had twice rescued the Apostle Peter from prison, smiting the chains from his hands and feet.

Moreover, it would seem he was especially zealous in matters concerning his churches. In Italy he had come to the Bishop of Siponto and ordered a church built in a certain cavern. In France he had come to Saint Authbert, Bishop of Avranches, and the result had been the erection of that soaring pile that is one of the monuments of the ages, Mont St. Michel. At Colosse in the suburbs of Constantinople——

Father Spinsky snapped to his volume. This was America and the Twentieth Century. He held in his hand a check signed "William Dunnigan." William Dunnigan was a slangy, rapid-talking individual in a flashy plaid suit whose "pay-to-the-order-of" might not even be worth the paper it was printed on. A convincing, likable chap, but then most confidence men were convincing and likable! Father Spinsky moved to his telephone, asked for the Nanticoke number that was the Miners National and was quickly talking with his friend, its president.

"I have a check for one thousand nine hundred and fifty dollars signed by a William Dunnigan. Is it good?" he asked, having made himself known.

"If the signature is Mr. Dunnigan's, it's as good as cash in hand," replied the president.

"He made it out in my presence. A tall man in a light plaid suit and a black derby. Talks rapidly and wears greaves—I mean spats—" said Father Spinsky.

"That is undoubtedly the gentleman," said the president.

"What do you know about him?" asked Father Spinsky.

"All we need to know. Connected with powerful interests. Wealthy. He has received a large cash credit here from the Manufacturers Trust in New York. Identified with motion pictures, according to the newspapers."

"This morning I also mailed for collection a savings bankbook on Brooklyn, New York, which this man yesterday assigned to me as security. The amount was five hundred dollars which I would not care to lose as I am responsible to—"

"Five hundred dollars!" broke in the Nanticoke bank president. Sometimes even he became a little impatient with his friend Father Spinsky's pettiness and suspicion and preciseness in matters financial. Since he was talking to a member of the clergy and a customer of many years' standing, he divulged more than he would have ordinarily.

"Listen, Father Spinsky, this gentleman has a credit of fifteen thousand dollars with us, and that after withdrawing five thousand dollars in cash. And we have just received another wire from his New York bank that we are to extend to him any additional credits he may desire. What are you doing holding up such a man for a five-hundred-dollar-savings-bank account! He should be treated with consideration. He could help this whole district. We could use outside capital. If Coaltown isn't interested, we in Nanticoke certainly are!"

"Thank you. Good-by," said Father Spinsky and hung up. What indeed had he been doing? Like undertaker Orloff's, his usually cast-iron stomach felt a dull pain. The vision of the shin greaves returned—and scraps of the conversation. "Great gallop it was over your high hills!" "Saint Michael the Scrapper!" "He's had a raw deal around here, but he's going to get a break!"

Could it be—could it possibly be——

And what was the meaning of the statement, "I only hope your big church doesn't burn down!" "I won't ask a refund if anything happens to you!"

Father Spinsky looked anxiously at his church through the side windows of his office. It was still there, of course. It was not in flames. It had not crumbled. Anyway, it was fully insured. He'd paid the policies only last week. Insurance policies, however, could not restore in a day fifteen years of labor and devotion.

He sat himself at his desk. For the first time he could remember he was not entirely satisfied with that self. For the first time a shadowy fear gnawed at his mind. For the first time his heart was troubled. His supreme confidence in his every action was badly shaken.

There had been a small matter that very morning that now assumed gigantic proportions, just as his attitude regarding the small matter of the savings bankbook was becoming a tragedy. Father Paul at St. Michael's was out of shrine candles. Father Paul had hesitatingly asked the loan of some, even offered to pay for them, and had been curtly refused. Come to think of it, the request had been phrased, "Could you—would you lend Saint Michael a few candles to tide me over?" *Lend Saint Michael.* It had given Father Spinsky an unholy joy to say, "No. I have no candles to spare."

He had them to spare and in plenty in his well-stocked storeroom. A shipment had arrived only the week before. And no matter what money Father Paul might have now, it would be several days before candles could be obtained from the supply houses in Philadelphia or New York. Unless—unless the presence of Saint Michael himself could miraculously turn dollars into shrine candles on the spot!

He, Father Spinsky, had been given his chance to supply this need. Perhaps it was an opportunity of atonement for many past slights—he remembered how, without saying a word but by a gesture, he had indicated to the salesman of one of these supply houses the uselessness of extending further credit to Father Paul. He remembered another time——

These were no longer pleasurable memories. They were a little terrifying! Father Spinsky called out to his assistant whom he had heard come in.

"There are ten gross of shrine candles that arrived last week in our storeroom. Father Paul up at St. Michael's has run out of them. Put as many of the boxes in my car as you can and rush them there at once. Tell Father Paul to let me know if he runs short again."

The assistant wondered if he had heard rightly! For that very morning, on Father Spinsky's return from the Dunnigan interview at the Wyoming Hotel, he had listened to a tirade against St. Michael's Church and Father Paul's absurd request for a loan of shrine candles!

"Do I understand——?" he commenced.

"You understand exactly what I said!" thundered Father Spinsky with a gesture of great impatience. "Be quick about it! There's no time to lose! Say they are a present from Saint Leo to Saint Michael the Scrapper."

"Saint Michael the What!"

"No matter. Rush the candles there!"

The dazed assistant hurried off on his surprising errand.

Father Spinsky again wiped his forehead and drew the handkerchief around inside his Roman collar. It was a shock to be jolted out of the complacency of a lifetime. He arose and paced the floor several times, then took off his coat and donned a cassock which hung in the closet at one end of the room. He stepped out of his doorway and entered his Church of St. Leo.

There, at any rate, his soul would have peace. There he could collect his thoughts. All within its sacred doors was right and strong and holy. He had made no mistakes about his church. God, himself, was there.

But inside, and standing by the marble holy-water font near the entrance, he had the most disturbing shock of a disturbing noon hour. God was not there! At least, so it seemed to the perturbed mind of Father Spinsky. Or if there (for the small red light was still burning before the tabernacle containing the Eucharist), God had turned his back on all that this church contained.

Father Spinsky's massive, white-marble altar rose imposingly at the far end. But no golden-hallowed Presence was beside it. Instead, the priest could see the obsequious, frock-coated salesman of the Philadelphia supply house and hear that man's aggressive voice:

"I tell you, Father Spinsky, you will have the most expensive altar in that part of Pennsylvania. We have just erected one in St. Mary's at Reading that is not nearly as magnificent. And our price includes all transportation charges and erection in Coaltown. You'll have something to brag about!"

And how many sermons of fear had he preached to obtain the money to buy it!

The great organ, now silent, was in the choir loft above him— some of its tall, gilded pipes were visible where their rows extended along the side walls. But no trumpeting Angels were near them. Instead, he saw the calculating face of the Cleveland mineowner, whom he had persuaded to meet that organ's cost, and heard his question:

"You are sure that if I do this, it will tend to prevent strikes— will make these ungrateful miners feel that their wages are adequate —that their employer is interested in their good?"

The great cone of a gold baptismal font at his left—sheer death-bed fear had persuaded the grocer whose money paid for it to change his will at the last minute in Father Spinsky's presence. He could see the man's terror-drawn face now, and could hear himself promising reward for this "generosity."

Each costly shrine, each stain-glassed window had some similar memory. Fear, self-interest, hope of reward. Nothing given in a fervor of love.

St. Leo's suddenly became a museum of expensive objects gathered by a selfish, unscrupulous collector—not a sanctuary of hope and prayer and consolation.

There was sincere pain in Father Spinsky's eyes. He had not meant to do any wrong. He had not, in every case, been entirely wrong. Fear and self-interest were the only emotions that would move certain people. But he had come to treat everyone that way, to distrust all men, to forget that great things could also be accomplished by love, by friendship, by understanding. He had pretty thoroughly eliminated all the basic teachings of Christ Jesus!

There was a small shrine by the door. It was a tarnished statue of Saint Joseph, repaired where an arm had been broken. He was intending to throw it out and replace it with a new and larger statue. At least this shrine had no disturbing memories—it was there when he had taken over the church. It probably had been brought from Poland. Father Spinsky moved to this shrine.

One candle was burning before it. He took a wax taper and lit three other candles. And he deposited the three dimes that was (in St. Leo's) the candle charge. One candle he lit to Saint Michael the Archangel, one to the dead girl, Olga Trocki, and one to her father for whom his bell was also tolling—the late Stanislaus Trocki. He knelt before this shrine.

He asked a simple forgiveness of Saint Michael. For the girl Olga Trocki, whom he did not remember except that he had once seen her assisting her staggering father to their home, he said the usual prayer for the dead. Stanislaus Trocki he remembered well. Who in Coaltown did not?

Other men of the town sometimes became intoxicated. Women also. And exhibited themselves in public in this condition. But none so consistently, so openly as the late Stan Trocki. Father Spinsky had no sympathy for such human frailty. And his casual annoyance as a citizen on seeing this gentleman negotiating his homeward journeys from the round of saloons on payday, became a very personal and indignant anger when one morning he had stumbled over Mr. Trocki asleep in a drunken stupor on the very steps of St. Leo's Church!

Father Spinsky had telephoned the sheriff, and presently citizen Trocki (still unconscious) was loaded into that official's car and taken to the jail in Wanamee. Coaltown had no jail. Not wanting to appear in the disgusting matter, Father Spinsky ensured that his name was not brought up, and the girl never knew who had caused her father's only arrest and the twenty-five-dollar fine that it took her Breaker earnings of a month to pay.

Father Spinsky had himself forgotten it till now. It flashed into his mind just as he was about to ask Saint Joseph to intercede for the sins of Stanislaus Trocki whose soul was without doubt being grilled in Purgatory.

Father Spinsky did not proceed with this petition. A windfall of over two thousand dollars had just come to St. Leo's partly because of this man. And he, Father Spinsky, had once refused him mere assistance—shelter—the simplest of Christian ministration. He could have carried the poor fellow inside his parish house. He could have sent for the girl. What would the Master, Christ, have done in a similar instance?

And there was another stabbing thought. *"In as much as you have done it unto the least of these, you have done it unto me."*

Father Spinsky arose and went slowly and wearily to his own great altar. High above it, above the top of the marble spires of the altar, was a life-sized figure of the Christ nailed to a cross. It, too, was an inheritance of the church as he found it. It had not been bought through fear.

The priest grasped hard the rail of his altar, so hard that the knuckles showed white through the heavy skin. He stood outside the sanctuary. He looked up at the suffering figure of the Christ. His own face was drawn. He repeated no Latin monolog—no one of the set phrases that he knew so well. He said very simply:

"Oh God—forgive me. Forgive me!"

He closed his eyes and stood there silently for awhile. He could not even pray. The cruel enormity of countless little things that he had done all his life paraded before his mind. How could he expect the compassionate Son of God to stand beside him? Was he destined to go on preaching sermons, repeating holy words in a place from which God had seemed to withdraw his approbation. Could he go on doing this?

He opened his eyes at last. He turned, still gripping hard the altar rail, to look again at the building his pride and sin had desecrated. He was afraid to look up at the Christ above his altar—afraid he would only meet with the same coldness that had reigned in his own heart. His eyes were drawn toward the humble altar by the door.

The three candles that he had lit before Saint Joseph were burning brightly, making a warm glow about the whole shrine. They were sending out a tiny glow that grew to an aureola and seemed to be embracing the whole edifice, seeking to re-sanctify that edifice, to change it from a museum back to a Church of God once more.

Father Spinsky took long, deep breaths as if to saturate his whole being with the light from his three candles. He did not feel that he was forgiven. But he felt that his church was again a holy place, and that he could start again from that humble altar, and by deeds, not words, merit the grace that should belong to the vicar of a church.

These plans for the town that Father Paul had tried to carry out. Some of them were good plans. Maybe they *could* be carried out. He would talk with Father Paul, put himself at Father Paul's service. If both parishes worked together, his and St. Michael's, a great deal could be accomplished.

And was there anything more that he could do immediately for St. Michael's? Besides candles he remembered that he also had some extra candle racks. Father Paul could use these if his church was to be crowded the next few days. He could even lend some racks from the front of his own shrines. He would do that before Father Paul's next Mass. He would announce Father Paul's early Mass from his own pulpit that evening, when he held a regular service. And he must locate still more candles. If means were provided, St. Michael's could, by this funeral, get well on its financial feet.

Father Spinsky squared his shoulders, but his head was bowed. Nevertheless, he walked from St. Leo's with the quick step of a younger man.

In the parish house his sister had his dinner ready and waiting. Father Spinsky ate his principal meal at midday.

"Well, did the man at the hotel come through?" Mary Spinsky asked bluntly as they sat at the well-laden table.

The words "come through" grated harshly on Father Spinsky. He was about to utter a severe reproof when he remembered that she was only quoting his own terminology. He had turned not only his church but his very household into a place of distrust and greed. Looking at his sister, he realized it would be easier to re-sanctify the church!

"The gentleman met his account promptly," he answered. "He is evidently a man of his word."

"And the funeral remains at St. Michael's?" persisted Mary Spinsky.

"It remains there—as it should," said Father Spinsky with some emphasis.

Mary Spinsky looked at her brother, but his set face gazed down upon his plate. He added nothing to this surprising qualification of his statement.

"Well, at least you can now throw out that old St. Joseph shrine and buy the new one you were speaking of."

"The St. Joseph shrine will remain exactly as it is," said Father Spinsky in the same firm tone. "There will be other use for this money."

"What other use?" asked Mary Spinsky.

"I do not yet know. I must have a talk with Father Paul."

"With Father Paul!" There was amazement in the sister's voice.

Father Spinsky did not answer. He felt it would be useless to answer at this time. And he was thinking new thoughts of Father Paul as he ate his plenteous, well-cooked dinner.

What about Father Paul's dinners all these months? The man lived alone. There had been no funds at St. Michael's for a housekeeper or a cook. Did he have proper food? Had he always had the money to buy proper food? Had there been days when he, Father Spinsky, was stuffing himself at this table and a fellow cleric a few streets along had sat down to bread and coffee! Perhaps only bread!

Father Spinsky suddenly ceased to take his usual satisfaction in his dinner.

He spoke abruptly. "Mary, do you know someone who could be gotten to keep house for Father Paul—come in and cook for him?"

Mary Spinsky did not understand this solicitude, but she would not fail as an information bureau.

"There is a woman in his parish whose husband died last month. She is a good cook. I think she would like to earn some money."

"I will get her name from you tomorrow," said Father Spinsky. "First, I will have to speak to Father Paul. I think he should have someone to look out for him."

This was not at all understandable, but something less understandable was still to come.

Mary Spinsky brought in a large chocolate cake which she had spent the entire morning making. It was her brother's favorite dessert. She was about to cut him a generous portion—one for herself, also—but Father Spinsky raised his hand.

"Wait, Mary," he said. "I want you to do something for me. I want you to do it yourself. The cake looks wonderful. And I know how good it will taste. Cut it in half. Take half to Father Paul at St. Michael's. Take the other half to the Wyoming Hotel and leave it for William Dunnigan. The food there must be pretty terrible. Say it is from Saint Leo—no, say it is from yourself, Father Spinsky's sister——"

"But I can't waste such a cake!" Mary Spinsky was horrified. "I have used a whole cup of butter and half a dozen eggs!"

"I don't think it will be wasted," said Father Spinsky, and directed a fixed gaze at his sister. He was looking at her and yet beyond her.

"Well, if you say so! But I can't take it till tonight. I have a meeting of our Ladies Aid this afternoon."

"Tonight will do."

What astute plan did her brother now have? He offered no further explanation, and the look in his eyes told her not to question further. There was some clever stratagem behind it, she was sure! So she offered no further protest.

But after the meal she heard him telephoning Philadelphia. "I want another shipment of shrine candles, and send them direct to St. Michael's . . . Yes, I know, but he is all right now . . . Very well, I guarantee the bill. Charge them to me if you wish . . . Not till next week? That will be too late . . . Please do the best you can. I will take full responsibility."

Strange words to be heard in the parish house of St. Leo! Mary Spinsky did not understand.

--- *41* ---

*Q*UITE INNOCENT of the turmoil he had left behind him in the mind of Father Spinsky, Bill Dunnigan quickly finished his business at the other three parish houses. As each parish house had become richer by nearly two thousand dollars (less the few hundreds they would spend on relief bell ringers and their regular sextons, the speeding Packard left only content and amazement in its wake. Two pastors did not wish to accept the increased rate, knew nothing of it, but Dunnigan was in no pinchpenny mood. Marcus Harris, in his telegram, disclaimed being classed as a piker. Far be it from his again loyal employee, William Dunnigan, to belie such an admirable attitude!

All pastors received the same amount as Father Spinsky.

He had a bone to pick, however, with his final creditor, Father Paul. Dunnigan had first to rescue the little priest from ten newspapermen, two newsreel photographers, and three radio reporters who had him surrounded just outside his church where he had been watching the ever-growing line of townspeople entering to view the coffin of the "famous actress," Olga Treskovna. The coffin to which undertaker Orloff had said no one would bother to journey for the purpose of paying their respects.

"I don't know what to do about it all!" exclaimed a breathless Father Paul, alone at last inside the parish house with Dunnigan. "A radio company insisted on putting a microphone in my bell tower to carry its sound 'from coast to coast,' as they said! They gave my sexton ten dollars to ring it faster while they were there! They're coming back at six to broadcast it again. My little bell that even Coaltown would not listen to!"

Father Paul was both disturbed and thrilled.

"You say they gave the sexton ten dollars?"

"Why, yes. I'm glad for him. He is a poor man who has been loyal. We were very far in arrears with his salary."

"What did they leave for Saint Michael?" asked Bill Dunnigan aggressively.

"Why—I don't know. I don't think they thought of that."

"They would not! And neither would you! But they'll think of it when they come back at six. I'll be here myself to prod their memories. And it won't be any ten bucks!"

"I tried to find you this morning, Mr. Dunnigan. I sent one of my altar boys to your hotel to see if you approved of all this— this public attention. It isn't turning out to be a private funeral as you wanted!"

"No, it sort of got away from me," admitted Bill Dunnigan with a solemn face, "I had to go to Nanticoke on business. But now I'm back, and everything is under control."

"And it got into the newspapers," continued Father Paul. "I haven't seen them, but they say both Wilkes-Barre and Scranton printed several columns about it. And all these reporters who have come this morning! I don't know what to tell them!"

"Don't worry, Father," said Dunnigan. "I'll handle them. There's one thing, however, that isn't hunky-dory. Do you mean to say you would have let that big lummox—excuse me, Father—that Father Spinsky put it over on you!"

"You mean his suggestion to move the funeral to St. Leo's?"

"I mean just that!"

"But he has a larger and finer church."

Bill Dunnigan exploded. "Look here, Father, don't *you* get to talking like the crazy place in California where I just came from!

Out there everything is bigger and better! Bigger and better, hell! Excuse me, Father. Size has nothing to do with fine things. Smaller and finer is our motto! Haven't you got the swellest church and the swellest Saint in this town?"

"I have tried to think so," said the priest with a glance at the picture of the victorious Saint Michael on his wall. He did not know quite what Mr. Dunnigan meant by "swell" as applied to Saint Michael and his church, but it evidently was a term of highest approbation.

"Then say so!" cried Dunnigan, and rose from his folding chair and paced the floor, with pauses in front of Father Paul at the end of each statement. "Say so to Father Spinsky and everybody else! Say it good and loud! Wasn't it your Saint who took on Kid Lucifer and put him down and out for the full count! Saint Michael was always tops! Remember that! And your church is going to be tops around here! Does the radio want to pipe the sound of anybody else's bell from coast to coast? No! Your bell is in a class with Big Ben in London—the Liberty Bell in Philadelphia! Because it's big? No! Because it's the bell that's started something fine! I wouldn't let you move this funeral to Westminster Abbey, if it were here! I forgot—that's a Protestant hangout! I wouldn't let you move it to St. Peter's of Rome! No, not even to St. Patrick's on Fifth Avenue!"

"I'm happy that you feel that way," said Father Paul. "I confess I really didn't want to do it!"

"This girl would have turned over in her coffin if you had! And I would have carried that coffin back here on my own shoulders if necessary!"

Dunnigan seated himself again. "But this Father Spinsky has done you a service," he continued. "He raised the ante on the bell ringing when I turned him down. Thought I couldn't make good, I guess! He didn't know the undefeated champion, no less and none other than Battling Saint Michael the Scrapper, was on our side!"

Bill Dunnigan looked toward the picture on the wall and shook his locked hands in its direction in proper prize-ring congratulatory fashion.

He noticed that Father Paul made a movement at the phrase "Saint Michael the Scrapper." "I meant no disrespect, Father," he explained. "Quite the contrary! That Saint of yours is the goods! *I know!*" He took the new Nanticoke checkbook from his pocket.

"I'm going to write you a check for one thousand nine hundred and fifty dollars—on a Nanticoke bank so you can get the dough in half an hour if you need it—a check to pay for the ringing of your bell up to and through the funeral service Friday. And you're going to have another thousand from those radio tightwads or I'll eat my shirt!" Bill's shirt that day was a rich lilac and really looked edible.

Father Paul got up and then sat down again. All this was too fantastic to be true! Money could not really be pouring from the skies in such a veritable deluge! Yesterday he could not even meet his candle bills. Today there was the means for paying every bill, for repairing St. Michael's, for doing all the impossible things he dreamed of doing! And yet he was disturbed, for he could not help but recall a part of Mr. Dunnigan's first conversation the evening before.

"Mr. Dunnigan," he said, "I don't understand. You told me this girl did not leave much money. I do not think you are a wealthy man, in spite of all the stories that are going around. You as much as told me you were pressed for money. You spoke of five hundred dollars in a savings bank, and I saw you turn over that bankbook to Father Spinsky. It isn't any of my business, but I must ask you about all this money."

Bill Dunnigan looked straight into the eyes of Father Paul. There was anxiety, fear, in the deep, honest eyes of the St. Michael's pastor.

"That's all right, Father," he said. "You have the right to ask. I ask you just to trust me. As I begged you yesterday to trust me. I haven't robbed a bank!" and he smiled. "It's honest money. This girl has powerful friends. Friends who have a lot of what it takes. They want me to carry out her wishes. Do everything she wanted done. If it comes right down to it, Father, the money really belongs to this girl. And a lot more besides! She would have had it if she had lived. She died suddenly—was working six hours before she died. Does that relieve your mind? Will you still trust me?"

"I will trust you," said Father Paul. His eyes had cleared of their distress. "But I cannot accept any more money from you—from this girl's estate, as you put it. Why, already nearly five hundred dollars has come to St. Michael's from the collection and the shrine boxes at my early Mass! And those boxes are being filled hourly as all these people go from the coffin to the shrines. I can hardly believe it has happened in one morning in my church! It is almost as much as we took in the whole of last year!"

"Father," said Dunnigan, "you want to do things for your church —for Coaltown. It will take more than just wanting and your own good work. It will take money. You're going to have that money now. You're going to earn it yourself."

"I forgot to tell you about the Mass at five forty-five," said Father Paul. "It had always been such a failure! Sometimes nobody came. It was like everything else I tried to do here. But this morning!"

"I know. I've heard all about it," said Dunnigan. "And it's grand! I was happy for your sake. I wish I could have seen it. But all your Masses from now on are going to be like that."

"I don't expect any such miracle," said Father Paul. "But I shall always remember and be grateful for this morning. Something happened, however, just before you came that *is* a miracle."

"What is that?" asked Dunnigan.

"Father Spinsky has just sent over many boxes of shrine candles, after refusing me this morning. You see, I was all out of them. And I probably can't get any for a week, even with the money to pay the bill. I offered to reimburse Father Spinsky this morning— now he sends them and refuses any payment!"

"You mean Father Spinsky would not take money!"

"The assistant who brought them would take nothing. Father Spinsky's orders. Said the Father had talked very strangely. That these candles were an offering from Saint Leo to Saint Michael the Scrapper! That didn't sound like Father Spinsky either. It sounded like you, Mr. Dunnigan."

And Father Paul waited with a quizzical smile.

"I give you my word I didn't pay for them!" said Dunnigan. "And I didn't ask Father Spinsky to send candles. I knew nothing at all about it. I may have mentioned Saint Michael—Saint Michael the Scrapper—that's just my way of thinking of him, Father—but I'm as surprised as you are! Maybe miracles do happen!"

Bill Dunnigan little guessed then what he was now prophesying.

He took out his fountain pen and wrote check number five. He made no notation on this check regarding "Paid in Full." Instead, he thought a moment, then wrote, "On account—to Saint Michael the Scrapper."

"Have you a bank account, Father?" he asked.

"I did have one. I haven't used it for quite a time."

"I have a hunch it's going to get active again," said Bill Dunnigan. "This will give it a running start."

Father Paul looked at the piece of paper handed him. Nearly two thousand dollars! But to him it was not a pile of dollars. It was a pile of hopes at last to be realized, a pile of dreams that would come true. He put the check in his drawer, but he did not lock the drawer. There was no lock on it. There was never a lock on the dreams of Father Paul.

"I do not know how to thank you, Mr. Dunnigan," he said. His voice was a little choked. "I think I'd like to step into my church. You haven't seen the inside of my church. Shall we go there now?"

"I think we will go there now," said Bill Dunnigan. "And by the way, Father, my pals all call me Bill. I don't know, you being a priest——"

"That's all right—Bill," said Father Paul. And he placed both hands for a brief moment and held firmly against the strong arms that were cased in sleeves of a pale red and blue check on grey.

They went out onto the parish house lawn into the sunlight of a perfect afternoon. The bells were ringing steadily. Their sound seemed to be a part of that sunlight, transmuting it into a paean of courage and joy. And its resonant beat no longer brought moments of terror to the hearts of these two friends.

42

MARCUS HARRIS was having a busy time at the offices of Super Pictures, Inc., in Radio City, city of New York. He interviewed a gathering of nine reporters representing all the

New York dailies. He talked with the newsrooms of the radio networks and with several stations of purely local outlet. He talked to newspapermen who had called him by long distance from Boston, Philadelphia, and Chicago. The New York special writer of the *Christian Science Monitor* phoned to ask how he could reach Coaltown. Two newsreel organizations and a national press photographic service had requested the same information. Never before had any star or any picture created such an advance furor.

He wondered if he had sent enough money to Dunnigan. Such expert exploitation was cheap at any price. The press agent might have some more inspired ideas that would require instant cash. He told Miss Feinberg to get the bank via the private wire.

"I ordered a transfer of money to a bank in Nanticoke, Pennsylvania," he spoke to the head cashier.

"We have already sent it, Mr. Harris. It is too late now to cancel it. Your own treasurer came and insisted on an immediate transfer."

"Yes! Yes! That's all right! I don't want to cancel it. I want you to notify that Pennsylvania bank that Mr. Dunnigan's check is good for any additional amount he may need. You understand. Any amount."

"Certainly," came the answer. Marcus Harris carried a very sizable business balance. His Wall Street backing was well-known. And that was why Father Spinsky had been told of the unlimited credit of his "apparition" of Saint Michael.

Harris also called his Hollywood Studios. They had heard the news already. The Los Angeles papers all carried full stories wired by the press associations.

"Good!" he told the excited studio manager. "Put 'Garden of the Soul' in the works. Start the cutting and editing. Start the musical dubbing. Rush us here as many stills as you can, and photographs of Treskovna. We are entirely out of them. And for God's sake, tell that crazy director and the crazier Victor George, if they don't know it already, that I've changed my mind!"

"They both know about it, Mr. Harris, and now they are worrying me as to their billing. The director wants his name——"

"Yes, yes! He wants his name twice as large as anyone else's, and Victor George doesn't see why anybody else's name but his should be billed at all! I'll be back next week sometime to face those headaches. They'll be a pleasure compared to what I have been through!"

I want to see an edited film when I return. And don't cut any scenes or shots in which Treskovna appears. We can't take more of her. We want every inch of her we have!"

To his head cameraman he sent a personal wire. He telegraphed:

TELL WHISTLER AND THE OTHER FELLOW YOU MENTIONED TO CHEER UP STOP I'LL GIVE THEM PERMISSION TO PAINT TRES-KOVNA FROM YOUR CAMERA SHOTS WHEN THE FILM IS RE-LEASED

The early editions of the afternoon papers were brought it. Every one carried front page columns, and photographs of Olga Treskovna. At two o'clock he again had Mrs. Harris on the private wire.

"You have been to the synagogue, Rachel?" he asked.

"I have been there, Marcus. It is all right. The Vilna Rabbi was there. He has offered prayers for you. He says Irving would wish you to do exactly as you are doing."

"It is wonderful, Rachel! Four hours ago I was in despair. I knew I had been unjust. I knew I was also ruining myself. But I was afraid. Now I seem to be on top of the world. I hope nothing bad will happen to spoil it."

"Nothing will, my darling—except I know you haven't eaten any lunch. You haven't, have you?"

"I've had no time," said Marcus Harris. "The bankers are coming here at two-thirty. That is the best sign of all, Rachel. When Wall Street will come to you! When you don't have to run down to them! It means they smell profits ahead."

"You take time to smell some food! That's more important than profits. Let the bankers wait."

"I will. I'll have something sent in. Did the Rabbi say he would make a prayer for William Dunnigan?"

"He will make that prayer also."

"Send out for the evening papers, dear. Mr. Dunnigan has accomplished wonders."

"I will. And you send out for some lunch."

Marcus Harris rang for Miss Feinberg. "Order me some lunch from the Rainbow Room grill," he said, "and take another wire for Mr. Dunnigan. Send it to Wyoming Hotel, Coaltown. Pay for a messenger to get it there if there's no office directly in that town. Say:

'DEAR WILLIAM, IF YOU NEED MORE MONEY, THAT NANTICOKE
BANK WILL TAKE CARE OF YOU.   HOPE IT IS A SOUND BANK.
PAPERS HERE NOT BAD AND EDITORS CALLING FROM ALL OVER.
FILM GOING AHEAD STARRING TRESKOVNA.   YOUR SALARY IS
NOW FIVE HUNDRED DOLLARS A WEEK STARTING DAY YOU LEFT
HOLLYWOOD.   PAY YOURSELF WHATEVER YOU NEED PERSON-
ALLY FROM FUNDS IN HAND.   HAVE SPATS ARRIVED?   IF NOT
TELEPHONE ME.   ARE YOU FIXED ALL RIGHT ABOUT CIGARS?   DO
NOT KNOW THIS FELLOW MAECENAS BUT THIS BUSINESS IS GET-
TING FULL OF FOREIGNERS.   WHAT COMPANY IS HE WITH?'

"Sign it 'Marcus,' " he added.   It was the first wire Marcus Harris
had so signed, except to his wife, in many years.

43

*B*ILL DUNNIGAN and Father Paul stood in a
side aisle of the church.   To escape the reporters and the crowds
they had entered by the rear door behind the altar.

The interior of St. Michael's was surprisingly lovely.   One would
never have guessed it from its dilapidated appearance outside.

The altar was simple—a plain, black marble shelf, but behind it
was a high, three-paneled wooden screen framed in fretwork painted
gold.   On the three tall panels of the screen were three paintings
which looked like the pictures in medieval illuminated manuscripts.
The center picture was of the Holy Mother seated on a throne, with
the Christ Child on her knee.   The side panels represented two
Saints kneeling in prayer, their hands clasped before them, and each
facing toward the Holy Mother.   Around the heads of these figures
were wide halos of gold.

Their costumes were blue and white and green.   They knelt on
steps of carpeted crimson on which white roses were strewn, and
the high back of the Virgin's throne was deep crimson.   In the
background was a distant landscape—mountains—trees—a monas-
tery on a hill.   This screen was, in truth, a priceless work.   Some
unsung Polish Fra Angelico had given it the breath of living beauty.
It had been brought from Poland by the first priest of the church.

At each side of the altar were two solid marble statues, larger than life-size. One was of Saint Michael. The other, the Virgin holding the Child. They also were well-carved and had come to Coaltown from the mother country.

High around the side walls were the customary Stations of the Cross—represented by paintings some three feet square set in narrow gold frames, with a small gold cross above each one. They were very quaint and foreign in design, and the reading on the lower border of each frame was in Polish. They started with "Jesus Is Condemned to Death" and carried through to "Jesus Is Laid in the Sepulcher." The side walls were a dull grey. Four small windows of stained glass were placed along and near the top of each side wall.

The ceiling was raftered and followed the slant of the outside roof. It had become a dark brown.

There was a wide aisle up the center and down each side. The side proceeding from the bell tower was of extra width, as the width of this tower continued back to the altar. Four shrines were placed here—four Saints in painted plaster set above small altars. These were the usual figures made in America, but they had been well selected and had character. They represented Saint Joseph holding the crowned Child in his arms; a figure of the dead Christ stretched in the arms of the kneeling Holy Mother; the bearded Saint Jude Thaddeus, and Saint Hedwig. Before them were the metal candle racks and the narrow altar rails. There were two more candle racks at the front of the church outside the altar rail. The marble statues were inside the altar rail.

The bare, brown coffin of Olga Treskovna was before the altar in the center aisle, guarded by its three tall candles on each side. The steady line of worshipers was passing before it. Probably a hundred people were inside the church. As some left, others entered.

The church had a small choir loft above the main doorway and the organ was playing softly. The blind organist had come to pay her respects to the dead girl. She played well—some sacred music that seemed to Dunnigan to blend with the ringing of the bell. He remembered how Olga Treskovna had told him she used to sit on the church steps and listen to this organ.

"Do you think it is all as your friend would have wished?" asked Father Paul.

"I am sure it is," said Bill Dunnigan. But he had a feeling that Olga Treskovna was not in that coffin. That the coffin there in the center aisle represented merely what the world had to think because she had "died." He did not know just where she was—but the Olga Treskovna he knew was not there, prone, without life.

They moved down the side aisle and out of the church by the main doorway.

"I am saying the Rosary and other prayers for the dead tonight at seven," said the priest. "Will you be here—Bill?" he added.

"Yes," said Dunnigan. "I will come. But you mustn't mind, Father, if I don't sit quietly all through. I—I may have to go out for a smoke. But I'll be at the back where I won't disturb anyone. You see, I always was a sort of in-and-outer—standing awhile at the front, ducking backstage, on the sidewalk for a smoke, then back in again! Maybe that isn't so good for a church service," he added doubtfully.

"Maybe I ought to have a section in the church—just for smokers," said Father Paul with a smile.

"It's an idea," said Bill. "But I'll be here promptly at six to see those radio people. I'll stay with *them* to a finish! That's right in my line."

Father Paul returned through the church to his parish house—his only escape from the curious and the newsmen. Bill Dunnigan stood on the steps. If Olga Treskovna could only see and hear all this!

There was a voice close beside him.

"Bill, isn't the organ music beautiful—just like I told you?"

She sat on the lower step. She did not wear the clothes in which he had known her. She was barefooted. Her dress was a faded cotton slip. Her long, brown hair hung over her shoulders and was drawn together at her neck with a green ribbon.

"Kid," he said, "I hardly knew you! Yes, it's beautiful. But now it's all for you, kid. The organist is playing just for you. The church bells are ringing just for you. The whole town is coming here just for you."

"I'm glad," she said. "I'm glad to bring more music to the town. It's been lovely to hear the organ once again! But now I've got to go home and cook supper for pop. Pop gets home early today. I'll be seeing you, Bill—on Forty-Second Street."

"But I have a car now, kid. I'll drive you home. You don't have to walk home any more."

"No. That wouldn't be right. Pop wouldn't understand if I drove up in a big car. He'd think something was wrong. So-long, Bill."

She arose and moved down the wooden steps and across the street. Bill Dunnigan watched her go and his heart felt a great ache again.

He pulled himself together. This would not do. She was not there, of course. It was just thinking back to what Olga Treskovna had told him about sitting on the church steps. Yet she had *seemed* to be there—living over again some moments of happiness.

Was that what happened when we "died"?

He lit a cigar. The Harris money had provided for a supply of the Coaltown Drug Store's best—eight centers, two for fifteen cents. He got into his waiting car—even for the half block to the hotel. He hoped she might be there beside him—he would ask her about it all—but she was not there.

He was just a little tired. He needed a bath and a shave. Father Spinsky's early call had cheated him of those customary day-starters. And he would take a nap before the evening service of Father Paul, which he had promised to attend.

In the hotel lobby were more reporters waiting. Two had come from Philadelphia. "Is it true that the film 'The Garden of the Soul' will be released after all? The New York papers say Marcus Harris has changed his mind."

"I do not know," said Dunnigan. "Such information must come from Mr. Harris in New York. I have no knowledge of his plans. I hope the report is true."

"Just when is the funeral to be?" asked a newsman from Philadelphia.

"It will be on Friday. Miss Treskovna wanted the Angelus to sound the final ringing of the Coaltown bells for herself and her father." And that wasn't a bad idea, mused Mr. Dunnigan. It was a touch he had not thought of before.

"Is it true that over two thousand dollars a day is being paid for the ringing of the bells?"

"The cost of this ceremony is not a matter of consequence or of public interest," said Mr. Dunnigan. "If Olga Treskovna saw fit to set aside a week's salary for this tribute to her father's memory . . .

Gentlemen, I would prefer not to talk of money. I must ask you to excuse me. I am a little tired. There will be a service at the Church of St. Michael at seven this evening. Father Paul's famous and most popular early Mass at five forty-five tomorrow morning will be held as usual. I especially advise your attendance at this early Mass to see the hold this great Saint—Saint Michael, the patron of that church—has on the hearts of this community.

"And if you have not already viewed the interior of St. Michael's you will find a surprising jewel hidden beneath its plain exterior. Note especially the painting of the altar screens and the Stations of the Cross, which are a bit of Old World beauty transported with loving reverence from Poland to America."

He must learn more about such things, Bill thought, if he was to press-agent St. Michael's! He paused before he got in too deeply, and stepped to the desk clerk for his room key.

The clerk handed him a telegram which a messenger had brought from Nanticoke. It was the second wire from Marcus Harris.

"Gentlemen," he said turning again to the newsmen, "I can now tell you that 'The Garden of the Soul' will be released. My friend, Marcus Harris, has just wired me. There had been a clamor for it from Maine to California. So the final masterpiece of this girl's artistry will not be lost. I will look forward to seeing you, sirs, at St. Michael's at seven—or tomorrow morning at the early Mass."

Having made the first announcement of a church service in his varied career, Mr. Dunnigan ascended to his room. He left word he was not to be disturbed. Events had overwhelmed even him.

44

TWO HOURS LATER Dunnigan sat by the open window in his room. It was about five o'clock. He wore his "sleeper-jump" bathrobe, a Sulka creation of broad crimson and white stripes. He had taken a nap, a shave, two baths, one before and one after the nap.

His slippered feet were on the window sill and he was reading again the telegram from Marcus Harris. He had needed just that. He knew, of course, that "The Garden of the Soul" would be completed when Harris had sent the money—knew that he was once more its official press agent. But it was good to have Marcus Harris say it in so many words.

Work—work for Marcus Harris, for Olga Treskovna, for Father Paul, for Saint Michael—work was the antidote to the loneliness that sometimes got the best of him. He had noted the form of the signature on the telegram. Marcus Harris was now not just his boss. He was his friend. If trouble came, and it probably would, he could count on Marcus Harris to stand by.

There were five of them now, *five* musketeers: Father Paul, Saint Michael, Olga Treskovna, himself—and Marcus Harris. It somehow reminded him of a bronze sculpture on upper Fifth Avenue representing a charging group of American soldiers of World War One. What a strange bronze group his five would make (thought Dunnigan's theater mind)—the Catholic priest in his cassock, the armored archangel, the barefooted girl as she had looked on the church steps, himself, and the little Jewish picture producer . . . But that was America.

For his part he must move carefully. He must not appear in Coaltown to be a press agent for a film. There he was simply the friend of Olga Treskovna. And matters were progressing so well that in Coaltown the news would speak for itself. Reporters could report on facts—not what he, Dunnigan, might say. "The Garden of the Soul" must only be mentioned as the finest of Olga Treskovna's work. New York must supply any other facts about it.

One thing he could "promote" from Coaltown—Father Paul and St. Michael's church. Saint Michael, also, for there was now in his heart a very sincere belief—a gratitude—that somehow he had been helped by this Saint.

Dunnigan was not religious. He had not been inside a church for years until that morning. He had not suddenly acquired "religion" in Coaltown. It was more a feeling of loyalty to his pals— Father Paul and Saint Michael. He thought of Saint Michael as a pal.

And he was not quite sure just what he could do. Just what he should do. You couldn't promote a priest, a church, a saint, as you would a musical show or Eddie Cantor or a feature film. Or could you?

One thing he knew. Father Paul, that most unselfish and un-businesslike of men, must get what money he was rightly entitled to. Here was the opportunity for funds to lay a firm foundation for all the splendid things the priest wished to try. Those radio people, for example—they must be made to pay. They would gladly pay. Perhaps a whole Mass could be broadcast? Dunnigan did not know. He had heard church services over the air. It had been done. Broadcasting the sound of the St. Michael's bell was something he had not thought of. That was swell! He must be certain it was announced as "from the Church of St. Michael the Archangel of Coaltown, the Reverend Father Paul, pastor."

He had spoken with such assurance of being a press agent for Father Paul; for the Church and its Saint; for God Almighty even —but it wasn't quite as easy as just saying it. Well, he had mentioned this early Mass to the reporters. That would help if they spoke of it in their news stories. After the success of that morning he didn't want this Mass to slip back and fail Father Paul. Five forty-five was a hell of an early hour!

Perhaps there were objects inside that church that held a story. That altar backing. Those quaint pictures. He'd manufacture a story if they didn't have one! Just how *did* you publicize a church! He must cudgel his brain to the very limit to help Father Paul.

There was a faint, hesitating knock at his door. The chamber-maid most likely.

"Come in!" he called.

The doorway was in shadow. It opened and a young man stood there. Evidently a local young man wearing a cap and dressed in his Sunday best. He looked awkward and uncomfortable in the thick, store-made suit and the tight collar. The face seemed vaguely familiar.

"Are you Mr. Dunnigan of New York?" said the youth.

"I thought I left orders no one was to come up—" commenced Bill.

"I know, sir. I hope you'll pardon me, sir—" The lad had taken a step inside the room and removed his cap. He stopped, mouth open, in the middle of his apology, staring with popping eyes at the man who lounged by the window.

"As long as you're here, come in," said Dunnigan. "What can I do for you, son?" The voice also of this lad had a familiar pitch.

"But I had no idea I'd see *you!*" gasped his visitor and looked as though he wanted to turn and run.

Dunnigan removed his slippered feet from the window sill and leaned forward so that he could better view his unannounced caller.

"You don't remember *me?*" the intruder now managed to say.

Dunnigan experienced that most absurdly elusive of mental graspings—trying to place a familiar personage seen apart from his customary background—the bartender away from his bar—the cigar-counter clerk away from his shop—the bellboy out of his uniform.

"I seem to remember you well," he said, "but just where——"

"I talked to you this morning! I'm sure it was you, sir! You were dressed differently, of course. But I cooked you your breakfast in Nanticoke! The Special—ham and eggs and coffee and toast. Forty-five cents! And you bought a Phillie and gave me your last —gave me a quarter to buy a flower for my girl!"

Dunnigan knew after the first sentence. The red hair was now bobbing as vigorously as it had above the lunch-room counter. The eager face with the upturned nose was as glowing. Only the white work jacket was missing. But the press agent lay back in his chair and laughed and let the lad finish his speeches.

"Sure! Sure!" he said cordially. "I apologize, kid! I've been through quite a lot today. Have a chair, my friend. So you've tracked me down!" And he laughed again. He needed that laugh, he felt.

The boy sat gingerly on the edge of one of Dunnigan's chairs. He twisted his cap in his hands.

"I—I wanted to see the millionaire like I told you. William Dunnigan the papers said his name was; and when the clerk only laughed at me when I asked to have my card sent up, I looked on the register while he wasn't looking and it said room 1-A opposite this name. So I sneaked up the stairs. I guess the millionaire must have gone back to New York for you're the man now in 1-A."

"Yes—I'm the man now in 1-A," said Bill Dunnigan with a broad smile.

The dejection on the lad's face was almost tragic.

"I've come too late," he said, and then, biting his lip, "Tell me,

mister, why do people always laugh at me? The clerk downstairs
laughed! You laugh! Am I as silly as all that!"

Bill Dunnigan regarded the unhappy countenance opposite him.
The lad who had served him with an extra cup of coffee when he
was down to his last eighty cents. The lad who had suggested that
if he were "short" the next day he might get a meal with the check
"held over." Thank God, Marcus Harris had come through!

Bill lifted himself from his chair and stood above the boy who
had worked in the Breaker at Wanamee and now wanted to own his
own Quick Lunch. The boy who always made people laugh. He
put a kindly hand on the shoulder of the cheap, ill-fitting store suit.

"Kid," he said, "don't you ever worry because you can make folks
laugh! There's damn few of us can do that. This world would be
a hell of a better place if some more of us could! And now you
and me are going to get down to brass tacks about this Quick
Lunch business. But first, kid—did your girl friend like the
flower?"

"Why, yes—" The face brightened a little. "I bought her a rose.
She thought you were awfully kind, sir—said she'd like to meet you
and thank you herself."

"Good. I'll meet her someday. Now just how much was it that
you two needed for this business start you want to make?"

"It is two hundred and fifty dollars, sir, but now that I've missed
out on the millionaire——"

Bill Dunnigan had taken the pale blue and red-checked coat from
the back of another chair. He removed a long envelope from the
inside pocket of that coat and unsnapped a rubber band from
around that envelope. He took out three one-hundred-dollar bills,
as the eyes of the lad nearly burst from his head.

"I think you'd better have three hundred, kid," he said. "Things
always cost a little more than you plan." He placed the money in
the boy's hand and closed that hand tightly around it.

"That's because you made me smile this morning when God
knows I had need of a smile!"

Bill Dunnigan replaced the envelope in his coat pocket and went
back to his chair by the window. The boy from Nanticoke wanted
to rise but something had happened to his legs. To his throat, also.

"But I—I don't even know your name, sir, and you don't know
mine!" he gasped at last.

Bill Dunnigan lit a cigar. "You know my name all right, kid," he said. "And if you want to tell me yours, you can."

"But you're not—you're not the millionaire William Dunnigan!"

"I'm the only William Dunnigan that I know of around here," said Bill, "or anywhere else for that matter. There used to be a cop on Delancy Street in New York with the same name, but he got himself bumped off!"

"But, Mr. Dunnigan, you had your breakfast in the Lunch where I work—I saw you counting your change!"

"Sure. We all have mornings when we have to count our change. And it isn't always we meet up with a pal who will push out an extra cup of coffee! I'm no millionaire, boy. That's just newspaper talk. I don't mind. I've been called worse than that lots of times!"

"But can you really afford to back me! You really want to do it!" The lad looked down at the bills still in his hand. He had never seen such large bills before. They crinkled when he squeezed them! They were real—not something he was dreaming!

"I work, kid, the same as you," said Dunnigan. "I'd lost my job when you saw me this morning. I guess you brought me luck for I got it back again, got it back with a raise, right after eating your Special! I'd made up my mind to back you, if things came through. I was going to stop in tomorrow for another Special, and to find out when you wanted to start that 'Quick Lunch Heaven—Two Cups of Coffee.' "

This time the boy got to his feet. He felt a little dizzy but he could stand. "I—thanks! Thanks, Mr. Dunnigan!" he stammered. "I can't tell you what this means to me, and to my girl! We can get married now!"

He dove into his pocket and produced a small card. "Here is my card, sir!" And he handed it proudly to his benefactor.

Dunnigan read:

ROBERT OMANSKY
EXPERT SHORT-ORDER MAN
NANTICOKE, PA.

This time the press agent suppressed his smile.

"You'll be needing some new cards now, Robert," he said. "How soon can you start?"

The answer came with a bursting rush. "I can start right away, sir! There's a place I can buy out, on the Main Square. I used to work there. It's a much better location than where I work now! I'll see them tonight. They want a thousand dollars but I can pay two hundred and fifty cash and the rest out of the profits each month."

"Maybe you can pay them all cash, so that you start clean," said Dunnigan. "You talk to them, kid."

"They might take less, if I paid it all at once!"

"Sure! Find out, and you can tell me tomorrow when I drop in for another Special. By the way, Robert, I've got an idea for you to work on."

"I'll do anything you want, Mr. Dunnigan!"

"No, you won't! I don't know anything about restaurants but eating in them. If I try to butt in after this, don't listen to me! It's your show, kid. But I want you to do just one thing for me that may help *my* show. Invent a special kind of sandwich." Dunnigan paused, searching for a word. "A wonder sandwich that will knock 'em for a loop!"

"You mean something to make my place famous! Something they can't get anywhere else?"

"You've got the idea exactly!" Dunnigan rose and looked out of his window. The crowd moving into St. Michael's had not diminished. It seemed to be larger than two hours before. He turned to the lad who was watching him with eager eyes.

"I want this sandwich filled with all the good things that can be put between two layers of bread—the bread that's sort of like our life—get me, kid?—so that right here in this one sandwich we'll give 'em everything good you could think of, or dream of, or pray for—in a lifetime!"

"Gee! That would have to be a smasher!"

"Smasher is right! A sandwich you'd want to be born for and live for and fight for and die for!"

"Every bite a banquet?" said Robert Omansky, coiner of slogans as well as "Short-Order expert."

"You're better than I am, kid!" said Dunnigan, and he laughed happily. "But what will you put in it, so that it measures up to all this!"

The lad wrinkled a freckled brow under the flaming crown of red.

"I think I'd make it of chicken and very crisp bacon and Virginia

ham and crab meat—crab meat will give it an unusual flavor—and
then some lettuce and tomato, a few slices of hard-boiled egg, just
a little garlic and a little mustard—I'll cook the ham in mustard—
that will give it zip!"

"Plenty of zip is one of the things we want!" said Bill.

"And I'll use a special bread—there's a kind called Irish Soda
that makes your mouth water when it's toasted! It has raisins in it
too!"

"Something Irish always helps!" smiled Bill.

"I'll work hard on it, sir—I'll talk to my girl about it!"

"That's the stuff! It wants to be so wonderful a customer will
never forget it! .Come across a continent to eat it again! Thank
God for the rest of his life he had met up with it!"

"Yes sir, Mr. Dunnigan, sir!" The lad's face was agog at the
glowing qualifications of this wonder sandwich to be!

"And here's the name for it," continued Dunnigan, "The St.
Michael Sandwich."

"You mean the Saint that churches are named for?" It was both
question and surprise.

"That's the guy. That's the lad we're naming it after. So you
see why it's got to be good! Your place will be 'Quick Lunch
Heaven.' Let's have a sandwich named after the swellest Saint up
there!"

"Gosh! That *is* an idea!" gasped the excited boy. "I could paint
that on the window also—

> Home of the St. Michael Sandwich
> Every Bite a Banquet!"

The lad gestured with his finger as he painted each magic word.

"You certainly could," smiled Mr. Dunnigan.

The boy was still holding the three hundred-dollar bills in his
hand. Their reality gripped him now.

"You'll want some written agreement, Mr. Dunnigan—maybe
you'll make it out? And I'll give you a receipt."

Dunnigan raised his hand. "No, boy. I'm not much on written
agreements. Never found I had to have 'em with gentlemen. You
just get things going pronto! My address in New York is Radio
City. You can write me there. But I'll be around here a few days
more. I'll be seeing you before I go."

"You're half owner then, sir——Mr. Dunnigan. My girl knows how to keep accounts and I'll send you a statement every week."

"Half owner isn't fair. What about your girl?"

"She and I will own the other half."

"No dice. We'll split it three ways, kid. You and me and your girl. I got a hunch that she's O. K. And you pay yourself and your girl a fair salary before you figure any profits."

"Gosh! Gosh, Mr. Dunnigan! I didn't know there were people like you around! There ain't——around here! When——when can I bring my girl to meet you?"

"Do you go to Mass?"

"Not often, sir. But my girl does."

"What time do you start work tomorrow?"

"I don't go on till seven tomorrow morning. My girl starts in her store at nine."

"Mind getting up early?"

"I'm always up at five o'clock. When we've got our own place I'll be up at four to do the buying at the markets. Once I overslept till six, but my girl and I had been to a dance. There'll be no dances when we're running Quick Lunch Heaven!"

"I hope there'll be a lot of dances!" laughed Bill, "but tomorrow, don't oversleep, and be at the Nanticoke Garage at five-thirty——you and your girl. I've got a car there. I'll tell my driver to bring you over for the five forty-five Mass at St. Michael's church up the street. He'll take you back after it's over. Tell the girl to say a little prayer for the new Quick Lunch Heaven!"

"She'll be doing that tonight, sir, if I know her! She's been lighting candles to it for a year!"

"Atta girl! I guess prayers do ring the bell! So-long, kiddo——see you tomorrow——don't lose your money!" For the excited lad still held the bills in his hand.

The boy pushed the money deep into his trouser pocket. "Mr. Dunnigan——thanks, Mr. Dunnigan!" he managed to gasp again. "I ——you——can I shake your hand, Mr. Dunnigan——we being partners."

Mr. Dunnigan put out his hand.

"Shake, partner," he said.

Another citizen of Pennsylvania was seeing a Saint, but Robert Omansky's version wore no armored shin greaves and mounted no black charger. His Saint just stood in a hotel room in a long crimson and white dressing gown and was smoking an eight cent cigar.

"I'll get back to Nanticoke to tell my girl!" the boy cried and ran for the door. As a "businessman" he did not wish another business-man to see the tears in his eyes.

"And don't forget to work on the St. Michael Every-Bite-a-Banquet Super-Sandwich!" Bill Dunnigan called after him.

Mr. Dunnigan felt a lot better. God, but he was glad that nice kid didn't have to be let down! And he was making a start with Saint Michael. It wasn't much of a start—still—a cigar named after her had helped glorify Anna Held! You never could tell!

A young man named Robert Omansky had entirely conquered the laws of gravity. He had rushed out of Room 1-A, down the stairs, across the floor of the lobby of the Wyoming Hotel, treading the thin air only, as he struggled with the much less difficult prob-lem of inventing an unforgettable sandwich that would amaze and conquer the universe!

BILL DUNNIGAN attended his first church service in many years from the St. Michael's choir loft. By seven o'clock it was the only space in the church, except the sanctuary before the altar, that was not solidly occupied. A standing-room-only house, he would have called it, and that other abused theater expression, "hundreds turned away," would have been literally true.

They were not exactly turned away. They stood outside on the lawn and in the street, and uttered responses along with those who could crowd inside. The wide, front doors remained open through-out the service.

He had entered the choir loft from the bell tower. In the tower he had interviewed the representative of the local radio station of the Green Network, and secured Father Paul the tidy sum of three thousand dollars for the privilege of broadcasting St. Michael's bell at noon and at six o'clock the remaining three days. Rumors of interest on the part of a rival network had not retarded consummation of the deal. For the sexton, also, Dunnigan arranged an extra payment of one hundred dollars as a "broadcasting service fee." St. Michael's finances were looking up!

The press agent next had business with the organist. He found her in the choir loft with a younger sister who acted as a "seeing eye" for the musician.

"I remember Olga Trocki," she said. "I remember her when her father died. She came to me and wanted that I play a Polish folk song her father loved—play it during the funeral. She sang it to me herself until I memorized its melody. But the old priest was very strict. He would only allow what he called sacred music in the church. So I played it like a hymn!"

The woman smiled at this remembrance. "Maybe I did something very wicked, but I wanted to please the girl. She seemed so desperately eager to have that song played! I've never forgotten it."

She sat at her organ and struck an opening strain. It was the song Olga Treskovna had sung to Dunnigan in Ming Gow's that Christmas Eve.

"I'm glad you remember that song," said Dunnigan. "I want you to play it again when her own funeral service comes."

"I hope Father Paul won't object," said the woman. "The old priest did. I nearly lost my job!"

"But it is as beautiful as any hymn!" said Dunnigan.

"That was not the trouble," smiled the organist. "Someone recognized it as a song Mr. Trocki used to sing in the saloons!"

Bill Dunnigan had an idea. "Do you know any other hymn-like Polish songs?" he asked.

"I know a great many," said the organist. "My mother who taught me music, knew a lot of them. It was just that one song that was new to me. It seemed that song was Mr. Trocki's 'musical signature,' as the advertisers on the radio say—his signature when he had been—when he had been having too jolly a time."

"But it is a sad song," said Bill Dunnigan.

"We Poles play sad music when we are happy," said the woman.

"This girl loved the old Polish melodies," said Bill pursuing his idea. "She once told me she wanted to give a concert sometime in Carnegie Hall in New York. A concert of such songs. She never lived to do it. You and I and St. Michael's—we'll give such a con-

cert! In her memory. We'll give two concerts. Tomorrow afternoon and on Thursday. You come and play for one hour. Play
Polish songs."

"I will gladly do it. But will Father Paul permit?"

"Would the people here like it?" asked Bill.

"It would bring memories to the older ones."

"Then I think I can fix matters with Father Paul. He won't object to giving the town some memories of romance and love of
beauty. At least no one can say they heard Olga Trocki sing the
songs in the saloons!"

"Just keep Father Spinsky of St. Leo's away! I always thought
he was at the bottom of the complaint when I played for her
father," said the woman.

"You find a Polish song about Saint Leo and we'll disarm Father
Spinsky!" laughed Bill. "I may even invite him to attend! Make
him co-sponsor of the concerts!"

And using the word "sponsor" another idea occurred to press
agent Dunnigan. Such concerts could be broadcast; some network
would pay to do it while the bell-ringing excitement was on!

"You'll never get Father Spinsky to step inside St. Michael's!"
said the woman, "but I wish I had done something like this for the
Trocki girl when she was alive. Now she is there in her coffin. Do
you think she will hear the songs?"

"She will hear them if we leave the church door open."

"The church door open?"

"Yes. I don't believe you know, but she used to sit on the steps
and listen to you when you were practicing. I have an idea—I think
you'll understand—that maybe she'll come and sit there when you
play the Polish folk songs."

"That is a nice thought," said the woman. "I shall try to play
them so that if she does come she'll not be disappointed."

"I want to pay you for all this," said Dunnigan, "and for playing
at the funeral."

"You can pay the five dollars, if you wish, for the funeral. That
is what I usually receive. The other things I'd like to do just for
this girl. I didn't know anyone in the town cared enough for my
music to come just to hear me practice! I wish I had known about
it then!"

"Perhaps it's better that you did not know. You would have asked her to come inside and I think she liked to sit out there—on the steps. Especially at night, for there was a star she loved."

"Ah, a star," said the blind woman and there was a sudden lift of her head. "You know, of course, sir, that I am blind. I have never minded. God gave me music to take the place of seeing. I'll never really see this world—I've never been farther from Coaltown than Scranton; but I've traveled to Hungary with Franz Liszt, to Paris with Debussy, to Vienna with Johann Strauss, to Prague with Antonin Dvořák. Oh, I've been all over with my music! They are such beautiful places to me now—I might be disappointed if I really saw them. But the stars!"

The blind woman paused a moment. "I love to travel, sir, and when I die, and perhaps really have my eyes, I don't want to stay in just one place, no matter how beautiful that place may be. I'm going to ask if I can't travel—travel among the stars! That's really what I'd like to see—the stars. My sister tells me about them—they must be wonderful! They could never disappoint!"

Dunnigan, strong, possessing all his faculties, looked at this woman who could not see, who never had been more than twenty miles from her home. And still she lived in faith and hope and had found joy. He thought that if he was ever again discouraged he would remember the look of her face as she spoke of journeying among the stars.

"I think I know what to tell Father Paul about our Polish concert—and Father Spinsky also. We will take the older people back to Poland—as the guests of Olga Treskovna and yourself. And I think I know how you can make sure of a trip to all the stars."

"You really do, sir?"

"You just ask for Saint Michael when you get there. Tell him you played all these years in one of his churches. Tell him——"

He was going to say, "Tell him you know Bill Dunnigan," but he checked himself. "Saint Michael will fix it for you. I know!" he spoke aloud.

He took out his manila envelope. He unsnapped the rubber band and selected a note, folded it and put it in the woman's hand.

"Here is the five dollars for the funeral and a little extra," he said. "I want you to accept it for—for steamship fare on this trip to Poland. You'll be taking a lot of people along, you know!"

The sister looked at the money and was about to speak but Dunnigan placed a finger on his lips. He had given her a hundred dollars but he felt even that was little enough. Never again would he quit, no matter what the setback.

The church below was filled. Father Paul and his altar boys appeared from the door at the side of the sanctuary. The service was about to start.

Dunnigan looked in some dismay over the railing of the choir loft at the solidly-packed crowd below. There did not seem to be a spare inch of space.

"Here is where I stay through a service whether I want to or not!" he said, and crouched on a small stool at one side.

It did not prove too difficult. Unseen, he was able to chew on a cigar. During a long stretch of "Hail Marys" he was about to strike a light but caught himself in time.

"Saint Michael," he smiled, "don't you mind, please, if I want to smoke. I got a lot of things to dope out for you and I can't think yet without a cigar. I'm just an amateur press man at this church business, you know!"

He watched the long-handled baskets start on their somewhat perilous rounds; but in the now expert hands of the druggist and the garage keeper and several volunteer assistants they did manage to pass from hand to hand, over shoulders from pew to pew. From his vantage point it looked as though the "take" was good. He found himself as anxious to learn the "gross" as he would have been if it were the box-office receipts of the second night of a new show!

But what worried Dunnigan, constantly shifting his cigar, was: *Why were all these people there and why were they giving?* He feared that it was curiosity. The coffin of an "actress." That coffin would be gone in two short days. Would attendance at St. Michael's then slip back to its old neglect?

He felt that it was up to him, Bill Dunnigan, not to let this happen. Saint Michael and Father Paul had done their part. Marcus Harris certainly had also. Now it was his turn.

To his theater-working mind it all was like a new production. Saint Michael had helped to raise the backing. Bill felt that somehow he would not have received that money from Marcus Harris but for his answered prayer to that armored Fighter of the church.

Backer Harris had come through. Stage Manager Father Paul was down there "putting on the show."

But how could you make a show "run" in a place that was not even a one-night stand, as Olga Treskovna had called it! And with the leading lady leaving in two days! It looked as though it would take a lot of chewing on cigars to solve this problem.

But either he *was* or he was *not* a press agent! A man who could *make* shows go! The top man in his trade! He'd just got to dope it out!

<hr />

46

*B*ILL DUNNIGAN and Father Paul sat on the steps of the Church of St. Michael the Archangel. It was nine o'clock and a full moon was low in the east casting its glow over the darkened sky and the town.

Bill had waited for the priest after the evening service. His Packard had returned from Nanticoke and it had been his plan to drive the Father to Wilkes-Barre or Scranton for a dinner at one of the hotels. But the priest had insisted that they have their supper —as he named it—in the parish house.

So Bill dismissed his driver for the day, with orders to pick up his quick-lunch friend early in the morning and return in time for the five-forty-five Mass. The driver had brought him the New York newspapers he had reserved that morning in the garage town, and he had read the story they carried. Marcus Harris would have been adamant indeed to have resisted their opportunity and appeal!

"I must stay near my church," Father Paul had explained, "so long as the girl is resting there. I really should have asked some Sisters from the convent in Scranton to keep a vigil by the coffin. They would gladly have come if I had sent word to them. And not having done that, I should myself sit by my altar during the night."

"She would not wish you that hardship," said Bill. "Or wish that the Sisters lose their rest. The bells are keeping her vigil."

"You do not think she will feel lonely?"

So Olga Treskovna was also becoming a living person to Father Paul! Bill said:

"I think that after the busy day—it has been a busy day for all of us—she will want to rest alone. Father, I don't know what you believe, but I think she was not there all day. She was with me as I crossed the hills in my car—she was on the steps of the church when the organ was playing this afternoon. She went home to cook a supper for her father. Is it very wrong that I should believe such things?"

"I think those nearest us know what we do," said Father Paul. "I often imagine my mother at her sewing. Your heart can be trusted when it speaks in such a way."

"Then I think that tonight she will sleep well. And in your church. In life she wished to stay alone after a day of work. I remember that."

So they had gone to Father Paul's little garden at the back of his parish house, cut bright green lettuce and great red tomatoes; then Bill read his newspaper while Father Paul prepared a salad of these and eggs which he had boiled hard and sliced. He had a dressing of mayonnaise.

"I live very simply—you are sure this meal will satisfy you?" he had asked.

"It is quite wonderful," said Bill and meant it. The salad, direct from a garden, had a different taste from those he had ordered in restaurants. Even his friend Oscar of the Waldorf would have approved that salad!

"Now I'll make coffee," said Father Paul. "My stove runs by oil —it's almost as quick as gas—the coffee will be ready very soon. And there's a big surprise for our dessert! A box was left at my door just before the evening service. Do you, by any chance, like chocolate cake?"

"Do I!" said Bill. "I've sometimes bought a whole one, and eaten it at one sitting back at my hotels! And if yours is homemade— You mustn't raise my expectations too high!"

Father Paul opened the box and placed the half cake that had been left at his door on the table.

"It's homemade right enough, but I don't know who sent it!" he said. "There was just this piece of paper inside," and he handed Bill a sheet torn from a ruled tablet. It read:

This cake is made with six
eggs and a full cup of butter.
I hope all this trouble and
expense has not been wasted.

"A generous soul sent it, even if there is no name," said Father Paul.

"I don't know about that," said Bill judiciously. "They only sent you half of it! And wanted to make sure you realized how much it cost to make. The action and the note are a contradiction They pose a veritable Ellery Queen who-done-it problem! Now if Sherlock Holmes were here! But it's just as well he isn't! Dr. Watson would be along also and with *his* appetite and Holmes testing samples for clues——"

Dunnigan made a gesture of complete annihilation.

"No matter what our vows, our resolution, we are all sinfully selfish at heart," smiled Father Paul. "A homemade chocolate cake is the acid test. I confess I, too, am glad Dr. Watson is not here!"

The priest started his coffee on the oil stove. Bill Dunnigan eyed the cake. Its exposed inside was a rich yellow, and the dark brown chocolate was a quarter of an inch thick between the layers. There was a forming of saliva around his tongue not induced by his cigar

"Do you mind if I try just a small piece?" he asked.

Father Paul smiled again and produced a cake knife from his pantry drawer. "I've not had much use for this knife," he admitted. "I cannot seem to acquire the grace to bake a cake!"

He had noticed a forming of anticipatory moisture beneath his own tongue. "I think I'll try just a small sample myself—while the coffee is boiling," he explained.

A chocolate cake—homemade—has power to stir the souls of boys —and men—who, in the presence of such glory, always become boys again.

They ate their samples in silence. Bill Dunnigan was back again near Houston Street where his mother sometimes made him such a cake. Father Paul was in the little house in Scranton where another mother also knew what would please a hungry lad.

Silently Father Paul cut another and larger piece and passed it to William Dunnigan. Then cut a slice also for himself. The coffee was ready and the cups filled, and very soon a third piece of Mary Spinsky's cake was rapidly disappearing.

"Ah-h!" breathed Bill Dunnigan with a deep sigh. "Now, Father Paul, we have a real problem on our hands."

"What is that?" asked the priest.

"To find out who *made* this cake! Among other unexpected adventures today, including my hearing your service, I've become a partner in a quick-lunch business in Nanticoke! I cannot rest till I get the recipe of that cake for a friend of mine there!"

"The accompanying note mentioned a full cup of butter, six eggs and trouble. And as you deduced, there is another half somewhere in Coaltown tonight," added Father Paul sagely.

"I hope it's not in the hands of a family of healthy men," said Bill, "or it's quite disappeared already. Suppose someone was trying to find our half! It would take a microscope to discover one crumb. We must make a house-to-house search quickly, Father, very quickly!" And they both laughed.

They went out presently to lock the church for the night. The druggist had just finished counting and sorting the money from the collection and the shrine boxes. Again it was nearly three hundred dollars. He departed taking the bills and silver to his store for safety. The priest extinguished some of the shrine candles.

"I would like to leave them all burning," he said, "but I fear it is a little dangerous. I would not want a fire at this time, or any time. I will pray for their intention at each shrine if you will wait for me."

"I'll be out on the front steps," said Bill. "Would I disgrace you, Father, by sitting on your church steps and maybe smoke?"

"I'll come and sit with you presently," said Father Paul, and that was answer enough.

When they were sitting there together, their knees hunched before them—just two boys it seemed to both of them—Bill said:

"I think the fellow who invented steps that face on a street did mankind a great service. I haven't sat this way for a long time. I'm realizing what I've passed up, tearing around the country."

"I've always loved to sit on steps," said Father Paul. "I sit here often. I know I have been criticized for doing it, but here one can meditate, as one should sometimes, above the world, and yet not too far above the world. Your fellow man is passing you—you can see his face—you are still one with him."

"It takes me back to a street on the East Side of New York," said

Bill. "At night in summer everyone sat on the steps or on the fire escapes."

"And you would sit there?"

"Not too often. I'm afraid I didn't do much meditating in those days! I wanted to roam around. To see the world. Go way up to Fourteenth Street or over to the Bowery! And there was a whole world right in front of me on Orchard Street, a world in one short block! Morgenstern's Fashion Center and next door O'Reilly's Fish Market. A lawyer's office was next to that—his name was Marcatto —then came the Great Textile Bargain House, James McNab, Sole Owner and Proprietor. Are you visualizing large emporiums, Father? None of them was more than ten feet wide! They were on the street floor of the tenement houses. And every house had a space of iron steps that ran down to the sidewalk. So step-sitting was born in my blood. I've often wondered why I liked to sit at night on fire hydrants outside the theaters where I worked. Now I know, Father."

"I've always just wanted to stay in one place," said Father Paul. "With one church—one parish. Do you think—Bill, do you think this success at St. Michael's is going to last?"

So Father Paul had also worried about that! Bill Dunnigan bit hard on his cigar.

"It's got to last if that is what you want most," he said.

"But you will be going away soon," said Father Paul, "and it is you, my friend, who has made my church a crowded place. It will be very lonely when you go."

"Father," said Bill, "you and I are going to stick together. You're not alone any more. I'm not alone either, as I've been most of my life. It's no good, being all alone.

"There's five of us going to see this through, Father—five musketeers—I was thinking this afternoon—and I don't just mean this funeral——"

"Five of us?" asked Father Paul.

"Yes, five. There's a guy back in New York that you don't know yet. A right guy! He doesn't know yet about you. But just wait till I see him again! Then there's this girl. She's not dead. She's going to help you. I know that, Father, though I could not explain to you how I know it.

"Someday I'll tell you about this girl and myself. A chance

meeting—an almost absurd chance—I did not see her again for over a year—I didn't even know her name. Then another meeting for only a few hours. I could count on my fingers the times I have been near her alone. Then came an opportunity for her that I helped to realize. She accomplished something that I believe is great and good. Then death. Or what we call death. And my life with her really began—did not really begin until she died!"

Father Paul placed his hand on Bill Dunnigan's arm.

"I think I understand," he said. "You loved her very deeply."

"I only told her of that love here in Coaltown," said Bill, "and you know that I brought her to Coaltown in the casket that is supposed to be the end of all."

"There is no end of all," said Father Paul.

They were both silent. Bill Dunnigan felt for a moment again a hand in his. On the side away from Father Paul. But just for a moment. It was gone before he could turn his head.

"Then there are we three men battling shoulder to shoulder in Coaltown," he continued at last, and lit a fresh cigar.

"Three men?" said Father Paul.

"You and I and Saint Michael. All for one and one for all! Maybe that's sacrilegious or whatever the word is, but I don't think so. I don't really care if it is.

"I won't be here all the time, of course. My work will take me to New York—to California. I guess Saint Michael had his other jobs too. Off there among those stars. But I'll return often and so will he. And you're coming to New York sometimes."

"I have never been to New York," said Father Paul.

"Always when I had to figure how to make a show run, I'd go out and sit on a fire hydrant in front of the theater. I'm thinking now, Father—sitting in front of your church—about *your* show. I'm thinking about that Mass every morning at five forty-five. That's your big idea in this town. I think we're going to 'bill' this town about that Mass!"

" 'Bill' this town?"

"You haven't any newspaper here. That makes it difficult. But suppose we have a newspaper! Suppose twice a week we get out a sort of paper. Just one page, maybe, but regular newspaper size. So they'll have to spread it out to read it. We'll tell in it what you are doing. What you want to do. What you hope to do.

It won't cost much to print. Perhaps it should be in Polish. Polish and English both. *Saint Michael's Coaltown Clarion!* Published from the Front Steps of St. Michael's Church!"

"I have always been afraid of newspapers," said Father Paul.

"So have I," said Bill, "when I've opened them the morning after a new show. But they are useful—sometimes. I'm going to dope it out someway. I believe our partner back in New York will meet its cost for an advertisement about his motion pictures. And then I'm going to print some window cards."

"Window cards?"

"That's what we call them. About as large as that moon looks to be. Only square. We'll print just one thing on them, in heavy type:

DON'T FORGET!
A MASS AT ST. MICHAEL'S
At Five Forty-five
EVERY MORNING!

That's our slogan, Father. Just that. I think the stores will place them in their windows if I ask them to. Maybe even the bus company will help us out. A card in every bus. They have a silly idea that I'm sort of a big shot. We'll make use of it. That's really the way I started in my promotion work for theaters. Going out with a bundle of cards under my arm, and putting them in store windows. I saved many a show that way. It will be fun to do it again for you!"

"You mean that you yourself will go around to all the stores!"

"All ten of them," said Bill with a laugh. "And where else do people here congregate a lot?"

"In the saloons," said Father Paul a little sadly.

"Great! Great!" cried Bill. "It couldn't be better! I didn't think of that and I've spent half my life in bars. Where were my brains! We'll put these cards in all the saloons!"

"But the owners would never allow that!" gasped Father Paul.

"Listen," said Bill, "I never met a saloonkeeper yet that wasn't a sentimentalist, and I've met hundreds of them. Thousands! In every town in America. Coaltown can't be any different from the rest. We'll have our cards up right over the bars—cards with a picture of Saint Michael like the one in your office. That guy's not afraid of saloons! If the miners must go to the saloon before they go to bed, they can come to your Mass before they go to work in the morning. I'll have every bartender saying with each night-cap glass of beer—'Going to St. Michael's in the morning?' We got to make it the best attended early Mass in America! Father Paul's Mass for Miners! I'll see the head of their Union. We'll even put cards in that damn Breaker! I'll tack some myself on the outside of it! You and Saint Michael and I are on the loose, Father, and this town is going to know we are around!"

They sat awhile in silence, listening to the bells, and to the crickets and locusts that were chanting a chorus beneath the bells and the rumble of the Breaker farther down the street. Two men who felt a great comradeship of spirit. Two men who wanted only to accomplish good.

Perhaps there was a third one there, also, who determined to take a hand. Saint Michael the Fighting Archangel might have been sitting on those steps, his hands clasped about his steel shin-greaves, making plans. Who could say he was not?

*   *   *

Back in his room at the Wyoming Hotel, Bill Dunnigan placed two packages on his bureau which the clerk had handed him. One, plainly marked "Frank Brothers, New York," he knew contained a supply of the beloved spats. He could now stride the streets of Coaltown properly clothed—attend the early Mass the next morning in fitting style! But it was the note, inserted under the string which tied the other box, that made him stare. It was written on ruled paper torn from a tablet. It read:

Mr. Dunnigan, Sir:

I am the sister of Father Spinsky of St. Leo's. Today I made him a cake using six best eggs and a full cup of butter. My brother has insisted that I send half to Father Paul at St. Michael's and half to you. I am carrying out my brother's request.

Sincerely,
Mary Spinsky.

"I'll be damned!" said Bill Dunnigan. He had no knife and tried to unfasten the stout cord with which the box was tied. No use. Mary Spinsky was a firm woman and tied a firm knot. At last he managed to slip the cord over the sides. Removing the cover, there indeed was the superb missing half of Father Paul's cake in all the splendid magnificence of its six eggs, its cup of butter, its generous chocolate.

First his altar candles, then a cake made especially for Father Spinsky's enjoyment and sent (in the obvious opinion of its creator) to two less worthy palates. Father Paul had called it the acid test of unselfishness!

What had happened to Father Spinsky! Was it guile or repentance?

Sniffing and viewing again such a culinary masterpiece, Bill Dunnigan did not really care. From St. Leo's, deep-dyed schemes might be plodding afoot or high-born reformation might be soaring overhead! The important thing was to win over Mary Spinsky and her chocolate cake recipe! Perhaps this Saint Leo of Father Spinsky's was a regular guy also, and worthy a place in Quick Lunch Heaven! The St. Leo Chocolate Cake! Could his young boy friend think up a slogan around that name!

Since Father Paul had shared his half with him, Bill Dunnigan felt honor bound to do the same. He would carry the cake to the parish house the next day. But he felt a great longing for just another taste, and there was an experiment he wished to carry out. He had not yet seen the sober face of the Wyoming Hotel clerk relax into a smile. He had always felt very sorry for unsmiling people.

He walked to the speaking tube and pressed the button that connected that tube with the desk in the lobby.

"Can you leave your duties for a few minutes and come up to my room with a knife?" he said to the answering "Yes, sir."

"With a knife!" came the clerk's surprised voice. There seemed to be alarm in its tone.

"Yes, a knife," said Mr. Dunnigan grimly. "The largest, sharpest knife you have!"

"Is everything all right with you, sir?" came the voice.

"Everything will be quite all right—when you and your knife are here."

"I have no knife, sir, and the pantry is locked for the night. I have a pair of scissors."

"Is the blade a long one?"

"They are quite large scissors, sir."

"We will have to make them do. Come quickly."

By the time the clerk arrived Dunnigan had taken off his coat and donned his long dressing gown. He stood by the cake box like a high priest at the sacrificial altar.

The clerk knocked—then entered warily. He held a pair of formidable office shears in his hand, but did not immediately offer them to the guest of A-1.

"Well?" said Dunnigan sternly.

"Mr. Dunnigan," said the clerk, "I must ask you what you wish to do with these scissors at this hour of night."

"That is my business," said Bill Dunnigan.

"Undoubtedly, sir, but I feel that I must ask you."

"Why?"

"I have had two very unfortunate experiences with gentlemen guests who sent for knives, sir."

"Really! What experiences?"

"One of them—he wore a dressing gown not unlike yours, sir—wished to attempt suicide. He had been here a week and was a salesman for the *Encyclopaedia Britannica*."

"And the other case?" said Dunnigan.

"That was even worse, sir. The gentleman *asked for* scissors, so I had no inkling of criminal motives. You see, he had lowered his window blind and was not able to raise it before retiring. He seized the scissors—they were the same ones I now have brought—and jumping onto a chair and before I was able to prevent it, cut the linen of the blind straight across the top!"

Dunnigan regarded the bleak, austere individual before him.

"Tell me," he said, "have you ever smiled?"

"Why, yes, sir, I believe I have, sir," said the clerk doubtfully. He still held tightly to his cutting tool of tragic memories.

"Would you smile," asked Bill, "if I gave you a sight and taste of something that would penetrate your very gizzard with happiness!"

The clerk shuddered. "Why, I suppose I would, sir," he said.

"Very well. Give me your scissors. I promise you I shall not attack either myself or the window blind. I am about to cut you a slice of Paradise that will restore your youth!"

He motioned the clerk to look inside the box on his bureau.

And solemnly, using the largest blade of the scissors, he cut two small slices of the treasure within, and passed one to his guest.

"I'm sorry to be so stingy about the portions," said Dunnigan, "I'm obligated to save most of it for a friend of mine."

The clerk cautiously bit into the piece of gold and chocolate he held in his hand. He paused as its taste struck his palate. He swallowed the bite.

The reflection of a great inner struggle tensed the muscles of the countenance that always was conscious of its resemblance to the sedate physiognomy of our greatest mass-producer of automobiles.

"I'm afraid—I'm afraid I'll have to smile, sir," it said and did.

Even Mary Spinsky was spreading joy in Coaltown!

47

*B*ILL DUNNIGAN had gone to sleep with the strong conviction that it was now up to him to carry the ball. But it seemed that Saint Michael thought otherwise—Saint Michael and an Ally even more powerful, no less than the Blessed Virgin Mother herself! For that night was the night of the miracle.

Bill's thoughts had focused on the five forty-five Mass. Ideas about this Mass flocked to his mind as he passed into slumber. That Mass was Father Paul's unique idea. That Mass set his church apart from the others. Unless they also adopted it, there was no reason why it should not draw an "audience" from *all* the Coaltown parishes. "Father Paul's Mass for Miners"—all miners—before they started their dangerous work each day!

So reasoned the press agent, and he must try to "organize" this Mass. It had been laughed at, neglected! Father Spinsky even said it had brought discredit on the whole Church body! Very well, it must be made to be the most successful religious service in the town! The shining glory of the faith. The "stone that the builders rejected" that became a corner stone—there was a line like that in some play—a line out of the Bible. A service the fame of which would spread beyond the town!

The Miners' Union—that was it. Bill was a union man. His

trade of theatrical press agent had a very strong organization. He must find out the "powers" in the Coaltown workers' Union and talk to them as one union man to another. Father Paul had plans for bettering their working conditions, helping their home life. The only Coaltown cleric who ardently wished to do something for them. Let *them* help Father Paul! Make him the official Chaplain of the Union! Just like in a regiment. And there would be a certain number of the men who would attend the Mass each morning. Fifty—a hundred—to take turns representing their fellows. Once a month an attendance of seven or eight hundred to completely fill St. Michael's.

They would come, of course, in their work clothes, with dinner pails, wearing the caps with the electric lights at the front. On the day that they came in a body they would gather at headquarters and march to St. Michael's with these cap-lights burning. It would almost be as if they carried candles. The candles of the workers! What a sight in the half light of winter dawns! He could land that picture in every rotogravure newspaper section in America! Saint Michael's Miners! Father Paul's Miners!

And perhaps there would be some place in the Mass—in the church service—where they could hold these caps before them—over their hearts—and suddenly have all the little bulbs blaze out in answer to the altar lights. What Bill could do with *that* picture and *that* story!

Let Father Spinsky and his grand organ be a friend of the mine owners. Father Paul and Saint Michael would take on the workers and make a "production" Flo Ziegfeld or Charlie Dillingham would have been proud to have created!

Bill Dunnigan only hoped the attendance at this early Mass would not fall off before he could put some of his big ideas into working order. He hoped there would be more than a scattered few the next morning, that the two services of the day just passed had not exhausted the present Coaltown interest.

He need not have been fearful of that astounding morning.

*   *   *

We have noted that at each side of the altar rail of Father Paul's church were two statues. Along with the screen that formed the altar backing, these statues were the glory of that modest house of God. They stood inside the altar rail, were somewhat larger than life-size—were of heroic size, in fact—and almost too large for so small a church. They were very old, possibly dating back several hundred years, and beautifully carved from pure white marble. They had been brought from Poland thirty years before by one of the early Polish priests.

One statue was of Saint Michael and the other that of the Blessed Virgin and her Man-Child. Saint Michael was sculptured in full armor, his sword (which was of bronze) upraised, his foot on the head of the defeated Satan. On his face was the triumph of the conquering warrior. Across the way, the Blessed Mother held her Child in her arms and on her countenance was a gentle, elusive smile which made the stone Madonna seem almost flesh and blood.

Father Paul loved these statues. They seemed to him to typify two basic principles of his religion: the spirit of endeavor, the spirit of love. Both statues, being very heavy, were firmly attached to bases going down through the floor into the foundations of the building, and both were set squarely so that they looked straight out into the body of the church.

It was two of his altar boys arriving for the early Mass on this second morning who brought the startling news to Father Paul—bursting breathless and wide-eyed into his upstairs bedroom as the priest was donning his cassock to come for the service.

"The altar statues!" they both gasped at once, "Saint Michael and the Madonna!"

The priest misinterpreted the agitation in the faces of the lads for alarm. "No one has injured the statues!" he cried in considerable perturbation.

"No! No!" shouted one of the boys, and the other crossed himself.

"They are moved!" cried this lad, and the other broke in: "Yes, Father, they are moved! They are not like they have always been! Come and see!"

"What are you two trying to say?" asked Father Paul. "You mean someone has taken them! But that is impossible!"

"No! They are both there!" The boys were again speaking at once and their excitement was so intense that the priest broke in.

"One at a time!" he said. "You, Thomas, tell me just what you are both talking about."

The older boy again crossed himself fervently.

"Both statues have turned!" he cried.

"Turned?" repeated Father Paul. Again there was apprehension in his question.

"They do not look out into the church! They are looking toward the coffin of the dead girl!"

And the lads waited, open-mouthed, for the effect of this astonishing announcement.

Father Paul regained his calmness. His statues were not harmed. No fanatical vandal had mutilated them. As for their being "turned," they were firmly cemented to concrete pillars that ran down through the church basement and into the ground. Their great weight had made that necessary, and whoever had first placed them had taken care to see that there could be no danger of their toppling and the precious marble suffering injury.

Father Paul had long since tested the solidity of their attachment to the bases. It was one of the first inspections he had made on taking over the church three years before.

"I think you must be mistaken," he said quietly. "The bells and the unusual crowds in our church are making you imagine things."

"We are not the only ones who noticed it!" reiterated the older boy, and the other broke in:

"The janitor's brother, who came this morning to relieve him at the bell rope, saw it first!"

"The sexton has already opened the church doors for some who were waiting like yesterday, and a lot of people are inside!" continued the other lad. "They say it is a miracle! They are all on their knees in the aisles! For God's sake, come quick, Father!"

Fully dressed by now, Father Paul followed the excited altar boys.

"Come to the front door!" cried one of them as soon as they were outside. "You can see it plainly from the front part of the church!"

Father Paul permitted himself to be guided by the straining lads and paced after them. They went by the grass lawn down the parish house side of St. Michael's and entered by the open front doors. As they entered two excited women were dashing out.

"A miracle! Father! A blessed miracle!" one cried. And the other, "The dead girl must have been a holy child! I am going for my son to come and see!"

"Peace, my children, peace," said the priest. "There can be no miracle. Some foolish person has started this story and you must all be dreaming quite impossible things. Perhaps the early morning light through one of the windows——"

But he was addressing the morning air. The two women had rushed down the steps and one was talking excitedly to a group of miners passing the church on the way home from the Breaker night shift. The other woman was spreading the news along the roadway to all she met. Coaltown's Main Street was not empty at that hour of sunrise—there were men both coming and going to their work, and meals were being prepared behind every lighted kitchen window.

Such part of Coaltown as did not work at night arose at five for the day shifts.

By this time the altar boys had seized Father Paul's hand and dragged him through the wide doors. Like the two women, they could not comprehend his denial of a visible fact!

Father Paul stood still at the end of his center aisle and looked. There was no doubt about it! The two statues had turned ever so slightly, but enough so that the face of Saint Michael and the face of the Holy Mother were not directed straight ahead, but at an angle toward this center aisle, at the exact point where stood the coffin of Olga Treskovna! Saint Michael's triumph was for her alone. The compassionate smile of the Madonna rested on the dead girl.

"You see, Father!" said one lad in an awed whisper, and the other boy had knelt and was repeating, "A miracle! A miracle!"

But the emotion that swept Father Paul was neither awe nor reverence nor amazement. It was sheer alarm.

One of his greatest worries had been the slight but noticeable sinking of one side of the church foundations during the past year. It was, he knew, because of the mine shafts below. Houses in Coaltown had been known gradually to sink as much as several feet because of this network of excavation that burrowed beneath the whole town. Occasionally a building would collapse.

Father Paul had long ago consulted one of the mining company's foreman engineers who was a member of his parish, and had been assured that in the case of St. Michael's there was no real danger. The shafts at this particular spot were several thousand feet underground. It was only shafts nearer the surface that brought on sudden disaster.

Still, the matter had been a source of anxiety, for even if the undermining simply cracked a foundation side wall or an entrance step, it would mean money that was not at hand for repairs.

Father Paul turned quickly. His way down through the church aisles was already blocked by a hundred or more worshipers who had been waiting for the doors to open for the Mass and who were now, as the altar boys reported, kneeling on the church floor and either praying or gazing in rapt adoration at the holy statues. They were crowded toward the rear of the church as if fearful of approaching too closely this new wonder. So the priest rushed out as he had entered, brushing past a group of mine workers and women from the neighboring houses who were flocking into the church doors.

He hastened to the rear entrance door behind his altar. Ordering the altar boys, who had followed him, to wait in their room there, he descended alone to the basement of his church.

The priest switched on the cluster of three electric bulbs in its ceiling. There was also a certain amount of light from the shallow windows along the strip of foundation wall above ground. The room was bare except for a stored table, a broken pew, some paint cans and garden tools in one corner. The low ceiling was beamed with solid, unfinished rafters which supported the floor of the church above.

It was toward the two sturdy and square-built, brick-and-concrete pillars which disappeared through the ceiling to support his statues that Father Paul directed his attention. It was as he had thought. The pillars themselves were very slightly turned. There was a small crack and a rounded bulge in the concrete flooring near one of them which extended across toward the other pillar. Some shifting of the soil, beneath and at their base, had undoubtedly occurred.

There was nothing miraculous except that this shifting had caused both statues to look toward the center aisle and hence toward the coffin of Olga Treskovna!

The priest had been on both knees by one of the pillars to better examine the telltale crack and bulge in the floor. Thank God the pillars were solidly intact! He had inspected them on all sides on first lighting the room. The statues were not in danger! Father Paul sighed with relief. And he knew what he must do immediately. He must hasten up and explain all this as best he could to the people in the church above—and to those who were coming in. Stop at once this talk of miracles and Holy Child, this hysteria before it got out of hand!

"I must hurry!" he said aloud to himself, "Thank God I know what has happened!"

"Wait, Father!" said a voice beside him. "Father Paul, please let me have a word with you."

48

S *O FRAUGHT* with consequence was this interruption it might have been Saint Michael himself! It might have been some other Saint sent by Heaven, as the Voices were sent to Joan of Arc! It was neither of these.

It was a Broadway press agent in new, spotless white spats, and a black derby at a rakish angle, who stood beside the priest. It was, of course, Bill (White Spats) Dunnigan.

Bill had decided the night before to attend Father Paul's early Mass on this morning. He must get that Mass "under his belt" if he was to publicize it—make it the key factor of a campaign for St. Michael's. Also, he would be one more worshiper if there was to be any falling away of the patronage given it the day before. Maybe he could now sit through a service without a hankering to smoke! And he had not forgotten that his young friend of the Nanticoke Quick Lunch would be there with his girl, and that he was expected to meet the girl.

So guest William Dunnigan had left a call for four forty-five, A.M. and had experienced the questionable thrill of the Wyoming Hotel clerk's alarm system. And although, not entirely awake, he had taken at least four minutes to find either the light cord hanging from the center of the ceiling or the speaking tube by the door to silence the alarm, and despite the fact that getting up at the crack of dawn was not exactly his life habit, the press agent was far from being in an ill humor as he shaved and dressed.

The untiring bells were ringing on. Were their ringers and relief ringers as untiring? Bill made a mental note that he must visit all the bell towers and distribute some sort of bonus to these faithful, unseen collaborators. They were like the behind-the-scene stagehands of a theater production and quite as necessary! Then he must go to Wilkes-Barre or Scranton and get a blanket of roses made up for Olga Treskovna's coffin. Also, he had forgotten to speak to Father Paul about the concerts of Polish songs. They should be announced at the morning Mass. He must tell the reporters about it, some of whom were still there, having registered at the Wyoming Hotel, and perhaps he would himself telephone the near-by city newspapers.

His own press campaign was moving of its own momentum, since every inhabitant of Coaltown was eager and willing to talk exhaustively of the late Olga Trocki—"the Breaker Girl"—stage name Olga Treskovna.

Yes, all up to this moment was well and good. The jinx seemed to have departed with the Brooklyn bankbook. Best of all for his morale, six pairs of immaculate white spats lay on his bureau. "Dunnigan can't work properly without them!" Marcus Harris had commented in New York when he had instructed Miss Feinberg to see personally to their dispatch. They did make a confidence-restoring difference.

Just before descending to the lobby Bill looked from his front window. There seemed to be unusual activity on the street below, although it was barely daylight! Groups of miners were pausing, talking, pointing toward St. Michael's! Leaning out, he could see that people were already going into the church. This early Mass had surely caught on! But there was something in the air that seemed to go beyond a mere church service. There was a new, hushed excitement in the mingled voices that reached him from the street. Bill Dunnigan hastily put on his coat and hat and descended the hotel stairs.

His friend, the cake-loving clerk, called the news from his reception counter.

"I was just coming up to tell you," he said. "Something's happened at St. Michael's church. I first heard of it at five-fifteen and one quarter. There's a lot of fuss and hubbub on the street about their big statues. I don't take much stock in religious doings, but everyone is talking about some sort of miracle."

"A miracle!" exclaimed Dunnigan. Like Father Paul he felt a sudden chilling alarm. His anxiety was for the safety of the coffin of Olga Treskovna.

"I don't know what it's all about," said the clerk. "I called you exactly at four forty-five on the dot, sir. That chocolate cake of yours was certainly top-notch, sir—I found myself smiling again at three-ten A.M.——"

But Dunnigan had left this gentleman whose interest in miracles would only have been aroused had his electrically controlled clock suddenly stopped or gone berserk and whirled its hands in reverse around its dial! The press agent rushed to the street.

The rest of Coaltown was not hearing events with such indifference! A fuss and hubbub indeed! The first groups just beyond the door were speaking Polish and Dunnigan could not understand the words cried to him or whispered among themselves from excitement-loosed or awe-tightened lips. But a few yards farther along English words were being hurled from mouth to mouth.

"A miracle at St. Michael's!"

"The holy statues are looking toward the coffin!"

"The Trocki girl must also be a Saint!"

And a woman rushed past crying:

"I have seen a miracle! We should all be on our knees! Perhaps it is the end of the world!"

Two nights before Bill Dunnigan had observed on this same street the mounting interest and agitation caused by his bell ringing. Observed it with the calm and detached mind of the expert publicist that he was. It had been his life business to stir people up! He had simply accomplished it again. The means, not the results, were to him the novelty of that situation. He had never before rung church bells!

But now something was taking place that he certainly had not instigated, something beyond his calculation and control, that was spreading a tumult of emotion quite different from the curiosity, the animal excitement of the evening when the bells had started.

For the story of this "miracle" was sweeping like a prairie fire, and no holocaust of leaping flame could have more rapidly emptied the homes and filled the street with men and women and children.

The inhabitants of Coaltown were almost entirely Catholic. The Faith had been born in the marrow of their bones, for it had been bred there for generations. It might have hardened or become afflicted with a tuberculosis of indifference, but it was there. The Communion of Saints was real to them—the statues which represented the canonized Saints in their churches were not mere legends. They were potent and alive.

The inhabitants of Coaltown were predominantly Slavic—deeply emotional when really stirred.

And now, in all faces, was an agitation of something more than curiosity. It seemed to Dunnigan that these faces were like so many lamps whose fuel had nearly burnt out and now were suddenly supplied with new, lifegiving oil. In every voice was a tone of quivering elation. They would shout or whisper hoarsely to each other, then push on toward St. Michael's church.

Bill Dunnigan hastened forward at top speed. Though subconsciously sensing the tremendous news value of what had apparently occurred, he did not smile. His face was tense and grave. What was this turmoil doing to Father Paul? Did the priest even know of it yet?

Bill managed to reach the space in the street before St. Michael's, but there was no getting into the church. The crowd already filled the roadway and the steps leading up to the structure. He pushed his way through the miners, the housewives, and dashed up the narrow parish house steps and down the lawn to the side door of the church. The two altar boys were there and several others, dressed for the early Mass, and talking in low, tense whispers.

"Where is Father Paul?" cried Dunnigan.

"He is in the lower basement, but said no one must come down!" replied one of the boys.

"He says it is no miracle!" said one of the lads who had aroused the Father. "But I have seen it myself! The Holy Statues are turned!"

"I must find him!" gasped Dunnigan and plunged through the rear church door by which he and Father Paul had entered the evening before. There was a stairway leading downward to a lighted space and Bill took it two steps at a time.

A short passage and he was in the basement room. Father Paul was intent on his examination of the floor around one of the statue-supporting pillars. Bill Dunnigan's quick mind grasped the meaning of this inspection.

"You have heard?" said Father Paul when he recognized the voice at his side. And he gathered the skirts of his cassock and stood up from the floor of his basement.

Dunnigan said: "I have heard. I have not seen the statues. It is impossible now to get inside your church from the front. But I have seen the crowd outside and the people who are still gathering there. I know what they say has happened."

"It is extremely unfortunate that such a thing should occur at this time. It is terrible!" said Father Paul. Grim concern looked from his troubled eyes.

"Why?" asked Bill Dunnigan. "Why do you say this miracle is terrible?"

The press agent was by now acutely aware of the amazing possibilities of this astonishing event. Possibilities of an undreamed-of publicity for Olga Treskovna, for her film, "The Garden of the Soul," for the Church of St. Michael the Archangel, for Father Paul! It was so stupendous it was a little frightening. But how could it be terrible? How could it bring anything but good?

Father Paul was answering his blunt "Why?"

"There has been no miracle."

"But these people——"

"The people have become unduly excited by the ringing of the bells. In that, I had convinced myself, there was no harm. They needed, perhaps, to be stirred from their apathy toward the church. But that they should now believe that by some divine act our statues have turned their faces to look toward the coffin of a mortal who has died—that they should believe a sacred miracle has occurred——!"

The priest paused. There was acute distress in his face, but his lips were very firm.

"I feared that you were thinking that way," said Bill. "When I found you in this basement examining these pillars, I feared just that. What are you now going to do?"

"I am going to tell my people the truth," said Father Paul simply, and moved to leave the lower room.

"Wait, Father, please wait," repeated Bill Dunnigan.

And he placed his hands on the shoulders of the little priest, as he had placed them at the cemetery that first evening, only now their grasp was very gentle.

"My friend, my very dear friend," he said, "are you sure that you know what is the truth?"

"Certainly. My church is above mine shafts far under ground. There has been some slight movement of the soil—enough to tilt and turn these foundation pillars a fraction of a degree. So the statues also had to turn. You can see it plainly here."

And Father Paul knelt again on the floor and pointed out to Dunnigan the crevice there and the bulging concrete.

"Is it not a miracle that it should happen just at this time—and to both statues?"

"A coincidence. Not a miracle."

"Even if you so believe, must you make this physical fact known? I know you are the soul of honesty, Father, but——"

Father Paul placed his hand on the arm of his friend. "It is not a question of my personal honesty. The Catholic hierarchy instructs us to give no recognition to so-called miraculous happenings, unless they are so proven by long and exhaustive investigation. I needed no investigation. I knew the cause at once. I must not remain silent."

Once more Bill Dunnigan was fighting for his chance, but this time it was free of self-interest. It was for St. Michael's, for Olga Treskovna, for Father Paul himself! And it was motivated by another burning urge. He did not agree with Father Paul about the miracle!

"Before you speak to them, Father, may I tell you of a play I once worked for?" he asked.

"Tell of it quickly then, for my Mass is almost due and I must first address the people and end this foolish and dangerous hysteria."

Bill Dunnigan spoke rapidly:

"The play was called 'False Gods' and was by some famous French writer. I never could pronounce his name! It was set in ancient Egypt, and about a young priest of their religion, who realized that the river Nile was not sacred; that the animals—the jackal and the bull—were not sacred; and being honest—and very young—he wanted to tell his people what he called 'the truth.'

"And there was a scene with an old, very wise priest, to whom the young student rushed with what he thought were his momentous discoveries. And the old priest said: 'You are telling me nothing we older priests have not known for centuries, if we chose to look at it that way. But it is best the people believe the Nile is sacred or they would pollute it, and we would have disease. It is best the people believe the jackal sacred, for he is our best scavenger. He must not be exterminated. The herds of Egypt must be multiplied, therefore our bulls must be held inviolate and not killed.' "

"But what has that to do with this so-called miracle?" asked Father Paul.

"I am coming to that," replied Bill. "This young priest also thought he had discovered that we do not live again in this mortal body—that careful embalming for a future life was all a fraud. And in spite of the older priest he insisted on preaching his 'discoveries.' Did he help his people with his 'truth'? He destroyed their faith—their hope of meeting loved ones after death. He took away their only real hope of happiness. They finally killed him."

"I do not think I will be killed by my parishioners if I tell them the truth about this turning of our statues," said Father Paul with a little smile.

"But they will not thank you," said Bill. "I do not think they will even believe you! And if they do believe you, you will have killed something in them."

"The miracles of the scriptures, of later centuries even, were a need of their times. Faith, now, is a matter of the inner mind, the inner heart. It is born in us. We need no outer signs."

"Don't we?" asked Bill Dunnigan and he held the priest with the sharp sincerity of his voice. "Are you quite certain of that, Father Paul?"

"What do you mean?" said Father Paul. The pulsing earnestness of Bill Dunnigan could not be brushed aside. Compared with that earnestness, his own argument sounded like something in a printed book.

"I mean this," said the press agent, "I found this town a deadly place; except for you, Father, filled with selfish, cruel people—either that or people with lead in their hearts and glue in their minds and souls. Their eyes did not see. They were a hundred times more blind than your blind organist! The faces that passed me on the street that first evening—dull, without hope, without joy. There was a change yesterday. The bells did that. If not joy, there was at least an awakening interest—something besides just to struggle for money, then eat, drink, breed, sleep! And as I rushed here this morning there is another change—a hope, a glow, a living flame in the faces—in the eyes turning toward St. Michael's!

"Go up and look at the people now in your church—at the crowd standing outside! There are hundreds there! The whole town is there by now. Some through mere curiosity, I realize; some are there who will scoff; but most of these men and women have literally been born again. That is the church phrase for it, isn't it, Father? For the first time since they were born, they live! They see! I don't know about your religion, but I would say that many of them have this morning found a new faith in it. A new belief! I would not hastily destroy that new faith, Father, if I were you."

"But they are saying the dead girl—your friend—must be a holy child—even a Saint!"

"Who knows?" said Bill. "Perhaps she was! Are you to judge of that—or I? As I told you, I did not really know her so very well, Father. But I can tell you this—she did nothing in her short life that would bar her from saintliness. She lived clean. She was kind. She was loyal. She was humble. She only wanted desperately to give the world some beauty—some happiness. She was not bitter and yet she had received from the world only ugly things—poverty, loneliness, frustration. Maybe it was meant that with death she could give what she was not able to give as a living mortal. There is the makings of saintliness in all that, is there not?"

"Who really are you?" said Father Paul, and he looked at Bill Dunnigan as if he had never seen him before. "Are you sincere in what you are telling me?"

Bill Dunnigan reached for a cigar. In so doing he realized the incongruity of his situation. Here was he, a man of no religious knowledge or belief, trying to expound faith to a man of God! But his inner convictions about what had happened were very clear, were very real. He continued to speak. He did not light his cigar. He held it tightly between his fingers. The presence of this very material link with his everyday life seemed to make even more *real* these events that bordered on the supernatural.

"I am what is known as a theatrical press agent," he said to the priest. "I am myself that man I told you that I knew. I had no religion. I have none yet, I suppose. I came here with a simple purpose; to bury my friend as she wished. I confess that purpose changed when I stood with you in your cemetery and heard your

Angelus; when I started these funeral bells with the idea of attracting attention to a motion picture this girl had just finished making.

"But even then, Father, it wasn't entirely a selfish idea. Yes, I did want back a job I'd lost. I did want to put over, as we say, my big stunt. But at the same time I wanted to do something for this girl; to make her great work, which was going to die with her, live. And I had met you, Father, and knew you, and wanted honestly to do something for you and for your church and your Saint Michael. I took a great fancy to that guy! I seemed to know him right off. I became your pal—and his, I hope.

"Well, we rang the bells. The crowds came. The reporters came and the newspapers fell for it. I stopped worrying about that motion picture. I began to worry about your church. What could I do for it? You were worrying also. Would the success of your Masses last? Now we've been given a break I never could have imagined in my wildest press-agent dreams! Would we have gotten that break if my motives were entirely selfish and bad? This 'miracle'—and who knows but that it *is* a miracle—will flash across the continent! It will be mentioned in newspapers tomorrow from London to Shanghai. It will leap across oceans. As a vendor of news stories I know that. It has already started. Neither you nor I can stop this story—if we call it a 'story.'

"But is it just a story? Think, Father. The other churches have mine shafts beneath them. Did their statues ever turn? Your church has been over mine shafts for years. Did its statues turn before? Don't destroy what can hurt no one—what can only bring new hope to a world that needs a lot of it!"

"But the skeptical; those who will not believe? Those who may even cry fraud?"

"Let them not believe! At least, in the face of this, they cannot remain indifferent. Indifference is death. I want your Saint Michael to live. I want you and your little church to live. I want that now, just as much as I ever wanted the film play this girl made in Hollywood to live. So let some shout, 'There is no miracle!' We, who know, can answer that."

"We who know?" said Father Paul.

"I'll tell you one thing more, Father. I did not mean to ever tell you. When I bargained to have the bells rung for four days I took a desperate chance. I had no money to pay for them. I did not know if I could get the money. I sent a telegram about it after the bells had started. Sent it with my last dollar. And I prayed, Father. Not to God. I don't think God ever heard of me. I prayed to your Saint Michael. For I'd met *him*. Met him through you. And as I stand in this room, I believe Saint Michael helped me get that money!

"So, as true as I stand here, *I* believe there *has been* a miracle. I told you last night there were five of us. You and I, the girl and Saint Michael—and a man you don't know yet. I believe Olga Treskovna has not died, though some part of her is in that coffin above us in your church. I believe Saint Michael, *our pal* Saint Michael, turned those statues, though you show me a thousand cracks in your basement floor! Are you still worried about the success of your Masses? Saint Michael has knocked that worry in the head! It's out for the count of ten! Good God! What you and I can now do for him, and for your church! Are we going to let Saint Michael down? Not carry on from here!"

Bill Dunnigan placed his cigar between strong teeth. He bit into its end. He spat out that end. He produced a match and struck it vigorously on the pillar that supported the statue of the fighting Saint in the church above him. He would have struck that match on the very side of God's throne, had he been defending a deed of Saint Michael's to the Great Commander.

And through the smoke clouds, Father Paul stared into the eyes of this man from another world. The man was sincere. The man was honest. In plain words he had told what the priest had suspected, not concealing selfish motives. This stranger to the Church saw the cracks in the floor, he had heard the explanation, and yet, *he believed!* And even if he, the ordained priest, could not believe that a miracle had taken place, was some great good to spring from all of it!

"I do not know—I truly do not know what I should do!" said the duty-torn pastor of St. Michael's flock.

"Wait at least till you have seen your people, wait till after your Mass," said Bill Dunnigan.

"I must wait now," said Father Paul, "for I am already late in starting it."

49

THAT SECOND morning's early Mass at St. Michael's—the second since the arrival of Bill (White Spats) Dunnigan, and destined to become known as the "Mass of the Miracle"—was held in an atmosphere charged with dynamic expectancy.

When the agitated Father Paul at last entered the sanctuary before his altar, one could feel the straining tension as well as hear the "Oh-h" of the intake of breath from worshipers jammed into every niche of the building. They had even found their way to the choir loft which reminded Dunnigan of a sort of first balcony.

The press agent stood in a doorway leading into the sanctuary. He could see but was not seen. He was in the wings, as it were, of the stage of this consecrated theater. But no mere theater ever held an audience so vibrating with hushed fervency.

And this tense excitation extended through its walls and out of the open doors, onto the lawn about the building; onto the steps and the street before it. That street was completely blocked for yards in each direction. All Coaltown had now heard, and had risen and come to marvel. During the past hour, even the bells had seemed to cry, "A Miracle! A Miracle!"

Over it all was the seemingly endless tolling of the bells.

And this great crowd somehow knew the instant the little priest entered the sanctuary, as Christ whom he represented, entered the Garden of Olives; stood at the foot of the altar; and made the sign of the cross; for those outside as well as in, crossed themselves, and many knelt, even in the roadway, as the words of Holy Mass began:

"In the name of the Father, and of the Son, and of the Holy Ghost. Amen."

Father Paul's voice was gentle but its timbre was resonant. And though he had forced a calmness as he faced the altar and commenced the Mass, though he had said to himself, "I will go on as if nothing had happened," he could not help but feel the surge of that new lifeblood in the throng behind him. Even though it was inarticulate, he felt it billowing up and rising around him, crying, "The Mass is real! Faith is real! God is real!"

And when, after reading Psalm 42, "Why art thou cast down, O my soul? and why art thou disquieted within me? Hope thou in God, who is the health and strength of thy countenance," he came to that part of the litany where the people could respond, then, indeed, he knew one could not lightly decide to say, "There is no miracle! Go back and be as you were!" For the responses came with an intensity no church in Coaltown had ever known before:

"Lord, have mercy on us! Lord, have mercy on us! Lamb of God, who takest away the sins of the world, grant us peace!"

And at the very end, after the sacrifice, when he prayed for first the intercession of the immaculate Virgin, and then that of Saint Michael—"Holy Michael, Archangel, defend us in the day of battle; be our safeguard against the wickedness and snares of the devil; do thou, O Prince of the Heavenly Host, cast into hell Satan and all his wicked spirits who wandered about the world seeking the destruction of souls," the *"Prince of the Heavenly Host, defend us!"* that came back to him was so vividly intense, he also felt that the fighting Warrior himself might have descended from Heaven and could even be at hand—there—in his very church!

Music had heightened the beauty of the service, had helped to stir the sensibilities of the worshipers. The blind organist was at her post and played as she had never played before.

Dunnigan had not understood any of the words repeated. They were chanted in Polish. But one need not know exact words to understand the deep passion of that audience. And he felt a humble pride that he had been some small part of this greater miracle—a flaming pride that his Olga Treskovna had brought it all about.

"Gee, kid!" he said, and he was unconsciously speaking to the girl, "maybe you've done something bigger even than 'The Garden of the Soul'!"

She was there by him before he finished the words, watching the closing of the service from the door into the sanctuary. Perhaps she had stood there since its beginning. She looked as she had appeared the afternoon before out on the church steps. The light from an altar candle was caught and reflected in her hair. It seemed to Bill it made a little halo about that hair.

"I'm afraid, Bill!" she whispered. "I'm not the cause of any miracles! I'm just Olga Trocki! I just wanted to bring a little happiness, a little joy. Not all this! This frightens me!"

"Hush! Hush!" said Dunnigan. "Just let me handle it, kid. Didn't you always believe in your star! And when you're shooting at a star, you shoot high, kid!"

"I'm glad I've got you, Bill," she said. "I don't know what I'd do without you!"

"You've got Father Paul—you've got Saint Michael—you've got Marcus Harris," said Bill Dunnigan. "One for all and all for one. You'll not fail us, kid, anymore than we'd fall down on you."

"All right, Bill. Just as you say. I leave it all to you. I'm going up to the cemetery. There's some goldenrod along the fence. (Dunnigan thought, *Again she's doing something she loved to do.*) I think I'll put some on pop's grave. Pop liked goldenrod, only he didn't call it 'God's prayer.' That was just my idea in the poem I wrote. Pop called it 'Devil's laughter.' Pop laughed at everything. He'd laugh now if he saw all this because of me."

"He'd be proud, too—down in his heart," said Dunnigan.

"That's the *Agnus Dei* the organist is playing now. It means the Mass is nearly over. I know the name of that music because pop can play it, too, on his accordion. Pop plays it beautifully. I'll be up at the cemetery if you need me—over by the fence where the goldenrod grows. I want pop to have the first goldenrod! Good-by —good-by!"

Bill Dunnigan wanted to follow her out of the doorway, but Father Paul had moved to the front of his altar rail and was directing words toward the coffin of Olga Treskovna. Was he speaking on the subject of the miracle? Was he denying that there was a miracle? Was he explaining the turning of the statues?

The Polish words brought no meaning to the ears of the press agent, but the worshipers had all knelt, and that atmosphere that always reflects and radiates the fused emotions of a great gathering was one of quiet and acquiescence. Dunnigan breathed more freely. Whatever he was saying, Father Paul was making no denial.

The priest was simply intoning a prayer for the repose of the soul, an old and beautiful prayer that he had once translated from the Latin into Polish.

Come to her bier, ye Saints of God!
Meet her, ye Angels of the Lord.
Receive her soul and present it to the most high God.
Let perpetual light shine upon her.

And having repeated this prayer, Father Paul moved again to his altar, wrapped his vestment about the covered chalice and other articles used in the sacrifice, and made his exit from the sanctuary as the organist played a lovely *toccata* of Bach.

In the passageway he paused a moment before the questioning eyes of William Dunnigan.

"I have said nothing, God help me," he spoke to his waiting friend, "but I am sorely troubled. I do not know if I have committed a very great sin or conferred a greater blessing. I wanted to bring just a little happiness, a little joy. Not all this. This frightens me."

Dunnigan was startled. They were the exact words of Olga Treskovna.

But he could not say to Father Paul. "Hush! hush! Just let me handle it, kid!" Nevertheless, he felt that it would be handled. He felt that behind this simple man of God was gathering an army with banners flying and swords flashing. And though this army wore the armor of a thousand Saint Michaels and carried shields of shining bronze, their helmets were miners' caps with the light-fixtures at the front, and there were tin lunch pails at their belts.

"I am going to my room to pray for guidance," continued Father Paul. He replaced the chalice in a cabinet, then moved, as Olga Treskovna had moved, into the open yard between the church and the parish house.

The priest could not, however, remain entirely silent; could not escape, on the few yards across his lawn, the questions of those crowded there—the questions of the half-dozen newspapermen who had remained all night in Coaltown and were already on the scene. The townspeople parted respectfully to make a path for him, but the reporters pressed forward and were not silent.

"Is it true a miracle has occurred?"

"Are both statues turned toward the coffin of the girl?"

"If this has happened, what does it mean?"

"Do you believe this dead actress to be some sort of saint, as your people are saying?"

And again the troubled Father Paul was on the point of speaking out the "truth," of telling the newsmen about the mine shafts and the "reason" for the turning of the statues. He imagined that he discerned in some of their voices a cynical challenge—a feeling on their part that he would break into some sanctimonious pronouncements of divine grace and show of power. How conclusively he could answer them, how surprised they would be if he flung back their questions with a brutal, matter-of-fact explanation.

But as he opened his mouth to speak he saw over their shoulders the eager, passionate faces of his parishioners, *his* people. What of them? They would not have torn him apart as happened to the student in William Dunnigan's Egyptian play, had he so spoken, but those faces would have changed to something akin to horror— they would have thought his words a dreadful sacrilege—thought him a Judas to his faith, a denier of the power of the God he preached, and in whom he asked them daily to believe. Along with this, a dreadful doubt of all faith might enter their hearts!

He replied to the interrogations of the newsmen: "The statues are turned. They are far too heavy and too solidly implanted to have been turned by human hands. As for the why, the wherefore, I do not know the meanings. Nor does any man. The matter will be investigated. Then only can we say. The Church does not recognize any so-called miracle without such an investigation."

Thus spoke Father Paul in a low, even voice that he hoped concealed the turmoil of his soul.

Just before entering his parish house he paused and looked out at the great throng that covered his grass plot—his flower bed too, alas —and beyond to the sea of faces in the sunken roadway and across the street. Though his Mass was over, they were making no movement to leave; there was instead a pressing toward the church from whose doors some of those who had been inside were coming out. And in all faces, in the movement of their shoulders even, was the reflection of the living flame that was newly burning within them, the flame that Dunnigan had noted.

St. Michael's was not just a building with a cross at its top—it was a symbol of God's presence on this earth—a shelter of Something God Himself had reached down and touched.

Could a whole believing town be told: "The day of miracles is over! We need no outer signs. I, your priest, tell you so. I, Father Paul, pastor of this church, do not believe!"

Just what, indeed, did he believe?

~~~~~~~~~~~~~~~~~~~~~~~~~~~~~~~~~~~ *50* ~~~~~~

*F*ATHER PAUL might doubt and hesitate; the church authorities might—or might not—in months to come, debate and argue and listen to evidence; but the people of Coaltown made a decision then and there. And it was the people of Coaltown who answered the telephone calls from near-by towns and talked now to reporters and radio announcers; the people who, if they were not in the street before St. Michael's pressing to gain admission, were gathered on every corner and porch and doorstep, and in every store and saloon.

Coaltown had no police force equal to regulating such an unusual throng. It did possess two uniformed officers of the law who spent most of their time in Orloff's poolroom. Their duties consisted mainly of stopping an occasional brawl in the saloons, or seeing that a car with a blowout did not block the roadway. These officers had appeared at about the time the Mass was finished, but stood gaping and wondering with the rest of the inhabitants. They had been busier than usual since the bells had started, seeing that alien cars were not parked so as to obstruct the "traffic" on Main Street. That was within their organizing ability. But such an outpouring as had now occurred was beyond their capability. Besides, it was no business of theirs to interfere with "miracles."

Coaltown was under the jurisdiction of the County. In the town, itself, there was a "Squire," duly elected, who, two days of each week and more often if necessary, held a sort of court in the "law office" he maintained in the front room of his Main Street dwelling. He notarized documents, settled small disputes. Any larger matter went to the County Court in Wilkes-Barre.

The maintenance of order, the enforcement of the law (if that were necessary), was in the hands of the State Police. State Troopers they were called. Their headquarters was the Wyoming Barracks just across the river from Wilkes-Barre. Originally a mounted service, some hundred and fifty of them now patrolled the countryside in less romantic but more efficient motorcars or on puffing motorcycles. Their routine task was to enforce the speed laws for other vehicles.

Dunnigan had noticed one of these black and white cars, with the large block-lettered S P painted on its rear, cruising through the street the first night of the ringing of the bells. He had seen one of its uniformed men in the gathering that had listened to his oration in the parlor of the Wyoming Hotel. His own driver, on that return dash from Nanticoke the noon before, had slowed down when one was seen approaching over the hills. As the driver had mentioned, the forty-mile speed limit was rigidly enforced.

Standing outside the rear door of St. Michael's and just as Father Paul disappeared into the parish house, the press agent again saw one of the Troopers approaching. He was on foot. His car had been left half a block up the street, since it was impossible to drive through the densely-packed inhabitants.

~~~~~~ *5 I* ~~~~~~

*H*ANDSOME AND NEWLY promoted Sergeant Dennis Patrick O'Rourke, Pennsylvania State Police, viewed the world as a rule with equanimity, content, and a lofty and condescending good nature. He viewed it mostly from behind the wheel of his speedy coupé, but when he dismounted from this modern chariot, he was conscious that he made a dashing figure in his natty grey uniform with black leather puttees and service hat whose wide brim was smartly turned up and tacked on one side, and had a black strap below the chin.

He had health, youth, authority, more than his share of good looks. What else could a young Irish-American desire?

Bad weather had no effect on him. There was a song in his heart when the rain poured so that the car slid dangerously on the asphalt of the turnpikes or ploughed through the mud of back roads. He did not swear when he had to change a tire in the burning sun. At twenty-two he had achieved the goal of his ambitions.

He was not, however, an entirely perfect character. He had three pet and petulant hates. He expressed an intensely bitter allergy to the presence of Protestants, Republicans and "millionaires."

The first two dislikes had been forced upon him as a small boy. He had had the misfortune to be the son in the family of the only Catholic-Democrat in a small town of Dutch Reformed-Republican worship.

Religious and political tolerance had no place in the code of the youth of that particular Pennsylvania settlement, though their fore-bears had come to America to find these qualities. Young Dennis O'Rourke was either bullied or snubbed. His bricklayer father was Irish, Catholic, Democrat. Spawn of the devil himself! The small lad would have been better treated had he been a Negro or a Chinaman. But a Catholic! The family moved to cosmopolitan (and largely Catholic) Nanticoke when the boy was ten, but the damage had been done. The impressions of childhood are in-delible, particularly the injustices.

The dislike of "millionaires" came later and was of his own devising. Not entirely perhaps, for his "old man" had spent con-siderable energy and time (in carpet slippers or bare feet and an easy chair while his wife did washing) cursing out the "pluticrats" who had combined to keep a good man down. And when young Dennis and his sister were through grade school and old enough to go to work, this gentleman had given up the one-sided struggle en-tirely.

O'Rourke senior could now devote his full time—about equally divided between the corner saloon and his home—to discussing the state of the nation under a tyranny of wealth.

Dennis gradually came to realize that a basic aversion to hard work had perhaps a little something to do with his parent's failure in the economic battle, but the hatred of "millionaires" had also taken root. Not that he knew any, but a succession of employers, representing to his mind the embodiment of intrenched plutocracy, said employers believing firmly in small wages and long hours, had a cumulative effect.

At fifteen he resented still pushing a handcart to deliver meats after seven P.M. (having started the pushing at six-thirty A.M.) while the boss quit at five and often passed him with his family, pleasure driving, in a glossy, gasoline-propelled Buick. Under those circumstances you might sing "Sweet Rosie O'Grady" at six-thirty with the sunrise, but by sunset its melody somehow stuck in your throat. The young man's salary was then twelve dollars weekly. At seventeen he did not see the social justice in sixteen hours a day for a stipend of fifteen dollars weekly as a helper on a delivery truck for the local "department store," the owner of which was building the new twenty-room mansion that was to be one of the show places of the town.

But since his work was outside and gave him a chance to take deep breaths and view the changing scene, the long hours and small pay could not sour him on the joy of living. Being alive was grand! He simply acquired, on his own, a hearty hatred for capitalistic employers.

He stuck to this department-store job because he was learning *to drive* the truck. That gave him a tremendous "kick," even if he were still working at it long after sundown. He liked the feeling that he controlled all the power of that truck. He was, in fact, soon promoted to be a driver at eighteen dollars. And this money, besides helping out at home, was putting his sister through a night-school business course. He was fond of that sister.

Young O'Rourke did not envy these "millionaire" employers. He didn't want to be one, God knew! He wouldn't have sat behind a desk in an office, during the best hours of the day, for all the meat markets and department stores in the state! He just wanted an active, outdoor life at such remuneration for services that he could live and help his mother, and at the same time not feel he was a wage slave (as his old man put it) of some grasping, mansion-building employer. And if, along with this, there could be some authority, some control of power——

At nineteen it suddenly dawned on him what should be his life work. It was right under his nose! He had been observing it for two years and had not realized! The black and white cars had speeded by his delivery truck which took him to outlying towns as well as purely urban districts—day after day. In these cars rode Freedom, Security, Authority—and a blessed chance to put some of these "millionaires" in their places! For he had observed tickets being handed out to owners of expensive motors, who in their arrogance often forgot that they also were subject to laws about the number of miles an hour you should cover, and the crossing of white lines on state roads.

He would become a State Trooper.

He made the acquaintance of some of them and learned the requirements. You had to be twenty-one years old. Well, that age of maturity was only two years off. No hardship to wait two short years to commence a lifetime of bliss. The wages started at sixteen hundred dollars a year. Very satisfactory! You had to pass certain examinations. He wrote to Harrisburg and obtained the papers setting forth the subject matter of these examinations. And he spent his spare time for the next two years "getting up" (with his sister's help) in these subjects.

The day after he was twenty-one he went to Wilkes-Barre and took this examination. He passed, as they say, with flying colors.

It was also necessary to have a character recommendation from three persons of standing. And it was here that young Dennis had his first eye-to-eye brush with intrenched capital. This brush solidly confirmed the truth and justice of his prejudice.

The priest of his parish church in Nanticoke readily gave him a letter. Dennis Patrick O'Rourke was a clean-living, hard-working boy, who attended Mass every Sunday. The owner of the saloon of which his "old man" was a steady patron (said owner being a power in local politics) gave him another. While young Dennis was not personally a source of revenue, an occasional glass of beer being his only alcoholic requirement, this owner knew that O'Rourke senior obtained his more generous liquor budget from the wages of the boy.

Dennis applied to the owner of the department store for his third recommendation.

He picked out a bad morning. The mansion-building merchant had had an argumentative discussion the afternoon before with a member of the State Police over a small matter of parking. Even the belligerence of "didn't the officer know who he was talking to" and the disclosure of his exalted name had no effect. The officer's exact reply had been: "I don't care if you are Bucky Walters or Bing Crosby himself!" Contempt for greatness could not be more conclusively expressed!

So, in that store owner's wallet burned a small ticket, requiring his presence at a county courthouse a week hence. Since it was his fifth or sixth offence, the matter might be serious. His daughter, also, had received a ticket two days before, because of speeding in her personal Lincoln Zephyr. That ticket likewise rested uneasily on his mind and in his wallet.

The innocent request on the part of truck driver number eight, the same being Dennis Patrick O'Rourke, for a recommendation to join the State Troopers, met with not only an explosive refusal but a profane tirade against that most estimable branch of the State of Pennsylvania's law enforcement. Dennis had to procure his certificate from his immediate boss, who, with a modest Chevrolet, was not addicted to traffic violations.

Naturally, this interview with the department store owner did not add to the young man's love of the wealthy classes.

One more detail. This Nanticoke merchant wore spats. He wore them not (as did Bill Dunnigan) for vain adornment, but to keep his ankles warm in cool weather. Dennis noticed these spats, for their wearer in his excitement came out from the sheltered recesses of the executive desk and paced the deep-carpeted floor. Watching those inexorable spats stride back and forth, Dennis had momentarily thought his life dream was going to be trampled to bits into that carpet under their ruthless tread. Their hard-cut lines, their unyielding stiffness, their glaring pearl buttons made a lasting impression. He had never before noticed a man wearing spats. Perhaps all millionaires affected them! Spats became sure insignia of arrogant wealth in its most detestable, tyrannic guise!

He passed his examination, went through a period of training which doubtless included a swift execution in filling in a "speeding ticket" against the side of a car, and was soon admitted to full, law-enforcing fellowship in the service of the state founded by William Penn. And when he presently was placed, first on a motorcycle and then, more recently, as a sergeant in a natty car with a companion, to patrol a specified route each day, no member of the force was more enthusiastically diligent in his duties.

He was not entirely heartless to road-law offenders. If the car were humble, if its driver were obviously a working man, he got off with a warning. But let a pleasure-driving, high-powered, custom-bodied motor in the hands of some individual of obvious means, male or female, break even a small fraction of the rules, that male-

factor's doom was sealed! The ones who tried to "fix" matters by
a display of their wealth (a five or a ten or even a twenty-dollar
bill!) found "attempted bribery" added to the violations on their
ticket.

An occasional wearer of spats who broke the road regulations
might even find himself charged with highway robbery and attempted murder!

— — — — — — — — — — — — — — — — *52* — — —

S UCH WAS the background of the particular
Pennsylvania State Trooper who was now approaching Bill (White
Spats) Dunnigan. It should, perhaps, also be mentioned that during the past year Sergeant O'Rourke had acquired still another
cause of grudge against "capital." His sister had met and become
engaged to a nice Catholic-Polish boy who wanted to start his own
business, and was prevented therefrom by lack of any co-operation
or understanding on the part of this same ogre—Capital.

On this particular morning, Sergeant O'Rourke was perhaps not
in his usual perfect rapprochement with life in general and his
job in particular. He did not sing "Sweet Rosie O'Grady" as he
started out. He had been aroused from his bed at the barracks a
full hour earlier than usual. There had been a telephone call from
the "Squire" in the settlement of Coaltown that there was some
sort of unusual excitement going on—crowds were gathering—a
police car had best be sent.

Sergeant O'Rourke was selected from the hundred or so men
then at the barracks, for Coaltown had been his route that week.
He was familiar with that town's unusual funeral doings of which
the papers had been full—he had in fact reported them the night of
the starting of the bells. But since they concerned a happening in
the churches—denomination mostly Catholic—and there was apparently no law violation and no complaints from citizens of the
town, the report had been routine.

He had stood (as Dunnigan had noticed) with the crowd in the
Wyoming Hotel and listened to the speech the press agent then

made for the benefit of the newspapers and the radio. He alone had not been moved by it. The career of Olga Treskovna, Coaltown's "Breaker Girl," meant nothing to him. Only when this wealthy city man had spouted about "America being the land of equal chances for success" had he become mildly interested. Interested to the extent of a sarcastic smile. Another millionaire shooting off his mouth. His comment as he left the place had been brief but conclusive. One word—*Boloney!* But the man was violating no traffic or other regulation if he chose to preach a lot of bunk in the hotel where he was stopping. He felt sorry for the gullibles who believed it. He, Sergeant Dennis Patrick O'Rourke, knew better.

He had driven through Coaltown several times the following day. The people were orderly. The line going into St. Michael's was orderly. There were no complaints regarding the noise of the church bells. Why should there have been by any Coaltown native when it was bringing extra business to every store and saloon, and creating an atmosphere of pleasurable and welcome diversion?

He had checked with the town's undertaker and the burial papers were in order. Asking about this alien millionaire in charge, he had been told by Mr. Orloff that the man was both very wealthy and very stingy. The usual combination, thought Sergeant O'Rourke. Being wealthy and stingy was as yet, unhappily, no crime!

But arriving at Coaltown this second morning at six forty-five, and without his usual satisfying breakfast under his wide, revolver-supporting, military belt, Sergeant O'Rourke found a different situation.

The State's thoroughfare was completely blocked. A violation of rule 261 that all public highways should be kept open and free at all time for traffic. Even the sight of a police car failed to move the solid mass of people. Still it was happening in front of a Catholic church. The Catholic Church could do no wrong. And the cause of this blocking was said to be a *miracle*. There was nothing in the rulebook about what to do in the event of a miracle.

Leaving the police car in charge of his companion Trooper, he pushed his way through the throng to the church. He would speak to the priest in charge and if everything was O. K., make some arrangement about regulating the people and keeping the roadway clear.

Instead of a priest (Father Paul having gone into his parish house, as we know), he came face to face with William Dunnigan.

And it flashed into the Sergeant's mind that the massed people— the blocking of the street—was this "millionaire's" doing! Perhaps there was no miracle at all. This man had devised something, O'Rourke did not know quite what, to attract further attention to himself. Perhaps he wanted to gather a crowd to make another speech about the "equality of opportunity." Wealthy and stingy and arrogant, also!

The rules required that you approach citizens politely and give an offender, even the most obnoxious ones, a chance to explain. So Sergeant O'Rourke planted himself in the path of William Dunnigan and started the conversation with the mild:

"So it's you again! What's going on here!"

"Again? I don't quite get you, officer!" repeated the amazed Mr. Dunnigan. His relationship with the police, the police of dozens of cities, wherever there were theaters or wherever the great Circus had shown, had always been cordial. But the tone of the question directed at him by this young Pennsylvania officer implied some previous entanglement with the law in these parts—of a magnitude no less than rape or arson!

It had occurred to Dunnigan during the Mass that he should communicate with the proper authorities for handling crowds, so that Father Paul and St. Michael's—Olga Treskovna's coffin also— would have protection. There might be a great influx of strangers. It never crossed his mind that the authorities would do other than co-operate about a matter connected with a funeral service. Especially as the crowds drawn by this miraculous happening in St. Michael's were an entirely unforeseen emergency.

"I listened to you spout night before last at the hotel down the street," answered Sergeant O'Rourke. He stood, feet apart, hands on hips, eyeing at close range this representative of a hateful class.

Dunnigan knew nothing of Sergeant O'Rourke's peculiar dislike for "millionaires." And even if he had known, he was certainly not at that moment thinking of himself as a possessor of great wealth! He was a press agent, elated over a gift from Heaven that would sweep across the country; worried about what his friend Father Paul would decide to do.

The verb "spout" gave him the only clue to this unexpected

antagonism on the part of the good-looking State Trooper before him. "Spout" was not exactly a term of enthusiastic approbation, especially when projected by sarcastically-curved lips from the corner of one's mouth.

"I'm sorry my little speech displeased you, officer," said Bill in his most friendly manner. He had long ago learned that it was extremely foolish to combat local authorities. When he had been ahead of the circus he had dealt with them constantly. Restraint, tact, an overlooking of any provincial prejudices or quirks was the system. The barking dog could often be won by a friendly word.

He continued: "I was just thinking that I must find out where I could secure the help of your well-known, efficient organization. The State Troopers of Pennsylvania are famous—our American counterpart of the Royal Canadian Mounties——"

That was as far as he got. Dunnigan's complimentary remarks about the "service" were not impressing Sergeant O'Rourke. They all talked that way when on the spot. A sure sign of guilt. And in the general looking-over, his eyes had reached the footgear of this soft-soaping, goose-greasing plutocrat.

He was not reminded of any Saints in armor. He was reminded of the smug department store owner who had sweated him for two years at eighteen dollars a week and then refused the courtesy of a character certificate. This "counterpart" (to use Dunnigan's term), whose spats were white and looked brand new, probably worked hundreds of people at starvation wages so that he could ring church bells, and get his name in the papers by orating to spellbound yokels. Rich and stingy, eh? There would be quite a fine for collecting a crowd to block the state road.

"You're under arrest!" interrupted Sergeant O'Rourke without further parley. One hand closed over the handle of the revolver in his belt while the other reached out to grasp the arm of William Dunnigan.

Dunnigan's dilemma was absurd but also loaded with possible tragic consequences. He could resist for he had done nothing to warrant being arrested. He was not exactly to blame if crowds gathered because of a miracle. He knew that he would quickly be freed by any proper authorities if this young and apparently prejudiced officer dragged him to a court. But meantime there would be publicity of a kind he must not have. There were a dozen reporters in that crowd, some only a few feet away.

And Father Paul? The arrest of Dunnigan would cause the priest to give immediately his "explanation" of the miracle—and perhaps so ruin all the magnificent opportunities that now lay open to advance the fame of St. Michael's. It might seriously hurt the "Garden of the Soul" campaign. It might even stop the ringing of the bells!

"My friend," said Dunnigan, and he put into his voice all the sincerity and good will and persuasion of which he was capable, "surely there is some mistake. I have committed no crime that I know of. The body of a member of this parish is awaiting her burial from this church. An unusual, unforeseen and not-to-be-explained event has happened. A miracle, no less! The whole community is amazed and wondering, but as you can see there is no disorder—on the contrary the greatest of awed respect——"

Dunnigan might as well have talked to a deaf mute. No words of his, no logic or explanation or ingratiating smile could overcome the prejudice created by those brazenly-new white spats.

"You have violated rule 261 in blocking a highway for through traffic, and ordinance 341 in unlawfully collecting a crowd," reiterated Sergeant O'Rourke coldly. "You can make your explanation and your speeches to the judge in Wilkes-Barre."

"Won't you please step inside the church," pleaded Bill. "I am sure we can arrange matters to meet all requirements of the rules."

He thought of the manila envelope in his pocket. Perhaps a show of money, not exactly a bribe, but a willingness to pay well for services rendered——

He took out the envelope and unsnapped the rubber band.

"I am quite able and willing to pay for any extra service in keeping the crowds orderly and the roadway clear," he said, and extracted a hundred-dollar bill from the envelope.

It was the most disastrous move he could have made. Sergeant O'Rourke's face flushed to bursting, then hardened. His jaw clamped like a vise on each word that issued.

"So it's money you think can buy me!" he exclaimed.

Dunnigan realized his mistake. He was in despair. He glanced about fearfully. Would he have to call Father Paul after all! The absurdity of this whole incident! This young bull wrecking the china shop of countless noble plans!

"Please come inside and talk it over!" he pleaded again.

"I'll not come inside and I'll not talk it over!" said Sergeant O'Rourke. "You're coming with me right now. If I have to use the handcuffs, so much the worse for you! And I'm telephoning the barracks to send a squad to clear out this mob——"

Was heaven indeed now on the side of the press agent? Was Saint Michael really there behind Bill Dunnigan? Thinking of it afterwards, that was the only way he could explain it.

For at that critical moment two people broke through the crowd, one making for and speaking to William Dunnigan, and the other rushing to Sergeant Dennis O'Rourke.

The one who eagerly grasped the press agent's hand was red-headed and his face was beaming.

"Mr. Dunnigan!" he cried, "I want you to meet—that is, my girl wants to meet——'

He turned to present the very pretty young lady who had burst through the throng with him. She was momentarily engaged with Sergeant O'Rourke and talking to him excitedly.

"Dennis," she was saying, "I've been trying to get you by phone ever since last night! We've got the backing! Robert and I have bought the Quick Lunch on the Square! The rich man who is the friend of the actress being buried from here has backed Robert——"

"Kathleen!" cried Robert Omansky, and seized her arm whirling her about, "Here is Mr. Dunnigan! Here is the gentleman that sent you the rose and has given us the money to start our own lunch-room!"

Kathleen O'Rourke whirled from her only brother. She was an impulsive Celtic girl. She had prayed and struggled and saved for that Quick Lunch for a year. She had almost given up. Then her Robert rushing in the night before with this tale of an Aladdin's Lamp came true! The actual money in his hand! Since that hour she had been in the clouds! After the rush to the Square and the negotiations there, she had hardly slept all night. She had been at the Nanticoke garage a full hour before the time. She now looked on the Arabian Night jinni who had made their dreams come true!

She was very much in love with Robert Omansky, expert short-order man, but Sergeant Dennis Patrick O'Rourke saw his only sister suddenly throw her arms about the neck of the culprit he was about to arrest; kiss him; release him just as suddenly and burst into a flood of happy tears.

"Denny," cried Robert Omansky, "this is my swell partner that's backed Kathleen and me!" Then, remembering formalities, he said with a labored attempt at correct usage, "Mr. Dunnigan, sir, please meet my future brother-in-law to be, Sergeant Dennis O'Rourke of the State Police!" As neither of the men made a move he added, "But maybe you've met already!"

There are moments in life when Destiny, Fate, what you will, can benumb the strongest of mortals. Both Sergeant O'Rourke and William Dunnigan were stunned. Sergeant O'Rourke was the first to recover. A member of the State Police must be equal to any emergency. But even Sergeant O'Rourke had to swallow hard before he spoke.

"I—I have just met Mr. Dunnigan," he said. He looked at his sister again. She was holding the hand of Robert Omansky. They were both gazing at Bill (White Spats) Dunnigan as if he were an angel from the morning skies.

Sergeant O'Rourke held out his hand. There were no handcuffs in it. He thought of that, for, being Irish, he did have a sense of humor. He smiled, the Irish smile that lit his face when he sang "Sweet Rosie O'Grady."

"I'm glad to know you, to meet you again, Mr. Dunnigan," he said. "I guess—I guess I made a slight mistake. Just tell me what you want done, sir. A miracle, is it? O. K. I guess my buddy and I—I left him back in the car—can regulate miracles. I handled the mob at the funeral of an ex-mayor in Wilkes-Barre last month so this is just in my department! If these people want to get into this church, we'll line 'em up. Three abreast will do it. Then they won't block the state road. And someone inside to keep them moving. I'll phone for half a dozen more men. You'll maybe be needing them to see you through the funeral of your friend."

Dunnigan had taken out the green silk handkerchief and mopped his brow. He had taken the hand of Sergeant O'Rourke. They both took deep breaths. Then they laughed.

"No hard feelings?" said Sergeant O'Rourke.

"No hard feelings, Sergeant," said Bill Dunnigan. "You were

only doing your duty. But I want to tell you sometime about that speech you didn't like. I don't like it now much myself. A lot of things have happened around here since that speech was made two nights ago."

So did the majesty of the law come over to the side of St. Michael's. And presently, under the able supervision of Sergeant O'Rourke, was started the blocks-long line, at first of Coaltown people but soon augmented by the entire countryside—by near-by cities even—the line, three and four abreast, moving slowly up to and through St. Michael's doors.

A line that was as much an item of news as the miracle itself. Father Paul's little church and this line were soon to flash as a part of the newsreels in every picture theater in the land.

53

*W*HEN FATHER PAUL had told Bill Dunnigan he was going to the parish house to pray for guidance, he did not mean that he would fall upon his knees in some secret room and so remain until he felt that he had been handed a solution of the problem. He did indeed ask for divine help, but he felt that we had been given an intellect by Almighty God and that we were expected to exercise that intellect. And he had discovered that he could best function as a thinking man when his hands were occupied with some humble and useful work—a task that he could automatically accomplish while struggling with the greater question at hand.

By some psychological twist this occupation of his hands seemed to leave his mind more free for right decision.

He had sometimes, indeed, wondered if Jesus, when on earth, had not kept His youthful tools of carpentry, and when there had been moments of doubt and fear (as there had been even for Him), if He had not labored over the fitting of a shelf, the cutting of a board, while reaching an all-wise determination. When there had been mention in sacred lore of relics of the Master—the pieces of the True Cross, a thorn from the True Crown—he had wondered why no one had thought to treasure a simple adze, a rule for measuring, some one of the implements of the trade practiced at the side of Joseph by that Son who was Divine. Would not one of these have been a thing very close to His heart—a thing of intimate connection with judgments that were to live forever?

Father Paul was one of those men with absolutely no mechanical ability. The driving of a nail usually resulted in a bandaged thumb. He sometimes thought St. Michael's would have been much better served had its priest been a first-class plumber, roof shingler or house painter. It had needed badly the ministrations of all these, not to mention those of a stone mason about the sinking foundations. And there had been no money to hire them from the laity.

He had managed to paint the crosses above the door and at the top of the roof apex—the latter at the risk of life and limb on a tall, borrowed ladder held by his elderly sexton. But even this small paint job had ruined one of his two black suits. White paint improved the crosses but not the appearance of a jet black suit.

He had learned a little about gardening, and (as Dunnigan had noted the first day), kept his lawn well trimmed; planted flowers in a circular bed between the parish house and the church. He grew enough vegetables in the small patch at the back to supply his simple needs in summer, though Japanese beetles and like insects had no particular respect for the clergy. They attacked clerical as well as secular gardens. In the growing seasons he worked out most of his sermons while bending over his lettuce and tomato vines or pushing the ancient lawnmower with one blade broken.

But in the autumn, when he wished to occupy his hands, he had to turn to another task diversion. He turned to one used by many another single, lonely man. He darned socks.

They always needed darning! The lining of his shoes was invariably worn through, and sharp edges of leather rubbing against soft cotton or lisle created a destructive friction. Tramping the hill streets of Coaltown gave that friction plenty of scope and exercise. The heels of some of Father Paul's socks held more darning than they did of the original material.

Working at this domestic task brought an additional comfort to Father Paul. It brought back his mother.

It was the dress-making mother who had taught the lad this highly useful exercise for the hands. She taught him before he went away to St. Joseph's Seminary. She gave him the white, short-handled darning egg which was placed inside the toe or heel of the worn item to give a firm base for the operation of the needle.

Next to a rosary, also a gift of his mother, this darning egg was Father Paul's greatest personal treasure.

He had become reasonably skillful in weaving the thread back and forth over the gaping spaces and giving the cross work, now and then, a sharp pat to make it set. He had never acquired the art of quickly threading the needle. Fifteen years of practice and determination had not improved his speed, his technique, his accuracy. It was a skill of accomplishment that heaven had denied him utterly. Threading the needle took longer sometimes than the actual work!

But, as we know, the priest was a persevering soul, and he never entirely gave up. The thread always, sooner or later, was projected through the elusive hole in that small steel instrument. Father Paul felt if he ever gave up in this bedeviling prelude to darning he would falter in greater tasks.

The needle was threaded quickly this morning of the miracle. Was that a good omen? Before him was a sock of many yawning holes. Inserting the wooden egg he attacked these holes vigorously while his mind debated the distressing problem of what had occurred to his altar statues. He was not interrupted in the parish house for he had stationed a choir boy at the door, placing a dollar in the youth's hand, with orders that no one was to be admitted during his meditation.

But ponder as he would, darn as he would, he could not reach a conclusion. The statues had turned because the pillars supporting them had turned and slightly tipped. There were the cracks in the basement floor. The pillars had turned because the earth at their base had moved. This could be explained by the mine shafts. But could it be fully explained? What power had caused mine shafts two thousand feet below to make this disturbance at this particular time of all the years they had been there, and in such a manner as to cause *both* statues to face the coffin of Olga Treskovna? Had Dunnigan been right in reiterating it was more than a mere coincidence?

The glorious lines of the old psalmist came to the priest:

For the Lord *is* a great **God**, and a great **King** above all gods.

In his hand *are* the deep places of the earth: the strength of the hills *is* his also.

The sea *is* his, and he made it: and his hands formed the dry land.

O come, let us worship and bow down: let us kneel before the Lord our maker.

For he *is* our God: and we *are* the people of his pasture, and the sheep of his hand. Today, if ye will hear his voice.

In His hand are the deep places of the earth. So it was set down in Holy Writ.

Over and over again the pros and cons of the event tore at the intellect of Father Paul.

And there was the very human problem of the effect all this had had, was now having, and would continue to have on the people of the town. When he pondered that, his *heart* was torn. To destroy this new faith, this new fervor! To cast, at the very least, the dark shadow of doubt across the bright glowing of that faith, doubt that the hand of God had been there! What would be gained thereby? And what never-to-be-regained faith would be lost!

Father Paul darned every hole in three pairs of badly damaged socks. It took him twenty minutes to thread the needles on the second pair. But the hardest thinking and the neatest darning of his whole life brought him only more confusion, carried him no nearer to a determination of his duty as a priest.

He put down the needle, the socks, the darning egg. There was a last resort. He must consult his Bishop; go to the near-by cathedral city—immediately—as soon as possible—for an older and more experienced wisdom. The whole matter would, in the end, have to be placed in this official's hands.

More than a full hour had passed. It was another half hour while he changed to his best black suit, his one good pair of shoes, brushed his non-clerical soft black hat, and heated himself some breakfast porridge so that he could make the bus journey, his body fortified.

But before he could go, before these and other tasks were consummated, his Bishop came to him.

~~~~~~~~~~~~~~~~~~~~~~~~~~~~~~~~~~~~ *54* ~~~~~

*F*ATHER PAUL'S Bishop was a genial Irish gentleman who believed both life and religion should be a cup of joy and happiness. Of better than medium height, wide and sturdy of face and body, he kept that body in robust health—and his mind also—by fine surroundings, good food, good wine, good cigars.

He lived nobly in the three-storied mansion adjoining and attached to his cathedral and built of the same excellent grey sandstone. He was a collector of good paintings and valuable first editions of both books and brandies.

The rugs, the draperies, the furniture of this mansion were of the finest, and many of the pieces of furniture were of considerable value. His dining table, for example, and its chairs and the massive buffet cabinet at one side had come from a palace in Venice. Likewise the great chandelier overhead. The china service had been especially made by the famous Royal Worcestershire potteries in England. His silver was solid sterling. His linen was from Dublin. The house was staffed by a number of capable servants and he had the best chef in the city.

Think not the less of him for this, for these surroundings gave that broad body and broad mind a tremendous energy. This Bishop abounded in good works done in the same grand manner in which he lived. Over that dining table and its perfect cuisine were formulated many plans for the betterment of his city. And the necessary money was raised alongside the rare brandy and the expensive cigars to carry these plans through. He labored with a tireless zeal on every civic committee that would help the town. He spoke well and with a blessed humor at every gathering of public importance. He maintained with his own purse a "Center" in the poorest quarter, with a day nursery, a playground, a gymnasium. He induced manufacturers to open new businesses so that there would be no unemployment. His great Cadillac car was as often before the door of a ward hospital or a tenement building as it was on the driveway of some wealthy man's estate.

He probably had more friends in every walk and condition and belief of life than any other citizen of his cathedral community. Catholic, Protestant, Jew, no faith at all—this Bishop was known and loved by all. Tolerance, that virtue of virtues, might be said to have been his middle name—tolerance and a belief that happiness and the good things of life were not the tools of Satan; that a long face and indifference to luxury did not necessarily denote sanctity.

Though born in Ireland, he was a staunch American patriot, who was devoted to his adopted country with a sincere and ardent belief in its democracy and in all that we mean by the American way of life. Freedom was blazoned on his banner along with the triple crown of his personal faith. He was a true liberal.

He knew about the ringing of the Coaltown bells, of course. How could he help knowing with the story in black headlines in both his local newspapers. He was not disturbed by it. His bishopric was dotted with a number of settlements of almost entirely foreign origin, where the sermons were in an alien tongue, and where many and often picturesque customs of the motherlands had been transplanted and nurtured.

Coaltown was such a settlement, and if they had chosen to ring their bells for a month it was a matter for the local clergy and the local civil authorities to decide. He *liked* the sound of bells, anyway, and could (and often did) as an amateur, play the chimes of his own cathedral.

His only thought about the Coaltown episode was that he hoped it would bring some joy into a drab neighborhood. He knew the sullen grind of the lives of the workers in the mines.

The Bishop was an early riser and had breakfast promptly at seven every morning. While eating he listened to the news broadcast from his console radio. After the enthusiastic announcement indicating that the salvation of humanity depended on a realization of the superiority of Simpson Ackerly maker-to-wearer clothes and a few other items of national concern, the entire ten minutes that morning was given to an event said to have occurred in the Roman Catholic Church of St. Michael the Archangel in Coaltown.

A reporter on the scene described the crowds that had gathered and the "miracle" that had allegedly taken place in this parish church where the bells had already been ringing for two days in connection with the funeral service of an actress with a Polish name who was born there.

Wasn't that the small church to which he had sent a Polish boy several years before whose mother had been so eager for her son to have a parish? One of the lads who had started in his own cathedral? The Bishop made a note that he must someday soon visit Coaltown.

As for this radio talk of a miracle, it was probably a reporter's exaggeration of some simple happening on a morning when news was scarce. These Poles were an excitable people. The incident would be over and forgotten by another morning. The Bishop had a busy day ahead—a meeting with the Mayor at nine, another meeting at ten with both Rabbi Solemann of the large synagogue and the Protestant Bishop of St. John's about the United Charities campaign, a luncheon of the Rotary Club at which he was the guest of honor. And his secretary had just placed before him a long list of afternoon appointments at the rectory.

"Remind me to drive to Coaltown the first free morning we have next week," he told his secretary. He proceeded to finish his breakfast, his mind on the business of the day.

Coaltown was not content to wait until another week. It waited scarcely ten minutes before it again projected itself on the conscience and consciousness of the Bishop.

His telephone started to ring. It did not ring with calls from unimportant Coaltown. They were at first from the editors of the newspapers of his own city and the city of Wilkes-Barre. Then long-distance calls from the city desks of the early afternoon editions of papers in Philadelphia, Pittsburgh, Baltimore, Boston, New York. The radio networks also and the Press Associations. All wanting an official statement from the Church regarding this first seemingly-authentic miracle to occur in America.

The Bishop was by this time repeating to himself, "Well, well! Well, well!" with a not unpleasurable accent. His secretary found that St. Michael's had no telephone. The only priest in Coaltown with a telephone was Father Spinsky at St. Leo's, and Father Spinsky the Bishop did not like.

If this newspaper and radio barrage against planned tasks were to continue—and it was continuing—he decided he had best post-pone the tasks and seek some facts at first hand. Besides, his own keen interest was now aroused. He instructed the secretary to rearrange the schedule of appointments—put off the Mayor and the Rabbi and the other Bishop till afternoon if possible, cancel the afternoon engagements at the rectory. If he started at once he would be back in time for the Rotary luncheon, at which the Mayor would be present.

By eight o'clock he was in his Cadillac and on the way to Coaltown fifteen miles distant.

He arrived just as Father Paul was emerging from his parish house to take a bus to the cathedral city.

The Bishop's car had had a deal of company on the drive. The usually little-frequented road to the hill country was spotted with many other cars. The whole countryside was wide awake and on its way to see a new wonder while it was fresh in the happening. Even as a growing cavalcade was speeding toward Coaltown, their car radios were telling more details. Two great marble statues weighing tons had miraculously turned toward the coffin of the screen star Olga Treskovna. This girl of poverty for whom the bells were ringing might be another Theresa of Sainthood. Some announcer had remembered that the canonized Carmelite nun had written a book called "The Castle of the Soul." Olga Treskovna's film was named "The Garden of the Soul." It was about a girl who became a nun. The Bishop was acquiring a very healthy curiosity about it all as he approached the great black Breaker that marked the beginning of the main street of this dingy, mining-country Lourdes.

This curiosity was not lessened by the triple line of several thousand people, men, women and children, extending several blocks to the door of St. Michael's. Or by the great throng that was still gathered around that church, although the roadway was being kept clear and free. It was only clear because a dozen State Troopers were on hand, regulating traffic, directing cars to side streets for parking, herding the people into the long lines, all under the direction of a particularly energetic young Sergeant. Motorcycle Troopers had whizzed by the Bishop's car earlier in the drive. Sergeant Dennis O'Rourke had telephoned for his reserves and was on the job in earnest.

The Bishop's car drew up in front of the small parish house just as Father Paul was emerging from its doorway. The still-waiting and ever-increasing throng, the reporters (some now with cameras) the State Troopers, the Bishop's great car (for Father Paul immediately recognized it) were almost more than the little priest could comprehend.

Father Paul halted on his doorstep in real terror, an almost physical terror.

The door of the car opened. A State Trooper whom Sergeant O'Rourke had placed in front of Father Paul's parsonage, opened the car door and stood smartly at one side in salute. Every Wyoming Valley Trooper knew that car well. It was the Bishop who gave so generously each year to their Recreation Fund, who never failed to attend their track meet and their ball games. Father Paul saw his Bishop step out—dignifiedly resplendent in a handsome black cassock with purple buttons and the purple tassel on his black biretta, saw him shake hands with the happily embarrassed Trooper and pass a friendly word. And now the great man was mounting the uneven wooden steps up the short embankment and coming toward the humble pastor of St. Michael's.

The Bishop—a smile on his not unhandsome face—started to speak as soon as he spied the startled parish priest.

"Well, well, my lad! You seem to have started something in your town! Don't look so worried! Congratulations! It's a grand sight to my eyes to see all these people flocking to a church. I wish the likes of it would happen at my own cathedral. I hope you're taking up collections."

Father Paul gulped. "You're kind, indeed, to speak of it that way, Your Excellency," he gasped. "I am terribly distressed and was just on my way to come to you. A rather dreadful thing— that is, it seemed dreadful at first and now I don't know—a dreadful thing has happened, and I badly need your counsel."

"Well, here I am after a fine morning ride across your hills, and we'll go inside the parish house and hear all about it," said the Bishop, taking Father Paul's hand in a firm and friendly grasp. "But cheer up! The radio reports have me all atingle. It sounded most interesting!" and he paused on the steps to again view the crowd from this higher vantage point.

But before these two could find the privacy of Father Paul's humble "office," a small tidal wave of newsmen swept around them. They had been waiting to get at Father Paul. Now they had also the Bishop of the district in their net, for he had, of course, been recognized. Even while he had been speaking to Father Paul a murmur was going through the crowd: "The Bishop!" "Bishop O'Conner!" "He has come clear from Scranton!" "What will the Bishop say!"

The reporters were not backward. "May we have a shot for the afternoon papers, Your Reverence," cried two cameramen at once, and one of them was already holding his instrument high up before him and adjusting a proper focus.

"Of course, boys," said the Bishop, "only wait! I want Father Paul of St. Michael's in it. He was one of my boys, and this is his party, not mine. Where are you, Paul? Don't back away! And smile, my lad, smile!" This to the now almost terrified pastor of St. Michael's.

"It's time the press realized what handsome clergy are right in their midst!" exclaimed the Bishop with the greatest of good humor. This excitement on a bright, sunny morning was a tonic he was enjoying to the full. He placed an arm about the little priest as the camera shutters clicked and clicked again.

The other newsmen were ready with their notebooks. "A statement! A statement!" came from several in one voice.

"Ah—for that, boys, you'll have to wait," the Bishop said. "You know more about it than I do. I'm just arrived, as you see. Off the record, I hope it's all true. We need a good, old-fashioned miracle these days to wake us up. And don't the bells sound grand! I'll see you all after I talk with Father Paul. It's his miracle, not mine, you know."

So Father Paul and his Bishop were presently alone inside the parish house.

"Do you wish to see the statues first?" asked Father Paul. "They have really turned. We can go there through the sanctuary door."

"I want your story first," said the Bishop. "I might not believe what I see. I can believe what you tell me. And I hope you don't mind if I smoke. I like to have my after-breakfast smoke sitting quietly. The newspapers sent me scurrying from my rectory this morning before I had barely finished eating! You didn't at all consider my comfort in timing your miracle!"

He produced from beneath his cassock two cigars of formidable size and color. One of these he handed to Father Paul.

"I—I don't think I'd best try one now," said Father Paul. "My stomach is already a bit on edge."

"You should smoke a pipe," said the Bishop. "Tobacco is one of the real blessings bestowed upon mankind. It has kept many a stomach from wrongly directing a disturbed mind. I shall send you a pipe that was given me last week by a great philosopher who masquerades at running a corner tobacco store near my church. And a can of Bond Street which will not burn your tongue."

He had by this time lit his cigar and inhaled several puffs of its satisfying fragrance. "Now, my boy, let's hear about it all," he said.

Father Paul took a deep breath. What a wonderful man his Bishop was! He poured out his troubled heart as to a confessor.

"It started as I was sitting just here Monday evening, very low in spirit, looking over my unpaid bills, which were like my life, Father—hopes and desires unsatisfied, bankrupt—and there was a prolonged jangle of my doorbell. A stranger I had never seen before stood in my doorway and demanded if I were Father Paul. A stranger I have learned to love and yet I wondered today if he had been sent by God or Satan!"

And he related to the attentive Bishop all we know had happened since William Dunnigan, press agent out-of-a-job, had arrived in Coaltown with the body of the unwanted, unknown Olga Treskovna.

The Bishop listened carefully. He did not remove his eyes from the face of Father Paul during the long narrative. Like all really important men, he gave his full attention if he talked with one at all. Only he wished Father Paul's chairs were a little more comfortable! He made a mental note to see that St. Michael's parish-house office was supplied with a large leather one that was in his storeroom.

"I'm not sure that your press agent gentleman isn't entirely right," he said at last, after puffing in silence for a full three minutes at the end of Father Paul's strange story. "Dunnigan you say his name is? Good. An Irishman. Sentimental and hard-headed at the same time. You Poles can't combine the two. Must be one or the other."

"But what shall we say about this so-called miracle?" asked Father Paul.

"So-called?" replied the Bishop.

"I have told you there is an explanation," said Father Paul.

The Bishop smiled. "I have no doubt our modern weather bureaus could have explained when Jesus rebuked the winds and the sea for His disciples and there was a great calm. The 'calm' had been moving toward that 'area' for sometime. I have no doubt modern medical science could explain many of the cures. Perhaps even the five loaves and the two fishes were near an explainable cache He knew of in the desert, placed there by the Roman Office of Price Administration! The name of the play this Irish gentleman mentioned—what did you say it was again?" he switched the subject abruptly.

"Why, I think he called it 'False Gods,'" said Father Paul.

"That was the name!" said the Bishop. "I remember it well. It was written by Eugène Brieux, a great writer. I don't wonder your friend could not pronounce it. We Irish, clever as we are, are no linguists. I'm not sure of it myself! But I saw the play in London when I was a young man studying there. Wonderful music it had too, composed by Camille Saint-Saëns. And a fine English star it was who portrayed the High Priest—Sir Herbert Beerbohm Tree. He had a strain of Irish blood. The scene you mention made a strong impression on me, also. I wonder why the movie people haven't made a film of such a play. I must speak of it to Max Goldstein who manages the picture theater nearest my church. The man might get a promotion if he suggested it."

"You think then that we should keep silent regarding any explanations?"

"Paul, we live a good deal by our illusions. I sometimes think that much of our happiness is based on them. Is your chronic skeptic happy? No. But your man who *believes*—not foolishly, of course—but who has faith that all is not meant to be torn apart and analyzed; there is your ardent worker, your contented citizen. And your good Christian, too. The greatest shock of my life was when, as a lad, a smart older boy told me there was no Saint Nicholas who came down the chimneys and filled the stockings at Christmas. He had his damnable explanations of the miracle of a child's Christmas. I never forgave that boy. And he was not right in the larger sense. Saint Nicholas is in the heart of every generous soul at Christmas time. As I grew older I discovered other things that I wished I had not discovered . . . When did you say is to be the funeral service for this girl?"

"It is planned for Friday," said Father Paul.

"At least we will make no comment until after that service," said the Bishop. "And even then we need not confirm or deny."

"But the rules of our Hierarchy——"

The Bishop for once interrupted. He arose and made a gesture of great impatience. The smile left his face.

"I pray God no complicated issue is made of it," he said, "with meetings of clergy, high dignitaries, conference and commissions to listen to the learned opinions of Dr. This and the Most Holy Reverend That! Learned indeed! What blunders have sometimes been made of such things. The Maid of Orleans—'Blessed Joan the valor of Lorraine'—Lorraine was her province—wrote sinner François Villon five hundred years before we canonized her! *We* burnt her, but the heart of the people knew even then. That voice of the people, Villon in his gutter, knew more surely than all our Hierarchies, our concordants, our Congregations of Rites, our Lord Bishops, our professors of theology—learned ignorance judging the handiwork of God! And what a mistake we made concerning that miracle at Lourdes. God spare us from all that! What I can and will say publicly is this: 'Who really knows? Two forces. God in His supreme wisdom. And the great heart of the common people.' That heart knows also. I believe that as I believe in Holy Writ."

The Bishop moved to the single window and looked out at the crowded lawn. He visioned beyond that lawn the packed street and the great line down that street.

"Your people are strongly stirred," he continued. "I think most of them needed that stirring. Maybe you needed it, Paul, my lad. Maybe I needed it. Many of those out there will realize again, perhaps for the first time in months, in years, the beauty of the Mass, that greatest miracle of all. Do we have to explain *that* miracle? The wine into Christ's Blood? The wafer into His Body? Those people of yours and mine will again feel the comfort and glory and happiness of communing with our Saints. The results of this occurrence can only bring good. Must we churchmen prate of 'explanations'?"

The Bishop sat again on his folding chair. The smoke of his cigar came in great puffs. Then the smile quickly returned to his face.

Father Paul felt that he must point out one other matter. The Bishop's smile helped him to mention it.

"I cannot forget that it was all started partly to promote a motion picture," he said. "I believe Mr. Dunnigan sincere; I respect his honesty, but can the Church lend itself——"

Again the Bishop held up his hand. "It is curious that a stage play should help point out the right path for us; and that another play should be at the beginnings of your miracle. And yet it is not so curious, Paul. The real Theater is like the Church—or should be—a source of guidance and wisdom and inspiration. I believe in the Theater. It started in our Church. The first English and French plays were sacred stories. They were even named *miracle plays*. Just as the first great paintings were all inspired by characters of the Testaments. I have dreamed often of a Theater more closely united to the Church. Working with the Church for good. I go to the theater whenever I can. I encourage my clergy to go. There are bad plays—yes. But then there have been bad priests in high places in our Church. Bad pontiffs even. That did not destroy the Church. I believe our America is morally sound and healthy and that most of the plays that last are good. The bad ones die of themselves, just as all evil dies."

"But this is a motion picture."

"A new art, but with tremendous influence—and so, tremendous possibilities for good. How they have improved in the last two years. I attend them regularly now. You should attend them. You will learn something new each time about your fellowmen—and you and I cannot learn too much of the human comedy—and tragedy—if we are to rightly help those who need us."

It was Father Paul who now rose suddenly from his chair. A change had been taking place inside him as he listened to his Bishop. A tide was swelling and rising in his heart. He looked straight at the lithograph of Saint Michael on his wall. The fighting Saint he, Paul, was supposed to represent as vicar of a church that bore that fighting name. A Saint who had even touched that stranger to the church, William Dunnigan. And the spirit of Saint Michael seemed, for the first time, to reach out to him extending the strength and courage and the will to face any danger. The will to fight and conquer for one's ideals!

He faced his Bishop, a new flame burning in his soul and in his homely but ardent face. The Bishop even was a little startled at what he saw there.

"You must know," said Father Paul, "I have always been afraid. There have been days of courage, but I have always returned to fear. I was afraid when my bells started ringing. I was afraid as I said my Mass this morning. I was afraid when I opened my door awhile ago and saw the crowds. I was afraid when I recognized your car—when its door opened and you were coming up my steps.

"But now, thanks to you, thanks to this strange man Dunnigan, thanks to Saint Michael and with God's help, I don't think I will ever be afraid again!"

"There you are!" said the Bishop. "Is not that a miracle? And when I've made a good pipesmoker of you—perhaps even a cigar smoker later on——"

The Bishop also rose and held out his hand. "I have two requests to make. We Bishops always want something! First, invite me to attend your funeral service Friday."

"I would be honored if you yourself would officiate," gasped Father Paul.

"No. I will not do that. That is your duty. Your privilege. This is your church. I will preside in your sanctuary. I'll tell you —I have some new requiem mass vestments—very lovely—black and silver and purple. I will bring them for you to wear. We must not let this theater man think that we cannot keep up our end of the spectacle."

"How am I to thank you?" asked Father Paul.

"That is simple. Remain brave. Remain strong. Banish this fear forever. Never return to it. Smile. We—you and I—are custodians of the greatest well of happiness ever given to mankind! See that your people understand this—see that they do not go thirsty simply because they do not know."

They were by then at the open door. The crowd was even larger than before. A newsreel camera straddling the top of a car started to grind as the Bishop again took the hand of Father Paul.

"I almost forgot my other request," the Bishop said. "Tell your theater friend his film must be shown in my city at least one week before it appears in New York. The Archbishop there always chides me that the films I try to tell him about have long since been seen by him. Here is my chance to put one over on an Archbishop! Good-by."

The Bishop purposely did not go inside the church. That he would do on Friday at the funeral. He had heard Father Paul and that was enough. To look seemed to him would mean that he had a doubt.

To the waiting newsmen he said: "I believe there is here a great stirring of the power of God. A miracle we may call it. I say this personally, not as an official of the Church. I can only speak now from my heart. Ask me nothing more at this time. Ah, I do like the ringing of these bells! They may be ringing for the dead, but life is here, gentlemen, and they are a joyful sound. Why do we in America always associate church bells with somber thoughts? Bells are happy! They mean happiness."

The Bishop looked up at the bell tower of St. Michael's. There were slatted windows around its top and through them you could see the small bell swinging back and forth. Its tone was very beautiful and had the quality of a voice. The eyes of the newsmen looked upward also.

"Is not that sound a miracle!" said the Bishop. "Our churches are filled with these lovely singing voices and they are too seldom heard. My own cathedral is a sorry example. A few brief moments on the Sabbath is their allotted time. We might have less preaching and more singing of those bells. I think I am going to propose that our bells be rung for several hours on Easter and Christmas— even on days of lesser moment in the church calendar. And certainly on our national holidays. The Fourth of July. The birthday of the great Lincoln. The very swinging of the bells means Liberty. Their voices cry Freedom! These villages do better than our cities—they still sound the evening Angelus. The daily call to prayer. The Christian prayer. I am going to sound the Angelus in my city from now on. I am going to ring my cathedral chimes on holidays for an extended period. I shall speak of this at a businessmen's luncheon I am now to attend. Think it over, boys. Maybe if you write about it, other cities will try it too!"

And the Bishop made the sign of the cross to the people, entered his car and was driven away.

55

THE BISHOP "in their notebooks," the reporter
moved on to the priest of St. Michael the Archangel. They foun[d]
a new Father Paul, no longer terrified and abashed. Not for himself but for Saint Michael he spoke up boldly and with purpose.

"The statues have turned," he said, "and they were not touche[d]
by human hands. That I can vouch for. Is it a miracle? I leav[e]
that for my people to decide. For myself, I know that Sain[t]
Michael, the patron of this church, is a potent Angel. He could[,]
I believe, accomplish whatever he chose to do."

"Just who was he?" asked a young reporter. Could there be [a]
story even in a musty Saint?

"He was the leader of the fighting Angels," said Father Paul[,]
and into his own eyes came a glint of battle. "He goes back eve[n]
before the advent of our Blessed Lord upon this earth. He wa[s]
the Prince of the Host guarding the temple of God. He drove th[e]
proud Lucifer from Heaven. It was written of his army, 'Thes[e]
are the Watchmen set upon the walls of Jerusalem, to stand in th[e]
power of the Lord round about His people.' He was a fighter lik[e]
—like Jack Dempsey or General MacArthur! A friend of mine ha[s]
named him 'Saint Michael the Scrapper'! The 'undefeated Cham[-]
pion'!"

The newsmen took a sudden interest. What they thought wa[s]
going to be just a preachment had a punch line. This little
funny-looking priest was a live wire!

"You mean they had a battle up in Heaven," said the youn[g]
reporter.

"The battle of battles!" said Father Paul. "Surely you me[n]
know about that. Saint Michael was the **General** of the army o[f]
our Lord. But he wasn't afraid of a personal scrap." He wa[s]
going to say "encounter." He changed the noun just in time[.]
And was it his voice that was speaking up so fearlessly to reporter[s]
for newspapers?

He continued with just the trace of a smile in his glowing eyes. "Saint Michael, himself, took on Kid Lucifer and put him down and out for the full count! He was tops, my friends! And he is still tops!"

Bill Dunnigan, himself, could not have said it better. Father Paul's Saint was emerging from a dim past into someone for a headline.

The priest continued. "My statue of him here—one of the statues that has turned—is a very grand one!" Again he was going to say "beautiful" but he changed the adjective. Maybe he should have said "swell" and so made it even stronger. "I will take you and show you. You photographers may take pictures if you wish. I do not think there is another quite like it in America."

"But this Saint Michael did his fighting a pretty long time ago," said the skeptical, very young reporter.

"Ah, there you are mistaken!" said Father Paul. And how good it was not to be afraid! "Saint Michael fights today! Do you not know he is the patron saint of aviation? I thought you did not. He rides in every fighter plane that takes the sky for liberty and freedom from evil. He rides in every battleship that plows the seas for justice, for he is also the patron saint of mariners!"

This was something new to all of them. They wrote it down. The most calloused, most irreligious felt the fervor of this country priest. And his humanity. They followed him through the chancel door and presently flash-bulbs for the first time crackled in a church in Coaltown.

Next day the tabloids carried something besides the likenesses of murderers and divorcees. Readers partial to sporting subjects were surprised to find above the caption, "The Undefeated Champion," a marble gentleman in armor, his sword upraised, his foot upon the head of a rival who was undoubtedly "out for the full count."

And next week the rotogravures had pictures of an altar of God as well as shots at race tracks and the latest fashions in slacks.

Thus did Saint Michael the Archangel—Saint Michael the Scrapper—break into the news, along with a film called "The Garden of the Soul," along with Father Paul, unknown parish priest, and Olga Treskovna, rapidly becoming-known motion-picture star.

But alone at last in his study, the little priest felt a trifle faint.

"I wonder—I wonder if I am doing rightly?" he said to his desk. But this wavering was only for a moment and for the last time. How was it his Bishop had spoken? *"Banish this fear forever!"*

Father Paul had drunk the blood of courage. Ten minutes later one of his vestrymen, who came to bring more than a thousand dollars in nickels and dimes and quarters, dollar bills and five-dollar bills (for the druggist and the garage owner, unable to pass among the people in the packed church, had taken up stations with their long-handled baskets at the door)—this vestryman was startled beyond measure to find his pastor puffing energetically, though a trifle pale of countenance, on a large and very brown cigar. The Bishop had left the one offered Father Paul lying on the little priest's desk.

"Why, Father, I didn't know you used tobacco!" the man exclaimed.

"I usually smoke a pipe," said Father Paul calmly, "but I have just had a talk with our Bishop and I think I will change to cigars. I hope you took up a collection at the Mass."

"And how!" replied the garage keeper. It was he who brought the money. And he dumped out a veritable mountain of currency on the desk of St. Michael's parish office, where candle bills two nights before could not be met.

56

*B*ILL DUNNIGAN was not at St. Michael's during the time of the Bishop's call. He had watched Father Paul cross the short space of his lawn, speak briefly to the several newsmen there, disappear into the parish house. The priest wished to be alone and Dunnigan had respected that wish.

Then came the adventure with Sergeant Dennis O'Rourke and the appearance of Robert Omansky and his girl. What a fortunate "break" that had been! The cold sweat broke out on his forehead as he thought of it. His quick-lunch partner had unknowingly repaid, with interest, that investment.

"A fine host I am!" he said to the boy and girl, "I invite you to early Mass and then am nowhere to be found. But honestly, I had no idea so many other people would decide to attend. It sort of swamped me and tied me up. I don't suppose you were able to get inside the church."

"My Robert got me in," said the girl proudly.

"He must have been a magician then!" said the press agent, remembering his own struggle to reach the side door of St. Michael's.

"I saw there was no chance by the main door," said the boy, "but there was a small door into the bell tower. We went up a flight and there was another door——"

"And we were in the choir loft!" broke in the girl. "We saw the Mass from there—and the holy statues that have turned and the coffin of Miss Treskovna. My Robert always gets what he goes after."

"I think you and your man are going to make a success of life," laughed Dunnigan. "I've noticed the O'Rourke side of the family also has a certain degree of determination. But I lose both of you your jobs if I don't rush you back to Nanticoke pronto!" He looked at his watch. Robert Omansky's hour of seven was irrevocably in the limbo of the past.

"I've lost my job already," said the boy gaily. "I went around last night to give the boss a week's notice—he's on himself at night —and he fired me. Said he always knew I was a fool and now he was sure of it." But this low evaluation of his intellect had not seemed to depress the new owner of a quick-lunch on the main Square.

"Now I'm sure you'll be a success!" And Dunnigan laughed again. "Great men are always fired at least once before their triumphs. Thomas Edison, Ulysses S. Grant, Benjamin Franklin— and there is another guy I could mention! But I was counting on your cooking me another Special for my breakfast. I'm hungry now and that's a fact."

Miracles had not lessened the Dunnigan appetite.

The three of them returned to the Wyoming Hotel. Dunnigan's Packard was waiting there. The press agent paused only long enough to pick up a box from his room. Father Paul was going to be cheated of his share of the Dunnigan half of Mary Spinsky's

chocolate cake. It was devoured and discussed by three famished
souls—four in fact, for the driver was given a share—on the first
few miles of the trip to Nanticoke. And added to the repertory
of Quick Lunch Heaven by a unanimous vote of all stockholders.
St. Leo's Chocolate Cake!

Bill Dunnigan had things to do in Nanticoke and he also felt
it best to absent himself from the immediate scene. With funeral
expert Dennis O'Rourke and his Troopers in charge of crowds, he
felt all would move smoothly around St. Michael's. Father Paul
must be given a chance to fight out his problem of the miracle.
Somehow Dunnigan felt that struggle would also come out all
right. And more than ever he did not wish to personally appear
in any way to be involved with these latest events, as indeed he
was not. Let Coaltown speak and let what had happened speak.
Here was a situation where the presence of a known press agent—
and there might be newsmen arriving from the larger cities who
knew him—would be a liability.

But his publicity brain cells were seething. The crowds, which
had so frightened Father Paul, were like heady wine to his spirits.
The man who had helped crowd a quarter of a million people into
Boyle's Thirty Acres, who had packed the Polo Grounds and
Soldiers' Field on more than one occasion, who had done his part
to make big musicals gross forty thousand weekly, season after
season, felt in his rightful element. Even there, on that hill road,
a steady stream of cars was moving by in the direction of Coaltown
and St. Michael's. He must not in any way muff this magnificent
opportunity.

As he rode along he tried to bring some order to his mind. He
had three labors ahead. Three obligations. They were interwoven
yet distinct.

First, the task for which he came to Coaltown. The simple
burial of Olga Treskovna. Simple? When her name would that
night be in every newspaper in the land, when already it was
doubtless being mentioned by every radio newscaster. When he
knew that he must now make that funeral the climax of this wave
of publicity that had rolled up with such amazing swiftness since
he had stood with Father Paul at the cemetery and conceived the
idea of ringing the Coaltown bells. Well, he would keep its spirit
simple. There should be the little girls "with wings" beside the

coffin, there should be the blind organist, there should be Father Paul at his simple altar in the little church. The crowds, both the curious and the adoring, should not change that.

"We're reaching for that star of yours, kid," he said to himself and to her, "and to get to a star you must ride a comet! You can't ride comets without the world looking up to see what's happening. But it will all help Father Paul and St. Michael's. They stood by us when there wasn't any glory, any money, any hope. Now we can repay that debt."

For Father Paul and St. Michael's was the second "labor" he had set for himself. The miracle had given it a tremendous lift. St. Michael's would not lack attendance for the Mass the following morning or the next. But what about when "the tumult and the shouting died"? Maybe even—the way things were going—when the Captains and the Kings departed? Dunnigan knew that the time to strike for a lasting success was while the iron was red hot. In the theater, when the newspapers gave fine reviews, when there were lines at the box office, then (he always felt) was a time to increase, not lessen the efforts of promotion.

One reason he was journeying to Nanticoke was to have his window cards printed, the cards with which he intended to "bill the town." The cards were to read:

DON'T FORGET
A Mass at St. Michael's
(Coaltown)
at 5:45 A.M.
EVERY MORNING.

FATHER PAUL'S
MINERS' MASS
AT ST. MICHAEL'S

He had elaborated somewhat on his previous copy. He would print the five forty-five in numerals. Easier to read. He would put "Coaltown" under the name of the church. Perhaps these cards could be placed in outlying districts. He would start calling it "Father Paul's Miners' Mass."

The prestige of the miracle would greatly help in placing these cards. No store, no saloon would now turn down this service.

And the Miners' Union. He must get after them while things

were booming. He must make the acquaintance of the head of
that Union. They must be persuaded to support Father Paul as a
body. Dunnigan could now, thanks to Coaltown's leap into print,
give this local Union also a boost that would not be without value
and acclaim.

He had neglected the concert of Polish songs he'd thought of
for that afternoon. But only for the moment. The miracle provided enough attendance for that day. Perhaps a concert the next
afternoon—the day before the funeral. And have it a memorial to
the father. They were *his* songs. That would please Olga Treskovna, he knew. Olga Trocki who had gone to gather the first
goldenrod along the fence. That was where she now was, Bill
knew. He would speak of such a concert to Father Paul when
he got back to Coaltown.

There was an idea simmering also that there could be a concert
of old Polish melodies every week. He believed he could make a
tie-up with the local radio station about it. Broadcast it to all
the near-by cities. Great Polish music in memory of Stanislaus
Trocki! Give Pop a break also! That would make her happy!
And it would help to keep the name of St. Michael's shining like
a beacon. Shining over the magic of the air waves. For each concert should start and end with the sound of Father Paul's bell—
the bell of St. Michael's! Another thought: Some team of the
several great song writers he counted among his friends would
compose a ballad and title it, "The Bell of St. Michael's!" Bill
would persuade them to assign all royalties to Father Paul and
dedicate it—on every song cover—to Father Paul of the Church of
St. Michael the Archangel in Coaltown.

Now to his third task—"The Garden of the Soul."

Only his best was going to be good enough for what Marcus
Harris had done! He was now drawing five hundred dollars a
week. More than twenty-five thousand dollars a year.' He, Bill
Dunnigan! It was twice the salary he had ever been paid up to
the time he met the picture producer.

He recalled his start as a "publicity" man. He had been hired
by a lower East Side dance hall. He was seventeen years old but
looked older. His title was "Assistant Floor Manager," but he
was really the bouncer. He had a reputation in the neighborhood
for being handy with his fists—had then thought seriously of becom-

ing a professional fighter. But the memory of his mother had caused him to forego that profession. His mother did not approve of prize fighters.

His dance hall task had been to tap the shoulders of gentlemen patrons who insisted on wearing their hats onto the dance floor, who ignored the polite sign:

> GENTLEMEN WILL AND OTHERS MUST
> REMOVE THEIR HATS WHILE DANCING
> By Order of the Management.

Or of requesting other gentlemen not to "expectorate" on the wax. Decorative spittoons were thoughtfully and conveniently provided along the wall by this same "management." But sometimes there were profane objections to this interference with customary ball-room manners. His abilities as a boxer often stood him in good stead when these principles of Emily Post were being violated.

This dance hall was waltzing and turkey trotting (so to speak) on its last financial legs. The "management" was about to throw in the sponge and the towel. Perhaps there was too heavy insistence on strict etiquette. Young Assistant Floor Manager Dunnigan wanted to keep that job. It paid twenty-five dollars weekly.

The rage of the dance world was then the great team of Vernon and Irene Castle, who had set the town to talking with their exhibitions in the ballroom of the old Waldorf-Astoria—with their appearances at the new Palace Theater way uptown in a place newly named Times Square. The tall Irish boy put on his best suit and hat one morning, gave his shoes an extra careful polish, and made a call at the Waldorf. He must have looked not unlike the quick-lunch lad who now sat beside him in the Packard. He accomplished the unbelievable. He got to the Castles in their apartment. He persuaded these great ones to come to this East Side dance hall for an exhibition the following Saturday night!

He had sold newspapers. People read them, he noticed. He journeyed around and told the newspapers about his "booking." He had laboriously written out longhand copies headed *Important News Item* telling in glowing terms of this coming "supreme event." He left these "news items" with the City Desks where they thought it a joke until several telephoned the Castles and found that it was true! They printed (somewhat edited as to adjectives) that first Dunnigan press notice.

The next week he interviewed a fabulous lady named Ruth St. Denis who was appearing as Salome at Proctor's Theater at Twenty-Third Street. She also succumbed to the enthusiasm, the hopeful ardor of this tall, good-looking Irish lad. She promised to come to the dance hall for half an hour with her act the coming Saturday. She kept that promise. It required police reserves to handle the crowds around the bankrupt dance hall.

The die was cast. William Dunnigan had discovered that he could not only make friends but influence people—and newspapers! He turned down a raise to a thirty-dollar weekly stipend. He moved on to greater tasks in larger fields. At forty dollars weekly he became the advance agent for a burlesque troupe. He was in show business.

Well, he was still in show business along with miracles and St. Michael's. Just how, at five hundred bucks a week, was he going to best apply miracles and a church to the aggrandizement of Super Pictures, Inc., and "The Garden of the Soul"? To accomplish that was also his duty now.

The story of the new film, thank God, was clean and even inspiring. It had a religious theme at its end. There would be no tarnishing of St. Michael's because of a linking of the two. It happened that Marcus Harris had always stood for "clean" pictures. As we know, he was a religious man in his own faith. His private life was upright. Without trumpeting about it, he had quite naturally kept away from the salacious and the harmful-sensational.

When Dunnigan, on inspiration, had started the Coaltown bells ringing for four days, he had not thought of where to go on from that. It had, for the inspired moment, seemed all that was necessary. But after the first excitement of the bells—the first news stories about it—he realized that something more must happen. News in America, at least news of national importance, was news for twenty-four hours only. Other happenings in a newsy world quickly drove a single event from the press and from the minds of the readers of that press. In that first boyhood effort he had instinctively climaxed the polite Castles with the sensational Salome dancer. Later, as a trained press agent, he had built his climaxes deliberately. What next in Coaltown?

The unexpected miracle had provided the second lift. Olga Treskovna (and that name was now inseparable from "The Garden of the Soul") was the central figure of a supernatural event. It would, he was certain, simply as news carry on and climax the ringing of the bells. It had the further advantage that it would cause talk—argument. That argument would last beyond that night when it would be read of at every dinner and supper table in America—or at least be there to be read. And at every breakfast table the following morning. All of which must create a desire to see the new film.

It also had a pictorial appeal to newsmen that the bells could not by themselves stimulate. He had seen the sudden influx of cameramen and several newsreel cars. Pictures sometimes spoke louder than words. Trust these sleuths of the cameras to make the most of a picturesque village church, two statues that had "turned," an actress, a cassocked parish priest (Dunnigan did not know that a Bishop had already been added to the gallery), and the crowds of a mining town. He hoped that Father Paul would not hide from the news-spreading lenses. He hoped the priest (if the church rules did not forbid) would permit the cameramen inside St. Michael's.

So—the next move? It was going to be mighty hard to top a miracle. He was like a playwright with a great second act, too great almost, for the third was bound to be an anticlimax. Heaven was not likely to drop another miraculous plum into his lap!

Saint Michael (as he firmly believed) had carried the ball for a grand touchdown. A sensational touchdown. It was clearly up to Bill Dunnigan to provide the next flare for the papers, and so keep "The Garden of the Soul" in the public eye.

The funeral itself was now the third act of this Coaltown drama. How could he keep it simple and sedate and yet have something happen of moment—surprise—acclaim?

He felt the need of consulting Marcus Harris. That was another reason he was journeying again to Nanticoke. He wondered how New York had received the miracle. The New York papers might even ignore it entirely. But that scarcely seemed a likelihood.

There were telephones in Coaltown but none that he could use were private. The Wyoming Hotel's equipment consisted of a pay station on the lobby wall, not even surrounded by a booth. He did not feel that the booth in the drug store offered much better protection. The ever-present wife of that merchant had ears tiained to pierce its thin partitions. Any plans laid from there would be public property in five minutes, possibly only four!

As he rode along all this passed through his mind much more quickly than it has been recorded. His companions, noticing his fixed gaze ahead, sat quietly. They were still somewhat in awe of the great man who had befriended them. *He* was the miracle of Coaltown in their eyes.

They had breakfast at a restaurant. There Dunnigan listened to their own excited plans about Quick Lunch Heaven. They had paid two hundred and fifty dollars down on the new place on the Square. Seven hundred and fifty more in small monthly payments would completely own it, or a further cash payment of five hundred dollars. Bill took out his checkbook and wrote a check for the latter amount.

He made it payable to the girl.

"This is a wedding present to you," he said. "You're putting it into the business, not me. It isn't even from me—it's from my boss back in New York. He'll be glad to do it when he knows."

In his checkbook record Dunnigan made a notation. The incorruptible Pennsylvania State Police would have been surprised to read it—could the meaning have been deciphered. It said:

"On account securing services and good will S. T. $500."

"S. T." stood for State Troopers. Where, indeed, would he and Marcus Harris have been but for Kathleen O'Rourke!

The girl went to her store where she must work out the week. The boy went to complete his deal. Bill Dunnigan went to find a florist, for he wanted a blanket of roses made up for Olga Treskovna's coffin. Also to find a job printer who could set up in type his St. Michael's Mass show cards at once. And by that time Marcus Harris would be in his office and he could talk with him by telephone. There was a general office of the phone company in Nanticoke. It would have impersonal, soundproof booths.

The picture producer should certainly be pleased with the morning's happenings.

57

MARCUS J. HARRIS would have forged to the top in whatever business he had undertaken. He had energy, resourcefulness, determination, but the spark plug of his success was a by-product of still another quality—concentration. He *believed* in what he did. The task to which he set his hand (the rest of his compact body, also, and his mind) was the most important task in the entire world.

This had and did apply equally to the pressing of a pair of pants and the making of a million-dollar film. While he was in the former industry, empires might rise and fall, a presidential campaign or a World Series come and go; they were not nearly as important as the delivery of a pair of trousers when promised, and the conscientious creasing of these trousers before delivery. Every picture he had made, whether a silent melodramatic serial or a great all-star spectacle with symphonic orchestra, was undertaken in the same thorough manner. Whatever work he was responsible for must be the best of its kind, because the world existed at that moment solely for the purpose of receiving that pair of trousers or that film.

So, had he remained in "cleaning and pressing," this same world, or some part of it, would doubtless have been (with the prompt delivery of and the perfect creasing of many of its trousers) a less irritating and more sartorial-beauteous planet. And there would have been a lot of trousers so groomed in many cities thereon! His ambitious nature would have expanded the East Seventieth Street basement shop into a nation-wide chain of such shops, all giving this superlative and soul-gratifying service. In fact, he changed over to motion pictures because he had journeyed to Fourteenth Street one morning with the idea of establishing his first basement branch in that business section—if he could find a vacant basement.

He desired a "business address" with the prestige of that center of metropolitan retail commerce, not only for his own aspirations, but because the father of the girl he wanted to marry seemed to look down on a businessman whose headquarters were on East Seventieth Street. This father owned a prosperous jewelry store on upper Broadway.

Very well, young Marcus Harris would go the father one better. He would enable himself to send out monthly bills from the great Fourteenth Street.

But arriving there by the Third Avenue Elevated, he quickly found there were more than enough basement tailor shops on that busy street. Several in every block! And walking along past the plate-glass-fronted stores, the young man felt a sudden, overwhelming urge to get up out of basements. But he knew that rents of above-ground locations were much too high for the twenty-five cents a pair that sponging and pressing then brought.

Suppose he and his brother went into some entirely new business? A business with big enough returns to warrant the renting of a store! They had saved a thousand dollars between them from three years of intensive industry and frugal living spent in pants pressing. Their father on his deathbed had left them another thousand. Two thousand dollars in all.

He was toying with this revolutionary thought when he paused in front of a vacant shop. The door stood open and an estate agent was showing it to a prospective renter. Marcus Harris stepped inside to see how far beyond anything he could probably pay its rental would be.

It was entirely outside the means of a pants pressing establishment. Three hundred dollars a month! He and his brother paid thirty dollars on East Seventieth Street. But it did not seem to be beyond the means of the vocation of the other space-searcher, a young Jewish fellow of about his own age. It was the noon hour and the two left together. They exchanged a few friendly words. They went into the next door Hartford Lunch for a sandwich and a cup of coffee. They commenced talking.

The stranger was from Brooklyn and he, also, was looking to establish himself in this heart of Manhattan. They found that they bore the same first names. It seemed to draw them together. They formed an immediate liking for each other.

The Brooklyn boy, to whom three hundred dollars monthly was

not an impossibility, was in an entirely different "line." Amusements. He operated two penny arcades in Brooklyn—those recreation centers for the proletariat where, for a copper in a slot and the turning of a small crank, you could see two boxers or a dancer or an acrobat appear to be in motion. It was accomplished by means of a series of photographs on tiny cards that flipped into view in such rapid succession as to give an illusion of consecutive movement. For the musically inclined, tube-like wax records would whirl on a cylinder beneath a curved glass (if a penny were deposited); and two black tubes inserted in the ears of the investor brought the thumping melody of the Sextette from "Lucia" or the sentimental "Down Where the Wurzburger Flows."

This young impresario for the masses wanted to bring the cultural benefits of such sterling entertainment to New York City proper. He believed that on a great money-spending thoroughfare like Fourteenth Street the price of these various delights could be raised to five cents.

He had a name to call his place of entertainment. A Nickelodeon!

Looking beyond even this, the stranger had an entirely new and startling conception. The large vaudeville theaters were showing, as a minor part of their programs of acts, short "moving pictures" thrown on a screen from a rapidly moving film projected from a sort of magic lantern. They were beginning to record stories—little plays as it were—on these films. To be sure, the pictures had to stop and words were in turn projected on this screen when dialogue was necessary, but the audiences did not seem to mind!

This stranger believed that people would pay a small fee—say ten cents, perhaps even fifteen—to see a whole program, lasting an hour or so, made up entirely of such "moving pictures." He believed that a regular theater could be used! The performance could be continuous so that the house could be filled eight or ten times a day, not just for a matinee and an evening. Patrons could come at any convenient hour and, if they missed the beginning of a story, they need only wait until it came around again in the film routine. There would not be much operating expense as the entertainment was mechanical. No stagehands, no actors. Just ticket sellers and ushers, and a couple of piano players to supply a background of "Hearts and Flowers" or "William Tell" accompaniment.

But to start this daring enterprise he needed more capital than he possessed. He needed five thousand dollars. He had three, which he had made from his penny arcades the past year.

His name, by the way, was one that later graced the marquees of seemingly countless "picture palaces" across America—this land of immediate reward for foresight and courage.

Marcus Harris listened. Here would be getting up out of basements with a vengeance! A Nickelodeon! A real theater! And a new business without the profit-crushing competition of pants pressing! The other Marcus could consider paying three hundred dollars monthly for the store space, because he took in as much as fifty dollars daily in each of his Brooklyn penny arcades. You'd have to press two hundred pairs of pants a day to do that. Marcus Harris and his brother were lucky if they pressed two hundred pairs in two weeks.

The two young men named Marcus agreed to meet next morning at the Hartford Lunch.

There was heated argument that night in the East Seventieth Street basement. The girl, whose name was Rachel and who had been asked to come over, was all for it. She knew nothing about penny arcades, but often went with her parents to a vaudeville theater at Fifty-Ninth Street. She liked the moving picture part of the show. It was the part she liked best. The older Harris brother was against it. To him it sounded completely crazy. They might as well throw their money into the near-by East River. Younger brother Marcus Harris was debating, but he knew he had made up his mind. Pants pressing had already lost this bright jewel from its crown.

The younger brother and his fiancée won out. The savings and the inheritance were to be risked in the new venture with this young man from Brooklyn, if the girl approved of him. Marcus Harris wanted her confirmation. As a compromise (and an anchorage) the older brother was to continue the cleaning and pressing place until there were tangible results from Fourteenth Street. A man would be hired as his helper. Marcus Harris would give all his time to the new enterprise.

This is not a saga of the motion-picture industry. Enough that the girl Rachel thought the other Marcus sincere, honest, dependable. By noon the next day the Harris brothers were partners in a Nickelodeon, to be opened as quickly as possible in that vacant store on Fourteenth Street on the south side of Union Square. And the search for a vacant theater and the larger plan commenced.

The Nickelodeon paid from the start. On that busy Square a hundred dollars flowed in the first opening day. The first Saturday brought nearly two hundred dollars. The two active partners felt they could pay themselves a hundred dollars weekly salary. It was more than Marcus Harris sometimes made during an entire month with the hardest kind of work on East Seventieth Street. He and his Rachel were married.

Beyond the salaries, a sizable surplus was piling up each week. The young man with the startling conception located an empty theater. It was right on Broadway but north of Twenty-Third Street. But then he felt the amusement center was moving "uptown." It might even jump as far as Herald Square! The partners leased this theater for six months with further options. They had to pay two months rent in advance. Four thousand dollars. They spent another two thousand dollars redecorating its dingy interior, cleaning and repairing the seats, putting up new signs outside. They installed a staff and the necessary apparatus for projecting a program of "motion pictures." They put advertisements in newspapers, such newspapers as would accept them, for the more conservative journals did not care to sell space announcing such a dubious form of entertainment.

In one way and another the partners were risking their entire capital.

The first day, less, much less, came in than down at the Nickelodeon. The gross receipts were twelve dollars and twenty cents. Hardly more than enough to pay the ushers. Brother Irving, who had now given up the tailor shop entirely and was selling tickets behind the grated window, was in a near panic.

But Marcus Harris and the other Marcus were steadfast. The audiences—the daring ones who parted with ten cents and ventured inside—liked the idea. These two young proprietors took turns tearing tickets at the door. They talked with the customers as they came out. Most of them said they would come back in three days to see the next episode in "The Perils of Pauline." They would not miss the next Tom Mix adventure. They wanted to see if King Baggott won the girl. The theater was changing its program twice weekly.

The second day receipts went up. Eighteen dollars and forty cents was garnered. And there were no complaints. The third day the "take" doubled. Twenty-nine dollars! Brother Irving was still pessimistic—*it was just a fluke—it would not last*—but the two boys whose names were Marcus felt "they had something."

They took a loss, however, for several weeks. The Fourteenth Street Nickelodeon paid that loss. Two of the partners went to the Hartford Lunch each midnight and over ten cents' worth of coffee and doughnuts made plans about hiring "sandwich men"—putting out a "banner"—distributing printed handbills in the neighborhood. Brother Irving spent his ten cents to journey up to East Seventieth Street and gaze sadly at a darkened basement.

Then, suddenly, the movie theater began to "pack them in"—to sell out from the middle of the afternoon till late at night. In two months there was a regular profit of over two thousand dollars weekly!

Thus humbly commenced a great empire of motion-picture show houses. Had Marcus Harris remained a part of it, he would have become a multi-millionaire. But accumulating wealth was not his goal. His personal tastes were modest. So were his Rachel's. They had only themselves, for Heaven did not grant them children.

Although audiences were soon filling two other theaters added to the chain by the energetic lad from Brooklyn, and competitors were springing up who also did exceedingly well, the instinct that partner Marcus Harris possessed for doing a single thing finely, kept gnawing at his content. He was not happy about the films they could secure. He felt that these moving pictures could be much better made—have better actors—better stories. And why must they be only one or two reels in length? Just as you got interested, they ended!

Why couldn't one great story take up two hours as a play did in a regular theater? And why not make a "serial" from a really well-written story—the serial stories that were published in the good magazines his Rachel bought and read?

He purchased the right to make into a film a great Broadway success that had before that been a great novel. He paid the fabulous price of ten thousand dollars for this right. Even then the owners did not wish to sell, feeling it would cheapen—maybe ruin—their property. He persuaded a well-known playwright to make a picture adaptation on condition that the matter be kept secret. He in-

duced one brother of a famous theater family to appear in the leading role. He had met a sympathetic director of serials who also
wanted to try producing on film an entire play.

Marcus Harris took over the staff and equipment of a large studio
in New Jersey just across from 125th Street.

All this ran into a lot of money. Much more than he had. He
sold back his interest in the three picture theaters to his Fourteenth
Street associate and plunged this small fortune into the making of
a great, spectacular movie. The brother, now simply looking out
for finance, went along with Marcus Harris.

It was, fortunately, a success. It got back in rentals the quarter
of a million dollars it eventually cost. It stayed in one New York
theater for three months! A film! It went on to make another
quarter of a million profit.

Marcus Harris had proven his idea correct. You *could* do a full
length play on film. Audiences *would* sit through it. And see
effects no theater could duplicate. A battle scene with a thousand
horsemen! The whole street of a town in action! At the other extreme, the most minute detail of the expression of the eyes or the
lips. With this taste of creating great picture plays in his mouth, a
man like Marcus Harris could never go back to simply operating
theaters, no matter what the profits might be. He became a producer.

As a producer he both won and lost. The man who creates takes
chances. The pictures could not all be successful. In producing
there was not the steady crescendo of sure profits that adding new
theaters in the right locations to his chain now gave the young
Brooklyn Marcus who had started with a penny arcade. For the
popularity of this new form of entertainment grew by unbelievable
leaps and bounds. It challenged and surpassed the patronage of the
regular playhouses.

Most of the films were still only a couple of reels in length and
cheap in story and handling; but Marcus Harris could not bring
himself to make pictures, short or long, in that manner. Nor did
he care to produce "wholesale," so that by the law of averages he
would always win. He tried that for awhile, just after the introduction of sound and its spoken dialogue, but he soon resigned
from a great corporation of which he was a partner. The same instinct that caused him to want each pair of pants that left the East

Seventieth Street basement to be perfect, and which pants he personally inspected if he had not actually pressed them himself, carried over into the making of a film. He wanted to make only as many pictures as he could personally plan for and personally supervise.

So while not the largest producer, he soon became known as one of the finest and most careful. When a Harris film failed, it was not because it was not well done. The subject matter simply did not have a wide enough popular appeal. He was always tempted to try new subjects. He made the first picture with a religious theme. He made several without the usual happy ending. He made one entirely about the life of a traitor to his country that had the best acting of its year. This pioneering sometimes cost him almost all he had made. But his integrity was of the highest, and he could go to Wall Street if he needed more money for the next one. Sooner or later he would turn out another box-office winner.

This expert knowledge of a new art, gained in the hard but thorough school of trial and error, was still hidden beneath a modest, almost childlike exterior. The casual observer thought him simply lucky, or that his success was due entirely to the clever people he managed to draw to his Studios. They did not realize that even these clever ones were guided by the brain of the onetime pants presser, the brain that wanted everything to be "the best," that considered each film he undertook the most important task in the world!

He was content, even when he occasionally lost all his profits on several unsuccessful stories. He and his Rachel did not covet yachts and country houses and racing stables. Many of the stars he used (and often made) who went in for such things, ended each year with much more money than Marcus Harris.

The producer had a sizable apartment on West End Avenue. He had a small farm in Westchester County where his wife's father and mother now lived. He and Rachel would sometime retire there, when he became too old to work and take chances. They wanted nothing more.

His home life was very happy. Their lack of children was made up for by a very great love of each other. Rachel's friends were in New York—her social life, her charities, her small clubs were there. So he did not move to California when the producing part of the great new business migrated to the West Coast. He preferred the inconvenience of commuting back and forth. At first it was a hardship, but nowadays with fast planes, it was not too tiring. They may not have realized it, but this constant separation had strengthened their affection. They had no chance to get tired of each other, or if not tired, to take each other for granted. They missed each other damnably in the separations, but it kept their love always young.

One last observation. With Marcus Harris, work was a thing for working hours. Outside of those hours he was not the pants presser or the picture producer. He was a husband who had found the perfect companion. To make *her* happy and proud of him—that was the great incentive. And he did not carry over into his own life any traits of his trade. As a presser of pants he never bothered to crease his own trousers. He liked them roomy and baggy! As a producer he did not go in for any of the glamorous life of his films. He did not even care much for attending the theater. He preferred to sit at home by the living room table and read his newspaper, then play pinochle or cribbage with his wife or with her friends who might drop in. Their flat on West End Avenue was simple and comfortable. It was only the office—the place where her Marcus met his business world—that Rachel wanted him to be in a magnificent setting.

She was very proud of him. She thought he was the greatest picture producer in the world. But she would have been just as proud had he been the world's best pants presser. She *knew* he was the world's best husband. She knew he could not be anything but the greatest in whatever work he did.

58

*M*ARCUS *AND* RACHEL HARRIS did not breakfast till about nine-thirty o'clock the morning of the miracle. Friends had dropped in the evening before and they had played gin rummy till a late hour. So the producer did not hear the radio news broadcast at eight-thirty to which he usually listened. He liked that broadcast, not so much for the news, but because its announcer, after the official weather report, always gave the "unofficial McCarthy reaction" in a pithy, humorous phrase. Marcus Harris wore his overshoes or left off his topcoat according to the advice of that phrase. It was seldom wrong.

So he missed the "unofficial reaction" that morning; he also missed the mention that a "miracle" was reported to have occurred in connection with his star, Olga Treskovna, and the bell-ringing church in Pennsylvania. There was nothing, of course, about it in his morning paper which had been printed before the turning of the statues was discovered.

He had not gone directly to his office. There was a meeting of the board of the Hebrew Sheltering and Immigrant Aid Society at ten o'clock of which he was a vice-president and active force. The Society's building was "downtown" and he went directly there, taking the subway at 103rd Street. In New York he still preferred this democratic means of transportation.

On leaving his apartment house his thoughts as usual turned to his business. Those thoughts were similar to the thoughts of William Dunnigan, except that they were concerned entirely with "The Garden of the Soul."

The news stories of the ringing of the bells had aroused the dramatic editors. Largely on request by telephone and wire (an unusual manifestation of interest), the drama departments were being supplied with such "still" photographs as were in New York of scenes from the new picture, as well as photographs of Olga Treskovna in the leading role. More "stills" were being rushed from Hollywood by airmail. Stories about the film and its new star were being mimeographed and dispatched to the lists every producer's office kept of all the papers of importance in the entire country. The Press would have full data about the new film.

But Marcus Harris knew too well that these releases would only be used if the news end of the promotion were kept alive. For, what with cutting, editing, inserting subtitles, synchronizing of a musical score, it would be a full month before the picture could possibly be playing in theaters. What could his press agent think of meantime to keep up the news interest?

It was nearly noon by the time he reached his Radio City office.

Excitement there was running almost as high as on the day before. This time Miss Feinberg was waiting at her employer's desk. She had heard about the "miracle" over the radio. When ten o'clock came and he had not arrived, she broke a rule and telephoned the Harris apartment. Both Mr. and Mrs. Harris were out, for Rachel Harris had gone, as she always did, to personally do her marketing.

Miss Feinberg could only wait impatiently. She did not wait idly for again there were telephone calls from the newspaper offices and the broadcasting newsrooms. Mr. Dunnigan had phoned twice from Pennsylvania but wanted to speak directly to Mr. Harris. At eleven o'clock the publicity department had advance copies of the afternoon papers. They were passed from hand to hand among the office staff and now awaited, on his desk, the arrival of the president.

These papers gave the answer to any letting-down of news interest on the part of Mr. Dunnigan. The alleged event in Coaltown, the excitement it had created, was recorded on the first page of most of them. Usually in a two- or three-column box which set it off even better than if the story were printed up and down a single column. *PM* had a photograph of St. Michael's church and the crowds outside it. Another paper carried one of the Bishop of the district and the parish priest of this church standing together. These photographs had been radio-wired to New York by a photo-press service.

A MIRACLE REPORTED IN PENNSYLVANIA TOWN WHERE BELLS ARE RINGING FOR LATE FILM STAR

was a typical headline.

One paper even said "the late Olga Treskovna" as if her name were now a familiar one to its readers!

Always there followed a graphic reciting of the discovery of the turning of the statues of Saint Michael and the Madonna in the direction of the coffin of this girl. In two papers the entire story of the bells was repeated, and one tabloid had a photograph of Miss Treskovna covering its outside page.

"Mr. Dunnigan is certainly on the job!" exclaimed Miss Feinberg proudly as she greeted the smiling Marcus Harris and spread out the news sheets before him. "No one but the one and only 'White Spats' could put on a stunt like it tells about today. It's magnificent! It's sensational!"

Since the hiring of Bill Dunnigan, Miss Feinberg was rapidly acquiring a vocabulary of superlatives.

Marcus Harris seized the papers, but the smile slowly vanished from his face as he read. He read them all, unsmiling and in silence. Having read, he did not burst into the expected approbation of his ace press agent's newest achievement. There was instead a decided look of worry on a strained and sober countenance.

"The inside theater pages all carry articles about Miss Treskovna and the film," the secretary added, as her employer, for some unexplained reason, seemed to be most unhappy! "The *World-Tele* gram has nearly half a page about her early hardships in this mining town, and how you gave her a chance in Hollywood—they must have sent a special writer to the town. But all this front page stuff Mr. Harris! I don't think any film ever made got such an advance build-up."

Marcus Harris remained silent. He did not seem to Miss Feinberg to be listening. He was regarding again the front-page headlines and he took up the paper which had Father Paul and his Bishop looking out from its left center. Miss Feinberg could see his jaw hardening and his thick lips forming in a tense line. A danger signal.

"What is wrong, Mr. Harris?" she could not refrain from crying. She felt she would risk her job to defend Mr. Dunnigan, if there was now some new reason for a prejudice against him and his latest inspiration!

"I don't like it," said Marcus Harris. "I don't like it at all! See if you can reach Dunnigan by telephone."

"He's been trying to reach you," gasped the mystified secretary. "Has phoned twice and will call again at noon. But what's the trouble, Mr. Harris? That picture of a Bishop and a priest is wonderful for us! And a church! Of course, it's not like as if it were a synagogue but 'The Garden of the Soul' is a Catholic story. know two grand priests up in the Bronx. They're not unlucky. You couldn't buy such front-page attention like Mr. Dunnigan has grabbed off for us today for a million dollars! Even the *Times* has telephoned you and I'm sure that in the morning——"

Marcus Harris looked up at his secretary. "I'm wondering just what it *did* cost!" he said.

"But Mr. Harris! If I may say so, it don't matter *what it cost*

ou told Mr. Dunnigan to spare no expense. You sent him twice as
uch as he asked for. You had the bank wire to give him un-
mited credit."

Let anyone ever again speak to Miss Feinberg of the inconsistency
f women. Women indeed! Men!

"I know what I said and what I did," snapped Marcus Harris
rimly. "Stop talking and try to contact Dunnigan at once. What
as that hotel? Wyoming. In Coaltown, Pennsylvania. Get him
n the phone immediately!"

"Yes, Mr. Harris," she said. But there was the glint of battle—
lmost revolt—in her eyes and voice.

Miss Feinberg did not have to "try to contact" Bill Dunnigan.
s we know, he was not at that moment in Coaltown. The tele-
hone from the office switchboard was buzzing. Pennsylvania was
n the wire again and wanting Mr. Harris personally.

"It's Mr. Dunnigan now!" said Miss Feinberg, so fiercely that the
icture producer gave her a second glance as he took the receiver
rom her.

Over the wire came a happy, confident voice. Still aggressively
tanding by the desk, Miss Feinberg could also hear it.

"Hello, Marcus boss! This is Bill Dunnigan! It's great news we
ave this morning for 'The Garden of the Soul.'"

"*What* great news?" asked Marcus Harris.

To the press agent, encased in a telephone booth in Nanticoke,
here was a surprising lack of enthusiasm in the producer's voice.
t didn't sound at all like the voice of the employer who had tele-
raphed twenty grand instead of ten. Or the friend who had signed
he second wire "Marcus." Could it be New York did not yet know?
ven so, without news of the miracle, the bells were still ringing.
hat exploit seemed to rate a better comeback on their first direct
onversation than an antagonistic, disapproving "*What* great news?"

"Perhaps the evening papers aren't out yet," said Bill Dunnigan,
or maybe you don't hear a radio during business hours. I think
f you'll send out for the papers, you'll find that maybe, perhaps,
our new star is given mention again. I'm in Nanticoke now, but
ur little Coaltown was bubbling over with big-time reporters when
left there."

"The evening papers are out and I have read them," said Marcus
arris. "You've made the first page again all right, all right."

"Anything wrong about that!" exclaimed the voice from Nanticoke. What did his boss expect and want? If this coldness was his idea of being funny, Dunnigan didn't relish its humor. There was just a little too much at stake.

"You'll be glad to know there's a picture of your church, and one showing a bishop and a priest," continued Marcus Harris. And it sounded to Dunnigan as if this commendable "flash" was to be construed as a great calamity!

"I don't know about any bishops," said the press agent, "but surely this is giving 'The Garden of the Soul' a boost no film I know of has ever had. Miracles don't happen in churches everyday. What's eating you, Marcus? I don't get you at all."

"What did it cost to pull it off?" said Marcus Harris.

"What did it cost! Good lord, are you joking?" exclaimed Dunnigan. Was the Maecenas who disclaimed being a piker now worrying about money? Human nature was unpredictable indeed.

"I'm far from joking. What did you pay to have it done?" came the stern voice from New York.

William Dunnigan nearly dropped his receiver. He was used to unusual reactions in a career devoted to instigating that same, but this was too much.

"You mean you think *I had it done!*" he finally exclaimed.

"What else am I to think?" came the voice of Marcus Harris. "Look here, Dunnigan. Your ringing of the church bells was a great idea, whether Olga Treskovna really wanted it, or whether, as I suspect, you cooked it up yourself. That don't hurt anyone. But this latest stunt! I'm a religious man. I go to my synagogue. I'm respected there. I don't give a damn about the money. I told you to shoot the works. But I didn't expect you to use that money to tamper with another religion—to hire someone to move holy statue in a church! I don't want to play that game. I *don't* play that game! I——"

"For the love of Mike!" came an interruption from the Pennsylvania end.

"Let me finish," continued Marcus Harris with deadly sternness. "It's tampering with something we have no right to tamper with. And it will surely bring us bad luck. It will bring Super Pictures, Inc., a retribution! It's dishonest! It's sacrilege! It will——!"

But the astonished Bill Dunnigan was now fully articulate. He broke in and there was undisguised scorn in the tone.

"Listen, my friend Marcus," he said. "Listen and use your bean that I didn't think was such a dumb one. Do you think that your Moses—or was it Elijah?—*paid* someone to push back the Red Sea? Do you read that your Daniel *paid* to get out of the lions' den? Did Jonah *buy his way* out of that whale? For God's sake, do you believe that money turned that Bible dame into salt—that a bank roll could——"

The picture producer interrupted this hectic enumeration of Old Testament supernatural occurrences. Fortunately perhaps, for William Dunnigan's limited knowledge was running out of examples.

"Are you telling me there really was a miracle in this Catholic church!" he broke in. "That it wasn't a job you thought up, and hired to be done?"

Dunnigan took a deep breath of the carbon dioxide of his phone booth. "That's what I'm telling you!" he said. And what sounded like a most profane ejaculation came over the wire.

"But such things don't happen now!" exclaimed a defensive Marcus Harris in a voice containing both relief and amazement.

"It happened up here without any help from your massive bank account or my massive brain! Get that straight, Marcus. I may not be as damn religious as you say *you* are! I don't go to any church or mosque or synagogue—no one knows or respects me there! I'm better known in barrooms and gin mills, but I play the game, I hope. And there's a priest, not to mention a Saint, at this particular Catholic church—you tell me you've got the pictures there—he's a little guy with a little church—that I wouldn't doublecross for all the motion pictures your cheap Hollywood fakers have made or ever will make!"

Bill Dunnigan sounded pretty sore. He was sore. He was about to slam down his receiver.

"Wait! Don't hang up, Bill!" cried Mr. Harris. Even across the hundred miles that separated them, he sensed the acrimonious mood of his press agent. And the great man looked up a little helplessly at his secretary. William Dunnigan must not go on the warpath at such a moment!

Miss Feinberg was equal to the occasion. She had saved situations before. She pointed to the tops of her shoes.

"Spats!" she tensely whispered. "Spats!"

Marcus Harris did not know exactly what she meant, but he made a guess and a correct one.

"Bill, did the new white spats arrive O. K.?" he spoke quickly into his telephone.

The man in the booth at Nanticoke stayed his hand toward the receiver hook. He had to smile. And there was a further thought Good old Marcus Harris! Wouldn't lend himself to a fraud on a church—any church!

Bill knew that he liked his boss the better for it.

"The spats arrived O. K. and thanks," he said.

"What do you want us to do next, Bill?" came in a humble tone Mr. Harris had just come from the solving of "what to do" about transplanting five hundred immigrants to mid-Western farms, but the turning of two statues in a country church was beyond his grasp "I guess we've got something pretty big on our hands! It's bigge than I am! You'd better be the boss on this job—I mean miracle—from now on."

"You're still the big boss and O. K.," said Dunnigan, "only don' get me wrong again, Marcus. And 'big' is right about what has hap pened up here! I'm in Nanticoke, seven miles away, and it's al even this place is talking of. Our Olga Treskovna and 'The Garden of the Soul' will be played up in every news sheet in the land, or don't know newspapers! The miracle don't worry me. It's ou next move—the funeral—that's got me buffaloed. I'm no expert o funerals!"

"What's wrong about the funeral?" asked Marcus Harris. Wa there some new trouble in the air?

"Nothing wrong," said Bill, "but it's day after tomorrow, and want to do something unusual.

"It's like this, Marcus. We've served up a swell news-meal so far Real Cinderella stuff for the cocktail! Appetizing bells for th entrée! A miracle for the solid meat course! I take no credit fo that. Now, what are we going to give 'em for dessert? You and mustn't fall down from here on. I like to finish what I start! S do you!"

"There's that Polish Ambassador," suggested Marcus Harris.

"We're not going backwards," laughed Bill, "backwards to the jinx or any other jinx!"

"You'll think of something unusual," said the producer with confidence.

"That's it. Something unusual! But I think too much of this girl, and this church has been too swell to me to pull any hocus-pocus. You use your bean, Marcus. I'm pounding mine. We've got to top a miracle for news values!"

"Maybe there's some other important people who might attend," said Marcus Harris without conviction.

"That isn't a bad thought. You don't by any chance know the governor of Pennsylvania?"

"I don't even know who *is* the governor," confessed Mr. Harris. "The leader of Tammany Hall is a friend of mine—and the New York Commissioner of Police."

"I'm afraid they wouldn't help," said Bill.

"I will come myself," said Mr. Harris.

"You're aces high with me, Marcus," laughed Bill again, "and you're a big shot in the industry, but you're not yet a national hero with the masses. Also, you're what they'd call in the law an interested party. I want you here, but for once I'll have to keep silent about you, Marcus."

Miss Feinberg, who had been called to the outer office, had at this point burst in again, and by gesture evinced a strong desire to speak.

"Hold on a minute, Bill," said Marcus Harris. "Yes, Miss Feinberg?" to the bursting secretary.

"The manager of the Music Hall is outside, and the vice-president of the Intercity circuit! I think they want to ask about booking 'The Garden of the Soul'!" she said in one breath.

Such great ones had never before come with their hats in their hands.

"Bill," said Marcus Harris, "stay right where you are! Give me the number. I've got to see a couple of the boys I don't want to keep waiting. I'll call you back inside half an hour. I may know something more by then."

"I've some things to do and I'll be here again at twelve-thirty. Main telephone office, Nanticoke. Same town as the good old Miners' Bank. Please don't be late in calling, for I must get back to Coaltown. The excitement there may be too much for my pal, the priest. I'm glad he let them take his picture, but I'm worried about that bishop fellow!"

"They're both smiling in the picture!" said Marcus Harris.

"That's good!" said Bill. "Thanks! That makes me feel easier. And it reminds me. There's one thing I want you to do at once. Send out and buy the finest altar cloth in New York. Buy half a dozen of 'em! I think Barclay Street is the Catholic supply district —or near St. Patrick's. The very finest, you understand. I wish there was one made of pure gold threads! No price is too much to pay. It's a small altar, about seven feet long. You bring them with you when you come Friday morning. Don't leave till then. The hotel is no Biltmore and there may be other things for you to attend to in New York. I'll stay close here. Remember—a Catholic altar cloth. Don't make a mistake and bring up a Jewish one!"

"I'm writing it down," said Marcus Harris. "Miss Feinberg—a Catholic altar cloth—seven-foot altar—to fit the priest in the picture —half a dozen of them!" Bill could hear the obedient Mr. Harris repeating. "Price no object. Don't make mistake and bring Jewish one." Then to Dunnigan again, "Say, do I ever buy cheap props?"

"Good lord! These are not theatrical props! They're the real thing! For the altar of this church."

"Right! Miss Feinberg, note *must be guaranteed the real thing!* I'll get them myself, Bill. I'll take my wife to help select them."

"Hold on!" said Dunnigan. "I think you'd better do it yourself, Marcus. This church is very quiet and simple. And it's a quiet, simple guy I'm getting 'em for, like you and me."

"Maybe you're right," sighed Mr. Harris, and glanced grimly about his private office. "Thanks, Bill. A man's taste is best for another man! But wait—I know a fellow who might get us some wholesale——"

"Not on your life!" broke in Dunnigan. "I once bought an overcoat that way! And Marcus——"

"Yes, Bill."

"Ever hear of Saint Michael the Archangel?"

"I've been reading about him in your miracle news. The priest seems to have given the Associated Press quite an interview on the subject."

"Great! Fine! Another good build-up for Super Pictures, Inc.!"

"For Super Pictures, Inc.!"

"You bet! You read up some more about this Saint. Get out your Bible and read! Go to your synagogue and find out! Because—" and Bill Dunnigan had at last hit on a real idea to promote Saint Michael "—you're going to make a feature film about that guy! Good-by, Marcus—talk with you again in half an hour."

"But wait, Bill! This Saint Michael's been dead a long time, and the public wants live, up-to-date subjects!"

"He's the livest, up-to-datest guy you ever met!" cried Bill. "All you and I have got to do is to try to keep up with him. Don't argue, Marcus. I'll make a real producer of you yet!"

"O. K. Good-by—boss!" said the voice from the blond desk in Radio City, with a happy laugh in it now.

The sharp click of the receiver being hung was a reassuring one. The Napoleon of the Industry was in top form again.

Bill Dunnigan emerged from his soundproof, airproof booth. He left word he was expecting a call in half an hour and would return. He would go to see the setup of his "5:45 Mass" cards, which were to be ready by night. And he turned over this new inspiration in his mind.

A film about Saint Michael! Not an ancient story, except as the background, but a Saint Michael that was still the fighting champion and took part in the destinies of living men! One might not have thought his mind was on such a subject as he emerged into the street. He was singing softly:

"A pretty girl—is like a melody——!"

But that was always Bill Dunnigan's Song of Victory.

If only he could now hit on a real inspiration about the funeral.

The funeral! For the world it was fast becoming a spectacle—he was doing all he knew to make it that—the burial of the film star who has caused a miracle to happen! What had he just said to Marcus Harris? It was all a news-meal, and they must now devise a stirring, world-shaking dessert! Thus thought the five-hundred-dollar-a-week press agent for "The Garden of the Soul."

But there was another William Dunnigan. The man who loved this girl. What would it really mean for him? When the coffin was lowered into the open grave—when the cold, black earth was shoveled back—when he heard the thud! thud! on the coffin lid—when Father Paul had repeated the final words.

Would Olga Treskovna be gone forever? Bill Dunnigan stopped his song abruptly. A chill gripped his heart.

As he stood silent on the Square in this strange town, the faint sound of the Coaltown bells reached his ears. And with those bells came a voice he knew.

It was just her voice this time—he looked to see but she was not there beside him.

"I'm still at the cemetery, Bill. You *know* I'm not in that coffin. I'll not be in it—really—when they bury it deep. I'll be standing with you—holding your hand.

"Sometimes, maybe, I'll go there—at night when you're asleep— when you're working hard during the day—when you haven't the time to think of me. I wouldn't want you going about sighing for me every minute! You have your work to do. But whenever you want me, I'll come to you. I told you I'd be with you always. I'll come back to New York when you need me there. I'll be in Holly- wood if you need me there. We're still going to do a lot of things together, Bill, my darling!

"I was frightened this morning, but I'm all right now. I'm glad the statues turned, for it will help Father Paul. I like Father Paul. I'm sending a little message to him, Bill. From up here at the cemetery."

"What message do you mean, kid?" he asked.

"He'll tell you when you get back to Coaltown. I'm telling you so you'll know I really sent it. Don't be unhappy, Bill. There isn't any death, when there is someone who loves you—someone you love——"

There was again only the sound of the distant bells. But Bill (White Spats) Dunnigan had been told the secret of immortality, that secret that is not the property of any race, any Koran or Bible, any creed. That secret only born of love in the human heart that can transcend Death itself! That new Dawn that must follow as bright Day succeeds the Night.

He crossed the Square to his printer. Several who noticed him glanced a second time at the radiance that seemed to spring from his eager face.

And he wondered what kind of message it would be that Olga Treskovna would send to Father Paul.

59

*B*ACK IN COALTOWN, Father Spinsky also had not failed to hear the news of the St. Michael's miracle.

He heard of it first at about six A.M. when his sister Mary shouted it through his bedroom door. The phrasing of the announcement recalled only too blatantly his former attitude of antagonism toward this humble building that seemed to be suddenly in the hands of a supernatural power.

His sister said: "Get up, brother! If you're going to get the best of Father Paul you'd better be on the move! They say a miracle has happened at his church! The whole silly town is on its way there already!"

She did not wait for a reply. She was provoked with her brother. He was the silliest one of the lot. What had gotten into him? Lying down to this weakling Father Paul!

And after eighteen hours of meditation, she was very angry with herself for sending the best chocolate cake she had made in weeks to the two people doubtless responsible for this latest act of upstart effrontery! For such it seemed to her. If miracles were to happen in Coaltown, they should occur in a church worthy of them, and where there was a priest worthy of them. St. Leo's.

She had the initial news from the brother of their sexton who had come to take his shift at the bell rope. This man had to pass Father Paul's church on his way to St. Leo's. He had passed it just at the exciting moment of the discovery of the statue turning. He had managed, with the first comers, to get a look at these statues, so he knew their turning to be a fact. He then hurried on, not to be late at his job of bell tugging, and to bring the startling tidings to the St. Leo's parish house.

Father Spinsky did not respond with his usual aggressive efficiency. He did not leap from his bed and stamp down to get further facts, then take appropriate action thereon. He arose very slowly. Subconsciously he had been expecting some untoward event. It had come! His anxieties of the afternoon before had not been ground-less.

He was always up at six-thirty. On Wednesday mornings he him-self had a Mass at seven. He commenced to dress slowly. From his window he could see and hear people hurrying past. Undoubtedly something quite unusual had happened.

He was anxious to know what it was, but he was almost afraid to know!

He would not have been surprised at anything. Saint Michael himself was abroad in the town. Walking and conversing with hu-man beings! Had a new, great cathedral risen during the night in the place of the tumbledown edifice bearing that name? He lis-tened a moment to the bells and could distinguish the high, sweet tone of Father Paul's metal clarion. St. Michael's bell, at least, was the same!

His own bell was tolling also. No avenging army of winged war-riors had descended to destroy St. Leo's. Destroy it as the evil don-jon that had sheltered one who in deed and thought had tried to blot out the rival chapel of the greave-clad Saint.

When he finally descended his stairs he still asked no questions.

He had come to the kitchen, as was his habit, to shave—that be-ing the only place where the water was hot so early in the morning. The sister was inwardly bursting with a full report, gathered not only from the relief bell-sexton but later from the neighbors. She waited for the eminent satisfaction of being able to answer every question in minute detail, but when no interrogation came from her tight-lipped brother she could keep silent no longer. She poured it out to him in a flood. Even then he made no comment except to say, "Thanks."

He was indeed thankful—relieved to hear that omnipotent efficacy had been satisfied with so simple a thing as the turning of two statues!

"What are you going to do now?" demanded the sister at the end of her voluble reporting. As she talked she had been viciously mix-ing eggs and butter and flour in a large bowl.

"I'm making another cake," she said, "and this one stays here for us! For our stomachs! Fine thanks we are getting for being gen-erous! Statues turning indeed! This man at the Wyoming Hotel and his money! You can hire anything to be done with money! If

I were you, brother, I would see him at once and demand an explanation. I would go to the Squire and tell him what I suspect!"

She was saying this, curiously enough, at the same moment that Sergeant Dennis O'Rourke was telling Bill Dunnigan, "You're under arrest!"

"Mary," said Father Spinsky heavily (he was now drying his face), "I must ask you, I must *demand* of you, that you voice no more such thoughts."

"I shall speak my mind and it's time you spoke yours!" said the woman with increased vehemence. As she kneaded the mixture for the new cake, the recollection of the hard labor put into the one of yesterday again rankled her soul. "When I think of my trotting up to that filthy St. Michael's parish house, going to that awful hotel, to deliver our food—*our food* to two ingrates——"

A sudden, blind fury seized Father Spinsky. A fury and a fear. He dropped his face towel; he strode to his sister and grasped from her hand the large bowl in which she was mixing the cake ingredients. He raised it above his head with his two hands and dashed it to the floor. The yellow mixture of the unborn cake and its crockery spread like Gluttony incarnate, disemboweled! The sister stood open-mouthed—too startled to resist.

"Evil!" cried Father Spinsky. "Only evil! A cake made with thoughts like yours is poison. It would poison this house! It would poison St. Leo's! Make no more of them. Cook for me no more until you have cleansed your heart!"

"Why, brother!" the woman gasped. She had seen him angry before—when he had first heard of Father Paul's five forty-five Mass —when he had heard that this priest had brought "visiting nurses" from Scranton—when he had learned about the "absolution" of a Jewish peddler—but never had he raised his voice in anger at herself.

Father Spinsky stared at the mess he had made about the kitchen floor. His anger fled as quickly as it had risen. He realized the absurdity of his act. Absurd, but perhaps it was the only way his sister could be impressed. He went to where she had sunk into a chair. Tears were coming to her eyes.

"Mary," he said, "I'm sorry. Forgive me. I am under a great strain. I am not myself. I should not blame you. For you have been living with an evil man for twenty years. That man is me.

Selfishness, hatred, revenge, pride have ruled my heart. I have taught them all to you. I have taught them perhaps to my whole parish! It is my fault entirely. Try now to understand. I am no longer seeking to 'get the best' of Father Paul. I am not worthy to be an altar boy in his sanctuary. And this man, as you call him, at the Wyoming Hotel. I have a strange fear and a strange premonition. Perhaps he *is* just a rich man carrying out the wishes of a dead friend. Perhaps he is something more than that. I do not know. But I do know he has shown me myself as I really am. I am angry at myself, and like all men so angered, I turn on those I love.

"I will go now to say my Mass, though I am unworthy! Maybe God will forgive me because I know I am unworthy. Cook for me still, Mary. Have my breakfast when I return. But try to prepare it with love—with charity in your heart. From now on, Mary, we live differently—or we do not live! God help us, we were better dead! We have been dead these ten years of my pastorage in Coaltown! And before."

Father Spinsky put on his cassock. He looked again at his sister. He moved to her and bending down, kissed her on the forehead. This woman had given up her life to his comfort. She had not married to take care of him. For the first time in his life he felt a tenderness toward this sister. He had accepted her services as his natural right. He had selfishly used her as he had used all others who had crossed his path.

"Try to understand, Mary," he said. "I ask your forgiveness for what I have done to you." And he went quickly from the room and across the lawn to his church.

Mary Spinsky did not entirely understand. Like her brother she was a stolid, granite type. A lifetime's habit of thought could not be changed in a single three minutes.

She was not discontented with her lot. She adored her brother. In spite of what he said, he was not "evil." He was great and good! He had kissed her. That was what mattered most. But he was certainly not himself!

She was no longer angry with Father Paul. Somehow she connected this new tenderness with Father Paul. The fear in her brother's heart was not apparently due to anything the pastor of St. Michael's had done. It was due to this stranger stopping at the Wyoming Hotel. This man William Dunnigan to whom she had taken the other half of the chocolate cake.

How had he managed to make her brother feel that his whole upright life was wrong? Who was this Dunnigan person to upset and disturb Father Spinsky? If she no longer hated Father Paul, a double measure of hatred welled up against this stranger in the town.

As she cleaned up the mess about her otherwise spotless kitchen floor, she made up her mind to personally see this man and demand by what right he had destroyed the even tenor of their lives. She determined to find out by what witchcraft he had caused a man of God to lose faith in the righteousness of his world and life!

She must protect her brother from whatever sinister spell this man had cast over him.

But she would move carefully. She must not let her brother suspect any such plan. When she had fathomed the cause of all this she would bring him back to his normal, confident self.

* * *

Meantime Father Spinsky entered his church. It was strangely empty. It was absolutely silent except for the great bell tolling above. The sound of that bell seemed to emphasize the silence. There were no altar boys to help him don his vestments. He put them on alone. When, promptly at seven, he moved into his sanctuary and turned to make the sign of the cross to the worshipers, there were no worshipers there! Not a single person sat in the spacious pews. The miracle at St. Michael's had drained the town.

Father Spinsky winced. He felt a strange dryness in his throat. He had never before had such an experience. He recalled how he had laughed, how he had gloatingly sneered when he had heard that Father Paul's early Masses often had not a solitary worshiper in attendance. He knew now how Father Paul must have felt the first time it occurred.

But perhaps Father Paul had not suffered! Father Paul was at peace with his God. Father Paul had no memories of cruelties, of petty injustices to mar his inner tranquillity. Content was from *within*. Strength was from *within*.

Father Spinsky went through his Mass. He did not hurry but

gave each word its full sonorous value. And he made each gesture
with a grace and solemnity not too often usual with him. Strangely
enough, he felt that he was acquiring a new strength. The strength
of humility. The joy of humility!

He had never known humility.

At the very end he looked out into his church. He looked again
and passed his hands before his eyes.

Three candles were burning at the small shrine of Saint Joseph
by the door! Just as he had lit three candles the afternoon before.
They had not been burning when he had commenced his service!
Of that he was certain.

There seemed to be a figure kneeling at this shrine. It was in the
shadow and he could not see it clearly. And as he looked, it arose
and moved toward the doorway.

The figure seemed vaguely familiar. It was a man in miner's
clothes. There was a bulge under the arm toward the altar, as if
the man were carrying a package.

The door opened, and for a moment the figure was silhouetted
against the bright sunlight of the morning outside. Father Spinsky
knew what the bulge under the man's arm was. It was an accordion!

And Father Spinsky knew who this figure reminded him of.
Stanislaus Trocki! The father of the girl who had caused the
miracle up at St. Michael's. The man *he* had caused to be arrested
for his drunken sleeping on St. Leo's steps. The man had been
clutching the accordion that morning, even in his stupor. Father
Spinsky remembered that the sight of it had increased his furious
resentment.

But Stanislaus Trocki was dead! He had been dead for more
than four years! The bells were ringing partly for this man's
memory.

Nevertheless, Father Spinsky called out:

"Stanislaus! Stanislaus Trocki! Wait!"

There was no answer. The door closed. The figure was gone.

Terror struck the priest's heart. But it was a terror urging action.
He rushed through the gate of his altar rail and down the aisle of
the church. He opened the great door. He half expected to find
Stanislaus Trocki lying on the steps. Heaven was giving him another chance to right that horribly unjust act!

Stanislaus Trocki was not there. He was nowhere to be seen.

People were passing, among them miners on their way to and from work. But no miner that his straining eyes could see carried an accordion under his arm. Father Spinsky stood on the church steps and called out a little wildly:

"Stanislaus! Stanislaus Trocki!"

Some people paused and looked up at the frantic figure in the bright robes of the Mass.

"Something wrong, Father?" one miner asked.

"No, no," muttered Father Spinsky. He forced control of his emotions. "I thought I saw someone I used to know," he repeated.

He turned and went back into his empty church. He closed the door.

He moved to the shrine of Saint Joseph. The three candles were surely burning. He passed his hand above them and the flame scorched his fingers. He made the sign of the cross. He sank on his knees in prayer before this shrine.

"Saint Joseph, Friend of the Sacred Heart, most chaste spouse, intercede for me! Pray for me!"

After a few minutes he arose. He had regained his composure.

There were, of course, other miners in Coaltown who played the accordion. It was a favorite instrument among the Poles. But they did not carry it abroad early in the mornings! If they brought it out into the street at all, it was in the evening.

Father Spinsky returned to his altar, took up the burse-topped chalice, and went out into the sacristy. His assistant, a part-time secretary, had by this time arrived. The assistant lived in Wilkes-Barre and came to Coaltown by bus each day.

"I have heard," Father Spinsky cut off the excited comments of the younger man. "There is no time for gossip. We have work to do!"

The assistant had never seen Father Spinsky laboring under such emotion. The stolid St. Leo pastor trembled once or twice as he issued his instructions.

"Gather together all the remaining candles in the storeroom. Take them at once to St. Michael's. Father Paul will need them all. There are also some extra altar racks. I meant to send them yesterday. Take them on a second trip. Use the car. Make as many trips as necessary. Tell Father Paul to use them as he thinks best.

And when you have done all this, if he needs your help about his church, remain. Tell him I will come to St. Michael's when I have had my breakfast. I wish to talk with him if he can spare me a few moments."

Father Spinsky returned to his parish house. He was a man of set habits and he would have eaten his breakfast had St. Leo's itself burnt down. But he ate that breakfast in silence. His sister served him silently. She had already eaten her morning meal.

As the priest finished, his assistant returned from the first trip to St. Michael's. He had more news.

"I left the candles with a sexton," he reported. "I could not talk with Father Paul for the Bishop is there! He came from Scranton!"

"I hope the Bishop is putting an end to this nonsense!" said Mary Spinsky.

"The Bishop and Father Paul had their pictures taken on the parish house steps—for the newspapers!" said the assistant.

But Mary Spinsky had an answer for that. She might have known! "Trust the Bishop to push himself forward!" she exclaimed, but a look from her brother silenced her. Mary Spinsky felt that her brother would long ago have been a bishop, had he been Irish instead of Polish. This Irish bishop was one of her numerous minor hatreds. The hatreds that made up the fabric of her life.

"A reporter said the Bishop was in great form!" continued the assistant with enthusiasm. He did not like Mary Spinsky. "Told the newsmen he hoped it was all true, and promised a statement when he finished with Father Paul. Father Paul can certainly use our candles! Hundreds are filing through the church! There's a line for two blocks passing into St. Michael's! The State Troopers are keeping it in order."

"A fine thing when the Troopers have to keep order about a church!" said Mary Spinsky.

Father Spinsky at last smiled. When a man who has not smiled for a day and a night, who has done little smiling in his entire life, can smile without malice at the thing that has just enraged him, can see the humor of our human frailty, there is hope for his eternal salvation!

"Mary," he said, "put on your best hat. We are going up to St. Michael's to see the miracle."

There was nothing in this world Mary Spinsky was more eager to do. But pride would not let her admit that eagerness. Father Paul had probably *sent for* the Bishop. He should have sent for her brother!

"I prefer to go when I am invited," said Mary Spinsky.

Father Spinsky again smiled. A little sadly this time. He realized those would have been his exact words two days ago.

"Father Paul has several times invited me to his church," he replied. "I never went. I went to his parish house yesterday morning on an evil errand—to try to rob him of this opportunity, this prestige, this lifesaving revenue. And he was willing to move the funeral to St. Leo's!"

"But why then—" said Mary Spinsky. But she knew why. The man at the Wyoming Hotel. Another Irish parvenu! Well, *she* was not awed by this man and his money, even if her brother was.

"We can all thank God that it was not moved!" said Father Spinsky with an unusual earnestness. He turned to his sister. Into his voice there came an unaccustomed gentleness.

"Are you coming with me, Mary? I would like you to come."

It occurred to Father Spinsky that in all the years he had never asked his sister to accompany him anywhere.

Curiosity was stronger than pride. The woman sensed also the tenderness in her brother's tone. But that, she thought, a further sign of his sudden weakness.

"I'll come," said Mary Spinsky. "At least we'll not have to wait in this police line!"

"I can take you both in by the side door where I deliver the candles," said the assistant.

"No. We will go to the foot of the line," said Father Spinsky.

"But surely Father Paul would not want that! And you might miss the Bishop," said Mary Spinsky.

"The Bishop came to see Father Paul, not me," said Father Spinsky quietly. "I go to St. Michael's as a simple pilgrim. As all the other people of the town are going. I take my turn."

He regarded his sister for a full moment. How loyal and able and efficient she really was! If these traits could but be redirected toward unselfish good.

"And as I have the handsomest sister in the town," he continued, "why shouldn't I want her at my side? God will forgive me that pride."

Mary Spinsky was startled. Startled and pleased. She *was* a handsome woman. But no one had told her so for a long time.

Mary Spinsky smiled. It was almost the first smile without malevolence that had crossed her face in many years.

"I—I'll be glad to stand with you, brother!" she said. "But I must change my dress and my shoes. I have a new dress that I bought in Wilkes-Barre last week. It will be the first time I've worn it!"

"Good!" said Father Spinsky. "But wear your walking shoes. We will not use the car. The car is needed to take candle racks."

And somewhat later it was noted by the wondering townspeople that Father Spinsky, in his non-clerical clothes, accompanied by his "uppish" sister, was in the line progressing slowly toward the door of St. Michael's! It was cause for almost as much comment as was the arrival of the Bishop.

Father Spinsky had never before stood in line to wait to see anything in Coaltown. And it was known that he had said he would not set foot inside St. Michael's Church, since the time Father Paul inaugurated his early Mass without consulting him.

--------------------------------- *60* -------

*T*HE TELEPHONE in the soundproof booth of the Bell Company's Nanticoke office was ringing, and the man with the black derby at an angle was told his expected New York call was there. Bill Dunnigan had been waiting some five minutes, having returned from inspecting the setup of his St. Michael's cards, and an appraisal of the rose blanket being made at a florist for the Olga Treskovna coffin. Both were to be ready by six o'clock that evening, were paid for, and could be collected by the Packard driver at this hour.

While waiting, Dunnigan's mind again returned to an unsolved problem. He did not like unsolved problems when they concerned the business in which he was supposed to excel. It irritated and depressed him. But cudgel his brain as he would, no inspiration came on how, for the sake of the new film, he could make the funeral service of Olga Treskovna a breathtaking news event. Breathtaking and yet having a proper dignity. Marcus Harris had suggested that prominent people be invited. Well, there were no grounds on which he could persuade either the President of the United States or John D. Rockefeller, Jr., to attend! Several champion pugilists even could be no help and he wanted no church dignitaries who would overshadow Father Paul. It was a knotty enigma.

Inside the booth came the voice of Marcus Harris. The voice was happy.

"Cheer up, Bill!" it cried, as if there were an understanding of his press agent's mood. "It's my turn to have great news!"

"*What* great news?" asked Mr. Dunnigan, and Marcus Harris smiled as he recognized his own glum words of half an hour ago.

"We're all set about 'The Garden of the Soul'! That is, we will be before night. And it's due to your publicity, for they certainly don't know how good or how bad a film we've made! I can sign the largest booking contract I've ever swung for a release of the picture, sight unseen, over the entire Intercity circuit! A top straight rental, plus a big percentage! They say if the picture is as good as the advance stuff, it will gross the biggest trade any film has yet known! And the Music Hall here will give us a first showing. They want to view it, but they're half sold already, and you and I know that the picture is a sockeroo! Grade A plus! And that Treskovna will come close to giving the award performance of the year!"

Halfway through this song of praise the Dunnigan brain was suddenly aflame again. Not for "The Garden of the Soul." An idea for the funeral! The problem of what to do regarding it! The answer had been right in his grasp all the time! He had not seen the forest for the trees, as the saying went. But now it was a forest fire!

Bill Dunnigan could never understand the insatiable interest of the public in the personalities of the stars of the theater. Why an article about the kind of lipstick used by some brainless, dancing ingénue should be more avidly read than a scholarly dissertation on the career of a great surgeon, for example. In fact, no one cared

When he at last emerged into the sunlight outside, he left his sister and knocked at the door of Father Paul's rectory. The morning before he had pulled the bell knob with almost as vicious a force as William Dunnigan had exerted on his first visit.

So now he sat with Father Paul. The Bishop had gone. The sexton who had brought the Mass collections had gone. These two priests of Coaltown were alone.

Father Paul was the first to speak.

"I am very grateful for the candles and the candle racks," he said. "That is kind of you. I want to pay you for the candles and I feel I should send you the money which your candle racks collect. I *will* send it, if I may."

Father Spinsky had a sense of the dramatic. He could not resist the framing of his next sentence.

"I want much more than that!" he said and looked sternly at Father Paul.

"What more?" said Father Paul.

"I want your forgiveness for my arrogance—my greed. For my antagonism through the four years you have been here." He raised his hand as Father Paul started to speak. "I want you to let me help you in the plans I know you have to help the town. I want no credit—I just want to help—if you think I can help!"

Father Paul looked hard at Father Spinsky. Father Spinsky smiled. It was a sad smile but it was sincere.

"Can you forgive me, Paul?" the St. Leo pastor said.

The pastor of St. Michael reached over and took the hand of his erstwhile enemy. "There is nothing to forgive," he said. "You had your church and I had mine. I suppose it was only natural——"

"It was neither natural nor Christian," said Father Spinsky. "And I also know that words are cheap and easily spoken. I have received some two thousand dollars for the ringing of my St. Leo's bell. I will send you my check for this money. I want you to add it to your funds for something you want to do. There was a plan about visiting nurses that you tried. It was a good plan. I did all I could to discredit it. Maybe you can start that plan again."

"*We* can start it again," said Father Paul. "We *will* start it!"

"And there is one other thing," said Father Spinsky. "You are going to be too occupied to cook for yourself, to take care of your parsonage. Your time is valuable to this community. I want you to have someone prepare your meals—my sister says she knows a woman of your own parish—my sister is a fine cook, you know, and understands about these things, as I am sure you will agree from her chocolate cake——"

"*Her* chocolate cake!" gasped Father Paul. And now he had risen to his feet.

"Why, yes," said Father Spinsky. "Didn't she send you half a cake yesterday? She said that she would, and the other half to—to William Dunnigan at the Wyoming Hotel."

"Good God!" said Father Paul and sat down again.

"What is the matter? Wasn't it all right!" said Father Spinsky.

"Yes, yes! Of course!" said Father Paul. He was on the point of telling Father Spinsky of the only message that came with that cake—the part about the "six eggs and a cup of butter not being wasted," but he stopped. He realized the real source of the gift.

"I mean—I forgot to thank you for it!" he finished. "It was grand! Swell!" and he smiled. "Mr. Dunnigan is most anxious to meet your sister. He wants the recipe she uses, for it seems he is backing a Quick Lunch in Nanticoke——"

"Backing a Quick Lunch!"

"Yes. A remarkable man. Helping some young Polish boy there. Goes about doing such things. Going to name their foods after Saints. I can't quite make him out. Sometimes I think he's almost sacrilegious and then, that he's a better Christian, would be a better priest than either of us, Father Spinsky! Why, he——"

He was about to tell Father Spinsky of the conversation in the church basement regarding the miracle, but he halted. That had perhaps best be left unsaid, at least for the present.

"So you also have noticed something strange about him!" said Father Spinsky. He leaned forward. "Father Paul—has it occurred to you——"

But he did not finish his sentence either. The tall, somewhat grotesque figure of Andrev Denko, the village "halfwit," was standing in the doorway.

Andrev seemed to want to speak to Father Paul.

*   *   *

Andrev Denko had reached Father Paul by way of the back door of the parish house. He had come from the cemetery.

He had not come by the roadway. You could climb the rail fence near the grave of Stanislaus Trocki, go down a steep, heavily-wooded hillside thick with briars and underbrush, and you would come out at the foot of St. Michael's parish house garden. The lad had a sense of direction like that of a wild bird. If he wanted to go anywhere he usually disregarded such things as streets and thoroughfares and even woodland paths and proceeded to that place in a straight line.

He had a message for Father Paul.

He never rang a doorbell or knocked. That humans should have doors and sometimes lock them was another of the absurd peculiarities of this species. Like getting drunk. The trees, the hills, most of the animals he knew did not so barricade themselves. Perhaps because they had no dark secrets to hide!

Father Paul was one human whose door was never locked. He was used to the lad's unannounced appearances. He had a keen sympathy and understanding of him. It was Andrev who helped each month clear the weeds from the untended cemetery graves, and along the fence borders. The boy was very expert with a scythe, but he would not use this symbol of Death in the cemetery. Not because he knew anything about or had ever even heard of the symbolic figure of the Grim Reaper. He would not use a scythe because it also cut down an occasional tall sunflower or shattered a cluster of wild arbutus. Andrev would bring a small sickle, and though the work took longer, there was not an indiscriminate destruction of both beauty and rank growth. It was this quite unusual sensitivity that had first caused Father Paul to be drawn to the lad—to suspect that under the crude exterior there was something fine and unusually good.

Andrev reminded him of the contradictory edifice that was his Church of St. Michael.

"Yes, Andrev?" said Father Paul. And Father Spinsky turned quickly and paused in the stating of his weird suspicion about the identity of William Dunnigan.

"I want talk with you," said Andrev to Father Paul, and the look he gave Father Spinsky meant, *talk with him alone*.

"I will go," said Father Spinsky rising. In a way he was glad of the interruption. Perhaps what he had been about to state would have seemed utterly absurd to Father Paul. Father Spinsky realized that he was somewhat abnormally moved by his reactions of the past twenty-four hours. The vision of Stanislaus Trocki was still disturbing him. He could see Father Paul later in the day, at a calmer moment.

"No, do not go," said Father Paul. "Andrev, you can speak before Father Spinsky. Surely you know him. My brother priest of St. Leo's."

Andrev knew Father Spinsky. Two weeks before, the St. Leo's pastor had ordered him to stop cutting the weeds along the fence of the St. Leo's cemetery which was just across the roadway from that of St. Michael's. The lad had finished his task for St. Michael's and had seen no harm in tidying up St. Leo's. And there was a particularly gorgeous sunflower growing there that he had paused to talk with, and he wanted to be sure it would be spared by whoever did the weed cutting.

Father Spinsky had been passing in his car. He had observed with irritation this halfwit working on "his property." A halfwit Father Paul had persisted in using about the St. Michael acre.

Father Spinsky's exact order had been, "What are you doing here? Get away! Get away and stay away! Don't trespass again on my cemetery!"

Andrev had hastily withdrawn.

Father Spinsky (as well as Andrev Denko) now remembered these words. Was there anyone in all Coaltown that the priest had not spoken to, at one time and another, in an unkindly manner!

"I know Father Spinsky," said Andrev. "I know something to tell him also. But I do not like him as I like you, Father Paul."

Father Paul was about to remonstrate at this frank statement of dislike, but Father Spinsky spoke first. This seemed to be his day for confession of faults.

"Andrev is perfectly right," he said and turned to the boy. "I am sorry for what I said to you at the cemetery. Will you forgive me?"

The boy obviously did not quite understand.

"I want to arrange with you to cut my grass along the fence each week," said Father Spinsky. "I will pay you for it. Will you do that for me?"

This the boy did understand. He smiled.

"I'm glad to do that!" he said. "And I want no money. There going to be the biggest horse chestnuts in Valley on tree in your cemetery! If I can pick what I want of them——"

Father Spinsky did not know what this was all about but Father Paul did.

"Andrev collects horse chestnuts," he said. "He has some very beautiful ones."

"Of course!" said Father Spinsky. "Take whatever you wish. I will pay you besides for the work."

"Thank you!" said the lad. A bright smile transfigured his long, homely face. "I need your horse chestnuts for my brightest stars!"

Father Paul had viewed this little drama of Father Spinsky and Andrev Denko. From the expression of Father Spinsky's face he felt it meant more than the hiring of a weed cutter to his brother priest.

"His brightest stars?" said the St. Leo pastor.

"He is charting the night sky," said Father Paul.

Father Spinsky looked at this halfwit whom he had despised. This lad whom he had once or twice—when he had noticed him— thought of taking steps to have placed in an institution. Which of them was the wiser? Which of them was the nearer Heaven? The answer to that question gave Father Spinsky a shuddering pause.

But the lad was reticent no longer.

"I have just been at cemetery," he said. The words seemed to carry more meaning than a mere statement of his whereabouts.

"I'm glad we cleared it last week, Andrev, for I'm having a funeral day after tomorrow," said Father Paul. "I am proud of Andrev's work. My graves all look well!" This last was addressed to Father Spinsky.

But the boy did not seem to hear the compliment. He proceeded with what was apparently his errand.

"I been talking with Olga Trocki, Stan Trocki's girl," he said.

"You have been talking—*who* did you say!" said Father Paul. The priest was startled, for the matter of fact simplicity in the boy's tone gave it a ring of truth that no excited declamation would have conveyed.

Father Spinsky was also startled. He had been about to retire, for the thought of what, but for the grace of God, he might have inflicted on this lad who "charted the night sky," was not quieting. The priest sat again in his chair and gazed transfixedly into the curiously earnest face of the boy who stood before them.

"With Olga Trocki," repeated Andrev Denko. "I did not see her for long time. We used to talk together at the cemetery. She went away, but she back now. We cut some goldenrod and put it on her father's grave."

Perhaps the day before Father Paul would have tried to explain to Andrev Denko that he could not possibly have talked with Olga Trocki. That Olga Trocki was dead. That the funeral he had just mentioned was to be for this same Olga Trocki. But explanations seemed trivial and profitless in the face of what was now happening in Coaltown.

Father Spinsky's thoughts were the same. A day ago he would have laughed at such a tale and told its bearer to go about his business. In the case of Andrev Denko, telephoned the authorities. But now!

Father Paul said earnestly: "Are you sure, Andrev, it was Olga Trocki?" And he had an eerie feeling, as he looked at the simple face of the lad, that the boy believed he was speaking truthfully.

"Me and she are friends," said Andrev. "I talk with her there lots of times before she went to Wilkes-Barre. She held a hurt robin while I fixed its wing the day before she went away."

"What did you talk about today?" asked Father Paul, and the strained eagerness that he met in Father Spinsky's eyes told him the St. Leo pastor was even more tense than he himself.

"We talk about the rain and the hills. It was mostly about the hills. She say she missed them terrible while she away! She say she wouldn't be going away for long any more again. She say she wondered always if the hills missed her, but she knew I was here to talk to them. They don't have hills in some places, Father, she say! 'Never leave the hills, Andrev,' she tell me. And I tell her how old Bald Top Mountain is complaining they cut off all the trees on one side. He say he'll be cold this winter with no leaves on his shoulders——"

"Andrev," said Father Paul, "did Olga Trocki say anything about a funeral?"

"Oh, that!" said the lad, as if it were not a matter of great consequence. "I tell her they are saying in the town that the church bells are ringing for her funeral, and she say 'Yes, I know! I am going to be buried there by my father, like I've always wanted.' But she's going to sit and talk with me sometimes when I come up alone. She say I must always be alone because the other people would not understand, and they would think me silly talking, because *they* could not see her! Just like they think I'm silly when I talk to old Bald Top! I promised to put goldenrod on her grave too. And she give me something to give to you, Father Paul."

Andrev had produced from the deep side pocket of his patched, weather-stained trousers a box such as school children use to carry pencils, and handed it to Father Paul. The paint on the box was peeled off. There were bits of soil still clinging to its edges.

Father Paul held the box in his hand. He looked at Father Spinsky and then up at Andrev.

"She gave you this herself?" he asked.

"We dig it up from the foot of her pop's grave. It was just under the grass. She say she put it there before she went away. There's some writing inside. She read it to me. It's what she call a poem. She say she wanted you to have it, Father, because some of the words are just like you speak to her friend here at the cemetery. To the man who's fixing the funeral. She was there when you talk to him. She say to tell you she was sorry she never knew you. You come after she went away."

Andrev Denko had never said so many words at one time. Now that he had said them he turned to go.

"Wait, Andrev," said Father Paul.

"Please wait, Andrev," said Father Spinsky, and pushed forward the other folding chair.

The boy sat down.

Father Paul opened the long lid of the box. It contained a single sheet of ruled tablet paper in a roll. There was writing on it in pencil. This is what was written:

HILL PRIDE

A Poem by Olga Trocki

Oh fair the hills of my country
Oh Fairer than the fair!

Their curve is like the Virgin's breasts
      (The Christ-head rested there)
I think that when God moulded them
      He took a special care.

Oh high the hills of my country
      Oh Higher than the high!
And from their tops a child can see
      The world's end meet the sky
And tall men bend their heads to let
      The storm clouds scuttle by.

Oh stern the hills of my country
      Oh Sterner than the stern
To frown on pettiness and greed
      And vice for which men burn.
The heart must seek nobility
      The soul for beauty yearn.

Oh sacred are my country's hills
      Like Altars in a church.
The pine trees stand like candlesticks
      Each dawn a lighting torch
That drips hot flame on altar cloth
      Of hickory and birch.

Oh strong the hills of my country
      Oh Stronger than the strong!
A ring of fortresses to fend
      A world of crushing wrong.
And we who stay—and are content—
      Find victory and song.

Father Paul read it through. His thoughts indeed! And his imagery about the pine trees being candlesticks and the hickory and birch trees forming an altar cloth! Only, she spoke of the sunrise and he spoke to William Dunnigan of the setting of the sun behind the hills.

Father Paul handed the paper sheet to Father Spinsky. As Father Spinsky read, the St. Michael's priest spoke again to the lad now seated on the chair.

"Do you remember what is here, Andrev?" he asked.

"I don't remember all," he answered, "though it was all beautiful. Someday I want you teach it all to me—I'd like to tell it to the hills. It would cheer up old Bald Top Mountain—the part about the hills protecting us from the world. He sometimes think he is no use to the world—he is so old—old Bald Top! And I like the part where it say 'tall men bend their heads to let the storm clouds go by.' I was on mountain one time and the black thunder clouds come all around me!"

Both Father Paul and Father Spinsky knew that Andrev could not read or write.

"It is beautiful," said Father Paul. "You are sure, Andrev, you have not shown it to anyone?"

"I bring it straight to you—right after I speak to her father——"

"Her father!"

It was Father Spinsky who asked the question. He looked up sharply from his reading of the composition of the dead daughter of this dead man. His voice was strained. He had the look of one suddenly struck full in the face.

"Yes," said Andrev. "Her father come at end of our talking. He come walking down the path. He have his accordion. He play a song she liked and she sing it. It was a fine song—about a dying Polish soldier who wanted to see his native land again! And he tell us he going to your church to light three candles, Father Spinsky. He say he once make a lot of trouble for you. May I go now? There is a bird nest that fall down yesterday. I put it up best I could. I must see if it is all right."

"You may go," said Father Paul. "Thank you for bringing me the poem. And Andrev——"

"Yes, Father?"

"I would say nothing about this to anyone, if I were you."

"I do not talk to people about my friends," said the lad scornfully. "They would laugh. I come to you because I know you would not laugh. You will teach me the poem?"

"I will teach you," said Father Paul.

The boy went as he came—through the back of the parish house. When he had gone Father Paul spoke first.

"I suppose this man he believes he saw might have been a passing miner who read him the verse," he said to Father Spinsky. "It is very strange, however."

He noticed that Father Spinsky was staring straight ahead. Looking through him—beyond him. The St. Leo priest glanced again at the verse he still held, then focused his eyes on Father Paul. Eyes that reflected a kind of fearful resignation.

"The man was no passing miner," said Father Spinsky. "Paul—I saw Stanislaus Trocki in my church hardly more than an hour ago!"

62

*B*ILL DUNNIGAN, gazing at the goldenrod on Stanislaus Trocki's grave, did not, of course, yet know about Andrev Denko. The lad had long since gone. By the time the press agent reached the St. Michael's parish house, Andrev had also come and gone from there. And Father Spinsky had departed.

Dunnigan got out of his Packard and for a moment looked up and down a new Main Street. There seemed no diminishing of the number of people in the line stretching for a block to St. Michael's church door. Three and four abreast they stood and edged slowly forward. On the opposite side of the street the Troopers had permitted cars to park, and they presented a solid, slanting front (or to be more accurate, a rear), for at least a half of the full mile of the town. Fresh cars were arriving each few minutes. Visitors and natives were milling about the street. The four lunchrooms were serving hungry strangers with more food than they had sold in months. Several Bars and Grills were actually making sandwiches!

The whole was not unlike some Western town in an agricultural region on the day set apart for marketing and trading. But the lure to Coaltown was not barter but a neglected church where a miracle had occurred.

Dunnigan also found a new Father Paul. The priest had taken an eager batch of newly-arrived reporters into the church through the side door, and was giving another talk about the fighting qualities of Saint Michael. A national photographic press service was taking more pictures of the two statues that had turned, of the altar screen, the line passing before the Olga Treskovna coffin. Standing in the same doorway where he had watched a fearful and uncertain Father Paul celebrate a Mass a few short hours before, Bill Dunnigan was happily amazed.

"What has happened to you, Father!" he exclaimed, when he and the St. Michael pastor were finally alone in the parish house for a humble lunch of coffee and cheese and jam which the little pastor, talking all the while, had himself prepared.

"Much has happened this morning," said the priest. "Most wonderful of all—my Bishop was here!"

"I heard that from New York," said the press agent, "and it had me worried for awhile."

"From New York!" gasped Father Paul.

"Yes," said Bill, "your fame has reached New York. Yours and Saint Michael's. Not to mention the Bishop's. All three of you made the front pages they tell me."

Father Paul put down his cheese and swallowed a large lump of sudden terror that rose in his throat. The first page of New York newspapers! But he took a deep breath. He took a firm grip on himself.

"The front page—good!" he said.

He was sure now he had conquered fear. And the next moment both he and Bill Dunnigan laughed.

Then Father Paul told of the visit of Andrev Denko. He recited the lad's words about Olga Treskovna. He handed William Dunnigan the paper that was in the pencil box, the paper with the poem called "Hill Pride."

Dunnigan read it through. His eyes were a little misty at the end. It brought back vividly that hour in the Hollywood hospital when she told him of her longing for her hills. He remembered her words in Ming Gow's Chinese restaurant—the first time she had spoken them—and the ardent, wistful look in her blue eyes. The blue of her eyes was of the distant hills rather than the sky, he suddenly thought.

"I love the hills!" she had said.

He remembered the poem she had sent him to New York—the girl who stood atop her mountain and looked at the star.

"Your hills were really her mother!" he said at last. "This verse is how she felt about them—and the handwriting is hers. She used to joke with me because I didn't like hills. I didn't know much about them then. I have learned. I think the hills have gotten under my skin too. Into my blood. And I knew there was to be a message here from her."

Father Paul waited but Dunnigan did not explain. After a moment the priest said:

"You knew one other thing I did not know—or did you? The name of the maker of the chocolate cake!"

"Yes, I knew that. In the excitement this morning I forgot to tell you. And I must ask you for an indulgence forgiving gluttony! I ate it all—that is, with some friends of mine. But when did you discover who made it?"

"Father Spinsky was here."

"Did he come to collect for the six eggs and the cup of butter?"

Father Paul arose and paced his floor. Then he turned to his friend.

"It is only natural that you should ask that. I also was sure he wanted something when he appeared. He did, Bill. He wanted my forgiveness. Mine! He wanted to turn over to me the money he has received for the ringing of his bell. For my plan about visiting nurses. Something out of the ordinary has happened to him! He believes that he saw Stanislaus Trocki in his church! Andrev Denko also says he saw this man—but Andrev is a child at heart with a child's imaginings, while Father Spinsky is a grown man, a very practical grown man!"

Bill Dunnigan was about to light his cigar. He let the match burn out in his hand.

"I was 'out ahead,' as we say, of another play once, Father," he said. "You'll get tired of hearing me talk about my plays! But sometimes I think there is really nothing new in life, if one is around the theater. It has all happened in the plays the great ones have set down! This script was by the greatest word artist of them all, I guess. With your education you know this play better than me. I never did see it all through. But Bob Mantell wore black tights and said:

> 'There are more things in heaven and earth, Horatio,
> Than are dreamt of in your philosophy.'

I always liked those lines, and remembered them."

"Yes, I know," said Father Paul. "It was spoken about the ghost of Hamlet's father."

"Only Olga Treskovna is not a ghost!" exclaimed Dunnigan. "I saw her just awhile ago in the bright sunlight of noon on the Square in Nanticoke. I have seen her here in Coaltown—on your church steps—inside your church—standing by me at the cemetery —kneeling there by you at her father's grave. I saw her in Hollywood after she died! She *lives*, Father! If I did not think she still lived, I would not want to live!"

"Knowing you, I cannot think your belief is other than good," said Father Paul. "And whatever it is that Father Spinsky believes —he seems to have some ideas about you, Bill, that are a little strange——"

"About me!"

"He has not said just what they are. He was about to tell me, I think, when Andrev Denko came. In his case I think it is a great fear! But if fear has brought about this change in him—it seems that you are the one who has changed him—perhaps great fear also can fathom the Beyond. In Andrev Denko's case it is a great simplicity. Perhaps I do not *see*," and the priest smiled a little sadly, "because I have achieved no greatness."

"I cannot believe that, Father," said Dunnigan. "Whatever good there is in all these happenings is because of you! It was your courage that set me going again—it is your example alone that brought about the change in Father Spinsky——"

Father Paul shook his head.

"It was not I who brought about Andrev Denko's keen perception, or any of the other unusual things," he said. "I shall perhaps know that I have achieved the grace of greatness when I, too, have a vision of the things unknown. And that, I'm afraid, will never be!"

"Don't be too certain! We shall see!" said William Dunnigan, press agent for Saint Michael as well as for "The Garden of the Soul." "But tell me, Father, what did your Bishop say? It worried me at first when I heard that he was in Coaltown. Then I was told from New York that he was smiling in the picture."

"You mean our pictures also?"

"On the first page!" smiled Bill Dunnigan.

"I'm glad the Bishop was there. Thank God for that!" But

Father Paul was also smiling. "I don't think I ever quite knew my Bishop before," he continued. "He is right with us, Bill—with you and me—and our blessed Saint Michael. He's coming to the funeral Friday and will preside in my sanctuary! He made one condition, however, that I don't know if you can manage."

"What condition is that?" asked Dunnigan.

"This film of yours—you've got to have it shown at least a week before New York in his cathedral city!"

"We'll show it a month before if necessary," said Bill with a laugh. "But what does *he* think about our miracle?"

"I think," said Father Paul, "that he believes a bigger and finer miracle than any mere turning of some statues is happening in Coaltown!"

63

THE ONE UNHAPPY soul in all Coaltown (if we eliminate the Breaker, who, black of countenance, growled defiance and disdain at all this talk of "miracles") was Mr. James Orloff, proprietor of Orloff's Funeral Parlor. His lot it was to see no visions, nor to experience any joy or anguish of regeneration. His not to share one pulse beat in the universal feeling of uplift!

Excitement in the town had reached a fever heat, but nobody died of it. On the contrary, everybody was gloriously alive. Invalids who had been bedridden for years, and might be expected to be customers any day, were up and on their way to St. Michael's! Money was pouring into everybody's coffers, except Orloff's. Restaurants and saloons were hearing a constant ring of cash registers as well as that of church bells! Half the townspeople were renting rooms till after the funeral! The Wyoming Hotel was filling up with newsmen!

Even the Orloff poolroom was deserted, for greater wonderings than the speculation of whether ivory balls would lodge in green pockets were in the air!

And a modern Midas, whom Orloff felt he might have had solely

for his own, was scattering gold in all directions, except the one
direction in which it should fall for a funeral!

Mr. Orloff could stand the strain no longer. He decided to call
on Mr. Dunnigan. He must report on the important matter of the
six pallbearers.

There the undertaker had pulled off a minor financial success.
He had found that instead of paying *them*, individuals were willing
to *pay him* to gain the distinction of lifting the coffin of Olga,
daughter of the late Stan Trocki. Mr. Orloff had collected ten
dollars each from six gentlemen of his acquaintance for that
privilege.

He also had thought of another idea which would add a few
more dollars to his lamentably small gain from this world-shaking,
chance-in-a-lifetime-missed transaction. Mr. Orloff did not know
of Maude Muller; had never heard of John Greenleaf Whittier
and those saddest words of tongue or pen; but *"it might have
been!"* was the gist of his poignant thoughts.

He located William Dunnigan shortly after lunch time at the
Wyoming Hotel. The press agent was reading a telegram his
"chauffeur" had sped back from Nanticoke to bring. The Nanticoke operator had hailed the Packard returning from the St.
Michael rectory—dismissed until it should bring, at six, the "Mass
show cards" and the coffin roses.

The smile on Mr. Dunnigan's face indicated that the wire
brought pleasant news.

There are individuals to whom the only ground for respect is
the possession of money. Mr. Orloff was of that ilk. He removed
his hat as he now approached the fabulous man that he alone
(and alas) held in his clutches two days before, as that man climbed
down from a day coach at Wilkes-Barre out of the West! Mr.
Orloff would never again judge people by day coaches.

Mr. Dunnigan was now asking the desk clerk for his room key.

"May I speak to you privately, Mr. Dunnigan, sir?" asked the
undertaker. He finished this respectful request with a slight bow.

A jovial Dunnigan looked up from his telegram. "Well, well!
If it isn't my old buddie, Jimmy Orloff!" he said. "I heard from
our mutual friend Father Spinsky that your health was failing.
I'm happy to see you up and about again! We don't want you
having to bury *yourself*, do we? No profit in that at all!"

Mr. Orloff responded to this hail-fellow pleasantry with a hollow, dolorous noise meant for a laugh. It was not entirely successful. The sight of the now quite immaculate Mr. Dunnigan was a sickening one to his eyes. He was acutely conscious of a cavernous void both in his wallet and the region of his stomach.

"I am feeling better, thank you, though not entirely recovered," he managed to say.

"Good!" exclaimed Mr. Dunnigan. "Very good! Then you'll be O. K. for the funeral Friday. That's the big day. It's turning out to be quite an event, isn't it? Should add to your prestige! But you look worried. Come right up to my room and unburden your anxious heart to me!"

The press agent reread his telegram, smiled again, placed the yellow paper in his side pocket. "Just wait with the car!" This to the Nanticoke chauffeur.

Mr. Orloff shuddered visibly. This further reference to affluence was more salt on open wounds. The Packard was already a much-pointed-out millionaire's chariot in Coaltown.

He followed Dunnigan up the stairs into the front A-1. Bill motioned to a chair, and himself sat on the bed. He adjusted his black derby at a little more jaunty angle than heretofore. Mr. Orloff sat down gingerly and held his soft hat in his hand.

"Well?" said Mr. Dunnigan.

"I've arranged about the pallbearers," said Mr. Orloff. "I've persuaded six friends of mine to serve. And what I want to speak to you about is the black gloves——"

"I paid for the gloves—a dollar a pair—six dollars in all," interrupted Bill sternly. "I have your receipt somewhere."

"Oh, that isn't what I mean," said Mr. Orloff, and he attempted to put a lightness—a "what is a receipt among friends" note—into his tone. "I wanted to say that I think the dollar gloves will be too cheap for such a funeral as you are planning. I'm afraid I did not at first understand how first-class you wanted things done. There is a make for four dollars that will look much better and——"

Mr. Orloff had worked out a neat two-dollar profit on the better gloves. Twelve dollars in all, as against a ten-cent profit only on each pair of the dollar kind.

But Mr. Dunnigan interrupted.

"Dear, dear!" he said. "I'm sorry you're put to all this worry! And on top of your ill health! You certainly have my interest at heart!"

Mr. Orloff made a deprecatory gesture. "I'm only trying my best——"

"Sure!" again broke in his sympathetic listener. "Rest easy, pal. You'll need to supply no gloves at all! In fact, I can cheer you now by the helpful news that you won't have to supply even the six pallbearers! I can imagine the difficulty you've been having in finding six reputable citizens willing to do that job." He got up and looked from the window to the street where he could easily see the tail end of the line progressing toward St. Michael's.

"But you have to have pallbearers!" gasped Mr. Orloff. He also arose. In spite of Mr. Dunnigan's smile and his unexpectedly cordial manner, the undertaker had a premonition of dire, naked disaster ahead.

"I know that," said Bill. "Coffins have to be carried somehow! They won't walk alone! Ha, ha! But I should not joke about so serious a matter! And I realize your devotion to an agreement and what a time you were probably having about it! Discouraging days! Sleepless nights! Being turned down by this one and that! Rebuffs on every side! A girl with no friends in the town. Her late father in ill repute. So I'm happy to be able to tell you that I just have word——" and he produced his telegram, "——that some fellow film players of hers are coming gallantly to the rescue. They fly here from California by special plane and will arrive at Williamsport airport Friday noon. I will have motorcars meet them. Let me see——" and he again consulted the telegram "——there will be——"

Mr. Dunnigan here read six names whose combined weekly salaries would have indeed equaled the semi-monthly pay roll of the Coaltown mines.

"I'm quite sure, with Hollywood thoroughness," he added, "they will be equipped with the proper funeral clothes, including black gloves!"

Mr. Orloff felt the need of sitting down again. He sought his chair with unsteady hands and legs. His stomach trouble had returned. Likewise a dizziness about the brow. His swarthy face paled, and he licked drying lips.

Not only more evidence of titanic wealth, but sixty good dollars to be returned for non-delivery of pallbearer jobs—front seats, as it were, at this funeral! Misery without end!

"But I've already hired six men," he gasped, "and paid them—in advance!" He added the last falsehood in a weak hope of warding off this colossal calamity!

"My God!" he continued—*it could not be true—he must not have heard correctly*— "You're telling me all these motion picture stars are coming to Coaltown as pallbearers for Stan Trocki's kid!"

By now Mr. Orloff had the appearance of a huge, over-stuffed fish out of water and sucking for air.

"So I am reliably informed, most reliably," said a calm Bill Dunnigan, and he gave the telegram sheet an airy flip. "But don't be upset. Since you've already paid out the money, I'll not ask a return of the twelve bucks you have advanced to your friends. I will not be unfair. I do think, however, that I should have back my six dollars I advanced to you for gloves. Especially as you apparently have not yet purchased this cheaper kind."

Mr. Orloff was trapped. ("Hooked"—thought Dunnigan—intrigued by the beauty of the fisherman metaphor.) Too late the undertaker realized his fatal mistake! He should have said he had already bought the cheaper gloves and wanted now to exchange them.

He thought momentarily of altering the story to that effect. Blood flushed his face under the need of instant and sharp mental effort. But he did not like the look in the city man's eyes. Eyes that had narrowed and for the moment lost their joviality. Did the "gent" suspect what the undertaker had already done? The gent did, if the truth were known. Dunnigan had heard certain rumors in a bar about the ten-dollar-a-pallbearer transaction.

Mr. Orloff slowly took out his billfold (did he produce it from a gill?) and sadly extracted a five-dollar bill and a one. He handed the bills to Mr. Dunnigan.

William Dunnigan was not a person to make a vulgar display of money. In his business it was no novelty to carry on his person sizable sums of currency to be expended for his employer's benefit. But he could not resist letting this mortuary gentleman have a concrete view of what his petty greed had probably lost him. And the press agent had not forgotten what Orloff had said about Father Paul and St. Michael's Church.

So he did not simply jam the two bills into his trousers pocket or toss them onto his bed cover. He carefully produced a large roll, smoothed it out, and placed the Orloff money in the inner sanctuary of its circumference. The glassy-eyed undertaker could not help but see that the outside bill was for five hundred dollars, and that there seemed to be quite a number of that pleasant denomination in the roll. There were about eight, in point of fact. And a sizable number of delectable hundreds cushioned these, and served as a core when the roll was refolded and pushed again into the pocket from which it came.

Thus did William Dunnigan figuratively strike the blow he had withheld when Orloff applied the brakes to his hearse and refused to move until Stanislaus Trocki's funeral balance was paid. The Manassa Mauler could not have landed more solidly.

"Well," said Mr. Dunnigan, "it's nice to have seen you again. Have your hearse and one carriage, as per our contract, at the church promptly at two on Friday. Get there early, Jimmy, for there may be a few more carriages in line!"

James Orloff died hard.

"I was going to speak of that," he said desperately. "Of course, you'll need more than one carriage for all these people, and I could arrange at a reasonable wholesale rate——"

"It's all being arranged in Nanticoke," said Mr. Dunnigan. "They're very accommodating to me there, and don't have to have their money in advance; although, as you may have heard, *I pay in advance*. Of course, they are not pressed for ready cash like yourself—have no relatives' dance-hall bars to meet installments on. Maybe they're not as kind to their families as you are. But that is the price one must pay for brotherly generosity. Good day, Jimmy! Chin up! Gills open! See you at the church Friday!"

And so it happened that an almost suicidally despondent James Orloff first spread the rumor that unbelievable notables of the legendary motion-picture world of Hollywood would carry the coffin of Stan Trocki's girl from the Church of St. Michael the Archangel some forty-eight hours hence. A rumor that the afternoon near-by city papers confirmed on press dispatches from New York and Hollywood itself.

64

*B*ILL *(White Spats) DUNNIGAN* started out
from the Wyoming Hotel with his "Miners' Mass" show-cards under
his arm—just as in the old days he had gone about the towns as
an "advance man," and planted similar clarion calls to attend the
theatrical attraction he was heralding.

It was a small beginning in his job as press agent for Father
Paul and Saint Michael. The next morning, his cards having
paved the way, he meant to locate the office of the Miners' Union,
talk with its head, try to put through the idea of the Union getting
solidly behind this Mass, making Father Paul its official chaplain.
He felt that now, at least, he would not have opposition from
Father Spinsky. And he could promise this union some swell
country-wide publicity! The first mine union to have an "official
Mass" and an "official chaplain"!

It was about eight o'clock in the evening. His Nanticoke chauffeur had brought him the show-cards and the blanket of roses. The
latter he had taken to St. Michael's, and he and Father Paul had
spread it over Olga Treskovna's coffin. As there were still people
in line, Father Paul was keeping the church open till nine o'clock.
Two nuns from the Wanamee Orphanage were coming to keep an
all-night vigil until the next morning's Mass.

The first card went up over the hotel desk. That took no
salesmanship, for Dunnigan's visit had filled the hostelry from
dusty lobby to leaky roof. Cots were being placed in the parlor
to accommodate the overflow. The day clerk asked for *two*
cards. He would place one in the dining room. The press agent
noted that the reporters in the lobby were reading the card and
jotting down its message.

He talked with several of them.

"This progressive priest," he said, "has wanted the mine workers
of the district to have a service at an hour which would come

before they embarked each day on their unusually hazardous employment. A Mass at 5:45 A.M. Like the 12:45 A.M. Mass established at St. Andrew's in New York for men of your own newspaper profession and other night workers. You all know about that famous service! And Father Paul's idea would seem to have divine sanction, for this blessed miracle was first discovered at this Mass at sunrise in Coaltown. Within twenty-four hours I hope to make an announcement from the Miners' Union here that will be real news," he continued.

"What do you know about these famous movie stars coming for the funeral of Miss Treskovna?" asked several newsmen.

"I only know what your news tickers have probably recorded," said Bill, for he had by then seen the afternoon Wilkes-Barre and Scranton papers. "A spontaneous recognition of an artist by the fellow workers of her craft! It is most gratifying, gentlemen, most gratifying!"

And news-innocent Mr. Dunnigan moved from the hotel lobby to continue his show-card distribution.

The placing of cards in the drug store and the next-door Acme Lunch, where business was booming, was also not a task that took persuasion. Or the adding of a card to the clutter of bottles in the window of Hilda Kubisac's Beauty Parlor with its legend on the plate glass, "Here Dwells Loveliness." Coaltown even possessed one of these! The neglected business of "hair-do's" was likewise whooping along. One notable result of the miracle was a sudden swerve of the feminine population toward personal attractiveness. Behind in her rent, and about to move to more appreciative environs, Miss Hilda had had a waiting line all day, and was working far into the evening!

So William Dunnigan, these preliminary sorties beneath his belt, entered the Bar and Grill of Mr. Koepke—he of the multi-colored juke box and the boisterous laughter and oaths. The press agent had been there before and sampled its doubtful liquor. It was the roughest saloon in Coaltown. It would be a test of his boast to Father Paul that he could place his cards in the saloons.

Koepke's place was cut to the pattern of all the other Coaltown drinking places. The largest perhaps, but at that it was simply a lengthy, narrow room—the long bar with its curved, shut-in end taking up one side, and against the other wall a waist-high shuffleboard game that extended some twelve feet like a bowling alley track. Beyond this, at the rear, small tables for card playing and relaxed drinking, likewise for private wrangling and fistbanging discussion of mine politics. Two washrooms radiating their odors led off from here. Koepke's had all the conveniences for a complete social life. Women could enter, but were seldom there except on "pay night," when the place became a gala scene of mixed-company festivity and bickering.

This being an ordinary day (except for the miracle), there were no ladies present, but due to the town's awakening, more miners than usual and several newsmen were having refreshment for body and mind. There were some two dozen patrons in the room.

Bill Dunnigan avoided the newsmen talking at the far end of the bar and stepped between two groups of miners. Heavy-faced, drink-serving Mr. Koepke (he attended his own bar) greeted him cordially, as he considered Dunnigan a welcome although a "single shot" customer. Since his arrival in Coaltown Bill had not gone in for any heavy drinking.

"I've got a special bottle for you, Mr. Dunnigan," said Koepke, "didn't know I still had it! Pre-war Vat 61. It will cost you sixty cents a shot, but it's well worth the difference!"

"Thanks," said Bill, "I'm a little tired and could do with a good drink! And I've got a big favor to ask of you."

"The house is yours, Mr. Dunnigan!" said Koepke. He had a feeling that the presence of this well-dressed stranger gave a lacking "class" to his emporium. Proudly he produced from a bottle-filled shelf the special one he had been saving since morning for this monied customer. He deftly loosened the cork and placed both bottle and a glass upon the bar. This in itself was an unusual mark of confidence. Most drinks in Coaltown were very carefully measured, and poured only by the seller thereof, the bottle being immediately replaced beyond the reach of the customer.

"Seltzer and ice?" he asked. "Or do you prefer it straight?"

"If it's the real thing I'll take it straight," said Bill, "and, Mr. Koepke, I want to ask you to put up a show-card behind your bar."

It was at this precise moment that Bill Dunnigan became conscious of the presence of a burly figure of a man at his immediate right. He became conscious of it because the left arm of that figure jostled him as it reached out across the bar and took a firm grip on the Vat 61 that had been placed there for the press agent's particular consumption.

"Pre-war stuff, eh?" growled a husky voice addressed to this bottle, now held up for closer inspection in a ponderous, mine-stained fist. "Been holding out on us, have you?" this to Mr. Koepke. "I'll have a shot of it myself, if His Highness the city gent don't object!"

The words "His Highness" and "city gent" had no friendly intonation. They were in fact exceedingly insolent, as was the manner and leer of the person who spoke them.

Dunnigan's entrance had not passed unnoticed. There had been a pause in laughter and oaths, a general looking in his direction when the tall, smartly-dressed, derby-topped figure had appeared. Next to the events occurring at St. Michael's Church, his own presence in the town as the "millionaire" friend of Stan Trocki's kid had been the chief topic of speculation and conversation. But as he had already been seen in several of the saloons during the past two days—he was no "damned prohibitionist"—had bought his drink (never more than one), drunk it quickly and departed in silence—local habitants had given him the courtesy of at least a pretended indifference that even the roughest of barrooms will extend to a patron who minds his own affairs. They would have been equally generous in friendly or unfriendly conversation, if the stranger had wanted it. Such is the understanding code of bars the world over, a code too little copied in nobler assemblages.

Bill turned slowly to regard this unexpected and uninvited sharer of his bottle. The man was really huge, a head taller than the six-foot theater agent. He was about Dunnigan's age with a dark, scowling, smooth-shaven brutishly-intelligent face; his clothes were those of a miner and a reddish-colored shirt open at the neck revealed a hairy upper chest. He did not wear a miner's cap, however, but a weather-stained slouch hat. He had been drinking, obviously.

Before Dunnigan could speak, owner Koepke interfered.

"Now, Jan," he said, "that is this gentleman's liquor. I've got plenty of your favorite brand the same as I've been serving you."

"I think I'll change my brand to a kind that's set out and left on the bar," said the giant pointedly. "I've always wondered what these millionaires like to gargle best. Nothing wrong with seeking some information, is there?" he added aggressively. "Or isn't my money as good as his?"

Bill Dunnigan was in a placid mood. The ex-bouncer of an East Side dance hall, the frequenter of saloons in every state in the Union had met up with the occasional quarrelsome drinker before.

"It's all right, Mr. Koepke. Give our friend a glass. I'm happy to have him sample my liquor, even if he seems to have forgotten his manners. And I'll pay for both drinks."

"I pay for my own liquor, and if you don't like my manners, you know what you can do about it!" replied the man called Jan. The look in his eyes changed from insolence to truculence. He glowered at the peaceful Mr. Dunnigan.

The press agent chose to ignore this remark and its accompanying scowl. He had more important business on hand than an argument with a flushed miner over a bottle of liquor. He motioned the hesitating but obviously relieved proprietor to set out another glass, and turned his back on this disagreeable bar neighbor who seemed bent on an evening of trouble. He produced one of the two dozen show-cards he carried beneath his arm.

"I want you to put up a card over your bar where all your customers will see it—an attraction I am very much interested in."

"Sure!" said Mr. Koepke, now especially anxious to accommodate, "I used to put up a show-card each week for a picture theater in Nanticoke. And I had a pass for me and the missus on my night off. What theater is it for, Mr. Dunnigan?"

Bill Dunnigan smiled. "It's not exactly for a theater," he said. "It's more important stuff than any show. And I can't pay you in passes for putting it up. It's just that you'll be helping two grand guys that want to help your town—that *have* helped you and your town a lot the past few days."

"What guys are them?" asked Mr. Koepke dubiously. Mr. Dunnigan was obviously not speaking of himself. And ten years in Coaltown had convinced the bar owner that no native of that settlement—much less *two* of them—was addicted to altruism of either a civic or a personal nature.

"Father Paul of the Church of St. Michael the Archangel is one of 'em," said Bill Dunnigan. "Here, read it yourself!" And he presented the "5:45 Mass" show-card to the shirt-sleeved dispenser of liquor.

Mr. Koepke's narrow eyes opened wide. He had no need to take his glasses from the top of the cash register to read Bill Dunnigan's bold, two-inch-high type. It was a striking, two-color job—the "DON'T FORGET," the "at 5:45 A.M.," the "MINERS' MASS AT ST. MICHAEL'S" in a flaming red; the other words in brilliant black.

"You'll be doing it for Father Paul," repeated Bill. "He and his Saint Michael are the lads I'm speaking of."

Saloon proprietor Koepke was not without religious sentiment. He wasn't, to be sure, in the habit of attending Mass at 5:45 A.M. or any other hour, but his "missus" went each Sunday, and an eight-year-old daughter had lately been confirmed at St. Adalbert's. He had always considered religion as a thing for women. He did not particularly care for the presence of women in his saloon, and there was a vague, undefined thought that his saloon was not a place for religion either, or for a card advertising a Mass.

He wanted, however, to please a gentleman as important and as genial as this Mr. Dunnigan.

"I don't know," he said. "I have nothing against Father Paul or his church, but I don't think a card here will help much! My customers don't exactly have their minds on religion." The explosive language at the shuffleboard game behind Dunnigan lent emphasis to this remark.

Bill Dunnigan spoke up, however.

"Of course not! There's a time for religion and a time for other considerations. But since you and Father Paul are both in the same business——"

"The same business!" gasped Mr. Koepke.

"Certainly! You're providing good cheer, aren't you?—a little happiness—escape from troubles—stimulation when one feels blue? Well, so is he. You do it for the body—he does it for the soul!"

Mr. Koepke's brow wrinkled in a process of thought. Then he smiled. "I never looked at it that way!" he admitted and was flattered by the idea. Another wrinkling of the brow and he said, "Perhaps you're right!"

"Of course, I'm right!" countered a determined Bill Dunnigan. "Take—take your juke box!" That instrument of the Muses had suddenly started to execute an aggressive rendition of the "Beer Barrel Polka." "The late Olga Treskovna told me how she remembered that juke box as a little girl. She only saw it from the street, but its music, its bright lights impressed her—she remembered them as a sort of magic!"

"Did this great actress say that!" There was a broad, pleased expression on the hard, fleshy face. Mr. Koepke was impressed.

"She sure did!" cried Bill Dunnigan, pursuing his advantage. "Be a regular fellow and put up Father Paul's card. It won't do you any harm. It may help him. Your place, I'm told, is the most popular in town with the mine workers."

Mr. Koepke was only human. And he was up against one of the best salesmen in America.

"I'll put it up!" he decided. "I don't know what the boys will say, but I'll put it up. I'm doing it for you, Mr. Dunnigan, and for this dead girl. She liked my juke box! Good music *is* a fine thing for old and young, isn't it?"

"Thanks a million!" said Bill, and lifted the bottle to pour his drink.

There had been curiosity, ever since Dunnigan's entrance, about the large cardboard placards he was carrying. The customers could now satisfy that curiosity. The card advertising a 5:45 A.M. Mass at the Church of St. Michael was placed in a position of prominence and honor—above the cash register itself, and there was a concerted craning of some two dozen unwashed necks. Those at the tables half rose to get a better look. The players of shuffleboard paused in the intricacies of their game. One newsman, leaning on the juke box, took out a notebook and started to copy the reading matter on the card.

But the audible reaction came from the man Jan who had by now taken a second liberal helping from the Dunnigan bottle and had thrown a five-dollar bill on the bar to pay for the same.

"By damn!" he said loudly. "By damn! It's reached a hell of a pass, Koepke, when a man can't buy a drink without a damn priest's name stuck in his face! Be hearing a sermon next, I reckon, when a guy wants his shot of liquor. A hymn and a prayer with every beer! Take that damn poster down! I say, to hell with it!"

The card players at the tables were by now on their feet in earnest. The drinkers paused in the middle of lifting their glasses. The shuffleboard addicts tore their eyes from the polished surface of their chute. All conversation in the room came to a dead and ominous silence. Even the juke box seemed to sense tragedy and ended as abruptly as it had started.

Those nearest Dunnigan moved back hurriedly. The anger and commands of this creature Jan were evidently not to be lightly regarded by those who knew him.

Proprietor Koepke made the first positive movement. He reached beneath his bar and took a firm grip on a solid police club that he always kept there for "emergencies."

Jan Rubel was the ugliest fighter in the Valley. A dangerous character when aroused and crossed. He had once killed a man with his fists in a saloon brawl and had got off on a plea of self-defence. Mr. Koepke had no desire to have the annihilation of as notable a person as millionaire William Dunnigan take place in his saloon. It might lose him his license! But like a higher placed exponent of corrective power, he spoke softly while he grasped his big stick.

"Go home, Jan," he said. At the same time he pushed back the bill on his bar. "Take your money. The drinks are on the house. Mr. Dunnigan is my friend and I'll do him a favor if I wish."

Simultaneously the saloon owner tried to convey to Mr. Dunnigan by look and gesture that he should step back, that danger threatened him.

But William Dunnigan did not step back. At that moment the placing of Father Paul's and St. Michael's Mass card above Mr. Koepke's cash register was the most important act of his career. He eyed the mountainous figure beside him with a quizzical gaze.

"I'll settle this," he said to Mr. Koepke.

"You'll settle what!" said Jan Rubel, and took off his coat and tossed it on the bar.

Mr. Dunnigan well knew the meaning of the shedding of a coat. It had happened before in provincial places he had visited, though he himself usually had not been the objective of the garment shedder. It brought back nostalgic memories of East Houston Street.

He lifted his glass and swallowed his drink. The liquor was good. He placed the empty glass on the bar. "Good whiskey!" he complimented Mr. Koepke. "Thanks for digging it up."

He then turned to the belligerent Jan.

"My friend," he said calmly, "you seem to be upset and unduly excited. It's bad for the blood pressure. I don't know you, never saw you before tonight; I shared my liquor with you; you can have nothing against me. But you evidently have it in for priests. Why, may I ask? What harm has Father Paul of St. Michael's done to you?"

Dunnigan's calmness infuriated Jan Rubel but at the same time he was momentarily nonplused by it. You couldn't strike a man who did not even raise his voice, much less his hands. Was this millionaire so spineless he could only parry insult with compliance, and challenge with a question?

Rubel would answer the question as insultingly as possible and repeat his demand. Then boot the softie out of the saloon.

"I don't know the bastard and don't want to know him!" he sneered. "Let him keep out of my way, that's all!" and he gesticulated toward the Mass card. "I want no part of him or his fake religious muck! I say, take down that card!"

"But why?" persisted a still cool Mr. Dunnigan. And for the first time in his life he framed the question that he never dreamed he, Bill Dunnigan, would ask.

"Don't you believe in God?" he queried. He wanted to get to the bottom of why any worker in the town should so hate Father Paul. Inadvertently he hit on the core of this man's social rebellion.

"God—hell!" shouted the Coaltown unbeliever. "God be damned!"

"You are then—an atheist—I think that is the word," said Bill and he viewed the man with a renewed interest.

"Why?" he repeated.

Here was something more than just a barroom gangster out for a debauch. Bill Dunnigan had never met an avowed atheist.

Jan Rubel was now itching to throttle this cool city dandy who stood leaning against his own favorite bar, viewing him, Jan Rubel, with a critical, half-smiling stare. A mere booting would be letting him off too easily. But there was time for that after he had seared the interloper with a few well-chosen words and expressed his utter contempt for one of the bulwarks of dandyism, who besides the arrogance of clean fingernails and polished shoes, thought all who worked with their hands devoid of mental capacity. Sooner or later these gentry fell back on a mention of "God"—"Divine Providence" they usually called it—to justify their superiority.

Rubel's views on the subject of religion were well known to all natives of the town. The stranger Dunnigan had surely put his foot into a hornets' nest. His head into a lion's jaw. Mr. Koepke took a firmer grip on his club beneath the bar, braced himelf for a quick leap over it, and again spoke placatingly in an attempt to avert a shambles.

"Now, Jan!" he commenced.

But Dunnigan again took command.

"Let the gentleman speak out and get it off his chest," he said. "It's a free country. I'm interested. It's a new breed to me . . . Well?"

And he turned again to his antagonist.

The word "breed" had not escaped Jan Rubel. Very well! A demonstration of mental superiority, and then——!

"I'll tell you if you really want to know," he said, and included a spellbound audience in his discourse. "I suppose, soft as you are, you have *some* brains! Only you don't think people like me have them too! Who invented God? God!" And Rubel's voice became a sneer. "People like you who wanted to live off the sweat of other men. Smart guys who wanted to live easy, who wanted other men to work for them. I've read. I'm not a dumb cluck like most of them around here. It goes way back. How could men be kept down! How could a few grab everything in sight? Fear! That was the racket—fear! So they set up a bogey God, set up a fake terror called religion, invented a Heaven and a Hell— 'you'll go to Hell if you don't knuckle under'—and along came priests—they were the worst rats of the lot—*they* saw that the poor dupes would pay money to keep out of this Hell—easy money—a living without doing any work or dirtying your hands—and in a lot of countries they seized on a faker named Jesus Christ—born illegitimate—their own Bible says he was—the old guy Joseph married the mother to save her reputation——"

There was a stirring in the deathly silent Bar and Grill of Mr. Koepke. Several men hastily crossed themselves. The miners there were not churchgoing men, they constantly violated all precepts of their faith, they blasphemed God hourly, but they were

Catholic and at least held the Christ in superstitious respect. They were used to hearing atheist Jan Rubel orate about the non-existence of a Supreme Being, but not before had he attacked the Immaculate Conception of the crucified Saviour of their Church.

Even Bill Dunnigan was shocked. He was more shocked than angry. He felt a pity for this blaspheming fellow man.

"My friend," he said, "I'm not a well-read scholar like you. I don't know much about religious history or who 'invented God,' as you say. I always thought that He invented us. I think that any mother, good or bad, rates a break from guys like you and me—and as for Jesus Christ—if we all lived as He taught—I remember at least that much from Sunday School—there wouldn't be all the rotten sorrow and suffering there is around us. But I'm not the guy to argue it out with you. I want you to do me the favor of talking with a pal of mine, Father Paul of your St. Michael's. I want you to hear about the great Saint—Saint Michael the Archangel—that is the patron of that church. You'll understand him— a fighter, as I take it you are——"

But Jan Rubel interrupted. He was in no mood to listen to pious argument and advice. And Dunnigan had opened another canker in the atheist's revolt.

"Saint Michael! Saint Fake! We'll leave out mothers. I can tell you plenty about that too. But Saints! That's another thing they invented! A lot of tin gods—Saints—so they could put up plaster statues in the robber churches they built with other people's money —stick boxes for more money in front of them and a place to kneel like a cringing slave—put the fear of more Hell into the poor saps if they didn't burn candles and pay nickels and dimes and quarters for forgiveness! Forgiveness!"

"But people don't only ask forgiveness," interrupted Dunnigan. "They pray sometimes for help—" The press agent had a very vivid recollection of his own prayer to Saint Michael on the bus to Nanticoke.

"Prayer!" sneered Jan Rubel in the same voice he had spoken "Forgiveness!" "The great come-on of the whole lying business! Pray hard enough, pay enough money into the coin boxes and maybe you'll get a new car, a new woman! You'll get 'em if you have the dough, or if you've got the guts to go out and take what you want. Tell me one person who ever had a lousy prayer answered."

"I have," said William Dunnigan. "And I think it was a pretty lousy one."

"*You* have!" Jan Rubel laughed and spat so that Dunnigan had to move back to avoid the tobacco-colored saliva. "You with your checkbook hiring bells to ring for a week—you with your sixty-cent whiskey—you with your priest pal that cooked up this miracle they're all yapping about, standing in line to see—right in my own town!—more priests' fakery—more Saint nonsense to get more dollars—to start more fear! I knew the nerve of your kind, but I didn't think you'd ever go so far as to try to spring a bogus miracle!"

"But have you no faith of any kind?" said Dunnigan. He had never before met a man so rabid, so bitter. He had never heard arguments against an Omnipotent Power so bitterly stated, so stressed with passion and hatred. The man reminded him of a giant cobra, writhing in a coil of loathsome malevolence. And being strangled by its own coils!

There, indeed, was a case for Father Paul and Saint Michael!

"Faith!" Jan Rubel was answering Dunnigan. "That is a real laugh! Ha, ha! Insanity and ignorance! The trick that was thought up to save the God-racket and the Saint-quackery! People started to ask questions. And because nothing could be proved in this fraud called religion, the priests hit on the idea of faith. Believe without proof! Take their word for it! And if you don't, you're eternally damned! The word of a crew of lazy, lying hypocrites! Why did this Christ of theirs stop being a carpenter and turn preacher? Because with honest carpenter-work he had to dirty his hands. Because with work he had to sweat! He hated to sweat! So he took on an easier job. Talk. Phoney talk. He deserved what he got for it!"

"Do you really believe what you are saying?" asked Bill Dunnigan. "If you do, I feel very sorry for you!"

Jan Rubel felt that he had argued long enough. He had stated his case pretty fully. There were no more words to be wasted on this patronizing advice giver. He rolled up the sleeves of his dark shirt, exposing a hairy, muscle-ribbed arm.

"You! *You* feel sorry for *me!* You cheap fraud, sticking up priest advertisements in the one place a man can still speak the truth! Don't try to tell *me* about a religion backed by statues of this phoney Saint Michael and the harlot Mother of this Jesus Christ turning toward the coffin of an actress tart you're burying! A 'holy' girl! I used to see her old man around here. A holy prostitute more likely, if she was in the theater business!"

"Just say that again," said William Dunnigan quietly. The eyes of the press agent had narrowed. The tall, relaxed body had suddenly become very tense. He removed the black derby and placed it on the bar. He also placed there the other show-cards he was carrying.

Jan Rubel accommodated. Repeated the words with a fierce unction. At last the stranger was going to fight! Rubel had not had a fight for a month. This one was going to be a pleasure!

"I say Saint Michael is a fraud—and Christ's mother and this actress girl—like all women—*tarts*—tarts for any guy with the price—that's what your church card stands for—what your lazy, rotten priest——"

"You low, filthy swine!" said William Dunnigan and he had not raised his voice. "Take it back! Apologize before I give you what I suspect you've needed for a long, long time."

The patrons of Koepke's Bar and Grill (including the two newsmen, one of them a former sports reporter) were never sure of just what happened next. Jan Rubel, snarling like an infuriated boar, started for William Dunnigan, both arms swinging. Owner Koepke, club now raised in full view, started to climb across his bar. The others stood rooted in fascinated horror to watch this stranger gentleman be beaten into a pulp before Koepke could possibly fell his attacker.

But the long, swinging arms of Jan Rubel struck only air. Mr. Dunnigan's face was not in their orbit. The city man had seemed to crouch like a professional boxer, his fists clenched before him, his elbows close against his sides; he had stepped inside the flailing blows; Jan Rubel ran into a jolt like that of a pile driver which sank right into his stomach, and as, too late, he lowered his own hands to protect that section of his anatomy, two other jolts coming up in lightning succession almost ripped his head from his sagging body. The man several fighters had tried to persuade to turn professional, the press agent they had preferred boxing with to any of their sparring partners, had not entirely forgotten an old "one, two, three" a certain champion of champions had taught him, and practiced with him many a spring day at the training camp.

Jan Rubel, greatest fighter of the Wyoming Valley, victor of half a hundred brawls, a man who had never even been knocked down before, lay stretched on Mr. Koepke's floor, completely and conclusively "out."

In a dead, gasping silence, Mr. Dunnigan straightened up and adjusted his tie. He inspected his knuckles and dabbed the green silk handkerchief against a clot of blood. He took up the black derby, brushed his hand around its crown and replaced it on his brow at its customary angle. He recovered his show-cards from the bar.

"When Kid Atheist comes out of it, give him some of my liquor," said the Church of St. Michael's card placer. "He'll be O. K., I think, in about ten minutes. Throw some water on him now. He could use a bath. By the way, Mr. Koepke, I want to contact the head of the Miners' Union here. I want to get the Union behind this early Mass of Father Paul's. It's a great idea, I believe. I hope all you boys will go, some morning soon. A little churchgoing under a right guy like Father Paul won't hurt any of us. Who is the man I should see?"

Mr. Koepke had only just recovered his power of speech. Crouching atop his bar—he had gotten that far in his rescue mission—he had been gazing open-mouthed between the prostrate Jan and the leisurely movements of Mr. Dunnigan in recovering his hat and cards.

"Why—why, I guess you've contacted him already—and how!" he gasped. "The District Chairman of the Wyoming Unions is Jan Rubel—and there he is! My God! How did you do it, Mr. Dunnigan!"

*　*　*

Placing the St. Michael show-cards in the other Coaltown saloons was not a difficult task. If the news of the miracle that morning had spread like a conflagration, the report of the fight in Koepke's whirled through the town like a tornado. Jan Rubel, head of the Miners' Union, giant, two-fisted king bully of the entire Valley, had been knocked out in a matter of seconds! Bartenders received Mr. Dunnigan with awed admiration in every worshipful greeting. Patrons respectfully moved aside to give the conquering hero a path to the bar, where a hand reached out for his show-cards before he could open his mouth to make the request. Several places asked for three or four cards—one for each of their windows—a couple to go up behind the liquor counter. A crowd was soon following the press agent from tavern to tavern.

The downfall of Jan Rubel in Koepke's Bar and Grill was even a greater phenomenon than the turning of the statues at the Church of St. Michael!

But the center of all this attention was not entirely happy. Dunnigan had set his heart on the idea of Father Paul being the "official chaplain" of the Union. He had already envisaged the march of these miners through the early dawn, their cap-lights burning like pilgrims' candles. He already saw them seated in the little church, filling every pew; he felt the supreme thrill the little priest would know with the realization that his early Mass had achieved its basic purpose, and was not going to slip back into an abrupt desuetude with the final funeral service of Olga Treskovna.

Now Bill Dunnigan had hopelessly antagonized the all-powerful head of this union. That man richly deserved his beating—there seemed a universal agreement on that score; but there also seemed little doubt that he had a stranglehold on the affairs of the workers' organizations in the vicinity, was greatly feared, never forgot an injury. Fat chance it left of getting him to agree to such a plan! The press agent could scarcely go to Jan Rubel the next morning and say: "I'm the guy who humiliated you and knocked you out last night. Hope you slept well and feel chipper and O. K. this morning. Now I have a favor to ask!"

Even a new and very interesting telegram from Marcus Harris handed Bill when (having "made" all the taverns) he returned to the Wyoming Hotel, did not restore the elation, the feeling of complete success the earlier events of the day had promised. Being the press agent for a church, a priest, and a saint was some tough assignment!

65

*B*ILL DUNNIGAN had a late caller that evening, a surprising one. The time of this call was partly the result of the fight in Koepke's bar. And the caller was a woman.

The news of the battle had reached the St. Leo parish house by a relief bell ringer. It was related in picturesque detail to Father Spinsky and his sister in the sitting room of the parsonage.

Father Spinsky had been again perusing his *Lives of the Saints* with special reference to Saint Michael. Mary Spinsky was darning a batch of her brother's socks—that priest had never been privileged to know the pleasures of this nerve-calming task.

"In one second—with a single blow—wham!—this millionaire gentleman had Jan Rubel stretched flat on his back!" Thus the bell ringer finished his vigorous recital.

The bell ringer was an elderly man, but he crouched and graphically gave illustration with a vicious if wavering uppercut, which was the accredited Main Street version of the Dunnigan knockout blow.

"Jan Rubel smacked cold! Stone cold!" he reiterated the incredible. "It took half an hour and a bottle of whiskey to bring him to. Three miners had to help him home. They say he was still in a daze."

"Disgraceful! Both probably drunk!" was the comment of Mary Spinsky. And she feared for the safety of her china table lamp as the bell man gave his gesticulating picture of Mr. Dunnigan in action.

"I never heard such sacrilege as putting up a notice of a church mass in a disreputable barroom," she added with pious indignation.

She looked across the table at her brother for confirmation.

Father Spinsky sat with his book open before him. He had just reviewed the triumph of Saint Michael over the Prince of Darkness himself. The priest seemed fascinated—fascinated and strangely perturbed. He spoke at last, and he spoke unexpected words, words that came from his depths.

"Jan Rubel had best be on his knees and thank God he is still alive!" he exclaimed.

"Why do you say that, brother?" asked Mary Spinsky. The recurring apprehension she noticed in that brother's eyes was very troubling to her.

Father Spinsky turned to the relief bell ringer.

"Thank you for stopping to tell us about this," he said. "Now go to your bell tower and keep St. Leo's ringing without pause. Do not weaken in your task! I will see that you and your brother receive a bonus for your faithful work. These are great times for God's voice in Coaltown! We must do our part without faltering."

When the man had gone, the priest turned to the still inquiring gaze of his sister.

"I say Jan Rubel should be thankful that he is not dead, because it is a dangerous venture to attempt assault on the Saint who led the army of our Lord," he said.

Mary Spinsky replied to this incomprehensible statement with irritation and concern.

"This disgusting saloon fight was with no Saint, but the wealthy man who has been swaggering about the district with his checkbook and his hired Packard. Brother, what has this man told you? What has he done to you?"

Father Spinsky debated with himself. Should he tell his sister all that he suspected? All that he believed? Would she understand?

"Almighty God moves in mysterious ways, His wonders to perform," said the priest. "He is a merciful God—that I believe, although I have not often enough stressed it—*that* I have cause to know! Let me pray that He will forgive my grievous fault. But there have been times when God showed the sternness of His justice. When He drove the first two of us who sinned from the paradise of the Garden of Eden—when He rained brimstone and fire upon Sodom and upon Gomorrah—when He smote the reason of the proud Nebuchadnezzar—and slew his arrogant son Belshazzar with His righteous wrath. Even the gentle Christ whipped the money-changers from the Temple in Jerusalem.

"And the blessed Saints. Their joy is to intercede for us. To help us in our sin. But the Saints, also, can know anger—can resent indifference, open antagonism. They also have interfered in the affairs of wilful men—as I have been reading here."

And he indicated the book in his lap.

"What are you trying to tell me?" asked the woman. She had never known her brother so obscurely earnest; she had never known him to speak with such obvious alarm in his inner soul.

"Belshazzar, king of Babylon, when his mind was hardened in boastful pride, saw the writing on the wall: ME-NE, *God hath numbered thy kingdom;* TE-KEL, *Thou art weighed in the balance and found wanting;* PE-RES, *Thy kingdom is divided, and given to the Medes and the Persians!* I too, sister, have seen a triple writing, only mine was three burning candles. But I have hope that the sign given me was one of forgiveness for my pride, my selfishness, my intolerance."

Mary Spinsky half rose from her chair, but sank back again. She knew what she must do and at once What she said was:

"Brother, you must not think such thoughts! You have done nothing wrong!"

"I know my fault—my sin," said Father Spinsky. "And in my case there is a greater sin than the blackness of my own soul. It is the blackness of this town—the example I have set for my fellow men. I see it—I see it——"

He was going to say, "I see it reflected in my own sister, before my eyes—now!" but the alarmed look of her face caused him to pause. Instead he arose. He closed his *Lives of the Saints.*

"I will say no more tonight," he said aloud. "I wish to talk again with Father Paul. Perhaps with the Bishop. My heart is troubled. I have most certainly been weighed in the balances of good works and found grievously wanting!"

He moved to the bookcases that lined one side of the room and replaced the volume. His sister followed him with anxious eyes.

"I am going to my room to pray," he said, turning to her, "then I shall retire. I need rest perhaps."

He noticed the look still clouding the woman's face. He came to her and again kissed her forehead. He pressed her hand.

"Do not fear," he said. "Thank God your brother has learned in time! I have taken heed. There is hope for me if I work and pray."

A recurrent thought crossed his mind. Troubled as he was, it caused him to smile.

"Jan Rubel—thinking he could best God's champion! I would like to have been there! Good night, sister."

He went from the room and she heard him mounting the stairs. His footfalls were slower than usual. Her brother had been aging before her eyes.

Mary Spinsky did fear. Not for herself. She feared for this strong man she loved not only as a sister but as a mother.

She had made up her mind, but she sat for a time and worked doggedly at the socks in her lap. She was listening carefully. She heard him moving about in his room above. Going to and from his closet—the impact of his heavily-soled shoes when he removed them and dropped them to the floor. Silence for awhile—he was praying—then, outside, the reflection of his room lights against the upper windows of the next-door church went black.

Her brother had gone to bed.

Mary Spinsky arose quickly and put the socks and her darning basket on the table. She stepped to the hallway and took up from a table there the hat she had worn that afternoon, and her handbag in which were her keys. She put the hat on quickly. She listened again. No sound from the upper room. She went out by the side door of the parish house. She opened and closed the door quietly. She locked the door behind her.

She hastened to the sidewalk and hurried up the street. She scarcely heard the bells and paid no attention to the chattering groups that she passed. The talk was about equally divided between the "fight" and the "miracle."

When she reached the business section of the town there were a great many people still abroad. The open-doored saloons were brightly lighted and crowded. There were animated gatherings of men and women in front of all of them. These were mostly speaking of Jan Rubel and the "millionaire" stranger who had knocked him out.

There was talk also of the "5:45 Mass" placards which had started this fight. No one in the town but knew *now* about Father Paul's "early Mass for miners"!

Among the younger element there was another topic of speculation and amazed debate—the names of the Hollywood stars which the evening papers said would arrive in Coaltown Friday for the funeral.

If Mary Spinsky now paid some heed to all this—and she could not entirely ignore it—it hardened her resolution. She remembered that she herself had helped spread the excitement the night the bells started ringing. She had contributed her full share in creating this Frankenstein named William Dunnigan who had in two short days caused the whole town to lose its head completely; who had in some manner instilled in her brother a horrible, mysterious fear. Underneath his civilized raiment this millionaire was assuming the guise of a hairy monster, a monster bent on the destruction not only of her brother but the sanity of the entire community. The reported outbreak of brute passion in Koepke's had been a momentary revelation of his true character.

It was therefore to her credit that she had not the slightest fear for herself. If no one else dared, she would rescue not only her brother but the whole town from the clutches of this suave, crafty devil in human form.

She felt as Charlotte Corday must have felt when that courageous patriot determined to call on the unspeakable Marat. Her stately figure did not look unlike that of the Norman maiden who marched to the Rue de l'École de Medicine No. 44 to kill a "savage wild beast" in the person of the "atrocious" signer of a thousand death warrants and thus give "repose to her country."

Mary Spinsky resolutely entered the lobby of the Wyoming Hotel.

She pushed her way straight through the crowd of newsmen and miners to the desk. It did not deter her that she was the only woman in this particular place.

"Is the man William Dunnigan in?" she asked in her firm, authoritative voice. "I want to see him at once!"

The clerk looked up in some surprise. He knew Mary Spinsky by sight. That the sister of the priest of St. Leo's should come to the hotel at this hour of the evening was an unusual occurrence. That she should come there at all! Mary Spinsky had not personally delivered her cake package to the desk the day before. She had sent it in from her brother's car at the curb by a passing boy to whom she had given five cents for the service.

"Mr. Dunnigan is in his room," said the clerk. "He came in at nine-thirty-seven and one-quarter," and he glanced up at his electric clock. It was now nine-forty-eight and one-half. A late hour for Coaltown!

"Is he expecting you, Miss Spinsky?" he added dubiously. He was regretting his haste in betraying the whereabouts of guest William Dunnigan. His passion for stating the exact time of events had outstripped his discretion.

"He is not expecting me!" said Mary Spinsky and there was scorn in her voice. That anyone should think she, Mary Spinsky, would come to a public hotel at night to see this stranger by appointment! Or any man!

"Tell him I'm here."

"I—I'll tell him," said the clerk, wavering before the woman's determined gaze. "I'll tell him myself." And he locked the cash drawer and came out from behind his counter.

He looked again at the clock—nine forty-nine and one-quarter—and went quickly up the short flight of stairs that led to A-1. He could have used the speaking tube to the room, but something told him he should not shout Mary Spinsky's name over a speaking tube. And the now "great" Mr. Dunnigan might not want to see "a woman" at that hour—a woman who appeared bent on no friendly errand. Even if she were the sister of the St. Leo pastor.

Mary Spinsky stood by the reception counter and waited. A newsman offered her a chair in which he was sitting but she curtly refused. She noticed the "Mass" card above the desk and read it. She looked about the crowded room and heard its rough talk and laughter. The talk was largely about the fight. What a place to put up something that had to do with holy things!

Father Paul should be in fear of divine wrath—not her brother! Father Paul needed a keeper—a protector—more urgently than he did a cook!

Bill Dunnigan opened his door to the clerk's knock. Unlike the atrocious Marat, he was not yet in his bath. But he had taken off his coat and vest and loosened his necktie. He had been sitting on the bed playing coon-can. He played this card game whenever he wanted to think. It cleared his mind.

He was thinking about the debacle of his great plan for the Miners' Union. What rotten luck that such a thing as this brawl had had to happen! Still, if the head of the Union felt as Jan Rubel did, there would have been little chance anyway of gaining his co-operation. He'd have to devise some new way to help Father Paul.

"The sister of Father Spinsky is in the lobby and asking to see you," announced the clerk.

"What!" said Dunnigan.

"If you don't want to see her, Mr. Dunnigan, I can say you've gone to bed," the man suggested. "That's why I came up myself. She don't look very friendly to me."

The sight of this room brought back sharp memories of the delectable chocolate cake of the night before.

"I sure can't forget that cake!" the clerk added and felt that he was making his presence and news a little less unpleasant. "I find myself smiling every time I think of it." He wondered if there was any of it still around.

Bill Dunnigan had recovered from his surprise.

"Father Spinsky's sister, eh?" he repeated, and the clerk nodded. "By the way, she made that cake, my friend. If she came to get it back, she's sure out of luck! It's gone to the last crumb. I'll see her! I'd get up out of bed to meet any woman who can bake a cake like that! Tell her I'll be right down. I'll see her in the parlor. I hope you took her there."

"I couldn't," said the clerk, "and I'm afraid you can't talk with her there either, sir. We've put cots in the parlor for our overflow. Four newspapermen from Philadelphia are occupying it. On account of the miracle, sir, and the movie stars that are coming! You've certainly brought us swell business, Mr. Dunnigan! And I guess what happened tonight at Koepke's will make this town really talked about!"

"Don't remind me of that silly affair," said Bill. "Forget about it, please! I wish I could! But what'll I do about Miss Spinsky? I'll have to see her up here, I suppose, if she'll come. Explain and bring her up yourself. Here's a dollar for your thoughtfulness."

"Thanks! I should have said you weren't in, Mr. Dunnigan," admitted the clerk.

"No. I want to see her," replied Bill. For the unexpected presence of Miss Spinsky had suggested an idea to his mind in the problem of helping Father Paul. But just having, with considerable difficulty, made a veritable "progress" through the lobby (his prowess as a fighter seemed to cause an unholy stir!), he didn't feel it quite the place to greet as distinguished and probably as confidential a caller as Father Spinsky's sister! And into the bargain, she was a lady he wanted a favor of.

The clerk left. Dunnigan hastily put on his necktie, his coat and vest. He stuffed a soiled shirt into a drawer. He tossed a half-smoked cigar out of the window. He pulled forward his two chairs and removed an extra pair of spats from one of them. He pushed the playing cards back on his bed.

There was another knock.

"Come in!" he called.

The clerk ushered in Mary Spinsky.

"Miss Mary Spinsky," he said formally and then, "Your cake was grand, Miss Spinsky! Mr. Dunnigan let me have a bite of it! I never tasted such a fine cake before!"

"Why—why, thanks!" said Mary Spinsky. Coming up the stairs she had been working herself into a fine mood of outraged indignation. The unexpected, spontaneous compliment somewhat shattered her grim antagonism.

But the clerk was a Coaltown man. This Dunnigan monster was the one she must do battle with.

She turned now to him. But there again she was surprised and baffled.

She had never seen Mr. Dunnigan, except to watch his back disappear into the Packard from her window, the noonday he had paid her brother for the ringing of his bell. That hour which marked the dreadful change in this brother.

But now that she met this monster face to face, try as she could, she could find no Frankenstein leer in the clear grey eyes, in the likable smile of the tall figure that stepped graciously forward. Neither was there the slightest trace of the barroom brawler that had been pictured to her as crouching like a jungle beast and "whamming" Jan Rubel. And the voice was quiet, friendly, well-modulated, sincere.

"I'm sorry, Miss Spinsky, I have to ask you to come up here! You see, they've rented out the reception parlor to extra guests. I would gladly have come to you had I known you wished to see me. And I want to apologize for not getting a word of thanks to you about your chocolate cake. With one thing and another I've been on the jump. What a cake! I got my first taste of it at Father Paul's! I didn't think anyone else in this world but my blessed mother could make a chocolate cake that tasted so good! But yours even surpassed hers, as I remember them. My good mother is long since making her cakes for the angels, Miss Spinsky. Father Paul and I ate all of yours—every last crumb—at one meal! And sighed for more! And the next morning the half you sent to me disappeared as rapidly! I can taste it yet!"

Mary Spinsky was very proud of her skill as a cook. That skill had been devoted solely to her brother. And that brother, until the last few hours, had never pronounced a single word of praise.

She was pleased. She was even thrilled! When you have been starved for years to hear a single word about that in which you know you excel, a laudatory speech has a heartwarming sound. Without premeditation, Dunnigan had pierced her Achilles tendon with his first word.

But she had her errand.

"My brother has always thought well of my chocolate cakes," she said defensively, trying desperately to crush back this liking she was beginning to have for this enemy stranger, "and it is about him——"

"Lucky man!" cried William Dunnigan. "Now I know the secret of his vitality and good health! Have a chair, Miss Spinsky. I'm afraid it's not a very comfortable one!"

And as Mary Spinsky hesitated, "You're not afraid to be alone in my room, I hope! You're safe—unless you have another chocolate cake hidden in your handbag!"

"I'm not afraid of you, Mr. Dunnigan," said Mary Spinsky, and although she attempted to put a menace in her voice and a look of outrage in her face, she knew that she was failing utterly in both! She knew that she was even smiling back at the man who smiled so humanly at her.

"Good!" said William Dunnigan. "For you and I are going to be friends. Partners, I hope, in a way of speaking! I was coming to see you tomorrow. I must have the recipe for making that cake! You see, I'm already a partner in a new kind of Quick Lunch over in Nanticoke——"

"You're in a Quick Lunch in Nanticoke!"

Another depth of Mary Spinsky had been plumbed. Curiosity. Not always a kindly curiosity. The newspapers reported this millionaire an owner of theaters. A shady business but one of importance. A Quick Lunch proprietor! That was a juicy morsel to be the first to know and spread!

"Yes! Sounds sort of crazy, don't it? But I really am! Don't get

me wrong—I'm not actively engaged in it. I'm not going to be behind the counter there! I'm not half clever enough! It's all the
idea of a young friend of mine. I guess it was the religious angle
that got me!" and Bill Dunnigan smiled at *that* sudden thought.
But strangely enough, it was the truth!

"The religious angle!" Mary Spinsky was completely mystified.

"Yes. He's going to call it Quick Lunch Heaven—isn't that a
swell name, Miss Spinsky?—because he wants to make it the best
public eating place in Pennsylvania—in America! We're already
busy inventing a St. Michael sandwich for this Heaven, and when
your wonderful gift came *straight out of Heaven*—I'll be thanking
you till my dying day for it, Miss Spinsky—I had the inspiration of
a St. Leo cake!"

"A St. Leo cake!" gasped Mary Spinsky. She did not know
whether she should be shocked, flattered or offended. The phrase
had a not unpleasant ring.

"Sure! A St. Michael Sandwich! A St. Leo Cake! For this Nanticoke eating Elysium! Miss Spinsky, you're going with me some
morning to try that boy's ham and eggs!"

"I make good ham and eggs myself," said Mary Spinsky, on firm,
understandable ground at last. "I use a bit of green pepper——"

"Yes?" said Dunnigan eagerly. Maybe there was some other neglected Saint whose name could be honored by a glorified ham and
eggs!

"That's all," said Miss Spinsky. There was more, but no reason
to give away an excellent recipe—a secret recipe.

"I want to pay for the cake recipe, of course. This is a business
proposition——" Dunnigan had sensed the woman's hesitancy. "Miss
Spinsky! I'll tell you what! We'll pay a royalty on every cake we
make! Like a patent, you know—or a copyright on a great song.
That cake of yours *was* a song! First time it will ever have been
done, I guess. Wait till I give that out to the newspaper boys!
They'll eat it up! The news, Miss Spinsky, not the cake! Come to
think of it, we needn't stop with my Nanticoke place. There's my
friend Oscar at the Waldorf-Astoria in New York! He told me a
hundred times he could never find anyone to make a real, honest-
to-God, homemade *American chocolate cake*. People ask for it—
will pay any price for it—and what do they get? One of those fancy

French pastries that are no more like a cake such as yours and my mother's than sawdust is like homemade gingerbread."

"I can make good gingerbread too!" said Mary Spinsky proudly.

"I'll bet you can! That makes my mouth water also! Gingerbread! Yum, yum! What is your first name, Miss Spinsky?"

"Why . . . Mary," faltered Miss Spinsky. And she realized that the hairy Frankenstein monster had receded and vanished beyond recall. The Nanticoke Quick Lunch had not impressed her—she was not quite certain that Mr. Dunnigan was entirely serious about that project—but the thought of her cakes at the Waldorf-Astoria! She had never seen the Waldorf, but in her avid society-news reading it was a synonym for all that was expensive, magnificent, luxurious.

"Mary! That's swell! My old pal George Cohan wrote his best song about that name. Mary! Couldn't be better! Sounds so honest! No phoney French pastry about Mary. The Mary Spinsky St. Leo Chocolate Cake! Sounds grand even before you taste it. Gee! Oscar will thank me a thousand times! And he'll make your name as famous as Melba's! You know, Peach Melba. Named after the great opera star."

"But—but I never thought of taking money for my cooking!" exclaimed Mary Spinsky. But even as she said it, the words had a pleasantly intriguing sound. Like fresh, warm rain pattering down on the tin roof of her summer kitchen. Money! Showers of money for her very own!

And this gentleman (Dunnigan had now become that) who could hire church bells rung for a week, in whose wake miracles occurred, gave the impression he was not now speaking idle words.

He could do what he said he could.

"Not money for yourself, of course, Miss Spinsky," Mr. Dunnigan was saying. "You're a church lady. I can understand that. But you must have a lot of church charities—a lot of good works that are dear to your heart and that you can use extra money for."

Mary Spinsky had to think hard.

"Our Ladies' Aid is raising money for a new set of altar-boy robes for my brother," she managed to recollect.

"Fine! That money is raised! Already in the till! We'll work out a plan that your Ladies' Aid receives so much royalty a cake—

and a good payment in advance against this royalty to cover these altar robes. You could go to New York, couldn't you, Miss Spinsky, and give Oscar personal instruction?"

"I was in New York once," said Mary Spinsky. She tried to keep her voice calm. Her heart was beating very rapidly.

"You'll be there a lot of times before we're through! And Miss Spinsky—Mary—I may call you Mary?"

"Why—why, yes—if you wish, Mr. Dunnigan."

Her brain was whirling like her giant-size eggbeater. She was already rushing through the countryside on the express from Wilkes-Barre—she was saying to the conductor, *"The Waldorf-Astoria sent for me!"*

"Look here, Mary," and Bill Dunnigan hitched his chair a bit nearer the sister of the St. Leo pastor, "I've got another idea also!"

"But Mr. Dunnigan!"

"Listen! It's a heap bigger than any restaurant stuff! All that's only the sideshow. Peanuts! It will take care of your Ladies' Aid —and Oscar's Waldorf and my Nanticoke place. But now we move on to the Main Event—into the Big Top with three rings and a brass band! You see, I was pounding my poor head when you were announced—what I could do to help my pal, Father Paul, because one of my big plans for him just received a swift kick in the pants—er—trousers. But I've something in mind—your coming suggested it, Mary—that won't fall down on any barroom floor if you will help me. Will you help me?"

"Why—I'll—I'll try, Mr. Dunnigan," Mary Spinsky heard herself replying.

"Father Paul is worried about the *cooking* in this town. The way the miners' families cook, I mean. He says it's part of the trouble with the people's health. Why so many children die young. Why there's so much illness. He tried to tell them when he first came here. They wouldn't take it from him, of course. I don't suppose they'd take it from *any* man. I can understand that. But they would listen to you. The sister of Father Spinsky of St. Leo's! Why, Father Paul says they even give young children—*sick* children —pork chops fried in lard! Hard-boiled eggs!"

"Too much fried food is bad for children," said Mary Spinsky.

"Sure! That's what my mother said. It's bad for anybody. If I eat much longer at this hotel I'll be in a hospital myself. Miss

Spinsky—Mary—" and Bill Dunnigan's mind was now galloping at full speed—"most of the people here have radios, don't they?"

"They have radios and cars, even if they don't have shoes," said Mary Spinsky censuringly.

"Good! That is, good for what *we* want! There's a local radio station in Wilkes-Barre—I made a deal with them about St. Michael's bell—they're going to be on my tail about this funeral— I've got some pretty big movie stars coming on! *You're going on the radio, Mary! Mary Spinsky's St. Leo's and St. Michael's Cooking Half-Hour!* Kind of long, but I've got to work the name of Saint Michael into all this! It's Father Paul's idea."

"But Mr. Dunnigan—I wouldn't know how to talk on the radio. I couldn't!"

"The hell you couldn't! You've got an excellent radio voice. I've been listening to you. I've had experience. I know!"

"But what could I talk about?" exclaimed Mary Spinsky. She did feel that she had a "cultivated" voice. She had attended a good convent school as a girl. And already she was hearing that voice issuing from the mahogany front of her brother's cabinet Philco!

"Cooking!" said Bill. "How to cook! What to cook! No subject in the world hits so many people! A friend of mine in New York has a food hour every morning—draws down five hundred bucks a week for doing it—a lot of baloney about vitamins—and I'll bet he couldn't even poach an egg properly himself. But someone like you! You know about all kinds of cooking, don't you, Mary?"

"Our mother was the best cook in the Valley, and I learned from her!"

"Grand! We'll start right back at the very beginning. That's what Father Paul says should be done."

Bill Dunnigan gave his chair another hitch. He leaned forward and raised his hand to signify the profundity of the next question.

"What's the basic trouble, Mary, in *your* opinion, with Coaltown cooking? *Is it lard?*"

Mary Spinsky gave her own chair a hitch. She leaned forward and raised the first finger of her hand.

"It goes deeper than that!" she responded with no thought of a pun, but with the grim certainty of expert personal observation. "They don't keep their utensils half clean! They never wash their coffee pots! *They never scour their skillets!*"

Dunnigan jumped up from his chair.

"Good! I mean, of course, bad! No— Good! Gee, Mary! *You're a genius!* I'm glad you came around tonight. You've got something there. Bigger than you know, you've said. You've solved the whole problem about the radio deal. I've got a friend in Cincinnati—a grand guy who makes a cleaning powder—Silas Bartlett —Bartlett's Cleanser——"

"It's a good cleaner," said Mary Spinsky.

"That's fine! I'm glad to hear you say that! That's all I need to hear. This man will sponsor our program! *'The Basis of All Good Cooking—Clean Utensils—Use Bartlett's!'* What a slogan for him! He ought to pay you five thousand dollars just for that! But he'll buy us coast-to-coast network time—he'll pay you every week. He's a churchgoing man, Mary—public spirited—I met him when he used to buy out a circus matinee every year for the poor kids of his city—he liked me—had me to his club to dinner—said if I ever wanted anything—I'll long-distance him in the morning! We'll double his sales, Mary! I'll bet he's already heard about the doings here—the miracle—though he'd never connect it with me!"

"But what then would I talk about?"

"Plenty! There must be a hundred different things to cook, and a dozen ways of cooking each one of 'em. Good ways and bad ways. That's it! You'll tell 'em about *both* ways! Take up all the foods—one at a time. Meats! Eggs! Fish! Vegetables! Salads! Desserts! And one meal at a time—a series about breakfasts— lunches . . . *Lunches!* There's an idea, Mary! There's our wallop! I see these men here all carrying lunch pails. *What's in 'em?* I'll bet there's no sandwich like you could tell 'em about! No fried chicken! No meat pies! No gingerbread! No homemade chocolate cake to make that noon hour seem like an hour in Heaven worth struggling toward! No coffee like you could tell their wives how to make! I'll bet they don't even *wash out* those lunch pails properly."

"They don't!" said Mary Spinsky.

"That's it then! There you are! *Mary Spinsky's Miners' Lunch Pail Suggestions!* A new Suggestion at the end of each program. For the glory of Saint Leo, Saint Michael, and Silas Bartlett's Cleanser! We'll make that series of Lunch Pail Suggestions ring from Coast to Coast—from Maine to Florida—before we're finished.

Not only miners' women, but the women folk of every working man in America will be listening for it. To give her husband's lunch pail next day the treats you, Mary Spinsky, can think up!"

"I *can* think up things! I've written out in a book a lot of new recipes I've worked on."

"Mary—we're in! We'll do it! Trust me. You just get busy about *what to tell 'em*. Your brother can help you write it out. All I insist on is that Saint Michael be mentioned every time. You see, Mary, I'm a sort of press agent for that guy—an Ambassador Extraordinary—a—" and Bill Dunnigan suddenly thought of a couple of grand words he had once heard in a play "—a Plenipotentiary Interceder Ex-Officio!" he finished with a flourish.

"I did not know!" gasped Mary Spinsky.

"But I don't mind giving Saint Leo a lift too," said Bill generously. "Your brother and I didn't see eye to eye at first, but I guess I had him wrong, just as he had me wrong. He's regular! I'm for him now. You tell him I want to talk to him. He's going to help Father Paul about a visiting nurse plan. He's turning over his bell money for that purpose."

"My brother is doing that!"

"Sure is! And it's corking! Father Paul just told me today. And now you're going to help. That's corking too! But gee whiz, Miss Spinsky—Mary—I've been talking my head off. You wanted to talk to me. What is it I can do for you, Mary?"

Mary Spinsky was suddenly jerked back to the errand for which she came. She opened her mouth to speak of it, and closed it as quickly. What was that errand? She couldn't even remember at that moment, except that she was going to berate a gentleman who had opened up for her a wonderful horizon—who praised her brother—whose only boast was that he held some sort of big sounding title connected with Saint Michael—was it something conferred on him by the Pope? She knew that wealthy laymen were sometimes made "Knights" of some sort or other. Maybe that was what had upset her brother. But whatever Mr. Dunnigan was, she couldn't now express anything but gratitude and thanks! *What could he do for her?* What wasn't he doing for her!

"I—I happened to be passing and just stopped in to see if you received the chocolate cake," she said, "and to ask if you'd like me to make you another one tomorrow?"

"Mary, if you'll do that, I'll be in debt to you the rest of my life. I'll share it with Father Paul. We're two bachelor guys, you know, and it's like an angel dropping from the blue to find a girl like yourself taking an interest in us."

Mary Spinsky rose. Bill Dunnigan rose.

"I'll see you home," he said.

A spirit of old-fashioned gallantry swept Bill Dunnigan. As they crossed the lobby he offered his arm. Mary Spinsky took that arm. So they walked out of the Wyoming Hotel. The clerk stared. The loungers stared.

They walked down the still crowded street toward the St. Leo parish house. People stared.

What new thing was up now! "What is cooking?" one miner's wife expressed it.

She came nearer to the truth than she knew. Much was going to be cooked as a result of the momentous interview of Mary Spinsky and William Dunnigan.

But these two were not talking of cooking recipes during that walk. Bill Dunnigan told Mary Spinsky about Olga Treskovna. He had had need to talk to a woman about it all. And this woman —love starved—confidence starved—victim of a dozen inhibitions— listened for the first time in her life with sympathy—without a trace of malice or contempt. Listened almost as a mother to a son.

They reached the front of St. Leo's. The great bell of the church tower tolled steadily. When one stood directly beneath it, its booming almost drowned out the other churches. But the upper room of the parish house was dark. Father Spinsky had been granted the blessing of sleep.

"Well, good night, Mary," said Bill. "Get to work on your radio talks. I can put it through, I know, just as soon as you are ready. Make it last fifteen minutes at first—we'll broadcast twice a week to start with. It's been good of you to listen to me!"

"I'll send your cake by afternoon," said Mary Spinsky. "I'll make two! I'll send one direct to Father Paul. And I'm going to get a woman to cook for him. My brother asked me about it today."

"You're a swell girl, Mary!"

She turned and went quickly to her side door. Mary Spinsky was crying. She had held back the tears until Dunnigan had gone.

Why was she crying? She did not entirely know.

Back in that hotel room she had felt elation. Trips to New York —new dresses—new hats and shoes—a new car of her own—fame— the envy of all the other women of the town! The passing also of the fear for her brother. This stranger was not intentionally harming him—held no ill will against him regardless of what differences they may have had at first.

But as she listened to the story of Olga Trocki—daughter of her own drab town—neglected—kicked around—blamed for her father's shortcomings—a girl without a chance—now back in Father Paul's church, her name on every tongue, her fame spreading with every hour! . . . Why?

Perhaps because this girl wanted to help people! Perhaps because she wanted to bring people happiness! Perhaps because her main concern had not been for herself!

And this man who had lost all nearest and dearest to him. He was finding happiness—a beginning, not an end.

Mary Spinsky was seeing a new light. A new way of living out one's days. A rectification of life's values was knocking at her soul.

Her brother had said they had not "lived." Perhaps that was what her brother meant. Maybe he, also, was groping for a different Way.

She must not forget, however, to ask him about the title "Plenipotentiary Interceder Ex-Officio." He would doubtless know its meaning. And if the Pope or some Cardinal in New York had conferred it on William Dunnigan, her brother should not let that upset and worry him. For Mr. Dunnigan was now their friend, and wearing his great honor humbly, and to the glory of the Faith and the Saint in whose name it was given!

*   *   *

Back in his room, Plenipotentiary Interceder Ex-Officio Bill Dunnigan, now in his pajamas, thoughtfully dealt out a new hand of coon-can. Ten cards to himself—ten to the dummy, the deck face downward beside them. And he started to turn over the top cards of the deck, one by one, to see if he could play out his hand successfully.

"I wonder," he said to himself, "I wonder what she really came to see me about. I talk too damn much. Well, at least I've got the cooking business going for Father Paul. If only I hadn't barged

into that crazy religious argument with the head of the Union.
Well, you can't have everything, I suppose."

─────────────────────────────────── *66* ───────

*B*ILL DUNNIGAN had thought of his friend
in Cincinnati as a sponsor for the Coaltown cooking talks. At
about that same time—the midwestern clock, however, being one
hour earlier than that of Pennsylvania—Coaltown and its doings
was the topic of conversation of two people in another Ohio city.
And it was to bring another woman actively into the affair of the
St. Michael miracle.

The owner of the Coaltown mines was a wealthy family that lived
in Cleveland. This family had inherited the mines from a banker
father who had lent money to the Wilkes-Barre company that
formerly owned them, and he had finally taken over the properties.
This astute banker had acquired many other properties in that
thoroughly legal manner.

The ownership of these coal mines meant in reality the ownership
of Coaltown. This family literally possessed that valley settlement.
Except for the churches and a comparatively few workers' families
who had bought land of the old company and built their own
houses, all Coaltown paid ground rent. Even when the company
had sold any land, it had retained the "mineral rights" of the soil
beneath the houses.

The mines were not so far distant in miles from this Ohio city,
but they might as well have been under the craters of the moon
as far as this Cleveland family's personal knowledge of them as a
physical entity was concerned—or any thought of the workers as
being human beings like themselves.

Coaltown to them was a series of monthly statements and monthly
cash dividends. Under a capable manager the place had constantly
showed a profit since the taking-over. It was simply one of several
shrewd loans manipulated (usually by foreclosure) into an investment. The late father was quite expert in such manipulation.

A bad year—interest not promptly met—and the property became his. He had gone in for mines. There were mines in their own state also. But this Coaltown property was by far the most lucrative; in fact, it was the family's largest single source of income.

This family, whose name was Hanover, now consisted of a middle-aged daughter and son, who lived alone, except for a retinue of servants, in a very large house on spacious grounds on Euclid Avenue. The son, Frederick Hanover, Jr., was now president of his father's Bank and Trust Company, and although quite unlike him in appearance, being short and rounded like his mother, he had inherited his male parent's shrewdness as well as jointly with his sister that parent's fortune. The daughter, Miss Grace Hanover, a tall, slender spinster of aesthetic appearance and taste, was likewise not without a money sense.

In fact, she was reputed to be the business brain of the pair. She was a director of the bank and various "holding companies." Her brother brought home all reports on outside properties for her to scrutinize.

Scrutinize them she did. If costs went up, if profits went down, it was she who wished immediately to know why. She did not like profits to go down. The robots of hired labor and owned machinery should not vary. Money had to be spent sometimes to repair machinery, but labor, thank Heaven, cost nothing to replace so long as the "lower classes" continued to breed like rabbits.

In Cleveland this brother and sister were considered "close." Not that they did not give to charity—such charity as was brought to their notice. They subscribed a sizable sum—duly publicized in the newspapers—to the community chest each year. They had built an art gallery to house the notable collection of paintings their father had with a ready checkbook seduced from Europe, and in a sort of deathbed atonement willed to the city. Unsubtly, the building was called the Frederick Hanover Memorial Art Gallery.

Miss Grace Hanover had inserted in the deed of gift that this gallery should be closed to the public one day each week. On that day she could proceed through it without the annoying proximity of gawking, sweating, art-ignorant fellow citizens and enjoy by herself the pictures, of whose technical perfections and beauty she had, to give her credit, a real appreciation.

She had studied painting in Paris.

When not critically contemplating business statements and paintings, the lady spent much time in the extensive, glass-topped system of greenhouses just back of the mansion, these also being a parental heritage. Here were grown, in and out of season, the most beautiful of flowers. Her father's passion had been—and hers was—for lilies and orchids.

But she enjoyed these flowers (as he also had, along with his pictures) as a miser enjoys the gold coins of his money bags. Except for her gardener and three assistants, they were created and bloomed and died for her alone.

She exhibited (as had her parent) at the local flower show each spring. But, again thank Heaven, the parent had not in his last will and testament turned the greenhouses over to the city. They and their equally priceless content probably did not trouble his dying conscience. He had "created" this beauty, not gained it by taking advantage of somebody's financial need or the spreading out of an insidious temptation of ready cash. So Miss Hanover could at least enjoy the flowers in unsullied solitude each and every day of the week!

The nearest this family came to contamination by the black dust of Coaltown and the Breaker was a yearly trip which the brother, accompanied by his attorney, made to Wilkes-Barre to consult with their manager and have the formal meeting of the Pennsylvania holding company as required by law. On one of these trips, in a year when there had been signs of unrest among the ungrateful robots to whom they had always paid "fair" wages, the brother had fallen into the clutches of Father Spinsky. It had cost him a church organ.

So this evening, the evening of the day of the St. Michael's miracle and the momentous fight at Koepke's, this brother and sister were having dinner alone as usual in the large, gloomy dining room of the Euclid Avenue house. A butler and a maid were serving it. A cook, an assistant cook and two helpers had prepared it.

The evening papers had been brought in by the butler and placed, as was customary, beside the sister. Father Paul, not to mention Bill Dunnigan, would have been interested to know that a picture of St. Michael's Church and its long line of the curious and worshipful, had a two-column spread on the first page of one of them. And an Associated Press story of the miracle.

"All this pandemonium in the newspapers—isn't Coaltown, Pennsylvania, where it is happening, the location of several of our mines?" asked the sister.

"It is," replied the brother, "and it's causing me considerable annoyance. In fact, I had to miss my golf this afternoon. You may as well know, you'll discover it on the next report—" this with a wry smile in his sister's direction "—Coaltown is behind on a delivery-or-penalty order. But the customer wants coal, not penalties. The contractor, who also banks with us, complained today directly to me. His information was that there was going to be some sort of holiday declared up there; that the miners weren't working full time all week, in spite of our being behind in delivery. I couldn't believe it, till I got our manager on the telephone! And he tells me the men are demanding a three-day lay-off for this bell-ringing funeral of some actress who came from the town, and that dozens of them have been staying away from the shafts all week because of the excitement. Today he had only a half-shift at work because of an alleged miracle in the church where this actress lies in a sort of rural state——"

"I thought so!" said Miss Hanover. "I knew you were keeping something from me the moment you came in. You never can deceive me, Frederick!"

She was two years older than her brother, and a head taller. It had always given her a feeling of superiority.

"Here it is, described in our own papers," she added.

She signaled the butler. He conveyed one of the newspapers to Frederick Hanover, Jr. It was quite a trip—the length of a ten-foot table.

"I was not trying to deceive you, Grace," said the brother with some irritation. "It's simply that nothing can be done about it. Our manager says he is helpless."

He was looking curiously at the telephoto of Father Paul's church and the scene around it. "It does look as though half the town were in this picture!" he exclaimed.

"The working classes are getting entirely out of hand!" replied the sister. "It comes from government coddling. I would like to tell the President personally what I think of the new labor laws.

Socialism! Communism! Open anarchy next! Isn't that the town where some priest hypnotized you into paying for a new church organ two years ago?"

This was an old subject of controversy. Frederick Hanover winced.

"He didn't hypnotize me," he said with asperity. "We've been all over that. We were having labor troubles. I thought it would be a good business move. It was the largest church there, and its priest seemed to have considerable influence with the miners. He promised me he would preach some sermons to quiet the unrest— 'put the fear of God into them,' he said. We had no strike. It seemed to work."

"And now he's letting all this nonsense take place in his church! A Catholic church, isn't it?"

"It isn't happening in the church where we paid for the organ. It's in one of the small, unimportant ones. Our manager says he has no influence whatever with the priest of that church—doesn't even know him. And even if he did, the town is so excited——"

"I can believe it!" said the sister. "The whole place is Catholic— so the papers say—and therefore rife with superstition."

Miss Grace Hanover was a Presbyterian.

"The stories about this miracle are positively fantastic," she added. She had glanced at the other paper, which, although it had no photograph, carried a column-long United Press report of the Coaltown happenings.

"The supposed miracle," said the brother, "seems to be one of the reasons why the miners want a three-day holiday—Friday, Saturday and Sunday. At first they only talked of one during the funeral, which is Friday. Then came this holy statue turning. And there's another thing. It's here in this paper in the second column. A lot of film stars are flying on from Hollywood for the burial of this girl—I never heard of her till lately—though I'll say she is damn good-looking! Here's her picture on the inside page—I must watch for the film when it comes—called 'The Garden of the Soul.'"

Miss Hanover expressed her scorn for such trivial deviation and comment with a wave of her hand. She returned to a favorite theme.

"I knew at the time it was a mistake to give them that organ. And if you had not taken up that silly golf and got your mind off business affairs, you would never have done it."

Her brother's reference to films, which she considered trash, also irritated her. She took a further dig.

"I think you look absolutely ridiculous in that golf playing suit you are still wearing. I wish you would at least have enough respect for my eyes to change before dinner."

"You wanted me to do something to reduce my waist line," the brother replied mildly.

"I didn't expect you to dress like a clown!" said the sister.

Mr. Hanover ignored this uncomplimentary thrust at his comfortable plus-fours. He was deep in the romantic story of Olga Treskovna as chronicled with all stops pulled by one of the special writers Dunnigan's skill had attracted to Coaltown. *Some girl this actress must have been!*

"What were you saying, dear?" he asked, when he had reached the end of his paragraph.

"Your clothes!" said Miss Hanover.

"Oh," said Frederick Hanover, Jr. He meant, "Is that all!" His golf playing, which he found he liked, had been a source of criticism before. He was getting used to the jibes at it. If his sister went in for paintings and flowers, both of which he considered useless, why should not he have a hobby also? In his reply he returned to a dig of his own.

"You thought at the time we gave the organ it might add to their culture," he said with a sharp twinkle in his mild eyes. And he gave a humorous inflection to the word "culture." He meant Culture with a large capital "C"—one of the several silly things women like his sister wasted much time about.

"Pearls before swine!" replied the sister. And then, in defence of the culture implication—"I've always found it's quite hopeless to try to do anything for these foreigners. We'll not make *that* mistake again!"

"They consider themselves Americans," said the brother tolerantly. The golf playing had given him several human qualities. There was a grand Italian-born chef at the Country Club who was the most rabid American patriot he knew.

"Foreigners and Catholics!" There was tremendous scorn in her tone. And having pronounced that completely damning classification, she felt she had triumphantly ended this family-difference repartee. She returned to business.

"I hope you were firm with our manager that there should be no further stoppage of work in Coaltown."

Mr. Hanover frowned. He put down his paper.

"That's it," he said. "The manager swears the town is in such a state of excitement the men might go on strike if we bear down."

They ate in silence for several minutes. It was the meat course and lent itself to pleasurable concentration. But from the firmness of her thin lips—lips like the father's before her—it could be deduced that the sister had come to some decision at its end.

"For some time, Frederick," she said, "I have thought of personally looking over our properties. A firm hand is needed here and there, and I'm afraid you haven't father's firm hand." She could have added "face" also, but she refrained. Her brother's face was like their late mother's—round, a little soft. And he smiled too easily.

"Also, as I told you," she continued, "I am thinking of writing a novel of American life. A part of it must necessarily deal with the lower strata, and one must know them by personal observation. The people that form it, I mean."

Her brother had difficulty then in controlling his easy-smiling countenance. He wanted, in fact, to laugh. But he was really fond of his sister and he did not yield to the impulse.

"I think I will go first to this Pennsylvania town," continued the sister decisively. "I will go at once. It cannot be more than a day's trip. I will myself settle this holiday nonsense, and I am curious to see how, in a civilized country, with free public schools, there can still be all this superstition. Miracles! No doubt the workers are of a very low order of intelligence. It may furnish material for the coarser side of my novel . . . James!—" to the butler "—have the Duesenberg ready for me at seven in the morning. Henri to drive. With an early start I should reach this Coaltown place by mid-afternoon. And, James, tell the cook the roast was too well done. My dinner has been completely ruined. Tell her Mr. Hanover and I don't expect it to happen a second time."

Frederick Hanover had found no fault with the roast. He thought it "damn good." But he had learned not to argue more than necessary with his sister. Besides, he wanted to read the sporting page of the paper. Bobby Jones had a column about golf each day. Frederick Hanover, Jr., was trying earnestly to improve his game.

67

*W*HEN HE RETURNED from his epic, card-placing round of the Coaltown saloons that evening, Bill Dunnigan had received another wire from Marcus Harris. It had come direct to Coaltown.

Bill did not yet know, but the influx of newsmen had caused two of the Press Services to establish a telegraph office in the drug store. Western Union had worked fast.

Ordinarily the press agent would have visited the drug store that night with his placards, but the saloons had taken all he was carrying on the initial venture with them and he had decided to cover the stores on Main Street the next day. So he did not know about this direct service and its tribute to the importance his work had given the town.

The first sentence of this New York telegram had been disturbing. It read:

HOLLYWOOD IN HOT TROUBLE ABOUT PALLBEARERS STOP.

And Bill Dunnigan stopped. His heartbeat almost stopped.

"Good God!" thought the press agent. Had something fallen down after what he had told undertaker Orloff and the newsmen with so much assurance.

But the remainder of the wire was reassuring. It had even caused Bill to smile broadly. It said:

IS IT POSSIBLE INCREASE PALLBEARERS TO SIXTEEN QUESTION MARK EVERY STUDIO THERE WANTS SEND REPRESENTATIVE STOP AM GOING AHEAD ABOUT SIXTEEN COMMA MAYBE TWENTY COMMA UNLESS HEAR FROM YOU TO CONTRARY STOP HAVE BOUGHT SWELLEST ALTAR CLOTHS YOU EVER LAID EYES ON COMMA TWO DOZEN OF THEM FOR SEVEN FOOT ALTAR AND SMALL SIZED PRIEST STOP ALL DIFFERENT COMMA ALL GUARANTEED STRICTLY CATHOLIC PERIOD NOT JEWISH ONE IN LOT STOP LOVE

MARCUS

Dunnigan was soon to learn that behind this wire from Marcus Harris was such a stirring as Hollywood had not known in months, in years! Not, in fact, since the passing of the beloved Rudolf Valentino!

If the newspapers of the country at large gave space to the ringing of the bells, the Los Angeles dailies had given it a special, wide-open spread—as much prominence indeed as in the newssheets of Wilkes-Barre and Scranton where the bells could actually be heard. And the following day these distant Pacific papers carried long write-ups about the film (the Coast Studios of Marcus Harris were not slow in seizing such an opportunity), and every employee from manager to office boy had a tale to tell of this new picture and its young girl star who had given her life for its making.

There were interviews with the name-director, with Victor George the leading man, with other members of the cast, even with technicians who had been on the lot or on location at Yuma. One enterprising reporter had dug out her studio maid. Another the woman Martha Monahan who took care of her flat. Every intimate detail of Olga Treskovna's struggle on the Coast was dramatized—her arrival with a burlesque troupe (it was said she carried about with her hundreds of books on acting and the theater)—the discouraging, heart-crushing daily visits to the casting offices and the agents—"Nothing today"—"You're not the right type"—"Try us next week"—working as an extra so that she could continue to eat, and keep service on the telephone that never rang—the stand-in job with the Gronka film simply because she was Polish looking—her sudden plunge into the star role of a million-dollar epic—all grist to the mill of the most sentimental, most motion-picture-minded city in the world. It became the talk of every Studio—every coffee house.

And it seeped out also—for quite a number of "inside" persons had viewed snatches of the rushes in the Harris projection room—that Olga Treskovna had been the greatest find in years—that her work in "The Garden of the Soul" was quite beyond the ordinary. Casting directors who had not even admitted this slim girl to their sacred offices, now remembered how they had "sensed" her talent—how they had intended "sending for her" at the first opportunity. Several aggressive agents tore their hair that they had not found her. Tore their hair and went out and got forgetfully drunk.

Of course, only one man in all Hollywood had had faith in her—
Bill Dunnigan. Perhaps tall, scholarly Constantin Stanislavsky who
wrote a book about a theater called the Moscow Art Theater, perhaps Richard Boleslawsky, a Pole who worked under him and set
down in a little volume some "principles of acting" when he came
to America, might have had faith; but they, alas, were not employed
in Hollywood casting offices. They had passed on to work under
the Great Producer.

So, besides Bill Dunnigan, only the walls of some cheap, bur-
lesque-catering hotels! only the shabby seats in a string of provincial
"legitimate" theaters now turned temples of burlesque (but seats
that had more than once gazed upon Sothern and Marlowe, Richard
Mansfield, Maude Adams, Joseph Jefferson, Minnie Maddern Fiske,
a young Ethel Barrymore) could testify as to the "why" of this girl's
sudden talent. And they remained silent through it all.

Silent also two other witnesses who understood. An accordion-
playing miner named Stanislaus Trocki who could hold saloon
crowds with Polish folk songs, and a certain medieval troubadour
whose name had been Trocki, and whose bony fingers had thrilled
and reached for the beloved lute buried with him in his tomb in
ancient Cracow, when Olga Treskovna had tried out for Marcus
Harris that morning in Hollywood.

But the bells of Coaltown were not silent, and on top of them—
the miracle! Sacred statues turning toward the coffin of a martyred
fellow artist! And the word from the Marcus Harris New York
office that *the people* of this Coaltown *did not know* of her greatness
—that pallbearers were having to be *hired* to carry her coffin to its
resting place! So inferring, astute Mr. Harris had telegraphed his
request for coffin carriers direct to the Metropolitan Studios—and
wired copies of his telegram to the Coast newspapers.

Pallbearers hired indeed! Emotional Hollywood arose in indignation. They would carry on high shoulders and with banners
flying the body of this cast-out daughter of this ungrateful town—
this daughter *they* had received and sheltered and recognized!

Marcus had wired Hollywood direct when the New York Metropolitan people, after first agreeing, had started to hem and haw:
they didn't know if six stars could be persuaded to come, even if
their theaters lost the booking of "The Garden of the Soul." Mr.
Harris was not such an inferior publicity man himself. And he had

an able aid in a little Jewish girl named Rose Feinberg. It was
Miss Feinberg who suggested:

"Wire Hollywood! To hell with these New York stuffed shirts!
We're not going to fall down on Mr. Dunnigan, are we?"

Miss Feinberg was due to receive a sizable raise in salary. Once
again she had saved the day.

For there was immediate and dynamic action in Movieland Capital. Meetings were hastily called of the Screen Actors Guild, the
Jewish Actors Guild, the Catholic Actors Guild, the Protestant
Artists Federation, the Screen Directors Guild, the Association of
Motion-Picture Technicians. Practically every male star in the
studio district volunteered to fly to Coaltown! The Harris Studio
telephones buzzed with a clamor to serve! Hesitant Metropolitan
was in danger of being squeezed out entirely!

The women were not going to be excluded from this tribute. At
the meeting of the parent Guild, a great star of a foreign name
known round the world was appointed to select five other leading
actresses who would fly to Coaltown with the men, to place a wreath
on the coffin of this symbol of Hollywood's opportunity to American girlhood for courage, genius, hard work.

No beams of radar ever flung back a more instant response than
that given to the Harris plea.

While all this was happening, William Dunnigan at a meridian
four hours later by the clock had gone to bed. He was dog tired.
He intended arising at five to attend again the early Mass of Father
Paul.

It seemed to him that he was hardly asleep when there was a
rapping on his door. He managed to find the light cord hanging
from the center of his room. It was really only shortly after midnight he discovered by his watch on the bureau. He opened the
door.

His caller was Father Paul.

Father Paul was laboring under great excitement. He held in
his hand a great bundle—fifty perhaps—of sheets that were obviously telegrams.

"Bill," he said, "I had to come to see you! The clerk was afraid
to disturb you so I came up myself. All evening—since about ten
o'clock—telegrams in bunches have been delivered to me! It seems
they now have an office in the drug store. They are addressed to

the Pastor of St. Michael's Church. Some of them to me—Father Paul—by name! I can't imagine how they know my name! And the people they are from! Just look!"

Bill Dunnigan put on his bathrobe. He took the sheaf of communications from the hand of Father Paul. He read them one by one.

It was the avalanche from Hollywood. The answer of royal Filmdom to the reported indifference of Coaltown. The sincere tribute also to a martyr to their profession—the girl who would not quit—the girl who gave her life to finish a film.

For they were all children at heart—these great ones of the magic world of Make-Believe—with children's faults but also with children's generosity, children's enthusiasm, children's impulsive, unbounded, unrestrained emotionalism when aroused.

A great Jewish comedian was flying on to represent his Guild. Dunnigan had helped popularize him when he had been for several seasons a star of Broadway revues. Another actor, known both through pictures and the radio, and probably America's most loved singer of ballads, would be present to represent the Catholic organization. One telegram was from the Committee of Women Artists signed by the famous star with the foreign name, and listing the other five women stars who would accompany her to Coaltown.

Four nationally-known directors were coming to represent their studios. The other wires were from individual luminaries. Condolence, praise, requests for reservations to attend the funeral. The collective names signed on these pieces of paper was a veritable "Who's Who" of motion-picture aristocracy.

William Dunnigan sat on the side of his tousled bed. Father Paul had taken one of the chairs.

The press agent looked up at his friend the priest. His eyes were wet. The hand that had slashed Jan Rubel without wavering shook just a little. But these signs of weakness were the weakness of an overwhelming happiness.

"Thank you, Father, for coming," he said. "I can't talk! I don't know what to say. Leave these messages with me. I'll answer them for you if you will let me. I'd like to show them in the morning to the newsmen. I'd like to keep them."

"I'll go now," said Father Paul. "I just thought you'd like to know."

"Tomorrow we will plan it all out," said Bill. "I'm coming to your early Mass. You must get some rest. I'll dress and tell the drug store not to disturb you any more tonight. To hold further wires till morning."

"They're closed now," said Father Paul. "They closed at midnight."

He arose and took the hand of his friend in both of his. "God bless you, Bill," he said. He turned quickly and went from the room and down the stairs. His own eyes were a little misty.

Bill Dunnigan sat on his bed for quite awhile. And again, as through a rapidly shifting kaleidoscope—as if it were *itself* a motion picture—passed the episodes of this girl's life, as it had touched on his.

The Venus Burlesque Theater on Forty-Second Street—that other burlesque house in the Middle West—the dinner at Ming Gow's—the day he received the letter in the Ziegfeld Theater office—the day he had looked at her through the camera lens on the Hollywood stage, the stand-in day—the dinner at her flat—the moment at the Studio meeting over Gronka's "kick-out" when he had thought of proposing her for the star role in "The Garden of the Soul"—her try-out for that role and his certainty that she was 'there" as a great actress—the day she became ill on the set, the day he found the lung x-rays in her apartment—the return from Yuma and that last day of the shooting, with the party on the big sound stage and she reciting the poem about the village girl who loved her father.

And then the hospital—their last talk there—the look on the face of the nurse when he had rushed back that night—the sudden touch of her hand as he had stood before her picture of "The Presence" in the empty flat—the dreadful, crushing interview with Marcus Harris—despair—the sullen trip to Wilkes-Barre—undertaker Orloff and Coaltown—then Father Paul! The road had led to Father Paul, thank God! And it was fitting that it was Father Paul who had brought him these telegrams to climax all his hopes and all his dreams for her.

"Kid," he said, "they're doing it now because of you! Just you! No booking pressure. No strings pulled backstage. I'm glad! I'm terribly glad! I love you, kid. I have always loved you. I will always love you."

He put out his light. He looked from the window, but not down at the Coaltown street. He looked up at the darkened, star-studded sky.

There was her star. Bright and glowing—like a lantern held by God Himself.

He went back to his bed and was soon in slumber.

Had he been awake he would have seen another visitor. This visitor did not knock at the A-1 door, but just quietly appeared. A slender girl sitting for awhile on his window sill.

She also looked up at the star.

She was strangely dressed. She wore the practice-clothes that girls put on when they tried-out in Forty-Second Street for the chorus of a burlesque show. Her bare legs, hanging from the sill, seemed all too slender—undernourished. But the face was beautiful —wistful.

The visitor moved from the window. She touched the derby hat where it lay on the bureau edge. She ran her hand along the top of the coat hanging over the chair back—the grey coat with the pale blue and red plaid checks. She took up one of the white spats that lay on the seat of the chair. She held it a moment to her heart. "I love you, Bill—I have always loved you—I will always love you," she said softly.

She was not seeing a figure asleep in a hotel bed. She cared nothing for a pile of telegrams on the bureau top.

She saw a tall shadow standing out in the semi-darkness of an empty theater. The shadow wore a light suit and a black derby that cut an angle across the forehead. The shadowy figure was speaking. "Tom, give the kid a break!" it said.

She returned to the window sill for a moment, then was gone.

The bells of Coaltown's five churches were ringing across the night. Bells that had now been heard and answered clear across America.

68

THE NEXT MORNING'S 5:45 Mass—on the day before the funeral—was like the two which had preceded it. Not more than half of those wanting to attend could crowd inside the church. A great throng stood reverently on the lawn and in the street in front of St. Michael's. As before, the doors remained open, and this overflow repeated the responses as they came; knelt in the roadway when those inside the church were kneeling. State Troopers stopped all passing traffic during the service.

Dunnigan arranged for the newsmen who wished to be inside to go to the choir loft by way of the bell tower. Many reporters, however, preferred to view the unusual scene from the street. The flash bulbs of the photographers gave an occasional brilliant lighting to the half-dawn picture.

The thing Dunnigan noticed was that there were many more miners in the crowd than on the other two mornings. Quite a number were inside the church. They came in their work clothes. They had their lunch pails. His show-cards were having an effect!

It was the fight at Koepke's that had stirred this sudden religious zeal among the workers. But Bill did not think of that. The one discordant note in his triumph was that fight. How could he now organize these miners so that the attendance of some of them each morning—*every morning*—in the days, the months, the years ahead, would be assured to Father Paul?

He himself watched the service from the room just off the sanctuary. To that room four excited vestrymen returned after the offertory with more than eight hundred dollars in the collection baskets, which they had passed also among the willing worshipers outside. The funds for Father Paul's good works in Coaltown were mounting hourly.

Again the playing of the blind organist lent a majesty to the service. Dunnigan had not forgotten his plan about the concerts of Polish songs. It had not been needed—there had been no time for it since the discovery of the turning of the statues, but he intended taking it up with the local radio station, along with his idea for Mary Spinsky's class in cooking. Marcus Harris could sponsor the program of Polish songs! It could easily be a dignified and unusual form of advance announcement for "The Garden of the Soul" whose heroine was Polish in fiction as well as fact. He intended keeping his word to Father Paul that the Bishop's cathedral city should have the initial showing in the East. After the run of this picture was over, he thought he could persuade several of the near-by city picture houses to continue sponsoring the broad-

casts. Father Paul had told Bill of the Bishop's friendliness for
film entertainment. Why not a co-operation there and then of
theater and church?

It was an extra altar boy who brought him word, as he stood
looking out at the celebration of the Mass, that a man wished to
speak with him at the church side door.

"Can't he wait till after the service?" asked Dunnigan.

"He gave me a dollar if I'd take the message to you right away,"
said the boy.

Such honest frankness was worthy of some reward. Dunnigan
flashed his ready smile.

"All right, kid. I'll make good for you! Who is he, do you
know?"

"I know," said the boy, "but I promised not to tell his name."

"A boy who keeps promises! Don't lose the habit when you grow
older," laughed Bill, who had now moved back into the room, away
from the doorway looking out to Father Paul's altar. He followed
the lad to the outside of the church.

It had reached a point in the Mass where worshipers were kneeling. Most of the several hundred who filled the lawn between the
parish house and the church were on their knees. They were
answering one of the most beautiful of invocations: *Lamb of God,
who takest away the sins of the world, have mercy on us.*

The man who waited just outside the church door was not kneeling. He was not repeating the responses—*"Have mercy on us."*
"Have mercy on us."—which the worshipers repeated twice, and
after the third Agnus Dei—*"Grant us peace."* He simply stood, a
figure apart, looking curiously about. He did remove his slouch
hat as Bill was emerging from the church. But he lowered neither
his eyes nor his head.

He was a very large man, heavy set and towering.

The man was Jan Rubel.

*   *   *

Jan Rubel had spent most of the night walking the hills. The
three miners had taken him home from Koepke's Bar. He lived
in a room alone, above one of the other saloons. When his mud-
dled brain had somewhat cleared, he had asked them what had happened—just as he had demanded this when he had first struggled

to his feet in Koepke's. He spoke like an angry child. They now told him briefly—bluntly and cruelly.

"He knocked you flat! Knocked the hell out of you!" was the gist of their replies. One of them added, "He's a *real* fighter, that guy!"

They all regarded Jan Rubel coldly and a little contemptuously. They were evidently eager to leave and to get back to talk about the fight. The loser did not interest them. What was the "millionaire" doing now? Would there be any more fights in the other saloons?

Jan Rubel understood their mood.

"Thanks," he sneered. "Thanks for bringing me home." Then anger swept over him. His voice became a savage snarl. "What are you waiting for? Get the hell out!"

They went. Through the open window he heard them talking on the street below. "That's his finish in Coaltown!" came up the words from one of them. "He had it coming to him!" said another.

These words, floating up to Jan Rubel as he sat with his head in his hands, did not especially impress him. "Scum!" he said and dismissed them. He spat in the direction of a china receptacle by his bed.

He could whip the three of them with one hand tied behind him. He would, when he got around to it.

His anger had not been against them. They were simply in his way. He brushed them aside as he would have brushed aside three lice found crawling on his neck. His anger was against the man who had beaten him up, back in Koepke's Bar and Grill. And, by a curious connection, against the dead girl, Olga Treskovna.

He sat for awhile nursing his throbbing head. There was a dull ache all through it. Both sides of his heavy jaw were sore. His cheek had been cut by his teeth on one side. His spittle was still slightly colored with red when he spat. He spat again as his mouth filled. There was a good deal of blood this time.

Suddenly his anger welled up in a cold fury. Christ! Why was he sitting there? He must go out and "get" this man—this cool city mug who, without even taking off his coat and by some shift of boxing, had knocked him down and out before he, Rubel, could get started! Why, the man had not half his strength. It was some trick. Some unfair advantage. All right. Anything was fair from now on! There was a way to beat this wealthy charlatan's mysterious advantage.

He got up from the chair. In his closet was a shotgun. Jan Rubel was a hunter. He went hunting every fall. Took two weeks off to do it. He had just renewed his hunter's license. He had the paper in his pocket: the right to kill two buck deer and any mountain bear he could track down.

He'd kill this stranger first. The idea obsessed him. It was like a stiff, fresh drink. Everything would be settled all right. He laughed aloud. He got up and went to the closet. He took out the gun. He broke it open. There were two empty shells in the loading chambers. He ejected them. He took from his top bureau drawer a box of fresh shells. They were loaded with buckshot slugs. He jammed two loaded cartridges into the gun. He closed the breach. He held it up and sighted along the black, double-barrel.

Once in the stomach and once in the jaw! That was how he would shoot Dunnigan—as Dunnigan had struck him. He would blast this dapper advertiser of priests and actresses out of existence. That quizzical mouth would ask no more questions about religion and the fraud called "God."

If he didn't find Dunnigan on the street or in some saloon, he would go to the Wyoming Hotel and wait. He knew that the "millionaire" stopped there. The whole town knew.

He reached for his hat where one of the miners who had brought him home had tossed it on his bureau. He caught sight of himself in the mirror of this bureau.

The sight sobered him. His face was streaked with dirt from the floor of Koepke's. There was blood around the corners of his mouth. His eyes were bloodshot. The whole top part of his shirt was wet. He remembered now. They must have doused him with a pail of water. He had shaken water from his eyes when he had first come to at Koepke's, when he had first blurted out: "What the hell is all this!" When he had got up and found that he was still too dizzy to walk steadily.

Jan Rubel was not a fool. To go forth looking as he did now—a shotgun in his hands—he wouldn't get beyond the first street corner! The town was not asleep as it usually was around nine. Main Street was filled with people—many of them strangers—newspaper reporters—and there were a dozen uniformed State Troopers about. The Troopers carried heavy loaded revolvers. Sergeant Dennis O'Rourke had increased his force since morning, and was doing patrol duty along the entire length of the town's main thoroughfare. Troopers were needed to keep traffic open.

Jan Rubel placed his loaded shotgun on the bureau and sat down again. He must work out a more sensible plan to accomplish his purpose.

He inspected his huge fists. He clenched them. He felt the muscles of his arms. He was as strong as ever. He would fight this man again, only now with care. He wouldn't be half drunk and rush in like a crazed animal. He had a brain. He'd use it next time. You could kill a man in a fist-fight and get away with it. Self-defence. He still meant to kill Bill Dunnigan.

He found a soiled handkerchief in his pocket and wiped his face. He looked at the handkerchief. He would have to wash his face presently. He would have to comb his hair. He would have to change to a dry shirt.

He'd do the job ahead like a gentleman.

There are deep within all of us the motivations to kill. Heritage of Cain. Revenge (the most futile); opposition (the most cold-blooded and brutal); frustration (the most insane); jealousy (the most terrible); possession (the most profitless); religious and racial (the most fanatical); threat of exposure (the most terrifying); be-trayal of trust (the most commendable). And to these primitive urges toward homicide, organized society has added other incite-ments—the payment of alimony, double-feature picture shows, loud playing of radios, chewing of gum, people who discuss their private affairs in elevators, non-extractable refrigerator ice-cube trays; all of which latter have much to commend them.

Jan Rubel's desire to kill Bill Dunnigan had two motives. The obvious one—revenge. But he was not entirely motivated by re-venge because Dunnigan had beaten him, had publicly humiliated him. That Rubel could remedy. Could the other motive be called religious? It was not because Bill had argued about and upheld religion, for that argument had given the mine leader a distinct pleasure, and he felt he had given the "millionaire" a sound drub-bing in the word combat. This less obvious motive was involved with a picture of Olga Treskovna dressed in the habit of a nun (her final characterization in "The Garden of the Soul"), which picture had been published in a Wilkes-Barre paper Rubel had happened to buy that day. This less obvious motive concerned a sacrilege!

Jan Rubel, atheist, defamer of Christ's mother, had been stirred to a killing hatred by this picture—the picture of an actress who "flaunted herself" as a Nun! Such is the contradictory complexity of the human soul.

And that was why a sudden consciousness at that moment, sitting in his room, of the ringing of the bells—the first time that evening he had noticed them—became a matter of consequence. For in the brain of Jan Rubel it was to lead straight to a long-buried memory.

During the last two days Coaltown had become used to the bell sound. It was like the constant rumble of the Breaker. It had become just a background to the movement of the town.

But now the bells—*as bells*—struck the brain of Jan Rubel.

Particularly one bell. His room was much nearer to the Church of St. Michael the Archangel than to any of the other churches. The other churches were at the farther end of the town. The sweet, high call of Father Paul's bell sounded very clearly above the others —like a solo voice in a quintette, rising above the accompaniment of the other four.

This bell now reminded Jan Rubel of something. He knew what. The bell of the Orphanage at Wanamee where he had been raised. It had the same clear, dulcet tone. Funny he had never noticed that before. But then he hadn't thought of the Orphanage bell for many years.

On this fateful night, Father Paul's bell, ringing for Olga Treskovna, commenced to say to Jan Rubel words that the bell of the Orphanage had always repeated.

69

*J*AN RUBEL had been a little boy once. He had almost forgotten that. He had not thought of it for a long time.

That boyhood had few happy memories. He had been taken to the Orphanage by officers of the law on a day his mother was arrested. She had been arrested for drunkenness and prostitution. The boy hadn't been told those words at the time. He was simply told that she was a "bad" woman. That statement confirmed his own observations. The small house in which they lived in Nanticoke had been no peaceful haven. Brawls—strange men—intermittent meals from unwashed dishes—he remembered days when his mother lay in a stupor and would prepare nothing to eat at all.

Other children had fathers who looked out for them. He seemed to have none. His own mother sometimes cursed him and called him "brat." He found out later what it meant.

He had no father. He was illegitimate.

The Orphanage put an end to days without meals, to being locked out at night, to cursings and the coming and going of men who drank whiskey out of a bottle with his mother and then told him to "beat it." There was a young nun at the Orphanage—Sister Elizabeth. She was the only one who ever tried to understand him, to explain things to him. He thought of her now because of Father Paul's bell. Her voice had always sounded to him like the Orphanage bell. Sweet, clear, restful.

Sister Elizabeth read the Bible to the sullen, bewildered, but rebellious boy. He didn't understand much of it but he liked the sound of her voice. The voice like the convent bell. The boy had blurted out to her his vague feeling of the injustice all around him. Why had other children avoided him? The actions of his mother and the men who came to their house. Why didn't *he* have a father? And he remembered what she had always said.

"Forgive. Forgive."

She said the word slowly, as if there were a hyphen in it. "For-give."

After that it always seemed to him that was what the Orphanage bell was saying when it swung back and forth in the early morning. At noon. At Angelus time. And when it struck the hours of the day and night.

But Sister Elizabeth was taken away.

The other nuns told him, "God has taken her." Just as the sheriff had taken his mother he supposed, though not for the same reason. No one said that Sister Elizabeth was "bad." But "God" became to the small lad a brutal, swearing creature with a badge, who came and dragged people away. Like the sheriff! He hated God from that day.

The Orphanage bell still said "For-give," but when he learned what that word meant, he could not forgive. He made up his mind to fight this God—to fight this world. He made a dreadful resolution to be formed in the heart of a boy. The resolution *never to forgive*.

When he was twelve he was "adopted" by a farmer. The farmer chose him because he had grown to be unbelievably large and strong for his age. The farmer—a widower with no children—wanted a helper on his two-hundred-acre farm.

The lad left the shelter of the convent-orphanage. There he had at least had education. Books. The nuns had a library that had been willed to them by the school-teacher father of one of them. Sister Elizabeth loved books and she had taught Jan Rubel to read, instilled in his mind a liking for printed words. When she was "taken away," the boy turned to these books for companionship. He acquired a passion for reading. He read everything he could lay his hands on. He liked especially a thick book called *Les Miserables*. He somehow felt that he was like a character in that book. Jean Valjean. He read some parts of it over and over again.

Had Fate decreed that he should especially know this book? Working for this farmer was not unlike the galleys of *Les Miserables*. You didn't have an iron ring forged to your neck, but that was about the only difference. He started work long before daylight. He was not permitted to rest till long after dark. His foster father intended to get his money's worth for the food the lad consumed. That was the farmer's only complaint. The boy ate a lot of food to nourish his already six-foot body.

This farmer was "religious." "God fearing," he called himself. He belonged to a Protestant sect. The lad did get somewhat of a rest on Sundays. The farmer believed the Lord's Day should be kept holy. He took the boy to church with him—though he sat him at the back of the church. He himself sat in the first pew directly under the preacher.

At this church the boy heard that all he had been taught at the convent-orphanage was wrong. Worse than that, it was wicked. Those who believed in it were doomed to hellfire. The only people who would be saved were those who belonged to that particular sect. Heaven would be populated by the hardfaced folk who sat stiffly in those particular pews. It confirmed the lad's suspicion that all religion was a fraud.

He had to contribute money to this fraud.

The farmer gave the boy a dollar a week for "spending money." He took out ten cents of this for the church. To be saved, you must give one-tenth of your income to the church. To be certain the boy paid in his percentage, the farmer himself took out the ten cents each week.

The farmer had no books except a Bible. All other books were "wicked." The lad missed books dreadfully. He had managed to buy, out of his spending money, a copy of *Les Miserables*. He bought it in Wilkes-Barre on one of the weekly market trips. It was in two small volumes that he could conceal in his pockets. The book at the Orphanage had been large and heavy.

He read in his room at night. He put the oil lamp on the floor and shaded it, so that the light would not be seen from the window. Also, he always waited till he was sure the farmer had gone to bed.

One night the farmer woke up. The lad had forgotten to shade his light. It was reflected on the snow outside. He crept up to the boy's room and burst suddenly upon him.

The boy leaped up from the floor. He was still fully dressed, for the room was cold.

"Burning good oil that I have to pay for!" the farmer stormed. He seized the book from the lad's hand. It was no Bible. He tore it from its covers and then tore the pages across. He had strong, powerful hands.

But the lad Jan Rubel was also big and strong. He was now as large as the farmer. He had endured enough. When he saw his only book destroyed he struck out blindly and he knocked the man down. He was as much surprised as the older man. But when the farmer got up, the boy knocked him down again. The man seized a chair but Jan Rubel wrested it from his grasp. He threw the chair into a corner and knocked the farmer down a third time with his fists.

The farmer retired, promising dire punishment the next day. That night Jan Rubel left the shelter of this farm house. Like Olga Treskovna, he put his few belongings in a bundle. He walked the ten miles to Pittston. Pittston was short of workers in her mine. He got a job at once.

The farmer managed to locate him inside of a week and had him brought back by the authorities. It was like returning to the galleys.

The lad stayed exactly one week. The argument this time took place in the barn. The farmer finally said: "What can I expect from a Catholic bastard brought up by nuns!" He qualified the word "nuns" with a foul adjective.

But Jan Rubel had discovered a way to end arguments. This time he had first to disarm the farmer of a pitchfork. It was not difficult. He threw the pitchfork into a far corner. He didn't need that. He liked the feel of the impact of his fists against things. They were better than any weapon! He knocked the man down, and when the farmer had staggered to his feet, knocked him down twice again. The last time the farmer was afraid to get up. There was a dangerous flash in the lad's eyes that he had never seen there before.

Jan Rubel said:

"I'm going now. Don't try to bring me back again. If you do, I'll kill you the next time." He hadn't struck the man with his full strength. He had held back a little. He felt that if he did strike him as hard as he could, he *would* kill him.

He had had the urge to kill, however, because of what the farmer had said. Not the "Catholic bastard" part. That didn't matter. But the part about nuns.

He hated women (because of his mother) but he had somehow never considered the Orphanage nuns women. Especially Sister Elizabeth. Gentle Sister Elizabeth would even have urged him to forgive this farmer! She was of some other world. She did not know what you must do in this one.

This time Jan Rubel was let alone. He went in the opposite direction to a place called Glen Alden, which was very close to Coaltown. He used at first an assumed name. He said he was Jan Valjean. It afforded him a boyish superiority to say that. The name meant nothing to the foreman who hired him. He didn't even write it down. "French, eh?" was his only comment.

"No, Polish," said Jan Rubel. He knew that he was Polish. He could speak that language as well as English.

"Well, bud, I can't spell in French. I'll mark you 'Big Jan,'" said the foreman. "How old are you?"

Jan Rubel falsified his age to eighteen years, for which he could easily pass. He became "Big Jan." When payday came around he forgot and signed the sheet "Jan Rubel." The foreman smiled. Runaway kids had funny ideas sometimes. An obvious Polack giving a French name. Since the lad heard no more from the farmer he continued to use the name Rubel. That was his mother's name.

It is not necessary to trace the career of Big Jan Rubel in detail. He had found his niche. Coal mining seemed to be in his blood. The unknown father had without doubt been a miner, as surely as (from the lad's Slavic features) he had been a Pole. Starting as a helper, he was soon a fullfledged miner in the technical meaning of the term. He loved hacking and blasting the great lumps of ore from the walls of the shafts. His huge, strong frame of a body was like a tireless machine. A machine to demolish. He knew that he loved coal mining because he was *demolishing* things in his path. He did not think of it as creating wealth. He thought of it as tearing apart the physical world!

He became quickly known as the best miner in the Glen Alden pits.

And the best fighter. He was as ruthless in his relationship with his fellow men as he was with the coal veins in front of his cap-light. He knocked down anyone who got in his way, and with the same joy as he knocked down the coal. "Knocking down the coal" sometimes seemed like hacking at a living body!

He commenced reading again. But not for companionship. He read so that he could demolish *ideas* as well as physical things. He read everything with a warped point of view—to discover power, weakness, the ease with which men were duped. Wanting it, he managed to find it in almost every book.

He read mostly history. The forgiving, the trusting, whether nations or men, always got the worst of it. He read some philosophy. Those who doubted found the truth. He read the Bible carefully from cover to cover. Ivan the Terrible was his favorite historical character. Voltaire his philosopher. In the Bible he revelled in the Old Testament passages where God ordered cities destroyed, children slain. If there was a God—which he doubted—

He was a God who hated men. To be godlike you should hate and destroy. With what delight he discovered—or thought he had—that the so-called Christ was illegitimate! Why, this "great" Founder of a soft religion that preached turning the other cheek was no better than he, Jan Rubel! And Christ's mother—like his own mother—a slut. Maybe he, Jan Rubel, ought to start a religion! What a joke it all was!

That discovery warranted getting very drunk one night and the beating up of half a dozen fellow miners in a street fight.

He hated and despised all women, anyway. He despised his fellow men. The women he found he could buy—and did when he felt so inclined. The men he could thrash—and did. He was respected and feared. No one called him "bastard" any more.

He discovered one other thing which added to his contempt for his fellows. With his knowledge of words he could make a fool of most of the men in an argument.

This word-knowledge was put one year to a practical use. The mines in the Valley were unionized by delegates who appeared from the Pittsburgh districts. They sought out the strongest men and the most intelligent. Jan Rubel was one of these.

And he found that by words he could sway gatherings—talk groups of these fools into anything he wished. They were just a lot of sheep. If an occasional ram arose, he used his fists. He was an efficient union organizer. Even the good which he accomplished for the men was accomplished with contempt. What a lot of weaklings they were!

For several years now he had been District Chairman of the Workers' organization in Glen Alden, Coaltown, and several other settlements. He continued to work as a miner and had transferred that work to Coaltown. He couldn't sit all day at a desk. His body craved the hard, shoulder-aching work. His hands craved the feel of the heavy pickaxes. Just as his mind craved the reading of human weakness overpowered by strength.

Brute force, brute knowledge, that was his life. Take what you wanted. Knock down everything that blocked your path. Glory in being feared, in being hated.

Above all, rely on yourself. Trust no one. Friendship, bah! Religion, bah!

From hating God he had come to the conclusion that there really was no God at all. As he had told Bill Dunnigan in Koepke's, it was all an invention of crafty men to dominate weaker men. But not believing in God, he also had no belief whatever in his fellow man. The ethics of some of the Union heads did not lessen this skepticism. They were using the Unions as the priests used religion.

Disbelief in God might not matter so much in this life, but this disbelief in any man, this contempt for all men, was heading direct to an abyss. An abyss that would someday suddenly yawn before him. For he also was a man, and had to live in a world of men.

This abyss is called Loneliness. Sooner or later he who determines to walk alone comes to its terrifying edge.

One thing only connected with religion and humanity, Jan Rubel respected. Whenever he passed two nuns on the street he touched his hat. He could not entirely forget Sister Elizabeth.

He had been vividly reminded of her once before that day. The picture of this dead actress, Olga Treskovna, in a Wilkes-Barre newspaper. Her sad, wistful, Slavic face resembled that of Sister Elizabeth. The resemblance was enhanced because that face was framed in a nun's head-covering. This "still" of Olga Treskovna as she appeared in the last scene of "The Garden of the Soul."

It had startled Jan Rubel. It had not pleased him. It had infuriated him. That a cheap "movie actress" should dare to dress like a nun, to resemble the one good woman who ever lived! It was proof to him that the miracle must be fraudulent. It was almost as if Sister Elizabeth were being used for this fraud. Being used by this Dunnigan person and the St. Michael's priest.

That was the thought at the back of Jan Rubel's mind when he had especially cursed Olga Treskovna and Father Paul to Bill Dunnigan.

Now, sitting in his room, strangely conscious of Father Paul's bell, it seemed to Jan Rubel that for the first time in years he heard again the voice of this good Nun he respected, and had come very near to loving. And the voice said with the bell: "Jan! Jan! For-give! For-give!"

The words came so strongly that he arose and shouted "No! No!" He picked up his shotgun, as if by the feel of it he could hold on to his resolution.

Another terrible thought entered his mind. How it got there he could not imagine. But there it was. *He did not entirely hate this stranger!* He had a sort of respect for him. The first man who had stood up to him in years! The first man who had ever knocked him down.

This man had knocked him down partly because he had slandered a dead girl—just as he, Jan Rubel, had knocked down that farmer because the farmer had slandered Sister Elizabeth. It was penetrating his consciousness that perhaps the dead girl the stranger was there to bury, meant to the man what Sister Elizabeth had meant to the embittered boy in the Orphanage. The boy that was himself, Jan Rubel. Olga Treskovna had the face of Sister Elizabeth—if the newspaper pictures were to be believed. What did he really know about Olga Treskovna—Olga Trocki? Nothing whatever. Make-up alone might not make these two women look so alike. There might have been *two* good women in the world! It might even be one and the same woman!

"Jan! Jan! For-give! For-give!"

The bell kept saying it over and over. *Sister Elizabeth's voice kept repeating it, in unison with the bell.* The bell that was now ringing for Olga Treskovna.

This would not do! It was destroying the foundations of his life. He had for a moment a mad desire to rush out and fire the shotgun at that bell in the tower of Father Paul's church. To break it somehow. To silence it. Would the voice stop speaking if he destroyed the bell?

But buckshot would not break the metal of a bell—as it would ruin, at close range, a human face, tear out the guts of a human body. He must get away from it somehow! He seized his hat. He held tightly to the gun. He did not stop to wash his face or change his shirt.

He did not go out the front door into the street. He went out a rear way, across the rubbish-filled backyard behind the saloon where he lived, climbed a stone wall and started up the side of the "mountain" that rose just back of this yard.

He must get beyond the immediate sound of that bell so that he could think with clarity. The bell that brought back the voice of Sister Elizabeth. Sister Elizabeth was dead, and forgiveness had died when she had died. This stranger was a fraud—his actress friend a cheap tart. He must continue to hate and despise or he was indeed lost!

Jan Rubel could not have exactly told how he spent that night. He only realized that shortly before three A.M., weary and distraught, he was standing across the street from the building that was the Orphanage in the dark and silent town of Wanamee. To get there he must have crossed two high mountains, for he had not come by the roads. He remembered slashing through underbrush, pushing aside briars, climbing over rocks. He had stood for awhile on the very top of one of these mountains and cursed the shadowy world beneath.

Some magnetic force drew him back of this three-story brick building on Wanamee's single street. A feeling that if he could start out from there once more, his philosophy of hatred would be justified. So he stood looking across at this building and tried to picture the black-covered box that was Sister Elizabeth being carried from its door. The end of all gentleness—the beginning of life's reality.

But instead, his eyes were drawn to a sort of arched recess above the doorway, where was a statue of the Virgin. The full moon was shining down on it, and made its outline almost as clear as day. This statue also had sometimes seemed to him to be Sister Elizabeth.

As he looked, the Orphanage bell itself rang out the hour. It spoke three times. It said: "For-give! For-give! For-give!" And the statue seemed also to be smiling and saying these words.

Jan Rubel had raised his shotgun. You could not destroy a bell but you could wreck a statue. A statue that pretended to be Sister Elizabeth. He took aim. He would destroy the memory of Sister Elizabeth forever and put an end to this hallucination.

Then he had suddenly crumpled. He had dropped the gun and sunk down on the steps of the store where he was standing. The enormity of what he was about to do struck him like a fever. The horror of what he realized himself to be.

Jan Rubel repeated dully, "For-give! For-give! For-give!" He did not mean that *he* should forgive. He meant that Sister Elizabeth should forgive. That life should forgive.

He sat there for quite awhile, his brain entirely numb. The physical beating he had taken from Bill Dunnigan still confused him. The trek over the mountains had exhausted him. The spiritual shock of what he was about to do to the memory of Sister Elizabeth horrified and stunned him.

He had no desire to pray. He still did not believe in any God. He had no recourse to any help outside himself. But he had lost faith in himself. He was afraid of the thing that self had come to be. Yet he had a desperate longing for counsel.

Out of a welter of uncertainty and loathing and dismay one answer came. He wanted to talk to one person. The man he ought to hate but could not. The stranger who had struck him down in Koepke's Bar and Grill.

*   *   *

When Bill Dunnigan stepped from the church side door and saw Jan Rubel, he stopped. He wanted no more trouble around Father Paul's church. He still felt a cold sweat whenever he thought of how near Sergeant Dennis O'Rourke had come to projecting a bodily conflict there.

But Jan Rubel's face did not now look belligerent. It looked tired and pale. It was clean, for he had washed it half an hour earlier in a mountain stream, shortly before a farmer, driving to early market, had given him a lift back to Coaltown as he had commenced his weary return along the road. He no longer carried his shotgun. He had thrown it as far as he could out into a deep gully. It had been a new gun the year before, but he never wanted to see it again.

So Jan Rubel stood by St. Michael's side door, and there seemed almost an anguish in the eyes that met those of the press agent.

Jan Rubel spoke first, in a low voice, so as, it appeared, not to disturb the worshipers kneeling all around.

"I can't remember your name." (He could not at that moment.) "I want to talk with you."

"What do you want?" said Dunnigan. "I frankly don't wish to talk with you. My name is Dunnigan, if that matters."

"You are the man who knocked me out at Koepke's, aren't you?"

"Why yes, I guess I am that man."

"May I say this," said Jan Rubel, "I'm not sorry for many of the things I said. I spoke the truth as I see it. But I lied in one thing. I apologize for what I said, Mr. Dunnigan, about the actress you're burying from this church. You did right to smack me down for that. I did the same thing to a man once myself—though it was long ago. Maybe your girl also was a good woman. Maybe she's even a saint—like mine."

Jan Rubel's eyes held such a plea in them that Bill Dunnigan could not entirely hate him as he looked into those eyes.

"Very well. I accept your apology for that part of our conversation," he replied.

"Now—will you come somewhere and talk with me—I—I am alone —I am afraid—I want your help!" said Jan Rubel. It was the first time in his entire life Jan Rubel had ever asked help from anyone.

He had not meant to say any such words. They had come out of his mouth before he realized. But having said them he knew they formed a truth.

He *was* utterly alone! He was terrified to be alone. He wanted desperately the friendship of the only man he had ever met whom he respected. The man who was strong enough to knock him down.

For looking now at Bill Dunnigan, he knew that this knockdown blow had been no trick, no unfair chicanery. It had been the result of the strength of a better man—a strength that seemed to Jan Rubel *clean*—that was the word—*clean*. He wanted to understand that kind of strength. As Bill Dunnigan had been drawn to Father Paul, Jan Rubel was drawn to Bill Dunnigan. The thing Bill Dunnigan called "palship." Jan Rubel had scorned any such emotion. He knew now that without it no man really lived. For him there was one bridge to that living. This man named Dunnigan.

These wretched people on their knees about him—the weakest of them (and they were all weak) had something denied to him. A comradeship. Even though it was the comradeship of a faith that was a delusion. They could say a common phrase: "*Lamb of God, who takest away the sins of the world, have mercy on us.*" He wanted none of that. But even if he did not want it, even if that phrase were a vain repetition to a non-existing God—these people could repeat it with fervor! Could hold on to it, and, by means of it, hold on to each other. There must be *some* faith not based on lies, on weakness. Jan Rubel felt that Dunnigan knew its secret.

To what had his own glorious, unforgiving individualism brought him? A triumph? No. To the desire to murder his one bright memory. And utter loneliness. He was as lonely there, that moment, in the midst of hundreds, as he had been, alone on the mountain top, during the night. He had arrived in his life's journey at no victory. He had arrived at the brink of an awful, gaping chasm. A chasm of Nothingness. In this shattering of all his standards he had not now a single worthwhile goal, a single hope. He could not go on!

Bill Dunnigan did not know this. He did not know of Jan Rubel's past. He recalled only the event of the night before. The drunken, blasphemous barroom ruffian. Sober now, and for some reason a little sorry for a part of what he had said. The press agent hesitated.

The bell in the tower above was ringing. To Dunnigan it was just Father Paul's bell. He also had become used to its sound. But to Jan Rubel it was crying more earnestly than ever before: "For-give! For-give!"

Again it did not mean that he, Jan Rubel, should forgive. It meant that this stranger should hold out his hand.

"Please!" said Jan Rubel. The look in his eyes was the most tragic, the most desolate Dunnigan had ever seen in the eyes of a strong, upstanding man.

Dunnigan moved to Jan Rubel. He placed a hand on his shoulder.

"Sure, pal," he said. "I, too, am sorry about last night. Damn sorry. I'll talk with you. Where shall we go?"

"We might go to Koepke's," said Jan Rubel. Ten years had dropped from his face. He felt like a galley slave whose iron collar and chains have suddenly been struck off. "Have you had breakfast?" he asked.

"No, I haven't," said Dunnigan. "Early Masses are a new thing for me and I'm damned hungry!"

He smiled. Jan Rubel smiled.

"Come on then," said Rubel. "Koepke's wife can fix a good breakfast. Best in town. He's open from six o'clock."

Miners who saw these two striding together down the main street of Coaltown stared. The two tall men were in earnest conversation. Some of the miners turned and followed them. Was there to be another fight?

At Koepke's side door Jan Rubel realized this following. He turned on it.

"Get the hell out!" he said. He said it very fiercely, but he smiled at Bill Dunnigan after he had said it.

The miners moved away. They were still afraid of Jan Rubel. Particularly if he had joined forces with "millionaire" Dunnigan.

Had he joined forces?

There was no report of what was discussed over the last table at the back of Koepke's Bar and Grill that early morning—a table surrounded by a sort of partition to make it into a private booth. Mrs. Koepke, who served the meal herself, heard snatches of a mention of Saint Michael and Jack Dempsey, and Rubel was speaking another time about a nun! Koepke told an intimate that he heard only these words as the two men paid their bill and left his place together an hour and a half later.

Dunnigan: *"Are you sure they will do it?"*

Rubel: *"They'll do it or else!"*

Later in the day, the news spread that District Chairman Jan Rubel had called a mass meeting of the miners at Orloff's Dance Hall for eight o'clock that night. That he had hired and paid for the dance hall from eight till nine for this meeting. And that William Dunnigan, the mysterious theater-owning millionaire who hired church bells to ring and put out cards advertising a Mass, who had been the victor in the short, quick, but town-shaking battle of Koepke's Bar and Grill, was to be the principal speaker.

~~~~~~~~~~~~~~~~~~~~~~~~~~~~~~~~~~~ *70* ~~~~~~~~

*A*T NINE O'CLOCK Bill Dunnigan and Jan Rubel came out of Koepke's Bar and Grill and crossed the street to the Wyoming Hotel. Rubel stood on the sidewalk and waited while the press agent went inside.

Dunnigan seemed very pleased. He was humming a once popular madrigal. It sounded very much like "A pretty girl—is like a melody——"

He emerged soon. He had a telegram. It was from Marcus Harris and confirmed what he already knew from Father Paul. Ten special planes were flying from Hollywood for the funeral the next day. *Have ten motorcars without fail at Williamsport airport by eleven next morning. Enough to transport some fifty people.*

The press agent also carried under his arm a bundle of his "Mass cards." But these he gave to Jan Rubel. Mr. Rubel was proceeding to Glen Alden and several near-by towns. He had some very special union business there (the Headquarters of the District Union) and would see that these cards were placed about. No reason why Coaltown should have a selfish monopoly! And Mr. Rubel wished to call on a number of foremen miners who worked in the night shifts and were now at their homes.

Dunnigan's Packard drew up as they stood at the curb. Both men got in. The car went through the town and to the cemetery. Dunnigan got out of the car there. Jan Rubel was to use it for his errands.

"Go wherever Mr. Rubel wishes," Bill told the driver. "He'll need you all morning. Come back to the St. Michael parsonage at about one o'clock. And tell your boss in Nanticoke I want ten motorcars to meet airplanes from the coast at Williamsport tomorrow—to be there by ten A.M."

The press agent had gone to the cemetery because he now had another acute problem. It was becoming obvious that Father Paul's church would not hold one-tenth of the people who wished to honor Stan Trocki's girl by attendance at her funeral. He had a mind to see if another service could be held out-of-doors. At the cemetery, in fact.

There would, of course, be a Mass at St. Michael's. There would be the six little girls "with wings" by the coffin. Bill had not forgotten that, and Father Paul was having his troubles over it. At least two hundred children wanted to serve!

And the blind organist was going to play Stan Trocki's "theme song"—the song the daughter loved.

But the crowds, thought Bill, could gather at the plateau above the town.

All was quiet at the cemetery. One heard the bells and the Breaker. One also heard the barking of a farm dog, the cry of the crows overhead. Nature still held sway. The thought and interest of the buzzing, swarming populace and newsmen had not yet progressed up the steep hill and around its bend. Not till the next afternoon would this spot pulse with the heartbeats of a living humanity.

Bill believed he was entirely alone as he entered the iron gate and started toward the corner where Olga Treskovna's coffin was to rest beside her father's. But as he drew near, there came the sound of a rasping spade, and fresh black earth was tossed up by an unseen hand to a goodly heap on the sod above.

The Coaltown gravedigger had started before daylight and was finishing his construction of "that abode to which we all will some-day come." The phrase that Bill remembered smiling at when he had heard it in some melodrama came to his mind. Could he smile at its reality?

He walked to the side of the new, open grave and looked down into it. He had never looked into an open grave. He had never met a gravedigger. Father Paul had arranged the matter. A very old man had paused in his work and was wiping his brow with the back of his hand.

At first, Bill Dunnigan had a feeling of *un*reality. He was look-ing at a "stage prop" that he knew had been ordered. A "prop" about ready for a new play to open the next day. He had looked at many such, for he had always been intrigued by these marvelous counterfeits of his theater world and the unsung sculptors and archi-tects in overalls who made them. He had been one press agent who had written about them, and there came to his mind some strangely diversified images—the solemn arch of a church doorway for Joan of Arc—a gay merry-go-round that really whirled for a revue—a tall gallows for François Villon—a gaunt silhouette of a horse for Don Quixote—a great shining chandelier in which the forms of beautiful girls were to recline—a steamboat for the painted background of the Mississippi. Here was something new in his experience, but it was a good "prop" and well made. The grave was already quite deep and its sides were as straight as if measured by a rule. As if it also were made of "profile" and papier-mâché that could be moulded at will.

Instinctively he complimented the maker of this new prop.

"I see you do your work early and well. It's a fine job! Good morning, sir."

The old man looked up into a face unknown to him.

"And who be you?" he asked bluntly. Here was a man whom compliments did not move.

"I'm William Dunnigan, Olga Treskovna's friend," said Bill. He had almost said, *"I'm the press agent for the show."* And he liked this blunt stagehand who wanted to know to whom he spoke. He then remembered that he, Dunnigan, had an obligation to meet for this excellent piece of work.

"I'm fortunate to find you here," he continued. "You have a bill against me. I can pay it now. It's the only bill I have not paid."

"Good morning then to you, sir," said the old man. "I'm Wadislaw Banek. Gravedigger for St. Michael's and the other cemeteries. The bill is seven dollars. The same to rich and poor. I expect no praise. Thank you for liking it just the same."

He ran his hand approvingly along the surface of his handiwork. "I'd dig this girl's grave even and deep whether you paid me or not," he added.

"Why?" asked Bill Dunnigan. He still felt that he was speaking of something quite outside reality—he had stepped onto a rehearsal stage and was questioning an expert technician about his work.

"Not because she was a picture star!" said the old man. "I don't go to pictures. They hurt my eyes. Or because of all this noise about her funeral. The more noise, the less the ones I dig for have usually been worth. But I knew Stan Trocki's girl. I guess I knew her better than anyone else in this town."

"Tell me what you knew about her," said Bill Dunnigan. He was still the press agent, and would perhaps gain some new information about his "star."

The man took a pickaxe and tore away more earth at one end of his "prop." He spaded it to the heap above before he answered. Bill thought he was not going to answer at all.

"Most of the ones I make a place for, I do not know," he said finally. "I know their names—yes—I have seen them every day for years. But know them? No. Since I became the town gravedigger, I did not want to know them. I'd likely have to dig their graves some day, and I'd do a better job if I didn't know. I wanted to dig no graves in hatred. I've been getting very disgusted with this town! Still—I wanted to give everyone their seven dollars' worth."

"And knowing Stan Trocki's girl well did not make it harder for you to make her grave a first-class, seven-dollar one?"

"It did not. Nor knowing her father either. His grave is there where you are standing. I made his grave the best I know how."

The old man paused and seemed to be listening. Then nodded his head and continued.

"Stan Trocki's girl used to come here and talk to me while I worked. I wasn't disgusted with her! She had sense. She was not afraid to watch a grave being dug. She would not be afraid to watch it now."

"She had courage," said Bill Dunnigan.

"And at just the right and proper time she died," said the grave-digger.

This abrupt assertion did for Bill Dunnigan. It shattered the unreality. "Final abode" was no overworked melodramatic stencil. This carefully made excavation in the sod was no stage property for a play of which he was the press agent. It had no kinship to papier-mâché church arches and profile merry-go-rounds. It was stark reality. The real grave of Olga Treskovna!

And this old man with the wrinkled face, the bent back, the gnarled and heavily-veined hands, the sharp retorts, was no theater technician, but a digger of graves for living people who *died*—as "Stan Trocki's girl" had died. Stan Trocki's girl was Olga Treskovna.

This, and the mention of the father—the old gravedigger seemed to think kindly of him—brought to Dunnigan in his grasping of reality the return of a militant resentment, a fierce anger even. This father of hers and the Breaker, the black top of which he could see from this spot, rising above the rooftops of the town below. To-gether they had done for her! They and the indifference of the wretched town. They had reached out even to Hollywood and snatched her from him before he had hardly had a chance to know her. Their senseless brutality had robbed the world of her amazing talent.

They had fastened to her the label of "Breaker Girl" and it had pursued her and claimed her for its own.

Then this old man could calmly say: *She died at just the right and proper time!*

The same bitterness, the same resentment seized Dunnigan that he had felt when he had first come to Coaltown—before he had met Father Paul.

"Damn this town and her drunken father!" he exclaimed. He was about to add, "Damn you also for saying the heartless thing you have said!" But there was a hand clasping his very tightly, and her voice at his side.

"Steady, Bill, steady!" she seemed to say.

For once he did not welcome that voice. He turned and spoke almost in hostility.

"How can I remain steady when you are dead!"

Her large eyes became very sad. She was as she had been the day of the party on the studio sound stage. She looked as she had when reciting the poem she'd made about the small-town girl and that girl's father.

"Have I lost you, Bill?" she said. "Are you going to fail me?"

"But you have died!" he cried. "This grave is for you! They'll bring you here tomorrow!"

"Bring *me* here? Bill, if I *live* for you, we must *both* believe!" There was a pleading in her eyes.

"Belief!" cried Bill Dunnigan, "When you are gone!" And it came to him for a terrible moment that it was all an illusion of his mind: her presence—her promise to be with him—this hope of life with her at his side, even though she were "dead." Was death indeed the end?

She had moved from him, stepping backward slowly toward the fence, no smile on her lips, no look of courage in her eyes.

"Olga, kid!" he cried, "Olga, how can I know——?"

"But I had told you," she answered.

The old man commenced to speak again. He had been working deep in his trench. He straightened up and paused in his work. If he had heard Dunnigan's words to Olga Treskovna he gave no indication.

"Most of them I dig for live too long," he said.

He looked at the anguished face of the stranger above him. "You were right perhaps to curse the town. But you are wrong to curse her father. You are wrong to think that this girl went too soon."

Dunnigan looked again toward his vision of Olga Treskovna. She now stood in the tall goldenrod that lined the fence. She seemed dim, almost a part of that goldenrod. Her voice came to him, but faintly.

"Believe, Bill—if you love me—if you want me still to live!" Was it she or the goldenrod? Was it God's prayer or devil's laughter? Again the old gravedigger spoke.

"This girl—she did something great, I read. And she goes now, while she *is* great. Before people forget."

"But she could have gone on to do more great things. Greater things!"

"She might. Then again she might not. Look at me. No one will care now when I go."

"But she was only twenty-two! All life was before her!"

"It isn't how long we live. It's what we do while we do live. And maybe some of us must die to really live."

Dunnigan looked again in the direction of the goldenrod. Once more she stood there clearly, as if the words of the old gravedigger had given her a hope. Her eyes were still very sad, but her lips smiled at Dunnigan.

"Listen, Bill," she said, "and have faith! He is old and wise. Tell him before you go that *I will care.* And if *you* have lost faith —good-by!"

There was only the bright sun on the goldenrod. She was gone.

Bill Dunnigan wondered dully if it were the end. He was still bitter. He knew if faith were to return, bitterness must be driven from his heart.

The old man was continuing. Bill listened, for Olga Treskovna had asked him to listen.

"It might happen to her as it did to me. As it did to her father," said the gravedigger.

"And how was that?" said Dunnigan. There seemed no possible parallel between these two men and Olga Treskovna, but he would listen.

The old man's keen eyes read Bill Dunnigan's thoughts.

"It's hard to believe, but I was young once. As young as her. Younger than you are. And I had my dream. I wanted to be a great gardener. I love this black earth."

He took up a handful and let it run through his fingers. His pale, small eyes seemed to see far away across many years.

There was such sincerity and longing in his voice, his ancient face, that Dunnigan was held.

"I had a garden back of my house," the old man continued, and he seemed to almost caress the words, "I grew the finest tomatoes in the whole Valley one summer. I took first prize at the County Fair. A long, blue ribbon, two inches wide it was. Printing on it in real gold. My picture was in the paper—the same as this girl's. The neighbors all came to see. I was a grand fellow!"

"You mean you should have died then!"

"Right then. That night."

"But why didn't you go on raising prize tomatoes? Take another prize the next year?"

"I had to work daytimes in the mines. I had to earn more money, for I thought I wanted to get married. I worked overtime. I was too tired when I got home to do gardening. I thought I'd take it up again the next year. But the next year children began to come. I had to earn still more money. I worked longer hours. The pay wasn't then like it is now. I never did go back to my gardening."

"But you raised a family." Bill somehow did not want this man to feel that he had failed. He had not failed, for Olga Treskovna had said that *she would care*. Olga Treskovna, had Bill looked toward the goldenrod, was standing there once more. Her eyes were no longer sad.

"Children! Children take no prizes!" continued the old man. "They're all gone now. Two died. I don't hear from the others. What good has it done me to live for sixty more years? I'm eighty now, mister. If I couldn't dig graves I'd be on the county. At the poor farm."

"But you dig good graves—maybe the best graves in the world!" And Olga Treskovna, by the goldenrod, was smiling now. Her Bill Dunnigan was himself again!

"Graves. Who cares?" Thus the digger thereof. "They don't take prizes either! Nobody sees them when they're open and fine to look at. Folks feel too bad, or they're superstitious and afraid to come like you and look into them. You'd be surprised to know how many of them are afraid! You're the first one in a long time that came to look at a grave the day before the funeral. The first friend or relative, I mean. Why did you come, mister?"

"I came for a special reason. But when I got here I also was afraid," said Bill.

"You didn't come to compliment me on my work, did you?"

"No, I didn't," said Bill honestly.

"There you are," said the old man. "No, don't feel sorry for Stan Trocki's girl. Feel sorry for those who are still walking around and should be dead. It's best to go while everyone thinks you're wonderful and grand. The world can be very lonely when they forget you. And very cruel. Take her father here. Stan Trocki."

"Tell me about him," said Dunnigan.

"I know what they say about Stan. What you've heard all over, mister. But Stan was the besthearted fellow I ever dug a grave for. The kindest in this town. He just wanted to make people happy. Like the girl that's coming here. He could play the accordion fine. The best at that in the whole Valley. He could sing. His playing and singing weren't much regarded—were a sort of joke—the serious things were who could load the most coal a day or start the best paying saloon—till there was a bad accident in the B mine shaft one year. Two hundred miners were trapped when a series of barriers collapsed. It took four days to get them all out. Three days to dig and blast to the nearest ones.

"Stan Trocki went home and got his accordion and came to where the women were waiting. He started to play the old Polish songs he knew. He sang them. He played almost steadily for four days. He didn't go home or sleep. He kept some of the wives and sweethearts from going mad. He kept up the energy and the courage of the men working at the rescue. It was like a drum or a bagpipe sending men into battle. I can see him now—always smiling Stan —pumping those small bellows and singing. Singing with God's hope in his voice and God's courage in his eyes.

"The second day they had managed to drill through and sink a long length of pipe so they could pour down liquid food. They had Stan pour down his music also. He played and sang for the men inside. The trapped men said afterwards that Stan's music did as much for them as the food."

"And he didn't die right after that," said Dunnigan.

"You've said it, sir. He lived on. He got to drinking too much. People bought him drinks because of his music. He bought them drinks. He was a miner also. He had to work. There was no money in playing an accordion, no matter how much happiness it made. How many lives it had saved. People soon forgot all about that anyway. They only remember what makes money. After awhile the drinking became more important to Stan than the music —or his job in the mines. I guess he just drank himself to death. Nobody cared at all when he went. Except this girl.

"If he had died the day those miners were rescued alive from shaft B, the whole town would have come to his funeral!"

The old man spaded in silence for a few minutes. Bill Dunnigan was thinking also. He was glad he had learned about Stan Trocki's hour of greatness. It partly canceled the bitterness he had felt toward the father who let his daughter work in the Breaker. He understood a little better Olga Treskovna's love for that father. And it was like her not to tell him about this incident.

"This girl of Stan's—" the old gravedigger was again speaking "—Stan made it very hard for her. He didn't mean to, mister. I guess he couldn't help himself. She loved him. He loved her in his way. They understood each other. I guess she got the talent they say she had, from him. Only she got away from Coaltown and found a chance with hers. When he died it was really a blessing for her, but she didn't think so. She'd been here yet if he'd lived. Cooking for him and taking him home from the saloons. So maybe even his drinking was for the best! He might be living still. What good would it have been for her to have been a great actress here in Coaltown?

"She stayed around quite awhile as it was. I used to find her sitting by his grave. She felt bad that there was no tombstone. I can see her now, sitting right there, making a cross out of two pieces of wood and putting it at the head of the grave. She had to keep making new ones, for the cows would knock them down."

"The cows?"

"Yes. There was a farmer over in the next field who had a herd of Jerseys. And the church let them pasture in the cemetery. You see, it kept the grass cut short on the graves.

"The cows certainly liked Stan Trocki's grave. Funny thing about the grass on the graves. I've noticed that when the dead person was good—really good, not just what the town pretended to think or what the priest said—the grass on that grave was always sweet and green. The other ones—the bad ones, the mean ones, the selfish ones, even if they had gone to Mass every day of their lives—couldn't to save their souls grow first-class grass! I guess the good earth understands.

"Find a grave that the cows liked and you had found a soul in Heaven.

"The cows knocked down Olga Trocki's wooden crosses, but she didn't mind. For some of the cows had bells. It nearly broke her heart that she didn't have the money to hire St. Michael's bell rung during her pop's funeral. I'd have paid for it myself if I'd known. I didn't find it out till afterwards.

"She used to say that the cows, who didn't want money for ringing their bells, were ringing those bells for her father!

"I'm glad you had the bells rung these four days, mister. Thought it was sort of crazy at first, but it's going to be awfully quiet around here when they stop. I like them. I guess everybody in the town likes them now. They're for a funeral, but they've cheered up this whole town. I'm not so disgusted with it now. I think Stan Trocki is liking the bells. They go well with his accordion."

Again the old man seemed to be listening. Again he nodded his head. Bill Dunnigan wondered what the gravedigger was hearing.

"She had a lot of funny ideas—Stan Trocki's girl. She asked me one day, 'Do you think they'll let pop play his accordion in Heaven instead of a harp?' She had no doubt he was in Heaven, no matter what the town said. I've no doubt of it either—if there is a Heaven. If that's where the good ones go. All Stan wanted to do was to play the accordion and sing. That didn't hurt nobody. Didn't make other people poorer. Didn't keep someone else out of a job."

"What do *you* believe happens to us when your good earth covers up the coffin?" asked Bill. He had a feeling this lover of black soil had found some answers in his spading of it.

The old gravedigger stopped his work. He was almost finished with Olga Treskovna's grave.

"I've thought about that a whole lot," he said. "I'm a good Christian, I hope, but I think some of the things in the Bible are just symbols, as they say. It don't mean exactly what the words read. And it says different things in different places. I think the useless people—the people that the bad grass grows on—just finish. They had their chance and they didn't take it. Like a plant that don't blossom. They're really dead. That's why the soil above them is dead.

"Look over there. That big plot with the cement posts around it, and the iron chains connecting them. There's the grave of the man who was the town's richest citizen. Before he died that man put in those posts and chains so the cows wouldn't walk on *his* grave. And the grave of his wife. He needn't have bothered. The grass that grew there was always coarse and hard and bitter. Like that man and his wife. No cows ever wanted or tried to eat it. The cows knew.

"But the dead people that left some happiness behind—did something to help someone—why, *they live*. They live right here, mister. I myself wouldn't want to live anywhere else but among these hills. Where could any Heaven be more beautiful? I think the buried ones know and answer every time we, who still live, think gratefully of them. Or if there is a tree, a hill, that misses them. The trees and the hills have better memories than men—and longer. I always imagine I can hear Stan Trocki's accordion when I think about that day of the mine accident. I've been thinking of it all week."

"Do you think that Olga Trocki will live?" asked Bill Dunnigan.

"Isn't the whole town talking of her? Grateful to her? Isn't everybody—well, happier because of her? I don't mean they're happier because she died. Maybe she *had to die* so they could really know her. This miracle at St. Michael's. Maybe she's almost like the blessed Christ—He had to die also before people knew Him!"

The old man crossed himself. "Maybe I shouldn't say that, mister. I don't really know. I know this. The grass on Olga Trocki's grave is going to be very green and lovely!"

Bill Dunnigan knew that also. He would not doubt again. The voice of the goldenrod was God's prayer.

"And I know I'll surely think of her gratefully," the old man continued. "I'll be thinking of her a lot because all this has set me to making plans. In the spring I'm going to start a garden again, mister. I'm going to put tomato plants this winter under glass. I'm going to see if I can again raise the best tomatoes in the Valley. If Stan Trocki's girl can make good I ought to be ashamed at my age to be a failure!"

Dunnigan took out his roll of bills. He handed the gravedigger a five-dollar bill and two ones.

"Here's for the grave," he said, "and many thanks. And there's something else. I'd almost forgot. Miss Treskovna—Olga Trocki as you knew her—wanted me to give you something you needed. Maybe you'll be needing special things to start growing these prize tomatoes. Here's another bill. It's from her. Please take it, to please her."

The old man looked in his hand. The "other bill" was for one hundred dollars.

"I can't take that much money," he said.

"Sure you can. Take it. Put it in your pocket. And she said to be sure to tell you she would care. Would care when you went, she meant."

"When did she say that, mister?"

"The last time I talked with her. It was not long ago," said Bill.

"Thank her—when you talk with her again. You will talk with her again."

Had he heard? Did he know? But the gravedigger had bent to finishing his task.

A final thought came to Dunnigan. He peered into the grave. "I want those tomatoes of yours to be the best ever! You can do something for me in connection with them. Got a name for them?"

"Why no."

"Call them the Saint Michael tomatoes. Only they must be the best! And I'll tell you where to sell some of them. A Quick Lunch on the Square in Nanticoke. I'll get you the address. They're friends of mine. They'll put a sign in the window that you grew them."

And so, still another miracle. A man of eighty was going to start making a forgotten dream come true. Make it so that *he* wouldn't be forgotten when he died.

And Olga Treskovna *lived*. Bill Dunnigan realized she was living in every life she had touched. This gravedigger's, Father Paul's, Father Spinsky's, the sister of the St. Leo priest, Jan Rubel—those and others he did not know and would never know. Her grave? She had no grave. It was just a "prop" in a piece we had to play for a little while in the eternity of living.

He listened to the bells. The voice he knew seemed to be saying with them, "Carry on, Bill! I'm depending on you!"

"It was O. K., kid, about your wanting me to give him something he needed?"

"It's O. K. by me—always—whatever you say! For I'm a part of you, Bill—or I would not want to live! What you wish—I wish. What you do—I do. I'm happy now again! Just carry on for both of us! Just carry on!"

And maybe it was an accordion that seemed blended with the bells and with her voice. Or perhaps it was just an echo in the murmur of the wind in the thousands of pine trees on the surrounding hills. The wind and the trees and the hills that did not forget, that had not forgotten a coal-stained, sleepless man who sat and played Polish folk tunes the four days his fellows were in need of courage and hope.

~~~~~~~~~~~~~~~~~~~~~~~~~~~~~~~~~~ *71* ~~~

*A*T *APPROXIMATELY* the same hour—the hour of ten A.M.—a discussion of a very different kind was taking place in an office of the State Capitol Building in Harrisburg. There was nothing spiritual about this conference, or about the two men who were concerned with it. They were notably successful in the art of popular government.

"Tom," said one of them who sat at a large flat-top desk, "weren't the votes in Wyoming County counted against us at the last election?"

"I believe they were," said the Tom addressed. He was a tall man lounging by the desk, wore a slouch hat which was pushed to the back of his head. He was lighting a cigar which he had taken from the mahogany humidor on this desk. He held no elected office, but was known about the building as a "confidential aide" to the Executive. He also headed a "contracting" business—what his firm "contracted for" depended on what the state was buying any particular month—paving stones, iron for a bridge, even labor. At that moment he was waiting for the right pause to speak of a bill just passed by a contumacious legislature that would reduce by half the fares on a transit system. He wanted that bill vetoed.

"You see, Governor," Tom explained, having carefully lit the cigar, "that county is a stronghold of the opposition party. Always has been. Mostly foreigners. Poles and such. So in spite of a considerable outlay for education, they failed to recognize your sterling worth, your democratic leadership, your devotion——"

"Forget the campaign talk," said the one who had first spoken, a stocky, solid man with an aggressive, but not unpleasant, round and ruddy face. "The county went against us. That is enough.

Do you think a personal appearance in that district would help us for the next year?"

"Your personal appearances have always helped," replied Tom, "especially when you wear a soft shirt and that black Stetson hat, and remind 'em how you started life as a worker in the mines."

"I am a simple man of the people," said the gentleman at the desk.

"Exactly. And the people can't be told that too often. But if I may say so, it's a little early to start on them for the next campaign. The people forget quickly." He almost added, "Thank God!" There was the matter of this transit bill.

"Have you been reading the newspapers the past few days?" pursued the man behind the desk.

"I suppose you mean about the bell-ringing actress funeral and the miracle that is supposed to have happened in a church near Wilkes-Barre." Tom's tone conveyed an amused tolerance of the gullibility of humanity. Thank God again they were gullible, or where would most of his political protégés have landed!

But his companion spoke with great earnestness.

"I mean the whole episode there. A famous daughter of our great state brought home for burial. Bells ringing for four days to carry out a promise to a dead father. This miracle that seems to have considerable foundation of fact. Anyway, it has caught the interest of a lot of people. Catholics vote, the same as Protestants and Jews. And now—in the morning papers—" he picked up the one on his desk "—it says a large number of great film stars are flying on from Hollywood. The names of the honorary pall-bearers are household words. It's probably a build-up for a new motion picture, but it's quite amazing!"

"Really? I didn't know about picture stars from Hollywood going there!" Tom reached for the newspaper. He read some headlines over its second column. His expression changed from condescending tolerance to a lively interest.

"H-mm. That will mean plenty of photographers and newsreels and reporters—radio broadcasts——"

"Exactly. But I was not thinking of that. I was thinking of my duty to the people of this state—my duty to give recognition to achievement—to the fact, as you mentioned, that I myself started in a very humble way, from a small town, and forged ahead, in spite of early handicaps and——"

"I get you, Governor," said Tom, without the trace of a smile. He was an expert "confidential aide." He knew when not to speak in jest. "Maybe all this is something to look into!"

He sat down and commenced to read the news story. "Good-looking gal too!" he commented, as he turned a page to study a two-column photograph of Olga Treskovna. Like Frederick Hanover, Jr., he added, "I must see that film when it comes!"

The hard-boiled, political dealer had his soft spot. He liked movies and read of the comings and goings of his favorites with the same childlike credulity he so taunted in his own political sphere. The man who doubted (with reason) all political pronouncements, swallowed with unbounded faith any item coming out of Hollywood. Thus did he exemplify the basic Anglo-Saxon need for some sort of faith in journalism. He had not believed the local reports that this Coaltown girl was a star. Every home-state product who migrated and was brought back dead had been a "leader in society," a "popular clubman," a "prominent citizen of." But now! If *Hollywood* said that the leading man of "Casa Banco" was coming to her funeral, along with two dozen others! . . .

Meantime the man behind the desk pressed a buzzer. A young male stenographer entered from an adjoining room.

"Take a telegram," said the solidly-built gentleman. "Get it off at once." And picking up his other morning paper for data, he dictated rapidly certain often-used sentiments.

"To the Pastor of the Roman Catholic Church of St. Michael, Coaltown, Pennsylvania. I am deeply moved by the stories in the press of the great loss to your community and indeed to our State and the entire Nation occasioned by the untimely passing of this talented daughter . . . What is the girl's name?"

"Olga Treskovna," said Tom authoritatively. "Shall I spell it out, Governor?"

The other man looked at his henchman and just the trace of a smile twitched his mouth. He had already found the name in his own paper.

"I have it here," he said, and then to the secretary—"this talented daughter, the well-known Miss Olga Treskovna, who I understand is to be buried from your church tomorrow. I myself know only too well the hard struggle that it is from obscurity to a position of trust, where one can serve his fellow man . . . say 'unselfishly' serve 'his or her' fellow man . . . I desire to attend the funeral of this star beloved by all America in special recognition of the unique honor this native-born Polish girl . . . She *is* Polish, isn't she?"

"So the paper says," replied Tom. "They're all Polacks up there!"

"We'll take a chance . . . This native-born Polish girl has brought to your community and to our State. America is proud of the children of her foreign born. My own father was an immigrant who came to these United States to find freedom of opportunity and religion. Please reserve seats for myself and staff of five. The newspapers say the service is at noon. Will arrive in time by motorcar. Please confirm.

"Sign it, my full name and the word 'Governor' . . . O. K.?" and he looked again at his friend Tom.

"O. K.," said Tom. "Here it says definitely her father was a Pole. 'A prominent citizen of the town.' Do I go with you?"

"You do. And pick out five of our staff who have the best official uniforms. The military aides would be good. It makes a contrast to my—er—soft shirt and Stetson—though maybe for a funeral I should wear a top silk hat. I'll think it over. See that copies of this telegram," he had turned to the stenographer, "are given to the Press at once. The people are entitled to know the whereabouts of their Executive at all times."

He turned to his "confidential aide."

"Well, Tom, that's that! I hope it gets us a few votes from those damned foreigners in the fall. What's on your mind?"

Tom's mind was at that moment on the non-political prospect of viewing the curves of the personable girl star of "It Happened One Evening" *in person* and at close range (the papers said she would be there), but he pulled himself back to more remunerative urgencies.

Romance paid no race-track betting losses.

"I hate to bring it up now, Governor, but it's this matter of the traction-fare bill. I know what we said during the last campaign, but a good friend of mine and yours, whose name I need not mention, wants it vetoed and——"

"Have I ever failed to be loyal to my friends?" said the Governor.

~~~~~~ *72* ~~~~~

*B*ILL DUNNIGAN walked back to the St. Michael parish house. There was again a line slowly moving into the little church. And a new topic of conversation for those waiting in that line. The names of the great motion-picture luminaries that the Wilkes-Barre and Scranton morning papers said were coming to Coaltown the next day!

The rumor had circulated the afternoon before that there would be six of them—six pallbearers. Now it seemed that Hollywood was moving there en masse!

Father Paul was already feeling the impact. More telegrams were arriving. And something not so easily handled as yellow-enveloped tributes. Flowers.

That morning might in fact be called, in the saga of the funeral of Olga Treskovna, the "Morning of Flowers."

In a horticultural sense, this funeral had started with Bill Dunnigan's terse comment to undertaker Orloff—"*No flowers!*" Her coffin was then resting in the bare room of Orloff's parlor. Nobody cared then where it rested except Bill Dunnigan. And he, in all likelihood, would not have the price of a single lily by the time he had finished his funeral arrangements.

Now flowers were arriving by the truck load at St. Michael's church. The bulging delivery wagons were marked with florists' names in Wilkes-Barre, Scranton, Nanticoke. Lilies, roses, camellias, carnations, hyacinths, sweet peas; bouquets, clusters, baskets, setpieces—made up of everything and anything that bloomed! By that magic of telegraphic transference the greenhouses and the floral shops and even the private gardens of the district were being stripped clean.

Sentimental Hollywood, that part of it which could not personally journey to Coaltown, was sending its tribute. And those who were coming telegraphed ahead these messengers of good will. Every studio, every organization of workers and artists, literally hundreds of individuals, were paying their botanical respects.

Broadway also was commencing to take note, and many of the identification tags were from organizations of this older amusement center. Film executives stationed in New York; the great Intercity Circuit that had booked "The Garden of the Soul"; the Music Hall; artists of the "legitimate" who had been touched by the newspaper stories of this girl.

As Dunnigan arrived at St. Michael's two large pieces were being carried in, the cards of which seemed particularly poignant. One read—"The Association of Burlesque Chorus Girls." The other was from "The Management" of the Venus Burlesque Theater on West Forty-Second Street. The stories of Olga Treskovna's humble beginnings had not gone unnoticed.

The assistant from St. Leo's, now helping Father Paul full time, was doing the best he could about this fragrant deluge. Sergeant Dennis O'Rourke detailed two of his Troopers to help. The entire front part of the interior of St. Michael's was being heaped with color and perfume.

"Poor little kid!" said Dunnigan to himself. He was thinking that she probably never had a single flower sent her while she lived. Even he had never sent her a flower.

Organ music was coming from the open doors, and Dunnigan climbed to the choir loft.

He had another talk with the blind organist. She had stayed after the morning Mass to practice her Polish songs. She had however no choir to sing. The lone singer she had formerly used had moved away.

There should be singing voices for the funeral Mass, both she and Dunnigan agreed. And if there was a special service at the cemetery, how would organ music be provided?

These problems gave birth to an inspiration that was to cause busy Marcus Harris in New York a bit of real headache. Later in the day the picture producer received this wire:

DEAR MARCUS ALONG WITH ALTAR CLOTHS BRING FIFTY CHOIR BOYS WITH A 1 VOICES AND REGULATION COSTUMES CATHOLIC NOT JEWISH STOP SEEM TO REMEMBER CATHOLIC CHURCH IN WEST FIFTIES THAT HAS BIG SUPPLY OF SAME I ATTENDED CELEBRATION OF ACTORS DEATH THERE ONCE STOP MUST BE REAL THING NO PHONEYS STOP ALSO BRING PORTABLE ORGAN HAD ONE IN AN OTIS SKINNER SHOW HIRED FROM ESTEY

PEOPLE NAME IN PHONE BOOK STOP CONGRATULATIONS ON
HOLLYWOOD RESPONSE MEETING SAME WITH CARS AT WIL-
LIAMSPORT AS REQUESTED STOP GET CHOIR BOYS HERE BY TEN
A STOP M STOP TOMORROW TIME FOR A DRESS REHEARSAL STOP
LOTS OF ACTION AROUND COALTOWN HOPE NEW YORK IS HAV-
ING DITTO STOP YOU ARE STILL THE BIG BOSS AND O STOP K
STOP WITH ME STOP LOVE AND KISSES

WILLIAM DUNNIGAN

*   *   *

After a brief talk with Father Paul and the arrangement to meet
later in the afternoon to plan about the cemetery service, Dunnigan
rushed back to the Wyoming Hotel. He had to answer the telegrams Father Paul had received. He had to telephone his friend
in Cincinnati regarding the sponsoring of the radio program. The
Bell Company had now hastily installed two pay-station booths in
the Wyoming lobby for the newsmen, and Dunnigan could talk in
privacy from his Coaltown residence.

These tasks accomplished, he took the remainder of his "5:45
Mass" placards and started placing them in Coaltown's stores,
wherever he had not called the night before. Like Andrev Denko,
Dunnigan believed in finishing whatever he set out to do.

It was from Sergeant Dennis O'Rourke that the press agent first
learned about the coming of the State's Chief Executive. The news
had been radioed to that officer's police car as he cruised about his
now very busy bailiwick. It meant that there would be a very
special detail of Troopers for the funeral.

"This is going to be bigger even than the planting of the Wilkes-
Barre mayor!" the sergeant enthusiastically exclaimed to Dunnigan,
as he ran his car to the curb where Bill had just emerged from
placing a Mass card in Sobeski's Meat and Poultry Center. "We'll
have a hundred uniformed men here in the morning! It will make
a tiptop showing for you, Mr. Dunnigan, sir! They'll wear their
new uniforms most likely—the ones with a stripe down the breeches
leg."

"You've been a real pal!" said Bill. "I'm told you have a Recreation Fund for your grand service. I'm mailing that fund a check
for five hundred dollars. In the name of Father Paul and St.
Michael's church. I hope you won't mind."

"The fund won't mind at all," smiled Sergeant Dennis, "and

neither will I, sir! The address is Wyoming Barracks, Wyoming. That's the name of the part of the town across the river. The Wilkes-Barre Police once got a fund check by mistake and we never got it back! By the way, Mr. Dunnigan, I wonder if you'd show me just how you K. O.'d a certain party in one of the saloons here last night? We don't know officially, of course, that it happened at all, but there was an argument at the barracks. I said it was a left-hand jab in the solar plexus followed by a right uppercut."

"But if I talk, I'll be admitting that it happened and you'll have to arrest me," smiled the press agent.

"I never take official notice of talk," said Sergeant O'Rourke, "and I wasn't here last night—rotten luck! If I had been, I'd been forced to use my authority—to make you show me *then* how you did it! I know the guy that was on the receiving end, and he's had it coming for a long time."

"Sergeant, I want you to like that guy," said Bill. "He's out in my car now, putting up these Mass cards in Glen Alden and Nanticoke."

"He's what!" said Sergeant O'Rourke. But he had heard.

"If you meet him, speak to him. Shake his hand. Tell him you've heard some nice things about him. That you're a friend of mine—and his."

"If you say so, Mr. Dunnigan!" said Sergeant Dennis. "This town's certainly been turned inside out since you arrived, sir! Jan Rubel putting out Mass cards! Holy Mike!"

"Nonsense," said Bill. "We're all right guys when we get to know each other."

"Give me a couple of those cards," said Sergeant O'Rourke. "I'll put them up in the barracks."

"Not afraid of trouble?" asked Dunnigan.

"Mr. Dunnigan, you *own* this district since last night! I told my young brother-in-law-to-be he'd better call your Quick Lunch 'Knockout Dunnigan's Place,' or at least put your picture in the window—in your fighting stance, sir. If I may say so, *that* would pull people there!"

"I was lucky I didn't get my damn fool head knocked off," laughed Bill.

"It was a left jab and a right uppercut?"

"Yes. Jack Dempsey showed me how."

"You know Jack Dempsey!" Sergeant O'Rourke said this in the tone in which you would say, *"You know Almighty God!"*

"I know him," said Bill Dunnigan.

"Say!" said Sergeant O'Rourke, "if you could get Mr. Dempsey to come to this funeral——"

"I'd thought of that," said Bill. "Do you think it would help —help Father Paul?"

"The hoi polloi," said Sergeant O'Rourke, snapping his fingers, "they fall for these movie stars. But me and my boys—and a lot of miners in the Valley——"

"Jack will be here—if he's in New York," said Bill.

"I'll give you another tip," said Sergeant O'Rourke. "You seem to want to help this little priest fellow. If you could get Jack Dempsey to pose with him on the parish house steps—same as the Bishop—for the newspapermen—and they'd publish it—every boy and man in the county would cut it out and paste it up! And they'd go all-out for that priest!"

And so, another sensational report spread about Coaltown. The most popular fighter of all time would likely be among those present the next day!

It quite took the edge off the news about the Governor, which in itself had caused a sizable stir.

*   *   *

Bill Dunnigan met, for a brief moment, another of his former antagonists that afternoon. He had driven to Wilkes-Barre and Scranton to interview the radio stations located there, and the large movie theaters. No difficulty in either place about his St. Michael's plans. The managers of the large Intercity houses in the two cities, on a promise of first showings of "The Garden of the Soul," would have agreed to almost any proposition. Sponsor a series of broadcasts? Gladly! One manager made Bill an offer for a "personal appearance"!

Both cities said the new film with Olga Treskovna would have at least a two weeks' run, where pictures were normally shown for three or four days at the most.

Father Spinsky had been humbly doing his bit. He was the only priest in Coaltown who possessed a motorcar. He now thanked Heaven for that car, but he would have walked barefoot at his task had that been necessary. He knew from his assistant that St. Michael's was constantly running short of shrine candles. None had arrived from the supply houses. Father Spinsky appointed himself an urgent collector of candles.

He had been ransacking the countryside. He had raided the surplus supplies of every Catholic church in the Valley. Brother clerics hid their last remaining tapers when they saw him approaching. He had even been seen emerging from the side entrance of a friendly synagogue with a suspiciously large box! The ever blazing racks before Father Paul's shrines must be kept filled at any cost. This was Father Spinsky's immediate penance.

Coming from a parish house in Scranton, he discovered a large Packard being parked directly before his Chevrolet. It had a familiar look. And it obligingly remained a motorcar and did not transform into a great black charger!

Two spat-encased feet emerged. Saint Michael's Plenipotentiary Interceder Ex-Officio was getting out to go to the near-by theater in front of which he had found you could not park.

"Mr. Dunnigan!" called Father Spinsky. There, in the sunlit, busy street, this tall figure seemed human enough. The spats were spats. The well-fitting grey suit was cloth, the black derby was made of felt. And yet——

Father Spinsky no longer trusted even a Board-of-Aldermen-ruled city street to provide explainable and logical events. He would not have been surprised had this cloth and felt all suddenly changed to a suit of shining armor; had Stanislaus Trocki with his accordion also stepped from that Packard!

But the St. Leo pastor was no longer afraid. That morning a sister he had hardly recognized had greeted him in her kitchen and unfolded plans this man—if he really were a man—had opened up for her.

"I want to thank you for my sister," said Father Spinsky. "Whether she can really do all this or not, I shall always be grateful that you talked with her, sir."

"Tell her it's all arranged," said Dunnigan. "I telephoned Cincinnati this morning. I'm to close the deal with my friend's advertising agency when I reach New York. You must help your sister write out her talks. Time them to last about twelve minutes, which will leave three minutes for what they call the commercial. How can she fail to make good with both your Saint Leo and my Saint Michael behind her at the microphone!"

The casual mention of the Saints again! But it reminded Father Spinsky of something else he wanted to tell this opener of new horizons.

"I would like those broadcasts to be entirely to the credit of Father Paul and his Saint," said Father Spinsky. "My sister agrees with me. It's Father Paul's idea. His should be the credit and reward. We are only here to help—if we can."

"That's mighty generous of her," said Bill Dunnigan.

"It's better than generous," said Father Spinsky, but he did not explain what he meant. Instead he said:

"She was busy making you and Father Paul—shall I say, a pair of the largest chocolate cakes I've ever seen!"

"Then I'd better hurry back!" laughed Bill. "There's a night clerk at my hotel that will have his eye on any package looking like a Mary Spinsky cake."

"Oh, she mentioned him also. She's going to make him a special one for Sunday! And I think in the matter of cakes she'd still like to have Saint Leo claim title. You won't mind that, Mr. Dunnigan?"

"Saint Leo's the cakes shall be!" smiled Bill. "Saint Michael shall have no claim to their glory, and I mean glory!"

"I've one other bit of news to tell you," said Father Spinsky looking hard at Bill Dunnigan, "though you doubtless know it already."

"Yes?" said Bill. "What news?"

"Do you recall warning me that my church might burn down—or something?"

"Good lord! Don't tell me——"

"No, no," said Father Spinsky. "St. Leo's is still there—or was when I left this morning. But I connected that warning somehow with a savings bankbook I was acting very childishly about."

Bill had to think. The savings bankbook and the jinx! It was only two days ago, but all that seemed in another century! As far away as this priest was now different from the man Dunnigan had then talked with!

"Don't tell me the money wasn't O. K.!" he exclaimed.

"It was O. K. and double O. K.," said Father Spinsky with a smile. "I fear you would have heard from me before if it hadn't been! But there *was* a fire in connection with that book of yours."

"A fire! Where?"

"The savings bank in Brooklyn had a fire. I happened to see the item in the newspaper and remembered its name. I had telephoned that bank, Mr. Dunnigan."

"Did this happen, by any chance, after you had sent my book back in?"

"The very day it was received by them, I should judge."

A fire, even in a savings bank, was no laughing matter, but William Dunnigan, Esq. (so his name had been written in a horribly perfect script on the jinx book) laughed one of those laughs that starts with a small "Ha-ha!" chuckle and proceeds to a crescendo of these monosyllables.

"Excuse me," said Bill between chuckles. "I have no doubt they carried plenty of insurance."

Somehow he couldn't feel sorry for that bank. It confirmed his diagnosis of his jinx. But to Father Spinsky it was another minor manifestation of the power of a certain greave-clad Saint—like the turning of two statues; the blasting of Jan Rubel; the miracle of the sudden change in his sister.

"And what are you doing so far from home, Father?" asked Bill, as the black-suited figure climbed behind his wheel.

"One might think I was trying to add to *Father Paul's* fire hazard," smiled Father Spinsky, "but I give you my word I'm only plotting to keep his altar shrine-racks blazing. I did my best to get some new candles on from Philadelphia——"

"I heard about you and your candle plotting," said Bill. "It's swell! You're a right guy, no mistake! I'm glad my curse hit the savings bank and not your church! And I heard about the bell money and Father Paul's Nurse Fund. I'll tell you what! When your grand sister comes to New York to meet my pal Oscar at the Waldorf—tell her I haven't forgotten that—you come along! We'll send her to a good show while you and I take in a good fight at Madison Square Garden. That is, if you like fights."

"I love them," said Father Spinsky, "and I never saw a real one."

"Great! It's a date! Now don't bring back any uneven-burning candles."

Bill Dunnigan was beginning to consider himself an expert on church supplies. And he watched the St. Leo's parish car push determinedly ahead in the direction of a large church a block away.

He could not quite understand the breakneck speed of the trans-
formation of this priest—unless Saint Michael had taken a hand.
The guy who invented the Sunday punch, Saint Michael!

In that car Father Spinsky was thinking. *So he is going to New
York from here.* Well, there were *two* churches of St. Michael the
Archangel in New York. He had looked the matter up. One in
West Thirty-Fourth Street and one at Ninety-Ninth Street.

Which church was due to have a jolt?

~~~~~~~~~~~~~~~~~~~~~~~~~~~~~~~~~~~~~~ *73* ~~~~~

*I*T WAS LATE afternoon when Bill Dunnigan
and Father Paul were again together at the cemetery. It had become increasingly obvious that a special service should be there.
Pray God the weather would hold good!

The telegram of the Governor, duly printed on the first pages of
all the State's afternoon papers, seemed to arouse a number of other
public-spirited gentlemen whose livelihood depended on votes.

Two Representatives of the district in Washington—due for an
election soon—wired that they also would, by their presence, like
to express the sorrow of their great state in its tragic loss. One
of the two Senators at the nation's capital had the same urge—and
for the same patriotic reason. The mayors of six not-too-distant
cities were immediately imbued with a like and laudable desire.
The judiciary—coming up for a ballot-box shuffling in two months
—did not lag behind, and no less than five elective judges of the
highest state courts sent telegrams that they felt it their duty and
privilege to make a personal appearance at St. Michael's.

Coaltown's near-by schools were going to close down for the day.
The mines were shutting for the first time in years—both day and
night shifts. The Breaker would not gloat audibly during the
funeral hours of at least one of its victims, Stan Trocki's girl. And
Olga Treskovna was going to "show" to a pretty full countryside
on her initial appearance as a star in the town and state of her
birth.

So this miraculous snowball rolled and gathered! A snowball that had been very tiny, almost non-existent, when Dunnigan and Father Paul had first stood together at the St. Michael cemetery.

Bill Dunnigan always held that it was no coincidence, but a miracle of the purest water, that caused a certain Duesenberg to break down at the very gate of that cemetery! His late employer of the famous girl revues had owned one, and it never had been known to go wrong. Other cars might sometimes sputter and balk, but not a Duesenberg.

Whatever the cause, divine or mere chance, this Duesenberg did come to a dead stop in the roadway just outside the St. Michael iron gates at about five p. m. It refused to go further. The steel heart of it had ceased to purr. No sit-down strike was ever more conclusively consummated.

The lady occupant of this car was in no pleasant frame of mind. The journey from Cleveland had taken hours longer than expected. On crossing the Pennsylvania state line it seemed there was unusually heavy traffic in the same direction she was journeying.

She "abhorred" crowds. The nearer she approached Wilkes-Barre, the more crowded the highway became. It was to escape some of this that she instructed the chauffeur to ask if there wasn't some detour by which Coaltown could be reached without the clutter of hundreds of plebeian, non-Duesenberg motors.

A tip of fifty cents to an enterprising seller of a liquid labeled "lemonade" at a crossroad sent Henri off the main highway along a narrow and little frequented stretch. It was harder on springs and tires but escaped the multitudes.

And that is how this aristocratic motor managed, in the first place, to get alongside the cemetery of St. Michael before actually passing through Coaltown.

"What now, Henri!" its irritated owner demanded through the speaking tube. The chauffeur Henri was decently separated from the upper classes by a germ-proof partition of steel and glass.

"The engine, madam, it stop!" replied the puzzled Henri, using the same completely sanitary means of communication.

"Well, start it again!" demanded Miss Hanover, and replaced her end of the communication system in its holder.

But inanimate objects like automotive engines did not understand that when Miss Grace Hanover of the Cleveland Hanovers issued an order, immediate fulfillment must result. Henri worked the levers, the pedals, the other gadgets in all directions. The Duesenberg did not respond.

He climbed out and raised the long hood of the motor.

After a period of foot-tapping Miss Hanover also descended. She was obliged to open the door herself, for Henri was by now completely under the Duesenberg. He did not even hear her order via the car's inter-communication system to open that door.

Then for the first time she noticed the bells. In the dustproof, air-conditioned, almost soundproof encasement of the car's custom body, she had not been conscious of their sound before.

She decided it was not unpleasant! It was in fact quite melodious. And she looked about the circle of hills—blue-green with just a touch of autumn coloring.

God is generous. He rarely leaves a human being entirely lacking in human qualities. Miss Grace Hanover responded to the beautiful. Those hills were magnificent, breath-taking. She would have made one improvement had she been consulted. She would have had the pale blue mountains that were beyond the hills just a little higher. The landscape would then have been the counterpart of a spot she knew in Austria. For America—it was better than could be expected.

The distant vista cared for, Miss Hanover turned her attention to nearer objects. Henri's feet, projecting from beneath the Duesenberg, were majestic but not magnificent. The roadway was cracked and dusty. But on each side of this roadway were small, well kept cemeteries—quaint, rural cemeteries with low gravestones, and only here and there an ugly stone angel or a clumsy shaft to spoil the simplicity. And the Christ-bearing crosses at their centers—most picturesque! Like roadside shrines in the Tyrol.

With the bells it reminded her of—oh yes—Gray's "Elegy"— though, of course, that was English. *The curfew tolls the knell of parting day*. There was no church in sight, but from somewhere these bells were ringing a curfew. Only it seemed a little early. Curfews should come at nightfall, she had always thought. She did not know that she was so near Coaltown, which must be a horribly ugly place with no such setting as this.

Well, Henri's boot toes were still pointing heavenward from under the Duesenberg. She noticed for the first time another car

standing a little further along. She decided that she would walk
into the nearest graveyard, the iron gate of which was open. These
country cemeteries sometimes had amusing inscriptions on the headstones. There might be one from which she could quote in her
novel. An author must introduce a smile here and there.

"Henri, have the car started in five minutes," she addressed the
feet of that unhappy (and if it must be known) baffled creature.
"I will walk for five minutes about this cemetery."

Miss Hanover entered the graveyard of the Coaltown parish of
St. Michael the Archangel. Two men in earnest conversation were
coming toward her. They probably belonged with the other
motorcar.

The shorter of the men wore a black priest's cassock and the
square biretta of his office. The other, who was much taller, wore
a light suit and a black derby set at a curious, rakish angle.

"We can't begin to get all the flowers inside your tiny church,
Father," Bill Dunnigan was saying. "They're covering everything!
We won't be able to see you at your altar—and I think I can promise an altar cloth tomorrow that will be a honey! *You'll want to
have it seen!* With a service here at the cemetery I wish we could
bring the flowers still coming in *up here,* and do something special
about them. Make a rose bowl of this spot! There'll be a lot of
photographers—what you've seen of the cameras is nothing to what
it will be when our Hollywood friends arrive—not to forget the
Governor and all these lesser political guys! I think Jack Dempsey
will attract a few shots. By the way, I'll ask him to tell you himself about that long count. A real pal, Jack. I had him on the
phone an hour ago. With all this, I'd like to give the camera boys
an unusual background to shoot at. It will be good for half pages
in the rotogravures, and the newsreels will gobble it up. Now we
got Saint Michael on the make, we mustn't let him down!"

"I don't think Saint Michael is complaining," smiled Father Paul.
He had just received a package of clippings from an out-for-new-
business bureau in New York that were hopefully addressed to the
Saint himself and indicated that this suddenly limelighted personage was considered a very live prospect! "We might make a great
angel's harp of the flowers," the little priest ventured doubtfully.

"No harp for Saint Michael and Olga Treskovna—both fighters!"

said Bill. "I wish we could think of something more different, and so do you. Something that won't look like an undertaker had designed it. Nothing is more awful than those funeral set-pieces! We've got plenty of 'em in the church. The trouble is—you and I are men! If there was only a woman about—that's what we need now—a woman's hand!"

"Our organist is the only woman here with any sense of the beautiful," said Father Paul, "and she is blind, as you know."

"I know of just the gal in New York," said Bill. "She does the town's most unusual department-store windows. But it's too late now to summon her."

It was at this moment they both looked up, to face, over a short intervening stretch of graveled pathway, Miss Grace Hanover of Cleveland, Ohio.

Miss Hanover was always faultlessly attired and today was no exception. She had for years been considered the best-dressed woman in Cleveland. Her ensembles, her color schemes, were carefully thought out, and gave an effect of almost too exact perfection.

She was also, to her gloved finger tips, the aristocrat. For a creature of the female sex, her clothes from the Rue de la Paix and her bearing Fifth Avenue, to suddenly materialize in this miles-from-nowhere Coaltown cemetery, seemed to impulsive Bill Dunnigan none other than an answer to an Aladdin's wish!

She even wore a corsage of flowers—the most beautifully tinted orchids he had ever seen.

He acted without hesitation before the phantom should vanish. He walked rapidly to the apparition and doffed his black derby. He almost felt he should drop on one knee! He spoke in his best romantic form, as culled from the watching of many plays.

"Madam," he said, "I don't know who you are or what Saint dispatched you here, and it doesn't matter. My name is Dunnigan, and that doesn't matter either. You are a woman and I am a man— a man desperately in need of a cultured woman's advice and succor! There are two of us helpless males here in fact—both equally dumb! If I may say so, my eyes and my heart tell me you are a lady of superlative artistic judgment, who can, if you graciously will, give us that advice and instant help we so sorely need. May I speak freely and hold nothing back?"

Miss Hanover was startled. The man before her was obviously

not a rural character. His pleasant face had a decided urban breeding. His clothes, though flashy in color pattern, were faultlessly made—she had tried for years to get her brother to wear garments of such perfect fit. She noted the polished shoes and the white spats. Spats for men was a British habit that she liked. She could never get her brother to adopt it.

"Why I—I—" She was going to say, "I do not know you, sir!" but instead she heard her voice projecting, "I will, of course, help you if I can!"

She glanced at the other male. He, too, had a kindly face, and although a priest, seemed harmless.

Bill plunged to his subject. Time was short.

"Do you know anything about arranging flowers?" he demanded, his glance dropping, had he known, to the finest orchids in America.

"Why—yes, I do," Miss Hanover found herself answering. "My arrangement of the roses from our greenhouses has taken first award at our flower show every year. By special invitation I am going to exhibit at Grand Central Palace in New York in the Spring——"

"I knew it!" cried Bill. "My hunches are never wrong! It's when I make *plans* that everything goes cockeyed! Kid!—" this to a Miss Hanover now debating whether she should shout for Henri or run "—I believe you have been sent straight from Heaven to two helpless guys! This is Father Paul of St. Michael's down over the hill—St. Michael's the Archangel. Just you come along with us and he'll pray for you the rest of his life!"

Bill had now taken Miss Hanover's arm in a firm grasp. It was too late. She could not retreat. She was being rapidly assisted over the grass toward a far corner of the cemetery, the priest on one side, the tall gentleman on the other. The latter's amazing flow of words had not ceased however.

"We're going to have a funeral service up here tomorrow that is going to be a lulu! Biggest ever held in this part of the country, maybe in the entire country! Movie stars—the Governor—a great champion—newsreel cameras—Associated Press photographers—the funeral of the century! It will be pictured in every theater, every newspaper in the land! And the good father and I have hundreds —will probably have *thousands* of flowers by morning—they're coming in by the wagon load—flowers of every color and shape and kind—and we don't know what the hell to do about them!"

By this time they had reached the Olga Treskovna open grave. *There were mad people about who pushed women into open graves!* Somewhere in some book she had read about fanatical mountain sects—the thought flashed for a second across Miss Hanover's mind——

But the two men released her at the grave side. As she was recovering her breath the tall one continued:

"We want to make this corner of this cemetery look like The Hanging Gardens—a Maxfield Parrish painting—St. Peter's of Rome —the Garden of Eden—a Ziegfeld setting—a glimpse of Paradise— the Grand Canyon—only much better; and we don't want it to look as if a damned undertaker had done it! For this funeral, kiddo, is a sort of happy funeral! An inspired funeral! Under the special patronage of Saint Michael the Archangel! We'll set up an altar for Father Paul right here—I've fixed it with his Bishop—there'll be an organ over there and a chorus of fifty choir boys—we'll have some ceremonial robes from the Cathedral in Scranton that have never been used and a new altar cloth—ditto—from New York; for God's sake, say quick you'll help us, lady, or I'll walk me straight to yonder ledge, where it's a sheer drop of five hundred feet to the town below, and dash out the brains I seem to be so lacking in!"

Dunnigan flashed the famous smile—the smile the news editors could never resist—the same smile that had long ago won the co-operation of the dancing Castles and Miss Ruth St. Denis of "Salome" fame.

In her protected life, Miss Grace Hanover had never been so manhandled, so addressed. Certainly no one had ever called her "kiddo," or for that matter surmised her starting point to be Heaven. A quite opposite springboard had been in the minds and faces of a number of boards of directors on various occasions.

But no longer fearful, she was liking it! Even the "kiddo" part! These words were honest. No groveling. No insincere flattery. For the first time that she could remember, her artistic sense was recognized and appealed to for that sense alone.

She had always known that when the local committee called on her to lay out the program for a concert, supervise the grouping of an art exhibit, decorate the church altar for Christmas and Easter, suggest the setting for the pageant on the lake front, it would be followed by a request for a sizable subscription to finance the event.

She strongly and rightly suspected that the very flattering invitation to exhibit at the New York flower show had a link with her family's Dun and Bradstreet rating, and would be presently followed by a request for money. Here was a stranger who could not and did not know her identity—didn't care in fact—appealing to her with an ingenuous even if flamboyant frankness, in which money could have no part.

It required no psychoanalytical expert on starved souls, no Dr. Sigmund Freud, to explain how forty years of protective snobbery was stripped away in the space of two short minutes.

Miss Hanover heard herself saying these (for her) incredible words, and meaning them:

"Where are the flowers—boys! I'll do all I can to help! And I believe, *by jingo,* I can help!"

Her late father had always exclaimed "By jingo!" when he'd made another hundred thousand, when he'd acquired a new painting, when he'd developed a new orchid. And once he had used it when he complimented her as a schoolgirl because she was good at figures. She hadn't thought of that expression in years!

Miss Hanover smiled at Bill Dunnigan and Father Paul.

"Atta girl!" cried Bill.

"God bless you!" said Father Paul.

Half an hour later she was riding the short distance to Coaltown between an unfumigated Catholic priest and an untamed theatrical press agent in a hired Packard car that apparently belonged to the latter gentleman. Her own Duesenberg was going to wait outside the cemetery. "The battery—it is dead!" Henri had finally discovered, and he was to be ingloriously taken in tow by Mr. Dunnigan's chauffeur to have it recharged in Nanticoke.

Miss Hanover had, of course, quickly discovered that she was helping about the very funeral she had journeyed four hundred miles to disrupt. She knew it when Dunnigan was flashing that smile. Which knowledge may have had something to do with a hurried and private conversation with Henri, charging *him* that their identity was not to be disclosed.

For when, around midnight, William Dunnigan was about to retire in the guest chamber of the parish house (having given up his A-1 bedroom and bath at the Wyoming Hotel to this lady, who wanted to be at the cemetery at daylight in the morning) and was

asked by Father Paul, "What is this charming woman's name?",
Bill had to reply, "I don't believe she ever told us."

"However, that isn't strange," Bill went on, "I call people Kid
and Kiddo and let it go at that. Sometimes I never do really know
their names. But I had to ask for hers when I came to write the
register at the Wyoming. She looked at me funny like and said
that you and I could just go on calling her Kiddo and Miss, but I
could put on the register Miss Grace Smith of Cleveland, Ohio."

"That's where the people who own these mines are from," said
Father Paul. "I must ask her if she knows them. She seems to be
so friendly and generous and kind; maybe she could get those
owners to loosen up and help a little about Coaltown."

"I shouldn't be surprised but she could," said Bill.

"I wonder how she ever came to be passing this way," said Father
Paul.

"I have a suspicion," said Mr. Dunnigan, "but no matter."

"What suspicion?" asked Father Paul.

"My chauffeur has been talking with her Henri. You know,
Father, that Duesenberg cost at least twenty thousand bucks! My
old boss owned one. And Smith is an easy name to think of
quickly, and the initial on the Duesenberg's door is not an 'S'. I
told you—you must not question miracles, Father. Just take 'em
as they come and thank God for 'em!"

74

AT EIGHT O'CLOCK that evening Mr. Dun-
nigan had begged off for an hour's absence from the task of sorting
and handing flowers to "Miss Smith of Cleveland, Ohio." The press
agent for St. Michael's had to attend a special meeting called at the
Orloff dance hall.

District Chairman Jan Rubel introduced him to the thousand
or so miners there gathered. Mr. Rubel spoke briefly and with an
unsuspected sense of humor.

"I give you the new champion, William Dunnigan, of Hollywood
and New York," he said.

When the applause subsided, Mr. Dunnigan spoke.

"My friend Jan is a good comedian," he said, "as well as a good fellow. As far as I'm concerned, he's still the champion. He has placed my St. Michael's Miners' Mass cards in every saloon in Nanticoke today and I'm told scored three knockdowns of stubborn critics of the cards. I only chalked up one K. O. and that, gentlemen, believe me, was just luck! I wouldn't be so fortunate in a return match.

"But we're here to talk about two better fighters than Jan and I will ever be. Two fighters who are battling every day to do a lot of things for you and your families. I want you to do just a little thing for them. I'm speaking of a scrapper named Saint Michael and his side kick, Father Paul. Both of 'em just up Main Street in a church named after the Saint battler. That guy who was the first charter member of the Fighters' Union!

"And this little fellow, Father Paul! Maybe you wouldn't think he was a fighter to look at him. Believe me, gentlemen, he's also a member in good standing. All dues paid and then some! And he's got more heart and courage and guts to the square inch than any ten of us rolled into one! Why, gentlemen——"

This meeting was declared to be a secret one. Special watchers had carefully checked at the door to see that no outsiders, including newsmen, slipped by. When the meeting opened, the doors were locked.

At this point in Bill Dunnigan's address a newsman was discovered. He had worn a miner's reefer and cap. Proceedings paused while he was escorted from the hall. It was this man who reported the first part of Bill's speech. The rest of it was forever lost to posterity.

Shortly before nine the meeting dispersed. All had been pledged to silence and would give no hint of its purpose and outcome. Everyone seemed happy including "champion" William Dunnigan. Ex-champion Jan Rubel also was in excellent spirits. These two adjourned to Koepke's Bar for a single shot of Bill's sixty cent whiskey. They talked alone at the far end of the bar.

The talk was quite uneventful except for a few moments when a bulky hardware salesman just arrived in Coaltown made a slighting remark about the Mass card above the cash register. Amid an expectant silence Jan Rubel paused in his drink, proceeded to the sales gentleman, swung him around, took him by the coat collar and the seat of his trousers and tossed him through the open door. Those who helped the hardware courier arise from the sidewalk advised him not to return.

Rubel dusted his hands, paid for the man's unfinished drink, and returned to Bill Dunnigan.

As Dunnigan and Rubel left, Dunnigan was heard to say: "About seven feet long—same size as the one in St. Michael's. It must fit some altar cloths coming from New York. You're sure you can make it tonight?"

"This head carpenter used to build saloon bars," said Rubel, "the finest damn bars in the district! He'll make it and do a swell job. I've got the key to the Glen Alden lumber storage."

"O. K.," said Bill. "See you at the cemetery in the morning. Don't forget—ten carpenters, and the lumber like the list I've given you. The Bishop will be there at ten to bless it. He's bringing a portable altar stone."

It is permitted to disclose that Jan Rubel was building the temporary altar for Father Paul to use at the cemetery. And his mine carpenters were to help "Miss Smith" about setting it up and erecting a certain backing she had designed.

As Mr. Dunnigan marched back to St. Michael's to continue his tasks under this "Miss Smith," he was singing. "A pretty girl—— is like a melody—" again competed with the ringing of the bells.

Suddenly the press agent paused and changed the tune. "That's it! That's it for sure!" he cried aloud, but to himself. "Maybe it isn't Catholic but it's on the street they'll use it!" He could only remember the words of the first line, but perhaps Miss Smith of Cleveland knew it all. Or the blind organist.

Bill started to whistle. The marching melody was a familiar one. It sounded very much like a stirring song written by another gentleman of the theater, Sir Arthur Sullivan of the team of Gilbert and Sullivan. A song writing partnership not unknown.

The tune sounded like "Onward Christian soldiers, marching as to war!"

*   *   *

At about this time—the hour being only seven P. M. in Cleveland —Frederick Hanover, Jr., was having his dinner and enjoying it.

He had removed his coat. He had unfastened his necktie. He had loosened his belt.

Open also at his elbow was a small volume he had purchased on the way home—a treatise of golf pointers by a very famous winner of many championships.

As he ate, he read. As he read, he pictured himself, driver in hand, making the powerful, rhythmic swings so graphically and minutely described and illustrated in the tome. He was therefore accomplishing his version of that highest goal of the ethical philosopher: "the greatest good to the greatest number." He was giving pleasure at one and the same time to his stomach, his mind, his ego and his external body. What more could any man desire, particularly as the cook—knowing the sister was absent—had made the roast well *overdone*. The cook knew *that* was how Frederick Hanover, Jr., liked it but the poor man never dared to say so!

In the very middle of a crackling mouthful of beef, done to a sizzling, autumn-leaf brown, while at the same moment he was driving a white ball at least four hundred yards straight onto the next green, and watching with pleasure from the corner of his eye the jealous consternation of his opponent (Frederick usually drove them less than a hundred, and invariably into one of the numerous sand traps), there was a loud ring at the bell that gained admission to the Hanover mansion.

"Damn!" said Frederick to the butler.

His shot and mouthful both ruined! A sarcastic grin on the face of his opponent!

"Who can that be at such an hour!"

Even golf had not yet broken down a lifelong habit of eating dinner in exclusive seclusion—or with his sister—at home.

He would have to start that swing all over again, and he cut himself another particularly invitingly crisp and ridged bit of outside roast to assist in the next attempt.

That also was doomed to interruption. The butler entered with the well-known, pale-yellow envelope of one of our telegraph companies on his silver tray.

Mr. Hanover greeted it with another "Damn!" But he took it. There is something compelling about a telegram. Even on the strongest of wills it makes an inexorable demand. It cries, "Open me!"

"Who on earth could be annoying me here at home?" complained the gastronomical golfer, as he reluctantly reached for the envelope.

"It might be the madam, sir," commented the butler, proficient in the art of deduction. "That is," he added quickly, "I don't infer, sir, that a message from madam is annoying——"

"You do, and it would be!" said Frederick Hanover. The butler was a privileged retainer. And, of course, correct in the identity of the sender of the message.

Only his sister would telegraph Frederick Hanover at the private residence. *Couldn't she let him get entirely through one meal in comfort?* It seemed not.

He pushed back his plate, closed his book, resigned himself to whatever harassment the yellow envelope contained. Damn business during his first relaxed dinner in months! The sister's wires were always business.

He opened the envelope. The message was marked as coming from Nanticoke, Pennsylvania.

RUSH OUR GARDENER AND TWO ASSISTANTS TO COALTOWN TONIGHT. HAVE HIM CUT AND BRING ALL ORCHIDS IN BLOOM IN GREENHOUSES. MUST HAVE THEM HERE BY EIGHT IN MORNING. DRIVE DIRECT TO CEMETERY CHURCH OF ST. MICHAEL ON HILL ABOVE TOWN. AM REGISTERED WYOMING HOTEL UNDER NAME GRACE SMITH ALSO KNOWN AROUND CHURCH AS THE FLOWER KID AND WISH REMAIN STRICTLY INCOGNITO. GARDENER BEST BRING ALL LILIES ALSO BLOOMING. USE STATION WAGON HAVE YOUR CHAUFFEUR DRIVE. HEAD FOR WILKES-BARRE THEN ASK DIRECTIONS. HENRI SENDING THIS WIRE FROM NEAREST LARGE TOWN FOR REASONS OF PRIVACY. LOVE

GRACE

Mr. Hanover swore now, but he changed the form of his oath. "I'll be damned!" he said. "I *will* be damned!" *Known around Church as the Flower Kid! His sister!*

"I hope it's not bad news," said the solicitous butler. "The madam isn't ill?"

"*That* would be a matter for debate," replied Frederick Hanover, Jr., sententiously. "Get me the head gardener and my chauffeur, and you pack my overnight bag quick! We're leaving in an hour for Coaltown, Pennsylvania—the station wagon and my Buick. Maybe those mines will still belong to this family if I can reach the place before the business day starts tomorrow!"

~~~~~~ *75* ~~~~~

*B*ILL DUNNIGAN stood at three o'clock the next afternoon near the open grave of Olga Treskovna in the cemetery of St. Michael the Archangel. He was not alone.

One newsman estimated that fully five thousand people besides Bill were in and about the cemetery that autumn day. They filled St. Michael's acre. They covered the roadway. They spread over into Father Spinsky's cemetery across the roadway.

All eyes were toward the altar Jan Rubel and his men had built. This altar was set at the far corner, just beyond the grave of Stanislaus Trocki. Behind it rose and extended some yards on each side, a great arbor of green-leaved cut branches which were massed against a miniature cathedral framework the mine carpenters had erected. The arbor climaxed in green spires, and just above the altar was a great cross of many colors flowering against the emerald of the maple leaves and the fir trees. This cross was formed of hundreds of orchids, the loveliest orchids ever grown in America. The bright sun made their amber, their rose, their purple, their yellows, their whites, blend into a rainbow cross that spoke of Hope—of life eternal. Not quite so high on each side, but also against the green altar background, were two great clusters of lilies—lilies that were also the loveliest in the land.

A border of pure gold edged the far sides of this background and topped its spires. The native goldenrod the girl had loved.

These colors were of a pattern of an altar front-covering—a handsome purple antependium brought by the Bishop, for on its satin damask was banded in metallic design golden sheafs of wheat that were not unlike the goldenrod. The sunlight also reflected from the gold of the crucifix and two tall candleholders resting on the pure and gleaming white of the altar cloth. Father Paul's robes of black with Roman-purple borderings (the Bishop's new funeral vestments) made the whole (thought Bill) a more glorious spectacle **than any theater had ever shown.**

But Bill's thoughts were still with the earlier, more intimate Mass back in the little church. The drama that the Catholic Faith enacts above the mortal figure of her departed children had moved him deeply.

He had listened to the solemn *De Profundis*—"Out of the depths have I cried to Thee, O Lord"; to the tender, pleading *Miserere*— "Have mercy upon me according to Thy great mercy"; to the *Subvenite*—"Meet her, all ye angels of God, receive her soul"; and the *Mass for the Dead*—"I will go unto the altar of God—our help is in the name of the Lord," with that greatest of hymns called *Dies Irae,* "Day of Wrath," which depicts the judgment scene and ends with the plea *Dona Eis Requiem*—"Give rest to them." Father Paul had elected to read *the prayers* of the service partly in English, partly in Polish, so that all could understand their wonder.

His top altar cloth in the church—reaching across the altar and to the floor at each side—had been of a purest linen that seemed almost to vibrate (so expertly was it woven), its silken, hand-embroidered, scalloped edges facing rows of silken Maltese crosses. Marcus Harris had searched all New York to bring the very finest. The violet antependium (another contribution of the Bishop) had golden bandings of the Seraphim—that stirring tongue of fire in a winged circle. Altar cloth and antependium could be seen by all, for Grace Hanover had cleared the altar space and placed the wagon loads of flowers about the side walls, the shrines, the Stations of the Cross; on the front of the choir loft, even on the rafters overhead. St. Michael's was a bower of the redolence of burning wax and the fragrance of Nature's lavish transmuting of sun and rain into the beauty of blossoms.

Life—not Death—was triumphant in the sanctuary that bade farewell to the coffin of Stan Trocki's girl.

Marcus Harris had also brought the boy choir by special train. Their white surplices and cassocks of dark purple filled the choir loft. The chant from the altar was answered by singing voices as well as the music of the organ.

The audience? The Governor and the Mayors of a dozen cities. The Archbishop from Philadelphia as well as Father Paul's own Bishop—these in the resplendent princely robes of their rank, and the tall, white miters of their office on their brows. The player folk from Hollywood (and some from Broadway)—the greatest all-star picture of all time could have been cast and directed and written from their number. Bill Dunnigan sat in a pew this time between two gentlemen as stalwart as himself—Jan Rubel and a certain great fighter and greater citizen.

But Bill thought that Olga Treskovna would have liked most the six children who stood each side of the coffin—the little girls "with wings." And of all the flowers she would have chosen the simple bouquet of mountain phlox which the blind organist had herself placed on the coffin.

Marcus Harris was there with Rachel Harris. He knew that the resourcefulness of a press agent had started it all. He knew that his money had made it possible. But as he listened to the chanting of the choir—to the words of Father Paul—he also knew that there was Something infinitely beyond press agentry and money in that church. A something that transcended any special creed or ritual. The Something that love and service can instill into the human heart and raise that heart to a communion with the Infinite.

His practical mind was not, however, entirely submerged. He said to his Rachel as they were leaving the church, as they viewed the hundreds on the lawn and on the street who could not crowd inside, "This priest should have a bigger church. *He's got to have one!* There should be more room to use up the two dozen altar cloths I brought."

Marcus Harris did not like things to be wasted.

So, passing through the crowds (Coaltown's Main Street was overrunning into the alleys)—the newsreels straddling the tops of a dozen cars—the funeral cavalcade moved up the hill, around the bend, and to its final goal. Even Undertaker Orloff had risen from his depression to an amazing gesture. He had hastily, that morning, purchased a new, shiny silk hat—the first in fifteen years of funeral services, rain or snow or shine!

Now they were gathered at the plateau cemetery.

There eulogies had preceded the religious service. The Governor spoke. But he did not say the words he had dictated to his "confidential aide" on the trip to Coaltown. He realized they would have been utterly hollow and cheap. Instead, he spoke with simple sincerity, "If we do our best, as it comes to us, who knows what reward may be in store?" He had decided also not to veto a certain transit bill on his return to Harrisburg.

The screen notables placed their wreaths, brought in the planes from distant California. Strange flowers that were almost tropical. The great star with the foreign name spoke briefly for them all. "We're very proud to honor her," she said.

The manager of the mines, a native of the district, spoke: "I think you should know two splendid people who have done their share to honor this girl—our employers and our friends, Mr. Frederick Hanover and Miss Grace Hanover of Cleveland." And these two stood bashfully as the cameras turned on them—bashfully but a little proudly also. They felt they were in a gathering of love, not fear or hatred. It was whispered that the holiday now given was to be with full wages—the gift of the lady member of the owning family.

The *Miserere* was once more chanted in the open air. The voices of the choir boys and the music of the little organ Marcus Harris had brought echoed to the distant hills. A great baritone from the Metropolitan Opera had sung the *Ave Maria* by Franz Schubert. A singer from St. Leo's had sung the Polish song Stan Trocki sang in the saloons, the song his daughter loved. Father Spinsky and his assistant served as Deacon and sub-Deacon by the altar under the cross of orchids—as indeed they had for the Mass at the Church of St. Michael.

Now the march to the grave, Father Paul repeating, "May the Angels lead thee to Paradise; may the Martyrs receive thee at thy coming."

The Bishop himself now garbed in a flowing black cope with a silver cross on the cape, blessed the grave: "O God, through whose mercy the souls of the faithful find rest, be pleased to bless this grave, send Thy holy Angel to keep it . . ." And then he sprinkled the casket and the grave with holy water and incensed them, and undertaker Orloff's men, who had placed their ropes and tackle in readiness, lowered the casket.

Father Paul now spoke the hopeful *Antiphone:* "I am the Resurrection and the Life," followed by the beautiful *Benedictus* which ends with "Eternal rest grant unto her, O Lord. And let perpetual light shine upon her . . . he who believeth in Me although he is dead, shall live; and everyone who liveth and believeth in Me shall not die forever."

A final sprinkling of the coffin with holy water; the pallbearers

tossed in their black gloves as was the Polish custom; Father Paul
sprinkled down the first spade of sod; the old gravedigger spaded
the symbolic half a dozen shovels of black earth.

The rites by the open grave Bill Dunnigan had not watched. A
sudden terror had once more clutched at his heart. An utter loneliness. He had moved to the edge of the cemetery where it overlooked the town. He was behind the altar screen of branches Miss
Hanover had arranged. He was "backstage" where he belonged,
he felt. That gave him a little comfort. But he had to clench his
hands until the nails almost cut the palms.

But Olga Treskovna did not fail him. She stood before him and
took both his hands in hers. She was the girl who had stood beside
him in the Hollywood flat the night on which she "died." The girl
who read for him the inscription under the picture named "The
Presence."

She held his hands perhaps just for a moment—for a time so brief
it could not be measured with a watch—but yet for all eternity.

"Bill, Bill!" she said, "I'm with you—always! Always! Even till
the end of the world! I'm going back now to the church. I can go
there, now that my coffin is up here. And then I must get supper
for my father. It's been a day for him! You must go to your
friends. They will wonder. I'll see you, Bill—soon—soon!"

She was gone. He looked across the Valley. The bells had
stopped. It all seemed strangely silent.

It had been a day of sunshine, but in the past half hour some
clouds had appeared, and now the sun was trying to pierce several
of them and sending great shafts of light to the stretch of rooftops
that was Coaltown. And as he looked, these shafts seemed to con-
verge and focus on the belfry of the Church of St. Michael.

Dunnigan knew that Olga Treskovna was not in the coffin beneath the black gloves and the black earth. She was kneeling at the
altar in the silent church of the Archangel.

*   *   *

Bill Dunnigan and Father Paul remained at the cemetery till after
the crowds had gone. These two men—so different and yet so alike
—had felt instinctively that it was fitting they should go back together and unaccompanied by others.

The final word had been said. *"May her soul, and the souls of*

all the faithful departed, through the mercy of God, rest in peace."
The final autograph of the great ones had been obtained by the
excited youth of the town. The gravedigger, having given the
coffin the protection of his "good earth," had removed his tools.

"The tumult and the shouting die," thought Bill Dunnigan.
"The captains and the kings depart," thought Father Paul. But the
two men were not depressed by the poet's lines. It was only the beginning, not the end.

"It's been a wonderful day," said Father Paul. "I have some more
news to tell you. Miss Hanover and her brother are going to build
us a hospital! Out there in that pasture land at the turn of the
road. They're going to establish a good doctor here at once, and a
dentist. They're going to help me with my visiting nurse plan.
And besides all this, they're putting new machinery in the mines—
they'll build a new Breaker where machines will take the place of
men in that dreadful, lung-filling sorting of the coal ore. What
fortune it was Miss Hanover stopped right at the cemetery just
when we were in need of her!"

"Not fortune. Saint Michael and your great heart," said William
Dunnigan.

"I think someone else had a deal to do with it all," said Father
Paul. And then, after a pause, "I shall miss you very much. I hope
you will not entirely forget me—and Saint Michael. As you said,
we both needed a press agent—and will need one still."

"Don't worry about that," smiled Bill. "I haven't finished with
you yet! I always try to finish any job—even when I'm fired!
You're not even through for today, Father. I'm taking you to
Wilkes-Barre as soon as we reach the parish house and my car. My
big boss, Marcus Harris, is having a little dinner there in another
hour, for the film people and the newsmen before they leave.
You're the guest of honor. I'll bring you back safely, for I'm staying over myself till tomorrow. I want to order headstones for her
grave and her father's. And I want to attend your early Mass."

At the mention of this Mass the face of the priest saddened just a
little.

"Ah, that Mass!" he said. "I know what will happen to it now.
I guess it was a mistake to have a Mass at such an hour. But I shall
always have my memories of the past three days."

"You're not going to give it up?" said Bill.

"No. I shall conduct it as long as God lets me serve the people here. And I appreciate all the things you've done about it. But I am afraid there'll be no more crowds of worshipers. It will fall back as it was before."

"Your heart is set on that early Mass, isn't it?" said Bill.

"I suppose we all like to do some one thing that is a little different, that we can call our own," said Father Paul. "I am still that selfish for my church."

"Well, at least *I* will be there tomorrow," said Dunnigan. And he hummed a phrase of a song he knew about a pretty girl.

They had walked down the gravel path and out through the iron gate. The hum of bees was again in the goldenrod, and a tiny thrush was singing its throat out from a fir tree. The man from New York's East Side, the man who had only looked at skyscrapers and listened to taxi horns, was beginning to notice things of this kind. And found that he was liking them.

"Father," he said, "I was born in your Faith. Then I drifted away. I hadn't been inside a church for years till I came here. Didn't feel any need for it. I've not suddenly 'got religion' as they say. I'm just the same guy that I was. But a fellow ought to have some church he can call his own. I needed you also. Do you think I could become a member of your parish—a sort of traveling member? I'll die someday—and they couldn't very well bury me from the Astor Bar or Gallagher's!"

"You're not going to die for many years," laughed the priest, "but it would be wonderful to have you as a parishioner of St. Michael's. Only there's some rule about having a residence in the parish——"

"I've got that figured too," said Bill. "I could save my salary—but not in a Savings Bank—" he smiled "—and build a little bungalow shack up here, where I could come for holidays and in the summer a month or two. You see, the little kid—Miss Treskovna—likes it here. She's promised to be with me a lot, Father—and I oughtn't to make her leave her hills the whole year round."

"I think that it can be arranged," said Father Paul. He questioned no longer things not dreamed of in his philosophy. His simply not yet the grace to see them.

But his earthly cup of happiness was full to brimming.

And the dinner at the hotel in Wilkes-Barre arranged by Marcus Harris added to that happiness. That he, the small-town parish priest, forgotten and deserted even by his own parishioners, almost ready to give up his pastorate, should be toasted by the Governor of the State, by the owners of the Coaltown mines, by the champion who had himself told him about the "long count," by the greatest names of a great industry, by his Bishop, by the visiting Archbishop, by the newsmen of every press service in the East! That was a happening quite fantastic—beyond belief!

There also had been a very practical side to this gathering of people who accomplished things. Fifty thousand dollars was subscribed to the equipping of the new hospital. The Olga Treskovna Memorial Hospital it would be named. "Without distinction of race, creed or color" was going to be carved along its wide foundations.

"I don't want the Presbyterians barred," said Miss Grace Hanover, as she smiled in a very graceful speech. "My brother and I are thinking of building a summer home on one of these lovely hills and we might get ill ourselves!"

The Packard brought Father Paul, Bill Dunnigan and Jan Rubel (he also had been there to represent his Union) back to Coaltown by eight-thirty. The motion-picture people had to leave for Williamsport to fly to California during the night. Marcus Harris and others were due back in New York. The newsmen rushed to their telephones and offices.

Bill Dunnigan and Jan Rubel declined the priest's invitation to sit on the church steps and talk awhile.

"Some other night," said Bill. "You're tired and have your early Mass. I'm tired myself, and Jan here has been up all night with your out-door altar and the cemetery timber. I think we should all be in bed."

But Jan Rubel and Bill Dunnigan did not go to bed. There was another Union meeting at the Orloff dance hall. One woman was present at this meeting—the blind organist. From the sounds that issued from the locked room it seemed that the men inside were learning to sing a hymn!

———————————————————————— *76* ———————

*F*ATHER PAUL had arisen from his bed and was dressing for his morning Mass. It was before sunrise and darker than usual outside, for after a week of sunshine the sky was overcast. It might be said to be a grey-black dawn instead of a grey-blue one. No morning star hung in the East like a lantern to guide the sun across the hilltops.

The hour seemed utterly silent. The ringing of the bells had ceased with the end of the ceremony at the cemetery the day before. The mine holiday had closed the Breaker, so that the monster's constant rumble was also absent. It was due to start again when the men returned to their work at seven. But now, at a little after five, the town seemed still in slumber.

It reached five-thirty and the street below was still an empty one, except for a solitary miner who plodded past like a shapeless ghost in the direction of the working-shafts. There was no excited gathering down around the doorway of his church, waiting for its opening.

Father Paul observed all this as he paused now and then in his dressing to look from his bedroom window.

The priest's thoughts were a mixture of elation and sadness. He was going to be able to work out all his cherished plans. The events of the past four days had not been a dream as he sometimes, on awakening, thought they must be. They had all really happened! The coming of Bill Dunnigan—the bells—the miracle—the crowded church services—the funeral of the girl—the money that had poured in—the promised hospital. But another few hours and Dunnigan would be gone, as the celebrities for the funeral had come and gone, and he, Father Paul, would be a lonely soul again.

He realized how much he had come to value this strange man from a world so far outside his own.

But he knew that the matter which really grieved him at that moment, the reason he constantly gazed from his open window, was the prospect of the empty church each morning at five forty-five. Regardless of how occupied, how triumphant the rest of the day might be, at five forty-five there would come a heartache, a disillusionment.

For four days now he had made himself believe this Mass would at last find worshipers. Not great throngs of course; but the new spirit which had stirred the town would induce at least some few of the miners to attend this "worker's Mass."

He looked out again. Not a single person on the street beneath him.

Perhaps he *should* give it up. Perhaps it *did* bring discredit to the Church—not only his church—all churches! To hold a Mass to which no one troubled to come, except under the impulsion of a clanging of church bells and a miracle.

But hark! What sound was reaching his ears from the distant, far end of the town? It came first in a low murmur, but a rhythmic murmur. It was not the rumble of the Breaker. It had the electric timbre of human voices. It seemed to be voices singing—the voices of many men.

It was closer now. It *was* the voices of men! And with these voices, the tread of men's feet—many feet in the unison of a firm, determined precision. As if all booted feet struck the hard roadway at one and the same time as each forward step was taken. And the singing was becoming louder. It resolved itself into exact cadences—a martial and inspiring cadence that made the blood tingle, that caused the priest's own feet to almost beat time with its rhythm.

Father Paul was leaning from his window by now, straining his eyes through the half-light, and surely—though still some distance away—down the main street of the town hundreds of tiny lights seemed to be flashing; lights that moved in time with the singing, that swayed slightly from side to side in quick, precise movement, while each second they grew brighter and larger! And behind these lights, which seemed about the height of a man above the ground, figures now became visible, stalwart, bulky figures that filled the roadway from curb to curb and were tramping forward like a swift tidal wave of flame-crested lava from some volcano at the street's far end.

The moving phenomenon was now a block away, but Father Paul knew well enough what it was. The lights were in the caps the

marchers were wearing, the miners' caps with the small electric
bulbs backed by polished reflectors. And although the figures were
still a blur, he sensed the miners' reefers, the trousers stuffed into
the heavy, high-laced boots. And he could hear another sound, the
metal clang of lunch pails as the men beat time to the singing by
striking them against the tools that hung from the belts about their
waists.

There was music also that now projected itself along with the
human voices and the clank! clank! of the metal lunch pails. Father
Spinsky would have recognized the quality of that music more
quickly than Father Paul, but Father Spinsky was not there. It was
made by accordions. No phantom accordions this time, but half a
dozen husky arms that could also play as well as march, toiled with
energy in the front line of the procession.

Coming up the street the men had been singing an ancient Polish
march—"Sons of Poland, on to battle!"—and its Slavic timbre
seemed to spring straight from the land where most of them had
been born. But as they neared the church the melody modulated
and changed. They were in the new land now—the land that had
given them opportunity and freedom—and in the language of that
new land they sang the hymn Bill Dunnigan had remembered.

"Onward, Christian Soldiers" rang out from hoarse, vibrant
throats into the dawn's dim awakening.

> Onward, Christian soldiers,
>   Marching as to war,
> With the Cross of Jesus
>   Going on before!
> Christ the Royal Master
>   Leads against the foe;
> Forward into battle,
>   See, His banners go!
> At the sign of triumph
>   Satan's host doth flee;
> On then, Christian soldiers,
>   On to victory!

The marchers were very close. The inspired words of the second
stanza smote the eardrums with the full impact of the thousand
throats behind them.

Like a mighty army
Moves the Church of God!
Brothers, we are treading
Where the Saints have trod!
We are not divided,
All one body we,
One in hope and doctrine,
One in charity!
Onward Christian soldiers,
Marching as to war,
With the Cross of Jesus
Going on before!

Religious fervor? No. Religious respect and belief and faith. But the fervor was a fervor of fellowship—of man shoulder to shoulder with his fellow man. Did not the Great Teacher say, "Love thy neighbor as thyself." The charity toward one's fellows that Father Paul had sought in vain to arouse—the charity that now breathed in the blending of the voices—that linked the powerful stride and swaying of the bodies—that was mirrored below the flashing lights in every strong-hewn face. The pulsing breath of comradeship that is more potent for good than a million solitary converts each locked in a selfish cell of righteousness.

Father Paul rushed down his stairs and out to his church steps. The wide doors had already been opened by his sexton. Crowds now were gathering across the way—women and children. Many newsmen also with their sound-cameras, and there was a flashing of light bulbs. They all knew what was happening. The secret had been kept only from Father Paul.

And now, when the front line was almost up to the wooden steps, the bell of his little tower rang out again and mingled its sweet, religious sound with the martial singing and the organ-like reverberations of the accordions.

They did not seem to notice the little priest who stood transfixed, and with leaping veins, at one side. They swept on into his church—two hundred—five hundred—eight hundred—the full thousand—and as each line entered they removed the caps with the sparkling lights and held them, still flaming, above their hearts.

Outside it had been growing darker, not more light. A storm was blowing up the Valley. There was a rumble of distant thunder and a play of lightning along the dark tops of the mountains. The priest's eyes were drawn there for a moment.

Perhaps it was just the formation of the clouds. Perhaps it was just a memory of what the servant of the prophet Elisha beheld when his eyes were opened—but to Father Paul it seemed that chariots and horses of fire were riding from those mountains. And at their fore a Saint in white armor with upraised shield and lance and a circlet about his brow from which a gleaming cross cast a flaming light, just as the bulbs in the miners' caps shone in the dawn as they swept through the darkened street of Coaltown.

Only for an instant and it was gone. But perhaps Father Paul had been given the grace *to see—to know*—that glimpse Beyond that greatness sometimes brings to men.

He felt a touch on his arm. He turned.

The man who stood beside him wore no armor or even a miner's clothes—just the grey suit with the pale blue and red checks, and on his head was the black derby at its customary angle.

"Father, you mustn't be late for your Mass," said Bill (White Spats) Dunnigan. "I think you're going to have a standing-room-only crowd this morning!"

~~~~~~~~~~~~~~~~~~~~~~~~~~~~~~~~~~~~~~ *77* ~~~~~~

*A*FTER THE MASS, Bill Dunnigan made one last trip to the cemetery. He went alone, as Father Paul was having a meeting with a committee of miners in the rectory, where he was officially informed that he had been appointed Chaplain of the Union—that the march to his church that morning would take place each month—that workers wished to come in rotation to each morning's service. This and other plans for the town in which the Union would co-operate were formulated by Jan Rubel and his fellows. Father Paul was being made a very happy man.

Many clouds were now piling along the hills, and there was an ominous and constant thundering. Bill hurried before the storm should burst. A moment by the grave, then back to his hotel where the Packard was coming at nine; a stop in Nanticoke to inspect a certain Quick Lunch there, then Wilkes-Barre and an eleven o'clock train for New York.

The cemetery of St. Michael the Archangel was silent and rural once more. The temporary altar had been removed; the flowers from it, as well as those in the church, had been distributed the night before to the hospitals of Scranton, Wilkes-Barre, Nanticoke— and an Orphanage in Wanamee.

Bill stood by the new grave, the derby in his hand. She was there and yet she was not there.

"Kid, we're only just beginning!" was his prayer to the mound of freshly-turned sod next to that other mound of Stanislaus Trocki.

A figure appeared climbing the rail fence that separated the graves from the steep, wooded glen to the town below. Its long arms were full of goldenrod. The face was bony and childlike but the eyes were very keen.

It was Andrev Denko, her friend.

Andrev had been pointed out to Bill by Father Paul, but the press agent had never talked with the lad who placed horse chestnuts in formations like the stars—the lad who also had seen and talked with Olga Treskovna since the coffin came home to Coaltown. The boy paused when he saw the tall stranger by the grave.

"You are Andrev," said Bill, "and I'm glad to know you. I want to thank you for the branches and the goldenrod you cut for the altar. Father Paul told me that was your work. I'm Olga Trocki's friend. I have to go away for awhile, but I'm depending on you to take care of the grave while I'm away."

"I bring goldenrod for it now," said Andrev. "She fond of goldenrod. I promised her I keep it on her pop's grave too."

"Andrev, you have talked with her?" said Bill.

"Just yesterday," said the boy. "I'm glad that she come back. And so is old Bald Top Mountain. I talk with him about it this morning."

"Talk with her often," said Bill, "so that she won't ever be lonely here."

The boy was arranging the long branches with their yellow clusters upon the two graves.

"When the goldenrod is gone," he said, "I plant tulips here. They won't grow up until the spring, but I put the bulbs down in the ground. I have some new ones that will be purple and red and black. I save them for her father's grave. Now I put them also here for her."

A sudden thought came to the man from East Houston Street.

"Andrev," he said, "there's room here for another grave. I'll finish up someday myself. I'll speak of it to Father Paul. And when I'm here—will you put goldenrod on my grave also—and plant tulips for the spring? Promise me—and I'll send you a lovely pipe from New York—I've already told Father Paul to pay you every week——"

"Three graves would be nice!" said Andrev, so seriously that Bill Dunnigan was forced to smile. "But if you want the black tulips on your grave, you must hurry up. This is the only year I able to find black tulips—I have enough for you this year."

Bill smiled again. Strangely enough, it would not seem so bad to lie there always in this peaceful spot protected by the circle of the hills! But not yet. There was much to do for Olga Treskovna, for Saint Michael, for Father Paul!

"I guess I'll have to miss out on the black tulips!" he answered. "But when my time comes, Andrev, don't forget."

"I promise," said the lad.

Again the thunder rumbled along the hilltops. And a play of lightning, like bright signals from hill to hill.

"It going to rain soon," said the boy. "But she always like the rain! She stand in it and let it wet her hair. She and old Bald Top over there. He'll like it too! He told me yesterday he was terrible thirsty. It not rain in the Valley for a lot of days."

Dunnigan knew that he should hasten, but the new, dark beauty of the Valley held him. The storm clouds had gathered low about the hilltops. Some more distant ones were completely hidden. He thought of Olga Treskovna's poem about the clouds that bent men's shoulders, and the verse about the pine tree and the storm. Perhaps such a storm was brewing now. But except for the rumbling thunder, which had almost a soothing sound, there seemed a great peace over all the world.

But suddenly another and quite different rumble broke the spell.

Bill had been thinking during the Mass that morning that all the villains of his adventure had been vanquished. Marcus Harris (he had been that for a little while), undertaker Orloff, Father Spinsky, the jinx bankbook, Sergeant Dennis O'Rourke, Mary Spinsky, Jan Rubel, Miss Grace Hanover—all but the bankbook won to comradeship! Well, it might not be so dramatic—one should have a villain to the very end! But it was a better "curtain" in real life. What an ending if it could happen thus to all the world!

So this sudden new clangor in the Valley startled him. And then he laughed. There was still one villain unvanquished and unreconciled. He had forgotten the greatest antagonist of them all!

The new rumble was not of Nature's making. It was seven o'clock, and the sleeping Breaker Beast was awake and once more sounding his tyrannic trumpeting.

For if Dunnigan had completely forgotten the Breaker, there it certainly was for all to see and hear, rearing its head like the antediluvian monster it resembled. And it seemed to say in answer to his frivolous laughter:

"You may laugh, silly mortal, but I am now in charge again! You and your Father Paul may think that you have changed the town, but I still rule! Humans' nature is a weak, weak thing! A fickle thing! I am not weak. I am not vacillating. I am strong and unchanging! I am the strongest thing in all the Valley! I will defeat your plans. I'll blacken your bright hopes. I'll scatter hate and jealousy and selfishness with every breath! I'll win out in the end. You'll see!"

So plainly did these words come from the huge, dark, wooden tower in the glen below that Dunnigan answered them aloud.

"You're wrong, old Devil!" he cried. "It's not going to be! Father Paul will not let it be. Olga Treskovna will not let it be. I will not let it be. And if we three are not strong enough, Saint Michael will not let it be!"

And now the Breaker seemed to laugh, a grinding, screeching, derisive laugh that set the teeth on edge, and then happened that which was the final miracle of Coaltown! The low rumble along the hills became a sudden, violent crashing like the bursting of heavy artillery in battle; abruptly rain commenced to fall, and a great, blinding, jagged streak of flame shot from the blackest of the storm clouds. There was another crash and a burst of fire from the monster's upraised head. Then silence, except for the beating of the rain.

With all the storms that had swept the Valley, the Breaker for the

first time had been struck and blasted! Had the murderer of Olga
Treskovna and countless others felt the staying hand, the piercing
shaft (as had the Dragon it resembled) of Saint Michael's lance?

The clouds opened wider. Rain swept down in great, whirling
sheets, for a wind now added its fury to the tempest. Dunnigan
and Andrev Denko rushed to the shelter of a tree at the cemetery's
edge. It had wide, heavily-leafed branches and offered a partial
covering.

And it was from here that he again saw her.

She stood some yards from them, out in the naked storm, as if
she really were a part of it and had been tossed there by that storm.
She was Olga Trocki now—in the faded blue dress—barefoot, hat-
less, her long hair loosened and lifted and whirled by the wind and
rain, so that it waved straight out like a silken banner. She held up
her arms to the hills. The rain drenched them and drenched her
slender form bent hard against the blasts that whirled about her.
Her glistening face was smiling—radiant. The light in her eyes was
more bright than the flashes along the hills.

"Olga! Olga kid!" cried Bill. He wanted to protect her from the
storm, but he knew that she wanted no protection. The wind, the
rain, was of her blood and sinew—as was the thunder and the flashes
that raced along her mountain tops.

"Do not call her—she love the rain," said Andrev Denko, more
wise than William Dunnigan.

The girl turned her figure toward the two men beneath the
shelter of the tree.

"I'll not be lonely, Bill," she called in her vibrant, throaty accents.
"Andrev will talk to me here—and I'll go often to Father Paul's
church to pray and hear the music of the organ. Sometimes I'll
kneel at the altar, and sometimes I'll just sit on the steps outside.
Father Paul will not see me as you and Andrev do, but I think he'll
know that I am there—and I'll know when he is there because he is
your friend. I'll guard him, Bill. I'll help him also! And whenever you need me—just call, Bill—call, 'Olga, kid!'—I'll always come
—and if I should ever be a little late, you'll know that it is raining
on the hills, and I am standing in the comfort and the glory of it."

Maybe the elderly gravedigger had the Answer, thought Bill.
Heaven was *right here*—if there had been a place we loved, and
hearts we loved.

She was gone, just as, suddenly, the storm was gone. Bright sunlight burst through a cloud. Trees and grass sparkled like emeralds as the rays caught a million drops of water. In the west a faint rainbow arched high from a pine-topped hill. A rainbow that reminded Bill of Grace Hanover's orchids. And a great fragrance arose from the refreshed and watered earth, the fragrance of eternal, pulsing Life.

The Breaker was speaking once more as Bill Dunnigan pushed back into the town. The heavy rain had quickly extinguished the flame in its tower roof. But its rumble seemed no longer to cry defiance. It seemed to know that its boasts of destruction were empty words. Perhaps even the Breaker had found a better way and a new battle cry: *"I serve!"* Another invincible Black Warrior once had taken that motto. The Black Prince of long ago, he of Crécy and Poitiers had chosen for his crest, not "I conquer!" but *"Ich dene!"—I serve!*

For the new machinery that the Breaker was soon to have meant an end of blackened lungs and shortened lives in Coaltown.

78

*T*HE NEW ROMAN CATHOLIC Church of St. Michael the Archangel and its new parish house stand on the raised ground that is the southern side of Coaltown's Main Street. The church is a somewhat smaller copy of a famous Twelfth Century church in Krakow, Poland. "The little kid would not want it too large," one of the three men who had planned its building had expressed it. But it is built of the finest limestone and has two square towers flanking its miniature but noble Romanesque central chapel. In these towers are chimes, said to be the most beautiful in all America.

It was most carefully built around two statues, Saint Michael and the Madonna, that face toward the center aisle. This central nave, in fact, is that of the older St. Michael's, and its altar has the reredos where sits the Holy Mother on a crimson throne, with the white roses at her feet, and the two Saints kneeling in worship from each side-screen. The reredos that was made and painted long ago in Poland.

This Catholic church, and its parish house and these chimes, as well as its fine organ, its mahogany pews, its lovely stained-glass windows of the two side chapels picturing the lives of Polish Saints— Saint Adalbert, Saint Stanislaus, Saint Hedwig (she was a queen of Poland), a dozen others—were paid for by a gentleman of the Hebrew faith. By a Jew.

For this is America.

Each autumn, on a certain day, about five o'clock in the afternoon of that day, a gleaming Rolls-Royce arrives at this church in Coal-town. It has been driven straight from New York, through the Holland Tunnel, across Jersey, up into the fragrant Poconos, over the near-mountains into the Valley called Wyoming. When it reaches the city of Wilkes-Barre it turns aside to follow a winding nine mile country road that one of its occupants first traversed in the front seat of a hearse.

In the spacious back seat of this chauffeur-driven car are two men. One is short and homey, and he has most likely—could we see them —forgotten to attach garters to his socks. The other (who has been coming here very often for radio programs, a class in boxing in the basement of the church, much business with a lady who makes chocolate cakes, and with an executive of the local Miners' Union) is tall and handsome in a rough-and-ready way, and garbed in a new suit of pale red and blue checks on grey, a black derby at a rakish angle on his greying head. Could we see his feet, they are encased in highly-polished black shoes, topped with spotless white spats.

The priest of this church, a little man, now called Monsignor Paul, in his best black silk cassock with purple buttons, is waiting at the top of the steps to greet his two friends. He has been standing there for a full hour on this day, looking eagerly toward Wilkes-Barre.

They shake hands and he gives them his blessing. Then the priest enters the car and these three are driven up Main Street, up and around the bend at the top of the hill, past a large, new hospital that has just been dedicated, to where the five cemeteries lay in rest and quiet on their plateau among the hills.

They enter the iron gate of one of them, walk down the gravel path between the simple graves, beyond the Cross and its crucified Saviour, over to a grave that is near the wooden fence. This grave is covered with fresh goldenrod, as is another by its side. The three men kneel at the first grave. The priest says an Our Father and Hail Mary.

By now it is six o'clock, and the Angelus bells of the five churches of the town below suddenly break the silence of the Valley. Just as they rang so fatefully for one of these three men on a certain late-summer evening. During this Angelus, St. Michael's still sounds its little bell that had hung in the older church tower. The bell that always reminds Father Paul's staunch friend among the miners, one Jan Rubel, of the Orphanage bell at Wanamee. The bell that always causes the tall man in the black derby to whisper to himself, "I love you, kid—I'll always love you!"

The Angelus over, this man turns to Father Paul.

"This season sure—if I don't get fired by Marcus—I'm going to put aside enough money to build that shack!"

"It seems to me I heard that speech last year—and the year before," says Father Paul.

But the stout man without garters interrupts.

"Don't you two start all that again! I know what to do. I'll build him the house myself and take it out of his wages, if he don't start on it this fall! But right now, there's something more important! I'm starved! Father, we go back to your place and eat. I've brought you some real kosher gefüllte fish. My wife, Rachel —she sends her love and she thinks you will like it."

For this, thank God, is America.